Wringing the Truth

*

Dorothy Michaels

PublishAmerica
Baltimore

At the specific preference of the author, PublishAmerica allowed this work to remain exactly as the author intended, verbatim, without editorial input.

ISBN: 1-4137-9651-6
PUBLISHED BY PUBLISHAMERICA, LLLP
www.publishamerica.com
Baltimore

Printed in the United States of America

For Mike, with love, love and more love...

Acknowledgments

Writing is generally a sole occupation; when the ideas are flowing you find yourself glued to your seat in front of the computer screen, the keyboard just a natural extension of your hands, not noticing that morning has become afternoon, afternoon night. It is a thrill to give life to words, and watch with wonderment when the characters, made up from your own imagination, dominate the pages with their dramas and events. Typing 'THE END' is tinged with relief and a little sadness—you, the writer, are no longer needed.

Now it is the time to become a jack of all trades and, in my case, master of none…in the field of technology, anyway.

So it is with sincere gratitude that I thank the following: my amazing and talented son, Mark, for retrieving the whole first draft, a two hour, late night endeavour made harder by the fact it was done by telephone. My youngest daughter Claire is a whiz kid too; not only is she a diligent proof reader, she has spent endless hours relocating files, and generally bringing order to the chaos I seem to create just by switching on my pc. Thanks too to Matt, his computer knowledge was shared magnanimously.

Kay, my eldest daughter; my inspiration, my number one fan; your hugs and support are unequalled. You are precious.

To Tara, and to Gwen: my girls, my pals.

Joanne Gillard and her editing red-ink pen: Yes, Joanne, you can wear a ball gown to my book launch. As a mother of five boys, and putting up with me, you deserve to be extravagant.

To Peggy Hampton for always being able to answer questions. Your knowledge is colossal.

To Mary Lou Burke, for spurring me on.

And to 'Sir' Mintz, my Primary School teacher of long ago, who stayed in touch. Maybe I can call you Cyril now.

To Ann and Joe Bibby, for everything.

And Mike…my husband. My world.

Finally to friends and family near and far who keep me in their thoughts.

Grateful acknowledgement is made to the Rights Department, Oxford University Press and Oxford Standard Authors Shakespeare for permission to use quotes from the Oxford Library of Words and Phrases 1993

To Anne

All good wishes

Dorthy Michaels

x

Disclaimer:

[Concerning bastards begotten and born out of lawful matrimony (an offence against God's and Man's laws) the said bastards being now left to be kept at the charge of the parish where they were born, to be the great burden of the same parish and in defrauding of the relief of the impotent and aged true poor of the same Parish, and to the evil example and the encouragement of the lewd life, it is ordered and enacted.]

Taken from the preamble to the Poor Law Act of 1576.

Prologue

[Montport, Rhode Island, U.S.A.]

The motorcade crawled up the gracefully curved, balustrade driveway like a giant black insect, lethargic in the heat of the late afternoon; the sombre faces hidden behind the glinting, darkened windows, its mournful captured prey.

The leading limousine glided sleekly to a halt outside the columned facade of Rockfort House: a late nineteenth century mansion house, designed and built by a wealthy businessman who had been inspired by the grandeur of the White House in Washington DC.

From her vantage point, the huge and arched staircase window that overlooked the lush front lawns and gravelled forecourt, the girl watched, unseen. Watched as the soberly attired mourners stepped from the various cars, the murmuring of their voices growing louder as they assembled, demurely, their usual prominent personae subdued for this lugubrious gathering.

On cue, the couple that had been waiting in the dappled shade of the marble portico moved forward and out into the brilliant sunshine to greet them. He, tall, athletic, his brown hair lifted slightly in the soft wind that was blowing in from the southern end of the island's rocky shoreline. As he shook hands with first one and then another, his well-tailored stance was dignified: some he kissed, exchanging the usual pleasantries, speaking low and confidentially, smiling with sincerity as he accepted their condolences with an incline of his head, before they moved on to shake the outstretched hand of the woman.

She, as small as he was tall, her petite dark suited figure haloed by a glossy crown of jet black hair, seemed more fragile than usual and, though she was gracious in her greetings, her grief was obvious.

The girl sneered as the woman came into full view. Mounting anger, intense and suffocating, glazed her dark brown eyes, and her thoughts leapt into action...*Ah, shit!*

No! What the...? Huh, yeah, look at her...prima donna...! And he's no better. Sick. The pair of them...like performing puppets...

The loathing for her parents intensified as she watched the unfolding scenario taking place below the window: the massing of family and friends for the memorial service of her late grandfather. A ceremony that the sixteen year old had thought would be taking place at St. Mary's Church later this evening. As usual, no one had told her that the gathering would begin at the house.

But the truth of it was, as she was now faced with the consequences, her behaviour these past few days had been so diabolical that few had wanted to be in her company. Even if they had informed her about the timetable of events, which in all probability they had, she had been too steeped in her own worries and miseries to be receptive.

And today, none of this had changed. Confused and shaken, the teenager turned from the magnificent window, her limbs stiffening with frustrated rage, her mind racing...*Oh God, no! No, no, no! What am I going to do? It's too late to speak to grandma now...*her agitated thoughts ignited her tongue, 'Bastard!' She was referring to her mother. 'Well, she can go to hell. They all can! They'll have to wait. I need Gran, *first,*' she hissed the latter word, her teeth grinding in her tightened jaw as she hurried up the remaining sumptuously thick, beige carpeted stairs, taking the steps two at a time, heading in the direction of her grandparent's suite of rooms on the first floor.

Those who knew the sixteen year old well would have raised their eyebrows, recognising the tell tale signs: the fury, the blanched face that was mottling red; the vile profanities uttered not quite under her breath; the rigid way she held herself as she tore down the wide, oak panelled hallway that led to her grandmother's apartment. She was having one of her infamous tantrums: a *paddy*.

What those who knew the girl did *not* know was how much she suffered, too. They did not know that she was tormented and terrified to exhaustion by the roaring venomous fray. Combustible emotions that seemed to have a life of their own, her slender body the vehicle for their survival. When a rage erupted it was volcanic, the lava, hot and thick, destructive, possessive, she was deafened by its roar. The heat seeped into her scalp, her skin, even her eyes. And when the surge slowed and steamed, a fleeting glimpse of another time, another place, flitting images, tantalised her mind, taunted her thoughts; an echoed voice willed her to be wild, directed her to hurt the ones who loved her most. Only in the presence of her maternal grandmother could these turbulent tirades be soothed and stilled.

And, even then, in the aftermath, they lurked, waiting to be provoked; a low rumbling, a simmering stock of molten grievances brimming close to the edge, always ready, a boiling force of lethal words and actions that threatened to destroy all that was good; to punish.

Why…? In the midst of these red-hot frenzies, even she wondered…*who is it…? Whose voice rules my mind? I know it's a woman…But who is she…?*

*

1

[1939, Liverpool, England]

'Come on, girl...knees further apart. Don't come the modesty now, it's a bit late for *that*.' Sniggering, the thin-framed doctor rammed his long bony fingers deeper, ignoring the girl's obvious distress.

Standing at the other side of the birthing bed the attending nurse, Hilda Johnson, watched the examination with mounting disgust. The doctor plundered the girl's body before abruptly withdrawing his hand and wiping it down the side of his trousers. Hilda could tell from his lily-livered expression, and his involuntary shudder that, as usual, the mediocre medic was repulsed by the vaginal fluids and gaping pubic exposure.

As she pursed her lips at his behaviour, the doctor tried to mask his nauseous thoughts behind more sly humour: patting the girl's thigh, he quipped, 'Not quite ready yet, dearie. But don't go anywhere...and certainly don't plan on going out *dancing* tonight.' With a contemptuous sneer at Hilda, he added, 'She's got *hours,* yet. If you were doing your job properly, *nurse,* you'd know that! I'll be back, later.' He minced out of the room, incapable of a manlier stride, slamming the door so hard that its frost-glass panel rattled in his wake.

The girl whimpered.

'Hey, come on, now. Never mind him, chuck, he's about as much use as a plug in the Titanic. Huh, come to think on it, I don't think he could plug anything. Come on, me love, don't cry. Let's get yer comfy. There, now, yer'll be all right, I'm not going anywhere's. Shush, shush...' Hilda spoke softly as she tended her young charge, very pleased to be left to her own devices. *Poor kid...*she thought...*she can't be more than sixteen.*

The midwife, more experienced and efficient than the duty-doctor could ever be, skimmed through the girl's medical papers. Reading them swiftly, she found the contents to be what she had surmised.

Rustling the documents back into order, Hilda mused to herself: she'd seen it all before, though that being so, she had never really become inured. Sighing sadly, she placed the medical report on the scratched, unsteady wooden table they used as a desk, before lowering her bulky backside onto the rickety wooden stool that doubled as desk chair and bedside seat, gazing thoughtfully, although not unkindly at her young patient.

The girl moaned, turning wide, frightened eyes in the midwife's direction.

Pity filled the older woman. She reached out and tenderly took hold of the girl's hot hand.

'Sh, now, shush! Relax a little, love. Try and stop all yer writhing around. Yer getting yourself all of a blither; it won't make it any easier, yer know, carrying on...There, there, calm yourself down. I won't leave you. No, old Hilda will be here for you, girlie.'

Leaning heavily, her dimpled elbows indenting the pale green counterpane that covered the bed, the midwife continued to ease the young woman.

'Now then, you've decided on the right course of action, love. It's no life for a youngster without a dad. Not that many of them are of any *use*. Still, I suppose it's better to have a rotten dad than be a bastard. There's a lot that do it, mind, bring these poor mites into the world, then make them pay for it by being selfish and keeping them. But, like I say, *you've* made the right choice. Do you know who the father is?'

The girl turned her face away, choosing to stare at the blank wall at her right-hand side.

'Never mind me, love, I'm just a nosey old woman. Come on, then, let's give your back a bit of a rub. You might think that things are bad, but believe me, Dr Walker's not that bad. Better than old Doctor Feeby. How he manages to still practice is beyond me. Always bloody paralytic! There, that feels a bit better, don't it?'

Hilda had worked at the nursing home for two years. Now, as she comforted and guided the girl through the hours of childbirth, she laboured herself with mounting disgust. *Nursing Home.* The two words galled the qualified nurse. A midwife on and off for the better part of thirty years, she knew only too well that this establishment was a den of iniquity, where inept and somewhat sullied doctors practised their shoddy business on incarcerated and defenceless teenage girls. Dispensing their suspect duties these doctors attended their charges in a building that was seeping deeper into decay with each passing day: freezing in the winter, humid and stifling on a late summers' day, as this day had the making of.

Still, it was a job, and Hilda stayed with the thought that in her own way she was useful to the young women: So many of them. What Hilda could not understand was the fact that some of them even came back for more. She herself had never found sex that important, or rewarding, 'A load of fumbling and panting for nowt,' she muttered. Shaking her head, her troubled thoughts continued…*some of these young girls don't even know how they've become pregnant. Bloody astonishing, aye, but true all the same. Take that little one last week. Twelve years old. Twelve years! Her sodding uncle told her that was what uncles' did. Had money though, didn't he, so he could pay his way out of it, hid her away, hid his shame…Bah…*

With every move of the labouring girl the rusting iron bedstead screeched its own annoyance. Ignoring the din of both the mother-to-be and the bed, the nurse busied herself, readying the crib, knowing that the time was coming close.

'I should think you're getting near now, me love, I'd better call doctor back.' As she pressed the bell button, the girl let out a piercing scream. Hilda rushed to her, aware that the final contractions *were* in motion. Watching the girl being tortured by a deluge of pain that juddered and crashed its force through her young body, she still felt the need to caution.

'Here, love, less of that! Doctor doesn't take to the noisy ones. When the pain gets too bad, bite on them here sheets, like this…' Demonstrating her words, Hilda bit onto the roughly starched, white sheet.

'Will you stay with me? Oh, God…make it go away…please, *oh, please…*' The girl panted, her body arching and bucking as another onslaught of excruciating muscle stretching marked the baby's hazardous journey into

17

life.

''Course I'll be staying, little one, you can't do it on your own.'

As the contraction passed, Hilda wiped the sweat off the girl's forehead, cursing the heat and the meagre resources of Sappleton House Nursing Home.

The birth was happening fast. The blood matted head, face dawn, came into view.

'Where *is* that sodding Doctor? All a big game to him! More important things for him to be doing on a Sunday bleedin' morning! It'd be a different story, mark my words, if they were to have the babies...' Hilda cursed men in general as the baby shouldered its way into the world. Red faced and drenched in sweat herself, she swiped the back of her hand over her own damp forehead, pushing back the grey strands of hair that had fallen from under her lopsided nurse's cap, panting for breath nearly as much as the writhing girl in her care. The temperature in the fuggy room was soaring, making matters worse. Never had a summer seemed so hot, or for so long!

However, with the girl co-operating as best she could to push and breathe on command, the midwife took charge. She would do this one on her own. She liked that and, afterwards, she always let them have a little look, a little hold.

And why not...she thought, as she watched the miracle of birth, a marvel she never tired of...*after all these lassies have been through, what was a little minute or two of mothering going to harm? Nay, I'm right*...she continued thinking, caught up in a fusion of emotions...*nothing wrong with one little cuddle to suffice them the rest of their lives. It helps them believe the fantasy. They daydream about their babies. See them living lovely lives: beautiful, handsome, and cared for in kind, luxurious homes. Growing up to be fine, well educated people: doctors, solicitors, lords and ladies of the manor. Huh! What a load of twaddle. When all's said and done, most of the babies'll have no better life than any of their young mothers! God help me, it's a bleedin' farce...All done in the name of religion. Done for the best, so they tell us. Bloody barbaric, that's what it really is. So, where's the harm in one little look, one quick stolen kiss from their real mothers. Surely to God, it had to help? It's monstrous to take the babies away without them being seen, all that pain, and for nowt. And who knows it's for the best, eh? Who the bloody hell knows? I don't...*

With a long grunting push, the girl, knees to her chest, eyes shut, tightened

18

her muscles to bear down for the last time, and the child was born, a lusty wail proclaiming its healthy lungs.

Hilda cut the umbilical cord and carried the crying, dark haired baby over to the other side of the small room to where an enamel basin of hot water and threadbare clean towels had been arranged on a low wooden shelf in anticipation of the moment.

'You did well, love; very well,' Hilda called over her shoulder as she worked on the baby, 'now just give me a sec. and yer can have a little hold. There now, we're nearly ready…' she turned as the door opened. 'Oh, it's *you*, Doctor. Yer a bit late, it's all but over,' The midwife was angry: she had been going to let the mother see the baby. Now, with the doctor's return, that wouldn't be happening. She clicked her tongue with disgust, muttering under her breath, 'Shame, the lass's been ever so good. Bloody rules…'

Doctor Walker examined his exhausted patient. 'Done a good job here, nurse, no tearing, no cuts. Trying to do me out of a job, hey?' he laughed.

Hilda fumed silently to herself…*sniggering, bloody fool. Done this young girl out of seeing her baby, more like…*

Placing the bathed baby into the prepared iron crib, the midwife shuffled across the room to aid the girl. Hiding her fury, she worked diligently before speaking up.

'I can manage now, Doctor. See? Have a look for yourself, no trouble with this one, at all. You get yourself away. I'll tidy up. Go on, Doctor, you've had a rough few days yourself. Go and have a listen, see if it's been announced yet.'

War. War was imminent and this young woman not getting to see her baby was also imminent.

'It's all right—I'll stay and do the paper work. Take the child away. *Now* nurse.'

'No. Oh no, please let me have a look. Please, *please*!' the young girl sobbed.

'Be quiet! You knew the rules. No contact. The child is not yours.' Doctor Walker, aware that his presence was objectionable in the cosy aftermath of this birth, enjoyed taking command.

*The swine revels in it…*Hilda thought, cursing the man under her breath.

'Can't you even tell me what I had?' the girl screeched.

'Take that child away. At once, nurse!' The doctor was loud in his insistence.

Before reaching into the crib, the midwife caught the mean glint in the doctor's eye: a malicious flash of peevish superiority. She seethed inwardly....*Just look at him...Enjoying every minute. Cruel. Men are bloody cruel...What with wars, pregnant young girls, and that drunken old fool at home, it's too much, too sodding much...*She snatched the baby up into her arms, 'I'm bloody well going. Keep yer hair on! I'll take this little girl out of yer sight, straight away.' Hilda's angry words were coupled with an anguished, unvoiced plea...*Dear God, when that young woman goes over it all, in her head, like, later on, please let her remember me last words to that bugger of a doctor...*

Carrying the snugly wrapped infant out of the birthing room, Hilda was met head-on by the stench of over-cooked vegetables that was hovering, as usual, in the dingy windowless corridor. Nausea added to her feelings of ineptitude.

Although the midwife had little control over her patient's dietary welfare, she was adept at ministering to their state of mind. A little word here and there often brought comfort to the young girls in her care.

And her words had registered this morning. The joyous smile that had swept over the girl's exhausted face was testimony to the fact. Nevertheless, it was a smile that was momentary; it was gone as quickly as it had come.

Left alone, she had only her thoughts for company. At first she had been delighted to have given birth to a daughter. But in the wake of this satisfaction, as she drifted into sleep, a bittersweet revelation flooded her senses. In a fleeting flash of insight the girl knew that her newly born daughter would be everything that she herself could never be.

Depression took hold again. She felt as she did before the birth. Except now there was nothing to keep her here. She wanted to get out. Be gone. Nine weeks was more than enough. Nine weeks of drudgery in the dreary rat hole they called a nursing home—humping her hateful, inflated body through the daily chores, set for them to earn their keep whilst, outside, the rest of the world was caught up in the excitement and anticipation of the inevitable coming war.

But it would be several days, days when she refused all food and fought off any medical attention, before her discharge would be granted.

'Well child, it's all done, now...' Father Carey had never known the right procedure, the right words at these times. In fact, on occasions such as this, he was usually in a state of total anxiety himself. What, indeed, was the right path? For him, the child was the important factor, and yet these young women were little more than children themselves. Sighing dolefully, he continued, 'I hear that you haven't been behaving yourself. Don't make it any harder than it is. The baby needs a good home, and Father Goodwin is a fine man. He'll have made *sure* the little one has a proper home. I can promise you that, at least...'

Still she wouldn't turn to look at him. Lying on her side, staring at the flaking, green painted wall, the girl made no attempt, no sign to show that she was listening to the young priest.

'A few more days and you'll be on your way. Starting again. A new life! A new chance! Take it, child. Use it as a challenge. You've been treated kindly, haven't you? You knew you wouldn't be seeing to the child. Look, turn yourself around,' he stood up, lumbering his perspiring, much over weight body closer to the girl's bed. Reaching out, he touched her stiffened shoulder. He spoke again, gently.

'Turn to me, so I can talk to you face to face. We'll say a little prayer for the babee, and you'll feel better. Come on now, you must want *something* to eat. It's been days, so let's get something down you...' Though he was cajoling with hope, he was nevertheless taken aback when he got a response.

Shrugging off the priest's hot hand, the girl jerked round, her face registering annoyance; her thick lashed, dark brown eyes glared into the innocent blue ones of the minister.

*Dear, oh dear...this one's really no more than a babe herself...*Father Carey's first, pitying thoughts were swiftly removed as the girl sneered at him, her own ugly thoughts more than obvious.

The cleric's round face reddened. Swallowing hard, he backed towards the wooden stool and sat, shaken and confused. He had expected tears, respect, and contrition: the girl, shrouded in an oversized off-white muslin nightgown, seemed barren of any of these emotions.

Looking straight at the flustered priest, the girl pulled herself into a sitting position and staring defiantly at him kept her thin-lipped mouth tightly shut. Very slowly she combed her fingers through her greasy and lank shoulder length dark brown hair, moistening her parched lips with the tip of her tongue. Hunger and thirst seemed forgotten when she finally spoke in a quiet yet threatening tone to the inept priest.

'Go on, then. Tell me about these *wonderful* people. Are they royalty...?'

Smiling tentatively, yet avoiding her now blazing eyes, Father Carey seized hold of his chance.

'No. Not royalty, but they *are* nice people. A couple not blessed with a family of their own, aye, as you yourself requested,' his voice became firmer as he took command. 'Now listen to me, young woman! That took some doing. We've abided by your wishes, now it's your turn. Sign the papers and put it all behind you. They've had the child for nearly a week, now. Play fair.'

He watched as she turned her head with indifference, her attention drawn to the room's iron barred, un-curtained window. A fly, idling its way along a cracked pane, seeking an exit, unwittingly seemed to add to her frustration. A moment or two passed as they both followed the fly's progress. Giving up, it flew back into the room. She seemed to take that as a signal and turned to the priest. He knew she had made a decision.

'All right, then, I'll sign your *important* papers when I'm dressed and ready to leave. If you can arrange it, that is...because if I can't get out of here...if you can't do it...I'll be signing *nothing*...' Raising her voice to muster the sarcasm was an obvious strain. The girl's pallor whitened further. She flopped back against her pillows, laying her hands on her empty stomach. She grimaced as though in pain. A pain that seemed to both fuel and feed her reactions. Pushing up into a sitting position, she faced Father Carey again, and this time there seemed to be tears in her eyes.

In a sympathetic gesture, he reached out to pat her arm. But the priest had misread her actions and emotions. The girl roared her disapproval as she elbowed his hand away.

'Get your *hands* off me. I don't need your pity. I've asked you to get the papers for me...If you can't, you can go to hell with the rest of them...you mean *nothing* to me. So you can forget the preaching and praying...and your *mauling*. From now on, I'll fend for myself. And I'm telling you—I'll be glad to be out of this sanctimonious dump! I'll bet you don't eat the slops they dish up to us, hey? No. Not by the look of you. And to think, they have the *audacity* to wonder why I won't eat...Well? What are you waiting for...?'

Shocked by the sudden ferocity of the girl, Father Carey stood up. Smoothing down his creased black cassock he turned his back on her and walked slowly, head down, towards the door. Overcome with a deep sense of failure, his step felt heavy. Weighted down. Pulling him, indeed, into the direction of hell...*Such hatred. And from one so young! Yet wasn't it his duty to try to understand, and in doing so, save peoples' souls...?*

At the door, he turned. His sad, watery blue eyes locked momentarily with the defiant dark ones of the girl. He was the first to drop the stare. Fumbling with his hat, a black biretta, its beige silk lining ruinously stained by the preparations he used to control his unruly ginger hair, the subdued priest thought long and hard before speaking again.

The girl watched him, her eyes blazing with unabated fury, her nose wrinkling with obvious distaste as his body odour wafted towards her. She fanned her hand in front of her face, and blew air from her lips.

More aware than ever of his inadequacies, the clergyman prayed for courage, and the wisdom to word his final sermon correctly. 'Child,' he stopped and coughed, clearing his throat before continuing, 'I will make it my *business* to see that you leave these premises by late this afternoon. You will be given an envelope. Inside it you will find a small sum of money, a few pounds donated by the good priest of your parish, who had your welfare at heart. To be sure, you'll be finding things a little different, now. Our country is at war with Germany; people will have their own troubles to worry about. It's a sad, bad world we're in…it is that. One day, though, with God's help,' the priest made the sign of the cross with his right hand, 'you may realise your own worth, and make amends towards your wanton life. You're a woman, now. Your, em…your *actions* have put your childhood far behind you. At least you have shown decency towards the child, by allowing its adoption, it most certainly is the best for the babee and…' he stopped mid-sentence, confused by the bitter laughter coming from the dishevelled girl.

'No, *Father*, you are wrong there,' she almost spat the words, her eyes shining with scorn. Languishing back against her soiled pillow, she continued to deride the unworldly priest, a cold, cocky mirth to her tone, 'Oh yeah, you've done what's best all right: what's best for *you*. Eased your conscious with your…*blood money*.' There was a menace about her now— her chuckle so out of place.

Father Carey turned his back on the hollow laughter, and walked out of the room. Defeat sagged his shoulders. The fetid air of the corridor seemed to encore the girl's words, mocking him and his beliefs. The young priest had thought his calling would be enough to see him through his ministering. In reality, he felt himself to be lacking of the essential ingredient: Understanding. He had passion, he had care, but…*oh, how can I understand how these young girls feel? What right do I have to tell them to give up their children, their own flesh and blood? How can I believe in the Virgin Mary, and yet advise these young mothers to forego, to give away, a part of themselves…?*

What Father Carey witnessed that September morning fostered within him for many years. He took the incrimination to heart. Indeed, the episode altered his beliefs and was instrumental in the eventual closing of Sappleton House.

Father Carey found his cross. Sadly, it came too late to help the girl whose hatred had been the catalyst.

*

2

'Stand still, Maureen! If you stopped fidgeting and ferreting about so much we'd be finished the quicker...' Through a mouthful of dress pins, Ethel berated her six-year-old daughter who, at that very moment, accidentally pushed her bony knee into her mother's right eye.

'That's it! Get down! I'll have to do the rest be guesswork.' Placing her hands around her daughter's waist, Ethel whisked her, rather more sharply than she intended, down from the kitchen table.

'I'm sorry, Mammy. I didn't mean to bang your eye,' her own young eyes, blue as a midsummer sky, shimmered with unshed tears.

Ethel looked down at her daughter, her irritation and anger melting immediately.

*Poor tot...*she thought...*I shouldn't have had her up there for so long.*

Overcome with remorse, Ethel crouched down, her actions more gentle now as she guided the dainty, dark haired girl out of the pinned-together pink satin, which was, vexingly, only halfway to being a dress.

Outside the house a cloud slipped across the afternoon sun, mirroring the dimming of Maureen's radiance. Stepping out of the material, subdued by her mother's outburst, she quietly dressed herself into her every day clothes: a navy blue sun-dress, which was white spotted, full skirted and sleeveless.

Busying herself with the satin, Ethel sat at the sewing cluttered table watching her daughter out of the corner of her eye. Guilt idled her hands; she pushed the dress fabric aside. 'Eh, now, come here,' she said, beckoning the sheepish child into a tight embrace. 'Don't worry your head, it were an accident. Mind you, I'd look a right one, wouldn't I, if me eye were to go black and blue and all the colours of the rainbow just as your dad comes home.'

They both giggled; Maureen with relief, her mother from nervous tension.

Ethel had been all of a dither, as she herself put it, ever since she'd received the letter telling of Bill's impending arrival. Well, it had to happen. He had to come home sooner or later. But Ethel was finding it hard to accept that, in reality, she would have preferred it to be later. Six and a half years was a long time, for both of them; and she would have to remember, Bill's time hadn't been as pleasantly spent as that of her own.

'…Any old rags…? Rag…bone. Rag…*bone*…'

Maureen left her mother's side, and ran to the kitchen's small side window, her attention drawn by the racket going on outside in the cobbled street. Pressing her face to the glass, she squealed with delight.

'Mam! He's here! The r*ag and bone* man: We *haven't* missed him. Can I go and get your donkey stones? Can I, Mam? Oh look, he's turned our corner already!'

'You can when you remember your manners, young lady…'

'*Please*, Mam. Oh, be quick, he's moving on, now, I won't be able to catch him!'

'Yes you will,' Ethel couldn't help but smile; Maureen had always been excited by the singsong call of the street trader as he trundled passed on his weekly round, his laden cart pulled by a tired old shire horse.

From her seat at the drop leaf, oak table, she reached towards the highly polished matching sideboard. Pulling open a long drawer, which topped three others, she withdrew a brown leather purse.

'Now remember, don't let him fob you off with white ones. I need brown donkey stones for doing me steps, and nothing else. Here, get two, you've got enough money. Go on! Be quick, else you'll miss him. And think on, now, no following him down street. Come back as soon as you get them, you hear me? Right, well, go on then…'

Placing the money into her daughter's small hand, Ethel propelled her out of the kitchen and down the narrow lobby that lead to the front of the terraced house. Street sounds filled the air as she opened the door, sounds which stole away Ethel's frustrations. Planting a hasty kiss on her chattering daughter's forehead, a surge of exhilaration swept all other thoughts away: the joy of motherhood was a tidal force.

Standing on the top step outside her opened front door, a wide smile on her face and her arms folded over her chest, Ethel looked like any other middle-aged mother who lived in the area, except, perhaps, that Ethel's attire was probably the cleanest and the neatest: her pale blue loose fitting cotton skirt was immaculately laundered, her short sleeved white blouse, trimmed with a sky blue braid, was crisp and fresh, showing no signs that the outfit had been made from jumble sale remnants.

Ethel Grady was a proud woman who kept a spotless home, and a good table; she was the sort of person who should have been blessed with many children; her wisdom was sound her discipline fair, and her love, boundless.

This afternoon, as on many afternoons, Ethel also wore the northern women's uniform: a pinny. Made from any material available, this item of necessary clothing—apron with bib, which was slipped over the head and tied into a bow at the back—was worn daily and, as far as Ethel was concerned, was the proper attire for a housewife.

Today, Ethel had chosen to wear a pinny patterned in a small blue check, one of her better cover-alls, worn in the afternoons, when the harder, dirtier chores of the day were behind her.

As she watched her young daughter skip across the cobbled street, shouting, seeking the attention of the old man who rode on the clattering, horse drawn cart, the fair haired and slightly built grey eyed woman felt choked with pride and then shame as her thoughts wandered... *What soft of woman am I? Not to want my husband back, and after all he's been through...*

Yet it was the truth. Ethel was not looking forward to Bill's return. Especially now, now with...

But Ethel refused to let the fearful dread that was brewing at the back of her mind spill over, concentrating her thoughts onto the here and now; dwelling only on what she had enjoyed and loved during the last six years. Six wonderful years, if the truth be known. Whilst all around her moaned and groaned, and rightly so, about the deprivation and loss caused by the war, Ethel had never been happier.

When Bill's call-up papers arrived, Maureen had been just a few months old. Now, that same infant was nearing her seventh birthday and barely knew

27

her father. In fact, she didn't know him at all; Maureen had no memories whatsoever of her sailor daddy.

Nonetheless, from the moment Maureen had uttered her first words, Ethel had brought the word *daddy* into her young daughter's vocabulary, creating, in all innocence, a fictional father: Ethel's anecdotal reminiscences had taken on a story-like quality: a fairy tale, where the handsome prince arrived and everyone lived happily ever after...

But it wasn't going to be like that. Wounded or not, Bill would still be Bill: the Bill who had not really wanted to adopt a child.

'Why?' he'd asked, 'aren't we alright as we are?'

For the first years of their marriage, Ethel had yearned to be a mother. Finally, after six long years, the penny had dropped; Bill had relented about adoption realising that unless they did, they really were going to be a childless couple.

Yet even then there were difficulties. Twice they had thought a baby might be coming to them, to have it all fizzle out to nothing.

Until the Reverend Thompson, who had taken their case to heart, had the good fortune to meet up with an old boyhood friend; the two men had been next-door neighbours and had grown up together before going their separate ways.

Rather ironically his friend, Dennis Goodwin, had also gone into the church, although his vocation had taken him into the priesthood: Catholics and Protestants had long since lived side by side, in harmonious camaraderie, in the back streets of Littleton, which was also home to many of the Jewish faith: McKenna's Grocery, Smith's Butchers and Liebermann's Bakery gave the narrow streets a *cosmopolitan* air long before most of the residents even knew what the word meant.

With Father Goodwin's intervention, Maureen was soon nestling in Ethel's arms. Little more than a day old, the newborn had been brought home to Littleton by the excited couple themselves: a telegram, sent on a day that would go down in history, had urged them to travel to Liverpool to collect the child.

Arriving there they had been told that the natural mother was in good health, and of good background and that she had also made it very clear, the baby was to be brought up by an older, childless couple.

That September day, the day the Grady's became parents, the day Ethel chose her daughter's name, had been hot and sunny. Britain, alert to the coming war, had been quietly basking in an Indian summer.

By the cold spring of the following year, Bill had been drafted; his days of being a father suspended, indefinitely: in the latter months of 1943 the Japanese captured him. From then on, very little was heard from him, or about him.

This silence did not deter his faithful wife. Ethel sent Bill letters every week, as she had done since he was first called to service. Her letters told of the fraught and dangerous months of late 1940, when Warrington Clough, which was directly on the bombers' route as they headed for the city and port of Liverpool, was hit, forcing his sister, Vi, and her young sons to seek refuge in Littleton.

However, this *safe-house* plan backfired: Littleton was also badly blitzed during the fierce bombing raids on Manchester, which coincided with Christmas 1940.

It was at this point that Ethel had locked the front door of number 93 Lupin Street, wondering whether she would ever return to the house again: rightly or wrongly she had decided to evacuate herself and the baby to a rented house in Warrington. Bombs or no bombs, she knew she would feel safer living closer to her in-laws, the Greenwoods.

But it seemed as though Ethel had gone straight from the frying pan to the fire by following Bill's sister home. The fear they all suffered during the terrifying months of March and onwards, through to the May of 1941, was difficult to put in words in the letters she wrote to her absent husband. Night after night, as she and countless others sat huddled in the Anderson air raid shelters (erected with great speed in any back garden big enough to take the galvanised iron, corrugated roof structure) Ethel berated herself for putting her young daughter in such grave danger.

Yet there were some happier times that made up for all the hardship and devastation. The companionship of Vi and Sid Greenwood, and the laughter and bantering that went on amongst her neighbours and newly found friends, was a great source of amusement and comfort to Ethel.

Wartime friendships were formed quickly in the cramped environment of the dugout shelters, where cats and dogs numbered as many as the children. Where Ethel was just one of the fraught and dishevelled weary parents who were worn out by their attempts to carry on with normal day-to-day routines of jobs, child rearing and housework, even though the previous night had brought with it little sleep or rest.

Pleasant natured Ethel had found herself useful; her days filled with child minding, and the endless preparations that went into making a home *bomb proof*. Home was very important to Ethel Grady for it was something she had gone long without during her teenage years.

At the tender age of fourteen Ethel had left the shelter of the Welsh village where she had been raised. The village, a grim place surrounded by mountainous black slag heaps, had been the place where she had lived since birth. Brought up by aged grandparents, she had always been aware that she was an unwanted lodger in their home.

Ethel's parents had died tragically young. Her father met his death, along with two of his younger brothers, in the trenches of Ypres, France. Less than five months later, her grieving mother had died giving birth to a stillborn son.

The orphaned girl's childhood had not been a happy one. Her grandparents were too old and deranged to properly care for a young child. Mercifully, the village school had a good teacher and Ethel was an able student. Her grandparent's austerity and growing dementia did nothing to sap the spirit of the yearning, eager youngster, who read by the light of a flickering candle anything and everything she could lay hands on: books, magazines, and newspaper advertisements.

Ethel had been a girl with imagination and dreams—dreams that, eventually, took her out of the grey-stone village and into service as a kitchen maid in the home of a prominent businessman who worked and resided in the city of Manchester.

Her employer was a kind man, devoted to his family, and fair to his loyal staff as they lived side by side, cocooned in upstairs-downstairs harmony which prevailed within his splendid Edwardian built home: a mansion house, which was one of many such properties gracing the long, tree lined avenues of Didsbury, a leafy, sleepy suburb a few miles south of bustling Manchester.

And it was here that Ethel blossomed; tying her wispy blonde hair away from her small featured face, dressed in well laundered, starched whites, she learnt to cook...and to socialise. Her many hours spent in the warm, well-lit kitchen brought a glow to her cheeks and a curve to her figure.

And it was from this house that Ethel had gone dancing, in the company of two other girls who were employed as parlour maids, and had met tall and gangling, sandy haired Bill Grady.

It was Bill's soft green eyes, his quiet and thoughtful manner that struck Ethel the most. Over the following weeks their love grew. They made plans to marry, and did so as soon as they found a room to rent.

In the attic bed-sit they had found in one of the cramped back-to-back houses of sooty and treeless Littleton, which was walking distance from the city centre, they shyly learned the rudiments of lovemaking, settling quickly and lovingly to married life, eager to begin the making of their own, perfect family.

Sadly this was not to be. Ethel fretted as the months passed by and her womb stayed barren. As both of them were in work, she as a cook, he as a ledger clerk, their savings prospered; soon they were in a position to rent a house. Here their luck was in: by their second wedding anniversary 93 Lupin Street had become their home. The six-strong family that had had the use of the rest of house had thankfully been evicted. Moving down from the bed-sit attic, they set about making the shabby un-loved terrace house into a proper home. All that was missing was the child.

A child did arrive, eventually. A child Ethel could not have loved more even if she had been her own biological daughter. With the adoption of Maureen, Ethel finally had the motherhood she had yearned for, but it seemed that life was withholding the final piece of jigsaw that brought full happiness.

With the worst of the bombing raids on Manchester over, Ethel had made her way back to Littleton where, in the comfort of her own home, and in the company of her growing daughter, Maureen, she had waited out the last, long years of the war, sending her absent husband affectionate, informative and often amusing messages from herself and their family in her long, weekly letters.

Maureen started her school life at the local primary school, St. Michaels. Daily, the child came home proudly bearing drawings and doodles, mementos that Ethel would have liked to have kept and cherished, but which she had resolutely sent to her imprisoned husband.

When at last the war had ended she was informed that Bill was safe, and back in England. Ethel learnt that Bill was in a military hospital on the south coast. His long incarceration had done great damage to his lungs. His rehabilitation, the slow mending of his health, was going to take many months.

Ironically, Bill's discharge date coincided with Maureen's birthday. The tea party Ethel had planned for her daughter was now going to double as a "welcome home" celebration for her husband. Ethel had invited Bill's two sisters: Nellie, who was his eldest sister, would arrive with her teenage daughter, Gladys. Vi would come accompanied by her five boisterous sons, and her equally noisy husband, Sid. Swelling the numbers even further, she had also invited a few neighbours and a couple of close friends.

With all this in mind, Ethel knew that her home would be full of good cheer. She also knew that people thought she was a very lucky woman; knew that she should be happy to have her husband returned to her. But she wasn't.

Now, as she stood awaiting her daughter, her thoughts creased her forehead. She was deeply troubled and more than a little ashamed.

'Mam. *Mam?* Are you listening to me? Here you are...I got brown ones, like you said. Can I go next door, now, and play with Betty? Can I, Mam, *please?*'

Pulling out of her reverie, Ethel granted her daughter her request, shooing her away with mock dire warnings that she was to, 'Watch her behaviour, or else,' knowing that the intelligent child was keenly aware that behind the usual banter, all was not well.

Running up the front steps of her home, Maureen had seen the worried, faraway look in her mother's eyes, and had been afraid. Yet, like any youngster of her age, the urge to play with her friends took precedence.

Sitting on the kerb-side of the cobbled street, Maureen and Betty played marbles in the dusty gutter, shouting out with annoyance when a battered and well-used football scattered the coloured glass balls each and every way...Ugh! Boys are awful, always spoiling everything...

For a few minutes the two girls traded insults with the gang of straggly lads, who were of a similar age to the girls.

And, as usual, Betty's threat to, 'Get me brother to beat you all black and blue' did the trick. With one last spit in the girls' direction, the five, bone-thin boys sauntered off, calling abuse over their shoulders, laughing and pummelling each other as they headed for the open spaces of the local park; they had time for one quick game of football before their mothers called them in for tea.

Gathering their marbles, stuffing them into the deep pockets of their near identical sun-dresses (both had been made by Ethel,) the two girls linked arms and went for a walk around the block. A walk that was difficult when you weren't allowed to stand on the cracks that separated the sun baked flagstones, 'If you stand on a nick, you'll marry a brick, and a beetle will come to your wedding.' Chanting this ditty, which was common practice with the girls of the area, a stroll around the block was an earnest matter, and could take anything up to an hour. No girl liked the thought of a *beetle* coming to her wedding.

As they walked, looking down all the time, the two girls chatted of this and that. The afternoon sun was warm on their shoulders, its rays adding a lustrous glint to their glossy hair: Maureen's, a midnight-black, club-cut and fringed, was in complete contrast to Betty's collar length, tumbling waves of gold threaded red.

The street they carefully stepped down, which was situated back to back to their own, also basked in the warming sun: children squealed whilst at play, dogs barked; gurgling babies rocked in their rickety prams, and women idled and chatted on their doorsteps. The high blue sky was unblemished as the late summer sounds filled the soft air, and the stench from the rubber works' chimneys polluted it. But neither girl was conscious of this historic, soon to expire setting. Only later, much later, would these days fill them with nostalgic longing.

Maureen confided her worries about her mother's mood to her friend, and was perplexed by the nonchalant reply.

'Oh, my mam's always miserable and nowty when she's in the *pudding club*.'

Maureen's head jerked up as Betty tittered and, not knowing what else to do, Maureen giggled too. Both girls knew that the pudding club had nothing to do with cooking—it was when a woman was having a baby—but neither knew why it was called that. *Maybe it's because their bellies look as if they've swallowed a pudding, and the dish as well.* This thought, when aired by Betty, made them both hold their sides with laughter.

And then Betty, who was more worldly than her friend, and who was probably feeling guilty for her betraying remarks about her mother, especially as her mother's last two pregnancies had been painfully miscarried, added a rejoinder.

'I *don't* think your mammy's having a baby, Maureen; she's too old. And your dad's never here. It's true it's men that make the babies, isn't it…?' Betty eyed her friend, probably hoping that Maureen might be able to shed some light on the question of where babies really came from. But as Maureen failed to answer, she decided to come up with an answer herself, 'I think dads' have to go drinking to give yer mam a baby. And my dad's always drunk! Mam says it's because he's one of the *left behinds*…says he feels sorry for himself. But me dad says it's because of his work at the pit, and the "bloody Bevin lads"…me da hates having to look after them, says they're all thick as pig shite.'

Maureen chuckled again. Betty was very rude—but very funny—especially when she was mimicking her father's Irish brogue. Maureen loved playing *out* with Betty; they always had such a laugh.

Maureen Grady was also keenly aware that even though her funny friend was not very clever at her schoolwork, she did know quite a lot more about life than she herself did. Betty knew about babies, and about having brothers and sisters. And she was always laughing about her dad—even when he'd been belting them all! Freckled face Betty never seemed afraid of anything, or anybody. Maureen was glad she had confided her worries: Betty seemed sure that no new baby would be coming into the Grady household.

Altogether, Maureen was pleased with the way the conversation had gone…Babies were nice, but she and Mam were happy as they were, weren't they…? Just the two of them…and Dad of course, when he came back…

As the two girls made their way to their own front doors, rain clouds scurried from nowhere across the sky. Large spots of rain dotted Ethel's newly stoned front door-steps. Maureen shivered as she went into the house; a foreboding thunderstorm seemed to be brewing. Maureen hoped it would pass; she also hoped whatever was bothering her mother would also disappear.

It had been another sweltering day. The threatened thunderstorm of the previous day had not materialised; the rain that had fallen had lasted little more than a quarter of an hour. Tonight, the September air was heavy with humidity.

The evening meal over, Ethel and Maureen had taken kitchen chairs into the back yard and were sitting just outside the back door, which they had left wide open allowing cooler air to drift inside before the night drew in. Ethel took a sip of her tea before speaking. 'Are you excited about tomorrow, pet?'

Maureen nodded, her mouth full of milk.

'Well, then, go and get yourself ready for bed. I'll be up to see you in two shakes of a lamb's tail.'

Ethel drained her mug and stood up, urging her daughter to do likewise. Carrying her chair back into the kitchen, Ethel blew out her breath, muttering about the heat: the opened door had made little difference and she was verbally thankful that they had eaten a cold supper: their ham and salad meal had left no tell-tale smells to further pollute the kitchen's sultry air.

Maureen followed her chattering mother inside, bringing the empty mugs with her. Rinsing them in the stone sink, she dawdled at the task, stalling for time.

'Shall I help you fetch the washing in off the line, Mam?' she asked.

Ethel smiled the smile of the knowing.

'Go on with you! Since when did you help with the washing? Eh? You just want to go back out there and peep into the shed, don't you, hey? Want to see if there's a three-wheeler bike in there—you little monkey. Go on; get going up them stairs. It'll be tomorrow soon enough, young lady, then your dad will be back and there'll be no more late nights for you then!' The minute she said it, she could have cut her tongue out. The look of dread that swept over Maureen's face made Ethel grow cold. She chided herself for her foolishness...*How could I have been so stupid? To start on Bill before he's even set foot over the doorstep...*

'Now then, don't look like that, love. I was only *joshing*. Your dad will spoil you rotten, for sure. Go on, then, up to bed. See you in a tick.'

But it had been said; it was out in the open, and no amount of cajolery could take it back. The unspoken fears had finally broken out—from Ethel's tongue—to across Maureen's face.

In her bedroom, Maureen slipped out of her navy and white sundress and her navy blue knickers (she hadn't worn a vest for ages, it had been so hot.) Pulling her pink cotton nightdress over her head, she tried to feel excited about her forthcoming birthday: the excitement, which had been present for days, had somehow vanished as she had made her way up the stairs.

As she settled into her bed, a little did return. She'd be seven tomorrow. And maybe it wouldn't be too bad having her dad back. Not all dads got drunk. Not all fathers shouted and took their belts off to hit their children. Her mam had told her that Bill wasn't like that. Not like that at all..."One thing I'll say for your dad..." her mother had whispered one cold night last winter, when they had stood together peeping through the white net curtains in the front bedroom, shivering in their nightgowns, as they watched Jack from the house next door throwing furniture into the street when he had come back from the pub "piss arsed," as a bruised Betty was to tell her friend the next day "...yes, Maureen," her mother had quietly confided, "there's one thing I can say about my Bill, he can hold his drink, that he can. I don't think your dad's ever been drunk. He's a better man than Jack Dwyer will *ever* be..."

Maureen remembered now the glow of pride she had felt for her absent father. Maybe if she prayed really hard tonight, her dad would come home tomorrow and make Mam smile again, like she used to.

Making herself comfortable between the cool cotton sheets, Maureen clasped her hands tightly together, shut her eyes, and prayed, with haste: she could hear her mother's tread on the stairs.

'I'm here at last, pet. Have you said your prayers?'

Maureen nodded to her mother as she wriggled down under the covers. The white cotton sheets smelled clean and fresh, and were a welcome cold against her bare arms and neck.

And then their nighttime ritual began. A few minutes they both treasured.

Ethel bent over the bed, placing a kiss on her daughter's forehead, and was pulled into a fierce embrace. They laughed together as Maureen peppered her mother's face with kisses.

With her small arms wrapped around Ethel's shoulders, Maureen wallowed in the comforting nearness of her mother, breathing in the aroma of the summer night air that had wafted in through the open window: an intoxicating mixture of mowed grass, dry earth, and bonfires. Her mother's greying fair hair was also tinged with this outdoor smell.

The child's anxieties were soothed away. Sleep beckoned. The sandman was on his way.

Pulling out of the embrace, her mother whispered in a conspiratorial manner, 'I'm just going down to fold the washing, and then I'll be up to my own bed. I need an early start in the morning, but you know what? It's clear slipped me mind *why*.'

At this, they both hugged each other again, laughing and kissing.

'Now then, get off to sleep, bugger lugs, before the sand man comes. Night, night, me love. Go to sleep now, and I'll see you in the morning...bright and early. Nos da, cariad.'

Ethel eased herself off her daughter's bed, careful not to show the pain she was feeling: the intense throb that was now a constant nag. Standing close to the door, she watched as Maureen snuggled under the cool comfort of her rose satin eiderdown, thankful for the child's ability to fall asleep almost immediately.

From behind the pink candy-striped cotton curtains, drawn against the late evening sun, noise floated in through the open window. Summer night sounds, the cause of enviable stirrings to the young children tucked up in bed against their will. Dogs barked and older children, mostly boys, usually loud and boisterous whilst playing football, muted their shouts and dusty scuffles in the age old custom of street playing, so as not to be sent to their own beds at such a demoralising, infant hour.

Closing the bedroom door softly behind her, Ethel gave way to her thoughts, her emotions. And the pain…*Dear God, what will happen to Maureen? What will Bill do? Will he learn to love her as much as I do? Will he keep her…?*

Blinded by her tears, Ethel edged her way slowly down the threadbare, faded-red carpeted stairs of her immaculately kept home, willing her mind to find an answer to the unanswerable. For weeks, Ethel had hoped the diagnosis was wrong. This morning, in the doctor's surgery, she had learnt that it was not: she was dying. How much time she had left she did not know.

What Ethel did know gave her no peace: Bill had been reluctant to adopt Maureen in the first place; he most certainly would not want to keep her now.

'Happy birthday, our *Maureen*…'

'Hip…hip…*hooray*…'

They clustered around, singing and shouting in tuneless unison: Stuart, Gerard, Barry, Bobby and Malcolm, were also tugging on Maureen's hair, a custom supposedly to count out the years celebrated, but which was being undertaken today with such an energy that the girl screamed with pain.

'Get off her, you daft clods! Any more of it, and you'll have her as bald as yer dad!' Vi Greenwood continued berating her excitable sons, 'Get yourselves into the yard and let off a bit of steam. Go on…before I *belt* the lot of yer.'

Turning to Maureen, who was rubbing her head, her eyes brimming with threatening tears, Vi said in a much softer tone, 'Sorry, lass, they don't means any harm, you know, they're just daft. Senseless! By the heck, what I'd give to have a daughter like you, me love.' Hugging her niece, Vi kissed the girl's glossy crown, enveloping her into a cuddle. Ethel's sister-in-law was immensely fond of Maureen, and had no hesitation in showing it.

'I'm telling you, Ethel, this lass is going be a corker, one day. She'll have all the lads after her then, *no* mistake.' The statement brought with it another fierce hug.

And Ethel, who was buttering bread at the kitchen table, laid down her knife and smiled warily; the concern for her daughter evident as she sought eye contact with the child: to be embraced by Vi was almost as dangerous as being attacked by her five sons. A cuddle from Vi could leave the recipient breathless.

Released at last from her aunt's ample arms, Maureen smoothed her full-skirted satin dress, timidly returning her mother's watchful smile before skipping off out to play in the back yard.

Ethel sighed as she cut and buttered more bread, relieved that all was well, for the time being, at least. Ethel was glad enough of the rapport that existed between Maureen and her Aunt Vi, indeed, she was thankful.

However, the look that had just passed between mother and daughter had said it all: Ethel's gentler ways suited Maureen's temperament best.

As Vi chatted on and on, busying herself between the kitchen and the parlour, it was this very fact which fuelled Ethel's worries even more. Maureen was suited to their quiet life. But her daughter's future welfare was soon to be in this brash woman's hands. There was nobody else to ask.

Much as Ethel loved Vi, she felt physically sick with anxiety...*maybe Vi would refuse; and what would happen to Maureen then...?* The smell from the hard-boiled egg she was shelling brought bile to the back of her throat. Wiping her hands on her floral pinny, she left the table and made her way to the open back door and took a deep gulp of air.

The sunny day was clouding a little. The vivid orange marigolds, which fringed her small patch of lawn, swayed in a gentle breeze. Vi's boys were leaping around, hiding behind dustbins, creeping round the shed: a game of *Cowboys and Indians* was in progress: Maureen was being tied to the washing-line pole.

'Maureen, love! Come in a minute, will you. I need to speak to you. Gerard...let her go, now, there's a good lad.'

Ethel was not too sure that her daughter was pleased to be rescued. As the youngsters groaned about their game being ruined, Ethel shook her head with disbelief; one way or another Maureen always seemed to avail herself for the boy's boisterous games...*Maybe things will work themselves out. Perhaps I'm worrying too much. She looks fragile, but who knows, maybe she's tougher than I give her credit for. She looks bonny today, though. The dress was worth all the hard work...Oh, Bill, please love her...please learn to love her...*Ethel fought back her thoughts and her tears as she guided Maureen indoors.

The house was filling with visitors. Ethel greeted them, sharing the banter, which always seemed present when Vi Greenwood was around. She poured lemonade shandies for the women, beer for the men, dandelion and burdock for the children, and tea for herself. Prettying the plate of egg sandwiches with thinly sliced tomatoes, she beckoned her daughter to come to the table.

'Your dad's taxi will be here in a few minutes, love, then we'll cut the cake your Aunt Vi's made, and have the tea party. Are you looking forward to seeing him? Remember what I told you to do, won't you?'

38

Moving to her mother's side, Maureen nodded in answer. Though she seemed to be listening, Ethel feared she was taking scant notice. The child picked up a piece of buttered bread and nibbled absently at the crust as though she wasn't the least bit excited or hungry; she seemed indifferent to it all.

But Ethel knew otherwise and her heart went out to her daughter, she bent to cuddle her close.

'It'll all be all right, love, you'll *see*. Now go and say hello to your Aunt Nellie. And be nice to our Gladys, too, pet.'

Idling before doing as she was told, Maureen rubbed her stomach with her free hand, whispering in a whiny voice that she had a tummy ache; she said her belly had a funny shaking inside, all squirmy like—was it because Gerard had tied her up too hard? She also told her mother that she actually felt a little sick.

But before Ethel could do much about Maureen's angst, Sid Greenwood came hollering into the house and a furore erupted around them.

'He's *here*, Eth…It's him, himself!' Sid shouted, for the fifth time no less, as he came running into the house, hitching his baggy grey trousers, which he had loosened for comfort, heedless to the braces dangling from each hip.

Vi's husband had been sitting on the front door steps, having a smoke and being the watch-out for the past hour or so, keeping out of the way, whilst the women of the family busied themselves with preparations for the party. Two other male guests, beer in hand, had joined him at his post, and they were as equally noisy with their jubilant calls of…'Bill's here!'

Now, as everyone rushed to the front of the house, the Gradys' small terraced home became jam-packed. The three up, two down house was tiny. On the ground floor, the two rooms came off the left hand side of the lobby. A steep, vertical stairway led upstairs to a back bedroom. To the left of the top stair, a short landing led to the master bedroom at the front of the house. And here, directly opposite this room, three further steps gave access to the attic room.

The downstairs front room, white distempered and darkly furnished in shades of brown, relief coming from the cherry red carpet, was known as the parlour; its doorway was positioned in close proximity to the fan-light windowed front door.

The small kitchen was at the end of the narrow, brown linoleum floored lobby, its doorway parallel with the staircase. Decorated in cheerful rose patterned wallpaper, it was the room most used. It was their living room and, though it was small, gave access to both the whitewashed back yard, and the rarely used parlour.

And it was from her position at the kitchen table that Ethel noticed, to her dismay, that Maureen had done as instructed: The ashen faced youngster sat squashed between Aunt Nellie and cousin Gladys, the latter who was Nellie's eighteen-stone teenage daughter. Looking decidedly uncomfortable, the pale-faced child seemed to have little desire to move from the tiny space she had channelled between her two portly relations.

With her heart pumping a pulse in her throat, Ethel moved quickly towards her daughter, she felt the urgent need to have her close: already a distance was growing between them. Ethel could sense it happening…and Bill had not even stepped out of the taxi…

Maureen was to always remember this day: the smell of scones baking in the oven; the parlour table, covered with the best white tablecloth, laden with jellies, fairy cakes, egg sandwiches. Bowls of salad stood on the sideboard, where a huge, honey baked ham waited to be carved; there were dishes of pungent picked onions and sliced beetroot; home-made crisps and bottles of pop…a cacophony of voices, and an excitement that tinged the very air.

The hazy afternoon sunshine filtered in through the white-netted window, haloing and soft focusing the room as if it were a stage. And then, when her father made his entrance, looking gaunt and yellowed, but taller than she had imagined, he became the star attraction.

Everyone rushed at him, except her mother and herself; they seemed detached from the scene, almost in the wings. But Maureen was aware of her father's eyes; his gaze held her transfixed…until he moved into her mother's open arms.

With the hullabaloo of Bill's arrival, Maureen thought everyone had forgotten that it was her birthday. Auntie Vi was crying, and Uncle Sid was blowing into a big white handkerchief. And their sons came running in from the back yard, barraging *Uncle Bill* with questions about how many Germans he'd killed, whilst she just sat and sat, head down, staring at her brand new, shiny black patent, ankle strapped shoes.

Then, all of a sudden, it had become quiet. Looking up, she had watched as people nudged each other out of the way so that Bill, hand in hand with her smiling mother, could come forward to stand in front of the sofa.

'Hello, Maureen…' he said, squatting down in front of her, '…did you get the bike you wanted?'

Face to face with the man who was her daddy, she stared into his gentle eyes, surprised out of her unusual sullenness by his question.

'No.' Her tongue wouldn't work properly; it seemed stuck behind her tightly closed lips.

She watched as her father looked up to her mother; they exchanged shy smiles.

'Perhaps you could step outside the front door with me, Maureen. I've got something to show you.' Standing, Bill held out his hand.

The small, slightly shabby front room, used only for special occasions and claustrophobic with all the visitors, was hushed again to silence. Maureen wriggled forward and slid as slowly as she could off the velvet cushioned sofa and, taking his proffered hand, walked with her father out of the crowded room and into the lobby towards the open front door.

The black taxicab, which Bill had arrived home in, was still in the street, its engine running. When the cabbie saw them, he opened the driver's door and jumped from his seat. The stoutly built, balding man sauntered round to the back of his vehicle, pausing to light a cigarette.

Maureen was stealing a quick, furtive glance up at her sandy haired father, when she heard her mother gasp. Turning her gaze back on to the driver, she saw that he was carrying a red and chrome three-wheeler bike.

The taxi driver swaggered towards them, puffing hard on the cigarette he held between his lips. Plonking the gleaming, black-saddled tricycle down in front of Maureen, he removed his cigarette and chortled, triumphantly, 'I believe this grand set of wheels is for you, young lady. And it's come all the way from Kent. Happy birthday, kiddo...and many of 'em.'

There followed a clamorous chorus of clapping and cheering, laughing and shouting of happy birthday and, out of the corner of her eye, Maureen saw Betty, and the look on Betty's face.

Glowing with pride, Maureen turned towards her parents to say thank you, but was startled to see that they were kissing. Kissing like they did in the films. The funny, shaking feeling that had been in her belly seemed to have dropped to her legs. But it did not stop her from climbing onto her bike and pedalling away up the cobbled street, heading towards the open spaces of Unity Park and its smooth pathways, with, to her added enjoyment, the envious Greenwood boys in hot pursuit.

'Mau...*reen*? Can I have a turn, next...?'

'Can I, after...?'

'What about *me*...?'

'No, Gerard, it's my turn, then...I'm older than you...'

'Maureen…wait for me. I've got no shoes on…wait for…me…'

And Maureen could also hear her Aunt Vi, who had also been standing outside alongside Uncle Sid, shout angrily to her sons, 'Give the girl a blooming chance, will you!'

*

3

'The little buggers; they're always showing me up...' Looking very vexed, Vi headed back into the house. Muttering to herself about the bad behaviour of her sons, she made her way into the kitchen.

Out of the blue, Vi was filled with an aching melancholy. As her eyes moistened, she bit her bottom lip. She had been so eager and excited with all the plans for Maureen's birthday and her brother's return, this sudden despondency, so unlike her, was disarming.

At twenty-eight, Violet, known to most people as Vi, thought herself to be middle aged. Married at seventeen to the first man that ever kissed her, she had been content with her lot.

Like many women, she got on with life, making the best of things. Sid wasn't a bad bloke—in fact, he was far from it. Older than her by some ten years, it had always seemed like she'd married another dad. Except for the bed bit, and that had been no burden.

Vi's lively and honest quick repartee made up for the lack of romance, and their coupled virility soon brought about her many pregnancies. With each birth her girth had widened and so had her magnanimous character.

Vi Greenwood was a mother born and bred, as a bunch of American GI.

stationed at a camp in a nearby village—whom she had fed with copious quantities of fish and chips—would eternally testify. The war years, although hard in many respects, had brought new faces and friendships into Vi's life.

This afternoon, suddenly and quite ferociously, standing arm in arm with Sid, her husband of eleven years, Vi had felt cheated. As she witnessed the homecoming of her brother, she realised romance was something she had never experienced and was caught, unaware, by an intense longing.

Yet she knew the truth of things more than others. The fact was, there had been little romance in Ethel's life, either. Ethel had been alone for over six years, raising her little girl Maureen single-handed, not knowing whether her husband was dead or alive for most of that time. It had been pity not envy Vi had felt then.

And now here I am, on today of all days, miserable and jealous of that same brave woman...

Ashamed of her thoughts, Vi hurried across to the sink, filling the kettle with water. Tossing back her bouncing mane of brunette curls, she tied a floral patterned apron around her thick waist, pitching the loathsome thoughts into a deep ditch at the back of her mind at the same time.

Vi Greenwood is an exceptional woman. And it would have surprised her to know, as she began brewing large pots of tea and crowding cups and saucers onto wooden trays, that she is thought of as quite a handsome one, too. Her long lashed wide eyes, a vivid shade of green that in some lights seem aqua, sparkle with a mirth and warmth that matches her girth. A smile romps constantly on her lips, even in anger, as right now her shouts and oaths are aimed at her retuning sons, as they come crashing back into the kitchen bemoaning the fact that they haven't even got one bike between them; her outburst is tinged with irony and grin achieving wit—the boys are soon laughing and larking around again, bikes and grievances forgotten. Sid often says that his wife's *gob* is only closed when she's asleep, and this is true, Vi doesn't know the meaning of *being quiet*. It isn't in her nature. Though some might find her brash, they would none the less accept that she is genuinely kind. Vi's personality is like an open book: no matter what time of day or night you come upon it, you can be assured of finding wholesome knowledge, coupled with humorous anecdotes; her husband, her family and friends know this and count on it. The worried, the lonely and the homesick, feel blessed to have been welcomed under its cover. But all of this is unknown to Vi; she believes herself to be an ignorant woman with little gifts.

Yet, later in life, this winsome woman will come to accept that she has the qualities and wisdom she had never even dreamed of owning. And because of theses attributes, coupled with an astute insight that as yet she has not had the need nor the absolute necessity to tap in to, Vi is already set to become Maureen Grady's lifeline. The seeds she will scatter into the girl's young mind, as she is unwittingly already doing with her sons, will take hold and germinate into strong roots. She will feed them and nurture them any which way she can.

And as the party guests sit replete, in the smoky atmosphere of the crowded front parlour, satisfied with the good food they have just devoured, and settled down with a cup of tea, a glass of beer, or in some cases, for medicinal reasons of course, a glass or two of whisky (Nellie's stomach will give her gip later, if she doesn't have a drop with a bit of water,) the children play outside: games of hopscotch, kick-ball-hide and the inevitable cowboy-style shoot-outs, the gloaming light of the coming evening making it all the more exciting,

The men folk of the party stand grouped together, their talk a little stilted—no one wanting to mention the war years that have been so wounding for Bill. Sport seems to be the topic: a new season of football already under way.

At the front door, Ethel looks to make sure Maureen is safe, and is pleased to see that the youngster has forsaken the rough and tumble business of playing with her boy cousins. Sitting on the steps leading up to their neighbour's front door, the girl is mindless of her mother, and deep in whispered conversation with her best friend, Betty.

Coming back inside, Ethel motions for Vi to follow her into the kitchen. With the door closed behind them, what they talk of is private.

With the babble of other voices, and the singing that has been initiated by Bill's tipsy eldest sister, no one really notices that the two women are missing. Until glasses need refilling, teacups topped up.

And if anyone notices that both Ethel and Vi, as they brew and serve yet more tea, seem to have been crying, no one mentions the fact. Northern people are like that: never trouble trouble until trouble troubles you. So they take their refills, their last, as no more is on offer, and the party winds down.

Maureen is shooed off to bed the minute the last revellers leave. She kisses her mother firmly, lovingly, but is a little shy with her goodnight kiss to her father.

The youngster tries to stay awake long enough for her mother to come up and tuck her in. But the battle with her eyelids is in vain. Maureen falls asleep without saying her prayers. For the first time, since she has been Ethel Grady's daughter, the nightly routine has not happened.

*

4

Sidney Greenwood suffered from a nasal problem. And the problem, when aired, usually brought with it a series of painfully bruised thighs. Bruises that would materialise over night: Bruises without apologies.

'I'm telling you, Sid, if you don't stop your snoring, once and for all, I'm out of this bed. You're like a bloody animal with all your snorting and blowing...' Vi would add pressure to her words with a swift whack to the back of his knees, using her own knee as a weapon.

Sid would sigh and toss himself over onto his right side, his body fitting the jigsaw-like hollow of the old feather mattress, his mouth tightly closed, but within seconds, as he dozed off again, the din that was ruining his wife's rest would restart, seemingly even louder than before.

Vi lay wide-awake, waiting for the pale light of dawn to invade the small bedroom. But the dawn was slow in its approach. Oblivious for once to the rasping snorts and repetitious blowing eluding from her sleeping husband, her thoughts far removed from such mundane piffle. Grief and guilt were her tormentors this hot and airless night: Grief at the grave news, whispered so quietly, as she and Ethel had washed the dishes, clearing away the debris left

by the afternoon's festivities: Guilt for the thoughts that had ensued—
thoughts that, even now, were ongoing, removing any desire for sleep.

The party to celebrate Maureen's birthday had been Vi's idea. Long
before they knew Bill would be coming home she had thought and planned
for the day. Bullying her sister-in-law she had said, "Go on Eth, don't be such
a stick in the mud, give the girl a party. I'll see to the food part; we'll sort it
between us. Go on, what do you say? One thing's for sure, we all need a bit
of cheering up."

Cheering up...Vi squirmed with the memory of her own brashness. And
with the memory came the tears. Hot tears leaked from the corners of her
eyes, seeping into her feather pillow.

'Vi...? Vi, are you crying?' Sid had woken when one of his longer than
usual snorts choked in his throat, causing him to cough. Heaving his body
over onto his left side, he propped himself up on his elbow, peering at his wife
lying by his side.

More awake now, it was obvious to Sid that something was amiss with his
wife.

Tentatively he plied her, stroking the hair away from the side of her face,
gently tucking it behind her ear, so that he could see her face more clearly.
Although Sid had the appearance of a tough, rather rough man, he was,
however, quite the opposite.

Having lost most of his dark brown hair in his late twenties, Sid looked
much older than his thirty-eight years. The years of hard labour in the
Warrington Clough coalmines had made Sid's body strong. His arms were
thick, his torso barrelled. This, coupled with his shortness, made his
movements lumbering and heavy-handed.

Yet his nature belied all of this. Sid was a tender and caring, good-natured
man, not given to outbursts of temper, nor malice. His children adored him,
and his wife, Vi, grudgingly accepted that, although he was by no means a
catch he was, nonetheless, a fair and honest man, who cared for his family to
the best of his abilities.

The only grudge Sid harboured was against the government. They had put
mining into reserve occupation at the onset of the war, denying him the right
to join one of the forces.

Further more, by 1943, when the miners' held a ballot, a ballot to draw one
man in ten to stay put in the mines, he drew that straw. The only action Sid had
seen during the entire war years was at the coalface. Vi had thought them to

be lucky; they had remained together: a family, and a useful family in many ways, yet Sid was constantly plagued with the thoughts of failure.

Now, with the war years behind them, Sid was at last beginning to see some sense in it all, and his good fortune. Perhaps he was a blessed man, after all.

So tonight, waking to the sound of his wife's sobs, he was dismayed to be so ignorant of what was troubling her.

'Here now, shush, *shush*. What's the matter, Vi? Tell me, lovey, tell me...' he stroked her shoulder, gently heeding her to turn to face him.

Vi sobbed louder. Turning over as requested, she buried her face into Sid's white vested chest.

It was Sid's turn to be distressed...*God almighty*...he thought, breaking out into a sweat...*is she pregnant again...?* He gulped at the idea...*But she can't be...I've been using the rubbers...I'll kill them bloody Yanks if they've sold me duds*...

Panicking at the mere thought of another baby, Sid continued more urgently to question his stricken wife.

'Vi, lass, come on, this is not like you, not like you at all. What's the matter, love...? How can I help, if I don't know what's wrong...?'

Vi pulled herself out of her husband's arms. Sitting up, she drew her knees up under the thin, white cotton counterpane, wiping her face with the palms of her hands. Sniffing back her tears, she tried to whisper; her words were croaky.

'Come downstairs, and I'll tell you.' With intermittent sobs, Vi threw aside the bedclothes and swung out of bed. Barefoot, she padded across the cold linoleum floor towards the door, with a bewildered Sid stumbling along after her, hastily pulling on his long white underpants. At the bedroom door, she turned, hushing him with a finger to her lips.

Quietly, he tiptoed behind his wife down the narrow landing, past the bedrooms of their sleeping sons, and down the steep wooden stairs that led straight into the kitchen of the old, stone built cottage. The cottage they had lived in all of their married life, rented from the colliery owner and badly in need of renovation.

Secretly, Sid had approached his boss in view of buying the house, but as yet, had not secured the deal he was seeking. He had the idea to surprise Vi, although in reality, he was finding it all a little too difficult to keep to himself. He did not have the way with words that Vi seemed to possess. Mainly, Sid was terrified of doing the wrong thing. Of paying too much for the run-down property and annihilating Vi instead of gaining her applause and greatly needed respect.

Closing the stairway door behind him, Sid looked anxiously at his wife, as she stood close to the well-scrubbed table that took precedence in their small kitchen. Vi looked a ghostly figure in her long, white nightgown, eerily silhouetted by the light of a full moon that shone in through the net curtained window. Her appearance unnerved Sid even further.

'Vi…for *God's* sake! What is it?' He moved towards her, pulling her into his arms.

'Aw, Sid, it's so awful. It's rotten. So unfair…After all this time…' She choked on her tears, burying her head into Sid's chest.

'What…*is*…?' Sid almost bellowed, his patience wearing thinner by the second. Holding her tousled head between his two massive hands, he lifted her face to his, asking her again, more gently this time, 'Come on, Vi. Enough's enough, now…you're frightening me, tell me what it is, love, what you're going on about…'

Vi sniffed hard, brushing at the tears on her cheeks with the back of her left hand. 'It's poor Ethel,' she said, softly. Taking a deep shuddering breath, she continued to speak through her tears, 'Sid, she told me something…something *awful*. Aw, Sid…she's dying: Ethel's dying. And I was jealous of her! This afternoon, I was so *jealous*. I'm rotten…a rotten person…'

For a long moment they stood in silence, save for Vi's sobs, each steeped in their own thoughts.

Sid had been overwhelmed by the drama of Bill's homecoming—in truth, he too had felt resentment: envy he was totally ashamed of the minute it raised its ugly head. He had spent the remainder of the day doing his best to accommodate and entertain the jubilant family, gathered together to celebrate Bill's return and Maureen's birthday.

Not quite believing what he'd heard, yet knowing it to be the truth as Ethel's severe weight loss came to mind, Sid gently pushed his wife aside, skirted the table and moved across the kitchen.

At the window he drew back the snow-white net curtains (which they had hung with such delight a few weeks previously in place of the grim black-out material,) and looked out. The night sky was high and black, the moon round and radiant.

Sid stared out onto the small plot of land that at one time had been a paved yard. Now, row after row of vegetables graced the small area. Vegetables he had begrudgingly planted, yet proudly harvested.

Sid had come to realise his worth during the interminable war years: A miner by day, a farmer by night. Each had its own merit. Each he was good at. Each fed and supported his family and, in doing so, helped Sid keep some respect for himself, even though he was not given the chance to fight for his country. At least he could, indeed he did, feed his fellow men. His war had been the war of the land. And he had won it, valiantly.

Turning his back to the window, he looked over to where Vi stood, and spoke quietly.

'Come here, love, come on.' Holding out his arms, he beckoned her close.

Vi rushed at him, and he was pulled into a tight embrace as her arms fiercely circled his hard buttocks, her mouth and lips meeting his.

Passion flamed between them, surging and soaring, as they kissed and caressed. The urgency of his feelings for Vi, and hers for him, took Sid by surprise. Guilt was somewhere at the back of his mind, but he had no trouble ignoring it with his wife's warm soft body under his hands.

'Come to bed, Vi. Oh, God, I love you *so* much. I don't know what I'd do without you...' Sid groaned into her hair, the very thought of losing her too much to bear.

Their united grief had brought about a mutual desire. It exploded from them both, sizzling the cool, early morning air.

Clasping, touching and tasting they mounted the steep stairs that led back to their bedroom, a sweeping erotic urgency putting aside all other thoughts.

Tumbling onto the dishevelled bed, they made love: fiercely, seeking, probing, gaspingly. Love like they had never made before, ardent and demanding, without care, wanton.

Entering her, Sid cried out his love, his need and was matched, move for move, word for word by his yielding wife; they found the rhythm, the passionate abandonment their marriage had been lacking. They became lovers.

Replete and now still, they lay in silence; though neither was sleeping. Sid spoke in a whisper, 'Vi? Are you okay? I didn't hurt you, did I?'

'No, Sid,' she touched his stubbly chin, answering in the same whisper, she too seemingly reluctant to break the aura that surrounded them.

The slight memory that his unshaved face had chaffed her cheeks brought a warm glow of embarrassment to Sid's own.

But Vi was convincing when she said, again, and more forcibly, kissing his scratchy jaw line as she spoke, 'No, love, you didn't hurt me. It was *wonderful*. I feel different—special. Do you?'

Sid snuggled closer, experiencing, for the first time in his marriage, his wife's reverence for him. A respect he was going to ensure of its continuation…

'I feel what I've always known. I love you, Violet Greenwood…mother of me five lads…mother of all love! You are *special*. And I'm going to show you. By *God* I am. It's took a long time in coming…but I'm going to show you what life can be like. If Ethel needs us, so be it. We'll manage. We've managed before and we'll manage again. Only better this time. You tell Eth that I knows what's worrying her—it's Bill. And if he don't want the little 'un, we'll have her. We had her during the blitz; we'll have her anytime; she's a good kid, is Maureen.'

As the birds began to bid each other good morning, the September dawn crept into the bedroom. And Sid's snoring was as loud as ever. Vi sighed at the cacophony, slowly shaking her head with resignation before turning onto her side: some things would never change.

But as images formed behind her closed eyes, as she drifted into a blissful sleep, she hoped that one thing would: Vi had longed for a daughter. With each birth she had wished for a girl, to no avail…*I love my lads…but a girl…Dear God, I'll do right by Maureen, if it comes to it…Yes, that I will. She'll think she's a princess. Poor Ethel…not to see her grow-up…* And with these compassionate prayers and pledges, Vi slept.

When at last the boys had been fed, dressed and shooed off out to play, Vi made two mugs of tea and walked down the path that led off from the back of their garden, a path that wound its way to the allotments.

'Morning, Vi,' Percy Fielding grinned his toothless salutation at Vi. The Greenwood's elderly next-door neighbour, glad of a moment's breather from his digging, obviously fancied a chat, 'it's a bonny day, again. I see your Sid been at it since the crack of dawn…'

Vi, knowing what Percy meant, smiled mischievously as she continued to walk past the man whilst giving her double-edged reply, 'Aye, he's been at it since the crack of dawn…and digging as well. He'll be in need of this cuppa, make no mistake.'

Sid grinned sheepishly at his wife as she handed him his steaming tea.

'Yer a cheeky bugger, Vi,' he mumbled, embarrassed, yet not mastering the fact that he was eye sparklingly proud of her quick witted humour; his face and mannerism showing clearly that she never failed to stun him, one way or another.

Vi laughed with delight at his discomfiture; she plonked herself down on an upturned wooden water barrel and continued to banter.

'Aw, stop fretting! Percy doesn't know what day it is, never mind out else. Blimey, it's hot out here!' She took a deep breath, lifting her head to savour the clear blue sky and the sweet smell that was all around her.

Vegetables were the allotments mainstay, although one or two of their neighbours grew flowers and plants. Sid had planted honeysuckle, which weaved itself into copious quantities around the gate area of their own, small garden, knowing that Vi found it to be one of the best fragrances in the world.

'Your dinner will be ready in half an hour or so. Do you think we should go back to Ethel's? I mean after the boys have been to Sunday school, Sid. Not to stay or owt, just to sort of *be there*?'

'Aye all right then; move yourself over a bit,' he said good-naturedly, nudging her, hip to hip, to sit down beside her.

Sipping his tea, Sid surveyed his handy work. He had been working on the allotment since they'd finished breakfast, save for an hour or so, and had completed numerous tasks.

'We'll have to do something about the rabbits from the fields yonder...' he laughed, elbowing her in the ribs, '...else they'll soon be better fed than you are!'

Vi joined in with banter, saying that he wasn't such a Slim-Jim, but there was a hurt in her eyes that Sid didn't seem to notice as they moved on to plan the afternoon's outing.

Sid Greenwood wasn't a man to help with housework. A woman's work was a woman's work was the way he saw it. Nevertheless, most Sundays it was he who washed the dishes after their roast lunch.

Today, as he cleared the plates from the table, he joked and jostled with his sons before putting a question to them...

'Fancy another trip to your Aunt Ethel's house this afternoon, lads?'

'Yeah. *Yeah!*' they shouted gleefully, clattering up the stairs to put on their best suits—for the second time in two days. The Greenwood boys felt very grown-up in their soft grey wool suits, even though they soon became much too hot and uncomfortable in the tight, badly made knee length pants. This discomfort was coupled with their mother's constant chastising: a lot of wriggling and fidgeting with their bottoms went on as they tried to ease the uneven seams into place, for Vi was blissfully unaware of her lack of expertise on the subject of sewing.

Indeed Vi was proud and delighted that she could turn her boys out well for Sunday School, making the little suits herself from the grey woollen blankets that she had willingly and gratefully accepted off the American boys: homesick young service men (General Infantry) who had found Sunday happiness, and the family life they were missing, within the Greenwoods' crowded front room: they brought the tinned peaches, Vi and her brood gave them the bantering and jollities that made up for the loss of home and sunshine.

Sunshine that the young men had taken for granted in the country were the peaches grew to ripe perfection: where every home had food in its larder and lights on its streets. A few blankets were neither here nor there, in comparison to a taste of the home life they were missing.

The youngsters were ready to go to Sunday school. One by one Vi knotted her sons' ties, tucked in their shirts and buttoned their jackets. Flicking a comb through their hair she instructed them of her wishes.

'Now be good lads for Miss Grayson. Do you hear me, our Gerard? You in particular! Afterwards we're getting the bus back to Ethel's. Dad and I need to have a little talk with your Auntie…and we're going to drop you all at our Nellie's place.'

At this news, the youngsters groaned.

'Now stop that! When we've finished at Ethel's, we're going take you all to the chip shop. Sit down, like…tea inside, I mean. Would you like that? We'll take Maureen, too.'

The boys cheered and ran around the house, shouting to their dad, pushing and pummelling each other in their delight.

Vi, happy at her sons' enthusiasm and thankful, for the moment, for her own blessings, propelled them one by one out of the front door and into the sunshine, watching them as they sauntered down the lane towards the village and the church hall: Gerard, eight years old and the most mischievous, held the hand of his toddler brother, Malcolm. Both of these boys had inherited their father's thin dark brown hair.

Sandy haired Stuart, taller and sturdier than most ten year olds, aimlessly scuffed his shoes in the dusty gutter as he ambled along, reluctant to spend the afternoon under the watchful eye of his Sunday school teacher when he could be playing football, like his friend Trevor, whose mother didn't fuss about going to church, or Sunday school.

Barry and Bobby, the identical, blond haired, six year old twins, squatted down for one last quick game of marbles, before they heard their mother call out to them, 'Get a move on, else they'd be late...'

Vi, content that the lads had finally taken heed and had dashed off in the direction of the church hall, didn't feel as content about her husband. Sid's remarks had hurt this morning. Though Vi would be the first to say that she was getting fat, it was another matter all together for Sid to keep rubbing it in. His joking had gone a bit far.

Vi knew she was too heavy; her weight had ballooned considerably since her pregnancy with Malcolm. It had taken her waist from a slightly large twenty-eight inches, to the immense girth of thirty-four. The morning's lovemaking had made her resolute to diet. A quiet resolution, which she knew she would keep to...*And besides*...she thought to herself, as she made her way indoors...*what's a bit of weight compared to what Ethel must be going through...? Unless, of course, the morning's antics have left me pregnant, again*...

Dampened by the fleeting nag of doubt, Vi swiftly removed it from the front of her mind in her usual fashion.

Vi worried only when necessary. A wonderful gift, that one day she would come to bless.

Returning to the kitchen, her thoughts and words were very much fastened on Ethel's needs, 'Listen, Sid, Ethel doesn't want Maureen to know she's adopted. She wants us to promise, like. Promise *never* to tell her. She thinks it's going to be bad enough not having a mam, without knowing she's adopted, and all.'

Sid had known his wife would come back inside the house in a worried frame of mind. Still working at the sink, he gazed out through the window at the rows of vegetables he had hoed so diligently before being called inside for lunch. There had been much more to be done, but he'd known better than to keep his wife's food waiting.

'Aye, and she's right. It's going to be hard on the girl. Poor kid!' He turned to look at his wife, reaching for the tea towel to wipe his hands.

'Hey, love, come here. I want to show you something. Look, come and have a decko at the shed...' his attention back on the window, he beckoned his wife to his side.

Crossing the kitchen with a weary sigh on her breath, Vi picked up the discarded tea towel in readiness to wipe the stack of pots, her body language showing that she was not the least bit interested in Sid's gardening *witterings*.

But when Sid put his arm across her shoulders, and tugged aside the net curtains to gain her a better view, she seemed to pay some attention: she too gazed to the left, to where the lopsided shed leaned adjacent to the back door (it was a nailed together series of planks and off-cuts of timber under a tarpaulin roof structure, a complete and utter eyesore that had always been far more hazardous than useful,) and, after taking a sideways sneaking glance at Sid's beaming face, she let out another long sigh.

Sid felt her body go tense under the weight of his arm and realised that his wife wasn't at all in the mood to listen to what she called his "barm-pot schemes." But ignoring the signals, and the sigh, he said, 'Can you see it, love, the shed?' Now he really knew that he'd lost her attention, especially when she shrugged out of his embrace. *Well, it was a bit daft, asking her if she could see the blooming shed...*he conceded inwardly. So he tried again. Quickly he went on, 'Well, aye, of course you can see it! But listen, love, it'll soon be knocked down. Yes, I'm going to build a lean-to...another room. And above it, a bathroom; can't have a growing lass in the house without a bathroom; and a room of her own...'

Vi, who'd already begun her plate-drying task, stilled her hands as she stared in a blatant horror at her grinning husband.

Sid knew he'd got her attention now, and was tickled—he could get used to this. But when the look became a head-shaking act of disdain, the smug feeling almost deserted him. But he went on, now in full flow and more than eager to inveigle Vi with his ambitions.

'You see, love, I was going to just build a bathroom onto the back kitchen, like, but now, if little Maureen's coming, I'm going to go up as well!'

'Who said you can, cloth-head?' Vi had made light work of the pile of dishes; she had begun on the cutlery, 'Sid, don't start on all that again, for crying out loud! It won't be happening. Not with your gaffer. He won't spend a blooming penny on this old house, and you bloody well knows it!' Vi banged the knife and fork drawer shut as a finale to the conversation.

Having also finished at the sink, Sid rolled down his sleeves and, moving with what he hoped was nonchalance, pulled a chair from the table and eased himself down onto it. Seated, he reached into his trouser pocket for his cigarettes, seemingly content for Vi to have the last word. Striking a match, he lit a cigarette and slowly puffed, letting the smoke rise long enough to hide his growing mirth: try as he might to be fair, he was enjoying this.

It was more than obvious that Vi was getting into a stew—crashing and clanging the pans about, as she sought space for them in the crowded cupboard under the sink, she even swore once or twice.

Waiting for her to finish, Sid inhaled again, enjoying his smoke, knowing his wife was getting even more het up by his silence.

When she was stilled from her storing, stationed with her back to the sink, her arms tightly folded across her chest, her face set for an argument, he picked his words with care.

'You're wrong this time, me love. And this time you're wrong by a *long* shot. I'll say whether we can spend a blooming penny or a pound. Or even a few hundred pounds! You see, Vi, I'll say it again...*I* said we can. Me! This time next week, the house will be mine...in *my* name. I'm buying it. I called into the gaffer's this morning. Struck whilst the iron was hot...Aye, once I'd made me mind up, there was no stopping me! So you see, love, it's up to me what I build...and *when*...and *how*...'

Sid was to always remember the incredulous look that swept Vi's face that sunny, Sunday afternoon in the late summer of 1946. The day he really became her man: the love of her life.

*

5

As Bill stepped from the train, an icy blast of cold November wind whipped the squally rain into his face and he gasped as the force took his breath away.

Huddling his chin deep into the collar of his overcoat, he hurried down the platform towards the exit, battling against the gusts of wind which threatened to take his trilby in the manner it had taken his breath, wishing that he could be somewhere, anywhere else, rather than Warrington Clough.

The journey itself lay behind him like an unremembered dream. If only it could have been just that. A dream: A tortuous nightmare to be released from upon waking. But then, apart from a few short months, the last few years had been a nightmare. But it had been a nightmare with hope. Now he was without that hope, he was finished.

Ethel. Ethel. Ethel...he repeated his wife's name over and over, step for step, as he made his way towards his sister's house, head down against the fierce gale, his mind jogging her name to the beat of his feet as they pounded the grey, wet pavement.

It was a game. A mind game he had devised in the prison camp: Changi Prison Camp, Singapore: where repeating the chant had kept him sane.

Five years of hell. A hell he had managed to live through helped by his strength of mind, and his dreams. Dreams that came to fruition the day he came home to Ethel and the little one, Maureen.

The five years had been intolerable. When his ship, a flagship of the Eastern Fleet, was torpedoed, he had thought his days over. Many times, later on, throughout the ensuing long years, he had fretfully, yet guiltily wished that to have been so, for to have been rescued by the Japanese turned out to be nearly as dire as to have perished in the bombardment.

The endlessly long days of incarceration, that were filled with pain-wracked hours, made worse with the harrowing sounds of tortured screams and the constant wails of his companions, treated like animals awaiting the abattoir, had made the task of surviving almost intolerable: The heat and the vicious bouts of malaria nearly costing him his sanity.

Before his internment, Bill had been promoted to Petty Officer; he'd been proud and excited to be in the thick of it. Yet December 10th, 1941 was the first and last time he ever used his new rank: both his ship and one other were sunk in Singapore harbour.

Of the six hundred taken from the sea, he was of the number rescued by the Japanese, captured and held prisoner until 1945. When he was finally liberated, he had become a ragged and skeletal reminder of the savage, wasted years.

Then, like many others, he had undergone several months of rehabilitation before being re-united with his family. The family that had kept him going; kept his spirit strong; thankfully knowing—only too well—that Ethel had been right all along: he had a daughter as well as a wife waiting for him at home.

And how he had yearned for that day. And when it had come, he had not been disappointed. But Ethel had looked different; something about her had changed. She was certainly softer spoken, older looking than her years, slimmer and...

Now he knew what that other difference was. Illness. Pain had etched deep into her features. Perhaps it had gone unnoticed by those who had seen her daily, weekly. But it had been there, and he had seen it from that first day.

Nevertheless he had shrugged it off, dismissed his niggling fears, content to enjoy his homecoming; wallowing in the comfort of being in a house: his home. A home that was not quite as quiet as he had remembered it. Not that Maureen was rowdy child. In fact, she was quite the opposite. Her huge blue eyes had followed him for days, watching and waiting. Waiting for the years to melt away. The years he had not been her father.

But then, just about the same time as Ethel had told him her grave news, Maureen had become more natural in his presence.

And it was then that he had to send her away. Away from the wasting illness that was wrecking Ethel. Wrecking and reeking havoc on their yearned for new start in life.

Reaching 87 Parkegate Lane, Bill stood motionless at its scuffed and dilapidated wooden front door. He stood for more than a minute before he knocked. In truth, he needed far more time to collect his thoughts, but time was not his for the taking. It had to be done. Besides, it was expected. The news he brought had been looming for over two weeks—two long drawn out weeks of absolute agony, of torment for Ethel; her pitiful whimpering, as tender hands administered her medication, had been harrowing to hear; her skeletal limbs had seemed ready to disintegrate whenever she was moved, her very breath adding further misery, crushing her fragile body.

Now it was over. Ethel was at last at peace; free from pain. Now he was suffering the full pelt of agony, the throes of grief, its merciless onslaught knowing no end. Everywhere he looked, people seemed so robust, so healthy, while he himself was submerged into the feeling that he was also afflicted by Ethel's grave illness.

Pulling himself and his thoughts together, as best he could, Bill rapped on the front door of his sister's house. Three times he hammered on the door. From inside he could hear squeals and shrieks followed by Vi's raised voice.

'I'm coming…I'm *coming*. Bloody kids! Can't hear a blooming thing with all their racket…' Vi opened the door, whilst at the same time scooping the wailing, runny nosed toddler, Malcolm, into her arms, 'shush, son, *shush*…let's see who's at the door, eh?'

Even when events are inevitable, the actuality, when it happens, is very different.

'Aw, Bill, love, come in. *Come in*. Oh, my God…Oh, *no*.'

Bill's haggard looks said it all, his face as grey as the trilby he wore on his head, his thin body seemed to have shrunk under the sodden grey gabardine coat. By his very presence at his sister's door, it was patently obvious that Ethel was dead.

Led down the narrow dimly lit lobby by his grieving sister, Bill entered the hot kitchen to be surrounded by clutching, sticky hands and a huddle of glowing children's faces. The air was thick with the smell of frying onions, and this, coupled with the intense heat, made him feel faint.

'Stuart!' Vi commanded her son, 'take them all next door, to Auntie Flo's...*Go on*...now, lad, now!' The look Vi gave her eldest son belied the harshness of her words. Stuart, older in many ways than his eleven years, understood at once and cast a pitying glance in his uncle's direction.

'All right, Mam; come on, you lot! You can take your crayons with you. Come on, I'll help you. *Mam*...? As our Maureen got to come too?'

They all looked towards the table where Maureen sat, crayon in hand, head down, intently colouring a picture of a clown.

Never lifting her hand from the paper, the girl continued her colouring with earnest, as though the talk was of somebody else. Only the stiffness of her back, and her lack of interest in the entrance of their visitor to show that she also knew what had happened.

'Maureen? Maureen, love, be a good girl and go with the others, will you? That's it...Good girl. You can take all your books and colouring sticks. That's right, Stuart, get their coats. It's chucking it down out there. Be quick, now. Go through the hole in the fence. Flo'll know why you are all there. Don't worry, go on, get going. See yer all a little later. And be good!'

Inwardly, Vi blessed her eldest son...*I'll make it up to him some day. Make up for all the hard work I put upon his young shoulders...*

Vi had been the youngest of her own siblings. Nellie was the eldest followed by Harry, then Bill. She could hardly remember Harry. He had died of diphtheria at the age of thirteen. The look Stuart sometimes wore on his face, like he had this afternoon, put her in mind of Nellie...*Poor Nellie...*Vi remembered that her sister had been both mother and father to them all for as long as she could remember. Their real father had died in the nineteen-twenties and their mother's death followed very shortly after that. Then Nellie had worked, slaved almost, to keep the family together and out of the workhouse. Worry lines had creased her face, making her older than her years.

And Nellie's luck had not improved: agreeing to become a widower's wife, she had suffered the trials of a bad marriage, brought to a head by the birth of their mentally and physically handicapped daughter, Gladys.

Frank Birch, Nellie's husband, flew the marital home soon after this event, never to be seen or heard from again.

*Stuart, Nellie...deserting husbands...*Vi realised she was letting herself think about anything rather than what was to come. But what could she do now? And what could she say...

Closing the back door on the exit of her noisy brood, Vi leant against it, burying her face in her hands: there was nothing she could do—and nothing she could say.

Bill eased himself out of the comforting fireside armchair with some reluctance. His face drained of any colour, he moved with a kind of reticence towards his sobbing sister, persuading her, with a grip to her elbow, a mild tug of direction, to take a seat at the kitchen table. Sitting down beside her, he let her cry. He said nothing. Vi's crying raised no emotion from him and so he sat, passive, now, to anything or anybody.

Finally, when the worst of her crying was over, Vi apologised, 'Aw, Bill, I'm sorry. I didn't know I'd take it so hard. I should be comforting you.'

'There's nothing you can do, Vi. Nothing anyone can do to make it better. She's gone.'

'You'll stay the night, Bill? We can put you up in the front room. I'll go and settle that, now—then I'll carry on with the supper. You must be starving...no, I suppose you're not. Bill, oh listen our Bill, I don't know what I'm saying half the time. I'm all of a *dither*. When did she go, love? Was it last night? This morning?'

They talked for more than half an hour. In between sobs, eventually mutual from them both, Bill told his sister of his wife's final hours. Ethel had died at nine in the morning, the day after Armistice Day.

'I thought she would have gone on the eleventh, each breath sounded like her last; but she hung on. How she did it, I'll never know. They said she weighed about four and a half stone. That's why I didn't let Maureen see her, these last couple of weeks. It broke Eth's heart, though, it really did. And I've promised her, Vi. Promised her...Maureen's *never* to know she's adopted, like. Never. Ethel made me swear to that. She wants for you to have her, you know that, don't you?'

Vi nodded, reaching across the tea-stained green clothed table, she took his hand into her own as she listened to him.

'You see, Vi, *I'd* be no good for her. What can I give her? What a mess...What a bloody, stupid...' he shook his head, 'we should never have taken her on in the first place!'

'Now come on, Bill, you don't mean that at all! This is just grief talking...Maureen's been a joy to Ethel. And to you, if I'm not mistaken.'

Bill conceded with a wan smile. 'I'm sorry, our Vi, I really am, lass. No, you're right, I don't blame Maureen one little bit for what's happened. It's what's going happen to *her* that bothers me so much...You can't manage with her, can you? Not permanently, like, not with all you've got already?'

But Vi shook her head, patting his hand to empathize her words.

'Bill, how many times have we to tell you! We love having Maureen! She's a doll. The lads love her too. Mind, you won't hear them telling her that...'

They both laughed a little.

'Anyroads, Bill, get your coat back on, and I'll take you outside to the back. You can see for yourself how ready we are to have Maureen. Come on, come and see what his lordship's been up to. It's a blooming mess, but he works at it every available minute. Say's it'll be ready by the spring.'

As Vi opened the back door, the gusting November wind came as a welcome relief from the charged atmosphere of the hot kitchen.

Huddled together, both without their coats after all, Bill and Vi surveyed the rubble and heaps of sand and stone chippings, piled up against the back wall of the cottage. Silhouetted by the bright moon, the foundations of the new bathroom looked like a disused quarry.

'He promises me faithfully that it will be a treat when it's finished. Looks more like a bombsite at the moment though, don't you think, Bill?'

And they both couldn't help but laugh again.

There was one thing that could be said for Sid Greenwood: he made people see the funny side of life albeit through his own, painfully hard endeavours, efforts that should not really be laughed about. But if Sid had been with them, it wouldn't have taken him too long to join in the laughter, even at his own expense.

'I suppose it'll be finished one fine day. Are you coming into Flo's with me, Bill? I think she's been tortured long enough, don't you?' Linking her arm through his, she leant close, planting a kiss on his cold cheek. 'Never mind, love,' she said reassuringly... 'I'll go myself. But think on! Ethel would be pleased to see you laugh a little. You go back inside, I'll get the kids. They'll be starving, it must be all of seven o'clock and they've had no tea. They'll have the blooming welfare after me...'

Later, when all the children were tucked up in their beds, Vi settled Bill onto the red moquette settee in the parlour: His bedroom for the night.

'I think you'll be all right in here,' Vi said, as she came back into the parlour, a mug of steaming cocoa in her hand. 'Here you are, pet, get this down your throat. I'll bank the fire up so you'll not feel the cold. We don't make a fire in here too often. Still, there's plenty of blankets, and an hot water bottle. Night, night, Bill. Sid'll be back soon, so I'll just wait up for him, in the kitchen, like. If you can't settle, make yourself a cup a tea. You'll be all right, won't you…?'

Vi was tired to the bone. She wanted him to agree with her. To agree he was settled and out of her way for the night, at least. It had been a long evening. None of the children had behaved themselves, including both Stuart and Maureen. Fretful at being sent to their elderly neighbours, and angry and hungry they had, one by one, voiced their objections; arguing, moaning and whining about one thing and or another. Then to crown it all, Maureen had refused to get into the bed she shared with Malcolm.

For three months Maureen had slept quite happily, contentedly sharing a single bed with her youngest cousin. Topping and tailing, they'd squealed with delight each bedtime. Now, tonight, Maureen was snug as a bug, curled up in the middle of the big, soft double bed her aunt and uncle slept in. There would be little chance of a quiet word with Sid when he came back from work: she would have to stay downstairs until he came home.

Defeated by the collaboration of events, Vi poked at the blaze burning in the grate of the fireplace in the kitchen, then sat sipping her own cocoa and awaiting her husband, battling with her eyelids in their efforts to close. Ethel's death had made her fearful for her own future. You could never be sure just what was waiting round the corner. And her brother's own ill health and depression alarmed her more than she had let show. But then, she thought, what could she expect? She needed Sid…Needed his support. Needed his strength… *Why oh why did he have to be on late shift today of all days…?*

Bill lay awake long into the night. At first he had dozed, to be woken abruptly by the slam of a door and the blasphemous, loudly whispered profanities uttered by Sid, as he came into the house and tripped over something in the darkness of the small hallway.

Then the constant murmuring of his sister's voice, coupled with the louder but indistinct replies of her husband, left him fraught and uptight.

Because he was still extremely thin he could find no comfort for his body on the hard settee that was his bed for the night; he remained wide-eyed with fatigue. Not only did his body feel sore, his eyes and, even more so, his brain felt fuzzy and red rimmed with the horrors of what he had been through and with the fear of what was to come. For Bill knew for sure that his own days were numbered.

In the small hours, his hosts had eventually crept up the back stairs to their own bed and the house was finally silent.

Bill's only companion was the crackle of the fire in the black grate as the red-hot coals disintegrated, falling into the ash pan below.

His thoughts wandered to the bedroom above him and he pictured the scene: Vi and Sid, both plump and healthy, strong of limb and strong of mind, with Maureen nestled, cocooned between them, warm and safe.

Tears of pity, pity for himself, unleashed a terrible anger from deep within him: resentment, jealousy, and rage—an anger fiercer than he would have thought possible, mounted and surged, flooding his senses with its bitter bile.

Finally, the tears and emotion took their toll; a fitful sleep followed for what was left of the long winter night.

*

6

Joan Bellingham glared across the classroom until her grey, rheumy eyes focused on the face of Maureen Grady.

Maureen wriggled uncomfortably on her wooden chair, knowing what was going to happen next, and dreading it.

'Maureen, perhaps you can enlighten this *heathen* bunch. Can you tell me what relation John the Baptist was to our Lord Jesus?' There was ice in the teacher's tone.

'Please, Miss Bellingham, he was his cousin.' Maureen's voice was low, although confident in reply.

'It would appear to me that Maureen Grady is the only person in this class who has a brain. But I'm afraid that she cannot carry on being the brain and the month piece for the rest of you. Every one of you, with the exception of Maureen, can write out two hundred lines...*I Must Listen To Miss Bellingham When I Am In Her Class*...Maybe then you will not be so content to sit and idle away this lesson, again. Now, get on with it, and watch your spellings, or else it will be five hundred!'

On the other side of the classroom, Gerard Greenwood also wriggled uncomfortably in his seat. Gerard had always enjoyed school...before. Before Maureen had come into his classroom and wrecked his life.

Although Maureen was younger than her cousin, her abilities and intelligence had earned her entry into the grade above: Gerard's class.

Prior to Maureen's arrival, Gerard had been a popular lad both with the girls and the boys. Now, his young life was plagued. Plagued with pity and something akin to love for Maureen, and a growing dread of coming to school.

Gerard knew it wasn't Maureen's fault that she was brighter than the whole class put together, but that had not stopped him from begging her to get a few things wrong, now and again.

Sighing, overcome with the misery of his school life, Gerard noted his cousin's life was not that much better: Beryl Wadson, who sat directly behind Maureen in the crowded classroom, was seeking revenge.

Gerard winced as Maureen's long plait of glossy black hair was violently yanked, firmly grasped between the grubby, nail bitten hands of the bullying Beryl. And as Maureen's head jerked backwards allowing Beryl to whisper into her victim's ear, he groaned, knowing what was to come.

'Mam! *Mam?* ' Gerard yelled as he opened the back door, and trooped into the kitchen with the wounded Maureen by his side.

Bobby and Barry, seated at the table, piecing together a jigsaw whilst enjoying a shared slice of hot buttered toast, gasped in awe at the sorry sight before them.

'Aw, Maureen! Who did that to you? Have you been beaten up? Did the gang get you?' The questions tumbled from their lips.

Vi, coming into the kitchen from the stairway, arms full with dirty clothing, bent to retrieve a sock that had fallen from the bundle. It was as she straightened that she suffered the shock.

'Oh...my...God!' Her outcry loosened the hold she had on the rest of the dirty washing causing it to tumble to the floor. Treading over it, she rushed at Maureen, 'Come here, me pet. Let's take a look. Who's done this to you? Who's done it, hey?' Vi turned to her son, 'Why didn't you look after her, our Gerard? I've told you till I'm *blue* in the face to look after her, haven't I?' Wrapping her arms around her niece, Vi pulled the girl into a tight embrace whilst admonishing her son, glaring her disapproval as Gerard protested his innocence.

'Don't blame me, Mam, it's her own blooming fault! Clever clogs here got us all in trouble with teacher. I *knew* they'd clobber her. Can I get me toast?'

'Never mind your toast! Why didn't you stop them, eh? A big strapping lad like yourself...' Tut-tutting, Vi turned her attention back to Maureen's face and the bruising that was fast forming around the girl's right eye.

'Come to the sink, and let's bathe your eye. It'll be a right shiner before the night's out, and no mistake...'

'I wouldn't worry too much about *Maureen's* eye, Mam, you should see Beryl's...' In the ensuing commotion, Stuart had also entered the kitchen. Grinning, he continued to inform his indignant mother, 'Right little tiger is this one, Mam. I wouldn't be worrying about having our Gerard look after her...' he tousled his younger brother's hair, 'from now on I think it's best *she* looks after him.'

Vi looked from one son to the other, taking in the news Stuart had just proffered.

In the stunned silence that followed, the boys watched Maureen's bottom lip begin to tremble, as she was slowly released from her aunt's grip: now it would be her turn to suffer their mother's wrath.

But they were wrong. Vi let out a bellow of laughter, which rang through the kitchen and out into the small back yard, assailing the ears of five-year-old Malcolm Greenwood as he sat whimpering on the floor of the new bathroom.

Malcolm was locked in. Try as he might he could not get the bathroom door to open. For well over ten minutes he had banged and thumped on the door, shouting for his mother to no avail.

Now, defeated, he sat on the cold, red lino, his bare knees tucked under his chin, quietly sobbing as he wiped his runny nose on the hem of his grey school jumper.

Malcolm Greenwood hated his dad. Hated him for making his young life miserable. The bathroom door always stuck, and nobody ever heard him when he called for help; he'd nearly missed his tea last night because of the daft door. When his mam had finally rescued him, his dad had just laughed.

And his brothers, they didn't care what happened to him, either; they called him "a whinging cry-baby..." or "Malcolm has to have his mum to wipe his bum..." they chanted, singsong fashion, whenever he got stuck in the lavatory, which sadly seemed to be every day of the week.

Malcolm thought it wasn't fair to be called names, because it wasn't true—he'd been going to the toilet on his own for years: And it was all his father's fault, his mother said so. His mam hated the "damn, bleeding place," too…Malcolm had also heard her telling his dad he should have "left well alone."

As Malcolm sat whining, he wished that his dad had left things as they were. He used to enjoy using the old outside toilet with its stable door. He had been able to watch the sky, count the stars. Sometimes, especially in the summer, he had sat for ages, picking the scabs off his knees, or looking at his comics. But all that was in the past—now that they had a posh bathroom.

The new bathroom, which should have taken pride of place was, in actuality, a disaster. The bath leaked, (Sid had accidentally made a small hole in the enamel when he was plumbing it in.) To flush the toilet was a performance. You had to stand on the lavatory seat to reach into the cistern and manhandle the ball cock into place, before you could pull the chain. And, as the cistern was far too high for Malcolm to reach, the youngster had to call for his mother's assistance. Assistance that she never gave quietly, always asking him, "Do you *really* need to go—right this minute?"

Now, as he lay on his back and kicked at the door, Malcolm thought that his father was the most stupid person in the world. You still had to go outside when you needed to use the toilet and, even worse, you had to go outside to have a bath. Gone were his childhood days of splashing in the tin-bath in front of a roaring fire in the kitchen. Malcolm's tears were tinged with nostalgia.

'All right, Malcolm, I'm coming. Don't kick the bloody door down, it's in a bad enough state as it is!' Vi pressed down hard onto the faulty latch that had imprisoned her youngest son—yet again.

'Malcolm, chuck, how many times do I have to tell you? Leave…the…door…open! No one's bothered about watching a little lad like yourself having a *biz*. There now, dry your eyes, and come on into the kitchen. Did you wash your hands?'

Whilst chastising Malcolm, Vi closed the lid of the lavatory's wooden seat, grunting as she pulled herself to a precarious standing position on top of it, clucking her tongue in disgust at the gymnastics involved in flushing the errant toilet.

The water realised from the cistern, Vi stepped down from the pedestal and pulled her dejected son into her arms. Placing a kiss on the crown of his head, she hugged him close for a second or two, before he wriggled out of her grip. Laughing to herself she thought…*poor little beggar! He's always getting locked in the lav*…But her humorous thoughts were tinged with anguish…*the young 'un will probably grow up with an inferiority complex where toilets are concerned. Sid will have to fix that bloody latch, else the little lad'll get constipated—holding onto it, instead of going. And I'll have to have a word with the others; there's been too much Mickey taking. Dear God, it's never ending; one load of trouble after another...*

Vi wiped the washbasin with a face flannel, and then turned to see that all Malcolm's *business* had been flushed away. And she remembered what the American lads used to say, "you've sure got your hands full, lady!" She grinned, ruefully...*by the heck, that's true...What with six blokes in the house, and a girl that can fight as well as any man...Is it any wonder I have trouble with me own femininity...?* And running her hands down the side of her trim hips, she thought, not for the first time, that Sid was thoughtless swine to say he didn't care what she looked like, as long as she was healthy...

It had taken Vi many months, months that had run into over a year, to shed two stones or more. Months of constant, nagging hunger, that suddenly disappeared (and that was what surprised her the most, the fact that she could not remember when the constant urge for food had vanished.)

Vi was delighted with her new image. And, whilst making new frocks for Maureen, had managed to make one or two for herself.

Indeed clothes had become a problem: Vi had very few items that fit her; most hung off her slimmer frame. But this did not deter her efforts. Especially as since her last scare, Sid had started taking proper precautions: he now bought his condoms from the local barber's shop.

Vi felt that at last she was emerging as a woman, not just somebody's mother, or aunt.

It wasn't that she didn't love her kids. No, she would never want to be without her brood; they made her laugh, they made her cry, they drove her to near insanity on a daily basis, but no, Vi acknowledged to herself, as she *flannelled* the floor, kids was what she was good at, save working in the chippy, where she had worked on and off for the past six years.

Vi's pleasant nature and sunny disposition was seen as a warm welcome to most of the customers that patronized *Jim's Plaice*. You could always be sure of a cheery word, a bit of a natter with Violet Greenwood.

But it had been difficult in the shop, trying not to be *snappy* serving the bags of aromatic fish and chips when she herself was starving in the quest for a slimmer, more youthful figure.

Though it hadn't been Sid or the chip shop customers that had noticed her trimmer frame; it had been Maureen. Whilst giving her niece a comforting cuddle, after the twins had been tormenting the life out of her, Maureen had cried bitter tears. Looking into her aunt's face, her eyes fearful, Maureen had solemnly asked was the weight loss the same as that of her own mother. Was her Aunt Vi going to die, like her mam had?

Vi had been ashamed to have so worried the child. As she had hugged and kissed her niece, reassuring her that all was well, she'd berated herself for her vanity...*poor Maureen, fancy her thinking me weight loss was to do with illness. She doesn't miss a trick...I should have told her what I was up to...*Being totally honest, and Vi invariably was, the thought that her weight loss was so noticeable to the girl brought a trickle of annoyance aimed towards her husband: Sid had not noticed an inch, let alone that she had dropped a couple of dress sizes.

So later that day, in the evening when all the children were tucked up in their beds, Vi had gone out of the back door and into the bathroom, re-entering the kitchen some two hours later after enjoying the pampering of a long hot soak.

Sid, engrossed in his newspaper, as he'd been before she had left the kitchen earlier, barely raised his head when she returned.

In a flash, Vi's petty annoyance became full blown, and seething, 'Sid? Can you see owt different about me?' she'd asked, hoping to have masked her anger by a bashful approach.

Dropping the evening newspaper to his lap, Sid had stared at his wife, quizzically, before shaking his head and resuming his earlier position: feet on the brass fender, newly adopted pipe in mouth.

Vi's fury had erupted, though she'd been tight-lipped as she'd stormed off to bed, without even laying the table for the morning.

Some time later Sid had followed, and, undressing in the dark, had slid into the big double bed, turning his back against his wife and instantly sleeping.

Vi's lonely anger had mixed with bitter tears. Tossing the blankets back, she had sat bolt upright in the bed and had berated her sleeping husband...what sort of man was he? Didn't ever look at her...He hardly ever kissed her besides anything else, these days. Only wanted someone to iron his shirts, make his dinners, slave after his kids...On and on she had raged. Not caring if she woke the sleeping children, so overcome by the unfairness of it all.

And Sid had taken it all, all the verbal abuse. Never said a word back in retaliation.

Nothing, until finally, depleted and exhausted, Vi had flopped back against her pillows and found instant sleep herself.

She had awoken to find Sid's side of the bed empty. Knowing that he wasn't on an early shift, she had fumed out loud again, 'He'll be on his bloody beloved allotment. He might as well pack his bags and move out there!' Flinging back the bedclothes, she had been about to leap angrily out of bed when the bedroom door had opened and Sid had entered, fully dressed in his smartest trousers, his best shirt—his stance awkward with the strain of holding a heavily laden tray.

'Good morning, me lady,' he'd said, 'get yourself back into bed, if you will, *please*.' Placing the tray on the small dressing table, which had been Vi's before she married, Sid had moved to the bed and his struck dumb wife.

Sitting down next to her, Sid had taken her hand in his, taking time to formulate his words. Words and deeds that Vi was to always remember.

'So! You think I don't notice anything, eh? Think I'm just a big thick coal digger, with no finesse, no feelings! That I care more about me turnips than I do you…But you're wrong there, Vi, 'cos I *do* notice, and I *do* care. Look, love,' he'd swung his legs onto the bed to cuddle up beside her, 'I've told you time and time again I loves you. I don't give a *monkey's uncle* whether you're as big as a blooming house, or as thin as a rake, as long as you are still my Vi…! Now don't go crying. All the kids are on the landing waiting to say good morning to you. They all love you too, even though you give them all a bad time with the manners and the learning's you want for them. *Come on in, kids…*' he'd bellowed.

And that was how they'd celebrated Vi's new look. First they all had breakfast in bed, Vi pretending she hadn't noticed the crumbs and spilt milk that was soiling her just changed sheets.

Mid-morning, as it was a Saturday, they'd all got on the bus, which took them into Manchester. There they lunched in a cafeteria before Vi had tried on some new clothes: off the peg. The first time Vi had ever had anything new that wasn't home made, save for her wedding suit. 'Where's the brass coming from to buy me these things, Sid?' she'd asked.

But Sid had just put his index finger to the tip of his nose in answer. Later she would learn that her brother Bill had given Sid the money; cash Sid had known his wife would toss back, "I'm not taking *money* for me own flesh and blood…" she'd have hollered.

So Sid had said nothing about the money, or the extra ration coupons, planning and listing instead: a few new clothes for his newly slim wife, albeit she'd moved his hand and timing with her outburst. Sid had also planned a few days away. Not that Bill's money had run to that: the holiday was being paid for out of a bonus or two he'd earned himself and had kept secret: At the Easter half-term he was taking the whole family (Bill, too,) to Wales; a caravan holiday. But Sid hadn't let on to Vi about that just yet, for they had Christmas to come first...

Maureen loved her bedroom. Not as much as she'd loved her Littleton bedroom when her mother was alive, but nearly as much. Her Uncle Sid was very kind. He'd wanted to make her a bedroom over the new bathroom, but a man from the Council had called telling her Aunt Vi that it wasn't possible. Her aunt and uncle had argued for days. Aunt Vi had called her husband, "stupid." But Maureen didn't think her uncle was stupid. No. Uncle Sid made her laugh; really laugh. He was like the funny men she saw on the films at the pictures...always making people have fun.

And because of her uncle, she was comfortably tucked up in a brand new bed in the parlour. Sid's latest idea; the parlour was now Maureen's bedroom. Her very own room. No more sharing with Malcolm. And Aunt Vi let her have a fire when it was very cold, like it was last night.

Maureen snuggled deeper into her cocoon of warm blankets and listened to the noise and bumps coming from the room above hers. The Greenwood boys shared bedrooms...and jokes.

However, along with the laughter there were the fights. And one such one was going on now; there was a thud that seemed to shake the house. Then she heard her aunt's footsteps, which brought about a deathly silence, before a yell, a yelp and a noisy outburst of tears. In the quietness that followed, the house settled once more into the early morning peace.

An hour later Maureen lifted her head to see the clock on the mantel. The gloaming light, filtering in through the dark curtains, made it difficult for her to see the small black fingers of the white alarm clock; but as she was straining her eyes, she heard her uncle's tread on the stairs and knew it was seven thirty. Time for Aunt Vi's cup of tea in bed. And Uncle Sid always brought her one in too, on Sunday mornings.

With glee, Maureen snuggled down again in anticipation of her steaming hot tea, and Sunday...After her cup of freshly brewed tea, there would be a bath, followed by bacon and eggs with fried bread, a fry-up breakfast that her uncle had taken to making, which was, as far as Maureen was concerned, better than anything else in the whole wide world—even her Aunt Vi occasionally conceded to the fact that it was nice to waited on for a change, as she tucked in to her own plateful with relish. Breakfast over, Maureen usually tidied her bedroom, dusting and sweeping, wiping the little ornaments that she'd brought with her from Littleton. Busy at her tasks, she often let her mind wander, and sometimes she'd think about Betty and wonder what was she was up to these days, not that she missed her one-time friend that much; no, there wasn't much time for missing anything since she come to live with Aunt Vi. Of late, Maureen found it hard to remember what her mother had even looked like, and she felt guilty then. But Aunt Vi would notice and holler at her, "Is that your face or the case you keep it in?" and then they'd laugh together and have a cuddle.

Her aunt had given her a shock a few weeks back with how thin she'd become.

But all that was sorted out...*And what a smashing day out in Manchester that had been...!*

As she lay awaiting her cup of tea, Maureen also remembered that her dad was coming this Sunday and her thoughts became subdued. It wasn't that she didn't like Bill (she always thought of him as Bill, though addressed him as Dad,) it was just that he was always so sad. He tried; she knew that. Tried to be all smiley and happy, like, but he never succeeded. And he was always asking her if she was all right? Did the lads drive her mad? Of course they drove her mad. But when it got too bad, Aunt Vi or Uncle Sid stepped in and gave them a clout. And now school was all right too. She'd made quite a few friends since *that* day, much to Gerard's delight. Now he didn't have to play with her anymore in the schoolyard at break-time, and so he was much happier, too.

With the thought of her father's impending visit, Maureen no longer wanted to idle in her warm bed. However, she knew she had better fox sleep so as not to disappoint her uncle when he knocked; Maureen was well aware of how much her Uncle Sid enjoyed this Sunday morning ritual..."Wakey, wakey, rise and shine, the sun's scorching your eyeballs out...!" he would bawl through the closed parlour door. Then, knocking lightly, he invariably would ask, "Are you decent in there, our Mo? Can I bring your tea in, me princess?"

A mischievous grin would light Maureen's face as she gave her usual answer, "One moment, Sir, whilst I put me tiara on...Now, you may enter." And then her carpet-slippered uncle would shuffle in, smiling his lopsided smile, bashfully awkward, but serenely happy. Sid had made it clear, right from the start, that he liked having his niece in his house, "brings us a bit of quality, lads, makes you watch your p's and q's...aye, like you *really* should treat your Mam..." After placing the tray of Sunday morning tea on her lap, he invariably said the same thing as he backed out of her room, "I'll run the bath for you now, Maureen. Don't forget to leave the water for your auntie, when you've finished, like."

She never forgot, but her uncle always reminded her, as he mooched off to get the bath and breakfast started.

Maureen often wished that she was as easy with her own dad as she was with her uncle. He was lovely, her Uncle Sid: she never had to worry what to talk to him about—there was always something. And she had no need to wonder why her Aunt Vi was so happy and jolly most of the time; it had not slipped by Maureen, the looks and smiles that passed between the married couple, even with all they had to put up with. Maureen was old enough to recognise that it was love that wrapped itself around Vi and Sid in copious quantities, with enough spare to spread around their offsprings...and herself.

It was after her feast of a breakfast, and whilst sauntering round her bedroom, cloth in hand as she dusted her few ornaments, a collection that had once belonged to her mother (an odd assortment of pottery that passed for china: a brown cocker spaniel, a pink crinoline clad girl, two black cats...all lovingly polished each and every Sunday,) that her Aunt Vi popped her head around the parlour door.

'Can I come in, love? I just want a little word with you...'

As Vi entered the room, Maureen felt her aunt's anxiety. And it was contagious; placing the last ornament back on the mantel, she dawdled at the task.

'Leave that for a minute, lovey. Let's sit on the settee for a moment or two...and have a little chat,' Vi beckoned her to the sofa.

'There, now, this is nice, isn't it? Have you been all right in here, Maureen? I mean, you've not been frightened on your own, or anything, have you love?' Vi's unease was plainly obvious.

Sitting down next to her aunt, Maureen remained silent, an inner voice asking other questions which needed to be addressed more urgently: She knew her aunt was troubled, and not by the questions she had posed. Her aunt's enquiries were just trivia, an opening...*But an opening to what...?*

Vi was lost for words. How was she going to tell the child? What should she say?

Sid had said she was *flapping* at nothing. But Vi knew different. Could feel it…and so would have to handle it, from the beginning. Yes, she would start from the beginning.

Reaching out to the earnest, intelligent eyed young girl, she pulled her into a fierce embrace, plonking a kiss on the crown of her freshly shampooed head.

'Now listen, me pet. You knows that your dad's coming the day? Yes, well…he'll not be on his own. Seems he'll have a visitor with him. A young lady, like.' Rooting into the pocket of her floral patterned apron Vi produced an envelope, and waving it in front of Maureen, she continued, 'Like I say, he' ll have this visitor with him today. He wrote to me last week telling me he'd be bringing this…er, woman. You see, Maureen, I think your dad's been a bit lonely, being on his own, like. And she's just a *friend*…you knows that your dad's got himself a little job? Aye, to help with his pension—his wounds pension's not much, you know—anyways, now that he works for a few hours a week, he's met this lady there. She's only young, but he seems quite taken with her. Still, we'll see. Now come on, don't go looking like that! Nothing will change here. But I thought I'd put you in the picture, so to speak. Now then, finish your dusting, and then come and have a nice cup of tea with your Aunt Vi…in the *kitchen*,' she emphasised her words with another firm hug. Then, moving from the settee, she hurried over to the door and her exit, repeating, 'Now as I say, there's *nothing* for you to worry about. But it's best you knows what's afoot. Hurry up now, and I'll see you in a minute! Lad's are at the park with their dad…so there's just the two of us, eh lass?'

Back in the kitchen, Vi swore, muttering quietly but angrily to herself, 'What the bloody hell is Bill playing at? Stupid bugger, just when things are improving all round, he has to write to say…he's in *love*…'

As Bill and Iris walked arm in arm down Parkegate Lane, the net curtains twitched both in the upstairs window and in the downstairs at number 87.

At the upstairs window, Vi unconsciously patted her unruly hair, seeking to tidy herself for the visitors, 'Tut-tutting,' vexed beyond words with her brother.

Downstairs, Maureen jumped back from the window, startled. The lady looked so pretty: So young. Her blonde hair so vivid and bright on this cold December afternoon; and her navy coloured suit and matching beret style hat looked very smart. Surely she couldn't be her dad's friend? Maybe her auntie had made a mistake.

Maureen finished her dusting chores with determination. This morning her Aunt Vi had said it wouldn't affect her...Dad having this woman with him, like. And while helping her aunt to get things ready for their arrival, she had said it again. In fact she'd been all smiley and a bit strange. She'd seemed shy of meeting Dad's friend...which was very unusual: Aunt Vi loved having company. But this person wasn't just company, she was her dad's new *friend*...

But before the afternoon was out nobody was in any doubt about who the woman *friend* really was. She was Bill's new wife.

This news was delivered at the same time as the bread and butter pudding was being served, to the youngsters seated round the card table and the grown-ups at the kitchen table, a pudding that nobody ate; the children having been sent from their table, to "Play upstairs," when, in actuality, they were standing on the landing, in bewildered silence, even the youngest, Malcolm, stunned and subdued and eager to hear more...

'Don't be like that, Vi! We thought it best. Why wait? It's Christmas next week, and we wanted to be together for Christmas. Come on, lass, give us your blessing.'

Vi remained silent.

Sid stood up, and, scraping back his chair, walked around the table to where Bill sat.

'Yer comes in here, Bill, and out of the blue announce that you're married...to this young *girl*, and you wants our *blessing?* Christ, man, I think you must have a hole in your head as well as yer lung! She knows about that I take it? Knows yer an invalid?' Sid's northern dialect was strong when his dander was up.

Bill looked bemused. Placing his arm protectively on his wife's shoulders, he answered his brother-in-law, 'Listen, Sid, Iris knows all there is to know about me, and she loves me. And I thought you all loved me, too. After all I've been through, surely you don't mind me having a bit of happiness now, surely not? Iris, here's, a good lass: A woman to be proud of. And by God I am proud of her! Proud that she wanted to be my wife; proud she wanted me baby...'

At this piece of information, Iris bowed her head, and Vi exploded at the sheepish looking Bill.

'You what? Your baby! What bloody *baby*? Surely you've not married a

77

woman who's carrying another bloke's child? Surely to *God* you've not done that, our Bill?'

'No he hasn't!' Iris spoke out, clearly angry at Vi's outburst. 'Bill has married me because he loves me. Do you hear: *Loves* me. And yes, I am expecting a baby…and it's Bill's. What do you think I am, eh? What are you implying…?'

Vi and Sid stared at each other, astounded and speechless.

Bill looked from one to the other of them, guessing their thoughts…'Come on, Vi, Sid. Congratulate us…Maureen is going to be blessed with a little brother, or a sister. Think of *that*. She'll have a family: A family of her own! You don't want to spoil that for her, do you? Bring her down. Bring her back in, so we can *all* celebrate.'

At this Vi stood up. She was shaken, but, at the mention of Maureen, she knew what she had to do.

'All right, Bill. I'll congratulate you, and Iris, but on one condition. You don't take Maureen back with you. You're to leave her here, with us. You two have a bit of time together, like. Get to know one another…God only knows, you can't have spent that much time together before you were wed! Maybe, maybe after the baby's born you can have Maureen over for weekends and the like. But think, Bill, think of Maureen. She's only just settled here…Now, to take her back, why it'd be monstrous! Tell him, Sid…tell him I'm right…'

But it was Iris who answered.

'I think your sister is right, Bill. Leave Maureen for a month or two. Let her get used to the idea of me being her new mother. It'll be hard for her. And me! And you know I haven't been feeling too good recently. Bill, do as Violet says, eh…? Leave the girl here, for a while at least.'

Upstairs, all the boys looked at Maureen. In their unnatural silence the audience of children had heard every word. Maureen's eyes glistened with tears as Stuart's arms went around her. The twins each held one of her hands. Malcolm clutched her skirt and Gerard blinked back his tears at the thought of losing his cousin, now, when all the trouble was settled, and she was as much a part of their family as he was.

*

7

Maureen was excited. She was going home. Her huge blue eyes shone with delight, and an overpowering feeling of joy made her squeeze the warm gloved hand that held her own.

Light hearted, radiant, Maureen walked with her stepmother, Iris, down the street that had been her home, and playground, for the first seven years of her young life. Lupin Street.

Lupin Street was like many other Littleton streets: long, narrow, and cobbled. A street where people lived side by side with the clothing industry.

Nestled between the slate roofed terraced houses, a handful of small, cramped garment factories thrived, the workforce being made up from the local community. The grey and sooty street was home to some sixty or so families as well as the *rag trade*.

As a toddler and young child, Maureen had skipped and played to the constant whir of sewing machines, dodging the endless streams of vans that scuttled back and forth carrying bolts of material and racks of newly made suits and coats, items of clothing that eventually took pride of place in the expensive shops that graced the city of Manchester.

Those few short years, of days happily filled with noise and laughter, were before Ethel's untimely death. Thereafter, on Maureen's infrequent returns to the street, to visit her widowed father, she had been more than happy to leave. The street was the same—the houses looked the same—but it was different, changed. Ethel was gone.

Even though Bill had kept his rented terraced home clean, it wasn't as before. A forlorn, barren atmosphere pervaded its shabby rooms; rooms which had been structured to allow as little light as possible to enter, which Maureen had never been aware of during her earlier, happier years spent in the company of Ethel. Then, the sun had seemed to shine nearly every day, filling the rooms with golden light.

And so as much as she felt sorry for her father, Maureen had been only too happy to return to Warrington Clough with her Auntie Vi at the end of each visit, feeling relief as she entered the Greenwood family home, even though it was overcrowded and untidy.

It was with these visits and thoughts in mind that Maureen had rationalised, in an open-minded almost adult way, the events that had led to her being brought back to live permanently with her father, Bill, and his new wife, Iris.

Today, nine-year old Maureen was more than ready for her new life. She was thrilled with the expectations of what was to come. Delighted at the thought of her old bedroom. Excited to know that she would soon have her very own brothers or sisters. And these emotions led her to voice a timid question, 'Iris? Shall I call you Mammy, now? Now that I'm coming home for good, like?'

The gloved hand let go its grip, and her stepmother's step faltered, almost to a standstill, but then it quickened to a pace much faster than before, leaving Maureen walking slightly behind.

'We'll see. Don't mither me with it *now,* for Christ's sake,' Iris muttered, 'for the time being keep calling me *Iris*. Let's wait till the babies are born; it won't be long, and then, like I say, we'll see. I'll be more used to the idea...the idea of being called...Mam, then, don't you think?'

Maureen didn't know what to think. Iris's manner was so different now that they were on their own. Perplexed by the woman's changing attitude, Maureen pondered on her dilemma, before thoughtfully dismissing it: Iris was tired, that's all...*Yes, that's it...Auntie Vi could be grumpy when she was worn out.*

As they walked on in silence, Maureen stole a quick glance at her young stepmother and was filled with pity. *Poor Iris*...she thought...*it must be very difficult for her to be so fat, when she'd been so slim and pretty at Christmas. And what a Christmas we had!* Maureen's spirits lifted as she remembered...

Bill and Iris had returned to Warrington Clough on Christmas Day, arriving by taxi. And with them they'd brought parcels and packages full of goodies and presents for everyone.

Maureen's Christmas present had been made by Iris and caused quite a stir. The gift was a beautifully tailored coat, camel in colour, with brown leather buttons that double breasted up to the neck. The coat's hip pockets and neat collar had been trimmed with velvet of a deep chocolate brown, and Iris had thoughtfully shopped for a velveteen beret in the exact same shade to compliment the outfit. Worn together, the effect was stunning.

So much so that Maureen had wanted to wear the coat today, but had been dissuaded by Iris who had pointed out that it was too warm a day for such a heavy garment. And Iris had asked her not to go on so much about it, the coat, she meant, not when they were back in Littleton, because she was only a button-hole machinist and people would begin to take liberties if they knew she had such a hidden talent.

Iris was near to tears in her misery as she neared her home. Earlier she had been forced to explain so much to the shiny haired girl by her side. The child was forever asking questions, and needing answers. The train journey from Warrington Clough to Littleton had been one long interrogation on Maureen's part. It being the first time they had been alone together, she had made a gallant effort to be kind and cheerful, and somewhat moderate with the truth: Iris knew that it wouldn't do for anyone to find out that Maureen's Christmas gift had been made by one of her stepmother's work colleagues at the factory where she did indeed work as a button-hole machinist.

Jimmy Dawson, the hot-blooded factory foreman, had ambitions regarding Iris; that being so, it had been only too easy to get him to make up the garment for Maureen. The coat she had taken credit for herself, and in doing so captured Maureen's adoration and a little begrudged respect from her new sister-in-law, Vi.

But now that Maureen was going to be living with her, and on a permanent basis too, Iris had realised that she had no choice but to put the innocent young girl a little in the picture—and with reason. It was very apparent that the kid had a memory and a gob on her the size of her Aunt Vi's...*Chatter, chatter...chatter...oh Iris, remember this, and remember that. And most of it a load of mindless twaddle*...Iris was finding Maureen's unexpected talkativeness and her unasked for devotion a little hard to handle, especially since she had no maternal feelings towards the girl in anyway.

In fact Iris had been seething with anger from the moment Bill had said he'd decided: she needed help, and who better to help her than their very own Maureen?

Iris's pregnancy *was* proving a difficult one. The never-ending nausea was intolerable, her heightened blood pressure had become a matter for concern; and then to crown it all, the doctor had heard two heartbeats upon her last examinations. Twins. Two babies. The reason her weight had ballooned: weight that brought with it an intense anger. An annoyance that crippled her thoughts today as she trudged down the long street, inspected by all and sundry, peeked at from behind net curtains, and being constantly nattered at by the nuisance by her side.

As they neared number 93, Iris's temper was smouldering fiercely, fuelled by Maureen's irremovable presence and the earlier remarks made by Vi. The thought that the *gormless* Vi had the nerve to say that "having twins would give them something in common," when it was more likely that the news of the expected twins had given Vi's conscience a twinge, made Iris red in the face with rage...*they say twins run in families...huh, my news soon put a stopper in Vi's big gob, didn't it just? Fat, stupid bitch...! And to think, the bloody fool thinks she's slim...*Steeped in her savage thoughts, Iris's indignation was becoming a roaring flame as she neared her home.

'Hiya, Maureen; are you playing out after tea?'

Betty Dwyer had been sitting on her own doorstep for most of the afternoon, eagerly awaiting the arrival of her best friend.

But it appeared that the red haired youngster had chosen the wrong time to issue the invitation. Her shy yet welcoming request blew the lid off Iris's brimming fury.

'Sod off, Betty! Go on...get in yer house! Sitting there on yer steps, spying on us, yer bloody Irish...*tinker*. Maureen will *not* be playing out tonight, or any night...Do yer hear me? I told yer not to pester Maureen, didn't I? She'll have things to do of an evening...her homework and her house jobs. Now get out of me sight! Go on, *shoo*.'

Maureen stood frozen to the spot, obviously shocked by the outburst from her stepmother. And humiliation was to follow as Betty flounced up the front door steps leading to her own Victorian terraced home, pausing momentarily to stick out her tongue in defiance of her tyrannical neighbour and her dumb-struck step-daughter.

And, as if this homecoming was not enough to make Maureen realise her happy childhood was over, the steps leading up to her own home was the final testimony. The three stone steps that led off the pavement up to the front door of number 93 were dusty, grimy and full of pigeon droppings and scraps of litter, dejectedly dirty against the freshly donkey-stoned steps of the neighbours' homes.

'Aw, Iris…Look at the steps…who's done that to them? My Mam would kill them, who ever did it!' The sight of the filthy steps had helped Maureen find her tongue.

'Never mind yer *Mam*…' Iris roared, as she put the key into the lock and opened the brown painted front door…'Get in here—at once! Get in, now!'

Slamming the front door behind them, she glared at Maureen as they stood close together in the dark and narrow lobby, with the only light coming in from the fanlight over the closed front door.

'Showing me up like *that*. What game do yer think yer playing, eh? Your Mam indeed! You *knew* Betty's mother was there, listening and nosing behind her bleeding front door: Listening and tut-tutting. *Bastard!* Like all the *other* bastards around here…what a fu…dump…'

Iris just about managed not to use the word. The word that would have spelt out that she had lost it. Really lost it.

Pushing past Maureen, she opened the door that led into the kitchen. Aware now that her distress was blatantly obvious, she battled to pull herself back from the brink: the vast canyon of despondency she had verged on falling into all day.

'Come on, Maureen, come on in to the kitchen. I don't bite, yer know! I'm just a bit hot and bothered with travelling and the like. Take no notice of me bark; it's like they say—me bark's *worse* than me bite…' With a brittle pretence laugh at her own shortcomings, Iris beckoned the wide-eyed Maureen to follow on into the kitchen.

'It's a bit untidy at the moment, the house, like. I've not been too good lately,' she waved at the mess in the room, before using the same swollen knuckled hand to rub her protruding stomach.

Maureen remained silent.

Beggaring for the girl's sympathy, Iris stood leaning her back against the sturdy frame of the cluttered sideboard and blew out a long, wistful sigh, eyeing the child and her reaction, searching for the words to put right the wrong she had done, 'Still, love, now that there's two of us, hey, two pairs of hands, like, we'll manage, won't we?' The challenge was coupled with a weak smile, one she found hard to wear, but hoped would do the trick.

Maureen returned the smile in the same manner. A fleeting up turn of the lips that did nothing to mask her obvious apprehension as she stood in the open doorway of the sordid kitchen: at her tender age the child was too young to know that her face showed signs of terror: a word that had probably never been in Maureen's vocabulary before.

But Iris knew the word, and the feeling. Hadn't she herself felt it as soon as she had realised that she was pregnant? Terror and depression, that was lifted only slightly when Bill, ecstatic at her news, suggested that they wed.

Looking over to where her stepdaughter stood, forlorn and teary eyed, Iris made a valiant effort to get herself and the situation under control.

'I said come on *in,* Maureen! Here, move this lot of the chair, and sit yourself down. You look dog-tired…Are yer? Do you need to go to the toilet? It's not been moved, yer know,' she tittered at her own attempt at humour, but quickly realised it was futile; Maureen's lack of response was humiliating.

Iris made a further effort at being friendly, saying, 'Soon have things ship-shape,' as she bustled over to the armchair, scooping newspapers into her arms, but then stood, aimlessly, not knowing where to put them. Defeated by it all, her shoulders sagged. She dumped the papers unceremoniously back onto the chair, and reached to the mantelpiece for her cigarettes and matches.

In the presence of the demure youngster, Iris had became totally aware of the state of the room, and of the penetrating odour coming from the sink area; not from the drains of the stone sink, but from the shelves that lay beneath, hidden behind a fringe of grubby, rose patterned curtain. Here, out of sight, cloths had become mildewed, and milk had soured. A jumbled mess of domestic waste that had not been cleared or cleaned for many weeks, added to the long list of other neglected cleaning tasks.

It wasn't the filthy state of the kitchen nor Iris's declining diction that made Maureen stay rooted to spot: it was the overpowering stench. The room stank. And the rank smell, coming on top of her stepmother's outburst, brought a weakness to the girl's thin legs. A drum beat in her chest, echoing through her body, bringing a tremble to her limbs.

Maureen did need to use the toilet, and urgently. As heeded, she moved into the kitchen and, without saying a word, quietly and confidently unlocked the backdoor before stepping into the yard: The yard that Ethel had kept so clean. The small flagstone area that each and every day her mother had swilled with used washing-up water, or the pine disinfected water from the copper-washing tub. Ethel had also lovingly tending the small patch of garden, which measured no more than eight-foot square—a grassy patch that just comfortably fit a spread blanket on a hot summer day.

Saddened to see the decline of her mother's garden, Maureen unlatched the toilet door and once again was assailed by a vile odour. The smell of urine attacked her senses. Deep at the back of her throat a wetness rose, soaking her mouth.

Holding her breath, she quickly tugged at her navy blue knickers in an urge to be relieved and out of the squat, foul smelling dungeon, for on closing the door she had reached for the light switch, automatically remembering exactly where it was situated, but the little room did not lighten.

Looking up to the cobwebbed ceiling, only the dangling cord was to be seen, no bulb. And instead of the crisp white toilet paper—which Ethel and Vi had hoarded and prized—torn pieces of newspaper hung from a dirty string that was knotted onto a rusting hook behind the wooden door of the toilet closet. No *donkey-stoning* graced the stone flagged floor, only the faint evidence that it had once been so. No fresh, dolly-blue whitewash, just water stained, flaking walls enclosed around her, threatening, menacing and doing nothing to mask the unseemly side of human waste, as this little room had always done before.

The outside lavatory had been a place where Maureen had often sat, swinging her legs and humming, the fresh, clean, disinfected air and bright light making it more like a private den than a privy. Ethel had joked with her that she "Spent so much time in there she'd better take her butties the next time." It had been a place to daydream and sing: practising Christmas Carols, the latest popular song…where she had listened to the murmuring of their next door neighbours as they chatted together in their own back yards, oblivious of any intruding ears.

On her return to the kitchen, Maureen went straight to the stone sink to wash her hands but, as there was no soap in evidence, she made do with just cold running water. Reaching towards the towel rail to wipe her hands her eyes widened at the state of the towel hanging there. Auntie Vi wouldn't even use such a cloth for her floors. Indeed, her Auntie Vi always boiled her cleaning cloths and hung them outside on the line to dry and blow away any lurking germs.

Iris was busying herself when Maureen came back into the kitchen and didn't notice the look on Maureen's face. In her usual fashion she was tidying the room by shoving old newspapers, books and other odds and ends, into the built-in wall cupboard that was on the right-hand side of the fireplace. A fireplace that had replaced the old black range that the house had been built with; a modern and fashionable tile design, muted grey with a hint of pink that had been the pride and joy of Ethel, was now full of cold ashes, the hearth dusty and littered with cigarette butts.

The fire companion set, consisting of small black bristled brush, shovel and poker, all with handles of heavy brass, which had always been polished to a bright lustre, reflecting the colours of the roaring fires that had nearly always graced the grate, had taken on a greenish hue, dull and unloved.

Squatting at the hearth, Maureen took up the small brush and swept the cigarette stubs into a cluster and in one sweep, collected them into the shovel.

'Shall I empty the grate, Iris? I don't mind, and if you can give me a couple of cloths, I'll wipe it down, like, give it a bit of a once-over...'

Iris turned from the cupboard, her face set in a stony glare as she looked at the kneeling child... *Thinks I'm not good enough, little shit! Still, why not? Let her do the bloody work...it's more her house than mine, anyhow...*

'If you like...' she answered, now not even trying to keep the sarcasm out of her voice... 'and while yer at it, you might as well get them front steps done. Yer knows how, don't yer?' Easing her swollen body into the fireside armchair, she continued, 'Your father feels the same way about them as you do...Can't understand what all the fuss' about myself. Yer do them, and then they're in the same bloody state again by next day!'

Maureen remained quiet, employing herself with the task at the fireplace, although it was apparent by her demeanour—the way her tongue worked over her bottom lip—that she was aware that Iris was studying her as she worked.

'And I've been thinking, Maureen. Perhaps you better had start calling me Mam...your dad would like it and maybe it would help us both to get along, like. Give you a feeling of being home again. Well, say *something*...has the cat got yer tongue?'

Iris was beginning to feel uncomfortable with Maureen's silence, a silence that threatened the older woman's authority.

'If you like,' Maureen answered politely, standing to full height... 'shall I put the back boiler on for some hot water, Iri...*sorry*, M...a...m, I mean?' Maureen stuttered over the use of the familiar name, and her cheeks seemed burnt red with embarrassment as she was pelted with her stepmother's scathing reply.

'Cold water will be good enough for you, young lady. Hot water costs money…so yer can stick Vi's high and bleeding mighty ideas where they come from! You're living here now, so remember that. And coal costs money here, too. Bucket's on the cellar steps,' she snapped.

Contrary to what Iris thought, Maureen did not know how to *stone* the front door steps. In fact Maureen had done very little housework in her ten years, except for a little dusting and polishing, for although her Aunt Vi's workload was heavy, with five children, six including Maureen, a part-time job in the local fish and chip shop and the weekly cleaning of her neighbours' house (Flo Fielding had suffered a massive stroke on Boxing Day,) she asked nothing of her children in regard to house chores, believing that children should be children and would be adult all too soon enough.

So it was Bernadette Dwyer, Betty's mother, who taught Maureen the rudiments of doorstep cleaning. The slovenly Bernadette (as Iris called her,) who could hardly believe what she was seeing with her own Irish eyes, when she spotted Ethel's idolised baby, on her knees, perplexed look on her pretty face, sloshing ice cold water and scrubbing the steps with all her might.

And that was how hollow eyed Bill found them when he trudged weary and cough racked down the street on his way home from work. Maureen and Bernadette, hip to hip, kneeling at his own front door steps, whilst inside number 93, his young wife, Iris, sat in the armchair in the squalid kitchen, blowing endless smoke rings into the air, adding further to the already tainted atmosphere, without regard for her ailing husband who found smoke filled rooms hard to bear.

*

8

Timothy and Christopher Grady were born at noon, two minutes apart, 28th May 1949. The babies were one month premature, weighing in at five pounds and five pounds five ounces respectively.

Iris had gone into labour during the afternoon of the previous day, although it was fourteen hours later before she was carried out of the house, on a stretcher, screeching and screaming, to give birth in the local hospital.

From her arrival at the hospital until the babies were born she continued to holler and bawl. The midwife and doctors attending the births heaved a long sigh of relief at the safe delivery of each child; Mrs Iris Grady had proved hard to handle: from her shouts of obscene profanities and verbal battering, they were left in no doubt that the babies had not been planned. Iris behaved in an appalling manner and, to the disgust of the hospital staff, without much dignity.

Two weeks later, when the taxi stopped at the front door of number 93 her temper had not subsided. With a baby in each arm she braced herself to be greeted by Vi Greenwood and Maureen, who had both been busy readying the house for their arrival.

As Bill (looking gravely ill,) assisted her up the three, freshly cleaned stone steps, Iris ground her teeth in an attempt to smile. Bill's over-zealous attention the last fourteen days being hard enough to bear without the added burden of his sister's.

Yet Iris had to admit to herself (within an hour of being home,) that she was glad to have someone of Vi's stamina at hand to assist them, for she knew that Bill was near the end of his tether with her hostile behaviour and his own fast declining health.

For one long week, in the middle of a very hot June, the Lupin Street house was submitted to some kind of order. Vi fed and changed the babies as often as she could allowing Iris to rest more and build up her strength. She also shopped, cooked and cleaned until the house shone a little under her painfully hard administrations.

Not only was the work hard, Vi found the patient to be almost impossible, especially where Maureen was concerned: Iris harangued the eager youngster incessantly whenever the girl moved to within an inch of the babies, a tirade completely unneeded—anyone could see that the girl was smitten with her young brothers; gentle and confident when handling them, her devotion was obvious. Vi had to bite her tongue on numerous occasions. But if looks could kill, one or two that she threw in her sister-in-law's direction were very much taken to heed, stilling Iris's harsh criticism stone dead.

Vi was deeply worried about Maureen's welfare. When she had first arrived to take over from the confined Iris, she'd been appalled by the state of the house and of her niece's lifestyle.

It transpired that Maureen had missed most of her schooling since her return to Littleton. Although Bill had agreed that Maureen should be enrolled into the school she had previously attended, Vi found out, from Bernadette, that no such arrangements had been made. Maureen had been kept at home to look after Iris.

So it was a furious Vi who marched Maureen into St. Michael's Primary School. And it was Vi who told Miss. Wade, a headmistress of some twenty years experience, that she had before her an outstanding pupil; one who had more brains that all her cousins' brains put together, and would the headmistress kindly keep eye on the girl's step-mother in view of the worrying absenteeism that the latter had done little about.

With the matter settled to her satisfaction, Vi left Maureen at the school, secure in the knowledge that she had enlightened the head teacher and set about to see what could be done regarding her brother's health. Sadly, this concern could not be handled in the same manner. Vi came away from the doctor's surgery more worried than when she had gone in.

Later that day, Vi returned to her own home in Warrington Clough eager to be back with her own brood, yet visibly and mentally worried at the circumstances she had left behind in Littleton. However, out of sight out of mind soon followed as she was swallowed up into the ongoing affairs of her own family and home.

It would be just before Christmas of that same year that Vi would return to the Grady household, unexpected and very much unwanted.

It was a freezing December morning, the sky low and grey. Vi shivered as she entered the front doorway of her home, glad to be inside and out of the cold drizzling rain that had drenched her as she had walked back from school after seeing Malcolm through its gates.

Malcolm had found school not to be to his liking. This had made life very difficult for his older brothers, who took it in turn to have sole charge of him as they journeyed, on foot, the quarter of a mile or so to the school building: when they eventually reached the school gates, no amount of persuasion, or blackmail, could coax the boy inside. Consequently, it fell to Vi to walk her youngest son the short distance to the schoolhouse. And with his vexed mother by his side, it did not take Malcolm too long to realise that school was not such a bad place, after all. This episode in Malcolm's schooling was now behind them but, nevertheless, Vi made sure her five-year old son entered the building and didn't lurk outside and unseen, for the long cold period until it was time for him to come home for his dinner.

Taking off her drab grey winter coat, but leaving her green paisley designed head scarf in place—a habit that was useful on two counts: keeping her head warm in a house that had no form of heating in its upstairs room, and as a useful fashion accessory that hid the fact that, as usual, in the mad rush of morning, she had not had the time to brush her unruly hair—Vi bustled into the kitchen, lighting the gas jet on the stove as her first priority: a hot cup of tea before she tackled her marathon of jobs: and a quick shufti at the mail that had just arrived which, to her pleasure, included the Christmas catalogue she had been waiting for.

As she settled herself at the table, a steaming cup of tea warming her chilled hands, Vi glanced at the pile of post; quite a bit with it being the beginning of the festive season. Amongst the white envelopes containing greeting cards there was a brown envelope addressed to her only, the writing spidery, childlike, and in an unknown hand.

Placing her cup back in its saucer, Vi ripped open the envelope, quickly scanning the short note that was written on a sheet of lined paper torn from a child's exercise book.

The few words she read left Vi in little doubt of what her priorities for the day would really be.

Two hours later she was on a train bound for Manchester after rushing round to the homes of various neighbours, who also had young school children, in an effort to secure a proper mid-day meal for her sons in her absence. This done, she had called into the colliery where Sid worked, leaving him a scribbled message, explaining her whereabouts.

Finally, with only a quarter of an hour left if she was going to catch the eleven o'clock train, Vi had hurried into *Jim's Plaice,* where she served on the evening shift, pleading for time off on family matters. And, as Vi was Jim's most reliable and efficient employee, he had reluctantly let her go, realising, as Vi babbled her story, how mean he would seem should he not concede to her earnest request.

Bernadette Dwyer was awaiting her visitor's arrival; as soon as Vi tapped on the door of number 91 Lupin Street, it was opened.

Half an hour later, Vi was hammering at the door of number 93; and it took almost as long before the front door was opened by Iris, bleary eyes and tousled haired, her face registering shock at the presence of her sister-in-law.

Vi was in no mood to offer pleasantries, nor to request entrance. Pushing the door and Iris aside, she entered the dark lobby and was assailed, immediately, by a ripe, pungent smell. Urine. Stepping into the kitchen Vi saw at once the cause of the odour. Placed directly in front of a roaring fire was a metal fireguard and, strewn over the guard's meshed sides, were stained nappies. Iris was drying out the small, heavily stained squares of towelling, and from the overpowering stench it was obvious a vital part of the process had been omitted. They had not been laundered.

'Dear God! You...you *vile* woman! What on *earth* are you doing? They need to be washed first...! Where are the children? Where's your babies...?' Vi had been prepared to be shocked, but this...She began to panic. Without invitation she turned, making her way out of the kitchen and running swiftly up the steep stairs, heading purposefully along the narrow unlit landing that led into the main bedroom at the front of the house.

The foul smelling room was empty, the bed unmade and the furniture cluttered with crumpled clothes, and an assortment of dirty cups and plates, feeding bottles and overflowing ashtrays. The blue brocade curtains, which hung limply at the window, were drawn together blocking out the mid-day light, casting a cold blue aura over the shabby scene.

Turning back onto the landing, Vi paced the few feet that led to Maureen's bedroom and, to her relief, found what she was looking for. The two wooden cots were side by side, each occupied by a sleeping infant. Vi felt herself relax, her fears subsiding, until she realised that something was missing: Maureen's bed.

Without further ado Vi closed the door on the sleeping babies, leaving them to their slumber, her fears now far worse than they were before she had entered... *Where was Maureen?* The small room where the babies slept held no evidence that her niece had ever slept there. Indeed, it held no trace of her at all save for the pink candy striped curtains, which Vi herself had made, as a present for her niece's sixth birthday.

Iris, who had climbed the stairs with angry intentions, made a grab for her sister-in-law's arm, but was thwarted: Vi's actions were quicker. Clutching at the neck of Iris's grubby, pink candlewick dressing gown, Vi hissed her question, the spittle from her tense mouth spraying the startled face of Iris.

'Where *is* she? Tell me! Where...is...she? Where's Maureen...?' Vi growled the words, her anger mounting: anger that was tinged with fear. Fear for Maureen's safety. And fear for what she wanted to do to the woman in her grip.

Iris made a massive effort to release herself from Vi's hands, protectively tugging the lapels of her dressing gown closer together. Surprisingly, she succeeded to pull herself from Vi's hold. Backing away from any further attack, she regained some of her old defiance, 'She's at school. Where *else* would she be...?' she blurted.

'No she's not.'

'Well, she *should* be. She left here hours ago! It's not my fault if she's buggered off somewhere, is it?' Iris retorted before turning and fleeing down the steep stairs.

Vi drew in a deep breath and followed. Re-entering the hot and smelly kitchen, Vi found Iris more composed.

'Get out of my house, Vi, *now.*'

'No! Not until I find out what's been happening here...I'll ask yer again, Iris. Where...is...our...Maureen?'

Iris threw a defiant glare at Vi. Then, reaching to the littered mantel of the tiled fireplace, she picked up an unopened packet of cigarettes. Breaking the seal on the packet of ten *Woodbines*, she expertly shook a single cigarette into the palm of her left hand before bending towards the fire, poking the end of the cigarette into the flames to light it. Sucking hard on the first drag, she straightened, inhaling deeply, before exhaling through her nostrils.

The cloud of cigarette smoke drifted towards the open doorway to where Vi stood, her frame filling the opening, her facial expression disgust, though her eyes were filled with fear.

A flicker of amusement crossed Iris's face; a sneer, an incitement that Vi found difficult to ignore.

'I don't know what you find so funny, Iris. You should be bloody *ashamed* of yourself. Look at you. Look at your house. Animals look after their own better...Now, for the last time, I'm asking you, Iris—where does Maureen go when she's not in school? She's not here! So, where the *hell* is she...?'

Iris took another long drag on her cigarette. Vi became more exasperated.

'I knew the minute I laid eyes on yer that you were trouble. I thought, now what would a young woman be a wanting with our Bill, eh...? And you know what? I *still* don't know! But what I do know is that you are wicked. For some reason or other you've used our Bill. Used us all...and I'm telling yer, Iris, I've had *enough*...If yer don't tell me where Maureen is...I'll bring the bloody police in, a will. Yes, that I will, because I happen to know that Maureen hasn't been in school for over two weeks! And I know that to be the truth because I've had a letter this morning from...' Vi managed not to blurt out the name of her informant, not wanting Iris to know whom the spy was, or how close they were situated. In a quieter tone, and mindful of her diction, she continued her questioning,

'Iris, you can wipe that grin off your face or I'll do it for you...so help me God, I mean it! I'm not moving from this house until I've seen Maureen. I believe she's got a black eye...Aye, now that surprises you, doesn't it? That I know that much, eh?' Vi could see the alarm in Iris's face.

'Who gave her a black eye, Iris...?'

Iris had a go at making light of what Vi had asked. Sneering, dismissively shaking her head, she took another drag on her cigarette before speaking with a lightness to her voice, 'Well, you know your *Maureen*...always the clumsy one. If yer must know...' she inhaled again, letting the smoke out in a short puff, 'she fell down the cellar steps when she was getting some coal up. It's a right shiner, and her legs have bruised up a bit. And, the truth is, that I thought it best she didn't go to school when it happened, in case the kids in the class made fun of her, like. I was going to take her to the doctors, but she said it didn't hurt. She doesn't like to be fussed over. She seems all right now, though, honest, Vi...'

'You wouldn't know an honest word if it bit yer, Iris! And what does our Bill say about it all? Does he believe she fell down the cellar steps?'

'Bill wasn't here at the time. He was at work,' Iris answered, dismissive again.

'Well, if Bill was at work when it happened, it must have been during the day—so, Iris, why wasn't Maureen at school? Answer me that...'

'She had the day off to help with Christopher, if you must know. He had colic...I'd been up most of the night. It were her idea. Honest, Vi! She's good with the babies; you know that. She really loves them and she said she'd look after them that day whilst I had a sleep...'Iris's voice trailed off when she realised Vi didn't believe a word of it.

Vi shook her head, pursing her lips; her stance was of stone, her voice steely hard. 'Iris. Just one more time—I'll ask one more time. I'm being polite; I've listened to your drivel. Now...where...*is*...Maureen?'

Defeat sagged Iris's shoulders, visibly shrinking her skeletal frame. Turning her back on Vi, she slowly moved towards the window. Heavy rain pelted the glass, vibrating on Iris's forehead as she leant against it. She turned, and buried her face into the limp grease-spattered curtains that at one time had graced the tiny kitchen window with their pristine crispness. Now, the once white curtains, patterned with pink cabbage roses, looked more like rags. Rags that Iris was using to shield her tear-stained face as she sobbed, her words a muffled whining, 'It's not...*fair*. Everything goes wrong for me...I've tried and *tried*...'

Self-pity was not what Vi wanted to hear; but needing an answer, she changed her tack.

'Iris! Come on; come and sit down. And for crying out loud, tell me what's going on, *will* you...' Vi urged her sister-in-law to compose herself, her own natural compassion reluctantly rising. Vi had always found her fast forming tempers difficult to sustain.

Taking control, Vi motioned for Iris to seat herself, thinking, as she glanced around the cluttered kitchen, that maybe she had been a little too harsh in her interrogations.

The fact was, although the house was dirty, and in obvious need of care, the babies seemed to be sleeping peacefully. She'd noticed immediately that they were plump and rosy cheeked, even though they lay in filthy surroundings...*Perhaps Maureen's bruises were accidental. After all, kids were naturally clumsy and, in truth, a pain in the backside from time to time. Maybe Bernadette's wrong...*Vi's thoughts were hopeful...*Maybe she's stirring up trouble for trouble's sake. The babies seem all right...Bill's at work...and Maureen must be at school if she left here hours ago...*

But the relenting of Vi's anger was short lived.

Iris, spurred on by her sister-in-law's forgiving tone, turned to face Vi. Giving full pelt to her feelings, her face contorted with self-righteous rage. Her neck reddened and blotched as the torrent of tears loosened her tongue, 'It's not my fault, Vi; it's *really* not. She just looks at me, and *won't* do as she's told...you know what she's like...she's *stubborn*. All she ever wants to do is go to school...and hold the babies...she's lazy, and *ruined*...' Iris gulped on her tears, choking in her eagerness to exonerate herself, to lay the blame elsewhere. 'She's spoilt, Vi. *You* spoilt her. You and her *bloody* mother...Maureen *hates* me...thinks I'm dirt beneath her feet...I can see it in her eyes...' her tirade was edging towards hysteria. 'She's in the *shed,* if you must know! Go on! Get out to her! Let her tell yer how *rotten* I am to her...! Take her *away*...out of my sight...her *and* her father! Yer might as well know this as well...' she lowered her voice a little as she imparted her other shocking news, '*he's* in the bleeding hospital. Been there a week...he's dying...'

Vi wasn't listening anymore, she was tearing out of the back door and down the wet yard to the shed and, as she unbolted the door, what she witnessed was to stay with her, always at the back of her mind, for the rest of her life.

At first she couldn't make out anything, the wooden hut was cluttered and dark. Rusted tools hung from hooks, boxes spilled round her feet, but then she saw movement under filthy sacks that were piled towards the back.

As Vi's eyes became accustomed to the gloom, she realised she was looking into another pair: The eyes of Maureen. Eyes that were dull and empty of emotion, yet the voice when it came was shockingly clear, 'Hello, Auntie Vi. Have you come to see my dad? He's very poorly, Auntie Vi. He's very ill and...' Whatever else she was going to say had to wait, for the cough that came from her convulsed her young body, a harsh, raw bark that jolted her to sitting position, causing her to flail her arms and cast aside the rough sacking she had been using to keep warm.

Vi knelt down by Maureen's side, utterly speechless for once in her life:

mute with shock. Slowly, Maureen's coughing subsided, which coincided with the entrance of Iris.

'Don't believe a word she tells yer! She's only been in here since this morning. Her bloody coughing wakes the boys. Night after night…first her bloody father, then her…I…' Standing defiantly in the doorway of the shed, Iris wasn't able to finish her sentence. Vi charged at her, incensed beyond reason, the full force of her body weight knocking Iris to the ground.

Wild-eyed, her fists clenched, Vi stared down at her sister-in-law as she lay whimpering on the wet flagstones, with the urge to do more damage to the snivelling, cowering woman mounting by the second. But her good sense quickly returned and, turning her back on the wailing, she squatted down to the frightened figure of her niece.

Softly whispering endearments, Vi gently lifted Maureen up, snuggling her deeply within her own warm, grey wool coat. Murmuring soft, comforting words, she stepped over the sobbing Iris and walked slowly up the yard and into the house.

Setting Maureen down onto the shabby armchair that sided the fireplace, she returned to the back door, closing it and swiftly turning the key in the lock.

Maureen lay in the middle of the big, rather lumpy double bed, fighting the sleep that threatened to overtake her. The warmth of the freshly laundered white sheets, weighted by several thick woollen blankets, cocooned her weary and aching limbs. Each time Maureen drifted into the much needed sleep her body jolted, bringing her back to a wakeful state, and she tensed with the effort of trying to make sense of the muffled voices that floated up through the flimsy floorboards of number 91, Lupin Street.

Bernadette Dwyer had had a very busy morning. Not being quite the slovenly woman that Iris believed her to be, Bernadette was also of strong character and blessed with a good heart. Although she was not the tidiest of people, preferring a good chat and endless cups of tea over her house chores, she could work fast and efficiently when need be.

And this morning had been one such time when the forty-year old Irish woman had indeed put a spurt on: as soon as her own family had left for school and work, she had toiled at the many neglected cleaning tasks of her household.

Plodding her way through the terraced house she had washed, cleaned, polished and dusted and, by some stroke of genius, had thought to change the sheets on the large double bed her three youngest children slept in.

Usually, Bernadette only ever changed the sheets when the youngest had a little mishap, a little leaking of the bladder. And, as that was fairly infrequent now that Sadie was six years old, the bedding was normally very soiled before she got round to changing it.

Bernadette wasn't lazy; she just didn't think to have a routine, preferring to do jobs as and when the fit took her. Although she was not a diligent housekeeper, she was a good mother, to all her children. They weren't the best dressed, maybe not the best fed, but they were loved and treated fairly and, as the years were passing by, one by one her children were leaving school, finding jobs, easing her load. Added to this, and to her amazement, Jack was laying off the booze…for the time being.

As an immigrant, Bernadette had realised long ago that she had to make the best of her life in England. There was no going back. To her credit that was what she had done. Her children were her jewels, and God was good to them, they all enjoyed good health. The boozing, pregnancies and lack of money being the only form of life she knew, she never thought to grumble…too much.

That was why Ethel Grady had made a friend of the happy-go-lucky Irish woman. Her house wasn't the cleanest, but her heart and mind were. Bernadette could be trusted to do her best and that was what she had tried to do, by putting a short note in the post to Violet Greenwood—a difficult task for Bernadette, who had had little schooling in reading and writing.

Nevertheless, Vi had arrived, so her letter must have made some sense. A letter she felt she had to write; for what she had witnessed over the few short months since Maureen's return had left her feeling angry, fearful and finally desperate. Bernadette didn't really believe in authorities, but she did believe in fair play and, with that in mind she had done her best to ensure that Iris's brutal treatment of Maureen would go no further.

Whilst Maureen dozed, the children of the house came home from school to be met at the back door by their mother, who, with a finger to her lips, hushed them into the kitchen. And as the afternoon merged into evening, the rain that had fallen all day was blown away by a fierce gale. The wind howled down the chimney of the Dwyer's home, and draughted in under the badly fitting back door.

But the noise was ignored by the two youngest children of the family who were seated on wooden stools, as near to the roaring fire as they could get, each wrapped up in their own thoughts.

Sadie was content to be home from school. Ravenous as usual, the freckled faced, red haired child, dressed in a high neck red jumper under a grey school pinafore, a replica of the elder sister by her side, had eaten her bread and jam and sat watching Betty dawdle with hers, hoping to be offered the best bit: the crusts.

Betty, fully aware of Sadie's greed, took small nibbles of her bread; her good appetite and natural generosity sullied somewhat by what she had been told by her whispering mother.

Turning her face away from Sadie's covetous gaze, Betty focused her attention on Bernadette. Her mother was better dressed than usual. A floral pinny covered her navy blue, box-pleated skirt and her neat lace collared white blouse. A green plaid headscarf hid her greying, rust coloured mop of frizzy hair. Seated at the kitchen table, Bernadette was peeling potatoes, the skins falling softly onto a piece of newspaper.

Watching her mother work Betty's eyes smarted with threatening tears and instead of biting the bread, she bit her tongue. The hurt, coupled with the falling tears unleashed her peevish thoughts...*it's not fair. All the exciting things happen to Maureen...*

Betty's vexed tears flowed freely as she thought of Maureen, lying upstairs in *their* bed...*tucked up and cosseted like a fairy tale princess...while we have to be quiet...sit and eat our tea in silence...whilst...she...she lies in our bed. And she hasn't even been to school! What a mardy-pants, just because that stupid Iris hit her...*

The feelings of jealousy were too much for Betty and, needing to release her pent up fury, she elbowed Sadie in the ribs, which caused the younger girl to yell and protest.

Uproar followed as Bernadette, forgetting her request for silence, jumped up from her chores at the table, berating her squabbling children. Then it was Betty's turn to yelp as Bernadette's hand cuffed the side of her daughter's head.

'Yer little devils, yer don't know when yous well off, that yer don't. There's that poor wee girlie up't stairs...Wit' all t'er troubles...Be quiet, now, the two of yous, else you'll be gettin' what for...Mother of God, what's I 'ave ter be puttin' up wit...' Bernadette always ended her sentences with a religious reference.

Now Betty knew for sure that she really did hate Maureen Grady. And in her petulance, hoped that it would not be long before the troublesome girl was back in Warrington Clough, where she belonged.

Sniffing back her tears, calm in the aftermath of the storm, Betty acknowledged to herself that Maureen had never been much fun, anyway...*we will all be better off without her*...With this thought, Betty brightened. The prospect of Maureen's departure coincided with the realisation that her own mother would then go back to normal. Betty didn't like her mother being posh. Turning to her sister, Betty grinned, and handed over her crusts.

In the house next door there was little to grin about: worry lines creased Iris's forehead as she sat smoking, although as usual, Iris's worries were for her own survival, her own future. At this present time neither seemed worthwhile. Iris wanted to curl up and die; be gone; be out of it. Wanted not to have to think, not to have to move, breathe, even. Tears leaked from the corners of her eyes, heavy tears that flowed down her cold cheeks, dripped off her chin and trickled down her scrawny neck. She sobbed and shivered, her limbs aching, her body throbbing, her anger, as usual, mounting at the unfairness of it all.

She winced as she moved out of her chair. Walking to the door which led out into the lobby, Iris stood for a moment, listening. Listening for signs that her sons were awake. Silence. The silence she had pleaded for. The solitude she had craved, settled around her. And it made her cry more. She was alone. On her own. Again. Even Vi had walked out on her...

After Vi had taken Maureen to the Dwyer's home, she had returned to deal with Iris. First, though—and leaving Iris shivering outside in the yard, whilst she got on with it—Vi had made sure the twin babies were safe and sound, bringing them down the stairs to the warmth of the kitchen.

Eventually Vi had unlocked the back door. Cold and rain soaked, Iris had re-entered her kitchen, timid and rather fearful of what was to come.

However, Vi's approach was not what Iris had expected. The older woman had spoken quietly, suggesting that Iris change her clothes, feed her sons. What she had to say could wait, Vi had said.

Vi had watched her every move and was silent, as promised.

It was two hours before either spoke again. The conversation which then took place made Iris shudder as she remembered: two hours of relentless questions, which had been peppered from each side with shouting and verbal abuse. Vi had not used physical violence during her outbursts but, nevertheless, had intimidated her sister-in-law with her insulting interrogations, before finally slamming out of the house.

Now that Iris's tears had stopped flowing, fury took their place. Crossing the kitchen, she made for the mantel of the fireplace where, amongst the litter, she kept her cigarettes. Lighting one, Iris settled back into her chair, brooding and reflective. One thing was for certain; she would not miss Violet Greenwood…*Good riddance! Busybody! Bloody know-it-all! Liked to walk all over people, did Violet Greenwood. You only had to take one look at Sid to see this to be the truth: henpecked sod that he was, and sex starved, no doubt*…Iris's reflections and harsh criticism helped dispel the guilt that had marred her afternoon.

Drawing deeply on her cigarette, Iris's mind trawled past events, and her marriage to Bill Grady…*Come to think on it*…Iris mused…*I've never been too keen on him either*…The war veteran had been useful, she could grant him that, although his usefulness had not lasted. All too soon she had become his nursemaid and that was something she was not cut out to be.

And Maureen…When Iris even thought of Maureen, her hackles stood on end.…*What a little bastard she turned out to be! All she ever wanted to do was to read her books, colour her pictures, when she could see there was work to be done. Defiant, too, the little swine…If she had done as she was told, there would have been no need to push her. I'd asked her a dozen times to bring some coal up from the cellar. It was her own fault that she had fallen down the steps. Should have done as she'd been told…! Any rate she was lucky, she could easily have broken her legs instead of just bruising them. And cheek! Christ, that kid knew how to give cheek…staring…stubborn cheek…it would make anyone want to smash her face in…gorge her big, blue insolent eyes out. Humph…daughters were supposed to help and care. Not her. Always comparing; always some comment or other…*

As Iris lit yet another cigarette, she remembered all too clearly the condemnations made by Maureen…

"Oh, you don't do it that way! Auntie Vi always *washes* the lettuce first."

"Do you think you should cook a bit of fish for my dad?"

"Auntie Vi says you should *never* leave babies to cry too long."

"My Mam always cooked fish on a Friday."

"Christopher's crying because he's got a wet bum, Auntie Vi says babies have to be kept clean"…*On and on she would go, like some damn old woman…not a nine year old…*

Iris also thought back to her own childhood. Her teenage years…*No. Not now! No, I mustn't think of that, now*...She shoved the thoughts aside, coaxing herself to stay calm, not to think too deeply. She had the boys now, Timothy and Christopher; and maybe, Jim...*he'll have to leave his wife, there's nothing else for it*...

Iris sat on. Reflecting, scheming, brooding. Her introverted thoughts, fuelled by the smoking of endless cigarettes, made her oblivious to the distant wails and whimpers of her infant sons coming from the room above her head.

And, as if they sensed their crying was to no avail, the babies drifted back to slumber, exhausted by their tears.

Downstairs, Iris continued where they had left off. Tears poured down her face as she involuntarily thought back to her early life. Memories she had pushed to the darkest recesses of her mind came tumbling forward: her mother, Moira, long since dead; of her brother, Michael, now the master of the family home and business: The stonemasonry business that had flourished under the austere hand of her father.

Her father, the cold-bloodied parent who had thrown her out like a bad dog: had flung her from all she knew. The door had been slammed shut behind her. No longer her home, the large stone house named Stoneliegh, which overlooked the sea, bolted against her. The house that he, Daniel Fairchilde, had built as a showcase for his work: his *shop window*, as he was proud to boast, as boast he did, when order after order had poured in for his reliable and outstanding workmanship.

Like father like son, Michael had followed into his father's trade. Both were hard men, not given to shows of affection.

After her mother's death, when Iris was in the final year of infant school, cuddles and kisses ceased to exist. And finally she'd been shown the door. Told never to let her shadow darken the doorsteps of Stoneliegh ever again.

And she had not done so. Not even when she knew her father was dead, for by that time it was too late, the funeral having taken place the week prior to her hearing the news that house and business now belonged to Michael and his wife, Rosemary...*Poor Rosemary*...was how Iris thought of her sister-in-law.

Even with all that had happened to her since that time, Iris did not envy Rosemary's lifestyle. Iris was aware that Michael had not changed his character with marriage. Far from it. Indeed, she had first-hand knowledge of how her brother conducted himself as a married man.

When the Second World War had ended, Iris had found herself once again without a home. Having spent more than two years in The Women's Land

Army she had been billeted as and where she was needed. With her demob orders came the invitation to share with one of the conscripts she had been friendly with, Molly Grafton.

Molly, full of fun and frivolity, was very much a *woman of the world*, her world being soldiers, sailors and airmen.

Iris joined Molly, sharing a two-room basement flat in Medlock, on the outskirts of Manchester city centre, an ideal base for Molly's trade. By day she was a seamstress, by night she was an escort.

Michael Fairchilde had used Molly's services on numerous occasions, unbeknown to the innocent Iris (Iris shook her head now remembering that innocence—naivety, really) who, at that time, unaware of her Molly's nocturnal occupation, had thought it was her friend's good blonde looks that made her popular.

However, it was after one of Michael's evenings with Molly that Iris was to learn the truth. After leaving a badly battered and bleeding Molly at the entrance to the local hospital, Michael had made a quick getaway. The next morning, at her friend's bedside, Iris received a double shock when she learnt of Molly's trade and the name of the *punter* who had put her into the hospital.

That same day, Iris packed her bags and left the flat, the words of her late father ringing in her ears..."Get out of here...get on the streets, where you *belong*..."

Suitcase in hand, and with yet again nowhere to go, Iris, reeling from shock, was only grateful she had found out in time. Molly's double life had distressed her, but that alone was not the reason she was fleeing. Iris had been deeply disturbed by how close Michael had come to finding her. Her brother had been her betrayer.

As his father's right hand man, Michael had been instrumental in her expulsion from the family home. Iris had pleaded with her brother, begged him. But he had been like the stone he worked with: hard and unfeeling, deaf to her pleas.

Only on the heel of the death of their father had Iris heard that Michael was seeking her, and knowing of his callousness, Iris was fearful of his motives for her return: Iris had witnessed her brother and his cronies savagely beat one of her father's employees, before bundling the wrecked man onto a boat sailing to Ireland, not knowing whether the man would live or die. Her brother's actions and her father's reaction had sealed her fate. And destroyed her love...

As Iris sat in reflective mood in the house in Lupin Street, Vi did the same in a side ward of North Hospital.

Vi sat censuring the events that lead to her being here. Her reflections and conclusions brought no hope. Deeply distressed, Vi waited in silence by Bill's bedside. Waiting for her brother's return to consciousness.

The Sister-in Charge had told her that Bill had suffered greatly during the day. His lungs had been drained twice during the past twenty-four hours. There was now little hope that he would survive much longer. Vi stroked his hand...*Oh, Bill*...she thought...*what a time you've had, lad*...

She'd been glad that Bill was asleep when she had first arrived at the hospital. It had given her time to calm herself. She had been negligent of just how ill her brother had been. Now that she knew how serious his condition was, she was deeply aware that it was neither the time nor the place to chastise him over the welfare of Maureen.

But what was to become of the child? Maureen could not be allowed to stay with Iris, that was a definite...At the mere thought of Iris, Vi's blood began to boil, to rage against the woman's wickedness...*She isn't human! That was it...It had to be. No human being could be so cruel, surely to God...?* Vi closed her eyes as she thought, her mind travelling back over the events of the day...

After settling Maureen in the surprisingly clean, big warm bed in the Dwyer's house, Vi had returned to her brother's home, unlocking the back door and allowing Iris to enter the kitchen. A sense of her own brutal behaviour towards Iris had rendered her quiet.

Vi's silence had given Iris time to compose herself, to change out of her wet night clothes; to feed and attend her babies. And whilst Vi waited, watching Iris move lethargically around the cluttered kitchen, she had noted the decline of the younger woman. A woman who had seemed so smart and in control not so many months before. Vi had been shocked by Iris's gauntness, by her lank hair and dirty clothes...*What had brought her to this?*

There had followed two hours of talking and shouting; moments when Vi had wanted to throttle Iris. Finally, the arguing had stopped. The babies had cried for attention. And, as Violet had watched her sister-in-law tend to her infant sons, she had felt a spark of relief. At least Iris could look after her own flesh and blood. Perhaps blood *was* thicker than water.

It was during those two hours that Vi had heard how her brother's health had steadily declined. And of how the babies had exhausted Iris. Bill's coughing had kept her awake, stopped them all from sleeping, save for

Maureen.

It appeared that Maureen could sleep through anything. At this piece of news Vi had to stop her face from twitching with mirth; it was obvious that the time spent in the noisy Greenwood household had put Maureen in good stead.

Iris had continued in her tirade, accusing Maureen of being lazy and stupid when her young vitality was needed the most: many nights, when Iris had needed the youngster to help nurse one or other of the twins, Maureen had slept on, dead to the world and her step-mother's cries. And then, to crown it all, the girl had come down with a very bad chest cold that had left in its wake, a barking cough. Between the bouts from Bill, and the bouts from Maureen, Iris claimed she had been driven to near insanity.

It was then that Iris had decided to put Maureen's bed into the attic, so that the babies, who shared the same room as their sister, could sleep for at least three hours in between feeds.

Moving the heavy iron bedstead had proved difficult for Bill and from then on his health had rapidly gone down hill: he had been admitted into the hospital. Iris had managed to visit him just once.

Today—(Vi found it hard to believe that so much could happen in the space of one day.) Maureen had insisted that she should be allowed to go to school. She had the chance to be in a nativity play and did not want to stay at home to care for the babies. She had argued with her stepmother and Iris had lost her patience, slapping the girl across the face, "She *deserved* it," Iris had stated. "She is an insolent, moody child, who needed to be put in her place and that place was the shed!"

Realising that she had listened to the whining excuses long enough, and fighting back the urge to slap a face herself, the sneering ugly face belonging to Iris, Vi had picked up her bag, adjusted her headscarf, tying it firmly under her chin, and had walked out of the house.

The good-natured night-sister made Vi a cup of hot, sweet tea, which Vi was sipping when Bill opened his eyes.

'Hello, Bill, love, how are you feeling?'

'Vi, girl… *Vi, w*hat are you doing here…?' Bill tried to sit up, but the effort exhausted him and he lay back into his pillows. Panting, he continued, 'Did…she…she…got in…touch, then? Did…' he mumbled on, breathless, his fingers fidgeting with the pale green counterpane that was tucked tightly across the bottom part of his chest.

Seeing his agitation, Vi moved out of her chair. Placing her cup and saucer on the bedside cabinet, she leant over her brother, hushing him, kissing his cool forehead.

'There, there, Bill, don't get yourself all het up, I'm here, aren't I? Does it *matter* who told me, eh…? Things will be all right from now on. Shush, lad. Go *on*, go back to sleep.' She stroked his head, and noticed how thin his hair had become. Her eyes filled with tears.

Bill remained awake. He needed to be alert. He knew the time was coming. The time he would close his eyes forever. And he was afraid. Not for himself: He was afraid for his children. His boys. And Maureen. Especially Maureen.

Tears leaked from his tired eyes, wetting the starched white pillow. Tears that were oddly comforting, warm and calming, and so he let them flow, unchecked. When at last he could cry no more, he looked towards his sister. She had continued stroking his hand whilst his tears had fallen. Silently, just being there. *Vi*…he thought…*she's a good woman. The best*…And then he wept some more before he slept.

The ward was all of a bustle when Bill woke again and, to his astonishment, he found it was morning.

'Well, good morning, Mr. Grady! Had a good night?' The nurse who had asked the question popped a thermometer between Bill's lips, so he could not have answered, even though he hadn't tried. So surprised was he to have slept the entire night, the only answer he felt capable of giving was a grin.

'We are feeling better, aren't we?' the nurse quipped as she removed the instrument.

'Fancy a light breakfast this morning? I'll see what I can do…a boiled egg? A slice of toast?'

Bill nodded before he dozed off. The next time he woke, Vi was there.

'Hello, love,' she kissed his forehead, 'I believe you've had a good night, not before time, eh? Things are looking up for you, Bill. And you seem a bit more like your old self today; your colour's better.'

He watched her plonk herself down onto the bedside chair. Chattering of this and that, he couldn't help but smile at some of her anecdotes: there was no one else like their Vi…that was for sure.

No one would have guessed the anguish Vi was suffering or the fact that she had not had even a wink of sleep herself for the past twenty-four hours.

105

The Dwyer's old sofa had been dreadfully uncomfortable, and the night had been long and fraught.

She spent most of the morning with her brother. It was true that he looked better. The Ward Sister had warned that he would have such a spell, but that it would be temporary.

'I'm afraid Mr. Grady is gravely ill. He might last another week—or go today. There's no knowing. Still, we'll do the best we can for your brother. He's had a good night, so you can go in and see for yourself. But please, Mrs. Greenwood, do not excite him. Placate him; tell him you have everything under control. And—oh dear, it's very hard to ask this, Mrs Greenwood, especially in light of what I've told you, but it would be better for your brother if his wife was to be kept away. She caused chaos last time she visited. Barracking my staff, upsetting her husband, no end. Is it possible you can keep her away? I gather they are not close?' Vi had assured the Sister, enlightening the dedicated woman of the situation.

Satisfied by what she had been told, the nurse had led the way to Bill's bedside, adding, 'Forget visiting hours, Mrs Greenwood. *You* are a positive tonic to your brother. Stay as long as you like. I'll get you a cup of tea.'

Bill died the following lunchtime. Only Vi was at his bedside. A dry eyed Vi. She had shed all her tears as she had listened to her brother's wishes. The conversations had taken their toll on the final hours of Bill's life, but at least he had died more contented with regard to the welfare of his children. Even on his deathbed, Bill would not concede to the fact that the twins were not his.

'No. No, Vi, you are wrong on that account. They're *my* lads.'

And Vi would have been a monster to have gone against him on this parentage issue—even though Iris had almost admitted that the boys were fathered by someone other than Bill…"Prove it, though," she had taunted Vi, during their marathon session two days previous.

During her long hours at her brother's bedside, Vi had reluctantly agreed that Iris was capable of looking after her own sons, remembering the adage that had already been in her mind: blood was thicker than water.

Satisfied with the welfare of his sons, Bill had conceded that it wouldn't be right to leave Maureen with Iris, and they agreed that there was only one course of action: Maureen was to be brought up by Vi and Sid. However, she was to be kept ignorant regarding her adoption, as Ethel had wanted. Finally, Bill had asked to see his wife. He said that he took some of the blame for her behaviour…she was too young…not a bad woman, really. He knew that her life had always been difficult and, by marrying him, he had made it much worse...

Vi had stilled her tongue. Yet, before anything could be done about notifying Iris, Bill had gone. Peacefully, whilst he slept—his last sleep of life.

*

**'Whither thou goest. I will go:
and where thou lodgest, I will lodge
thy people shall be my people, and thy God my God.'**

Taken from the Book of Ruth.
1.16

9

Stuart sighed. Kicking out his long legs he crossed them at the ankle and leant backwards in his chair, easing his tense body. Yawning, he stretched his arms high above his head lacing his fingers together, before bringing his joined hands back down to rest on the crown of his head. Tilting his chair, he rocked backwards and forwards and sighed again.

Littered across the kitchen table lay the cause of Stuart's fatigue: his homework: his nightmare. Facts and figures that left him cold, or rather, in a cold sweat. Double line entries that was as foreign to him tonight as they had been at the beginning of the course. A college course which, when completed, would give him a profession. He would be a *somebody*. He would be a bookkeeper. And that was someone everyone needed, at least every business. A proper job that would line his pocket and feed his bank account. Well, that was how his parents saw it.

For Stuart it was like slowly sinking in quick sand. And at present, he was up to his shoulders. It seemed that the more he was taught the less he knew, and his exams were exactly one week away.

As Stuart sat alone, brooding on his impending failure, the rest of his family worked in harmony, some in the two-acre field that backed the cottage, others in the newly erected greenhouses.

1952 had been a momentous year for Violet and Sidney Greenwood. Their eldest son had left school, and they had become business people.

Greenwood's Nurseries and Market Garden had opened its doors on the fourth of April.

Today had been the venture's first anniversary. However, there had been no celebrations. It was business as usual: the busy Easter period being only a week or two away.

'Flipping heck, our Stuart—you've not even done the bloody pots!'

Stuart straightened in his chair, startled by Barry's outburst. So steeped in his misery, he had not heard his brother enter the kitchen.

For his part, Barry looked immediately sorry for his outcry. Keenly aware, as most of the family were, of Stuart's anxiety, Barry busied himself removing his out-door coat, stilling the hum that was always on his lips. Known for the softness of his heart, and his love of out-door pursuits, Barry had said often that he pitied his elder brother. And it was probably a pity mingled with relief—relief that the workload, scattered in front of Stuart right now, was not his own.

Crouching down in the open doorway, Barry pulled off his muddy boots as he spoke again, 'Never mind, Stu, I'll do them. You carry on with *that* little lot.' Leaving his size twelve black Wellingtons outside, Barry stood to his full height, nudging the kitchen door shut with his solid backside. Whistling softly, he rolled up his sleeves, and tackled the dirty supper dishes.

Watching him, Stuart smiled for the first time that evening, before buckling down to his own work, thankful for his brother's arrival, and doubly thankful for the latter's good nature.

One of twins, and just turned fourteen years old, Barry was massive in build. His twin brother Bobby was equally as tall, well over six-foot, although not as well built.

The younger of the pair (by three minutes) Barry's gentle ways and kind nature set him apart from his more aggressive sibling. "Big and soft," his mother called him. And in fairness, it was an apt description of Barry.

Unlike their eldest brother, both of the twin boys were great athletes, although Bobby was the most competitive. Their good looks and sunny dispositions made them many friends and already girls were losing their hearts to the two blond hunks.

Their mother, Vi, often shook her head in amazement at the astonishing duo: their vexing antics, followed by their bellowing laughter, seemed to be always in evidence. Many frantic moments, which had come along with the new enterprise, had been eased by their humorous viewpoint, even though the nursery held little appeal for either young man.

Bobby and Barry Greenwood had decided upon a career in the Merchant Navy. But that was in the future. For now the teenagers were happy to help their parent's build their dream. A dream that brought with it a great deal of hard, back breaking work.

Each day before and after school the boys toiled at their set tasks, usually the heavy work of lifting and shifting, digging and hoeing, working side by side with their father, who himself was putting in an eighteen hour day.

The women of the family, Vi and Maureen, saw to the seeding, the *pricking out*, the boxing and crating of the many plants the steady workforce cultivated.

Stuart's role in the family enterprise was somewhat different. His task was to use his brain not his brawn. Upon leaving school, Stuart had set his sights on becoming an apprenticed carpenter. His parents did not agree. Brains. Brainpower. He had it, and he was not going to waste his life chopping wood. He was to learn bookkeeping, become a businessman: A man in a suit, with hands that were not hardened and calloused: Hands that would be a pleasure to shake.

Stuart had reluctantly conceded, his parent's vision of the future implanted firmly in the fore of his brain, blocking his natural ambition for another line of work.

And, at various times during the year that had followed, when the rest of his family, who rose at dawn to dig and plant and hoe in the most inclement weather imaginable, he had actually been thankful to play his part. Taking a bus into town, spending the day in a warm college building had been pleasant enough. Only now was Stuart becoming aware that it had been a year totally wasted.

Gerard Greenwood, who was in the process of hosing mud off the van this evening, had ambitions that were never aired. His mother and father were in the dark with regard to this son's aspirations.

As the second eldest, much of what Gerard thought or said was ignored. Known as the naughty one of the family—he had been in the most trouble at school, and the one usually caught up in any scraps—Gerard had learned to keep his own counsel and had become the watcher and listener of the family.

And it was a family he dearly loved. The trouble was, he didn't have the verbal word power the others' seemed to possess. Whatever he had to say was usually drowned out by the more forceful voices and personalities of his siblings, and his mother.

Gerard had never stopped being in awe of his cousin Maureen. He thought she was the most beautiful girl in the world. He admired the way her coal black hair swayed as she walked. The way her eyes smiled. He'd never seen that in anyone else's eyes. It was magic. Like her skin...so pale and smooth, he felt he could almost see though it, it was so clear, transparent, almost. Not like his own, which was pimpled and angrily sore looking. And the way she had come through everything—losing her mother, her father, her brothers, all the trouble with that Iris—yet she still seemed so serene, so thoughtful and caring...and so much more a friend to every one else except himself.

But Gerard knew that he was to blame for this. In Maureen's lone presence he usually was completely tongue-tied. He feared that she thought him to be stupid and ignorant. All the things he wasn't. Perhaps it was because they were of the same age. Perhaps it was because he had always felt responsible for her.

Gerard was a writer: A secret scribbler. He had written story after story, some better than others. If he was not good verbally, he certainly had no trouble with the written word. He hoped that one day he would be able to write for a living. For now, he had to work with his parents, digging in dirt, and building muscles to match those of his father's.

In truth, he was biding his time. As soon as Stuart had finished with college, and was working in the business, Gerard had every intention of making known his own ambition. He too wanted to work with books: as a travel writer and journalist. At night, when his family were fast asleep, Gerard worried that any of his hopes would ever come to pass.

Malcolm Greenwood had no such worries. The youngest member of the family rejoiced in his role: Malcolm much preferred to be knee deep in mud rather than go to school. The accolades he received for being helpful from his hard working parents (he'd been thanked for offering to go inside and make everyone a cup of cocoa; though the reality was, there was a comedy show on the wireless he didn't want to miss) made the rest of the outside working boys, which again included Barry who, after washing the dishes and putting them away—keeping his eldest brother out of trouble—was now back at his task of stacking heavy wooden pallets, fume at the unworthiness of the praise: Malcolm wasn't knick-named s*not-nose* for nothing. Always on the *whinge,* tonight Malcolm had been complaining that the cold April night was giving him a sore throat.

Now, as Malcolm smugly went about his duties in the warm kitchen, the radio blaring, he fuelled Stuart's sense of failure even further: the nightly comedy sketch show, with its rude repartee dialogue, was hard to ignore; and the clattering and banging, as his young brother moved from the sink to the stove, was fast making his task at the kitchen table twice as difficult.

Maureen seemed the least affected by the family squabbles and the never-ending workload of the market garden business than any of them. Though it had not been really by choice, she was set to become the family secretary: her chores within the newly founded enterprise entailed anything that did not dirty her hands, too much.

Indeed, Vi pestered Maureen to looked after her hands: creams and lotions graced window ledges and sink tops, and she was made to wear protective gloves even in the hottest months of summer.

Nevertheless, tonight, in the humid greenhouse, as she chatted with her aunt and uncle about the planned hours-of-opening for the forthcoming Easter weekend, Maureen was hopeful that within the few months she still had left at school, she would be able to change her aunt's mind. Maureen had no desire to spend her life in front of a typewriter. And even though Vi had listened to her niece's protests, she had turned a deaf ear.

As Stuart had, too, when he heard where Maureen's real ambitions lay. And to her dismay, he had been obstructive in his role as her chosen councillor. Normally her ally, this time Stuart could not understand why someone who had been brought up in the midst of a large family would voluntarily choose to work with children. Even worse, screaming babies. He'd annoyed her even more when she'd gone on to confide that she wanted to be a qualified nanny…uniform, hat, the lot: No, she wasn't *bonkers*, as he put it, she just liked being with little children, that was all.

Stuart failed his exams. His results came as no surprise to him or his tutors. His parents blamed themselves: he should have been given more time and space to revise. Arguments flared daily. Stuart refused to go on with his studies, preferring to take up the offer of a job in the offices of Shawton's Paint Factory; an office junior position that had been proposed by the astute despatch manager, who was a neighbour of the Greenwoods and who had known the lad since birth.

And Stuart, thankful for any placement that would lead to a wage, suggested a night school course to further his bookkeeping studies.

In the weeks that followed, the young man was relieved that his parent's attention had been grabbed by other, more pressing problems. Enjoying his new working environment, he hoped that the idea of night school would fade from his mother's mind. At least night school for accountancy: Stuart had his sights set on a carpentry course, which was due to commence early in September.

One of Vi and Sid's other problems came in the form of a letter. Correspondence from Chuck Vicente usually brought with it mirth, gifts and well wishes. However, his latest letter, although it was a blessing in disguise for Stuart, was a distraction for Vi and Sid: they were fretted by its contents.

Charles Vicente, know to all as Chuck, hailed from San Antonio, Texas. Chuck was one of the American boys befriended by Vi and Sid during the latter end of the war years.

A huge man of immense character and charm, the crew-cut GI had married his childhood sweetheart before being drafted overseas. Overseas leading him to being stationed at Warrington Clough, a posting that led him into the home of the Greenwood family. When the war ended, the food parcels began.

Chuck never ceased to amaze his *adopted* British family by his kindness. A kindness they had wanted to repay, but did not know how…until now.

Mary Louise, Chuck's wife, miscarried each time her pregnancy reached its third month. With so many miscarriages behind her, her physician had advised against further attempts at trying for a family, "Take her away for awhile, Chuck. Let her rest. Build up her strength. Engage her mind elsewhere. Get her to focus on something different," the doctor had said.

And Chuck had decided that nothing could be more engaging than a trip to England: England in June. And the coronation of a queen.

'Oh my God, listen to this!' Vi read out the telegram, 'Docking at Southampton. *Stop*. Taking train to London. *Stop*. Staying at The Strands. *Stop*. Meet us outside hotel 9.00.a.m. June 2nd. *Stop*. Chuck.'

'Meet *who* there?' asked Gerard.

Malcolm answered. 'Someone called *Stop*, I think…'

Everyone around the table sniggered. Including Malcolm, but he only laughed because everyone else did.

Bobby liked nothing better than to get at Malcolm and to goad Gerard.

'You're *so* stupid, Malcolm. And it's Chuck and his wife who are coming, *cloth head.* Who did you think, Gerard? The blooming Queen?'

Sid was getting fed up with his sons, 'All right, that's enough of that. We've got plenty to contend with, without your pennyworth, clever Dick! Come and sit down Vi, and let's think about it. Maureen, love—finish serving up, will you lass?' Sid motioned for his wife to take her place at the table, and for his niece to take over at the stove where a pan of frying chips were turning a golden brown.

It was Friday teatime: fish cakes and chips, bread and margarine, and endless cups of tea. The usual Friday meal enjoyed by all before they went their separate ways; Stuart and Maureen often went to the cinema. Bobby, Barry and Gerard to the Parish Hall for Scouts, grumbling about having to tail Malcolm, as he made his way back to school to attend Cubs.

Sid went down to the miners' social club most Friday evenings, and Vi stayed home to do her bookkeeping.

But this Friday evening the meal had begun with measure of excitement and intrigue and brotherly snipes brought about by the reading of the telegram.

'We'll *have* to go, Sid, you know that don't you? He's been good to us has Chuck...and he'll be expecting us. I told you he would, didn't I? Hey? Yet you thought we could ignore his letter! Well, we can't ignore a blooming telegram, can we?' Vi sipped her tea, her eagerness showing, though she was trying hard to mask it.

'Look at Mam, she's gone all red!'

'Shut up, Malcolm, and eat you tea,' Vi snapped back, annoyed that her hot cheeks had been noticed.

'We can't go, and that's *final*. I told you, Vi, when his letter first came, that we can't spare the time, nor the money. Besides, how'll we get there?' Sid, hoping that would be the end of it, continued eating.

'You could go in the van, Dad. I can just see it parked outside The Strands. They'll think you're an eccentric royal, or a barmpot millionaire,' Stuart quipped, to the amusement of all.

'The Strands! Chuck really knows how to do things, don't he, Sid?' Vi mused to herself more than to her husband.

Scraping his plate, Sid answered in his usual truthful manner, 'Aye, he's all right, that one, for a *Yank*.' His meal finished, Sid paired his knife and fork on the plate with a sigh of satisfaction: Sid enjoyed his food. He ran his tongue or his front teeth, thoughtfully, before saying, 'Maybe we had better think about going. But one thing is certain, before you get any grand ideas in your head, Vi…we're *not* staying the night in London. And I'm not driving! We'll go by train. There and back same day. Just you and me Vi…'

Uproar followed: The twins didn't want Auntie Nellie coming to look after them. Malcolm wanted to go with his parents. Maureen didn't want to be in charge of whining Malcolm; she had been chosen to sing in the school choir at the coronation celebrations, and didn't want to have to take him with her. Stuart said he had arranged to go out with his work pals (he was looking forward to his first ever drinking binge.)

Only Gerard was quiet, and he had his reasons. He was the only other person in on the surprise. A surprise that Sid had been looking forward to giving; he had ordered a television set to be delivered in time for the coronation.

Gerard eyed his father, willing him to speak up. And was rewarded for his silence with a knowing wink.

'Now just be quiet, the lot of you! Listen on…come on, *shut up* and listen. Right, well, I've got something to tell you. None of you will want to go out on Coronation Day. Don't look like that…even your Mam doesn't know what I'm talking about…' Sid was pleased by the look on Vi's face. '…You see, it was going be a surprise, like, but now I think I'd better tell you all. Nothing ever goes as planned, not in this house! Anyways, the thing is—we're getting a television set…'

Much later that evening Sid and Vi sat side by side on the sofa in the front room of their cottage. A front room that was no longer the bedroom of Maureen: she had moved into her rightful room over the bathroom. Since the girl's return to Warrington Clough, many alterations had been done to the Greenwoods' cottage. The lean-to bathroom had been torn down, replaced by a professionally built brick extension: a two room costly addition, an annexe that had been greatly needed.

However, the bank loan to do the building had long since been repaid, securing the necessary funding required to bolster the nursery venture. Sid was proving himself to be creditworthy client, and an adept businessman.

'I wish we could take Maureen and Stuart with us, Sid. Chuck always enjoyed the lad's company, took him fishing and whatnot. And it would break the ice, like. What have we in common?' Sipping her cocoa, Vi hoped she could get the matter of the London trip settled once and for all. With her husband mellow after his couple of pints of beer, she had seized her opportunity.

'Well love, I think he just wants us to meet his wife. He's written so much about her, I feel I know her—without knowing her, and it's sort of embarrassing, isn't it? Knowing all about her private whatsits...'

Vi laughed with her husband. *Men... she thought... they don't like talking about pregnancies. Don't like to mention when a woman's showing a bulge... just like to make it happen...*

'And that's just *why* I think it'd be good to have the two eldest with us...we wouldn't feel so shy, then, would we? Not with the kids with us...'

'Vi! We can't afford *four* fares...'

'I know, I know, but I've been thinking; we *could* drive there couldn't we, Sid? I mean it would be a wonderful day out for us all: A day to remember. It's not every day of the year a queen gets crowned, now is it?'

So it was the four of them that travelled through the June night on the long road journey to London. As they reached the capital, all tiredness was forgotten.

Everywhere was decorated with posters of the new, soon to be crowned queen. Buildings and houses proudly flew the Union Jack flag, their windows peopled, their front doors ajar. Red, white and blue bunting and banners hung from lamppost to lamppost, roof-top to roof-top; thousands of people thronged the streets, and music floated the air as the bands played their well practiced melodies and anthems: Londoners were proud to be Londoners, Scot's were happy to be from bonny Scotland, and Irish eyes were indeed smiling.

The capital was alive and expectant this dull weathered June morning. Arm in arm, caught up in the excitement, Vi and Sid, Maureen and Stuart walked down the crowded Strand, after parking the dark blue Bedford 5cwt. van well out of sight.

Vi was surprised by the ease in which she strolled into the grand hotel with her family close to heel. And how easy it was to greet and kiss Chuck and his pretty, dark haired wife, Mary Louise, who begged all of them to call her Mary Lou.

It was even easier to stand in the pouring rain, eight deep in the crowd with family, friends and strangers to cheer Her Majesty and wish her well; easy to dine in an opulent restaurant that backed onto the Thames and sip champagne as though she had done so all her life.

And, as she noted her own ease, she noted the same of Maureen, and felt deeply proud of the young girl who was blossoming into a fine woman. Vi loved Maureen as if she were her own flesh and blood. Indeed, it could be said that Vi adored her niece.

Vi was doubly proud of her husband and son. Sid was good company; Stuart, tall and handsome, though somewhat shy, came up to scratch for the occasion. Later, Vi was to regret only one part of the day. The part when her tongue, loosened by more than three glasses of champagne, took to having a mind of its own: it invited Chuck and Mary Lou to travel up to Warrington Clough and to stay for a few days.

On the long nauseous journey back north, Vi had hours to berate herself for her foolish generosity...*where would she put them? How long would they stay? What would she feed them...?*

By the time the van pulled up outside number 87, she had all the answers: They would stay as guest should stay, in the best room of the house: Her own bedroom. She and Sid would sleep in the front room; they'd done it before. And she would feed them as she always fed people...*the best I can, and, if they didn't like it, well...*

Chuck and Mary Lou *did* enjoy their stay in Warrington Clough. So much so, that they took all the youngsters of the Greenwood family with them when they travelled further north to the Lake District, staying in a large chalet on the shore of Lake Windermere.

There, by the shimmering lake, Chuck and Mary Lou spoke endlessly about their life in America, to the delight of both Stuart and Maureen. The teenagers learnt how Chuck's construction business was booming, and how he needed able and enthusiastic young people to help forge the way ahead. Chuck had plans to move his business to Florida, where houses were being sold faster than they were being built. As he listened, enthralled by what he heard, Stuart knew he wanted to have a part in this future.

When the three day holiday was over, the visitors deposited the Greenwood children back to their parent's care, and, after brimming eyed farewells, and prolonged hugs and chaste kisses of thanks (even from the boys, Vi noted) they had travelled back to London and their flight home not knowing that they were to become responsible for many hours of rows, pleadings; and tears.

Maureen was saddened to learn that Stuart was to go to America. What would she do without him? Who would she talk to? Stuart had always been stalwart in the advice he had given his cousin; also, during the years she had lived in Warrington Clough, he been her constant companion.

She cried herself to sleep the night he promised to stay for no more than one year. She wept openly, alongside his mother and father, when they waved him goodbye from the Liverpool dock, as he set sail for America upon the Cunnard liner, *Parthia*.

During Stuart's absence Maureen left school, taking up a place at secretarial college, putting her own ambitions on hold in the manner her cousin had before her.

Being a sensitive girl, in tune to other peoples' feelings, Maureen was aware that both Vi and Sid were still traumatised by the steely determination of their eldest son. Stuart's departure had left a hole in the Greenwood family. Maureen did not want to responsible for any more trouble. Time enough to think of nursery nursing, first she must become a competent typist, by way of a thank you to her guardians.

Stuart wrote often, to his mother, father and brothers, and long, descriptive letters to his cousin: Letters for her eyes only. Letters describing how fabulous his new life was…

Maureen, you'd love it here. So much of everything: food, music, sunshine; great opportunities. I'm learning loads. Mary Lou is getting stronger. She's great, real kind and thoughtful. I miss you all—but honestly, Mo, I wouldn't have missed this chance for the world. Maureen, stand up to Mam and Dad, tell them what you want to do. Tell them you want to go in for nursing. You'll regret it if you don't. Stand up to them. I know my mother and father have been wonderful with you—but it's your life, and don't forget it.

Maureen read her letters over and over again. She knew Stuart was right, but the time never seemed right to go against her aunt and uncle—an aunt and uncle who had never asked anything of her before.

It was fate that made the time right. Mary Lou was pregnant. Although she had passed the usual miscarrying month, complete bed-rest was prescribed. Chuck wrote to Vi with their request…

Could Maureen come for the summer? Just to help Mary Lou during the latter months of her confinement? Would it be possible? They'd make sure she was back for the beginning of the autumn term at college. And they'd pay her fare. Stuart knew they were writing and had his fingers crossed. It would be nice for him to have someone visit from England…

The other letter Vi and Sid received were from their son, begging them to agree.

Vi and Sid also begged. They pleaded Maureen not to go, 'For heaven's sake, surely to God Mary Lou can find someone else, someone who lives closer…'

Yet, at the back of their minds, both knew they were being unfair: A great trip missed because of their inability to let go?

Finally, after much soul searching, they agreed…

'Just for those few months, mind—until the baby's born. Are you listening, young lady, you are to come back, then…!'

Wide eyed with excitement, Maureen promised to return, and, with Stuart by her side.

In July of 1954, Maureen set sail for New York on another of Cunnard's liners, *Media*. As the ship made its noisy departure, Vi waved a frantic, teary goodbye, knowing in her heavy heart that life was changing, irretrievably.

*

10

'Gerard?'

'What?'

'Where is Boca Raton?'

'You know, Malcolm...it's in Florida.'

'Do you think they'll ever come back?'

'Of course they will. Now finish your soup before Mam gets back.'

Gerard was tired. Bone tired. Moving to stand by the bedroom window, he gazed out. Rain whipped the glass, gusted by the howling wind: rain that had fallen in torrential torrents, without interval, the entire day. A miserable and dark February day, far removed from the sunny climes of Florida.

'What time do you think Mam and Dad will get back?'

'Soon, I should think...' Gerard glanced at his wristwatch, '...the funeral service was two hours ago. Mam said there wasn't going to be much of a do after. Percy can't afford it.'

Florence Fielding (who'd been more of an aunt to the Greenwood family than a neighbour) died on the first day of February. Her husband, Percy, had been more relieved than sad. His wife had been a burden the last few years, suffering stroke after stroke. Nursing her had put a great strain on the elderly man. Now, after more than fifty-five years of marriage, the widowed Percy had little energy left, and even less money.

The funeral arrangements had been organised by Vi, although Percy, as proud as ever, would take no handouts; he'd bury his own, and pick up the bill for the funeral tea, no matter what it cost.

This being so, Vi had been only too pleased to leave her sons out of the scenario. Her boys could eat anyone out of house and home.

However, even if he had been invited, Malcolm Greenwood would have declined the invitation. The youngest member of the Greenwood family had been bedridden for over two weeks suffering a severe bout of bronchitis. It had fallen to Gerard to be the invalid's carer during this long, bleak afternoon of his mother's absence, and he too was feeling far from well.

Later, when his parents returned, Gerard excused himself from his evening duties in the greenhouses.

'I've a headache, Mam. I feel rotten. If it's all right with you, I think I'll have an early night.'

But sleep and rest was hard come by. Gerard's eyes refused to close. He felt strange. He ached everywhere. A hammer beat in his head, the thumping rhythm making him nauseous.

Switching on his bedside light, Gerard reached inside his nightstand and withdrew a large envelope. Easing into a sitting position, he pummelled his pillows to form a backrest, and shook out the envelope's contents.

Photographs spilled onto the blue eiderdown; a few slid to the floor. Gerard winced with pain as reached to retrieve them. Tears formed behind his eyes. He felt so unwell, so miserable. The photographs made him feel worse. The snapshots, which his mother would not acknowledge, made him want to weep: Stuart looked so tanned and fit. Leaning against a white wooden fence, he was smiling at the dark haired girl by his side. Maureen looked radiant, the sunlight glinting her black hair.

The next photo was Chuck and Mary Lou, standing proudly on the porch of their new home, with toddler daughter, Lydia, playing at their feet.

Then came a lovely shot of Maureen, Lydia and Mary Lou, laughing into the camera, as they sat side by side on a wooden swinging hammock seat, shielding their eyes in the glare of a bright Floridian day.

Another of Stuart; he too shading his eyes with a saluting gesture as he stood, naked to the waist, his chest tanned and muscular.

The last one was of them all: Chuck, Mary Lou, Lydia, Maureen and Stuart, sat around a wooden picnic table, Maureen's hair shorter than before;

smoke curled from a barbecue; the blue ocean the un-designed backdrop.

Clutching the last photo to his chest, Gerald flopped back against his pillows, wishing he felt better. Wishing he belonged to such a life. Wondering would he ever see his brother and his cousin back in England— and knowing the answer. *Why? What for? Why should they come back...? National Service? Grey skies...bleak, rainy days?*

Tears ran down Gerard's cheeks. He slid down his pillows, turned on his side, and wept.

It was Vi who found him; Vi who had wondered why he hadn't come down for breakfast; why he hadn't answered when she had called up the stairs. And it was Vi who ran to the telephone box on the corner of their road to call the ambulance, knowing in her heart that it probably was too late.

At the hospital, with her ashen-faced husband by her side, Vi heard the prognosis. Prognosis? What did *that* mean?

'Talk in proper English, will you! Say what you mean...'

They did. Then she knew what her heart had already told her...

'Spell it out...' she had flared, and they had. Poliomyelitis. Polio. And there was added complications: Gerard was dying.

Two funerals in as many weeks; Vi was coping. But then, didn't she always? She had coped when Stuart had gone. She had coped when Maureen had followed. Coped when the twins had joined the Merchant Navy: Cope, cope, *cope.* That was her life, wasn't it? Cope with this—deal with that. Lose your mother, father and brother. Take in another's daughter...cope with six children. Smile when they whinge "they want *more* out of life." Run a business...smile when people say "Aren't you the lucky ones...holidays in America for you for you next, eh?"

Cope. Show Sid you can manage. Don't let on. Don't say a word. You are strong, Vi. You can do it, Vi. You can cope with life...so you can cope with death. Think of the others, Vi...you're good at it. Big Vi can cope with the death of her son.

The doctor clattered down the steep wooden steps that led into the kitchen. Pulling out a chair, he sat down next to Sid at the cluttered kitchen table.

'She needs a break, Sidney. You both do. The strain's been too much. Take her away, Sid, if you can. For a few days, though a week or two would be better. Can your lads get compassionate leave?'

Sid nodded, knowing the doctor was right. Vi was getting worse not better. Sinking lower with each passing day. Placing his elbows on the table, he lowered his face into his hands and wept. Tears and spittle dripped onto the soiled green tablecloth as he sobbed.

The doctor, a kindly man who knew the Greenwood family well, tidied the kitchen as best he could, made a pot of tea, then let himself out, thankful that at least Sid was grieving openly.

*

11

'Repeat after me: I, Iris Grady, take thee, Declan Patrick Fitzgerald, to be my lawful husband...'

Declan was an early riser, born from sharing a bed with three massive brothers. Topping and tailing, Declan had always been the first to be booted out of bed: the runt of the litter, the small framed younger brother who didn't fight back. But the harsh treatment at the hands and feet of his siblings only fuelled the young Irish boy's dream: Declan intended to become a jockey— an ambitious vision of the future that was annihilated by under nourishment and rickets.

However, although the rickets deformed the bones in his legs it did not deform his mind: Declan had inherited nothing from his big boned father, save his name. Declan was the only son with the genes of the other parent: he had the quick witted intelligence of their diminutive mother and, like her, used this power against the empty headed brawn of his father and brothers to his advantage.

Leaving Ireland at the tender age of fourteen, Declan had tried his luck in the building trade. His first placement was in the city where his boat from

Ireland had docked.

Working long, back-breaking hours, he soon realised that the arrogant man who employed him only wanted empty headed mules. Declan defied the man at cost, and was dismissed for insolence.

Nursing his swollen pride, along with his swollen and badly beaten body. Declan thought to try his luck again, this time in the city of London. And for Declan the streets of the capital were indeed paved in gold, or rather the roofs were.

The year of 1957 saw Fitzgerald's roofing business booming. Known in the trade as *Monkey Legs,* Declan had spent his apprentice years on the bombed, derelict roofs of inner city London. A never-ending job, thanks to the Luftwaffe, and a career that suited his small build; he could scramble and work quicker than any other roofer.

Soon, contractors were asking for him by name and, sooner than he could ever have dreamed, Declan was running his own company.

And it was through his company's involvement with a contractor in Manchester that he had met up again with Iris, though it had to be said, he would never have recognised her. Notwithstanding that Declan was the love of Iris's life, he had forgotten all about the young woman he had briefly known during his sojourn in the north west of England.

Iris woke to find herself alone in the huge bed. She stretched and smiled: she always woke smiling. Now.

Turning onto her side, she snuggled into her soft pillow, and her thoughts pictured Declan. She knew where he would be: on the beach, walking along the sea edge, dodging the lapping tide; plotting, thinking, scheming of how to make more and more money. And how she liked that. Iris liked every minute of being Mrs. Declan Fitzgerald. She liked her solitaire diamond engagement ring that now was so enhanced by a broad gold wedding band: The golden band that had been placed on her finger five days ago. Their wedding day: Valentines Day to be exact.

Iris liked being in Sorrento in the middle of February. She liked the way the Italian men glanced at her…again and again. But that side of her life was over. She was going to be a good wife to Declan. She had waited long enough. Nothing would spoil her life now. Declan was going to adopt the boys. They would become Fitzgerald's, too.

The only sons of Declan Fitzgerald, though Declan did not know that yet, and Iris would never be telling. No, Iris would not be acknowledging to her new husband that a recent backstreet abortion had destroyed all chances of her ever having another child. Not that it bothered her. Pregnancies were a curse anyway...

But Declan had declared that he wanted children, 'To be sure, I'll adopt the boys. What's yours is mine...and what's mine is yours. And soon we'll have another strapping son, or a wee daughter! Me darling, we'll not have to wait. I want a family around me as fast as possible, I does that! A family of me own I can be proud of. A family that will carry on with me business, a millionaire's business, eventually...'

Declan returned from the beach to find his new wife still in bed. Joining her, they made love, then ordered breakfast and showered.

They ate on the terrace of their hotel suite, enjoying the view, making plans for the day, and the future. Declan was in fine form and eager to include his new wife in all his plans.

'I've taken a lease on a grand house in Old Kensington. The place needs a lot doing to it, been neglected, like. But the roofs sturdy, for sure...' he took a sip of fresh orange and laughed, '...did the work on that myself a couple of years back.'

Not being a big eater, Declan watched Iris as she tucked into her scrambled eggs and smoked salmon (as though she hadn't eaten for days,) with an amusement that was slightly tinged with annoyance. The disdain was fleeting; lighting a cigarette he continued...

'The boys can go to the local school, its a good one, in a good area. I want them to use their brains. Go on to university. Become professionals. You—me lady—you can furnish the house. And engage yourself some help. Find an Irish woman that can do the lot, and who'll look after the kids, too. You'll be travelling with me, in between yer pregnancies, of course. I've many plans, me flower, many plans,' he patted his wife's busy hand and looked out to sea, his words bringing a shine to his eyes as he saw the future stretched before him, bright and exciting.

Iris just looked out to the sea; the last piece of salmon seemed lodged in her throat.

Declan's new wife enjoyed looking at herself in mirrors. Of late, as Declan's fiancée, she'd had plenty of opportunity to do so with two appointments booked each week at a top beauty salon in Manchester city centre.

As a pampered and cosseted newly-wed, Iris was aware that she no longer looked her thirty-four years. Her slim frame carried her newly acquired tailored suits well, and her hair, softly permanently waved and coloured a sleek platinum blonde, enhanced her brown eyes. Iris was also aware that brown-eyed blondes were rare; she looked different, and the difference pleased her.

However, her elegant reflection seemed out of place today. Standing in the front bedroom of the grimy house in Lupin Street, Iris had no time to preen. Nor did she have the time to reflect on the memories which crowded in around her. She shuddered to clear her thoughts before she set about the task of clearing out what and what not she would be taking with her...

This was the first time Iris had been inside the Lupin Street house since the week after meeting up with Declan: He had been appalled to see how she living, and had not hesitated in finding her and the boys a better home.

The flat he had moved them into was in the Great Park area of Littleton: An entire top floor of a house that overlooked the well-kept park. The twins had thought that they had moved into a palace, especially when they realised they would each have a bedroom of their own.

And Declan had been thrilled by their delight. So much so that, on honeymoon, after one of his early morning beach strolls, he'd told Iris he couldn't wait to see the boys reaction to their new home. Iris heard that the Old Kensington property would be magnificent when her husband's workforce had finished the refurbishment: set in an acre of prime London, the imposing house was being readied to become their main family home. Iris was to expect to be moving south by as early as the end of February.

After their short five day Valentine honeymoon, Declan had not returned to Manchester. His London businesses demanded immediate attention, and so Iris had train journeyed back alone.

Indolent of what needed her immediate attention, Iris decided to complete her honeymoon week by booking herself into the Shireland Hotel for a couple of nights. Though the thought of going back to her flat wasn't unpleasant, other tasks that needed her attention could wait. And that included collecting her sons from their minder. They were being well cared for where they were; Iris concluded she would be back with her sons soon enough.

On her first evening, devouring a three course dinner in the hotel's splendid restaurant, she'd enjoyed the experience of being the only lone diner, revelling in the glances she received from the other tables occupied by well-dressed business men. Downing two glasses of port, she'd signed her bill and ordered a taxi to take her to visit her sons.

Christopher and Timothy were in the care of Iris's good friend and work colleague, Sylvia Baden. Sylvia, a hostess who worked in The Peers Club, Piccadilly, was acting as surrogate parent to the two boys, and was being well paid for her efforts. Indeed, Declan had paid Sylvia twice the amount she would have earned at the club.

At least he thought he had. Iris's new husband was unaware that Sylvia had another occupation: The oldest of occupations. And he was also blissfully unaware that it had also been his wife's line of business.

Iris had told Declan that she did bar work in the evenings so that she could be home during the day for her boys. The latter part was true. Unbelievably, Iris was a good mother to her schoolboy sons; but her days were spent pandering to the needs of older boys whom she met doing her evening bar work. The Lupin Street house was well known by the taxi fraternity, the numerous fares boosting their daily lunch-time trade…

And that was why today, two days after arriving back in Manchester, she had demeaned herself, travelling by bus to her old home in Littleton. Iris had been fearful of taking a taxi to her old address. Now, as Mrs Declan Fitzgerald, there was too much at stake for any knowing nods.

Dressed in some of her less expensive clothes, she had walked quickly down Lupin Street, hoping not to meet any of her one-time neighbours. Being a generous, thoughtful man, Declan had continued to pay the rent on the house leaving Iris time to settle her affairs: to take leave of the house at leisure. He had suggested that perhaps she might like to sell one or two of the better pieces of furniture.

In reality, Iris had telephoned from her suite in the four star hotel and had engaged a clearance firm to take the lot away…

Back downstairs now in the damp smelling house, she paced the floor of the room they had called the parlour, willing the removal people to arrive. Already half an hour late, Iris fretted that they would arrive at all. The house gave her the creeps, always had, but today more so than ever. With her changed circumstances she was becoming the person she felt she was meant to be; the person she had always wanted to be, and nothing or nobody was going to ruin her second chance at life.

And who would have thought it possible…? Iris lit yet another cigarette as her thoughts turned to the night she had been reunited with Declan…*to think, I nearly didn't go to the club that night…*

131

Timothy had been so poorly with the mumps, and Iris hadn't really wanted to leave him with Sylvia's mother, 'Go, girl, get going, now!' Myra had said, 'I needs the money, if you don't. Go on, Tim'll be all right with me...you know I loves your kids.'

And that was true. Myra Baden had been heaven sent when she moved into the house next door. The Dwyer's, who had gone so far up in the world (Iris still found it hard to believe that the Irish family's fortunes had turned for the better since Jack had signed the pledge,) that they were now the owners of a large terrace house in a better part of Littleton, had been *sharpish* in the speed of their move: the decline of the Lupin Street houses went hand-in-hand with the moral decline in their neighbour's home. Though it must be said, Bernadette Dwyer was distressed to say goodbye to the little boys, of whom she'd become very fond: Timothy, Christopher and Maureen Grady were always given a special mention in the caring woman's nightly prayers. Not having seen or heard anything of Ethel's youngster since the death of Bill Grady, Maureen still got a mention each and every evening, for that was Bernadette's way.

The Baden family, consisting of Myra, the mother, (no father ever came on the scene, or was talked of) three daughters and two sons, (they shared the house in between jail sentences) who had taken over the Dwyer's old house, were a jolly lot, not given to preaching to others the right and wrongful way of living. Number 91 was kept tidier and cleaner than Bernadette had kept it, and the front door was always open.

And, although Myra's daughters belonged to a seedy world, she herself lived like a saint, helping and aiding those in need. Her eldest daughter, Sylvia, had moved into a flat of her own, but still came to her mother's house each and every evening to share the gossip of the day, and the laden tea table.

Lonely boys at heart, Timothy and Christopher Grady had grown to love their next-door neighbour, whom they called Auntie Myra, and their mother, Iris, found the woman to be very useful...

It took just over one hour to clear number 93 Lupin Street of its furniture and tatty carpets. One hour to empty the home of the late Bill and Ethel Grady. Iris fumed at the price she was paying the clearance firm: twenty-five pounds, plus what they would get for the price of the furniture once it had been sold. It didn't seem fair to Iris, not when she thought of how hard she'd had to work for half of that sum.

But as she mounted the steep stairs, heading for the attic, Iris smiled, her annoyance forgotten; money problems were behind her. All she had to concentrate on now was the future. And the future looked rosy. The only cloud on the horizon was the subject of children.

Declan had made it quite clear that he intended having a large family. Iris knew that he would not be satisfied just being a father to her two boys. And she also knew, deep at the back of her mind, that he would never adopt them. Not until she produced a few children of his own, and that would not be happening.

It seemed so unfair: So unjust. She thought again of how he had not remembered her...*how could he not have remembered...?* When she could recall every single detail. She could ever remember the smell of him when they were teenagers: a peppery, leather scent, a masculine odour that she had not be aware of in any other man since.

Although petulant that Declan had scarcely recognised her, Iris had been sensible enough not to tempt fate, nor to jog his memory too much; bad enough that he'd found her working behind a bar, without stirring too much of the past into their new future.

True, Declan had seemed overjoyed to renew their acquaintance. Pleased even, that through her father's high handedness he had sought his fortune elsewhere—and had found it.

During their short courtship Declan told her of Michael Fairchilde's failure: the business was on its knees. Although Declan had no kind words for Iris's brother, he would not find fault with her father.

It appeared that Michael had been the one instrumental in Declan's dismissal, and it became clear to Iris, as she had listened, that Declan was without ill feeling regarding his brutal departure...

'Michael never liked me, Iris,' he'd stated, 'I think I was a too quick witted for him. He was on the take, you know! And like all fools, your brother Michael has little to *no* brain. He blamed you, aye he did. Said he didn't want me anywhere near you. Made out that he was protecting his little sister from an Irish ruffian. But he was jealous! Aye, he were jealous of me and the way I was getting on with your father. The pity of it is that perhaps we'd have been married the sooner, eh? And then them there lads would have been mine instead of old man Grady's...'

Iris was fearful of entering the attic. The small, dingy room at the top of the house had always un-nerved her. As she pushed open the rickety door her thoughts flew to Maureen. She hadn't thought of the girl in a long time.

Stepping gingerly under the sloping eves of the room her conscience began to twinge with guilt...*the girl must have hated it in here. Still, she deserved all she got...caused no end of trouble did little Miss Goody-Pants. She'll be a teenager now. Married off no doubt, fat Vi wouldn't want her hanging around too long...*

With these thoughts, Iris got straight to work. The afternoon was drawing in. Cold February air penetrated the dusty room as Iris decided on the bits and pieces she would take with her.

Mostly it was Ethel's belongings she was rifling through: books and letters. Photographs. Neat bundles tied with string, some with ribbon. Faded newspaper clippings, detailing news from the war front. Death certificates, mourning cards, song-sheets and music scores, and an assortment of cinema/theatre ticket stubs.

So much stuff—much more than Iris had accumulated over the years. Iris never thought to store memorabilia...*and who would want it? Not the boys...*

Iris thought of her sons, realising that they would have no recollection of Maureen. Were not aware that they even had a sister. Iris had made sure of that when Vi had written requesting for Maureen to visit her brothers. She had written back, spelling it out in no uncertain terms that the boys were not Maureen's brothers. That Christopher and Timothy were not Bill's children, putting paid to Vi's notions of keeping the children in touch.

But the twins *were* Bill Grady's sons. And if Violet Greenwood was to set eyes on either of Christopher or Timothy she would see the truth at once, as Jimmy Dawson had done when the boys were less than two years old.

Iris's twin sons were the image of Bill Grady: sandy blond hair and green eyes, the very image of Vi's own twin sons, Barry and Bobby. Once seen, there would be no mistaking the family likeness...*Perhaps that was why Maureen's on my mind now...*she thought...*this house belongs more to her than to anyone else...*

Iris pictured the girl: her small dainty figure and jet-black hair, nothing at all like her father's colouring...*she obviously took after mother, Ethel...*

She bit her bottom lip, guiltily. There was no getting away from it. She'd been a swine to the girl...*Still, Vi will have made it up to her...Vi was like that...*

In different circumstances, Iris conceded to herself, she might have made friends with Vi. At least Vi knew how to have a laugh...*not like her dour bloody brother! It's a pity that Vi was so frumpy, and old before her time...poor sod...*

Iris's mind kept wandering as she opened box after box, invoices and bills that had been labelled and stored in neatly tied piles. She wondered whether Vi was still battling with her weight. Looking back, she realised that Vi had been very young. Must have only been in her late twenties, but did indeed look so much older.

And Iris went on to wonder how life had treated Vi. Whether she was still married to Sid...? *Probably*. Did she have more children...? *Probably...there would be no abortions for the likes of Violet Greenwood...!*

She shivered, and pulled at her collar against the cold. The room was freezing...*I must get going...*

Still she rooted: papers, photographs; letters. Iris skimmed through some of the lose ones. Others were bundled. One of the bundles was a collection of six written by Bill to his first wife. No mention of love, just facts...statements, declarations. Iris read from the top one:

Glad we have our Maureen. You were right, Eth. But then, aren't you always? Look after Vi. I know she barges into everything full steam ahead...

She read from another, written whilst Bill was in convalescence on the south coast:

Dearest Ethel,

Good to be back in England. I expect you thought I was dead.

Did they send you a telegram? I've been thinking (I've had a long time to do nothing but think, ha...ha...ha) Anyway, you are right not to tell Maureen anything. Write and tell me what she looks like, now. What does she want for her birthday? I'd like to get it, and bring it home with me. I can't believe she is nearly seven. Send some photographs. And tell me what she talks about— who her friends are. Does she still play with Bernie's girl? There's so much I want to know, so much time to make up for...

She stood up, realising she had been crouched in a cramped position for too long. Wincing, she stretched her arms, bent and unbent her knees. The room was growing darker. She flicked the light switch on. A single, dusty light bulb cast a yellow glow around the paper-strewn attic.

Iris returned to a crouching position and searched for more letters, more notes from Bill. But found nothing of interest. In truth, she was looking for insurance papers. Money. Anything she could claim.

She opened a shoebox crammed with birthday cards, Christmas cards, and amongst these she found birth congratulations:

To welcome your new baby, with love from all in Didsbury...

Congratulations! Happy for you, thought it would never happen...

Babies bring love...

Hope all is well. See you at Maureen's christening. I enclose photograph:
The latter message came in the form of a notelet in amongst the cards. The photograph was in a cream coloured folder, pristine in condition and obviously much prized.

Iris opened the folder and stared at the photograph: a smiling Bill standing next to Ethel. Ethel, smiling down at the white bundle in her arms, their new baby, Maureen.

Iris turned the black and white photograph over, read the inscription on the back of the folder: *September 4th. 1939. Bill, Ethel and Maureen.*

Iris looked closely at the photograph again. Behind Bill and Ethel was a stone fronted building; wide, shallow steps led up to a massive front door.

Iris gasped, lifting the photograph closer to her face. She saw that standing to the left of the happy couple was a man in clerical clothing...*Vicar? Priest...?* Iris strained her eyes, willing herself to make out the man's features, knowing by the thud of her heart, the pressure in her chest what he was. And who he was. Father Carey.

The photograph slipped from her hand as the dirty floorboards beneath her seemed to give way. The cluttered small windowed room closed in on her as a long, piercing wail came from deep within. Her heart seemed to want to burst its way out of her chest, choking her breath. She thought she was dying. And didn't care if she was...

But no! She wasn't dying. She was going mad. She was going insane in Ethel Grady's attic. Iris ripped at her clothing, pulled at her hair, shrieked, '*Bastards*...it was *you*...! You took my baby. *YOU.* My baby, my baby, my *baby*...You two adopted her...Oh, God...Oh, my *God*! *Let it not be true. Bill?* How *could* you trick me...? What have I *done*...? *Oh*, let me die...let me die...let...me...*die*...what...have...I...*done*...'

Sometime later she woke from the blessed slumber that had followed the deluge of frenzied tears. Woke to find her face pressed against the dusty floorboards, her limbs stiff and cold. For a moment or two Iris could not remember where she was. Then she remembered, and in the sober calm of her waking moments she knew herself to be wicked: as evil as anyone could be. Knew that something inside her had died the moment she had given birth.

She remembered the emotions she had felt for the child: the infant she was never allowed to see, to hold. The fleeting joy she'd felt when she had heard that it was a girl, which too soon was replaced by jealousy: a resentment she had endured as the baby, her baby, had been taken to a loving home—to become somebody else's daughter.

That jealousy had turned to hatred and rotted inside her, spewing out its badness randomly and without mercy. She had been a dreadful wife to Bill, an uncaring mother to her two sons. A whore with men...*and a monster to Maureen...*

'*Maureen,*' she whined, pitifully calling out to the empty room, a room that she had made almost a prison for the girl that she now lamented.

'I wanted you, really I did. Oh, *so* much...! I was going to call you Moira, but they wouldn't let me see you, let alone *name* you...all these years I didn't know your name. My baby. You were *my* baby...and I never knew your name. I gave you away because they made me...they *made* me! But I got you back. *I can't believe it.* No. *No.* It *can't* be true! Surely I'd have *known* it was you...? My very own baby...and...I...didn't...know. I *swear* to God, I *didn't* know!' She was screaming again now, 'Oh, God, *how could You do this to me*...? I was *so* cruel...So cruel to my baby...*Maureen*...? It's a *nightmare.* It's not real. It can't be...! What have I done? How was I to know? Oh, God, why have You let this happen to *me*...why...*WHY*...?'

Iris struggled to her feet. An overwhelming fury tore through her, savaging her thoughts. She riled at God: blasphemous gibberish and vile profanities. She ransacked the attic, frantic rage giving her manic strength; indiscriminately she ripped and shredded. Lovingly bound scrapbooks lay torn and scattered at her feet. Ornaments were broken and glass was smashed.

Then, as quickly as the fury had started it abated, leaving her to crumple to the floor, a sobbing wreck. And next to where she fell lay further proof of the adoption of her child: A letter, as if by fate untouched by her vehement destruction, flaunted its bold handwriting, the professional curve of the italics, the evidence of an educated hand: A letter that would leave Iris with no doubt. The writer beckoned Mr and Mrs William Grady to journey to:

Sappleton House,
Cosby Road,
Liverpool.

Dear Mr and Mrs Grady,

The child is born! You will be pleased to know that it is girl, born this very morning Sunday, 3rd September. The sixteen-year old natural mother is in good health, and from good stock. The father is unknown. There is a need to evacuate the premises of infants as soon as possible due to impending restrictions brought about by the declaration of war.

Do come as soon as possible. And would you please give my regards to Reverend Thompson; it is good that we have been able to work together on this matter, he speaks very highly of you both. I pray all goes well.

May God be with you both and the infant.

Father Goodwin.

Iris read the letter over and over again, her mind taking in just two words...Father unknown...Father unknown...Father unknown.

Maureen's hair was so very black. Coal black. Her build, small, tiny: Petite. Her eyes blue, so very, very blue—her character, her nature, *so* strong.

Iris knew there was no mistake. Maureen *was* her own child. And she was also Declan's. Maureen was Declan Fitzgerald's little girl. And she had given her away...

Daniel Fairchilde had placed his pregnant daughter in the care of the Catholic Priests. The last words he had spoken to his daughter Iris was to tell her that the father of her child had gone away. That he didn't want her, or the brat she was carrying. That she was nothing but a whore who let men use her: Irish navvies. Anyone.

The door of her home had been sealed against her. She became the church's responsibility. Owned by them. Had lived in an unmarried girls' hostel until the birth and subsequent adoption of her child...

Now, in the freezing cold attic in Lupin Street, the truth dawned on Iris. No one had told Declan of her condition; he had been kept in the dark. Both her father and brother had collaborated. Declan had not been informed of her pregnancy. And, the many years later, when, to her hearts delight, she had met up with Declan again, neither had she...*Why should I...*she had thought, as they danced into the small hours that first night of their reunion...*He hardly remembers me, let alone a baby...I'll let him mention it first...*

But Declan had never mentioned the pregnancy and, as the weeks and months had gone by, and Iris had gotten to know Declan well, she had wondered why. It had nagged at her. Surely with Declan wanting a child so badly he'd have asked what had happened to the one they had conceived so long ago? Now she knew why he had never asked. He had never known...

In the eerily lit, paper strewn top room of the house in Lupin Street, Iris sat hoping for insanity. She had the need to become crazy, lunatic, *anything at all* that would stop her brain from working, thinking, screaming. But the hysteria had passed. All she was left with was her painful thoughts.

The phone in the bedroom was ringing. She had heard the shrill clamour and had ignored it; didn't want to emerge from her steaming bath.

Iris had been in the hotel room's bathtub for over an hour, adding more hot water each time she sat up to a swig from the whisky bottle: Hot water and fiery liquid. Melting her body, though her mind could not find the meltdown oblivion she was seeking.

Nothing would obliterate what she had done. Nothing. She was living the worse possible nightmare of all time, and all by her own hand. She had wanted to kill Maureen. Yes, really, that is what she had wanted to do. To get rid of her; had wanted the girl out of their life. She had hated the girl's brilliant blue eyes. Hated her sleek, glossy black hair, her pert, intelligent face. Hated her very own daughter. And all because she was mourning the lost one: one and the same.

But how could she have not have known? If Bill had been truthful... *if he had told me that Maureen was adopted, maybe I would have been kinder. Yes, I would definitely have been kinder...But Bill told lies, blatant lies...And because of it, I made Maureen's life wretched. Punished her...beat her...tormented her...I even spat on her...!*

'Dear God in heaven *please* let me die,' Iris wailed, through drunken tears.

'Hullo...' Iris finally answered the telephone. It was three a.m.

'Iris? *Iris?* Is that you? Where have you *been*? I've been ringing and *ringing* for hours! Are you all right?'

'Yes. Yes, Declan. I'm fine. Huh, I've got a bit of a cold coming on...that's all...'

'I rang at ten, eleven...then midnight...it's three o'clock in the morning! Where've you *been*...?'

'Oh...' Iris gulped back the tears, sniffing, she tried to make her voice sound as normal as possible...'I went to Sylvia's...to see the boys...we got talking, Sylvia and I, once the lads were in bed...and then it was an *age* before I could get a taxi to bring me back here to the hotel. Declan? I've cleared the house—when shall we come down...? Saturday?'

'No, no, me darling...that's what am ringing about. The house is not in a fit state for us to move into yet. Be towards beginning of March before we can move in. I wouldn't have let your bloody flat go, if I'd had known. You'll have to stay in the hotel for now. Come down for the weekend, though. I've tickets for a show. Don Sommer is in it. You like him, don't yer? Iris? Are you all right? You sound, *lonely*...Oh, I'm *missing* you like crazy. Missing me beautiful wife…Come on down. Can you sort it with Sylvia? Can she keep the young 'uns longer?''

'I don't know, Declan. She's a worried about her job. She said the boss is getting a bit narky with her for taking too much time off. I'll see what I can do, though. Oh, Declan, I'm missing you, too. I'm *really* missing you. I wish we could all come down now. Are you *sure* it's not possible?'

Iris could hear her own voice. She didn't sound drunk. And her diction was how it had been…so long ago…the way her mother had taught her to speak…

Declan sounded disappointed; but his sincerity was fierce, 'Am sure, flower. And I'm *sorry*. But I want us to start off the right way: as a family…in our own home. On the bright side of things, I've been to see the boys' new school. They start the first Monday in March. That will give you time to sort out their uniforms and the like. It's a *grand* school that it is. Aye, a grand school; wouldn't mind going meself! Anyway, you sound a bit strained, I can tell that you're poorly, me darling. Get back into bed. Have a wee nip of the hard stuff…that'll put a *bloom* back into your cheeks. I'll send you some more money…don't worry about your bill at the hotel, I'll settle that…Goodnight, Mrs Fitzgerald. Sleep tight. I love you.' The line clicked, and then went dead.

'And I love you too, Declan, more than you'll ever know,' Iris whispered down the empty line, her voice cracking with the onslaught of fresh tears…*I've made such a mess of things*…she cried to herself…*And there's Declan, doing the best he can*…

As she climbed into the large and luxuriant hotel bed, Iris knew one thing for sure: Declan was *never* to know that he had a daughter. A daughter she had given away. A daughter, who had been given back…and had been driven away by her own mother's cruelty…No, she would not be chancing losing Declan. Not a second time. Not for anything or anybody.

*

12.

Vi gazed at the photographs. Gerard had been wrong in his assumption that his mother had never acknowledged their existence. Quite wrong. Vi had looked at them secretly, and often, battling with her emotions of jealousy and longing: a fierce resentment towards Mary Lou, who now had what she herself had lost, coupled with an intense longing to reach out across the ocean to be a part of her children's new lives.

With Gerard in his grave this past month, Vi had openly spent long hours gazing at the snapshots of her eldest son, Stuart...and her darling Maureen. Gazing into their open, smiling faces, noting how the sun shone on their healthy hair; the roundness of their cheeks...And it came to her...*they are right to be where they are...*

This knowledge, this acceptance had a profound effect upon Vi. Maybe it was because she had almost crossed the threshold into a depression that would have been treated as insanity, that now, feeling so much stronger, she could see everything more clearly. Not that she would ever understand why Gerard had been taken from them. Not in a million years would she ever reason with that loss.

Gerard's short illness and subsequent death and taken a heavy toll on the family: His mother probably the worst. Gerard was the closest to her in personality, a kindred spirit. And because of this, their likeness, he was the one who had irritated her the most. If there was anyone to chastise, Gerard was the one. Anyone in trouble, look in Gerard's direction. Mischief had been his second name. And Vi had recognised all the traits.

Looking back, Vi could see that her behaviour towards this precious son of hers could have been misconstrued. She had never told a soul of her feelings for the boy: how she had been vexed with herself time and time over for her heavy-handed approach towards him.

But that had been the very problem. Vi had not wanted anyone to know: she didn't want people to see Gerard in the same light as she did: had not wanted them to recognise how very like his mother he really was: the joker, the one with the loudest voice, the one with the daftest schemes, the one who could think-up the most precocious pranks or ideas.

That was why she had vetoed most of what he wanted. She had tried to quieten him down; to lessen his popularity, turning his many pals away when they had called, saying he had better things to be doing. Vi had so wanted to kerb his natural tendency to play over work: Gerard had liked nothing better than to go fishing with a gang of mates; play football until his shoes were in tatters…and to scribble and then read out the most amusing of stories of long sea voyages and safari expeditions…that always had a twist in their tale.

Gerard had never been aware that his mother knew of the latter. Never knew that she'd known it was his outlandish and uproarious story-telling and cartoon drawings that caused the booming laughter late at night, when they'd all been tucked up in bed, and should have been asleep. Had never known that she had read every word, studied every picture, first crossly then, later, as he got older, with an admiration that was coupled with fear.

Although Vi had recognised that her son had a certain talent (indeed she had been told both by his English teacher and his Art tutor,) she had worried that he was wasting his time and energy on a past time that would not bring in any cash. And Vi had known, only too well, that it was her job to make her sons into men, capable men, who could earn their crusts.

But clearly, now, she could see that she had been wrong. Wrong. Wrong. *Wrong*. Nobody could change another's personality. And should never try.

That had been her problem, always trying to make everything right, everything run smoothly: Peoples' behaviour; even their lives. But the life plan had been just her *own* idea for a better future—no one else's. Vi wasn't a stupid woman. And neither was anyone else. She would have to remember that. She could not always make decisions just because they were her flesh and blood.

It had been the sound of Sid's keening tears that had finally pulled her from the brink. The doctor, who had visited daily after Gerard's death, had told her in no uncertain terms that if she did not pull herself together, well, then, she would have to be hospitalized. He'd said that Sid needed her. Needed her strength. Needed her love...'and young Malcolm? Aren't you she still *his* Mam? Even the twins, home on compassionate leave, that strong capable duo, who've quietly taken over in the nursery...they still needed you...and Vi, your Sid is inconsolable without you by his side...'

The doctor had also told Vi that most parents, who had lost a child, felt guilty. It was the natural emotion. But Vi knew hers to be different. Hers was guilt about his life—not his death.

Listening to Sid's sobs coming from downstairs in the kitchen, she had known that her husband didn't understand any of this. Yes, he knew that his wife was mourning, but Sid would have no idea of what for.

She found it hard to get out of bed that first day. Sid had looked up in amazement to see her standing in the kitchen. And then they had sat together, her on his knee, and both had wept, and hugged, and wept some more.

Little by little, during the rest of that first day, she had tried to tell Sid about Gerard. How she had felt about their second eldest son. How he had annoyed her on so many occasions. How she had fumed with him...and his behaviour.

And Sid had surprised her. Sid had said that he felt the same way about Malcolm.

Their youngest son irked him no end. But Sid thought this to be a natural run of things in life.

'You can't expect to like everyone, Vi, not even your own kids. It's the way it is. But not liking them doesn't mean you don't love them! I love Malcolm; I'd give my *life* for him. I would have done for Gerard, given half a chance. As you would have done, too...Besides, love,' Sid had grinned a little with his next words, 'I'm not that sure that any of them like you, much! Think on it, love, why *should* they? But I knows something far more important...I knows that they love you to pieces...'

It was then that Vi began to make more of a recovery. Sid always seemed to have something up his sleeve to motivate her...*and fancy...fancy him not liking their Malcolm. She'd have to be watching for that...*Still, she could understand it a little. Malcolm was a lazy little blighter.

Suppertime. This would be the way it would be from now on: Malcolm, Sid and herself. Bobby and Barry could have theirs later...*we'll start as we mean to gone on*...she thought, as she placed the sausages, burnt almost black, as they all liked them, and great mounds of mashed potatoes onto the four men's plates...*there's only the three of us now, living at home...better get used to it...*

Vi smiled as she piled the plates with food: This meal, bangers and mash, with thick onion gravy, had been one of Gerard's favourite dinners. She wasn't going to pretend that he hadn't existed. No. Gerard would be spoken of...laughed about...cried about, but never, never forgotten.

And Vi said as much, to Sid and Malcolm, as they looked down at their plates and remembered, repeating the same to her twins sons when, later that evening, she had re-heated their dinners.

'Eat. Eat and enjoy. And remember our Gerard for all the good things, even if it makes you cry. Gerard's kindly ways, his funny stories...aye, and his rude drawings!' She had trouble not grinning when the lads wide-eyed each other at her knowing about the comic strips, 'We all know how much bother he caused, his getting into trouble at every turn, and we're never to forgot it, do you hear? Not a minute of it. He could be a little swine...but he was *our* swine. So, eat your dinners, and cry if you have to—just don't push your feelings under a carpet of grief.'

As no tears seemed to be coming, (Vi was aware that all her men-folk had wept copious tears when Gerard had passed away) Vi went on to tell the well-built young men, as she watched them gobble their food (feeling ever so slightly guilty for her lack of care the previous meal times over the last month or so,) that she and their father had been having a bit of a talk. And they'd decided: they were going to do a bit of travelling. At the end of the summer season they were going to go visiting: In America.

*

13

America. Vi talked of nothing else. For the long week since she had made up her mind, her family were saturated with the subject. Vi could think of little else. The floodgates had opened. Strategic planning was needed. The twins were obliging: they would spend their next leave working the nursery. Malcolm groaned, though he finally consented to having his Aunt Nellie and cousin Gladys living in the house with him during his parent's absence. Percy Fielding, still quite active, would take on the onerous job of watering the many plants, aided by his younger pal, Harold, a mere seventy-one.

And Sid had decided, if ever there was a time to take on more staff, it was now, and had taken steps to engage a school leaver to assist him in the greenhouses. Further more, a delivery driver needed to be found, but that had been put on hold till nearer the time.

So it was a forward thinking, although a still much-bereaved Vi, who opened the front door that chill morning on the last day of February.

'Hello, Vi, can I come in for a minute? I have some things for you.'

Vi was so astonished to see Iris standing there, that she was rendered speechless.

'I know it's been a long time since we last met…but I didn't want to post…didn't want…Oh, look, Vi…could I come in? I'll not stay long…?'

Vi was furious so see Iris. She'd never thought to set eyes on her again, especially not on her own doorstep at nine in the morning.

'Whatever it is you want to give me, I'll not be a needing it! So, if you don't mind, I'll be shutting me door, now. If you're nippy, you'll be able to get back on the same bus you came on!'

'I came by train, actually. And Vi, I would like to talk to you, for a minute or two; for old time's sake, if nothing else. I *was* Bill's wife, you know. He'd like you to have some of his things, wouldn't he?'

Vi was now shivering as much as her unwelcome guest; she took a step backwards to allow her entry. Closing the front door, she nodded for Iris to move down the lobby in the direction of the kitchen.

'Well, it better had be a minute! I've better things to be doing than listen to your twaddle.'

Ignoring the insult, Iris walked into the kitchen, making straight for the roaring fire.

'Brrr…it's very cold outside. I see you've decorated since I was last here,' she warmed her gloved hands before turning to face Vi, and the woman's harsh tone.

'Never mind the small talk, we've never needed it before. What do you want, Iris? As I said, I'm busy, so be quick. What have you got?'

Iris took a moment to glance round the room, pulling off her black leather gloves at the same time.

Vi could almost read the woman's thoughts: the kitchen was untidy—the breakfast dishes still in the sink. Having been in the process of preparing the food they were to have for lunch, there was pastry rolled out on the table, and a pan of meat and stock simmering on the cooker.

Vi would never have guessed that Iris was finding the scene very comforting, a homeliness that she herself could never manage in any home of her own.

As if she really could read Iris's thoughts (though in reality, she had followed the woman's gaze,) Vi's attention was drawn to the gas stove. Stewing steak bubbled and boiled wobbling the lid of the pan it was cooking in. Gravy flowed down the side of the pan, hissing as it hit the flame.

Rushing to rescue the meat, Vi simmered with fury, she had intended to spend a quiet morning catching up on her baking. The stewing steak was being prepared as the filling for a pie: plate meat pie, Sid's favourite and her speciality. Clamping the lid back down firmly on the cooking meat, Vi hastily cleaned the side of the hot pan with a dishcloth, burning her hand into the bargain. Her temper fuelled further, she turned on Iris.

'Well, you can see I've things on the go, so get on with it! What do you want?'

'I've brought you some photos of Bill, and Ethel. And...*and* some papers belonging to them both. Thought you should have them. I've married again, yer see, Vi. I've been married a week or two, I'm Mrs Fitzgerald now...an' I'll not be living in Lupin Street anymore...' she hesitated, her diction had been become fraught mainly because Vi had rudely turned her back on her and was focusing her attention on the bubbling pan whilst, at the same time, sucking on her smarting knuckle.

Visibly swallowing hard, seeming to allude to the fact the Vi *was* both busy and in pain, Iris paused, momentarily. Then she said, in a rush, 'I'm going to live in London, Vi. My new husband has his businesses there...and...'

'You new *idiot*, you mean...' Vi had turned from the stove, her green eyes blazing, 'another bun in the oven, eh, Iris?'

Iris blanched.

'You don't have to be so *crude*, Vi. No! There's no baby.' Managing her own flaring temper, Iris tried again. 'I'm sorry, Vi. Sorry that you don't like me...but I understand...I wasn't very pleasant, was I?'

'*Pleasant,*' Vi roared, 'bloody *pleasant* was the last thing you were. You were a devil to our Bill. And Maureen. Good God in heaven...words...words *fail me.*'

And so had her strength. Pulling a chair out from around the table, Vi flopped onto it.

'Sit yourself down, Iris; give me what you want me to have and then get going...You make me sick...the very *sight* of you...'

Promptly seating herself opposite Vi, Iris open her full-length, black barathea coat, making it known she was uncomfortable with the heat in the steamy, food fuggy kitchen.

But Vi only had eyes for the expensive coat. She became sarcastic.

'I see this one can kit you out better than our Bill could?' Vi's temper rose again as she thought of her dead brother, and of her own much used grey wool coat that she had worn at Gerard's graveside.

Iris seemed to sit straighter; pride came into her voice.

'Yes, Declan is very successful. Mind, he's worked hard for what he's

147

got.'

'No harder than our Bill...' Vi retorted, indignantly, 'I suppose you've married a man much older than yourself. That's your style, isn't it, Iris?'

'Actually, Vi, Declan is not that much older than me. And I've known him for *years*. I knew him when I was a teenager. And...'

'I don't want you life story, nor your childhood memoirs! What do you *want* Iris?'

Iris delved into her large, black leather handbag. She placed a bundle of letters on the table; photographs came next, followed by a smaller bundle of certificates.

'I want to know why Bill didn't tell me that Maureen was adopted? Why he kept it a secret?'

Vi was not to know that Iris had rehearsed the question umpteen times; wanting to sound vexed, her question full of hurt innocence. And it worked.

Startled beyond measure to have had the question put to her, just out of the blue, with no preliminaries, no build up, Vi was, once again, rendered speechless. Her mind jumbled the possibilities of what she could answer. When she found her tongue, denial was her response.

'Don't know what the bloody hell your talking about! There's no *secret* about our Maureen...'

'No, Vi...Don't give me that. It won't wash...you *knew*. You can't be telling me they kept you in the dark, too...I just don't believe *that*.'

In the silence that followed again, the two women stared across the table at each other. As the fire crackled in the grate, and the aromatic stew bubbled on the stove, the air in the kitchen became charged.

The cause of Iris's questioning lay bundled in front of them. Each knew it; each wondered what would happen next.

Iris, aware of the contents of the letters, waited for Vi's reaction.

Vi, hoping that Iris was bluffing, that the woman had heard a whisper and was making the most of it, stuck to denial; she broke the silence to do so.

'Iris, I don't know where you're getting your information from...Maureen was...*is* Bill's and Ethel's daughter...'

'Well, Vi, if you cast your eyes on some of these papers...this *letter*...' Iris pushed them across the table towards her one-time sister-in-law...'you'll see where I'm getting my *information* from.'

Vi read slowly, aware all the time of the other woman's presence. She read what she already knew, using the time to formulate a plausible answer: An answer that would pacify. Lifting her eyes from the papers, she could see by

Iris's demeanour, that to continue refuting the truth would be a mistake.

Vi placed the letter back on the table, and sighed, deciding how best to approach the truth. How best to explain her brother's reasoning for withholding such important knowledge.

'It was their wish to keep it quiet. They wanted the best for the girl. And they would have given her the best, had they lived.' As she spoke, Vi remembered that Bill hadn't really done his best. Indeed, by marrying Iris, he had done his worse. With this in mind she added an appendix, '...At least, that would have been *Ethel's* intention, had she have lived. Ethel *loved* that child.'

'I'm not disputing that, Vi. What I *want* to know is why Bill didn't tell me? After all, I was his wife.'

'In name only.' Vi retorted. 'He didn't love you...no more than you loved him. He was using you, just as much as you were using him!'

Silence returned, each battling with their own thoughts.

Vi got up from the table and walked to the stove, turning the gas-tap to the off position, lifting the lid of the pan to check the cooking meat.

'Have you told Maureen, Vi?'

Vi spun round. 'No! And I won't be. And you'll not. Else you'll have me to deal with, make no mistake!'

'Why should *I* tell her, Vi? What's it to me, *now*?' Iris's composure was slipping.

Not noticing this, Vi moved back to the table. Sitting again, she picked up the photographs, flicking through them one by one.

Iris watched, but stayed silent.

'She knows *nothing*, Iris...Nothing except the fact that her mam and dad loved her; and that her mam and dad are dead. Maureen's a good girl. She's happy. And that's how it's going to stay; right?'

'You might have to tell her one day, Vi,'

'That as might be...But for the time being...'

'What about her birth certificate, Vi? Surely she'll want that when she marries. Is she married already?'

'No, she's not married, though why I'm telling you anything about her beats me! Anyroads, her birth certificate states Ethel and Bill as her parents...you get a new one when your adoption goes through. But all the same, she didn't need to see it when she went to...Anyway, enough! I'm not discussing another word with you...Thank you for bringing these...' Vi pointed at the photographs, 'it's probably the kindest thing you've ever done for our Maureen. I'll let her know you've been.'

Standing, Vi made it obvious that the meeting was over.

Iris also stood. From the table, she picked up the photograph of Ethel and Bill, as they stood outside Sappleton House, proudly displaying their new baby for the camera.

For some reason or other, Vi found herself explaining,

'That was the day they got Maureen. They were thrilled. I never saw them looking happier.'

'Yes. I can tell. And Father Carey looks pleased, too,' said Iris, taking one last look before handing the photograph to Vi. Fastening her coat, she bent to retrieve her handbag from the floor before extending out her hand. A hand that Vi ignored—refused to touch let alone shake.

'Well then, I'll say goodbye, Vi. I really am sorry about Bill. I can understand why you've not asked after the twins…but I'll tell you anyway: They're lovely boys. I've been very lucky with them. Vi…? Would you do me *one* favour, please? Would you pass a message onto Maureen, when she comes home from work, like…I presume that's where she is now…? No, I didn't expect an answer from you…Still, will you tell her that I'm sorry. *Really* sorry for what I've done. More sorry than she'll ever know…and that I wish her…the…*best*…'

Iris hurried from the hot kitchen, fled down the lobby and was out through the front door before Vi had time to draw an indignant breath.

*

14

Snow had fallen. Thick snow that covered everything in sight: Quiet and magical, it beautified even the most hideous eyesore. And there had been many cluttered around the cottage and the adjacent yard: boxes and crates, barrows and wooden pallets, piled high with refuse, waiting to be recycled. Sacks of soil and compost, and umpteen other implements and tools, used daily in the busy garden nursery, huddled together, fighting for space. An essential assortment of necessities needed and relied upon in a growing business with limited funds at its disposal: nothing was ever thrown away. Every thing had its use, and its day.

Now, as the full moon floodlit the gravel path that led to the greenhouses, Vi felt the thrill that snow always brought with it. Momentarily her troubles and sorrows where forgotten and she was a child once more as she made first footprints in the snow.

The air had lost its chill, as often happens when threatening snow finally falls, and the night sky twinkled with a million stars.

Looking up into the inky *diamond*-studded sky, Vi experienced a moment of peace and contentment. A renewal of her spirit, an ease of her aching heart. Tomkins, the sleek black cat that lived in the greenhouse nearest to the cottage, meowed, brushing itself against her boot clad legs, whining for attention. The tranquil moment passed.

'Don't you like the snow, puss…?' Vi bent to the cat, scratching the back of its warm neck before standing and resuming her short journey to the greenhouses: Vi was in search of Sid. And she found him.

'Sid…it's nine o'clock. Are you coming in soon, love?'

'Yeah, I'm coming. I just wanted to make sure the boiler was stoked up. It's going be a cold night, tonight. Still, I've everything done. Field is finished. And these mums are nearly dry enough to start the cuttings.'

The *mums* Sid was referring to were chrysanthemums, the garden plant that flowered in the autumn months and was fast becoming his trademark.

Widely used for Christmas decoration, and other less joyful occasions, the brilliant colours of the hardy flower had always fascinated the one-time miner. Growing the gracious blooms had turned from a hobby into a lucrative living, along with the many vegetables he also grew in the field that backed onto his home; a field that was now planted with spring cabbage, leeks, sprouts and the ever-faithful rhubarb.

Standing next to her husband, Vi sniffed the warm air and the closeness of her husband. The earthy, claustrophobic atmosphere of the greenhouse had penetrated his clothing: his baggy, home knitted bottle green coloured pullover, a previous and much used gift, hand crafted by his sister-in-law Nellie, was caked in dirt. His heavy-duty work dungarees, one time a dark navy blue, were now blackened and shiny at the knee area, filthy everywhere else.

Sid reeked of sweated hard work, but the smell did not offend his wife…far from it. As they gazed out through none too clean windows of the greenhouse, each felt a measure of comfort. The field, wholly visible now with the covering blanket of pure white snow, held the promise of a good living; a secure future. God willing.

As they stepped out into the night air, Sid was satisfied that everything was under control. Linking his wife's arm, he stared up at the sky in much the same manner as she had done earlier. Although the snow had stopped falling, save for a flake or two, it lay a couple of inches deep.

'Happen there'll be more to come; it'll be ankle deep by the morning, you'll see,' he said, inhaling deeply, filling his lungs with luscious air.

Once up the path, Sid and Vi stood in quiet contemplation outside the closed backdoor of their home, before realising they were chill and more than eager to kick off their boots and get inside to the warmth of their cosy kitchen.

Later, cocooned under many blankets, Sid lay wide-awake knowing that his wife, lying by his side, was also finding sleep difficult to come by.

'Are you still thinking of *her*?' he asked the question quietly, the whisper to his voice born from years of having to do so: whispering and hushing each other had become second nature, even when making love (which had been often, and good,) in a house where the walls were as thin as paper, and its rooms overflowing with their extended family and numerous friends. Yet now this home was more often quiet than rowdy. And in truth, both Vi and Sid were beginning to get used to it.

Tonight, though, as he lay in his bed, Sid was feeling uneasy with the silence, especially the unnatural silence of his wife. Vi had, once again, lost her boisterous chatter. She had shown a spark of her old self with her decision to visit America, but that had gone as quickly as it had come, once the plans had been made.

Sid was worrying that the bleak depression that had held his wife in a firm grip was returning. Vi was still mourning, as he was, some days more than others, but he had hoped that the despair had lessened.

Whenever Sid had the time to think, think deeply, he also became aware of how easy it would be to give in—Gerard's death had been almost impossible to bear; the first few days afterwards, he could have quite easily gone down the same road himself. But he hadn't. Thankfully, Vi had pulled through. She was carrying her load, her grief, better with each day. As they all were; life did have to go on.

But tonight, Sid was well aware that something else was burdening his wife besides her sorrow. And that something else had to have been brought about by the fleeting visit of her sister-in-law, Iris.

When told of the morning's episode, Sid had become vexed with the situation, and had fervently wished he'd been at home: Iris would never have gained entrance with him around.

Hearing the anxiety in her husband's voice, Vi turned on her side. Facing him, she stroked his arm before answering, stalling for time, pondering on how much to tell him. But then, what was there to tell? That she had a niggling feeling something was wrong? That she wished she'd never let Iris step over the doorstep…? *Of course I wish that! I must have been crazy letting the bloody woman in…*

Vi sighed, a long weary sigh before she spoke.

'You mean Iris? Yeah, she's bothering me. I don't like her knowing about our Maureen. Knowing that the girl was adopted. She's an evil one, is that Iris. How can we be sure she'll say nowt to nobody? I mean, when was she *ever* trustworthy? It's stupid, I know, what with Maureen being on the other side of the world, and all that. But you never know, do you, never know what'll happen next…Aw, Sid… l can't stand anymore…I can't…*I can't…*'

She was relieved to have Sid to cradle her; pull her closer, shushing her. She felt his lips brushed hers. Kiss the salty tears from her cheeks.

Their breath mingled, warm and familiar, inviting escape. Locked together in the heat of their bed, and of desire, their limbs entangled.

As the weather worsened outside their bedroom window, they found solace in each other's body. Knowing how to please, knowing where to touch, hands and mouths found an abandonment that obliterated all other thoughts. There was an urgency to their lovemaking. Each took greedily, with little thought to giving. The abandonment, which mounted quickly, surprising them with its voracity, vanished as swiftly as it came.

As they eased away, reclaiming their own side of the bed, the real world came surging back in: Guilt: that they could have forgotten their grief, even for those few moments: Resignation: which settled around their shameful thoughts…Life was going on.

With the first snow of winter falling thick and fast, settling more than a foot deep around the cottage, Vi and Sid kissed goodnight, turned back to back, and slept.

Two weeks later, whilst the snow still fell, to everyone's consternation, Vi battled with herself and her thoughts…*what is it? Something she said…I can't put my finger on it…but there was something, something she mentioned…What…was…it? What did Iris say…?*

Sid had been correct in his assumption that there was something more than Iris's visit worrying his wife. Toiling at her daily chores, made even harder by the cruel winter blizzards, frozen pipes, and icy footpaths, Vi went over, again and again, the conversation that had taken place between herself and Iris, her recall adding something different each time, until she couldn't remember what was a real memory and what was imagined.

What she did know was that Iris had not come to swank. Sid believed that had been Iris's only intention, to gloat about her new, obviously far richer, lifestyle. Vi did not agree. Gloating had come secondary…*But what had come first? Why, after so many years, had Iris come at all…?*

Even though Vi and Sid were not truly religious in the church going sense (though they had made all their children say their prayers and go to Sunday School,) both did believe in a higher power: they did, more often than not, believe in God...How could they not? They had thought themselves to be well blessed, until Gerard died.

Now, slowly, slowly, they were picking up the pieces, and in all fairness, had stopped blaming God. Whatever the reasoning behind Gerard's death, whatever the high order of things, the bereaved couple needed faith, the faith to continue living themselves. And gradually it was coming back.

Their children had been taught the same. God was good. God was loving. God was all seeing. God picked you up and carried you during the bad times...*Really? Had that happened to them...?*

In reality they found that bereavement made them more caring, more thoughtful. Something *had* carried them during the dreadful days of mourning...and was still carrying them.

Andrew Prentice, the vicar of St. John's Church hoped he was carrying his share, too, hoped he was of some help to the couple he had grown quite fond of.

The Greenwood children had attended Sunday school until they were in their teens. Maureen had been the only one to continue: her involvement with the church choir and her duties as a Girl Guide made sure of it. Occasionally, Stuart had accompanied his cousin to services, and the other boys had gone, under sufferance, when they had to turn out for church parade: a once a month obligation *if* you wanted to continue in the Scout movement.

So, all in all, the Greenwood/Grady family could be said to be members of the local church. And this being so, the Reverend Prentice felt it was his duty to call weekly upon the grieving household.

Reverend Prentice had, like many others, been fond of Gerard. Stories of the boy's kindest and good deeds had filtered through to him from his congregation, and in turn, he had relayed the information to the young man's bereaved parents. Parents the vicar thought to be...*a little rough around the edges.*

Now, with six weekly visits behind him, the rector picked his way down the icy, snow clogged lane eager to be inside the warm and friendly kitchen of the Greenwood home.

His mouth watered as he thought of Vi's rich fruitcake, thickly sliced and smothered with butter, and the steaming mug of tea that was always proffered along with it.

Violet Greenwood had altered Reverend Prentice's outlook on life these past few weeks and, it would not be untrue to say, that the stout, ginger haired, middle-aged man of God was more than a little in love with the comely mother of five.

Andrew Prentice was always falling in love. The trouble was, his affections were always for the married women of his parish. The rake-like single women, who batted their eyes at him each and every Sunday, left him cold. And besides, he didn't really need a wife...a mother would be better, for that was what he had never known, his own mother having died giving birth to the ten pound, ten ounce baby, who had torn bottom first into the world...him.

'Have you more thoughts on your journey to America, Violet?' The vicar asked, rather rudely whilst his mouth was full of cake.

Vi watched him, the greedy, self-indulgent man who came for his own comfort rather than to give it. Still, that he came at all was something. And it did give her the chance to talk of Gerard.

'We're looking into it at present,' Vi answered as she sipped her tea, watching the rotund man gobble his second piece of cake, 'and there's no rush, Vicar. After the summer, probably, we're waiting on a reply from Florida. We don't want to inconvenience Mary Lou; she's expecting again, you know. We've written to them first—before we tell Stuart and Maureen any of our plans. Thought it best that way; more polite, like.' And she also thought, as she spoke, that it all depended on money. They would have to wait and see what the bad winter had done to their profits before tearing off to America. But she wasn't going to let the vicar know this. Vi had her pride.

After he had eaten two thick slices of cake, and had emptied the teapot, Reverend Prentice glanced at the photographs laid out on the table before him.

'So! This is little Maureen's mother and father, eh? They look proud.' He turned the photograph over and read the inscription on the back:

'Looks like it was a sunny day...Not like today, eh? Will this snow *ever* end? The rectory isn't as warm as your own place, Violet. No, it's a bit bleak in the winter. Let's hope this weather doesn't last too much longer,' he gazed at the photograph again.

'Was your sister-in-law...er, Ethel, a Catholic, Violet?'

'No, Vicar, she wasn't. Why?'

'Oh, well this chap, standing to the side...see...here...He's a *priest*. I can tell by his hat...'

Vi snatched the photograph out of the vicar's hand.

A rather bewildered vicar huddled his chin deep into his chest as he hurried through the driving snow back to the cold rectory. Violet Greenwood had hustled him out of her cosy kitchen as fast as she could, claiming she had forgotten an important errand. And before he had stepped off the front door step, he had heard her at the back of the house, hailing her husband...like a fishwife. Women were funny. He was better off without them. Still, perhaps next week he'd visit Mrs Johnston...she was looking bonny these days...since she'd given birth to her triplets.

Sid said she was stupid going out on an afternoon like this.

'Why do you want to go into the city, today?'

'Because I want to see to getting the passports; I know I said there was no rush, but with the vicar going on about America so much, I thought I might as well get it done. Why wait! Besides, I need a breath of air. Been cooped up here for days. I can get the three o'clock train. I'll be at the office before it closes at five...and I'll bring fish and chips back for tea. I should be well back by seven.'

'All right...Okay, then, have it your own way. I'll run you to the station in the van. But I don't know, Vi, once you get a notion in your head, there's no stopping yer, is there?'

Vi planted a kiss of thanks onto her husband's cold cheek and thought...*you don't know how right you are. But please God, let me be wrong...*

They were very helpful at the library, directing her to the town hall. From there she went by taxi to the office where registration took place, arriving close on five o'clock.

'Can I help you, Madam?'

'Yes...er...I've lost my daughter's birth certificate. And I needs it, like, because I'm emigrating abroad and I want it with me. A keep-sake.'

'And she was registered here?'

'I *think* so...But it's so long ago...I didn't do the registering.'

'Couldn't you ask her father?'

Vi gulped. 'There was no...father, no. I mean, he wasn't registered...I don't think he was, anyway. Look, I'm not used to this...' Vi leaned close to the counter and whispered in what she hoped was the right way to go about her task, 'you see, I wasn't married back then…I was *very* young…and my daughter was adopted afterwards…'

The assistant sniffed, backed away a little.

'Well, yes, I see. But was your…er…daughter…was she born here?'

'Oh, yes! Yes she was! Sappleton House…er…September 3rd, 1939.'

'What name was she registered under…Do you *know?*'

Vi let the condescending remark go; her nerves were shredded enough with all the lies…But she'd come this far…As soon as the vicar had mentioned the man in the photograph, Vi had realised what it was that was bothering her about Iris: it was her knowledge of the name of the priest. Because it was most certainly something she had not known…

Now she bit her top lip, her green eyes enormous with the strain of what she was doing. She felt criminal when she said, 'Iris…er…Fairchilde.'

'Well, then, I've got all I need to know. And seeing that you know she was adopted, I'll see what I can do. Can you come back tomorrow? It's getting late now; we close in a few minutes…'

'Oh…I can't! It's *vital* I get it tonight. I really want it with me…for posterity, like…you understand, don't you? It's all I have…'

'Wait here, then. I'll see what can be done. It's most irregular, though.'

The clerk went out through a door at the back of the office, her high heels squeaking on the highly polished wooden floor, her body language making it quite clear what she was thinking…*Common as muck*…Vi could almost read the woman's mind. A mind which went with her appearance: small darting eyes, large nose, tight mouth, drain-pipe thin, unmarried and as thick skinned as the lens in her glasses.

The minutes passed. Vi's thoughts went back to when Maureen had been readying herself for her trip to America. It had been very hard keeping the girl's birth certificate away from her eyes when the teenager had been signing the papers to get her first passport. But they had managed it, albeit she and Sid had suffered a sweaty moment or two in the process of being so furtive.

From another room a clock struck five. Placing her shopping bag on the high mahogany counter, Vi adjusted her green, paisley patterned headscarf, tightening the knot under her chin, wishing that she had thought to dress more smartly than her old grey coat. Noting, with the same distain as that of the assistant, her grubby, snow sloshed Wellington boots.

'Miss Fairchild…is it?' The bespectacled man asked without preamble. He had come so soundlessly into the wood panelled room, using a side door for entry, Vi was caught unaware of his presence and was hesitant in reply.

'Er...yes...that's my name, *was* my name, back then.'

'Indeed. Yes. Well. As you said, there is a record of your daughter—she was registered here. But if you want a copy, you will have to write to Somerset House. And there is a charge. But...*er*...Miss Fairchilde...*Mrs Fairchilde*. Are you all right? You look as though you're going to faint...Here, sit down on...'

Vi didn't wait for the elderly, bald headed man to finish his sentence.

Outside, the cold wind helped her breathe more easily. Steadied her trembling legs, her palpitations. But not her thoughts...*Dear God in heaven, she's her mother. Iris is Maureen's natural mother...! Lord help us...it can't be true...How much more can I stand...? How many more shocks am I supposed to take...? Did our Bill know all this...? Lord God keep that evil woman away from our Maureen, I beg you, please...*

*

15

'Do you think we'll need to use these bags, Vi?' Sid's whispered question was followed by a low chuckle as he looked down at the white paper *sick* bag which had been placed on his knee by their air hostess: a smart, extremely blonde young woman in her mid twenties, whose smile and radiant complexion had dazzled the inexperienced travellers into an unusual shy silence.

'You'll need more than one bag if you drink any more whisky…you almost drank the bloody airport bar dry!' Vi retorted, finding her voice, her sober voice; fuming about Sid's slightly drunken demeanour, his drink glazed eyes. With vexed adrenaline flowing, she clutched her own paper bag to her chest, tensing with fear as the aeroplane taxied down the runway.

As the plane lifted off the tarmac, soaring onto the high blue sky, it was Vi who made use of the sick-bag, her sober stomach finding it had no head for heights.

Sid, elated by each elevated mile, loosened his collar and tie, aiding his vomiting wife by handing her his own unused bag.

Ten minutes into the flight, Vi, dressed inappropriately for the long journey, was languishing in her window seat, wondering how on earth she was ever going to manage the next seven or so hours.

Wanting to make a good first impression upon arrival, Vi had chosen to wear a canary yellow, full-skirted dress. The bodice of the frock was buttoned shirt style. Now these buttons refused to stay fastened over her ample bosom, and the stand-to-attention collar chaffed at her neck incessantly. To be the epitome of fashion, she had also been persuaded by the assistant in the pricey dress shop to complete the outfit with a white patent leather belt. Fastened today on the very last hole, the belt was far too tight for Vi to find any comfort, let alone breathe.

Her elaborate hairstyle did not help matters much, either: Vi's thick glossy hair had been pleated into a coil then twisted into a topknot. The front section of her brunette curls had been backcombed and teased, creating a beehive shape on the crown of her head. The hairdresser had wanted to compliment the results with a white Alice band, but Vi had deferred to this final adornment.

With her eyes closed, her brow pale and moist and her lips parched, Vi listened listlessly as Sid gave a non-stop commentary on the pleasures of air travel.

And, as her mind was tortured by thoughts of food (for some sadistic reason, she couldn't get the picture of fried eggs sizzling in a pan out of her mind) and Sid's inapt ramblings, she caught a whiff of what was being prepared in the galley, and her stomach climbed to greater heights.

By the time they reached New York, Vi was without the belt and settled into a comatose sleep brought about by Sid's remedy for a weak constitution: five shots of whisky.

It was mid-August, 1958. Although one year later than planned, Vi and Sid were at last on their way to visit their son, Stuart, and their niece, Maureen, the air fare having been made possible by the two youngsters' generosity—savings that had been gladly donated to ensure the arrival of the much loved couple the teenagers had sorely missed.

A day and a half after their first flight had taken off from London (it had taken two air journeys to reach their destination) Vi and Sid were reunited with their Floridian tanned children.

Through tears and laughter they kissed and hugged, talking at once: questions and answers, a babbling of high spirits—they all had so much to say—so much to catch up with.

Chuck and Mary Lou, with their toddler daughter, Lydia, and infant son,

161

Roy, stayed discreetly in the background, until they were beckoned forward for greeting. A greeting that had mixed feelings, on both sides.

Vi eyed Mary Lou: How tormented she had been over this younger woman. How jealous of her hold on Stuart. And now this person had Maureen in her power, too.

And in turn, Mary Lou was somewhat hesitant in approaching Vi: Mary Lou was well aware that she herself was totally responsible for encouraging Stuart, and Maureen to stay on in America.

To everyone's relief the meeting went well: each woman held out a hand, proffered a cheek; awkwardly at first, and then, as they looked deep into each others eyes, without restraint; for each realised their own worthiness, and an alliance, a connecting of souls, which would go on for many years to come.

In the mellow light of late afternoon, Mary Lou, clad in pale blue cotton slacks and a matching sleeveless blouse, led a much fussier dressed Vi around the single storied house she and Chuck had made their home.

Vi had never seen anything like the colourful bedrooms that belonged to the Vicente's two infant children. The adjacent magnificent bedroom, that was Maureen's, took her breath away. Decorated in lemon and white—the furnishings, the bed and the walls—the room was massive. A full-length window, where white voile curtains fluttered gently in a pleasing breeze, overlooked the garden. An en-suite bathroom completed the girl's sleeping quarters. Vi couldn't believe how deep the gleaming white bath was, or why the room needed so many mirrors. Never before had she seen them wall-to-wall. As for the gold etched glass shower cubicle, Vi was left speechless.

Sweating in a long sleeved white cotton blouse, which she had teamed with a navy blue box-pleated skirt, Vi wiped the moisture from her top lip with her already soaked handkerchief, and marvelled at such luxury—as she had also done when she had entered the bungalow's expansive kitchen.

The lavish kitchen had made Vi swell with pride when Mary Lou explained that it had been fitted-out by Stuart: hand crafted, in bleached oak, it was his own design from conception to installation. It was a kitchen containing every possible gadget and appliance. The numerous cabinets, some high, some low, displayed fine china, everyday crockery and plentiful glassware. This generous sized room, basking in the sunshine of late afternoon, had also been permeated by a tempting, lingering aroma: the spit-roasted chicken they were all to enjoy later for dinner.

Leading off from the kitchen, the dining room held a french polished table that could seat twelve. This immense room, that was further furnished with gleaming mahogany side tables and drinks' cabinet, was enhanced by two long and comfortable looking burgundy and cream stripped sofas. Textured rugs of maroon and cream haphazardly graced the wood laid floor, and a wall of glass doors opened onto a terracotta tiled patio.

The rest of the house was just as luxurious. The lounge, (great-room as Mary Lou called it,) which was entered by way of an archway from the dining room, was finished in light coloured woods. Vibrant oranges and turquoise-greens spread their hues in the soft velour's of the sofas and chairs. Plump cushions carelessly graced the sumptuously upholstered seats, and parquet flooring gave the room its cool ambience. Through a full length picture window came the inviting vista of lush green lawns, and white garden furniture.

Vi was awed by all she saw, as they moved on outside, and into the welcome cool of the evening breeze: Mary Lou chatting all the time explaining and directing Vi's gaze.

The patio, or deck as Chuck called it, was where they ate their six o'clock dinner: a deliciously moist herbed chicken that was served with potato salad and crisp greens, followed by the creamiest vanilla ice-cream Vi and Sid said they had ever tasted. Stuart and Maureen looked at one another, and beamed their own pleasure.

After coffee (tea for Vi and Sid,) Mary Lou suggested that she and Vi take a stroll.

Vi, still not quite used to Mary Lou's company, was quiet as they walked, until they came to a halt at the perimeter of a huge hole; an excavation that had been dug in the shape of the letter *L.* and was more than six feet deep and which was soon to be sided with concrete, then tiled and filled with water: The swimming pool. The Vicentes' *L*-shaped bungalow would soon be sporting a matching pool. Vi couldn't help but say she was impressed.

Standing by Mary Lou's side, Vi looked back towards the house to where, behind the glass of another floor to ceiling window, Sid could be seen.

With twilight now falling outside, Sid, Chuck and Stuart, dressed in open necked shirts and cotton trousers, their feet sandaled or bare, were seated round the television set in the room they called the family den.

In the blue light of the TV screen, Sid seemed completely at home and very comfortable in a green leather armchair, talking and laughing with his companions as they sat watching a game of baseball. As the game was new to Sid, with rules that obviously needed a lot of explaining, re-enactment debate and shaking of heads, waving of arms was evidently taking place.

Both smiling indulgently at what they saw, they waved an unanswered greeting to their men folk, and walked on.

Mary Lou linked her arm through Vi's, chatting amiably, naming the various shrubs and bushes as they crossed the garden, passing through a wooden archway, heading on down a sandy path towards the shadowed bulk of two other properties.

Two small houses, built in a cottage style, nestled side by side with a direct view of the sea. The Vicente's newest venture: Guest Villas. The villa nearest to the main house was where Stuart lived: the other, only recently completed, now was home to Vi and Sid.

Each villa had a small lounge area, a double sofa bed amongst its furnishings. With a twin bedded bedroom, a large bathroom, and a well planned kitchenette, the single storied dwellings could each easily accommodate four holidaymakers.

'Stuart always eats with us…' Mary Lou was saying…'but since the villas were finished, he's lived here. Before then, he slept in the den. I hope you'll be happy, staying with us, Vi. I'm mighty glad to have you here. And it sure goes without saying that Stuart and Maureen are just *thrilled*. They were beginning to think you'd *never* get here…'

Mary Lou chatted on, gaily, her Texan generosity knowing no bounds. Her gentle drawl lulling Vi into a passive mood, softening her focus, blending her thoughts…*no wonder they don't want to come home. Who would? It doesn't seem real, though, not any of it…it's like being in the bloody films…*Vi's thoughts were broken by the sound of Maureen's voice, as the girl came into the villa with the Vicente children in tow.

Cradling Roy in the crook of her left arm, Maureen guided Lydia into the lounge with her free right hand.

'Hey, be careful, Lydia, you'll knock your mommy over…' Maureen laughed, as Lydia rushed at Mary Lou, clamping her arms around the woman's legs, begging to be picked up and hugged.

'They're worn out, Mary Lou. Shall I take them back to the house for their baths?'

With her question, Maureen squatted down to Lydia's side, moving the chubby cheeked baby to her knee as she did so.

Mary Lou bent to her children, coming eye to eye with Maureen. She smiled, shaking her head in answer as she took the cherubic gurgling baby from the girl's arms.

'No, honey, it's okay. I'll see to them tonight.'

Roy, dressed in a nappy only, pulled at his mother's dark hair, his strength and his weight causing her to wobble backwards.

'Ouching,' and laughing, Mary Lou regained her balance, tucked the wriggling, blond haired youngster under her arm, and stood. Taking Lydia's hand in her own, she smiled again at Maureen then bent from the waist to plant a kiss on her daughter's dark, glossy crown.

A typical well cared for youngster, Lydia took the affectionate kiss as a signal to complain and get her own way: she wanted to stay with Maureen, and Maureen's Mom. Her tired whining continued.

'I want *Vi* to bath me tonight...Can she, Mom? Can she...*please*, Mommy?'

Mary Lou hushed her daughter, 'Not tonight, sweetie, *Aunt* Vi's tired. And she needs to spend some time with Maureen, don't you think? Come on, now; I know, let's play monkeys!' Pulling a face at her daughter, Mary Lou began making monkey noises, which made Roy squeal with infectious laughter, and Lydia bow to the inevitable.

Not a naughty child, Lydia dropped her sullen attitude and, mimicking her mother, said her goodnight's in monkey fashion.

'Hey, where's my kiss, Lydie?' Maureen bent to receive a fierce embrace.

Then, knowing what else was expected of her, Lydia stood, her hand clutching her mother's, looking picture-book-pretty in a sleeveless pink and white striped summer dress, smiling shyly in Vi's direction, swinging her left leg backwards and forwards and, in the process, dodging away from baby Roy's outstretched hand that was, as always, in search of her hair.

Vi found herself smiling back, warming to the lovely looking child who reminded her of Maureen when she was a little girl. It was she who made the move to say goodnight to the girl...and to the baby.

Kisses given and eagerly returned, Mary Lou quickly took charge.

'Right, well, we're off, aren't we, *monkeys*? You should take your Aunt for a walk down the beach, Maureen.'

Turning to Vi, Mary Lou added, with a note of concern in her voice, 'There's always a breeze this time of night, Vi. You'll enjoy it. And then, perhaps, you'll sleep better tonight. I *do* hope so.'

Vi did enjoy her evening stroll, but not because of the breeze, which was barely in evidence, anyway. She enjoyed it because it was the first time she had been alone with Maureen since they had arrived. Though that had not been Maureen's fault. No. The fault lay with Vi herself. Not being able to tolerate the heat, Vi had stayed in the villa for the best part of the day.

Sid, happy go lucky as usual, had not been deterred by the humid heat of Florida, spending most of the day out of doors. And, as he had busied himself around the Vicente's growing estate, playing with the children, helping Stuart and Chuck, Sid had known the real reason behind his wife's reluctance to leave their rooms: She was hiding. Hiding from her son, her niece. Bewildered and confused; Stuart and Maureen had changed so much, both in appearance and manner, Vi felt they were strangers. Even though they had hugged and kissed at first, chatting twenty to the dozen, the ease had soon worn off. Within a few hours of being in her family's company, Vi had ceased to have anything to talk about, anything in common.

That first night, lying wide-awake by Sid's side, she had been miserable and overwrought. Finding the heat oppressive, and her family distant, Vi felt their visit was a mistake. With sleep eluding her, the tears had come easily; she had wallowed in self-pity...*why had they come? It was a mistake...they would have been better to carry on corresponding by letter...*

As Sid slept, snoring loudly as usual, his wife had lay wide-awake. Only her thoughts for company...*I'll tell them tomorrow...we're going home! We don't fit in here...I'll explain; they'll understand. Oh, God, I want to go home...I'm no good here. My clothes are wrong...I'm wrong...I couldn't wear shorts, not with my figure...Oh, why have we come...?*

With the pinks and greys of dawn creeping into the morning sky she had finally fallen into fitful sleep, unaware that her husband was up and about, thoroughly enjoying himself in a climate that suited him as much as his hosts.

Tonight, Maureen, knowing something of how her aunt was feeling, (having herself experienced the same emotions when she had first arrived in Florida) threaded her arm through Vi's, steering the older woman past the gaping, rubble strewn pit that would soon be the swimming pool. They were, at last, heading for that promised stroll on the beach after having returned to the main house at Lydia's begged insistence.

Now, with the many hugs and kisses, and "night, nights" finally and exhaustedly over (Lydia had loved trotting between Maureen and Vi; especially when they had held her hands tightly, aiding her to swing her legs instead of walking...to which she had giggled and kept on asking "again, again" every step of the way back to the house,) Maureen could sense that her aunt was thawing.

'Do you remember when Uncle Sid was building the lean-to?' Maureen asked. And with that question, laughter and humorous memories stole away any lingering awkwardness.

Arm in arm, aunt and niece ambled down the dusty, sun baked pathway which led to the sea, giggling and chatting as though they had never been apart.

As the colours of sunset left the sky, they sat on the soft white sand, listening to the gentle lap of the tide. The ambiance brought with it a more sombre mood.

Vi and Maureen sat, arms wrapped round each other, cheek to cheek, and shed copious tears for Gerard, directing their thoughts and their eyes heavenwards, into the vast ebony darkness, hoping, praying, that Gerard could see them and feel their love.

It was one week later before Vi had the chance to spend some time alone with Stuart. A week that had been full of sunshine, swimming, (Vi had conceded to a swimsuit) visits to Miami, with its towering splendour, its shops, hotels, restaurants and wonderful beaches. She had been in her first ice-cream parlour…and her first beauty parlour. There, in a salon where the men assistants pranced effeminately, her hair had been tinted, her nails polished.

Later that same day she bought her first pair of slacks and, egged on by her husband and son, purchased two pairs of shorts and a swimsuit.

Now, as she sat on the soft padded swinging hammock, enjoying the cool of the evening, comfortable in cream coloured cotton trousers, and a sleeveless matching top, she seized the opportunity to speak with Stuart.

Sitting next to his mother on the swing, Stuart, very much at ease in a cotton, green and white striped tee-shirt and khaki coloured shorts, sipped from a glass of ice cold lemonade, with perhaps an inkling of what was to come…

'You know, love, you could come home for a bit. Now that you're qualified, you'll have no trouble getting a job at all.'

Stuart looked down into his glass. Tilting the ice that floated on top of his drink, clinking it from side to side, he was thoughtful before he spoke.

'Mam, this *is* home! I've made it my home. *Please* understand, Mam, I want to be here…need to be here. It's where I belong, now,' he placed his arm around his mother's shoulders, moving nearer…'what is there in England for me, Mam?'

Vi flared at him, 'What is there! For God's sake, Stuart…there's *everything*. Your dad, your brothers, your *proper* home…'

'Don't get upset, Mam, please. *Please*? It's got nothing to do with not wanting to be with my family, it's just not…Mam, I've made a place for myself here, a good place. I can become anything I want here. I work—and work hard, and I get paid for just *that*. Working hard pays well here, Mam. It's such a new country. It's exciting. It's everything I've *ever* wanted. Look…look around, Mam, and tell me what would I be coming home to, eh?'

Vi didn't answer. She sipped her drink, put her head back, and rocked. The sway of the hammock stilled their words. Neither of them wanted to argue, neither wanted to spoil their few quiet moments together. The night air was soft and balmy, calming, almost melodic in its lulling quality.

Deep within her, Vi knew Stuart was right…*but I had to ask; what sort of mother would I be otherwise…?* She stared up at the sky that now twinkled with shimmering stars. From the big house she could hear the murmur of a television set. Turning her head, she could see into the kitchen to where Mary Lou and Chuck stood side by side. Deep in conversation, her amiable hosts were busy at the after-dinner cluttered sink: it was their turn to do the clearing after the evening meal: their turn to wash the dishes, see to the garbage (Vi had fallen into using the American lingo.) Everything was worked out. Shared. Everyone doing their part in the making of this new life.

At length, Vi broke the silence that had walled up between mother and son.

'And what about Maureen…does she feel the same way, do you think? Is this where *she* wants to live…?' Vi so feared the answer.

'Ask her, Mam, not *me*. Maureen and I haven't been getting on so well of late. In fact, for quite some time.'

Stuart's answer was sullen. His mood had changed. Sitting forward, he leaned his elbows on his bare knees and spoke again. Quietly, confidentially, 'Mam, I might as well tell you. Before you came, well, you see, Maureen and I had such a flaming row. I'm thinking of moving to another part of Florida. The Gulf Coast; there's so much building going on there…Chuck seems to think it's a good idea. But Maureen, she went *nuts*. Thinks I'm stupid, can't see why I can't stay here…Oh, Mam, it's so *difficult*. My feelings…' he gulped, and stole a quick glance at his mother before continuing, 'Mam, I've got to tell *someone*…I love Maureen, Mam…I asked her to come with me…told her I loved her, proper like, not as a cousin, I mean. And she went mad at me. Stark raving mad! Said it *couldn't* be true. That I was crazy to say it…that I'd spoilt everything. And she cried and cried. Mary Lou tried to talk to her. Tried to find out why she was so upset. She even told her that it was O.K. for first cousins to fall in love. And Chuck, he said he'd wondered when we'd realise our true feelings…wondered when we'd admit it. But Maureen, she wouldn't hear *any* of it. Shut herself in her bedroom and screamed that it was wrong…that I was *stupid* and that I'd spoilt everything…especially with you and Dad coming…To be honest, Mam, we've hardly spoken since then! She avoids me. Haven't you noticed? She spends most of her time with the children. And she glares whenever she sees me. Huh, she only talks to me if she has to. I think, Mam, I *think* she will probably go back with you, if you ask.' Stuart dropped his head into his hands; his shoulders shook.

As her son quietly sobbed, the crickets chirped, and Vi's mind went into overdrive…*so that was it! That was the underlying feeling…the atmosphere I've felt since we arrived…*

Vi knew that what she was about to say would alter everyone's life, irretrievably. But she didn't care. She looked up into the high night sky knowing she was going to break a promise. And that she had no choice. Fate had seen to that.

She touched Stuart's shoulder. Hesitantly she spoke…

Slowly, Stuart lifted his head, turned to his mother, and listened. And possibly could not quite believe what he was hearing.

And, if it *was* possible, really possible, that Gerard was above them, in the high heaven of that brilliant star lit sky, he would have been glad to see and overhear what his mother had to say to his eldest brother.

Gerard would have been glad to see his fine, handsome brother shed his troubled frown, throw back his head and laugh, really laugh, a laugh resplendent with joy. Glad to see him run across the lush lawn, skirting the sprinkler, yet not caring if he got wet. Glad to see him escort the bewildered, rather angry, night-dressed Maureen out of the house to join his mother on the hammock. And he would have been happy to see the three of them cry, and then embrace. Three, which soon turned to six, as one by one Chuck, Mary Lou, and Sid came out of the house to see what all the commotion was about.

Vi had broken the promise she had made to her brother and his wife. But there was one promise she would never break. The promise she had made to herself. No one, not even Sid, would ever get to know the name of Maureen's natural mother.

Stuart and Maureen married in the twilight of September 18th, 1958. The ceremony took place on the lawns of the Vicente's house, with the gentle lapping tide of the blue Atlantic Ocean making up for the loss of a larger congregation.

Vi and Sid returned to England the following day and, much to Vi's consternation, her husband also made much use of the little white bags.

*

'All the world's a stage,
And all the men and women merely players:
They have their exits and their entrances;'

William Shakespeare: 1564-1616
139

16

Maureen moved slowly. The heat was oppressive and she was suffering, although she tried hard not to show it.

'Maureen, go home! I can manage; how many times do I have to tell you?'

'I'll go in a minute or two, when the rain stops. I want to put some of this stock on the shelves.'

'I can do that later. Now *go*, else I'll have that husband of yours after me…again!'

Mary Lou stood with her hands on her hips, flaunting mock annoyance as she chided Maureen.

It was July, the hottest and most humid month in the year: The month that most Floridians' dreaded. To be in the final month of pregnancy at this time of the year was tantamount to torture; from the first light of dawn there was rarely any respite from the intense summer heat. Even though rain fell like clockwork most afternoons, the humidity that followed the torrential down pouring was relentless. And the night air, when it finally came, was usually without mercy.

Yet Maureen rarely complained; the baby she was carrying was worth all the hardship and discomfort. And, during her ongoing pregnancy, she bravely laboured under both. Sickness, constant nausea, threatened miscarriage, blood pressure, each had raised its ugly head, and each had been mastered by the diminutive tigress—for that was how Stuart saw his wife: A tigress.

Stuart had long admired Maureen's strength, her strength of mind, of commitment. Her strong and compassionate character had lured him from the beginning, when they had been mere children. Her tiny frame, all five foot two of it, had always belied this strength. But as she was nearing full term of the difficult pregnancy, he was becoming very alarmed by his wife's ballooning and excessive weight, fearful for the expectant mother's long-term health. His concerns had been aired this very morning: he had forbidden his wife to go into work; had told her to stay at home and store her reserves of strength for what lay so soon ahead: the labours of childbirth.

Now, as Maureen stood side by side with Mary Lou, putting the finishing touches to the beauty salon that was soon to open, she gently patted her protruding stomach, smiling thoughtfully at her friend's last remark and also feeling extremely guilty...*Mary Lou is right...Stuart will be cross when he hears that I've been back in the salon...though how could I be expected to stay away from the opening of my own business...?*

Bad timing. That's all it was. Bad timing. But then, nothing had ever been timed. Not since she had first arrived in Florida...

The sunshine state had been wilting in the hottest July on record that year; Maureen's arrival had coincided with the birth of Mary Lou's child, and temperatures that beat all previous recordings.

Because of the baby's untimely birth, Maureen's daily chores within the new household were taken up with haste, leaving her little time to acclimatize; thrown into the deep end, as was wont to be her lot in life.

The Vicente's much longed for baby was named Lydia in memory of Mary Lou's deceased mother. During the infant's first three months of life, Maureen became Mary Lou's lifeline; under her constant and thorough care, both baby and mother began to thrive. Mary Lou slowly began to gain back the health she had lost during her many miscarriages and the subsequent full term pregnancy.

Later, as that first Christmas had neared, Mary Lou had been rewarding for all Maureen's hard work. The tables were turned: it was Mary Lou who had begun to plan, she who nurtured. During the festive season trips were taken to the coast's many unspoilt beaches and its enchanting towns, to the Everglades, crocodile spotting. To Miami, film star spotting. Mary Lou and

Chuck Vicente were enthusiastic about their new life in Florida, enthusiasm that had been contagious. With very little coaxing, Maureen agreed to stay longer.

By the spring of 1955, Maureen had been enrolled into college; the same college her cousin attended. Whilst Stuart worked with wood, learning the carpentry trade, Maureen worked with hair, a two-year night-school course that would eventually lead to her becoming a fully qualified hairdresser, emulating her role model and sponsor, Mary Lou.

Maureen's days were spent in the Vicente home. Fulfilling her first ambition, she was Lydia's nanny. This arrangement suited both women: Maureen enjoyed being with the contented infant, and Mary Lou was able to continue along her own career path.

Mary Lou was a talented stylist. After the long months of confinement and poor health, she was more than eager to get back to the work she had so enjoyed: the position she sought was as a beauty technician in an elegant salon in West Palm Beach.

Her application accepted, Mary Lou, with her southern belle good looks, infectious enthusiasm and talented fingers, soon became every one's favourite in the salon that was much frequented by wealthy and influential clients: her initial three days per week soon escalated into five.

Chuck's construction company grew steadily, but slowly. Suffering many teething problems with various legislations, the well-built Texan man found the snail moving pace of Florida frustrating.

Chuck was eager to build houses. His plans were well thought out and well structured: superior detached dwellings for the rich middle class, who were fast becoming the backbone of future prosperity in Florida. Chuck had done his homework and was sure that his good name, and his abilities as a builder, would bring his own riches…given time.

And, by the time of the birth of his second child, Chuck had built, to his credit, two small estates: Clusters of houses, single storied, with open plan lawns, nestled round an open air swimming pool. Each house had ample parking for two cars, with a back garden (yard as they were called in America, which really tickled Stuart and Maureen) that sported a barbecue pit, and space for a growing family to thrive and play.

As Chuck had envisioned, the newly rich were swarming into the Palm Beach area of Florida. The houses, once built, sold fast. The forward thinking businessman had also foreseen that busy people needed to be looked after: the exterior of the houses, paintwork and lawns, were maintained by his company too. This ensured the estate's manicured look. And it proved to be a look that sold.

His own home had benefited from the sales: a swimming pool graced the back lawn. And the two villas he had built in the grounds proved popular: Rented out on a weekly basis, to tourists seeking the sun and the pleasant climate that Florida was famous for, the idyllic properties were always occupied throughout the winter and, to every one's amazement, even during the hottest months of summer.

Stuart, before his marriage, had been only too happy to inhabit one of the newly built villas. It had been the most logical move: the main house had fast become overcrowded with Mary Lou, Chuck, their two small children...and the guest bedroom occupied by Maureen. The move had also given Stuart the solitude he had needed to untangle his mixed emotions. Especially when Maureen had begun to date various local boys. Chuck Vicente's involvement with the local rugby team had brought many big and handsome American boys into Maureen's life at that time.

As she dated a few of these young men, Stuart had also tried the mating game, but found the American girls to be lacking in the feminine qualities he sought. The bubble-gum smacking teenage girls seemed to all come from the same mould: pony-tailed, sneaker wearing sirens, who teased though did not please; the score card always ready, sex offered, then refused. Stuart, brought up in prudent England, was overpowered by their feisty talk...and their rules.

Confused and unhappy, it was at this point that Stuart had decided to move to the Gulf Coast. Newly qualified as a carpenter, he had been aware that finding work would not be a problem. But Maureen had been horrified to hear that her cousin was leaving the Boca Raton area. Arguments had flared...

'You're not being fair, Stuart! I've stayed on here because of *you*...' she had shouted.

'Why?' he had asked, wanting to hear the truth.

Maureen had been silent.

'I *love* you, Maureen. As I *know* you love me,' he'd finally said.

And she had taken her fists and had beaten at his chest, denying and crying.

Chuck and Mary Lou had intervened...It was *okay*. There was nothing wrong with the way they felt...cousins could fall in love...But Maureen had not listened to what anyone had to say; she had seemed so angry; and sad.

When they had heard of Gerard's death, their own troubles had been put on a back-boiler. Their grief had been mutual. Though they had barely spoken any words of comfort to each other.

Stuart had not spoken to her again until just before his grieving parents were due to arrive, 'I'll be leaving after their visit,' he had told her. She had shrugged and gone about her business, ignoring his presence, although in all fairness to her, she had pretended to be his friend when his parents had finally arrived.

Stuart had known that Maureen would continue to show her best face, her courageous face to Vi and Sid whilst they were in Florida. And he had not been mistaken. It was obvious that both of his parents had been in the dark regarding the sour state of Stuart and Maureen's friendship.

And then the miracle had happened. Stuart would always believe it to be a miracle. A miracle, that Maureen was not his cousin. No relation what so ever. His mother had stated it so calmly, first to him and then, gloriously (and loudly) to Maureen. Slowly, cautiously, Maureen had taken it all in. Had whispered that inside, deep inside her, she had always known that there was more to her life than what she had been told. Then she had turned to him...and smiled. Really smiled, the first time in many months. She had looked radiant, her blue eyes dancing with the joy of what was to come.

And come it did. There and then, in front of his mother, Stuart had fallen to his knees and proposed. Had proposed marriage to the girl he had always loved. And Maureen had accepted.

After the wedding, their honeymoon had had to wait. It seemed only fair to be there on hand to wave goodbye to his parents: Their parents.

His father, Sid, left Florida looking happier and healthier. And Vi? Only Stuart knew that although his mother was more than delighted to have Maureen as a daughter-in-law, that there was something worrying her, niggling her. Stuart knew his mother well, and only hoped that whatever was troubling his mother had nothing to do with his new wife.

But as they waved their goodbyes, Stuart had put all thoughts of his mother out of his mind. Another woman, whose hand he held tightly, was at the fore of his thoughts: And his desires.

However, Stuart and Maureen had been married for nearly a week before they made love.

Their wedding night had been spent in the small villa that had been Stuart's home before they were wed. With his parents in the villa next door, Stuart had felt unable to consummate the marriage.

Although his father had celebrated to oblivion, Stuart had known that his mother would be wide awake, angry at her husband's antics, and worrying over the return journey back to England, which would be undertaken the following day.

As they had cuddled close, Stuart had been apologetic, until Maureen had put her finger to his lips, and whispered that it was okay, that she had the same reservations about starting married life with her aunt and uncle so close by.

It was four nights into their honeymoon before Maureen truly became his wife.

Fort Lauderdale had been chosen as the setting for a perfect week of married bliss, the bridal suite of the Riverside Fort reserved to ensure their comfort.

Stuart had chosen the hotel for its incomparable position overlooking the calm river. Its excellent standards and fine culinary qualities were well known, and its rooms were well furnished and comfortable.

Stuart had known of the latter for certain: Chuck's company had undertaken the many improvements that had only recently been completed.

That fourth night, their second in Fort Lauderdale, they had dined early, and had walked hand in hand along the promenade before returning to their hotel.

As his naked bride climbed into bed, Stuart claimed her for his own. And the urgency had been mutual. Both had waited long enough.

Long into the early hours of that lingering, warm night they had quenched each other's desires and yearnings; learning each other, exploring, seeking, finding; freeing embarrassment, shedding their youth. Kissing they had become used to: they had kissed at every conceivable moment since the night Maureen had learned of her adoption. But their lovemaking had been put on hold. Not really spoken of, except on their wedding night.

When they had first arrived in the palm tree thronged resort, they'd been content to kiss and fondle. A courtship had begun. A deep understanding between them, a comprehension that needed no words, had given Stuart and Maureen the space to adjust to their new status as man and wife before they could become lovers.

And after their romantic honeymoon they returned to Boca Raton, and their new life. One that started in the villa in the grounds of the Vicente home, until Thanksgiving week-end of the following year, when they moved into a home of their own. A two-bedroom bungalow on one of the small estates Chuck's construction company had built in the town of Larson, a few minutes drive from Boca Raton.

Maureen had qualified as a hairdresser and, upon Mary Lou's insistence, had taken a junior position in the opulent salon where she was manageress.

Now, two years on, Maureen, heavily pregnant with her first child, was thrown into the deep end once more: the opening of her own beauty salon. A business that had the backing of her one-time employer, Mary Lou…"Go for it, Maureen. I'll help you all I can!" As Maureen had dallied with problem of being in the first stages of pregnancy *and* the possibility of owning her own shop, she had known this statement to be true. Mary Lou Vicente was an exceptional woman, a woman not unlike Violet Greenwood: A woman who got on with things. Never let anything stand in her way. Who was generous to a fault—and more like a sister to Maureen with every passing day. There had never been, nor would there ever be, the employer/employee status.

This being so, it was entrepreneurial Mary Lou (Chuck's wife was fast following in her husband's footsteps) who saw to the recruiting of staff for Maureen's new venture. Whose daily visits ensured that the clientele of the small salon grow in numbers within the first weeks.

It was Mary Lou who put many hours in at the thriving salon whilst July blazed into August and Maureen was busying herself in her other venture: Motherhood.

Beth Greenwood was born on the first day of August, a day that had dawned without the constant humidity that had marred the long month of July. A day during which Maureen, unbeknown to her husband, had spent entirely on her feet: her hairdressing salon, newly opened and two weeks into its stride, was showing signs of being popular.

The small shop, although situated in a quiet back street, was elegantly appointed, and its client list was growing longer with each passing hour.

Maureen's beauty salon was fast becoming the *in place*: her English mannerisms, her softly spoken voice and quiet dignity was thought classy. And the American women liked class…

Feeling anything but classy, Maureen had been glad to see the last of her customers leave the shop that evening. The salon's hours were nine until one, opening again in the late afternoon at four. The shop closed as promptly as was possible at around seven in the evening. These hours had been arranged with the hot summer months in mind, and because of the baby she was carrying. Maureen was determined to spend as much time as possible with her expected child.

Beth must have taken notice of her mother's wishes, waiting until the last client had left the premises before arousing the first pains of her forthcoming arrival.

As the sinking sun cast its fierce red rays across the panoramic Floridian sky, Maureen had time to calmly drive herself home, arriving exactly at the same time as her husband.

And Beth had also waited whilst Maureen phoned Mary Lou; waited whilst the frantic father-to-tie dashed from room to room, readying his wife for the hospital, though forgetting to put the packed-in-advance suitcase into the boot of the car, before speeding his labouring wife to the hospital.

Beth was born two minutes before midnight on August 1st, 1960. Weighing in at seven pounds and nine ounces, the dark haired infant was the image of her mother, Maureen, though her lungs put both of her doting, jubilantly grinning parents in mind of those belonging to her grandmother.

Whilst his wife slept after her labours, Stuart cradled the new born child, eager to spread the news of her birth: Beth Greenwood was Violet and Sidney Greenwood's first grandchild, and Stuart was happily aware that his daughter's birth would go a long way to restoring his bereaving parent's well being.

*

17

The telephone was ringing. But this evening its constant shrill was being ignored.

When it had first been installed, there had been a rush to be the first to pick up the receiver, a delight in being able to say... 'Hello. Warrington Clough 764512.'

These days it could ring for more than a minute before someone answered it, grudging the intrusion the instrument had brought with it. Business hours had spilled over into the evenings, as orders were now phoned in by day and by night. This, coupled with the growing number of personal messages, left almost daily, and needing to be relayed to near and distant neighbours (telephones were a bit thin on the ground in the back-waters of this Cheshire town) brought little peace to the busy Greenwood household. All in all, the installing of the telephone was more of a nuisance than a gain.

The prime reason for its introduction had been the impending arrival of the Greenwoods' first grandchild.

'We're having a phone,' Vi had stated. 'I'm not going to be the *last* to know when me own grandchild's born!'

And so it had been done, installed, and indeed Vi and Sid had been the first

181

to know of their granddaughter's arrival.

However, seeing as that was well over a year ago, this evening the telephone shrilled—and was ignored, even though Vi, Sid and Malcolm were seated in the same room as the intrusive instrument.

It was Friday, Friday night: Television night. More importantly— *Bonanza* night! This was the threesome's favourite television programme:

The star of the show was chastising his youngest son—the storyline in the much loved western running true to form; a format that drew thousands of other avid viewers, along with the Greenwoods.

But this Friday night, the very moment the telephone ceased ringing, unanswered, the programme was further interrupted by a news flash...

'President Kennedy has been shot. The President was in Dallas. Mrs Kennedy was with her husband at the time of the shooting...'

Sid was the first out of his armchair, kneeling in front of the television set as if by doing so he would hear more.

Vi and Malcolm looked at each other in a sate of shock. Was it true? Had they heard right? Was it part of the show...some pretend President?

When it was announced again, they knew it true.

President John F. Kennedy was dead.

And, as the awful truth settled around them, in the snug warmth of their coal fired parlour, the telephone rang again, and Vi rushed over to the walnut veneered sideboard, where the black telephone sat in pride of place.

'Hello? Warrington Clough...er, 764512,' she spoke hastily into the receiver. Sid and Malcolm watched her.

'Oh hello, Maureen *love*...! Sorry, chuck, it's a bad line...What did you say? Are you ringing about the President...? *What?* I can't hear you. *Maureen.* Are you crying...? *He's what...?* He *can't* have...! *Our Stuart?* Maureen, tell me *again*...Our Stuart's had a heart attack...Good God, *Maureen*...! Is he...? Oh, *thank God*...Thank God. Oh, Maureen, love...'

*

18

'It all depends on you, Stuart. You can get over this, put it behind you...or you can carry on as you have been doing, and bring on another. As I said, it's up to you.'

It was Maureen who answered, 'He'll get better, Doctor Sneldon. I'll make *sure* of it.' She stretched her hand out to the doctor, as firm in her handshake as she was in her convictions.

Stuart also shook the doctor's hand. Although his grip was not as strong as it had once been, the warmth of his gratitude was.

Closing the front door, after waving their goodbyes to the doctor, Maureen linked her arm through that of her husband's and steered them both through the lounge of their home and entered the kitchen.

Seating themselves on the pine bench seat, which fitted neatly under the yellow gingham curtained window of the room's breakfast alcove, they looked out onto their small garden to where their young daughter played happily in the safety of her wooden playpen.

'We have to talk this through, Stuart. The doctor *means* what he says...you will not be able to work as many hours as you used to do. You understand that, don't you?'

Stuart sighed. It was becoming a habit, sighing. Sighing with disbelief, sighing with anguish; sighing at his thoughts, thoughts that were in a permanent state of disarray...*how did it happen? How could it have happened? Heart attacks inflicted the old, not people in their twenties...*

Nevertheless, a heart attack is what he had had, like it or not. And there was probably more to follow.

He would have had to have been blind not to see the anguish in his wife's blue eyes; the deep concern on his friends' faces. He'd clearly heard the warning in his doctor's voice. But how could he face life with the constant worry of another attack?

"Take things easy," they told him. But they hadn't told him how, how he was supposed to do that...? *I had so many plans. So much work to do; so much to maintain...! How can I just sit around and do nothing...?*

Stuart sighed again, and turned from the window, not wanting to watch his young daughter any longer: The baby daughter who was a miniature version of his young and healthy wife. The heart attack had ruined everything. Tears brimmed his eyes. Tears that were always there, always ready to surface, to leak. Like the tears of a weak woman...*That's a laugh, though, isn't it...? I don't know any weak women. Indeed, all the women I've ever met, all the women in my life, are strong. Especially this one by my side...My wife. My Maureen. Oh, I've got find my strength again...I've got to.*

While all of this was swirling round in Stuart's head, Maureen moved from the bench seat. Busying herself at the sink, she spoke without turning, pretending she had not seen her husband's tears.

'What should we have for lunch? Oh, blow it! We'll think about that, later. Come one, let's take this coffee out onto the patio, enjoy the morning sun...'

Chatting was easier than thinking. As she stood in her sunshine yellow kitchen, pouring Columbian coffee into chocolate brown mugs, she talked of this and that, anything rather than Stuart's health problems.

Her pleasant stream of conversation and energy brought a certain amount of normality back into their lives.

After their coffee, Maureen whisked Beth into her arms, in readiness to put her down for her morning nap, persuading Stuart, at the same time, to stay outside and take some air. She was also planning to go back into the salon, just for a few hours. Maureen was aware that she had to keep things under control; and she didn't want idle time. Time to think. So that was the key. Keep busy. Don't have any spare time left for thoughts. Thinking too deeply brought questions. Questions to which she had no answers: *Why? Why Stuart? Why...?* Maureen battled with these questions: Other people worked hard, including herself, without having heart attacks! *Was it the heat? Was he missing England? Did she press him too hard with her own worries...?*

On that beautiful blue skied mid-morning, as the palm trees swayed gently in the soft Floridian breeze, Maureen did indeed keep herself busy: she made lunch, and also readied the evening meal: chicken, salad, fruit, a light diet of easily digested meals.

As she gave the baby-sitter her afternoon instructions, she watched her husband amble listlessly back into the kitchen clutching his mug of coffee, and battled with the growing anger that knotted in her chest... *Whoa, whoa, there...* she thought, chastising herself... *Get to grips, girl. Find a way to make things right. Don't worry yourself into a blooming heart attack, as well! You still have your husband. He's alive, isn't he? He'll get better. You have a daughter, a home, and a business to see to. You've got to be strong. So move, ugly black thoughts! Come on, shift...* Maureen fought for more positive thoughts... *Staying strong will help Stuart to recover. If I help myself, I'll be helping him to be positive, too...*

They got through Stuart's first full week out of the hospital and, within the month, it was if the heart attack had never happened. Stuart took his pills, and took his care. Chuck saw to that. Saw to it that Stuart's energies went not into the labour of the new houses but into their maintenance planning and expenditure.

A forte was revealed; a talent that surprised Stuart. And pleased him, too: His bookkeeping days (his mother's *insisted* book-keeping days,) coming into their own under the blue skies and soft climate of east-coast Florida.

A year passed, and then two. The heart attack was forgotten. They began to thoroughly enjoy their busy thriving lives living next to the ocean in the small community of Larson, only a few minutes outside of Boca Raton.

The mouth of the rat: that was the English translation of Boca Baton. Such a strange name for so lovely a place, a place of beauty and simple elegance, where the temperature averaged throughout the year at 75 degrees Fahrenheit: The Gold Coast, and aptly named.

From Palm Beach down to Fort Lauderdale, the white sandy beaches of Boyton, Delray, Boca Raton and Deerfield brought thousands of visitors. Some to stay for a week or two, some to stay for ever.

The *forever's* became Stuart's business: the houses they needed, and the golf courses which would attract them, were built to order; plans drawn, targets set, monies secured. As Chuck's company thrived, Stuart became one of its directors.

Maureen had both the tourists and the local community as her clients. Each had the need for a hairdresser.

And so the young couple, who had exchanged their wedding vows with the Atlantic Ocean the fitting backdrop, and who had conquered ill health, were now part of a thriving network of people who had chosen to work and live on the sun kissed eastern coast of Florida.

And Maureen's good friend and mentor Mary Lou Vicente had not been left behind in her own ambitions. With more and more hotels being built, she had realised the need for dress shops, boutiques as they were soon to be known. Mary Lou owned two such shops, both frequented by the rich and famous; people who spent money as though it was going out of fashion.

Maureen, however, was content to have just the one shop. It was doing well, her clientele book overflowing with appointments. Nevertheless, Maureen did have one other string to her bow—a very lucrative string, which had come about quite by chance.

One of Mary Lou's most frequent clients ran an advertising agency; the forerunner to what was to become a model/actors agency.

During one of her forays in Mary Lou's Palm Beach shop, this client mentioned she was looking for someone to do hand modelling. There was a new product coming on the market: false nails.

Cynthia Paton, the agency owner, was on the lookout for the right pair of hands. Elegant hands with long slim fingers and small, perfectly shaped nails. Attractive hands, which would photograph well, and enhance the product.

Mary Lou knew of such hands. She had always admired the hands she had in mind. The hands of Maureen Greenwood: The same hands that Violet Greenwood had also admired, and had gone out of her way to protect.

The flamboyant agent had been delighted to sign Maureen Greenwood onto her books. And one year on, Maureen was used to seeing her hands on bill boards and in television commercials for soap products, for Cynthia had gone on and on finding work for the hands that looked as though they did very little work.

Today, though, Maureen was a little fraught as she journeyed to her latest modelling assignment: a mother and child advertisement for a liquid soap.

Cynthia had been convincing when she had said that five-year old Beth would be just perfect for the child part. Who could be better? Especially as the little girl would be working with her own mother...

But as Cynthia drove them into the studio's parking lot, chatting nineteen to the dozen, Maureen glanced at the energetic youngster playing with her toys on the long back seat of the station wagon, and her reservations were confirmed; Beth would find it impossible to sit still for the long camera session...

'Cut! She's a natural; just like her mother!'

Everyone in the studio clapped; Cynthia beamed, and Maureen hugged her daughter close.

'Bethy, sweetheart, you were such a *good* girl.'

'Will I be on television. Mummy, will I? *Will I...?*'

'Yes, love. But not just yet, it takes quite some time before everything is ready. They have to record the jingle first.'

'What's a *jingle...?*' Beth giggled.

'It's a rhyming song, honey babe. Like a nursery rhyme: the cow jumped over the moon, that kind a thing,' Cynthia answered as she walked, jauntily. Swing-hipped, she sashayed out of the studio alongside Maureen and Beth.

Harsh sunlight greeted them as they hurried to the parking lot to where Cynthia's brown coloured station wagon waited, its paintwork glinting, baking under the intense heat of the blistering noon sun.

Entering the car was like stepping into a furnace. Within seconds the three of them were soaked in perspiration, even though they were clad in cotton, lightweight clothes: Maureen in a pale pink tee-shirt and matching slacks: Beth in a polka dot sundress, a crisp apple green and white, with a matching short sleeved bolero: Cynthia, with knock-out glamour always in mind, was dressed in a sleeveless, figure hugging shift of vivid scarlet.

Even with the car windows rolled down, the light breeze blowing in was insufficient as a cooling agent.

'Phew! It sure is hot today.' Glancing at her hands on the steering wheel, she added, 'hope it doesn't melt these here nails of mine.' Cynthia had become a devotee of the talon style false nails, which today she'd painted a deep red to match her dress. Checking that her nails where still glued to the nail base, taking her eyes off the road to inspect them, made her front seat passenger almost pass out from holding her breath.

Mercifully, Cynthia seemed satisfied that the nails were safe and, as they were nearing Boca, asked, 'Where shall I drop you, Maureen? At the salon? In the sea?'

Maureen chuckled as she answered. 'No, Cyn, we're going home. Home to Daddy, eh, Beth?'

'Yeah! We're going on Uncle Chuck's boat this afternoon, to Singer Island. Do you wanna come...?'

'Beth! You say—would you like to come. Anyway, it's not your place to invite people. And besides, Cynthia's probably busy this afternoon.' Maureen admonished her daughter, fearful that Cynthia might take up the invitation; Maureen was well aware that the hard headed, though humorous business woman never missed an opportunity, whether it was by invitation...or not.

Thankfully, Cynthia had other things to do, and so she said her quick goodbyes before dropping Maureen and Beth off at the end of the short driveway which led up to the Greenwood's bungalow.

Stepping into the blessed cool of her home, Maureen shooed Beth off to her bedroom, urging her young daughter to shower and change so as to be ready for their afternoon trip, feeling slightly perturbed that her husband was not waiting to greet them.

Unease accompanied her as she entered her own bedroom: Stuart rarely worked on a Saturday afternoon...*where is he?*

It was some two hours later before Stuart came home and, when she saw him, his sickly grey pallor frightened Maureen, the solicitous concern of Chuck, who aided her husband into the house, confirming her worst fears. Stuart was ill again: chest pains were making him breathless and weak.

Within the hour, Stuart was to be admitted into the hospital in West Palm Beach where he was to undergo tests.

Beth cried as she was scooped up into the arms of her Uncle Chuck. Having changed into a bright pink swimsuit in readiness for the afternoon trip to Singer Island, she was cranky and bewildered by the grave atmosphere pervading her home.

After previously being so excited about the forthcoming adventure, Beth now wanted nothing more than to stay home with her mummy and daddy. The normally compliant child rebelled: she did not want to play with Lydia. She didn't like Roy anymore; didn't want to go to her aunt and uncle's house...or on the boat to the *silly* island.

Pale faced, Maureen came to Chuck's side. Reaching to take hold of Beth's hand, and looking earnestly into her daughter's face, she assured the youngster that all would soon be well.

Not placated, Beth leaned down to kiss her mother, whimpering she wanted to stay home.

But Maureen was insistent. Urging the troubled child to go with her uncle as planned, she had to turn away from the youngster's brimming, pleading eyes, knowing it was for the best that Beth should not see her father being carried into an ambulance.

Just as Chuck's car sped away, the sirens could be heard.

Jack and Ruth Silverstein, both in their mid-sixties, shook their heads, commiserating with each other as they watched Stuart being wheeled down the driveway towards the waiting ambulance. They had grown very fond of their next door neighbours...*it's such a shame...he's a fine young man...wonderful neighbour...But they both worked too hard...And the little girl was crying when she left...did you see? And Chuck looked mighty grim...Things must be bad...*

As Stuart was undergoing the first of many-to-come medical tests, Maureen stayed by his side, willing the doctors to say that indeed all would be well.

On Singer Island, Chuck and Mary Lou played with the children, took them sailing, encouraging an unusually sullen Beth to join in the fun, though their own hearts and minds, and their silent prayers, were with their young friends back in Palm Beach.

The prognosis was bad. Stuart would never work again.

Still, as Maureen told him over and over again...'For the umpteenth time...so what! It's *not* the end of the world, darling. Given time, you'll get better, stronger. We still have each other, and Beth; *that's* what counts. The salon's managed now, and I only need to be there for three days of the week. We have a lovely home, friends...money in the bank. And our Beth...Stuart, don't you find it exciting that she is so much in demand in the advertising industry?'

It was the latter which was disturbing Stuart the most. 'Is it right?' he kept asking. He asked everyone who visited him in the re-fitted bungalow, and they all answered the same: Yes! Why not? Beth was young, bright, and very intelligent. She was having singing lessons, dancing lessons, all paid for by the agency. She never went anywhere without her mother or her Aunt Mary

Lou by her side. And wasn't it true that if neither of them were available, Cynthia stepped into the breach…? Even when schedules were tight, and Beth couldn't be in school, she had her own tutor, didn't she? And, of course, there was the money. Not many youngsters had such a nest egg for the future, now was there…?

In Stuart's presence Maureen was calm and efficient. Never did she let him see that she was fretted by everything in her life. By the severity of her husband's illness; by the workload within her busy salon; by the advertising agency and the never-ending demands it made on her time: the busy scheduling of her daughter's auditions and appointments, running here, dashing there. And, whilst all of this needed to be seen to, dealt with, the re-fit work of the bungalow had also required her constant supervision.

But she had done it all, and done it well. Stuart was back home in the bungalow he loved, determinedly roaming from room to room unaided; the widened door frames accommodating his bulky wheelchair and the ramps enabling him easy access to the front and back doors of his home.

Beth was thriving, doing well both in her schoolwork and in her modelling assignments. The child was well mannered and helpful, whilst at the same time thoroughly enjoying her many activities and social outings brought about by her growing fame. Beth was not only a blessing and a joy to both of her parents, she seemed to be liked and regarded by all who knew her.

Those very same people who admired and respected Beth, were worried by the decline of the girl's mother. Although she had always been slim, Maureen's weight had dropped considerably. Her shrinking frame brought a gaunt look to her face. Worry lines creased her forehead and wrinkled around her blue, sad looking eyes. Her black hair, that was always immaculate, short bobbed and fringed, was fast becoming streaked with grey.

And through all this daunting period of health issues, hard work and hectic timetables, the sun shone and the skies were blue. As the flowers bloomed their riotous colours of spring, then summer, Maureen knew with more and more certainty that she needed help. She needed the help of the woman she dearly loved. The woman she so very much missed: Maureen needed her mother-in-law: her Auntie Vi.

*

19

Vi travelled alone. *Fancy...*she thought...*fancy me going all this way by myself...*

It was October 1970, and Vi was at last on her way to Florida. She had boarded the plane clutching her prized possession: a studio photograph of Beth. A publicity shot the studio had sent to her. Sent to her personally. A picture of her ten year old granddaughter, a colour photograph showing Beth in a red velvet dress, frilly white ankle socks and shiny, black patent shoes. Beth's hands were tucked out of sight, tucked into a white fur muff, and she was smiling. Smiling up at the handsome man stood next to her.

And everyone who was on the New York bound plane that October morning soon learnt that the man in the photograph was a very famous singer, and that Vi's granddaughter had been chosen to sing in a *Christmas Special* with the talented, and very good looking entertainer.

The passengers and crew also learnt that the *Christmas Special* was being televised on Christmas Eve. A show that would be seen the length and breadth of America.

In a quieter voice, Vi told her immediate companions of her son's grave illness. And as she spoke of Stuart, she wept, gaining their sympathy, although it must be said, they had begun to wonder what they had let themselves in for the next eight hours.

Disembarking at New York, Vi's fellow travellers hurried away to their own destinations, their own flight connections, carrying a mental picture of a beautiful, dark haired child and an ailing, sandy haired young man who was her father, wondering how the mother and wife of this duo would ever manage to get through the coming months: Vi had let it be known to all and sundry that she would be staying in America for a prolonged visit.

Vi's connecting flight brought her to Miami. Tired by the long journey, she slept as she was driven through the Miami suburbs heading north.

Comfortable in the back seat of the black Plymouth, Vi hardly spoke more than a few words to the driver, as the deluxe car and professional chauffeur, (booked and paid for by Chuck Vicente,) sped through the night quiet roads.

Beth, however, was finding sleep very difficult. She could not contain her excitement. She was going to see her grandmother: at last.

Since infancy, Beth had spoken regularly to her grandmother by telephone. The grandma who had such a funny voice—who laughed a lot, and said funny things, like: "Give yer dadda a big smacker from me," and, "Help yer mam with the pots and pans."

It was a good job her parents knew the same kind of English because they could always interpret what she was saying, laughing together as they did so.

Now, when she woke up in the morning, grandma would be in the house…*actually here…in this house…*

But after being awake for most of the night, Beth was to sleep through Vi's arrival.

The sleek black Plymouth pulled onto the drive at five forty five a.m. In the dusky light of dawn, Maureen opened the car door, leaning in to hug Vi before the weary traveller had time to open her eyes properly. As Vi became fully awake, Maureen had to put a finger to her lips in order to hush the flow of greetings that bellowed from her disorientated aunt.

Smiling from ear to ear, Maureen ushered the whispering, over excited Vi into the bungalow, leaving the bags and packages to be brought into the house by the driver.

Vi's high-heeled shoes clattered on the parquet flooring of the lounge and, fearing the noise she was making, she tried, in vain, to tiptoe behind Maureen into the kitchen. Turning and seeing this, Maureen had to smother a nervous giggle.

They sat at the kitchen table. Behind them, through the window, the sun was rising, pinking the sky, promising the beginning of a beautiful day.

On the bench seat, Maureen snuggled closer to her aunt, savouring her special smell; a familiar, long lost odour filled her nostrils, pierced her senses with nostalgia.

'Oh, Aunt Vi, I can't *believe* you're here! Oh, hold me…hold me…' And the tears fell. Tears that Maureen had wanted to shed for so long.

The quiet weeping brought great gasping sobs from Vi, as she too cried, rocking her darling girl backwards and forwards.

'Well, you're a fine pair, aren't you?' Stuart had wheeled himself to the kitchen doorway. His voice was full of emotion, 'Hey, Mam,' he swallowed, 'hope you haven't brought all the River Mersey with you…there's plenty of water around here, you know.'

Vi pulled away from Maureen, almost leaping from her seat. Crossing the kitchen in a flash, she fell onto her knees and into the open arms of her son.

And that was how Beth first saw her grandmother: on her knees, her clothing dishevelled, milky-white thighs on show, her bouffant beehive of tumbling brown/grey hair a lopsided mess. Tears streamed down the smooth, unlined face that didn't seem very old, not *grandma* old at all. In fact, her father's mother was nothing at all like Beth had expected! And she had a funny smell about her. Not a bad odour, just different.

As Beth found herself enveloped into a hug that lifted her off her feet, the kitchen seemed to be filled with the woman's scent: a mixture of lavender, talcum powder…and food.

Breakfast was a laughing, loving affair that morning. Her father's mood was better than it had been for months, his eyes sparkled, his laughter strong.

And her mother was relaxed, too: sipping her coffee, smiling all the time, joining in the chat that flowed endlessly.

After the initial shyness, that had been lessened by repeated kissed, bear like hugs, and more than a few tears, Beth too had soon shed her reservations: the glowing child could hardly take her eyes off Grandma Vi

Joining in the frivolity that accompanied breakfast this morning, Beth wondered why her school friends thought the English had soft voices. Grandma Vi's voice boomed louder than any American.

Indeed, even though she was used to her parent's English accents, Beth found it hard to understand most of what her grandmother was saying. And it didn't help that she seemed to say everything with a chuckle in her voice.

But Beth didn't mind about any of this; there was so many conversations flying round the table, she couldn't possibly understand it all. She was pleased just to sit and spoon her cereal and smile and listen...and watch.

Grandma Vi seemed real nice, and her loud laugh made everyone else laugh, too. Not for a long time had Beth seen her mother and father so happy, so carefree. And the way they kept looking at one another...their eyes kind of shining...it was as if they knew a secret. Maybe they did...but maybe it was just having grandma here...Yes, all in all, having grandmother here was going to be good.

Beth could remember the time before her father became ill. She could remember how her mother was then. How happy and jolly—always smiling. Now, it was only infrequently that Beth had a glimpse of her mother as she used to be. And that was when there was just the two of them, maybe out shopping or walking, for a short time her mother could seem almost like her old self. When they returned home she would be quieter...busier. The ten year old loved her mother; loved her with all her heart. And she loved her father, too. But that was a love filled with pity, and a feeling of claustrophobic helplessness.

An onlooker this morning, Beth watched her parents become animated and so lively within her grandmother's company. Because of what she saw, Beth's knowledge of life grew. For the first time she noticed how ill her father really was. Though he was obviously delighted by his mother's visit, Beth was aware that the brightness of his eyes, the articulation of his speech this breakfast time, did little to mask the thinness of his limbs, the greyness of his skin and the deep hollows dug into his cheeks. And she made herself a promise. A promise she knew she would keep...*I'm going to be the best daughter in the whole wide world...I'm going to make them this happy all the time. From now on, I'm going to make them laugh and smile at one another...just like grandma can!*

Maureen had spent most of the week in the salon: A week that had given her the time and space to relax a little and reflect. With Vi installed as Stuart's carer, Maureen was able to give her clients her full attention: this full-day week had also made her realise just how neglectful she had become with regard to her business.

The client she was attending to at this moment had been one of her first customers. Now a regular, the middle aged woman was pleased to have the owner to herself; and the conversation taking place reflected this satisfaction.

'It's good to see you back at the helm, Maureen; *you've* been missed.'

The plump, grey haired customer glanced in the direction of Vera Malone, the manager of Maureen's salon, and the sniff that accompanied her statement spoke volumes.

'Thank you, Ida, I hope you don't think *too* badly of me, but Stuart has had to come first.' Maureen reached for the hand mirror as she spoke. Holding it slightly at an angle, she held it so that Ida could see the back of her newly styled hair reflected through the larger mirror which covered the wall directly in front of where she sat.

Ida seemed delighted by what she saw and, as she fingered her silver rinsed hair, and felt it's silky bounce, she smiled with pleasure: the hairstyle made her look years younger.

Seizing her opportunity, Maureen was earnest now in her compliments, and her explanations, knowing that Ida was a nice woman, as well as a much-valued client.

'It suits you shorter, more sporty, and it will be easier for you cope with. Next time you shampoo, leave a conditioner on for a minute or two before you rinse out. And then you can let your hair dry naturally; the layers will fall into place. It's much better than a perm. Enjoy it!'

Removing the protective white towel from Ida's shoulders, Maureen lowered her voice as she continued, 'I'm sorry if Vera's a bit abrasive. She's a good stylist, and a good worker. To be honest, Ida, I'd have been lost without her this past year or two.'

And Ida, herself a mother of five and a widow for more than a decade, conceded to this fact: good help was indeed hard come by. She could remember her own hardships: ill-health brought a lot of misery. Good friends and a good family was as essential as drawing breath during these difficult times. Ida was also pleased to know that Stuart's mother was visiting.

'Will Vi be coming into the salon, Maureen? I'd just *love* to meet her, she sounds a *doll*.'

Maureen laughed. 'She's been already. Her first day! Had her hair done, her nails, too. But maybe you'll see her next week. At the moment, she likes to spend her days with Stuart, and Beth when she gets home from school. But I'll see what I can do. We're going out to dinner next Tuesday, with Chuck and Mary Lou. We're having a bit of a get-together, kids as well...and I'm *sure* Vi'll be having her hair done for that...Come in on Tuesday morning, Ida. I'll introduce you. And honestly, Ida, it's been real nice to see you again;

and don't worry, I'll have a word with Vera...'

Maureen had to wait till the close of day before she had that *word*—and Maureen chose it with care. Vera Malone, a native New Yorker, could sometimes be a little harsh with the customers. A trait that Maureen had to try and curb...

'In Florida, Vera, they *expect* relaxation to be the order of the day. You have to give them your time. Chat to them. Spoil them a little...be kind.'

'It's okay for you, Maureen, it comes natural to you, to be kind, you're a real lady...Me, I've had to fight my way up. You learn quick when you're raised in the Bronx.'

'But you're not in the Bronx now, are you Vera? You've *chosen* to live and work in Florida. And Vera, you'd be surprised to hear what I had to put up with during my childhood...honestly...you'd be surprised.'

But as Maureen made her way home from the salon, she mused to herself that perhaps Vera was right. The American way of life was different—especially in New York. Life must have been quite hard for Vera, the seventh daughter of a large immigrant family.

Driving with the car windows rolled down, Maureen felt a frisson of contentment; she was lucky. Lucky to have a business, neglected or not. Lucky to have Stuart and Beth...and good loyal friends like Chuck and Mary Lou. Tears smarted at the back of her eyes as she thought of her friends. She was really going to miss them both.

Chuck's construction company was a great success. To date it had built four estates, each complex consisting of twenty-two houses. On the newer estates, some of the houses were two storied and double garaged, but even these had a Mediterranean quality about their white-stuccoed walls and arched porches.

Golf courses had been added for the communities' enjoyment and a further two were in the pipeline.

The company had two partners, Chuck Vicente and his wife, Mary Lou. Until his second debilitating heart attack, Stuart Greenwood had been the firm's Sales Director.

However, from its conception, most of the company's business had been undertaken by the two men and, latterly, their fast growing workforce, allowing Mary Lou free time to care for her children and to pursue her own ambitions.

Finding that she herself was an astute businesswoman, Mary Lou's ambitions had been fulfilled: she was the proud owner of five boutiques. Her elegant shops sold expensive items of clothing and accessories: quality designer wear, much in demand by the fast growing clientele of the many, newly built hotels, which were springing up in great numbers, on and around the south-east coastline of Florida.

Now, with most of the hard work behind them, Mary Lou was saddened to be leaving Florida. Yet they had no option: they would not have been able to achieve half of what they had without the help they had received from Chuck's father, Roy Vicente.

Himself a master builder, it was Roy's money which had first enabled Chuck to move himself and his new family to Florida. Although the loan had been long since repaid, Chuck felt it was his duty to return to Texas when he learnt of his father's declining health. A family man at heart, Chuck knew he had a lot to be thankful for: now, it was his father's turn to come first.

And Mary Lou, reluctant as she was, had to agree, especially after watching Chuck age before her very eyes; she had soon realised her husband could not possibly continue commuting between Florida and Texas, as he had been doing for the past year. Renting an apartment in San Antonio seemed the most logical idea. They were to spend seven months of the year in Texas. Their own businesses in Florida were well managed, well run, and so the remaining months of the year, in which they would return to the sunshine state, would be time enough to sort out any major difficulties.

With these arrangements in place, the Vicente family were due to leave for Texas the week before Christmas, and Maureen was not looking forward to their departure: the two families had become very close over the years and, being very grateful for all that she had received from the good natured Texans, Maureen had masked her own bitter disappointment when she heard that they were leaving.

In truth, Maureen was terrified of being alone, she had always relied heavily on the couple's ability to cope; their help had been immeasurable. Once Vi had also returned home, Maureen knew that she would feel isolated.

Now, as she turned the key in the lock of the front door of her home, Maureen hoped that Stuart was not aware of how she felt.

'What time's it on?'

'You've asked that twenty times, already. For the twenty-first time, Mam, *eight thirty.*' From his place at the table, Stuart shook his head in his mother's direction.

'Have I got time to phone Sid? What time is it in England, now? I can't work this blooming time difference out, no matter how I try…'

It was Christmas Eve. Hot, sunny, and totally strange to Vi: The Christmas tree in the lounge looked out of place. Having breakfast on the patio, listening to Christmas Carols on the wireless, under a cloudless sky, seemed bizarre.

'Don't think I'd ever get used to this heat. Not very Christmassy, is it? Still, I suppose it's better having sunburn than frostbite…Hey, love, you don't mind if I phone him, do you Maureen?'

'Aunt Vi, while you are here this is *your* home! So use the phone whenever you like. Do you want to call Barry as well?'

'No, I'll do that in the morning, pet. That won't be long distance, will it?'

Maureen shook her head, chuckling quietly, still delighted to be in Vi's company. As she stood at the sink listening to Vi bellow her 'Hellos' into the phone mouthpiece as if she had to project her voice at full volume to be heard across the Atlantic, Maureen rinsed lettuce in preparation for lunch and felt a colossal wave of happiness sweep through her…*it's Christmas…!* Maureen had always loved this festive season. And, as she chopped onions, tomatoes and cucumber, she smiled to herself…*Cold cuts and salad, followed by sherry trifle. What a combination…*Maureen had secretly made the trifle to please Vi.

'We *always* have trifle on Christmas Eve. And hot-pot.' Vi had mentioned this menu more than once. *Well…*Maureen thought…*she can have her trifle. But hotpot: a pan of meat and potato scouse…? No way! All the same, I'm glad she's here. Who would have believed it? Who would have believed that she would have travelled here, alone, and stay for Christmas…?*

'Yes,' Vi had told them last Easter Monday, when she had telephoned at her usual time, 'I'll be coming on me own. I want to see me first grandchild. See her in the flesh before me other's born. Sid said he'd be all right. And Patsy said she'd bob in each day.'

Patsy was Malcolm's wife. Patsy and Malcolm lived in a cottage they had rented, a cottage even smaller than Sid and Vi's, and the cottage was at the bottom of Parkeside Lane. And red-haired Patsy was pregnant. Patsy had also been pregnant when she married Malcolm; at least she had said she was. But there was no baby. Patsy miscarried on honeymoon.

'It's a funny-how-do-you-do if you ask me,' Vi had flatly stated when she had phoned to tell Maureen and Stuart the latest news: Patsy had gone on honeymoon pregnant, and had come back seven days later looking radiant…and very pleased with herself…'Aye, Cornwall must be the best place to lose the baby your carrying, from the look of her—that's if there *ever* was a baby. Our Malcolm's been *had*, make no mistake! That Patsy's taken him for a fool…'

Fool or not, Malcolm seemed to be enjoying married life, and Patsy's latest pregnancy was due to terminate in early March.

They all spoke to Sid on the telephone. One by one they had a few words, talking loud themselves, caught up in the infectious bellowing of Vi.

'Mam! You don't *have* to shout…' Stuart chastised his mother from his wheelchair.

But Vi carried on the conversation with her husband in her usual fashion: loud.

Maureen had her turn on the phone, 'How are you, Uncle Sid?' she asked, guilty that they were keeping Vi away too long.

Sid answered in his usual fashion—deadpan:

'I'm alright, don't worry your head about me, love…I've been missing Vi, of course, but listening to her big gob a minute or two ago, giving me her blooming instructions, I don't know why. Yes, I'll be having a Christmas dinner; Malcolm's bringing it round between two plates. *Why*…?' he sounded agitated now, 'I'll tell you *why*…it's because I don't want to spend Christmas in the company of Patsy and her bloody mother…! Yes, of course I'll be all right. I'm a grown man, aren't I? Have you heard from our Barry? No…you've not spoken to him yet? Oh, er…then…I just thought…Yes, night, night, Maureen. *What*? You mean it's still day there, is it…? Oh, right, then, that explains it. Well, then, God Bless…And Merry Christmas…Stuart? Is our Stuart there…? Put him on, lass…Are you there lad…? Listen, son…I love you…you knows that, don't you…I love *yer*…' Then he was gone, the line burred.

Vi cried. Maureen cried. Stuart lost his colour, and then the doorbell rang. Beth ran to answer it.

'Mum…*Mum*…' she squealed, 'it's Uncle Barry…!'

Blond haired Barry Greenwood, all six foot four of him, strode into the lounge, his arms full with gift-wrapped packages.

'Well who the blooming hell did you *think* it was? Father Christmas?' he asked his astonished family.

Beth would remember it as the best Christmas she had ever had. At eight thirty on Christmas Eve they had all sat around the television set in the lounge watching the *Christmas Special*. Everyone had whooped with delight when Beth had come on the screen. Her grandma kept shouting, 'what did I tell you? She's going to be famous.' And her dad kept shushing his mother, telling her to be quiet so that they could hear the singing.

When the programme had finished, Beth told her gathered together jubilant family all about how the fake snow had been added after the recording. And of how nice everyone had been to her, including the show's main star, who had patted her on the head, praising her singing and dancing abilities, saying that she was a "a good little professional who'd go far."

Beth had indeed enjoyed taking part in the programme, and had thoroughly enjoyed watching it. Her Mum had been right: Cynthia's agency *was* the best; she always got her clients a good deal. It was also true that Beth liked being with Cynthia, but not as much as she had liked it when her mother had travelled with them.

Christmas Day had been wonderful. They had all gone down to the beach, even her Dad. Uncle Barry had put the wheelchair in his car. And Uncle Barry had been great fun in the sea, even pulling Mum in and giving them both piggyback rides through the white, frothy waves. Grandma Vi had paddled, staying near the water's edge to be near Dad. Then they had come back to the house and had eaten a huge dinner: turkey, roast potatoes, followed by mince pies and chocolates.

And then Cynthia had come with her surprise: A Piano. A baby grand, black as black and shining new. Two of Cynthia's men friends helped her to carry it into the house. Dad said they all seemed a little drunk, and that they wouldn't be able to get the piano through the doorway. But no, they got it in. Cynthia said the piano was for her "star client." And then she told them the news; told them that Beth had been chosen for a part in a film that was to be made in Hollywood and Ireland; she would play the daughter of the star of the film, and that the film was called *'Blood's No Thicker Than Water'* and Grandma Vi had said...'Tell me something I don't know!' and had looked all kind of funny. Then her mum had asked who the star was, and Cynthia had said it was Don Sommer, and then they had all squealed with excitement.

Christmas week seemed to go by in a flash. Uncle Barry had to go back to Key West, that's where he had been living; working in a bar since he had left the Merchant Navy. But he had plans to start a restaurant because he had been a cook in the navy.

Uncle Bobby was still in the navy, but he was getting married quite soon. To a German lady, but Grandma Vi didn't want to talk about it. Not for the moment.

And then it was time to go back to school...time to tell her friends her news, time to sort out a tutor who would travel with them to California…and it was also time for Grandma Vi to go home.

Her dad had looked very sad, or maybe he just felt ill, he often felt ill. But anyway, that was the way Beth would always remember her dad the day his mother returned to England, which was two days before she was due to go to California.

It was whilst Beth was in California, in the care of Cynthia Paton, that her father died. But nobody told her until she had finished in the studios. When they did tell her, Mr. Sommer said they should wait awhile before going over to Ireland. Mr. Sommer was a very nice. He was also very kind. He even sent flowers to the funeral.

*

20

Julie Veronica Greenwood was christened on the last Sunday in August 1971. As the Reverend Prentice stood at the font, the squirming, flame haired infant cradled in the crook of his left arm, he stared thoughtfully into her tear filled blue eyes as he blessed her...*Life has been hard for the Greenwoods*...he thought, as he trickled the holy water onto Julie's forehead...*I hope this little one will help them come to terms with Stuart's death...I wonder which newspaper the photographers are from? From them all, I shouldn't wonder. Perhaps they'll take one with me on. It's all rather exciting...*

Handing the wailing baby girl back to her mother, Andrew Prentice was quick to return his attention back towards the front pew, acknowledging, with an incline of his head and a smug smile, his pleasure in having Beth Greenwood amongst the congregation...*maybe she will become a really famous film star...*The vicar was an avid cinemagoer.

Not everyone was so delighted by Beth's attendance. Patsy, Julie's mother, was seething: The christening had been put on hold because of the girl.

And now, as the celebratory hymn was being sung, praising everything great and small, Patsy made her way back to her own seat, her anger turned to scorn as she saw that Vi and Sid looked as pleased as anything to have Beth stand between them, their grief so obviously forgotten this day as they stood hand in hand with their American granddaughter; their pride and pleasure clearly visible as they turned to smile at one another, lifting their voices to sing their praise.

Hushing Julie close to her chest, with difficulty because of the infant's lace trimmed long christening gown, Patsy felt her own eyes prick with unshed tears...*it's not fair. It's Julie's day, and she's ruining it...Beloved bloody Beth...*

'We can't have the christening without our *Beth!* Let's wait till she's back from Ireland...' Vi had been insistent that the christening ceremony should wait. And, being totally out-numbered by the Greenwoods' wishes, Patsy had conceded.

As the last chorus of the hymn was sung, and the congregation seated, Patsy stole a glance at the child seated further down the wooden pew. Intently listening to the preaching vicar, Beth's features were still. Her black hair shone, its club cut a perfect frame for her small, upturned nose and full lipped mouth. *She is pretty; I'll give it that. And she does seem to be a nice kid...*Patsy thought, as shame began to replace the unwarranted jealousy, momentarily...*but no prettier than other children of her age or background...Huh, Florida...land of plenty. The land of milk and honey! Well, the kid doesn't look that well fed. A bit too scrawny for my liking...*

But Patsy had to concede to herself, concede for the second time with matters regarding Beth, that the youngster had been as good as gold since her arrival. She was well mannered, affectionate, and totally unaffected by her stardom.

And to her added discomfort, Patsy remembered something else as she sat nursing her newly christened child, her husband, Malcolm, by her side, and her own family seated around her: Patsy remembered that Beth was fatherless.

Although unaware of his wife's feelings, Malcolm was also close to tears: the lump in his throat always came when he thought of his dead brother, Stuart.

Stuart, whose ashes had been scattered on the well-tended lawns of the Garden of Remembrance less than a month ago; scattered at his widow's request...

I'm sending him back to England. Sending him back to you all, Aunt Vi, Maureen had written...*to where he belongs. I have the memories, memories to cherish. You can have his grave in England, where you can go and visit, where you can sit and talk awhile. Plant a rose bush for me. I'll be over soon. Promise.*

Malcolm wiped his eyes as he knelt to pray...*Dear God...Maureen's a grand woman. She made our Stuart really happy...Please take care of her, Lord. Give her strength and hope for the future. And will you bless our Julie, and young Beth, here...*

Malcolm opened his eyes and glanced to his left. Beth too was in prayer, her head bowed, her small hands clasped. *Who'd have thought it...*Malcolm marvelled...*our Stuart's girl...a blooming film star...*

Cynthia Paton was fed up. Fed up with being in hotel rooms in dismal Ireland, and in dreary England. The dark ages—Cynthia thought that both countries were still in them.

Nonetheless, Cynthia's misgivings were kept to herself. A true professional, Cynthia loved her job, no matter where it took her. And, to be continually in Don Sommer's company, she was prepared to put up with anything.

Now, as she paced round her room in her hotel in Liverpool, she was desperate to get back to the rain-drenched shores of Ireland. Cynthia had tried everything possible to ensnare Don Sommer, to no avail: the gentleman was just not interested.

Don Sommer's thoughts were on getting the filming finished and returning to his home on Rhode Island. He'd been away from his wife since early summer and he felt guilty of neglect. A guilt that was not justifiable: The singer had done everything possible to ensure that his wife's needs and comfort were attended to in his absence.

Elizabeth Sommer was in the advanced stages of leukaemia. Don's wife of twelve years was gravely ill. Dying whilst her only child, her eighteen year old son, Jake, his stepson, was in a rehabilitation centre in California. Don feared that the press would get hold of this news before he himself had the chance to tell Elizabeth.

Cynthia Paton's flirtatious company had become trying: Don had been glad to see her leave Ireland, if only for a few short days: Cynthia had flown over to England with little Bethy, the sweet kid who had just lost her daddy...*Life's a bitch*...Don thought.

Deeply troubled by his wife's declining health and his stepson's drug addiction, Don had a growing empathy for 'little Bethy' who, besides being a talented actress and a surprisingly good singer, was stealing everyone's heart, including his own.

Beth was enjoying her stay with her grandparents. Meeting her grandfather for the first time, she had been embarrassed by his tears. He said that he was like a "blubbering old woman" and had soon had his granddaughter laughing. So far, laughter had played a great part in her stay: Beth's grandparents were an amusing and entertaining couple: their banter, their wit, as razor sharp as ever. But Aunt Patsy was another story; there was little laughing when she was around. Uncle Malcolm's wife shouted a lot, and smiled rarely—and when she did, it was only at her own daughter. Yesterday, she had railed at Beth for picking Julie up without asking, 'You can take her out of her pram when *I* tell you to, not before!' She had scolded. Grandma Vi had pursed her lips and glared at Aunt Patsy, which in turn had only made the woman more vexed.

Uncle Malcolm was nice, though; he was always smiling. He didn't say very much. Grandma Vi said he was shy.

Beth could not believe that a grown up person could be that shy and, telling this to her granddad, he had replied that Malcolm 'Couldn't be so grown-up to have married a woman like Patsy.'

But grandma told her husband to 'Hush his mouth...be quiet,' and then, when she had thought Beth had not been looking, she had seen her wink at him.

After the christening, Beth was going to see her daddy's grave. It wasn't a grave, really. Grandma had planted a red rose bush where his ashes had been scattered, and there was a brass plaque with his name on. Beth was going to take some photographs for her mum. She felt sad for Mum, all alone in Florida.

But as she prayed, Beth put that thought out of her mind, quickly, before the prickly tears fell. Beth knew that it would not be fair to cry at her cousin's christening. She liked the baby girl; liked holding her, liked pushing her in her big brown pram. Julie had ginger coloured hair, and very white skin. Grandma Vi said Julie might grow prettier if she stopped crying...for once.

*

21

Maureen found it hard to believe that Beth was nearly eighteen. But then, there were many things about Beth that were hard to believe. The girl had turned into a woman practically over night. And her success had been phenomenal.

Alone in the house, Maureen slipped out of her synthetic-made, soft pink coloured coverall, that she had worn all day in her salon, feeling very tired, and sticky-hot. Rubbing at her neck where the mandarin collar of her hairdresser's uniform had chaffed her neck, she looked at the bed and decided to lie down in her underwear for a little while; perhaps take a nap. She'd had an exhausting day. And the heat of it was still very much present.

Outside the drawn blinds of the bedroom window she could hear the sprinklers quenching the thirst of the back lawn. She knew she should be out there, tending the borders. Stuart had planned their plot well; even in the humidity of summer, there was abundant foliage from the many shrubs and evergreens he'd planted with the fierce sun and heavy rains of a Floridian summer in mind. As her eyes closed, she brought her wedding ringed hand to her forehead and stroked her fingers across her brow, down to the bridge of her nose and then up again to her hairline. She needed this massage, and she let her fingers roam to her temples in an effort to soothe away the nagging ache she had suffered from for most of the day. The ceiling fan above her head was smooth in its operation, the noise minimal. That was another good thing Stuart had done—every appliance in the house had been checked for quality and reliability. He'd been very thorough at his job. And Beth was proving to be pretty brilliant at hers, too.

Maureen smiled when her daughter came to mind again. Beth had received three Grammy's for her record sales: Three songs that had gone almost immediately to the number one spot in the U.S...and number five, nine, and three respectively in the U.K. charts: it was a spectacular achievement. Her acting ability had brought similar accolades: Beth had made three blockbuster films, and had appeared in two musicals on Broadway. Maureen, understandingly delighted and proud of her daughter, was even more awed by the latest news: Beth had been chosen to sing the opening number at the forthcoming Variety Proms in London. This honour was indeed the icing on the cake for the young woman, especially since she had heard that royalty would be in attendance. Beth was more excited about this forthcoming role than of anything that had gone before it.

Maureen was thrilled for her daughter: she knew that Beth would give of her best and make the most of this very special time in her life.

Beth's career had blossomed almost as quickly as she had grown to be a striking looking young woman. It was hard to believe that so much had happened these past few years.

Now, more relaxed but as yet not asleep, Maureen had a serene smile on her face as she continued to think of her daughter, thankful for the one thing that was so very true: Beth had never changed; she was still their own Beth. A lovely person, both inside and out, who never got uppity or rude, who was continually kind and thoughtful to the people around her; and to her many world-wide fans.

Beth was a daughter to be proud of in every way; Maureen knew that Stuart would have been equally as delighted to see that his daughter had grown up unspoilt by the trappings of fame. And of this Maureen was eternally grateful...

As Beth travelled throughout Europe, the Far East and Australia, Maureen had been by her side. The fantastic experience of touring the world had been made possible by the talents of her only child. They had just returned from their second visit to Australia. Beth had wowed them in Sydney with her voice, and her looks: the tabloid press acknowledging that the young

American singer was fast becoming a very beautiful woman.

During their extensive travels, Maureen herself had received many compliments on her own beauty, demurely accepting the praise, but rebuking any further advances.

In the eight years since Stuart's death she had barely looked at another man. With memories of her husband still deep in the fore of her mind, his spirit never seemed far away. And although from time to time Maureen felt lonely, isolated, she felt no inclination to embark upon another personal relationship. *Besides*…she thought often…*who could come up to Stuart's standards? No one*…*!*

So when Vi had asked, in a telephone conversation not many weeks back, 'Is there anyone new in your life?' Maureen had balked at the question, the very idea.

Yet the same idea seemed to play on Cynthia's mind: time and time again Maureen refused to meet the various men Cynthia had lined up for her.

'Well, honey…what do you do for sex?'

Only Cynthia could have asked this question. And only Maureen could brush it off without an answer. In all fairness to the woman, she seemed to have realised that, even from her, the saucy question had been a question too far: she had not pressed for an answer. But she had gone on to say, 'for the life of me, *hon,* I can't make out how you English women tick! Gee, Maureen, if I had your looks, you wouldn't find *me* being a wall flower…'

As easy as it had been to evade Cynthia's probing, Maureen found it hard to do the same with her own questions. The questions that were always formulating, always there…*Who am I*…*? Where do I come from*…*? Who is my mother*…*? Father*…*? Is this life, the life I'm living, right here in Florida, is it my life*…*? Is it the life I should be living*…*?*

In her early years, her years spent with Ethel, she'd felt different. Listening to the bantering of the Dwyer family, who'd lived next door to them in Lupin Street, she'd known she was different.

Later, in the midst of the boisterous Greenwood family, she had thought the difference was due to being the only girl in the household. Then the inner probing would be fleeting, at odd moments.

And later still, when she was impelled to follow Stuart, for she had always acknowledged that she had been fated to be by Stuart's side, she had put all her inner thoughts on hold; she had been joyous; her life had become an unbelievable adventure.

When the truth had come out about her adoption, her thoughts had settled into place, their rightful place and she had been truly content to be so very lucky. The happiness she then felt overshadowing any thoughts regarding her natural parents, for didn't she know in her heart that Ethel had loved her as her own? That Bill had felt true affection for his adopted daughter? And Vi Greenwood? She'd been the best.

As for Iris—Maureen believed that the dreadful experience, the months she had been under the despicable woman's care, obliterated any desire to seek another *mother figure*...No way!

Besides, whoever had given birth to her must have thought long and hard before giving her child away for adoption. Yet the fact that throughout the ensuing years, her natural mother had never tried to find her, to seek her out, to claim her, had made Maureen resolute not to do any searching of her own.

But as she had cradled her own newly born baby, her darling Beth, she had wondered how any woman could give away her child; a child that had been part of her own body; a child she had nourished with her own life blood...*How...? And more importantly...Why?*

These thoughts had been roaming inside Maureen's head again for months, years, maybe. Probably since Stuart's illness and subsequent death. She didn't know exactly when they had started, again.

And the *voice* was back with vengeance: the tyrannical tirade that came and went at its own choice; in the middle of the night; whilst she sat driving in her car, sometimes when she was watching her daughter perform.

The voice in her head had always been there. In her teenage years she had asked others did they suffer from the same and, with their replies—some had said that they did battle with their inner voices daily; even Reverend Prentice had acknowledged that he too was plagued (it had taken Maureen many attempts to pluck up the courage to ask the vicar,) she had reasoned that it was, in all probability, just her conscience, her own inner voice.

But it wasn't. She knew what her own voice sounded like, and the one that plagued her was most certainly not that of her own. And though Maureen was used to its presence, she had never spoken of it to anyone since she'd become an adult. Stuart had never known of its existence. In truth, during the years her husband had been alive, it had rarely made its self a nuisance.

It had become most problematic recently. Always there: a lament; a whining, really; never very audible, irritatingly just out of reach: exhausting. She suffered daily: while she chatted and laughed with her customers in the salon; whilst she gardened, guarding the plants Stuart had eagerly sowed, and even whilst she spoke with Vi, during their mammoth weekly trans-Atlantic conversations. But she couldn't ask Vi for help. Couldn't say, 'Oh, by the way, Aunt Vi, there's this woman's voice in my head that won't leave me alone. And can you tell me who am I, please…? Do you know who my mother was? Where she lives? And why? Why she gave me away…?'

And if she didn't ask Vi—and there was no chance in this world that she was going to pester this courageous and caring woman—then there was no-one else to ask.

So she tried to conquer the nagging questions and fears, putting her attention on to the here and now, for what good would it do, for anyone, to rake up the past.

As for the voice, she had begun to believe that it was an ear problem: she had read about something called Tinnitus. Her appointment with an ear specialist had been made for August…

Sleep was not going to come. Maureen opened her eyes and sighed. From outside she could hear her elderly neighbours park their car in the joint driveway: they had obviously been out to dinner. She sighed again, and felt the prickle of tears smart behind her eyes. She was lonely. The sighing punctuated the truth of her situation…

'Mum, don't sigh so much.' Beth would admonish.

Now, Maureen recognised that it was a habit she had picked up from Stuart: Stuart had been alone. He'd told her once that he felt like a prisoner, a prisoner on death row. And no one could take that aloneness away from him: no amount of love or care. This evening, she realised that even though she was not facing death, she'd made herself a prisoner. A prisoner to the past: *how stupid…stupid…stupid…stupid.*

And suddenly she knew she would have do something about it. Right now. She had sighed her last sigh. As her Aunt Vi was wont to say, 'enough was enough.'

'Oh, Mum! I was *hoping* you'd say that.' Beth expressed her delight down the 'phone line.

'Good. Well I've made all the arrangements. We leave on the 31st. Halloween night. Just you and me, Beth, so don't mention it to Cynthia, not just yet. I want us to travel alone, like we used to. What do you say…?'

'That's just *great* with me, Mum. And I know Don will be more than pleased. He's terrified of Cynthia. Says she wants to eat him *alive…*' Beth chuckled, her giggle infecting her mother on the other end of the line.

'She is pretty scary about Don,' Maureen laughed with her daughter.

'Still, that's *Cynthia*...she never gives up, on anything, does she? Actually, she's been having a go at me...want's me to start dating. She's been doing it again—fixing that *special* date for me. I'm running out of excuses. She means well, and I do feel rotten not letting on that I've made all the reservations for our trip. Anyway, Beth love, leave it to me. I'll tell her. I'll tell her we just want to be with the family.'

'Whatever. Gee, Mum, last night was *fantastic*. You should have seen this place! There must have been well over three hundred guests...I thought I was used to grand parties, but Mum, wow! The gardens were lit by flame torches, right down to the beach...three bands: one in the ballroom, two in the grounds. The food was glorious...and Jake jumped into the swimming pool, fully dressed...and then a few of the others followed...'

'Who's Jake?' Maureen's eyebrows arched with the question.

'Don Sommer's son; didn't you know that Don lived in Montport too? He's one of the Howarth's neighbours. Well, anyway, Jake's not really his *son* he's his stepson. He was a hippy, or something like that. Writes some good stuff; some good lyrics...Don says he's writing a book, a book about his experiences in San Francisco. He had a breakdown. Anyway, Mum, I'll have to go now. Sonia sends her love...And Julia her best regards. I'll be back Sunday...Will you be at the airport, Mum?'

'Sure will honey; can't wait! Take care now; be careful in the boats...you know I worry when you're out sailing...'

'Forget it, Mum, it's wonderful here. The wind, the air...you'd *love* it...Bye, Mum. I love you.'

'And I love you, too,' Maureen whispered into mouthpiece, pursing her lips into a kiss as the line went dead.

As Maureen readied herself for bed she felt more alone than ever. But she checked herself—she didn't sigh. Wandering into the kitchen she didn't bother to switch on the over-head light. Bending to the refrigerator, she opened the door and closed it without having taken anything from its stacked, well-lit shelves. She wasn't hungry, or thirsty, just restless.

Moving over to the window she looked out over her garden that was bathed in silvery shadows. Lights twinkled in the distance heralding the clubhouse of the golf course that Chuck had established some five years previously.

Maureen could imagine the hub of voices floating through its many rooms and verandas, and felt a stirring of envy. Not the envy of wanting to be one of the *crowd*, that would be easy enough, but an envy of their companionship, for that was what she was without. Companionship. Soul companionship. Oh, she loved her daughter with all her heart. Wished her well. Wished her the best. Didn't begrudge her happiness…didn't begrudge her lifestyle…far from it. She herself could have been with Beth in New England, celebrating Sonia's eighteenth birthday that was turning out to be a weeks' long string of fabulous parties both on and off land.

It was true; the invite had been there for the taking—Julia, Sonia's mother, had asked personally. Maureen had declined, explaining to the charming, intelligent woman that she wanted Beth to explore and enjoy time by herself, without her mother always being in the background; she had gone on to further explain that Beth's life had been rather different than that of most of her young peers due to the early start in her career.

And Julia had understood, explaining that Sonia had also been brought up in the limelight of television cameras and newspaper reporters: having both her parents in high profile positions working in the Senate was not exactly a normal upbringing for a youngster…'I can't tell you how glad we are that Sonia has such a good friendship with Beth. They are both such sound, down to earth girls; they could be so spoilt…'

Julia Howarth had stated this on numerous occasions regarding the school friends.

A friendship that had been ongoing since they had shared the first day in their new school: Larson Academy For Young Ladies. A friendship that saw them both enjoying their many open-air pursuits, swimming, boat sailing, horse riding. The much needed giggly-time when they stayed over at each other's homes. The dark haired ethereal beauty of Beth complimenting the blonde haired, Scandinavian good looks of Sonia. The two girls had a friendship that could be re-established easily, down telephone lines, as Beth travelled, promoting her latest song, her latest film, rubbing shoulders with other well known stars.

The very fact that Beth was unaffected by all her own stardom came from the way it started: that Christmas Eve, the Christmas when she was ten years old and had been given the news she was to star in a film. Later that night, when Beth was bathed and ready for bed, Stuart had pulled her onto his knee as he sat in his wheel chair. Quietly and gently he had explained to his young daughter that her life would soon be very different—and in many ways; that most things wouldn't be quite the same as before, but that she had to stay the same…'Be true to yourself, always, Beth. Never lie to yourself, never change what you are today. It's because of who you are, right now, that you have been singled out...singled out from all the rest. Remember this. Remember it always.'

And Maureen, who had witnessed that scene, who had heard her husband's hushed words, could report faithfully that that was what Beth had done. Beth had never changed, save for growing into a woman. No, it was she who had changed. His wife. And the change was something she would have to work at...

Maureen had thought that to stay living in the same house, to keep on working at her salon, to live her life as though Stuart was still around, cocooned in the gentle world of their small, tidy bungalow, was the way forward; the way to endure the remaining days of her life.

But she'd been wrong. She could see that now. She had stopped living as much as Stuart had done. She had made herself an invalid to the past, whilst encouraging her daughter to move forwards and onwards.

Now it was time for her to move forward and onwards. She could change where she lived, she could change where she worked, who she saw, who she shared her life with, without it changing her.

Maureen went to bed and sleep came immediately. As she lay alone in the quiet, neat bungalow, the July moon cast a silvery shadow over the small cluster of houses. Shadows in their proper place; the one that had been with Maureen both night and day had disappeared, even the voice was stilled.

She slept soundly, knowing her eight-year bereavement was over. Knowing she would love Stuart eternally, yet also knowing that she could move on, unchanged, into the future; all that mattered was to be true to herself, no matter where she came from; no matter her demons; that in some way, we are all different.

*

22

'Perhaps Madam could do with an inch or two letting *hout...*' The pompous shop manager had been using her... *I'm more of a lady than you'll ever be...* voice since Vi and Patsy had asked to be shown something special.

And, as that had been well over two hours ago, the haughty inflexion to the woman's speech was becoming noticeably difficult to maintain.

In the background, the other assistants were making eye contact with each other, smirking openly as they listened to their superior's exasperated tone, each knowing that the younger of the two women, who had been trying on the various designer clothes, had caught on, too.

Maria Blackwell, who had managed *Style Fashions* long past her prime, hailed from Blackburn and had a strong Lancashire accent. An accent to be proud of, for had she had used it wisely she would have come across as a very capable and efficient woman.

Sadly this was not to be. Maria, who long ago had been told she favoured the actress Margaret Lowood, had ideas above her station. Her home taught elocution lessons had brought a clip to her voice that was both pretentious and preposterous. Putting aitches where there weren't any, and missing those that were, brought mirth to the faces of her subordinates, and a look of disdain

214

from the shop's ever dwindling clientele.

'*Madam* would like to be left in peace to make her own mind up, thank you very much! Come on, Mother. I told yer we wouldn't find anything in here. Tomorrow we'll go into Manchester: make a day of it. We'll find what we want for London all right there without having to deal with a rude *upstart* like this one for sure.'

Pushing, none too gently, the startled Maria out of the blue curtained cubicle, Patsy urged Vi to dress herself quickly, using the privacy of the small enclosure to let off steam.

'Bloody snob! Think's she owns the bleedin' place, just because she works in a fancy dress shop. She's been lookin' down her soddin' nose at us ever since we came in…They've got the stuff we want in the back of the shop, but will she bring it out…? *No.* Well, she can stick it! I wouldn't spend a bloody penny in this shop if they *paid* me.'

Patsy fumed as she struggled with the zip on her brown tweed skirt, her temper heightened further by the soaring temperature inside the airless, clothes strewn changing room.

And Vi's presence in the cubby-hole only made matters worse: Vi seemed oblivious to what was going on; the excitement of going to London, of Beth being billed along with other famous singing stars, filling her head and thoughts, stilling her tongue and her movements.

Becoming fully aware of her mother-in-law's irksome and vague behaviour, Patsy felt close to despair…*Good God in heaven, not her as well! I can't take anymore, I really can't. If she's going the same way as me mother, and Sid, I'll go round the twist…*

Patsy's life as a member of the Greenwood family had never been easy, but now, since Sid's stroke, her workload had become massive.

Although the stroke was behind him, Sid was still slow and lumbering in his movements. His speech had taken over a year to re-establish itself. Patsy's own mother had Alzheimer's disease and, after being found wandering naked down the main road in the village of Birtwood, where she had lived all of her life, had been installed into the cottage home of her daughter and son-in-law.

Daily life for Patsy had become a round the clock endeavour: Her mornings where spent running herself ragged looking after her own mother's welfare, coupled with her jobs in *Greenwood's Nursery*. The afternoon hours where given over to aiding Vi with the nursing of Sid and looking after the needs of her own child, Julie. Her evenings, and some times the early morning hours were probably the most trying: her mother's worsening dementia saw

215

to that. So it was no wonder that Patsy had been unaware of her husband's straying affections...

Malcolm Greenwood had finally grown-up. This happened after the death of his eldest brother, Stuart. His parent's grief had somewhat disabled their abilities within the nursery. Malcolm had taken over. And had found his niche. He loved the work. He enjoyed the social contact with the suppliers, the banter in the early morning markets, the pride in meeting the needs of the local greengrocers. The nursery bloomed; and so did his love life: But not with Patsy.

Whilst Patsy was bogged down with responsibilities in the home, two homes, the once shy Malcolm took his freedom. Took it in the back of the van, took it three afternoons a week in a seaside hotel that faced the grey sea in Southport. Took it until the object of his freedom, Marilyn Holmes, stole it away by telling him she was pregnant, which added to Patsy's hell.

It was Patsy to whom Malcolm turned to when, in terror that his girlfriend's life was in danger after being taken care of by a back street quack, he had come begging the impossible from his wife.

It was a grim faced Patsy who sat with her husband's mistress whilst the latter miscarried his child. Patsy who, beset with so many problems, had held her head high, convincing herself that she could manage.

And manage the lot she did, at great cost to her own wellbeing. However this was soon slightly restored, for it was Patsy who overheard Vi telling Malcolm, 'If he ever did anything to hurt his wife again, she'd swing for him!' From then on Patsy's life had been a little easier. Her relationship with Vi on a better footing, though how Vi had found out about Malcolm's affair Patsy had no idea: It hadn't been from her own lips; Patsy had been too ashamed of the whole sordid affair to tell anyone.

But Vi had found out and had stood by her daughter-in-law and, as far as Patsy knew, Malcolm was back on the straight and narrow. Patsy's own mother had been taken into a home for the elderly, two minutes away from the house the old lady had lived in all of her life. And Julie, their eight-year old daughter, was thriving. What more could she ask for...?

Even the impending arrival of the famous Beth and her mother, Maureen (as yet, the latter's intention to accompany her daughter was not widely known) would not too much dampen Patsy's newly found, though rather fragile contentment.

'I knew it! I knew it!' Vi waved a piece of pale blue writing paper into her daughter-in-law's face. Airmail paper.

'What *are* you going on about, Mother? Come on in, off the doorstep; you're letting a draught in.'

Vi followed Patsy down the narrow, whitewashed-walled lobby that led into the kitchen of the small cottage: the dilapidated cottage Patsy worked hard to keep warm, for even in summer, the rooms were cold. Now, as the October winds gusted, the house rattled. The front door fit badly, the sills of the windows needed repairing and the frames replacing. The list was endless, as was the list of Malcolm's faults.

Vi was not surprised to be greeted by Patsy's surliness; she had long since realised that Patsy found it hard to grin and bear her role of being Malcolm's long suffering wife. And the consequence was plain to see: her face (that could have been called pleasant at one time, although her nose was too sharp for her to have been pretty,) sported a mouth that turned downwards, and steel grey eyes that stared long and hard, as though she didn't believe a word that was spoken to her: Patsy was cynical in her approach to most people and, when she spoke, her words were often harsh.

'Sit down, Mother, and I *suppose* you'll be wanting a cuppa?'

Vi, eager to tell Patsy her news, quickly sat as she was told, placing the letter on the faded red and grey Formica table.

'Ta, love, in a minute…Hey, pet, just you read this. It's from our Beth. Oh, I'm so excited! Can you believe it? I still can't. The Variety Proms! They're coming in two weeks time. Not here, like, coming to London…Staying at The Strands Hotel. And guess what…?' she waved the letter again, like a flag, 'our Maureen's coming, too! *I knew it*, you know. I knew it all those years ago. She fit in, she did; I'm telling you. Oh aye, like a proper *lady*…and she was only a kid…'

'Who? *Beth*? Has Beth stayed in London before? If she did, yer kept quiet about it, because I don't remember that. She always comes here, don't she?'

'No. *No*. I'm not talking about *Beth*. I mean our Maureen! She fit in a treat, in them swanky places, like. Aye, I knew it then, at the coronation, you know. Felt it in me bones, I did. She's different, that one. Different from the rest of us…'

'Well,' Patsy sniffed as she turned to the stove, picking up the kettle and taking it over to the sink unit. 'Well…' she repeated, as she filled the kettle with water '…if *I* had her bloody lifestyle, I'd be *different*.'

Vi was silent for a moment or two. Thinking. Thinking of how odd it was that the only son left in England was the one who brought so little pleasure to their lives.

But as was wont was her way, Vi put the thought to the back of her mind. Malcolm's shenanigans were a great worry to her, and Sid…*Mind, if he'd have listened to us in the first place, he wouldn't have married the lass that's po-faced in his kitchen right now…*

Yet as Vi watched Patsy potter around her small, tidy kitchen, that was newly wall papered (Patsy had chosen a repeating cherry tree pattern with a white back-ground,) she felt a wave of pity for the younger woman. She'd had it rough with Malcolm, had Patsy.

True enough, Malcolm worked hard in the business. But at home, he was a dead loss: neither use nor ornament. Patsy did all her own decorating; and all the washing, ironing, cleaning; the bit of gardening that was needed at the back of the cottage. In addition to all that, she helped in the garden nursery, manned the telephones, visited her own mother three times a week, had a part-time job as a school cleaner and, in between, was a good mother to Julie.

No wonder, Vi mused, that the once vibrant red hair, that was bluntly cut to just below the jaw line and hung as straight as curtains, was now more of a washed-out brown.

'Have you got time to have a cuppa yourself, pet?'

'Aye, Mam, I've a few minutes,' Patsy said with a sigh, sitting next to Vi at the table.

They sat quietly, each with their own thoughts: Vi of the coming event. The event they had known of for some time, which was now nearly on top of them, but would be made even more special with Maureen being part of it.

Patsy sat sipping her tea, surveying her kitchen. Through the window she could see the washing she had spent the morning on billowing and blowing on the long rope line; a glimmer of satisfaction crossed her face, softened her tense features, as she leant back wearily against her vinyl padded chair.

'It might surprise yer to know this, Mam, but I actually *like* Maureen. And I know what yer mean—her life can't have been that *easy*. Some times I think of her, all alone in America, and then me own troubles seem…so small. At least I still have a husband, for what he's worth! And our Julie's a good 'un, and I'm thankful for that. But I tell yer, I wouldn't mind having a bit of her money…a bit of her life…'

Vi was defensive, 'Our Maureen works very hard, I'll have you know! Bloody hard…always has! And she *is* a lady. Make no bones about that, our Patsy, Maureen was, and always will be, a bit special. Like I was saying, she fit into that posh hotel like royalty. It startled me then. And I had a

218

premonition. I knew she'd make good. By the heck, if only our Stuart was still here…he'd be right proud of them both.'

Patsy and Vi sat in reflective mood.

Sipping her tea, Patsy looked hard at Vi and marvelled that the woman could be so stoic…*what must it be like to lose two sons? Five lads…all that work, all that time and effort…to be left with Malcolm, only! Oh, Barry's good. Sends letters regularly, money, sometimes. But even he's been a disappointment. One of them…Who would think it, just looking at him? So handsome! Still, we don't have to live with it here in England. Loves it in Key West, he says. Loves his bar, loves the life, the people in Florida. I wouldn't mind him coming again, though. I liked Barry. More than I liked Bobby. What a snob he is. And Liselle…Stuck up bitch. Glad they won't be coming to the show. Glad they're too busy. And I'm glad they can't have kids…*

'I thought you might be in here, Mam,' Malcolm entered the kitchen from the back door, struggling with a large brown paper parcel in his arms. Nudging the back door closed with the back of his heel, he nodded in the direction of his wife, who had swiftly moved from the table to the sink, making no acknowledgement of her husband, turning her back to him and his parcel.

The atmosphere was immediately hostile. Malcolm was quick to see the way his mother had eyed his beard. A beard that Patsy had requested he didn't grow, but which he had grown to spite her anyway. And it turned out that Julie didn't like the ginger tinged fuzz either, said it tickled and scratched her when he kissed her.

And as Malcolm didn't like being pushed away by his only daughter, the beard was another thing he was regretting. Malcolm was always regretting one thing or another.

Now he was regretting not letting Julie come find her grandmother: He'd left the youngster *minding* her grandfather this wintry Saturday morning.

'This came to your house a few minutes ago,' Malcolm dropped the package onto the table in front of his mother. 'Don't know what it is. It's got your name on, Mam, and it's from London.'

Curiosity must have got the better of Patsy: she returned to the table to watch Vi tackle the opening of the parcel.

Vi stared at the parcel until she was urged to take up the proffered scissors and to cut the strong straw coloured string. Then her hands were ripping at the thick brown paper that was protecting a large white box. Lifting the lid off the box they saw a wad of white tissue paper. Vi slowly removed layer after layer, before she gasped and leant back in her chair.

Malcolm delved into the box, his hands stroking the soft fur that nestled within the folds of the feather light paper.

'It's a fur coat, Mam!' he said, lifting the heavy garment out of the box. The dark brown fur gleamed.

'Good God! It's a mink!' Patsy shrieked louder than she would have intended, in Malcolm's presence.

Vi covered her mouth with her hand, overcome with emotion as she looked at the three quarter length fur coat. She leant forward; timidly touched it, before Malcolm held the coat up, splaying it against his own body.

'Don't just *stroke* it, Mam. Come on, get yourself up and try it on.' Malcolm urged her to stand; the laughter in his voice was infectious.

Vi's eyes shone with anticipation.

Helping his mother into the silk lined coat, Malcolm's attention was drawn back to the box. There was something else there. Under another wad of soft paper nestled a lighter coloured fur. Lifting the garment out, he whistled.

Then all three gasped. It was a mink stole.

Malcolm handed the second fur to his astonished wife, before reaching back into the box to retrieve a white envelope. He opened the envelope, pulling out a small white card edged with gold. Slowly he read what was written:

Dear Grandma and Aunt Patsy, I am sending you both a little gift. The coat for Gran, the cape (I believe in England you call it a stole,) for you, Auntie Pat.

I hope you both enjoy your gifts as much as I have enjoyed buying them for you. Wear them with my love, Beth. xxxx

Patsy wept. Malcolm went to her side; hesitantly, he put his an arm around her shoulders. Gently he pulled her into an embrace. She resisted at first and then she seemed to sway, pressing her weight into his hard body. He kissed the top of her head.

As Vi headed for the back door, the gleaming mink held tight to her chest, she heard Malcolm say, in a broken voice...'I'm sorry, Patsy. *So* sorry! I'll make it up to you. Don't cry, pet, *please* don't cry anymore...'

Vi kept Julie by her side for the rest of the afternoon, letting the youngster admire and stroke the mink coat, which she modelled over the new violet coloured suit that she had bought from Manchester, especially for the theatre date.

Vi was elated. The suit and the coat were the finest clothes she could ever wish to own, just as Maureen and Beth were the finest people on God's earth.

But as she proudly paraded, to claps and cheers from Sid and Julie, Vi's thoughts were with the couple in the cottage down the lane...*I'm right, by God I am! Maureen and Beth are very special people...as those two down road have found out today...Please God, let them find some happiness with one another. If not for themselves, though they could do with it, then for this solemn little mite by my side...*

Julie Greenwood was a solemn child. As a baby she had cried endlessly. Nevertheless she became an enchanting toddler. Later, when she was a little older, her parent's constant arguments and abrasive natures dulled her bright spirit and, although she was always pleasant and well behaved, Julie lacked the natural boisterousness of childhood.

Julie's long auburn hair was thick and luxurious. Patsy made her daughter keep it braided into two long plaits. Only on Saturdays was she allowed to have it loose. So today, with her hair softly framing her face, and with the added excitement that had been brought about by Beth's gift, she was more exuberant than usual. And this brought further pleasure to Vi.

'Tell you what, Julie. Shall you and I go to the pictures tonight? Just the two of us, like? Your granddad will be all right for an hour or two. And you won't have to ask your Mammy...' Vi was quick to see that although Julie liked the idea of a trip to the cinema, she was wondering what her strict mother would say to the idea. So Vi continued speaking, stroking her mink at the same time as she tried to put the young girl's mind at rest, 'Your mam and dad have a little business to see to today,'...*please God...*'So they said it would be all right for you to stay the night as well, so there. No need to worry your head.'

Later, as Vi sat in the darkened cinema, licking an orange iced lollypop and laughing at the antics of a car that could talk and sing and dance, she silently prayed that Malcolm and Patsy were enjoying themselves as much.

Vi had long feared that Malcolm and Patsy's problems were of a sexual nature. Remembering that it had taken Sid and herself many years before they reached a plateau where they could freely make love to one another, any way they chose, knowing nothing that brought pleasure within a close relationship was taboo.

Now she hoped that her son and daughter-in-law would at last reach out to each other in the same manner, finding, as she and Sid had, the love and joy of sharing a life together.

So, as she watched the vehicle do its amazing stunts, Vi reminisced her love life with Sid, not that it was completely over, yet. Sid could still teach the young ones a thing or two, stroke or no stroke.

*

23

Iris trembled. Downstairs she could hear Declan enter the hallway of their home. She could hear him talking with Samuel, their butler, and knew that very soon he would be coming up the stairs to get ready for his evening out. She took one last look at herself, tilting the rosewood framed cheval glass, taking in the whole of her appearance, before opening the door of her bedroom and stepping out onto the landing.

She watched Declan mount the stairs, her confidence waning as she noted his jaunty stride and the soft smile that played on his face. She marvelled, yet again, that he had hardly aged.

Declan, who had never been what you could have called handsome, was now, at the age of fifty-seven, becoming so. His constant good health, that matched his ever-increasing wealth, had filled his scraggy stature. His well-tailored clothes, his immaculate black hair, that was only slightly tinged with grey and worn to collar length, gave him a youthful dignity.

'Hello, Declan...I need to talk to you,'

Declan pushed past her as he stepped onto the soft, pale blue carpeting of the wide landing.

Iris grabbed at his arm.

'Get off me, *woman,*' he snarled. The smile he had worn as he had climbed the stairs vanished at the top step when he had seen his waiting wife.

'Please, Declan. *Please*…It will only take a minute. Please come into my bedroom…'

He turned. His eyes scanned her face and then slowly took in her appearance, looking her up and down.

'Why, *Iris*…' he said sarcastically, '…can it be at all possible that you are sober, for once?'

'I haven't had a drink for nearly a week. Declan we *have* to talk…'

Declan glanced at the expensive gold watch that graced his slim wrist. 'Five minutes! But not in *your* room! Come into my study.'

Declan retraced his steps, leading the way down the wide sweeping, rosewood balustrade stairway, across the black and white marbled front entrance hall and into the dark oak panelled room that was to the left of the hallway. The room he used as a study.

Iris closed the door behind her as she entered, but waited before she sat. Waited to be invited to sit.

Declan went to the drinks' trolley and poured himself a glass of iced water. Declan Fitzgerald did not drink alcohol.

'What do you want, Iris?'

'I want to come with you tonight.'

'Why? You didn't want to when I first asked you, a month ago…If I remember rightly, you told me to go with one of my floosies…'

'I know…I…it was *wrong* of me. I was drunk. Look, Declan, I'm sorry…'

'Too late, Iris; too late for *sorrys*…' He took a sip of his water.

'Declan, *please*. Don't make this any harder for me. I've not had a drink for more than a week. I've been to see Doctor Barnes. I've asked for help. *Please* give me a chance. Don't shut me out. *That's* what started it all. All my drinking in the first place…'

'Don' t whinge,' he glugged his water, thirstily.

'I'm not! Believe me, I'm not.'

Declan drained his glass and stared at her. Then in silence he moved to sit at his desk. Placing the empty crystal glass onto a silver coaster, he leant back in his high backed leather chair and surveyed his wife.

Iris knew that she looked sober. Her hair had been professionally styled. It was still a lovely platinum colour, still shiny. Amazing really, when she had neglected herself for so long, that when she tried, she could still look quite attractive. Her face, carefully made-up with expensive cosmetics, held the slight puffiness of a drunkard, but only if you were looking for it. She was still slim. Too thin, really, she would have to start eating better. As the seconds ticked by, she felt herself perspiring. She knew that Declan would be wondering if he could believe her...

Why now, for God's sake...? Declan's thoughts were troubled. He watched as Iris seated herself, without being asked to. She sat next to the long french windows that, when open, led out onto the two acre landscaped garden. The chair she perched herself on, a high backed burgundy leather, matched the one he himself was seated comfortably on behind the mahogany desk.

Declan's study was furnished to a high standard: deep padded burgundy leather was the theme throughout and, besides two wing chairs placed either side of the white marble fireplace (that in winter boasted a log fire,) two three-seating sofas, set facing each other in perfect conversational mode, were softened by velvet cushions that in turn co-ordinated with the cream velvet drapes gracing the south facing windows. It was a room he usually enjoyed being in: But not today.

'I don't want to lose you. Declan. I've lost the boys...' Iris seemed intent on making her case.

'They're grown men, so they are. Not little boys! How can you *lose* grown men?'

Declan was angry, angry to be in the room with Iris in the first place. Angry. Angry. *Angry.* Especially when he saw the tears glinting behind her thickly mascara-lashed eyes.

'Declan, they won't be coming back.' She sniffed back the threatening tears, 'you know it, and I know it. They've gone. Oh, don't look like that Declan, it's *true.*'

Declan shook his head, denying her words.

'All right, then...where is Tim? Do you know?'

Declan remained silent.

'No. You know no more than I do, do you? Is it San Francisco? Mexico? Australia...? Do we *ever* hear? And Christopher. Huh, he's right here in London...But do we ever see him? No...'

'You're *cracked.* Aye, that's what you are. You *know* why, Iris! You know why we never see them anymore; the reason we've never set eyes on them for months! It's because of *you.* Because of *you* that they left home as soon as they could...' Declan shook his head again; the memory of his wife's drunken rages all too vivid. The drinking that had thwarted any resemblance of family life.

Now, leaning forward in his chair, Declan chronicled, with mounting distaste, the episodes that had driven both Timothy and Christopher Grady from their home.

'You've never been anything but a *drunk*...and a screaming mad one at that, too. You...You...*You!* That's all we ever heard. Why? *Why...?* What have you done without? What *haven't* I given you? Look around, *woman*. A house in the best part of London...a car and driver always ready for your needs. Clothes. Perfume. Jewellery. Money in the bank...Holidays, if you were ever sober enough to travel. What *haven't* I given you, hey? You've lived in the best parts of Old Kensington. And now here...here in Hampstead Vale! What *have* you been deprived of, you *stupid* bitch? Answer me *that...*'

'You,' she whispered, looking down at her hands.

'You're a lunatic; that's your trouble, so it is. You're *crazy*. Me, you say. *Me*...You've had *me* for years, and thrown me away. Thrown away *all* your chances. I wanted everything with you, Iris. *Everything.* And what have *I* had? Because let me tell you, I've never had...*you!*'

'I've always loved you, Declan, you know that.'

'Do I? *Do I?* You don't know the *meaning* of love. Christ, since the day I married you, you've cut me out. Yes, cut me out! There's always been the feeling...the feeling that there's something missing...Always! Well, Iris, I've made up my mind, so I have. We will part. I'll be moving out next week. I was going to tell you at the weekend. You can keep the house. I'll not be for divorcing you...'

Iris whimpered.

'Please, Declan, *please*...let's try again...*please...*'

Declan leant more forward in his seat, straining from his waist. Placing his elbows on the desk he linked his hands together resting his pointed chin onto his steepled index fingers. And thought again...*why now? Why? Just when I thought I could leave her. Leave her without any remorse...*

Declan watched his wife quietly weep. But it would do no good. He had to go. He had no choice. A baby. That's what Cathy had said, 'Oh yes, Declan, I'm *quite* sure. I'm nearly five months gone. I've been to the doctors. You, my darling man, are going to be a daddy.'

A child: A child of his own. After all these years of hoping to have one...And it had finally happened now, when he was going on fifty-seven. But Cathy was not his wife. Iris was his wife: and Iris couldn't have his babies…*And I'd thought it was my fault…Iris already had the boys. Now Cathy's having me baby. And I wants to be with her. God, I think I love Cathy. I thought I did before, but now…now I'm sure! At last, my own child, my own flesh and blood. My daughter! I don't want a son, no to be fair I have Tim and Chris…they'll do. But dear God, let it be a girl child. Please give me a daughter: A daughter as soft and lovely as Cathy. But what do I tell Iris…*

Declan lifted his head and watched Iris wipe her tears.

'Is it *that* important to you that you come with me tonight, Iris?'

'I would like to. *Yes.* I know how much you have looked forward to meeting Don Sommer. I know how much work you have done for the Leukaemia fund he set up. You *need* your wife by your side tonight; if you will let me…' a thought seemed to strike her, 'unless…*unless* you've invited someone else. Have you, Declan?'

There was fear in Iris's voice. Declan was aware that she knew of Cathy. Knew that he had been seeing her longer than her had ever seen anyone else. He straightened in his chair, pulling his short stature to its height. She was his wife. He owed her this last night. And in truth, he hadn't asked Cathy.

'No. I was going alone. I'm going backstage after the show. That *has* been arranged. I had thought to invite Don out to supper…but then…well, something has come up…maybe I won't even be going myself,' he was exhausted by the day's events.

The backstage meeting had at last been organised. After all the years of being one of Don Sommer's greatest fans he was to meet with the legendry singer: Declan was to hand over the a huge cheque that would go towards the funding of the English branch of the Leukaemia research programme. The programme that Don Sommer had lent his name to after the death of his wife, Elizabeth, and that Declan had so generously donated to.

And it had been later that very same day, the day he had heard that he would be meeting Don Sommer, that Cathy had asked to enter his office. She had been with the company for two years and his lover for sixteen months.

Normally, the dark haired brown-eyed young Scottish woman avoided the office of her employer and lover, discretion being the keynote in the environment of their mutual workplace. In fairness to Catherine McDowd, she had never sought the affections of her boss: it had been he who had chased her, as he had chased and bedded others. Nothing serious: Until now. Now the comely young woman of twenty-nine had stolen his heart and was about to give him his heart's desire: A baby: A child of his very own.

When the relationship had begun he had told Cathy that he would never divorce Iris. And she had understood. Understood so well that she had hesitated too long in telling of her pregnancy. Yet, as Declan had hugged her to him, his delight had been obvious. The only problem on the horizon was Iris; Declan was still insistent that no divorce would be forthcoming.

However, he was going to give his expected child his name. And he was going to live with them. Openly. Didn't care *what* people thought. He was intent on starting a new life with Cathy and the baby. Had instructed estate agents to find him the perfect house needed to fulfil the needs of a growing family. For with the news of Cathy's pregnancy a dam had burst within Declan. This baby was going to be the first of many. He would have his dynasty, marriage or no marriage. His children would bear his name. Their mother would be well cared for, well loved. He didn't need a slip of paper this time. And he knew in his heart that he would be happy to stay in the bed of Cathy. His straying days were over.

Nevertheless, these dreams of such happiness, which had filled his thoughts and days for the past week, had soured as soon as he had reached his home tonight. Iris, his wife of twenty-one years, wanted back what she had thrown away.

Iris had been his wife in name only for more than eight years. He had been unfaithful during that time. In truth, he had enjoyed himself. As Iris sought the company of the whisky bottle, he had sought the company of young women.

Now it appeared he had found what he was looking for, ironically at a time when Iris was prepared to make an attempt to stop drinking.

'I'll be leaving at 6.15. It's black-tie. Can you be ready?'

Iris beamed her reply. And even Declan managed a smile.

Perhaps all is not lost. Perhaps I can get him back. Tonight...Tonight...I will tell him...I will tell him! I should have told him years ago. Please, God, give me the strength to tell him what I have done...

Yet in her heart, as Iris travelled to the theatre, seated next to her husband as he navigated the ice blue Jaguar through traffic clogged city streets, she knew that if she was to tell Declan about his daughter, and of what she had done to the girl, she would lose him. Forever.

There was an overriding aroma of perfume. It tinged the air. Perfume, mingled with expensive aftershave. In fact, there was an overpowering ambience of wealth. Good leather, silks, fur, the clink of jewellery, the murmur of high-class voices.

The theatre filled quickly and soon they were standing to salute the royal party as they entered the Royal Box. The national anthem struck up. Vi could hardly sing she was so tense and excited. Beside her, Sid stood proudly, without the aid of his stick.

Head held high, Maureen stood at Sid's other side next to Julie and, continuing in the row came Julie's mother and father, Patsy and Malcolm.

Malcolm had whispered into his wife's ear just before they stood up, 'You look *gorgeous.*'

And Patsy had acknowledged the compliment with an enormous smile, whilst gripping his hand and that of her startled daughters.

Julie, dressed in bottle-green velvet, looked surprised by her mother's show of affection; she had already voiced to her grandmother that her parents were acting very strange these days.

Maureen was dressed elegantly in a sleek black velvet dress that had long, tight fitting sleeves; her Floridian tan was enhanced by its high neckline which tapered to a V at the back, ending near her waistline. Fondling her long strand of pearls—a gift from Beth—she settled herself into her seat feeling a great wave of affection towards her daughter. Beth was so generous, to them all. Vi and Patsy had been truly delighted with their gifts. Malcolm, who had been in on the surprises, had been more than a gentleman since arriving in London. It seemed that at last Malcolm was growing up. Maureen felt a true contentment at having her family by her side. She wasn't even bothered that they hadn't taken up the offer of a box: Vi had wanted to be in the front stalls, 'I don't want to miss a thing,' she'd stated. And so the theatre box, furnished with gilt framed chairs, had been taken by Cynthia and her invited guests.

As the orchestra played fanfares from various popular shows, hushing the expectant audience, Maureen smiled to herself… *Vi does look rather grand in her mink coat, and the stole has done wonders for Patsy.*

The music stopped and, to an explosion of applause, the show's Presenter came on to the stage. He spent a few minutes cracking jokes and warming up the audience before he announced, 'Your Royal Highnesses. My Lords, Ladies and Gentlemen, may I introduce, from America, the beautiful, sensational, songstress, Miss Beth Stuart…!'

The red velvet curtains parted. The lights dimmed. A spotlight picked out Beth, dressed in a shimmering white gown, her black hair framing her artistically enhanced face: her eyes were the colour of the ocean; her cheeks and lips the soft glow of the setting sun. Sapphires set in a circle of diamonds twinkled from her ears. She threw back her head as music filled the air. Her voice was smooth and strong, the notes high.

The audience murmured their pleasure. It was a favourite number, and one Beth enjoyed singing: *Twilight Love* was a song that had been written specially for her. She moved around the stage, in command of the massive orchestra. The scenery, the backdrop resembled a twilight sky, not unlike the ones they had back home in Florida. As the tempo of the song soared, the backdrop darkened, until a million twinkling lights portrayed the night sky. She finished on the highest, longest note possible, and the audience went wild.

Maureen watched proudly as Beth bowed low, bending from the waist. Her hair swung down, itself like black silk. She curtsied towards the Royal Box. The diamond bracelets on her tanned bare arms caught the light, casting their radiance. She was enchanting. Bowing low again, the curtains closed, removing her from view.

Maureen looked to her family: Vi had tears running down her cheeks. Sid had his hanky to his nose. Julie was totally mesmerised, eyes forward, not wanting to miss anything, and both Patsy and Malcolm where splitting their faces with smiles.

The show went on: Comedians and magicians. Bands, dancers, pop groups Then it was the interval.

Sid said he didn't want to go for a drink. Patsy and Malcolm took Julie for refreshments. Maureen, Vi and Sid stayed in their seats. Most of the other people seated in the front row moved to stretch their legs.

'How can you watch her so calmly, Maureen? Honest to God, girl, I thought I was going to *faint* with nerves. Isn't she *wonderful*? Where did she get that voice from?' Vi chatted on before Sid interrupted her. Speaking slowly, as he always did now, he formulated his words with care,

'You've done a grand job, little Mo. Aye, a *grand* job. I'm so pleased she uses Stuart's name. It's fitting, that's what it is, fitting.'

Agreeing with this sentiment, Maureen nodded and Vi murmured that he was right. The three of them sat silent. Content to be so. They remained silent as they watched the others return to their seats, quietly just happy with their own thoughts, this very special night.

Sid was the first to speak; he asked when this *fellow* called Don Sommer was going to come on?

When told it would be at the very end of the show he looked a bit crestfallen: and Maureen knew that it was all a bit of a strain for the man...by this time of night, her uncle would normally be tucked up in bed.

Maureen looked around her. Cynthia, who had taken the first tier box, that had been intended for Beth's party, seemed oblivious to anyone save for the man sat by her side: Her latest beau. This time, from the business world and reputedly to be worth millions. Maureen smiled. There would have been none of this without Cynthia.

The lights dimmed and the compere came back on stage. A true professional, he knew his stuff and soon the audience were laughing and clapping, eager for more. Vi leaned forward a little, scanning the row they were sitting in. Celebrity spotting.

However, she didn't spot a celebrity...far from it. She leant back in her seat, a perplexed expression on her face. The next time the audience clapped, she leant forward again, and gasped.

Both Maureen and Sid turned to look at her. Vi sat still, unaware that she was holding her breath. The seconds passed. Maureen and Sid turned their heads back to watch the stage.

Vi was in agony. The sweat run in rivulets down her face, down her back. She wriggled, trying to get herself more comfortable. Trying to put the worry of whom she had seen out of her mind...*it couldn't be? Could it? Could it really be her? After all this time...! Did she know...? Is that why she was here? God in heaven...*

Vi's heart thumped hard, thudding her chest, in her throat, pumping the perspiration. She swallowed.

Maureen whispered across, 'Take your coat off next time we applaud,' Vi nodded.

Sid nodded. Not as an answer, he nodded in his sleep. Vi feared he would snore, which added to her misery.

Thankfully, as she struggled to take the mink coat off, Sid woke, and shook himself in an attempt to stay awake.

Cooler now, Vi tried to settle. The scene before them was taken from a long running West End Show. The audience laughed loudly.

Vi sneaked a look again along the row to her right, this time noting the man who was sat next to the woman she thought was Iris; and it was at this point that Don Sommer made his first appearance on stage.

The man, sat with the Iris look-alike, leapt to his feet, clapping and cheering as Beth too walked on to the stage from the right wing.

Vi watched as the man stood still, as if mesmerised. And Vi's world came

231

tumbling down. As the deafening applause rang around her ears, Vi knew at once who he was. This man, standing while all others sat, was Declan Fitzgerald. Next to his vacated seat sat his wife: *Iris.*

The man continued to stand. He was not very tall. He had a small stature and dark hair. Vi knew all about Declan Fitzgerald; how could she not; the businessman's face had been pictured in the newspapers often, recently; his donations to needy causes legendry.

Vi looked to the stage. Her granddaughter held hands with the tall, silver haired, strikingly handsome Don Sommer...

Don was telling the audience about the first time they had worked together, he and Beth. And of how many other times their paths had crossed. He addressed the audience,

'This little lady, here...this young woman has the finest voice I have ever had the privilege to hear. Not only that, she is also privilege to work with; Beth and I have been teamed together on a couple of film sets. May she go onto even greater things. Dear Beth...stay as sweet as you are...' he brought Beth's hand to his lips. Then his rich American voice boomed around the theatre, capturing every one. His charisma never waning, he continued...

'We'd like to sing this little number for you, Beth and I. The last time we sang it together was nearly a decade ago...I once had the honour of playing the part of her father in the film *Blood's No Thicker Than Water.* This song we are going to sing bears the same title. But before we begin, I'd like to make a dedication to one lady in the audience tonight. I think she *knows* who she is. This song is dedicated to her.'

Vi watched as a smiling, simpering Iris reached out to Declan, pulling him back into his seat.

Vi struggled with her breath...*It is her! It's Iris. I never connected that this Fitzgerald man was her husband. God in heaven, it never occurred to me who he was. But why should it have done? It's been years since I last saw Iris...and our Maureen's not clapped eyes on her since she was a little girl of what...? Eight? Oh, I feel so sick...Maureen is sat four seats away from her own mother...I can't breathe, so help me God, I can't find my breath...Dearest Lord...I've only done me best. Now she's going to find out...she's watching own granddaughter. Does she know? Is that it? Is she going to rush on stage and claim her? God help me...will Maureen ever forgive me for not telling her? Am I dying now...? I feel as though I am? Are you taking me, Lord? I thought you only took the good? Dear God, I'm not good...but truly, I've only done what I thought best...*

In her panic, Vi reached across her husband's lap, grabbing at Maureen's arm.

Maureen's face registered shock at the distress her aunt was in. She leant forward a little, desperate to attract Malcolm's attention, she whispered, quite loudly, over Julie, 'Mal, we've got to get your mother *out*. She's *ill*. Quickly. Stand up. Help me...'

Beth sang on: a true professional. She saw her mother, her aunt and uncle struggling with her grandmother. She heard her grandfather mutter 'What's going on...?' as he followed his family out of the theatre, through the side exit doors.

As soon as the song was finished, Don, who'd also noticed what was happening on the front row of the stalls, whispered, whilst smiling, nodding acknowledgment of the applause, 'Go, *quickly*, no one will notice. They will think you were only going to do one number with me, anyway.'

Beth curtsied and bowed and fled the stage.

From her seat, Iris watched the exodus of the noisy family...*Fancy making such a fuss; and being on the front row. Tut...terrible...*

But as the old man followed them out, muttering to himself, Iris had the vague feeling that she knew him.

The doddering elderly man was the last to reach the exit doors; and by that time a member of staff had come forward to aid him.

Iris gripped the arm of her seat...*I don't believe it...It's not possible, surely? But I'd swear it...Am right, that I am...it is Sid Greenwood! What's he doing here? That must have been Vi he was sat with: The big woman, in the mink. But then, it couldn't be. A mink coat...Vi...?*

As Beth left the stage, Iris excused herself to Declan,

'I'm going to the Ladies,' she whispered in his ear.

Declan nodded, his eyes furious.

In her haste, Iris was unaware of her husband's wrath. By the time she'd reached the foyer, there was no sign of the party of people who had unceremoniously left the auditorium. She did catch of glimpse of Beth Stuart, though, as the young woman gathered the long white skirt of her dress from trailing the pavement as she jumped into the back of a black taxi aided by the younger man who'd been sitting with the elderly couple on the front row.

Rushing outside, Iris was just in time to see the singer's cab speed away into the night.

Back in the quiet of the foyer, Iris approached one of the theatre staff.

'Excuse me. Can you tell me what happened to the family that just left the theatre? Was one of them ill?'

'Well, actually, Madam, one of the party had become rather unwell and has been taken to the hospital.'

'Was it the older woman who was unwell? The one in the mink coat?'

'Yes, *Madam*, I believe it was Miss Stuart's grandmother...but I didn't have time to see what she was...*wearing.*'

'Do you by any chance know their...Oh, I mean the woman who was ill...do you know her name?'

'Why yes...*Madam*: I believe she was called STUART, too.'

'Thank you...*Thank you...*'

Iris could see the contempt in the young man's face, especially when he sent a rolling eye signal to his colleague at the confectionary counter. It didn't bother her though. She was too relieved, and too thirsty...*Declan is right...*she thought to herself, somewhat bashful at her mistake...*I am stupid! Fancy thinking I'd seen Sid Greenwood. It must be because I've been thinking of them all day. Now Declan will probably be furious with me. He'll think I've gone to the bar. But, I can't face walking back inside the theatre. Everyone will know where I've been. I need a drink...I'll just have a tonic. No harm in one tonic. Yes, I'll go to the bar and wait for Declan. He thinks I'm there, so I might as well be. One tonic...*

As Iris, clad in midnight blue taffeta, made her way up the stairs she could hear Don Sommer belting out one of his old time hits—one of Declan's favourites: *Windfall Days.*

'How many Scotches do you think that old tart had down her neck..."Can you tell me her name." Silly star-struck *cow.* And the stink on her...she reeked of booze.'

The foyer staff sniggered together as they watched Iris hitch her full length, tight fitting skirt, and teeter up the stairs, heading for the bar.

*

24

'But you missed the royals...'

'It doesn't *matter*, Grandma.'

'Of course it does! I'm so sorry, love. After all you've done, I've spoilt it.'

'Grandma, *Grandma*, listen to me...*please?* All that *really* matters is that you are well. Maybe I'll get to meet them some other time. Tell her, Mum. Tell her I'm not bothered.'

'Beth means it, Aunt Vi. We *all* mean it; we're all glad there's nothing seriously wrong with you.' Maureen, leaning over the bed, kissed her aunt's forehead.

'Now then, you get some sleep. It's been an exciting day: For all of us. And remember, if you need me, just pick up the phone and dial my room number. That *easy*. You must be tired, too, Uncle Sid. Get yourself into bed as soon as we go. You will, won't you? Look, just in case you forget, I've written our room number down next to the phone...' Maureen walked to stand in between the couples' twin beds, pointing to the note pad that sat next to the telephone on the lamp-lit bedside table.

From the comfort of his wing chair, Sid nodded that he understood the instructions. Seeing as he had been readied for bed since they had returned from the hospital, he was drowsy and more than eager to be left alone: fussing had never been Sid's style, but even he had to concede that Vi's *attack* had given them all a shock. Sid was now bone tired and in need a good night's sleep.

Giving her grandmother a last cuddle, Beth noticed the drawn pallor of her grandfather's face, and hurried her farewells, 'Night, night. Grandma...' she moved across to Sid and bent to kiss him goodnight, too, 'Mum's right, Grandpa, if you need us in the night, *call*.' Beth joined her mother at the door.

'Before you go, loves...' Vi struggled to sit up again; there was something she couldn't remember; something the doctor had said, '...will you tell me again what they said I had...'

Beth laughed as she spoke, 'Hyperventilation, Gran. It means you forgot to *breathe*.'

They watched Vi snuggle down onto her soft white linen pillows, saw a mischievous smile playing at her mouth. Her grandmother had been such a worry tonight it was good to see her so much better.

And as if to prove that she was indeed on the mend, back to her old self, Vi said, 'That young doctor said I was overweight for my height...Seems I'd be better off forgetting how to *eat*...'

As they closed the door of Vi and Sid's room, Beth and Maureen chuckled quietly before they linked arms and walked down the corridor that led to their rooms. Adjoining rooms, no more than fifty feet away from the rooms of their family: they were all housed in The Strands Hotel for what was left of the night.

Later, as Maureen and Beth lay in their own twin beds, sleep eluded them. Maureen turned onto her back and sighed. Beth heard it...

'Are you still awake too, Mum?'

'Yes, darling, I'm going over everything that happened. Are you?'

'Yes. I can't get to sleep. It's been a strange night. Did you see the way people were looking at us in the hospital?'

'Well, we were a *strange* party, weren't we? Dressed up to the nines...Still, I'm glad we brought her back with us. She wouldn't have been happy in the hospital. And I'm sorry to say this, Beth, but I think it was the mink's fault.'

'I know. I *know*. Why did she keep it on?'

'She said she wouldn't be able to wear it again...' Maureen smiled into the darkness.

For a time, each was silent with their thoughts.

'*Did* you mind...? Not being in the line-up after the show? Are you terribly disappointed?' Maureen asked of her daughter.

'Yes, a little, it was, after all, what the night was all about...' Beth sat up and pummelled her pillow as she answered.

'I'm sorry darling...'

'Mum! Don't be. It wasn't *your* fault. As you said, if anything was to blame, it was the mink. I should have thought...' Beth lay her head back down again on the cooler side of the pillow.

'Beth...' Maureen sat up, as restless as her daughter, her tone of voice showing this, '...your Grandma was *thrilled* to wear it. Maybe there will be another time to meet the...'

'No, Mum, no...' Beth interrupted, 'I've had my chance. It won't come again. Really, it doesn't matter. Gran's health is *all* that matters. I honestly mean that, Mum.'

And as Maureen pummelled her own pillows, seeking comfort, she knew Beth's statement to be the truth. Beth took things in her stride...*but she must be disappointed. Who wouldn't be...?*

Maureen felt a surge of pride regarding her daughter. She really was so special. She hadn't hesitated in her actions. Her grandmother had come first. Family first. And Don Sommer...He had sent his own car to the hospital for their use. Had telephoned the hospital as soon as he had left the stage of the Castle Theatre. Furthermore, he had telephoned again, two thirty in the morning, to make sure all was well—informing Beth that the royal party had sent Vi their warmest wishes for a speedy recovery...*Wow. What a night it had been...*

As if Beth was reading her mother's mind she said,

'Don sang *Blood's No Thicker Than Water* for you Mum, you know that, don't you?'

'Me...' Maureen eased herself up onto an elbow and looked across the space between their two beds. She could just about make out her daughter's face, silhouetted against the snow-white sheets that covered her bed.

'*Why*...?' Maureen was astounded by her daughter's statement.

Beth turned in her bed, facing where she knew her mother was lying.

'Because. Just, well, *because*...'

'Because of *what*, Beth? You are being very *mysterious*.' Maureen was slightly angry.

'You'll be cross,' Beth spoke tentatively.

'Why should I be *angry*,' Maureen's voice was raised.

'Okay. I'll tell you; in rehearsals, I told him about you. About how wonderful you've been. He's asked about you before, a few times in fact. The first time was when Dad had just died...And when Elizabeth died, he asked about you again. Asked how you'd coped. You know, Mum...with the grief...the aloneness of it all.'

'You spoke to Don, about *me?*' Maureen was incredulous at the very idea.

'See, Mum? You *are* angry, aren't you? I didn't betray you; I didn't say too much. He needed help—someone to identify with. It helped, that's all...it *helped*. And he was good to us. Remember, Mum? When I was in Ireland? So when Elizabeth died, I tried to help him. Last summer, in Montport, we had quite a good long chat. He said he would like to get to know you...*Mum?* Would you mind?'

Maureen lay back against her pillows...*Don Sommer wants to get to know me...Why?*

She voiced her question again. And the answer, when it came, made her tingle with indignation, surprise...and finally, rising pleasure.

'Because he *knows* about how you came to live in America, following Dad. And he knows that you were adopted, and how you and Dad came together. Of Vi's love for you...He thinks it's an *incredibly* romantic story. Thinks you are one smart lady; and that it's sad that you lost Dad. He understands how you must feel; because of Elizabeth.'

They were both silent again. Maureen had thought Beth had fallen asleep.

'Mum?'

'Er, yes, Beth, I'm still awake,'

'Mum...Don's going to call you. He wants to invite you out to dinner, or a show. Will you mind? Will you go?'

Maureen swallowed. Her heart beat faster. She tried to answer casually,

'I don't know. We'll see what happens. I'm going to be busy looking out for Vi and Sid. We'll see...'

The dawn had crept into the sky before Maureen slept.

Don Sommer did telephone. Did ask to speak with Maureen. Did request, to the tongued-tied recipient, that she have dinner with him that evening. And it was the same recipient of the invitation who ground her teeth with embarrassment and held both hands to her burning cheeks as she related, to her daughter, the gist of the conversation.

'Oh, Beth! Not that I could call it a conversation; I was like some

dumbstruck *schoolgirl*. I thought it would be you, calling from the studio...'
Beth had taken advantage of being in London and was recording for her latest
album. Recording two songs written for her by Danny Rhoades, who had also
written her last American hit. Danny, a true cockney, knew how to write
powerful lyrics, which he set to unusual melodies. Beth Stuart's voice
interpreted both almost operatically. The storytelling songs were set to
become, yet again, chart topping hits.

Beth laughed gleefully as she bounced down onto her bed.

'So! Are you going...?' her eyes shone with merriment.

'I have to! I couldn't think of a single excuse! Not now Malcolm's taken
the others home. And Don knew that, seeing as it was *his* car and *his*
chauffeur that had taken them to the station.' Maureen fell backwards onto
her own bed and groaned, although the groan soon became a throaty giggle.
Sitting up, she picked up one of the cushions that graced her bed and threw it
across the space that divided her from her daughter's. Beth gasped as the soft
padded cushion hit her, then rocked herself, laughing louder than ever as
Maureen dived after it, launching herself onto her daughter's bed. Beth
whooped uproariously.

Writhing with her jubilant daughter, Maureen playfully hit Beth again
with the cushion, admonishing her at the same time as each blow.
'How...could...you...have...set...me...up...like...this?'

'Because it will be good for you.'

'Good for me! Look at *me*. I'm like a blushing teenager. I'm terrified...'

'Why? You've spoken to him before. You *know* he's nice. Go! Enjoy
yourself. What can happen to you? You're only having dinner. Most women
would die to be in your shoes, tonight.'

'That's it, Beth. That's it. I think I will *die*. Of embarrassment...' Maureen
moved away from her daughter's bed, her light-heartedness disappearing as
she sat herself down at the dressing table...

'Honestly Beth, I'm worried. I don't want to go. Can you understand? I've
not had a date, gone out with a man, in years...'

Beth sat up; the frivolity had dispersed. Adjusting her clothing, a heavy
knit, cowl neck sweater that was the palest of blues, and hip-hugging blue
jeans, she swung herself off the bed and joined her mother at the dressing
table. Resting her hands on her mother's shoulders she spoke reassuringly,

'Listen, Mum. You will have a great night. Believe me. Don's special.
He's...oh, *Mum*...he's kind, generous, *fun*: exactly what *you* need, right
now.'

Maureen looked into the mirror and smiled into the blue eyes of her daughter. She reached up and took hold of Beth's left hand, kissing the open palm.

'What would I do without you, huh? Okay, Beth...so, I'll *go*. I'll go on the date, if it pleases you so much. You' re right, I *should* be flattered...' Maureen groaned again, not believing what she had uttered.

The gaiety returned. Beth spun her mother round, urging her to stand; amid much banter they raided their joint wardrobe, seeking something suitable for the dinner date.

The wardrobe search was not successful. Nothing was suitable. Maureen's stomach churned: she feared she had lost her senses. Her nerves were already shattered by the phone call...now, the very thought of the date with Don made her tremble...*Why, oh why have I agreed?* She felt sick.

Beth said she had an idea, 'Listen, Mum,' she looked down at her leather-strapped wristwatch, 'it's only two-fifteen; have you had lunch?'

Maureen shook her head.

'No, I thought as much. No wonder you're shaky. Come on—get your coat. We're going out. Don't look like that, Mum! You know...*Out*...As in putting on your coat, opening the door, getting in the elevator...Excuse me, *lift*, and walking in the cold of London. We are going to Knightsbridge. After-noon tea, and shopping...Come on, Mum, don't dawdle so...'

Maureen allowed herself to be bullied. Allowed herself to be bundled into her warm camel coloured coat (Maureen always chose this colour for her ankle length winter coats...the only good legacy of her years with Iris,) zipped into her calf length brown suede boots—which were a perfect match to her fawn coloured, jersey wool, slim-fitting sweater suit—and escorted out of the bedroom. Link-armed with her chattering daughter, she then allowed herself to be ushered through the hotel, out onto the busy street.

The air was chill, though the sky was blue. They walked quickly, Beth having refused all offers of the hotel's doorman in seeking a taxicab.

'We'll walk.' Beth had stated, though soon they realised that it was too far to walk to the Knightsbridge shops.

Reaching Trafalgar Square they stood at the kerb of the busy street like any other tourists, watching the heavy traffic and waving their arms in their search for a vacant taxi.

Laughing and chatting, exuberant to be together in London, they spent a very happy afternoon, returning to their hotel at six o'clock loaded with their buys; numerous rope threaded shopping bags held the swag. The green and gold bags carried black satin shoes with the highest of heels, matching handbag with a delicate diamante clip, and in the third bag, an exquisitely tailored cocktail suit. The charcoal black, figure hugging silk brocade two-piece: jacket with three-quarter length sleeves which fastened with diamante and pearl buttons, and sleek skirt that was knee length and fit Maureen's trim waist and small hips like a second skin, was the perfect outfit for a lady who had been invited out on a very special dinner-date.

'We've been thinking of selling the Rhode Island house, too…' As he spoke, Don Sommer twirled the stem of his empty wine glass between his index finger and his thumb, before placing it back onto the white linen covered table.

Instantly, the over-diligent waiter, who had been standing to attention behind Don's chair, refilled the glass, glancing at the same time to where Maureen's crystal glass sat, the wine almost untouched.

As the waiter retreated, Don turned and spoke quietly to him: the surprised man removed his presence.

Don continued his conversation with Maureen.

'This place was recommended to me for its seclusion and excellent cuisine, both of which seem to be so. However, I cannot *abide* the constant hovering of the staff. And I can see, Maureen…' Don leant forward, and whispered, 'that it's made you slightly uncomfortable, too.'

Maureen nervously smiled whilst nodding her answer, showing that Don had been right in his assumptions, more embarrassed than ever that her frayed nerves were so very evident.

The first course of the meal was under their belt, or rather stuck in Maureen's throat. *Coquilles St. Jacques,* normally one of her favourite restaurant dishes, had been a mistake on her part as a first course choice. Although quite delicious, Maureen wished she had ordered something a little lighter; Don had finished his *Parisian Salad* long before she had even eaten half of her own. And Don had done most of the talking. Although Maureen, frantic for something specific to talk of, had mentioned that she was selling her Floridian home. Then panic had filled her, because that was not quite true. She had *thought* about selling her bungalow, though why she had stated she was actually going to do it, had come as a surprise to her, adding to her unease.

Yet within an hour she had to admit to herself, as she finally sipped her Montrachet wine, that Don was easy to be with…*If only I could stop acting like an over anxious school girl.*

Nevertheless, she remained that awestruck schoolgirl as they were served their main course; it took four waiters, resplendent in black tailcoats and stiff white shirts, to stage this event.

Two arrived at the table trundling a brass edged trolley; mutely, they awaited the arrival of another duo, a duo of obvious senior rank. With precision timed hand signals and eye contact, the silver domed dishes were lifted off the trolley and presented onto the immaculately laid table.

Thus far Don and Maureen sat in quiet wonderment, although a glint of merriment in Don's eyes reflected the same in Maureen's.

The quartet of white-gloved waiters stood to attention; then shuffled into twos: each pair raised their right hand; each duo brought their right hands down onto the silver domes; each duo of hands raised the silver domes; each duo of waiters bowed to the two diners; two diners eyed the masterpiece upon their respective plates, and two diners burst into laughter.

The waiters' brought the dinners; the laughter brought the ease. Maureen actually enjoyed her *Boeuf en crou'te, gratin dauphines* and *sauté courgettes,* although she did ask for a quarter of an hour delay before they were presented with the *crème brulee.*

Don ordered a cognac, Maureen declined.

'No thank you, Don, I couldn't eat or drink another thing, though maybe I could have a glass of water? Iced water?'

Don sipped his brandy and Maureen her water in companionable silence. The Belgravia restaurant slowly emptied of other diners and the soft piped music became slightly louder. A younger man, who had been sitting at the next table, sidled up to stand beside Don's chair.

The man spoke.

'Excuse me. I'm sorry to interrupt. I'm sure you have quite enough of it…But, if you would be so kind…For my wife, actually. It's our wedding anniversary. Our first. Do you think you could sign our menu card?'

Don reached into the breast pocket of his jacket, brought out a pen and with a flourish, signed his name, smiling across at the man's embarrassed wife.

'We came up to London for the show. Thoroughly enjoyed it. Seeing you in here, tonight…Well, it's been the icing on the cake, so to speak.'

Don beamed his famous smile.

'That's real nice to know. It *was* a good show,' he leaned conspiratorially towards the man. Nodding in Maureen's direction, he continued, 'Did you enjoy Beth Stuart…?'

The man, now joined by his pink-cheeked wife, nodded, but before he could speak Don added,

'This lady here, this lovely lady is Beth's Mom…'

'Really. Well, it's very nice to meet you, er…Mrs Stuart. Very nice indeed…Jane? Did you *hear* that…?'

Arm in arm the young couple walked out of the restaurant, ecstatic to have so much to tell of their anniversary of a lifetime.

'That was nice of you, Don.'

'Why not? Without the fans I'd be out of a job,' he joked.

'It's time that *I* thanked you, too, Don. I'd like to thank you for being so kind to Beth. And to my family…to *me*…' She added the latter, quietly.

Don leant forward. Reaching across the table he touched Maureen's left hand. Gently he lifted her wedding band finger, the finger that held a thin plain gold wedding ring.

'You still wear your ring…?'

'Why not?' she answered.

Don let her hand sit back onto the table.

'Why not indeed…were you happy together, you and Stuart?'

Maureen hesitated. Not sure that she wanted to discuss her life with Stuart. It seemed disloyal. She fought the feeling.

'Yes, we were *very* happy…but *so* young. It had seemed we were also so very lucky, until, well until Stuart's first heart attack. We had good friends. The Vicentes. It was through the Vicentes that we came to America in the first place. Not that I see much of them, now. They've moved back to San Antonio, Texas. Chuck is very involved in a building project. I'm sure Beth has told you about Mary Lou and Chuck?'

Don murmured he knew of them, adding,

'Beth tells me they sold their property in Boca Raton for a small fortune.'

Maureen smiled, nodding that it was the truth.

'Yes they did. Chuck always had an eye for a good bargain; a good purchase. He's a *brilliant* businessman. He bought a small plot of land near Boca, right on the water. He bought it in 1953 for a couple of thousand dollars. We lived there, for a while, Stuart and I, in one of the small cottages Chuck had built next to the big house. Stuart worked for the Vicentes. Even when he became too ill to work, Chuck made sure he never felt useless. Later, Chuck's father's business required urgent attention. The family, they have two children, two children that I was nanny to, moved with him back to

Texas. And well, they've kind of settled there again. It was their home in the first place. And, as you know, Chuck sold his shorefront property for *millions*. We keep in touch. Beth visits them. Often. They want to buy a property in Palm Beach...And that's where I'm thinking of moving to. So, I guess I should be seeing more of them, in the future.'

Maureen found it easy to talk with Don. Before they knew it they were the last people in the restaurant.

Don's hired Bentley was waiting for them as they stepped out into the chill of the night.

As Maureen was without a topcoat, Don tucked the car's plaid rug over her knees as they settled into the back seat of the limousine.

The Bentley purred along the quiet streets of Belgravia coming out onto Park lane.

Don was quiet, thoughtful as he gazed through the cars windows.

Maureen sat quietly too, wondering what she would do if Don asked to go back to the sumptuous Dowager Hotel with him for a nightcap drink.

They were cruising down the Mall before either of them spoke. And then they both spoke together.

'Ladies first,' Don laughed.

'Oh, I was just going to say that, well, it's been a lovely night, Don.' Maureen looked into Don's silver grey eyes as she spoke.

'And one *I* don't want to end. You are a very beautiful woman, Maureen. You look more like Beth's sister than her Mom. I know that sounds like a cheap line. But it's *true*. Hey, and that's another thing. Why does she call you, *Mum?* Its sounds royal...'

Maureen grinned at the royal bit, then turned her head to look out of the window as she answered.

'I wanted her to be a little English. Though she was born in America, and is proud of the fact, we, Stuart and I, were British. And I wanted her to know her roots...' Maureen hesitated before continuing. Turning to face Don, she wondered how much he *did* know of her life...

'I was adopted, Don, you know that. I had a wonderful *mother* until I was eight. Her name was Ethel. Had she have lived, I probably wouldn't have gone to America. But she died. And, well, before I went to live with Aunt Vi I had a stepmother. Her name was Iris. I'm afraid she fell into the category of *wicked stepmother,*' Maureen laughed a little, lightening the air, 'you can believe me, they *do* exist, these women. Anyway, let's just say that I had a lot of experiences of *not* belonging. And I didn't want that to happen to Beth.

When I went to live with Aunt Vi and Uncle Sid, I made one good friend. Her name was Beryl. We'd started out as enemies—enemies that became the very best of friends. I never told Aunt Vi this…but, you see, Don, I *missed* having a mother. And Beryl always called her mother, Mum, not Mam or Ma, like most people do in the north of England. And I kind of liked it: *Mum.* So I made my mind up. My daughter, should I ever have one, would call me Mum…And. Well. She *does*…'

The Bentley pulled up outside The Strands. The chauffeur came round to Maureen's side and opened the door. As she stepped out, Don was there by her side. He walked her into the foyer of the hotel. They shook hands. Don never took his eyes of Maureen's face. Bending forwards, he whispered her name, '*Maureen*. It's been a wonderful evening. Thank you. I have been very proud to be by your side. Good night…' He turned and walked out of the hotel.

As Maureen stepped out of the shower, she was startled to hear the telephone ringing. It was three thirty in the morning and Beth lay asleep in the adjoining room. Hastily wrapping herself into one of the large white towels that hung on the heated towel rail, Maureen dashed into the bedroom.

'It's for you…' sleepily, Beth handed the telephone receiver to her mother, adding, '…what time is it…?'

'Three thirty, darling, who *is* it? Is it Sid?'

Beth shrugged and lay back on her pillows, turning her face from the shaft of light that came in from the opened bathroom door.

'Hello?' Maureen suffered a twinge of fear.

'Maureen? Look, I'm *so* sorry. I didn't *think*. Is Beth sharing with you…?'

'Yes. We have…a…twin suite.' Maureen answered, her voice quivering with cold. Or was it excitement? The caller was Don.

'Sorry. Sorry to have woken her, and I won't keep *you*, Maureen…I just wanted to say…*goodnight*…'

'Don,' Maureen whispered, 'there's an extension in the bathroom…Hold on, I'll go to it.' Quietly, she replaced the receiver. She peered at her daughter. Beth appeared to have gone back to sleep. Tiptoeing, Maureen crossed the room. Entering the bathroom, she closed the door behind her as softly as she could.

From her bed, Beth listened. She could hear the murmuring of her mother's voice. With a smile on her face, she snuggled deeper under her blankets and slept.

*

'Tis strange but true
For truth is always strange:
Stranger than fiction.'

Lord Byron: 1788-1824
c.X1V.st.101

25

They were married at Marylebone Register Office. As both were widowed there were few formalities and, as Don was a lapsed Roman Catholic, and in Maureen's case that the Church of England did not really approve of second marriages, a registry wedding in London seemed to be the best option. An option that brought all round approval—it meant that the English side of the bride's family were able to be in attendance.

Rain had been predicted, as had the crowds. However, that forecast was made for Saturday 19th May. A subterfuge that paid off handsomely on Thursday the 17th May.

The sun shone and the crowds were made up from family and friends as Don and Maureen walked out of the register office as Mr and Mrs Donald Seymour Sommer.

The late morning traffic crawled passed as the glowing newlyweds accepted the warm congratulations from their invited guests. Guests who inveigled the radiant couple to step forward towards their waiting flower decked car, so that they, the exuberant well-wishers, could shower them with colourful confetti.

Amid much laughter and shouts of good wishes, the car sped the beaming husband and wife towards to The Strands Hotel and their wedding breakfast.

'Happy?' Don gently kissed his wife as he asked.

'Mmm, yes,' she answered.

The kissing continued as the luxuriant car inched its way along Oxford Street. The noisy, busy street was thronged with lunchtime shoppers and dark suit clad business people. An ordinary May day for most, although, as the silver grey Bentley came to a forced halt, caused by the bumper-to-bumper traffic, a number of passers-by smiled and nudged each other, their attention drawn to the car and its occupants.

But the back-seat couple, telltale rose-petal confetti covering their shoulders and decorating their heads, were oblivious to the hurrying pedestrians, or the few kindly, stop-for-a-moment stares.

As the noon sun glinted the car's windows this late spring day, Don and Maureen had eyes only for each other. They wallowed in their first few moments as man and wife without a glance or a care to the rest of the world.

Camera bulbs flashed. The news had broken.

Don and then Maureen stepped from the car to face a pose of photographers. The noise was deafening. The shouts and whistles bore instructions and pleas.

Don squeezed his wife's hand: an apology.

She smiled back, nodding her head: consent.

So, before they entered the hotel, the newly-weds turned and, hand-in-hand, posed for the mob.

Don bowed his head, whispering into his wife's ear, 'It was too good to be true, eh? But I don't mind, if you don't.'

Maureen looked up into her husband's tanned face, her smile wider than ever, though her words were a little troubled, 'No. But Don? Do you *ever* get used to this...?'

His answer was lost in the melee...

'Look this way. And *again*. Perfect.'

'A little to your left; hold it. Put your arm round her waist, Don...'

'Another kiss...Please. Just one more, Don...Yeah, nice one.'

'Where will you honeymoon?'

'Have you been back in London long...?'

'When will Beth's new record come out...?'

'Maureen? How does your daughter feel about your marriage...'

'She's *here*...'

With Beth's arrival, the press swarmed towards the black and grey limousine that carried most of the Greenwood family along with its more famous passenger.

Inside the hotel, Maureen and Don posed for their own wedding album. Conscious that she was fast nearing her fortieth birthday, Maureen had chosen her wedding dress with care, keeping her maturity very much in mind. And she looked stunning. Her ankle length sleek dress was made of oyster coloured silk. The long sleeves of the dress were of pure lace the same shade of oyster, a sweetheart neckline allowing a mere hint of cleavage. The style was timeless and elegant, and very flattering to Maureen's petite frame. Her small bouquet of gold roses matched the single gold rose that adorned her well-cut, jaw length black hair. She looked radiant and smelt wonderful— Maureen always wore floral based perfumes, today lavender—and every inch of what she was: a film star's bride.

The famous man himself, resplendent in black morning suit, held his top hat in one hand, his wife's hand in the other as they smiled for the cameras.

As Maureen posed, smiling and laughing, her family and friends chatting around her, jostling each other into position for the family snapshot, a fleeting thought stole her smile... *Whose name will be on my lips the day I die: Stuart? Or Don...?*

'Hey, Mrs Sommer...*I love you*,' Don's whispered devotion, as he lifted their joint hands, kissing her knuckles, brought tears to her eyes.

'And I love you, too, *Mr Sommer*: my husband.'

She did love Don. Was truly delighted she had married him. As she looked into his gentle blue-grey eyes, her troubled thoughts faded and her smile returned, lighting her face as the camera's bulb flashed and the moment was sealed for eternity.

The informal wedding breakfast was a gourmet feast. The enormous cold buffet table of the private dining room was decorated by gold roses and trailing ivy, and laden with silver dishes of every size. Huge platters held fresh fruits from around the world. Ripe avocados were filled with salmon mousses and were surrounded by the largest and pinkest prawns and the greenest of garnishes. Lobster, shrimp cocktails, smoked fish and caviars were temptingly displayed alongside breads and biscuits; glazed hams, tender chicken and turkey were waiting to be carved; pates and French breads, quiches and vol-au-vents were in abundance. A huge salmon, nestling on shaved ice, had been dressed to take centre stage and was surrounded with colourful salads and rices, spiced and delicately aromatic.

And the dessert tables groaned just as equally. From simple crème caramels to three layered gateaux and delicate cream or vanilla filled dainty pastries. British cheeses nestled next to French, and there was even a good selection of American—*Monterey Jack* being Maureen's favourite.

However, it was the magnificent wedding cake that made everyone gasp. The cake had been made to resemble the pillared white stone house that was soon to become Maureen's home: Rockfort House, the Rhode Island mansion.

White royal icing had been used to cover the huge cake and the master confectioner had addressed every detail of the house using his secret recipe for a dark rich fruitcake, with imaginative usage of gelatines and marzipan. Even the lush front lawns of the house had been copied exquisitely. Gold rose bushes (marzipan had been coloured and used again) lined the candle-lit driveway that led to the columned portico, and piped white icing resembled the balustrades that surrounded the house and its manicured grounds.

When it was time to cut into the cake everyone was a little dismayed, until, of course, they had sampled its taste: the dark fruit cake was moist enough to melt on the tongue and rich enough to satisfy the most discerning palate. It can be safely said that the sumptuous cake was demolished much faster than it had taken to been made.

As the wedding party, seated at round tables set for six, celebrated with the excellent food and fine wines, a five-piece orchestra played from their repertoire peppered by many requests.

'Enjoying yourself, Aunt Nellie?' Beth crouched at the side of her elderly great-aunt's chair.

'Oh, aye, I am that love. More's the pity your granddad couldn't be here to enjoy it.' Even after all these years, Nellie still missed her brother Bill.

'I know, Auntie, I know…' Beth stroked the older woman's hand as it rested on the arm of the straight-back gilt chair.

Truthfully, Beth didn't miss the grandfather she had never met. Maureen's adoptive father had died long before Beth had been born.

'Mum looks wonderful, don't you think?' Beth gazed across the room to where her mother stood chatting to Don's brother, Harry. The orchestra began playing a mellow version of one of Don's well-known melodies.

'She always does, pet!' Aunt Nellie shouted…'our Maureen always had a way with her…who's the fellow she's talking to?'

Beth told Nellie that it was Don's brother, and then the two women fell silent and just listened to the music and watched.

Maureen and Harry seemed comfortable together. Easy. Harry Sommer, two years older than Don, had his younger brother's height, but the similarity stopped there. Harry lost most of his hair in his thirties. Now, at fifty-six, his stature stooped from his daily routine in the office chair at his accountancy company, Harry looked older than his age.

Watching him chatting with her mother, Beth found it hard to believe that the two of them had just met. It was obvious Maureen found her new brother-in-law comfortable to be with and vice versa.

Maureen was indeed pleased by the presence of Don's brother. The man was intelligent and charming, and without prejudice: He seemed to be delighted with Don's choice of bride, and had no hesitation in saying so. He was without doubt a very nice man and seemed remarkably unaffected by his brother's fame and fortune. He was also very flattering when Beth's name came into the conversation, and it was he that told Maureen they were being spied on.

Waving across the room to her daughter, and laughing when Harry blew kisses, too, Maureen patted the man's arm affectionately and then made her way over to her daughter and aunt.

Squatting down at Nellie's vacant side, Maureen kissed her aunt and asked the same question that Beth had asked previously.

In her normal brusque manner, Nellie grunted that she was a bit too old for all this malarkey, really. Yet the old lady's watery blue eyes sparkled a little now that she had the company and the ears of the younger women. And it seemed she wasn't going to waste the opportunity…

'Oh, but I'm having a grand time of it, all the same. I were just saying to our Beth, here, it's a right shame your own Mam and Dad couldn't be here today. By, lass, they'd have bin right proud of you, no mistake. You know that, don't you?'

Maureen gave the expected reply, knowing that she would have to spend at least another five minutes chatting to her reminiscing aunt. Then, ashamed of her thoughts, Maureen urged Nellie to stand and to walk with her around the room.

Arm in arm with the elderly woman (who was having difficulties walking in the heeled court shoes that Vi had insisted she buy to co-ordinate with the

253

navy blue polyester dress and jacket that, along with its matching pill-box style hat, had cost Nellie more money than she spent on groceries for a month; an outfit which she was hoping she'd be able to take back to the department store she bought it in the moment she got back to Manchester—well, the receipt did state refund available for up to twenty eight days,) Maureen introduced her to Don's close family, and the few mutual friends who had flown over from America for the occasion.

With the band playing a tune with lyrics about being in a mood to be worshipped and loved, Maureen stopped to speak with Beth's agent, Cynthia. But within seconds of introducing heel-sore Nellie, Maureen felt her hackles rise and her cheeks burn: as usual the agent's questions were racy: Cynthia wanted to know what the newlywed's plans were. And she also speculated on what would be happening later, behind the closed doors of the honeymoon suite.

However, though Maureen was embarrassed by the taunting questions, she could see that Aunt Nellie was having no such problems. The look on her aunt's face was very similar to the one on Cynthia's. Both were in awe. And it was at that moment that Maureen realised that most of Don's other fans around the world would be thinking the same thoughts...*what would it be like to have Don Sommer for a lover?* And she, Maureen Sommer, already knew the answer...*Wonderful.*

By three-thirty, most of the guests had drifted away. The toasts had been drunk, the food devoured and the telegrams and cards read. Only immediate family remained.

Beth, standing next to an open window, was chatting to a tall young man with sandy coloured hair and a fresh though rather pale complexion. The young man's stance was confident and relaxed although his eyes, the colour of dark chocolate, held a hint of sadness.

'Anyway, that's about everyone, I think...' Beth had been explaining a little of her family tree, and had laughingly told her companion about her aunt's intention of returning her wedding attire...including the offending shoes,

'Poor Aunt Nellie! I shouldn't laugh; one way or another she's always suffering. Her life story is a sad one. She was *devoted* to her daughter, Gladys. I only vaguely remember her. I was ten the only time I met her. And then she died, just after my dad. It must have been a terrible year, for them all.' Beth had been talking with Jacob, on and off, for most of the afternoon.

'And who is the pregnant one? I keep forgetting…'

Beth followed Jacob's gaze, yet she knew already whom he meant. She answered his question with amusement in her voice, 'Oh, that's my Aunt Patsy. And guess what? The baby is due the fourth of July!' Beth took a moment to sip her orange juice before continuing, 'Huh…I never used to like her. She's very stern, a bit gruff. Still, Grandma says she's more bark than bite. And, well, if she likes her…then I guess Patsy *must* be okay.'

'And does your grandmother like *me*?'

Beth looked up into Jacob's face; she grinned a wide, mischievous grin. 'Why? Is it important that she does?'

Jacob grinned back his answer, 'Sure is. I've got to pass muster. That *is*, if I am taking her granddaughter out on the town. Or would she think I was cradle snatching, and lock you up?'

'Hey, you're not old, Jake! You just look it. It's because of your *hard* life.' Beth pummelled his arm playfully, teasing.

Beth was unaware of Jacob Adier's past troubles. Had she had known, no way would she have joked about his hard life. Her choice of words had been innocent. Innocent fun. And though Jacob laughed along with her, he most certainly would not have wanted Beth to know the truth behind those words…

Twenty-eight year old Jacob, mostly known as Jake, as Beth had so easily slipped into calling him, had indeed had a very hard life, brought about, mostly, by his own stupidity, by nothing less than rebellion. Thankfully, he was one of the few who had survived the drug crazed years in the hippy communes of San Francisco.

Jacob's father had died at an early age. He left behind a young wife, Elizabeth, a two year-old son, Jacob, and a vast fortune.

Elizabeth Adier, believing she was doing her best for her father-less son, sent him to a military academy school at the tender age of seven.

That school, severe in handling the young boys' in its charge, destroyed Jacob's natural boisterousness. In turn, he became a wilful teenager, resenting everything and everybody.

When his widowed mother married the young singer-songwriter, Don Sommer, Jacob turned his affections and affinities elsewhere: Drugs.

During his drug-using years, misted in memory now, his mother, Elizabeth, became more and more debilitated by the illness that was destroying her body: Leukaemia. As Don's career had soared, Elizabeth's life had ebbed away.

Protecting his ailing wife, Don had kept the seedier side of her son's life hidden from her as much as he was able to. But because of her new husband's fame, she had known, had read, about her son's dug addiction.

It was on her deathbed that she had made Don promise. She begged him to stand by her son. Made him promise to guide the young man any way he could.

Elizabeth's death, when it finally, blessedly had come, was catastrophic for Jacob. Knowing that it was too late to amend his lifestyle for his mother's sake, he sank lower and lower.

Don's pledge was made even harder when Jacob over-dosed and for a day or two it was unknown whether the young man would live or die.

Yet live he did. And, with the constant support of his stepfather, the man he now called his closest friend, he went into rehabilitation and got his life back on track.

Jacob Adier had survived, although he was thoroughly ashamed of what he had put others through during his wild addicted years...

And now, as far as he was aware, Beth Stuart, whom he was growing more and more fond of, had no inkling of his past misdemeanours...

'Well, talk of the devil! Look who's here! Have your ears been burning, Gran?' An impish grin on her face, Beth leaned forward to kiss her grandmother's cheek.

Vi tut, tutted, and was glib with her reply, 'Oh, aye, I could see you were having a fair old natter about us,' she nodded her head in the direction of where she had left her son and daughter-in-law on the opposite side of the room, 'I said to our Patsy, "just look at them two titterin' on over there. And I *bet* they're talking about us. Think I'll go over and give them a piece of my mind"...'

Vi's eyes, which shone today as vibrantly as they had done when she was younger, sparkled with imminent laughter. Especially when it was Jake that answered. 'You are quite right, Vi, we *were* talking about you. I was asking Beth if she thought Sid would mind if I were to ask his beautiful, elegant wife to accompany me to a nightclub later this evening.'

Vi was quick with her own banter.

'Sid? Who's this Sid?' Vi took a long glance around the room. 'Do you mean that old fellow sat in the corner over there? The bloke that's supped too much champagne, looks like a drunken sailor...? Nay, lad, don't worry your head about *him*. He like's me to enjoy myself. So listen on, as long as I can wear me mink, I'll go anywhere's with you. And without anyone's consent!

I'm over twenty-one, you know. Although to be honest, I'm not surprised you *didn't* know. You can never tell with us English women...we wear well, that we do. Don't you agree, our Beth?'

The laughter and affectionate bantering was infectious. Maureen and Don, who had finally found a moment or two to sit together, eavesdropped with amusement.

Don linked his hands into his wife's, and squeezed gently. 'Seems like they've all enjoyed themselves, honey.' Don snuggled closer to his wife of four hours. Nuzzling his face into her silky hair he whispered, 'I think it's time for us to disappear. You sneak off now and get ready. *Go on;* I'll hold the fort.'

Maureen turned her face to his; a quick kiss was snatched.

'Okay...*I'm going.*' She kissed him again. 'I'll just saunter over to the door. No grand exit.' Her voice was lowered even more when she added. 'I'd like to have a minute on my own...' Maureen was stopped mid-sentence by Vi's arrival at their table.

'Are you going to get changed, pet? I thought you had to be at the airport by five thirty?'

'Yes...er, I was actually. Okay, *okay*, I'll go now...'

Besides a long sigh, there was nothing else for Maureen to say. Her time alone was not going to happen. She smiled at her aunt. And then the smile became wider and more genuine: Vi looked very nice today. Dressed in a suit of emerald green shot silk, and styled to flatter the fuller figure, Vi looked elegant. Her greying hair had been tamed by the softest of perms; cut to jaw length, its springy curls were both fashionable and neat. Maureen let her pride and her love for her aunt be known. She told her she looked wonderful.

'Ta, love, glad I've not let you down. Now come on; let's be having you out of your wedding togs! Well, Don,' Vi's attention was turned onto Maureen's bemused husband, 'you've certainly done us proud today, lad. I hopes you're going to make my little girl happy. She *deserves* it you know.'

Don stood, and his stature dwarfed Vi's.

'I can promise, Vi, Maureen and I will be the happiest couple in the world. You can count on it.'

Vi enjoyed the rapport she had with Don Sommer...*Don Sommer...Bloody hell...Who'd have thought it? He's practically my son-in-law...*

Don's good-natured teasing went on for a moment or two; he

complimented her on her outfit, and her youthful appearances. But the latter comments made her feel a little uneasy about herself, especially when, stroking his clean shaven chin, he stood back to take a better look at his wife's aunt, pondering, aloud, on the fact that she reminded him of someone.

Pulling in her stomach, Vi inwardly groaned...*Hell's bells. Not him as well...! I'll have to do something about me weight...*She put a hand up to her stiffly laquered hair...*and this prim and proper perm as well...*

As she waited for Don's coming, 'Hey I *know* who it is,' Vi's thoughts went back to the morning, and her preparations for the wedding...

The silk suit had cost Vi a small fortune. A fortune she had not begrudged, that is until she had been dressing in the hotel bedroom.

'You know who you put me in mind of, Vi?' Sid had said as he watched her spray perfume onto her wrists and neck.

'No. But I can tell from the grin on your face I'm not going to like it. Go on then, who is it?'

Looking very smart in his morning suit—Vi had taken great care helping him to dress and be well groomed—Sid chuckled from the comfort of his wing armchair, a chair he had become rather used: their suite of rooms were the same they had enjoyed six months previous when they had been guests of Beth for her Castle Theatre début. Keeping his wife in suspense was great game for Sid.

'Well, you might as well tell me. You will do anyhow, at some point. So, go on. Spit it out. Ruin my day.'

'Nay, lass, it'll not spoil your day. It'll make it. Pity we can't run to a tiara...'

'Why would I want to wear a tiara, Sid? Are you going crackers or something?' Vi had little time for Sid's wanderings, this day of all days. Besides, she had thought all that was behind him now...

'Because, love, you look like royalty. That's what I'm trying to tell you! Aye, you look like the Queen Mother. And that's a fact!'

Vi's enthusiasm had deflated with the remark—Sid had done it. He'd ruined her day before it had even started.

She had walked to the full-length mirror, twisting this way and that.

'Ah, *Sid,* do I really look that old?'

Sid had seen the look on his wife's face and had been quick to retort,

'Old. *Old.* Who said owt about *old*? I was complimenting you, you daft beggar. You're not old, Vi! Still nothing but a girl to me; a bonny girl at that!

You look regal, yes, that's it...*regal*. I'm right proud of you, lass. That I am.'

Vi had turned to face her husband of forty-three years, pity filling her eyes. A pity that surged with love, 'Are you, Sid? Are you *really*? I want Maureen to be proud of all of us today. Aw, *Sid*...all that's happened over the years—sometimes it's hard to believe, isn't it?'

Vi had made a valiant effort not to let her tears fall when she had crossed the room to Sid, flopping onto the twin bed nearest to where he sat.

'Aye, love, it is. We've come a long way.'

'But I don't feel any different, I'm still...oh, you know what I mean...I'm still...*Vi*.'

Sid had chuckled a little, and then had asked, 'Why would you want to be *different*?'

'Why? How can you ask, *why*.' Vi had felt her patience and her willpower not to cry evaporating, 'Sid, we have two of our sons dead and buried...a film star for a granddaughter. And now, *now*, our Maureen, *my girl*, is getting married to DON SOMMER! *Why* you ask? *Why*...? *That's why*. That's why we should have...changed. We *should* be different...that's *why*...'

'And would they love you still, those that are left? Would you *changing* help them? Not likely...'

Vi had just sat. Quietly, save for the sniffing back of her tears. Her hands played with the silky material of her skirt, whilst her thoughts ran amok: nothing had come of her fears, her terror, from the night of the Castle Theatre. If it *had* been Iris seated near them, well, it had been a narrow escape. And a blessed one...*having the likes of Iris in her life would be catastrophic for Maureen...especially now. Now that she was marrying Don*...

Sat on the bed, dressed in her finery, she had actually been wringing her hands with the terrible worry of it all. The strain of the wedding, Sid's health, and trying to keep the truth about Iris away from Maureen, was an enormous burden—and the latter problem was one she was carrying alone. And it had to be that way.

It had all seemed so very trying; her nerves had been in tatters as she had watched Sid edge himself almost out of his chair. He'd reached out to her.

'Come on, love, this won't do, will it? What's brought it all on? I'm sorry, *love*, if it were my fault. Come on, Vi, this is not like you...Buck up, hey?'

His cajoling had gone further. 'Tell you what, Vi. You get yourself out of them fancy clothes, and I'll get out of mine...' he'd made to get out of his chair, '...let's get *cracking*. We've got time. I'll show you neither of us is old. Not for what I have in mind. Go on; lock the door! Like we used to, hey?'

Sid had practically flung himself onto the bed, knocking Vi backwards. Laughter had exploded from her.

'What you *laughing* at? Don't you think I mean it? Listen, I've always had an eye for the Queen Mum,' he'd hugged her fiercely, 'that's better. Give us a kiss.'

Vi had obliged, her brimming eyes full of adoration for this man—her lovely Sid. Who always made things right.

'Hey, now, no more tears, right? You were *made* to laugh, Vi. Come on; help me up…we've a wedding to go to, your *royal highness'*…

Now, with the excitement of the wedding celebrations waning, and remembering the morning and Sid's comments, Vi braced herself for Don's verdict.

'Tell me, then. You'll not be the first. Tell me who I put you in mind of…'

Don stroked his chin again, his eyes glinting.

'Well, I'm a big *fan* of hers, so I should know…Shirley DeWinter…Yes. Definitely: Shirley for sure. Vi, you are *just* as gorgeous…'

Beth heard the comment and was quick to say she agreed; that Vi was, indeed, the image of the glamorous, vivacious actress. The look of pure delight that swept her grandmother's face was reward enough for her words: it was good to see her looking so well again.

With Vi engrossed in conversation with Don, Beth gave her mother the eye signal that it was her chance to slip away. But the plan misfired: Vi didn't miss a trick. It was she that called across that Maureen should really get going if she wanted to change into her going-away suit. Quietly leaving the reception to ready herself for her honeymoon was no longer an option for Maureen. To claps and cheers, Beth escorted her mother up the stairs, with her grandmother close at heel.

The chatter and great whoops of merry-making that came from the three of them locked inside Maureen's suite made it impossible for Don's knocking to be heard. He had to almost hammer on the door before it was opened.

When Beth finally heard him, she greeted him still laughing, apologising for the bedlam and then, threading her arm through that of her stepfather's, she coaxed him back down stairs to wait with the rest of the family: her mother was at least ten minutes away from being ready. Mary Lou's fault: the generous woman had sent, by special delivery, the most gorgeous suit for Maureen to wear to her honeymoon, but unfortunately, due to its long journey, it needed to be pressed

'Okay then, Beth. But before we go back into the others, I'd like to have a quick word with you. Let's go into the lounge...' he glanced at his wrist watch, '...not that that we'll be wanted *afternoon tea.*'

As they stepped down into the lamp-lit lounge area of the hotel, people stared, recognising the famous singer.

Steering Beth towards a vacant corner and a comfortable looking sofa, Don confided his thoughts about the stares and whispers, 'It's *you* they're excited about, Beth...'

'I don't think so, Don. I'm sorry to say that most of the people here would not recognise a *pop* singer.'

The other lounge residents were indeed more in Don Sommer's age bracket than they were of hers.

'You do yourself an injustice, young lady. I'm telling you; no one can take their eyes off you.'

Don's perception was correct: the afternoon champagne and tea drinkers were indeed focused on the beautiful young woman who was Don Sommer's companion.

But Beth was also right in her assumptions: the party of four seated nearest to them elegantly quaffed back their drinks their excitement palpable as they whispered to each other: Don's name was on the women's lips...

'Yes, it is *him*... Wasn't he supposed to be getting married?'

'Oh, today...? *Here? Really.* Who's he with, then? She does look familiar...'

'It's that *Beth Stuart*...Isn't Don supposed to be marrying her mother...?'

'Yes he is marrying the mother. Did you catch her at the Castle Theatre? Oh, yes, we had tickets. The dress circle...*Wonderful* voice...It was rumoured it was her he was interested in...always been very fond of her...said so himself.'

'Her suit is stunning. The colour certainly flatters her. What colour would you say...Baby blue...Powder blue...'

'Does it *matter*? She looks fabulous, she could wear *anything* and look good...'

'*I* could, at that age. But have you seen her eyes? Have you *ever* seen eyes that blue...?

As if Don could hear the whispers, he added to the compliments with some of his own. 'You *do* look very beautiful today, Beth. You take after your mother. I just wanted to tell you how very happy I am—and that I'm going to take great care of your Mom. And that's a promise: She's one very special lady.'

Beth was as earnest with her reply, though she was aware there was something else in her tone. For some time unease had been creeping into her friendship with Don. One that she had trouble masking right now.

'Thank you Don, I know you are both going to be happy. I suppose I'm glad, *really*, that you talked her into marrying you so soon; not waiting.'

'We had no reason to wait. But you know your *Mom*, she wasn't sure if it was the right thing to do. Said she wanted a longer courtship…hey, though, she didn't take too *much* persuading, not in the end.'

Beth shook her head, closing her eyes. She leaned back against the soft upholstery of the comfortable sofa. She knew that Don had relaxed too. The silence between them was companionable. Beth, with her eyes still closed, smiled. The unease was unravelling. Aware that Don was watching her, she decided to go for it…

'How could she have refused, *Don*? You asked nearly every minute of every day! You wore her down, that's all. And finally, well, she probably felt she had *no* choice.' Beth now looked at Don. And saw that he was crestfallen by her words. But she'd had to say them; they had been festering within her for months. Pity of it, it should be this day they'd seeped out.

'How can you say that, Beth? Or even *think* it. Your Mom had already agreed to marrying me…she just wouldn't set a date…'

'So you set out to make her, hey? Don, she was *trapped.*' Beth's hackles where rising again as she remembered the New Year's Eve performance. 'Don, I'll never believe that what you did in Vegas was the right thing…*never.*'

'I really don't understand where this is coming from, Beth, your Mom was *delighted.*'

'I can say it because I *know* she wanted to wait awhile…get used to the idea of being married again…especially with you being who you are. Don, it's not *easy* living in the limelight all the time. You of all people should know that…'

They both stared at one another, each knowing the truth of what was now out in the open: Beth's reservations.

The tea-drinking women were ignorant of what was being discussed, but were aware that a heated discussion was taking place.

'So, you are saying that I railroaded her? Yeah?'

'Of course! Mum had *no* idea you were going to do it.'

'But she wouldn't name the day!'

'And you thought that getting her to join you on stage...forcing her to set a day...her *wedding day*...in front of a packed audience, was the right way?'

Don tugged at the gold brocade cravat at his neck. When it was loose he looked at Beth and asked, 'Have you been smarting with this all these months?'

Beth couldn't answer.

Don's eyes never left her face as he took her hand in his own. He spoke with sincerity when he confirmed that he had only done what was best.

'We're married, now, aren't we? Your mother had already waited long enough, don't you think? I'll *admit* she was cross with me at the time. But, hey, she did name the day...And she *did* stick to it.'

Now it was Beth's turn to look contrite. 'It's just that I love her so much.'

'I know you do, Beth. And I promise you, *again*, Maureen will *never* be sorry she married me.'

Beth's anxiety melted. She saw before her the Don she knew; the Don she had always known. She smiled at him with a relief that made her shoulders relax. Mischief slipped onto her tongue. 'Okay, okay, *okay*. But I want one more promise...'

'Just *one*? Am I off the hook that lightly?'

'One: A big one. No...more...railroading. Promise?'

'I promise.'

'Good.'

'Good.'

'Shake.'

'Shake.'

Their handshake and subsequent laughter was good: For both of them. The pair had always enjoyed each other's company. And now that they were father and daughter they had set a foundation of mutual respect. A respect that would grow into a strong relationship based on the love they both shared for Maureen.

'Hey, look,' Don glanced at his wristwatch, 'it's time to go. They'll all be wondering where've we got to...but *before* we go, I'd like to give you something.' Don delved into the left-hand pocket of his trousers. He produced a small, blue velvet box. He gave it to Beth.

Beth accepted the box with one hand; the other hand went to her chest. 'For *me*?'

'Yes, for you. A welcome present, for my blue-eyed...*daughter*.'

The people sat closest by craned their necks to see what she had been given. And they too smiled when they heard Beth gasp.

Don beamed his pleasure as Beth said, 'Oh, Don! They're *beautiful*. Thank you…Thank you *so* much…I'll treasure them, *always.*'

Don Sommer had presented Beth with the first of many gifts. However, the perfectly cut sapphire earrings would always be one of her most cherished possessions. They were a priceless gift from a prince of men.

As the pair left the room, arm in arm, all traces of discontent was left behind in their wake, as were the many smiles of congratulations and the hand-to-mouth exclamations of pleasure from the hotel's afternoon tea guests. The well-known singer had not only nodded his head in their direction when taking his leave, he had also bowed low from the waist, acknowledging their very presence.

Making her way upstairs to her mother's suite, Beth chuckled to herself. Don, who had gone to say another quick goodbye to his stepson and his brother, had certainly made the afternoon-tea ladies day one not to be forgotten. Gripping the velvet box in her hand, Beth was delighted by the thoughtful gift she had so unexpectedly received. But what pleased her most was the knowledge that her mother's life would now be bestowed with the greatest of happiness.

Twenty minutes later, accompanying her radiant mother back down the stairs to where her smiling new husband welcomed her as though she had been gone for months, not a mere three quarters of an hour, Beth too was glowing—with relief: for it had been she who had orchestrated the couple's meeting in the first place. And it had turned out that she had been exactly right: the newly weds were indeed a perfect match.

*

26

At last they were alone save for the chauffeur who sat up front behind a glass partition. Professional and discreet, the experienced driver drove the Bentley without looking through his rear view mirror, relying on the perfectly aligned side mirrors when he switched lanes en route to Heathrow Airport.

Both Maureen and Don had changed into comfortable travelling clothes before their departure from the wedding reception.

Maureen looked stylish and ultra modern in a lemon coloured linen trouser suit. A long black silk scarf was knotted loosely under the collar of the short-sleeved jacket and, although at this present time she was not wearing it the chic outfit was complimented by a large floppy black hat, ribbon trimmed at the crown, in colour of the summery suit. Maureen had been surprised and delighted when the outfit had arrived, by special delivery, two days ago. And today she was pleased to be wearing something that had come directly from Mary Lou's flagship boutique in Palm Beach.

Don had chosen beige cotton twill slacks, a casual short-sleeved shirt, cotton again and in the same beige as his trousers; his tan coloured sports jacket, tailored to perfection in heavy linen, completed his outfit.

Their exit from the hotel had been bedlam. Hundreds of Don's adoring fans had crowded the street that led to the hotel. With the added melee of clamouring photographers, and the cat calls and cheers from the few family members who had braved the flashbulbs to wave their goodbyes to the newlyweds, the echoing din, the shrieks, cries and whistles were still ringing in their ears some ten minutes later.

Don had been kind to a lucky few of his waiting fans: he'd signed autographs, accepted the odd kiss or two. But when he realised that he was going to be mobbed if he didn't get into the car, he'd climbed into the Bentley without haste. And that was when the crowds had turned a little more enthusiastic. Some women banged on the closed windows, begging for Don's attention. And when that was not forthcoming, they were loud in their admonishments. As the car glided slowly away from the hotel, careful not to knock anyone down, run them over, both Maureen and Don heard some of their snipes…'Why's he married *her*?'

'Why did he tell his Fan Club *lies*?'

'He's *never* done that before!'

'Well, if *that's* how he wants it…'

'Rotten trick to tell us the *wrong* day…'

'She must be to blame!'

'She'll not last *two* minutes!'

'It's Elizabeth he loved…!'

Don told Maureen to take no notice. She'd get used to it.

And though the shouted ugly comments brought a little sourness to the proceedings, she instinctively knew that she would have to put them behind her. Indeed the whole episode was something she really would have to get used to. Being Mrs Don Sommer would have its downside along with its good. She took notice of what Don was saying, but inwardly she felt sickened by the fans' contemptuous outbursts

Ten minutes in to the journey, and with her equilibrium somewhat restored, she nestled her head against her husband's shoulder and relaxed her own. As the car purred along the busy highways, heading towards the airport, Maureen could feel the warmth of his body, his masculine firmness.

Closing her eyes, she savoured Don's nearness, her body alert to his every breath. And her stomach muscles contracted as her thoughts leapt forwards: thoughts that were filled with desire. A desire that always surged deep within her whenever she was close to Don. It was a desire that surprised her, and its insatiable capacity was becoming slightly disturbing.

But for now, with the heady excitement of the day behind her, these sexual yearnings blended with the pull of sleep. The speed and comfort of the luxurious car lulled her eyelids shut. But her mind was still on Don—and the magical days, weeks and months that had led up to this day...

From the beginning of their courtship Maureen had been sexually conscious of Don. She had wanted him in a way she had not thought possible to want any man. When he had telephoned, the early-hour call that had followed on the heel of their first date, she had hugged the receiver close to her mouth, knowing without doubt that she was attracted to him. Had wanted him to be her lover. Had known, instinctively, that him being so was only a matter of days away. And when it had come she had not been disappointed. Her celibate years, and there had been many, were over.

Don had felt the same way, although he was genuine enough to tell her of a number of one-night-stands. Don had stated, categorically, that he wanted her to know everything about him...

These confessions were whispered to her as she lay in his arms in her bed in the brand new condominium she had bought in Palm Beach. The two-bedroom ocean view apartment she had moved into just before Christmas. Maureen's first home of her own. A home that truly was just for her, Beth having decided it was time to flee the nest, and had taken a lease on a small apartment in the West Miami area.

Beth's new condo was closer to Miami's International Airport and consequently the various capitals of countries she needed to fly to promoting her latest recording: *Love Power*, an aptly titled ballad for Beth's rendition of the song was both emotional and powerful. The recording, finalised whilst Beth was in London for the Variety Proms, was tipped to reach the number one spot in the English Charts before the fast approaching Christmas. It did. And stayed in place until well into the New Year.

Maureen and Don had spent Christmas together. Their first of what they hoped would be many. Beth had joined them for a sumptuous breakfast, which they had eaten at the marble-topped table on Maureen's white-railed first-floor terrace that overlooked the rolling waves of the Atlantic Ocean. The weather had been warm and pleasant, as was usual in December in the sunshine state of Florida.

Earlier, when Beth had first arrived and they had been exchanging gifts (nothing too elaborate, trinkets and useful items that they had agreed on a couple of weeks before, when the house moves had been both fretful and time consuming,) Don had suggested that they dine out for Christmas dinner. But as Beth had other commitments (she was slightly coy about with whom…and no name was ever mentioned) Maureen and he had stayed home to enjoy each other's company and a turkey salad complimented by a chilled bottle of champagne.

The day Maureen signed the final papers that meant her Boca Raton home was sold to its new owners, she also took Beth to the airport for her flight to London. And Maureen had valiantly kept her spirits high—any maudlin feelings were banished in view of the fact that Beth was beside herself with excitement at the prospect of her first appearance on British television, set to be aired live on New Years Eve. With her record still being in the number one spot, Beth was going to sing on the programme called *Hits of the Charts*.

Returning somewhat teary-eyed from the airport, Maureen had then had to dash around to make sure she herself was ready for her evening flight to Las Vegas: she was to accompany Don, who also had a New Year date booked: Don Sommer's *Televison Special* was set to be broadcast live across the entire United States directly from his sell-out concert date in Las Vegas; the fabulous dining/theatre auditorium in one of the glittering town's finest hotels being the venue.

During the long haul flight between Florida and Nevada, Don had proposed. And Maureen, totally overwhelmed by all that had happened to her in the past few weeks, and by the speed of which her relationship with Don was moving, had bit her lip, turning her face to the plane's window as her tears had finally fallen. Her weeping was a mixture of joy, trepidation, anxiety…and disloyalty

However, Don, fully aware of the tumult of Maureen's emotions, had gently requested that she turn and face him. Tenderly wiping the tears from her cheeks, he had then put his arm around her and hugged her close.

Don spent the remainder of the flight telling Maureen just how much she meant to him. That he loved her, and was quite certain she felt the same way about him. He had gone on to say that he had known from their first date that they would marry. In fact, when he'd come to think about it, and he had thought about it, often, he had been aware of her presence since Beth was a young child on the set of *Blood's No Thicker Than Water*. And wasn't that true? They had no blood ties, but the love he felt for her, *had* for her, well, it was what the world had been made for…it was everything he sang about. It was the feeling and emotion behind every song he wrote.

As the plane had flown into the cobalt-blue skies of early morning Nevada, Don had said that he understood Maureen's worries: her feelings of disloyalty. And he told her that loving him had nothing to do with the way she had loved Stuart. Stuart would always be etched into her heart, for had he have lived, they would have had a lifetime marriage—as he himself would have done with Elizabeth. But now they had to face facts: The two people they had loved had gone. Never coming back. Nothing could bring them back. And nothing could ever mar the precious memories both of them held in their hearts and minds...

Maureen had listened and had marvelled at Don's understanding. She had agreed with everything he said. But still—she wanted time. Time to think. Time to decide. Don had agreed that was okay; but he vowed he'd be asking her again on New Year's Eve. And that he thought that was giving her plenty of time: two full days.

On New Years Eve, just before Don was due on stage, true to his word he had taken her into his arms and asked her again: asked her to be his wife. In answer she had lowered her head and remained silent. Don had moved away from her, taking his cue in the wings.

And that was when Maureen had suddenly realised that her actions and silence had been very wrong, totally wrong; finally she found the courage to let her heart have its say.

With only seconds to spare before Don had to step onto the stage she was ready to rush to him—but was only in time to see him pull back his shoulders and, microphone in hand, walk out into the glare of the spotlights.

It was with a feeling of despair and misery for what she had done, and what she feared she had lost, that she joined her guests at the front row table reserved for Don's party.

The applause for the singer's appearance on stage was deafening. Chuck and Mary Lou were up on their feet, cheering and clapping. Maureen had joined them with a smile pinned to her face, for their sakes pretending that nothing was wrong. She owed Don that, at least. For it had been Don who had issued the invite to the Texas based couple. It was he who went secretly to the airport to meet them. It was he who made the unusually shy couple shed their inhibitions about being in the famous singer's company; to feel right at home in the town of bright lights and extravagance.

And it had been Don who had said he had a very, *very* special surprise for her that night, and had taken so much pleasure in seeing her face light up when he had first walked her to the reserved table where, besides a huge bouquet of flowers and iced, pink champagne, waited her dearest and most beloved friends.

When Don was half way through his repertoire, Maureen found herself clapping and stamping her feet along with the rest of the audience: Don's talent was wowing everyone.

With several of his well-know songs already sung, to the rapturous approval of the audience, Don was well into singing his last number when Maureen made a decision: *She* would propose to Don. If possible, she would do it on the stroke of midnight. The new year of 1979 would be the start of a whole new life.

As she clapped along with the melody she mentally said her goodbyes— and her thanks: *Stuart, I loved you so much...Thank you for loving me...and for letting me go now. Aunty Vi and Uncle Sid...have a good year. Hope you are going to be happy with my news...Thank you for taking me, and shaping me; for showing me what it is to belong...Beth, my darling girl, may God Bless you; have a Happy New Year, a happy life, sweetheart...*Her thoughts had brought a sheen of tears to her eyes, but she was not feeling sad. She turned towards her friends seated at the table with her. Saw the radiant look on their faces; their enjoyment of the night was total. Chuck's thick dark hair had turned grey, which added a certain dignity, although he would benefit from losing a pound or two from round his waistline. Mary Lou, attractive as ever, still with ebony black hair, hid her added pounds under a beautifully designed halter neck black evening gown, its bodice shimmering with a million black sequins.

Lost both in the admiration of her friends, and in her at-peace-now thoughts, Maureen was unaware that Don had stopped singing. It was only when the harsh glare of a spotlight made her blink, that she realised that whole auditorium was in silence. And that she alone was bathed in light. She turned to face the stage, and saw that Don was beckoning to her. Grinning from ear to ear, Chuck urged her to stand, and then he escorted her to the steps leading up to the stage.

All Maureen's *at peace* thoughts had left her. Anger had taken their place. A rage so strong that she felt she was suffocating with it...*I'll kill him...! I don't want to do this...I can't go on stage...I can't do this...I'm going to faint...*

But she hadn't fainted. Although her breathing was erratic, though she was concerned that her long black dress—the one she had worn to the Castle Theatre the previous month...*could it have only been last month? My brain must still be in working order if I can think about what I'm wearing...now...*wasn't by any means glamorous enough for what was about to happen, she made a graceful entrance onto the stage helped and aided, of course, by eager stage technicians and the firm shove in the back from Chuck Vicente.

Don had kissed her, whispering that she looked beautiful. Then, taking her hand in his had walked her to centre stage.

The audience had hushed, expectantly. And were not disappointed.

For the third time in as many days, Don proposed. He asked her to do the honour of becoming his wife.

And Maureen had nodded. Her cheeks burning, she had wanted to hide her face by burying it hard against Don's chest. But she didn't. Just like she didn't faint. And like she didn't stop breathing. What she did do was to say, very loudly, and very confidently, repeating it three times to be sure. 'Yes. *Yes.* YES...'

As she and Don had embraced, the audience had once again come to their feet, clapping and cheering, calling-out congratulations. Bells rang, whistles blew, horns honked, blowers hooted. New Year 1979 had arrived...

The Bentley came to a standstill. It was a quarter to six: their journey to the airport had taken a little longer than anticipated because of the volume of traffic.

'Wake up, sleepyhead. We're *here.*' Don lifted his shoulder, dislodging Maureen's head.

'Mmm...?' Maureen was a little disorientated. She hadn't thought she'd slept...*but maybe...* 'I haven't been asleep, Don, just resting my eyes.' It was a statement she had heard, and had not believed, many times herself: it was taken from Sid Greenwood.

'Some rest, huh? You've not spoken a *word* for the best part of an hour.'

Although Maureen was aware that Don was being playful in his reproach, she was contrite as the chauffeur ushered her from the car. She inwardly admonished herself...*Dozing on the way to my honeymoon...Good heaven's, I'll have to watch what I'm doing...Stop going off in my daydreams...*

As an airline representative led then towards the V.I.P. suite, a score of photographers jostled at their side.

'Maureen! Look this way.'

'Where will you be staying in Madrid?'

'Don? Will you be touring Spain?'

'Where's Beth? Is she pleased about your marriage...?'

Only when they were safely inside the secure lounge did Maureen realise that she had been holding her breath. Being Mrs Donald Sommer was taking some getting used to. She hoped that she would, eventually, because at this moment in time she was finding it very intimidating, very trying. And it was starting to mar this special day.

But later, aboard their first class flight to Madrid, when Maureen was much more relaxed, and sipping her second glass of chilled champagne, she voiced the question that had been at the back of her mind for most of the day. It wasn't something that had truly spoilt the proceedings, like the photographers had nearly done, but its nag had left its mark. She related this to her husband, secondary to her question.

'Why do you think Chuck and Mary Lou declined our invite to the wedding? I really can't *believe* it was because they were too busy. Can you? It's saddened me, Don, them not coming...'

'I don't think they would have missed it deliberately, Maureen. Not them.' Don looked out of his window as he spoke.

'Well, I don't believe their reason for not attending. There *must* be something else.'

Don chuckled. Which annoyed his wife.

'*I* don't find it very funny, Don. I mean, they are supposed to be my best friends. *Our* best friends! Being busy has never stopped them before...'

Don turned to look at her, but sipped his drink before speaking. 'Chuck has responsibilities in San Antonio. He just couldn't get away. Don't make too big a deal about it, Maureen...'

'Don! How can you say that to me? Everyone else turned up. Everyone else made the effort. They of all people knew we were planning to get married...'

'But, my love, they didn't know when...No more than we did, until a couple of weeks ago...'

Momentarily this explanation satisfied Maureen. It was true that the wedding plans had moved swiftly, once the licences had been granted.

'Hmmm. Maybe you're right. And perhaps they didn't want to leave Lydia...and the new baby. I suppose *that* would make sense...'

Their evening meal being served to them put a stop to any further discussion. Maureen declined the offer of wine. And Don took that to be a sensible option and did the same. Between them they had probably quaffed more that a dozen glasses of champagne and wines both during the wedding reception and on board this flight. Not that either of them were showing any signs of inebriation. As the ate their light meal of poached salmon and the tiniest of buttered baby potatoes and mange tout, they both took long drinks of mineral water which was followed by tea for Maureen and coffee for Don.

Maureen felt sleepy again after eating the dinner. But resolved to stay awake this time, she brought the Vicente family back into her conversation. This time, though, it was to talk about their married daughter, now Lydia Landon, and the baby she had recently given birth to. 'We must buy something nice for the little boy. He'll be nearly three month old, now. At the interesting stage.'

As Don was agreeable to her sentiment, Maureen relaxed again; the rest of the air journey was pleasantly spent. They sat joyously, hand in hand. And Maureen stayed well awake. She had so much to look forward to. Their talk of babies and family life brought Beth into the conversation: Beth was going to spend the summer months in England, which was a plan that had Maureen's full blessing. Maureen still found it hard to believe that her daughter no longer needed her mother's constant support and care. Which, indeed, was the way it should be. And Maureen enjoyed the buzz of pride when Don said that she had done a real good job in raising Beth on her own.

As Maureen buckled her seatbelt for landing, she reminded herself that she had also done a good job in her tutoring of Vera Malone: Vera had taken over the day-to-day business of the hairdressing salon in Boca Raton. The New Yorker had turned out to be a very good manager, and the shop was thriving under her capable control.

All told there was nothing to stop them enjoying their honeymoon: Don's schedule of concerts was for later in the year. For now there was two months of exciting travel in store for them. Starting in Madrid, the couple were intent on covering as much Spanish ground as they possibly could. And that also meant its Balearic Islands. And Mallorca, the largest of the isles, had been chosen as the island for their longest stay.

Their hotel in Madrid was situated near Retiro Park and the world famous Prado Museum. Maureen and Don were shown to an exquisite suite of rooms that boasted hand woven carpets and antique furnishings.

After unpacking their personal belongings they showered, put on bathrobes and settled on top of the huge and magnificently canopied bed in the suite's master bedroom. Chilled champagne had been left on the lamp-lit bedside table, and they decided that one more glass would do them little harm. They toasted each other, although one sip was enough. Enough for them to shed their robes and entwine their soap scented limbs.

Maureen initiated the lovemaking. Straddling her right leg over Don's naked torso, she sat on his muscular thighs.

Leaning forward, so that her full breasts caressed his chest, she kissed his name to his lips; and then to his eyes, to his nose and then his ears. Four times she said Don's name, nailing her hungry kisses at the same time. And then, when she leant backwards and eased herself down, they moved as one. A rhythm, ages old but so very new to them, built to an urgent crescendo.

And when they were finally stilled and silent, they settled and lay close, spooned together for what was left of their first hot Spanish night.

Madrid proved a worthy city in which to spend the first five days of their honeymoon.

Each day they ate breakfast in their suite; then visited the many museums and galleries. They walked and shopped, dressed casually in shorts and tee shirts. They ate lunch al fresco, swam in the hotel's magnificent pool and made love in the late afternoons.

In the cool of the evenings, they changed into their finest clothes and dined in the city's many and splendorous restaurants. They ate late and they ate well. They laughed, they sang, they danced into the small hours. Few people recognised the handsome couple and those who did, seemed to have the foresight to leave them alone.

On the last morning of their stay, Maureen was petulant about leaving the city she had come to love. As she watched Don finish his breakfast she toyed with her own, and let her feelings be known. 'Oh, Don. Why do we have to leave…?'

'Because the island of Mallorca beckons, my darling.'

'Is it all arranged? I mean, couldn't we cancel it, and leave at the end of the week instead?'

Don shook his head and laughed. He drained his coffee cup and indicated for Maureen to do the same, 'Come on…eat your breakfast. It *is* all arranged, and no we can't cancel. So stop looking so miserable, eat up and lets get going. We still have a few more hours left here, so lets make the most of the day, whilst there is just the…I mean whilst we still have some time.'

Maureen looked up from her half eaten bowl of fruit and muesli. Don seemed flustered. But when he moved to her side and bent and kissed the nape of her neck she put her moody thoughts aside. The reason for Don's flush made obvious to her now as they made their way back to bed.

Walking down the metal steps from the aircraft, waves of warm heat greeted them to Palma de la Mallorca.

Outside the airport terminal, they were greeted by the driver of their hired car, 'Buenos Dias, Senor, Senora, welcome to Mallorca.'

The black Mercedes pulled away from the kerb, its back-end dragging lower with the weight of the four heavy cases that travelled with Maureen and Don.

The car's radio blared: a well-known, chart-topping American song, and singer. But it wasn't Don.

The driver sang along, out of tune and then, much to his passengers' consternation, turned his head to say, 'I lika this man. Gotta gooda voice. Do you like him, Senor?'

Don was mighty quick with his reply, though he had to almost shout over the blare of the radio and the noise of the traffic coming in through the driver's opened window. 'Yep, I like him. He has got a good voice. Different; his lyrics tell a story.'

Maureen looked out of her closed window, a mischievous smile flashing her face, dimpling her cheeks, before she quickly admonished her thoughts: Don had been successful in the music business for so long, it was hard for him to admit that he had been toppled in popularity by the brilliance of the younger, Bronx born singer-songwriter.

'You Americano, Senor?'

'Yes. We both are.'

Maureen glanced quickly at her husband, and thought... *why do I still feel so British? After twenty-five years in the States, you'd think I'd agree that I was more American...*

The driver had a lot more shouted questions.

'Not a been to Mallorca before, Senor?'

'No!' Don yelled back. Though the traffic was not too heavy, it was extremely noisy caused by a conglomerate of exhaust spluttering farm vehicles, trucks and a constant stream of small motorbikes and mopeds. Honking horns seemed to be a national past time.

Not that any of this bothered their jacket-less driver, who drove with his white shirt sleeved elbow resting on the sill of his fully opened driver's window, his thick black hair, which he wore collar length, blowing in the wind, wafting the citrus smell of the oils he used to keep it under control and glossy, in the direction of his back-seat passengers.

Totally unaware of his bad driving habits, the chauffeur's commentary was non-stop…

'This is Inca, now, see…? You buy a plenty good leather at this place. I take you, tomorrow…next day. When you like, *si*?'

Maureen and Don looked at each other, raising their eyebrows. Neither of them answered, though both looked out at as the town of Inca sped by, a cloud of dust following in their wake. They were being driven far too fast.

'How long before we get to Pollensa, Senor?' Don asked, still having to raise his voice above the music blaring from the car's radio: once again it was the deep toned rich voice of Don's rival, and by now both passengers had come to realise they were listening to a cassette tape that was set on repeat.

'Soon, Senor, very soon! You like a countryside? It is a very butiful. Mallorca is the most butiful island in the world. *Bonito.*' The driver kissed the tips of his fingers to emphasize his words.

Maureen and Don had to agree as the open rolling countryside and the mountains of northern part of the island came into view.

Don's arm was round Maureen's shoulders as they sat close together, listening to the music that made them both want to tap their feet, and impulsively sing along with, whilst at the same time gazing out through Maureen's window in wonderment of the majestic mountain range that sided the left of the car.

'These the Tramuntana Mountains; we nearly Pollensa, now. You very much a like Pollensa: Very butiful. See, we are here. *Magnifico!*' The driver kissed his fingers again as he enthused about the beauty of the town they were passing through that nestled under the shelter of the mountainside.

'I thought we were staying in this *Pollensa* place?' Maureen posed the question to Don as the medieval looking town dwindled from view and was left behind.

But the driver—who now informed them his name was Miguel, as was his father's name, as was his grandfather's name and now, now that he was blessed, was also the name of his very own three month old son—said that they were indeed staying in Pollensa, but Pollensa was more than just a town, it had different areas. They were going to stay in a place known as Font la Mer.

Getting the gist of what Miguel was telling them, Maureen and Don realised that even a small island like Mallorca had suburbs and, like anywhere else, some were probably better than others. Maureen silently mouthed to Don that she hoped Font la Mer was one of the best. She got an affectionate pat on the arm in answer and immediately began to feel a little worried that

Don had no idea of where they were actually going, either.

Miguel's commentary was now fully on the subject of his new son. His pride was obvious. Like most Mediterranean's, Miguel was fond of children. Maureen was beginning to wonder if he would soon be in tears, his voice had become so emotional. She also wondered what that show of emotion would do for his driving.

But Miguel's next question took all thoughts of bad driving from Maureen's mind.

'Do you have childrens, Senor?'

'No!' Don answered loudly.

Maureen felt deflated by her husband's decisive reply. She would of course have answered, yes. And thinking of Jacob, who Don treated exactly like a son, she was puzzled by his statement. She stole a quick glance at him, and immediately knew why had said what he said: Don was an honest man. In truth, Don did not have children. He had never had a child of his own. And never would. On their second date, Don had told Maureen that he was sterile... 'It used to bother me,' he'd said, as they sat side by side in his sumptuous hotel suite in London, after having had dinner down stairs in the restaurant and had returned to his rooms for a night-cap... 'Heck, a man wants a kid of his own. But after I married Elizabeth, well, I got to thinking it wasn't too bad, me not being able to father a child. Jake was a good kid at that time, you know, when we were first married. He was a whole lot of fun, too. And then, after, when he was in so much trouble, I was kind of glad I couldn't have any. I sure was.'

Don had been thirteen when he suffered a severe bout of mumps. The infection, coupled with the onset of measles had nearly taken his young life. Though he was spared, the grave illness had left him sterile.

'We a here!' Miguel called out excitedly. The Mercedes turned into a long, gravel-laid driveway. The heady smell of flower blossom filled the car.

Stretching forwards in their seats, Don and Maureen rested their arms on the back of the front seats, watching with mounting interest as the driveway ended and what looked like a large farmhouse appeared.

'Casa Blanca.' The name of house flourished of Miguel's tongue.

Maureen and Don looked at each other, and burst out laughing.

'The White House!' They both said in unison.

And indeed the large stone house was painted white. It was also very beautiful.

Don began to tell Maureen all he knew about it...

'The original farmhouse dates back to the 15th century. It has been wonderfully restored. It has six bedrooms, all with bathrooms and some have terraces, or balconies. There's a barbecue area, a swimming pool. You are going to *love* it, Maureen.'

And as soon as she stepped out of the car, she agreed that she would. The courtyard area at the front of the house was fragranced with a mixture of orange and lemon blossom. The silence, the very air around them, was awesome. And, although it was three in the afternoon, the climate was cool, brought about by a light breeze: pure and mountain fresh.

The house, surrounded by many citrus, olive and almond trees, and with what Miguel told her (with great pride,) very ancient evergreen oaks, was two storied and had an imposing oak doorway set under a stone arch. All the windows that looked over the cobbled courtyard were framed with wooden shutters and magnificent blossoms of purple, sweet scented bougainvillea.

Maureen was enchanted by it all, and threw her arms around her husband's neck, kissing and hugging him with squeals of delight.

Inside the house was cool and fragrant, too. The entrance hall was furnished like a sitting room. Lush plants had been earthed in stone pots, some in copper. A large stone fireplace, its mantel dark oak, displayed a huge floral arrangement in its wide grate. The walls were stark white, a fine backdrop for the many paintings of Spanish landscapes and ancestral farmland. Comfortable looking, dark-red leather armchairs were very much at home on the polished dark wood floor. And further colour had been added by the use of handcrafted rugs and fleecy animal skins. Filled bookcases invited exploring, and on side tables quality magazines were piled aplenty.

The rest of the old farmhouse was much the same. Thick, dark red tapestry curtains hung at most windows. And panels of white voile were also used at the many terrace doors.

The dining room held a gleaming dark oak table that would seat ten people with the utmost ease.

In the kitchen, cream coloured worktops displayed useful utensils, its pinewood cabinets storing groceries in abundance. Two refrigerators, one for food and the other for wines and soft drinks, were well stocked, and a very modern looking oven and hob had obviously been newly installed. The scrubbed pine table (that took centre stage,) was surrounded by ladder-backed matching chairs and, once again, could quite easily seat a large party of people.

Today, for Maureen and Don's arrival, it was set for two with colourful ceramic side plates, dishes and drinking mugs. A large bowl of fresh fruit sat invitingly in the middle of the table and, within an hour of their arrival, both of them had devoured the ripest of plums, the freshest apricots they had ever tasted, the very fact that they were all home grown making them all the more tempting. The lemons in the fruit dish were as large as grapefruit—and both Maureen and Don had said they were looking forward to testing them later with their gin and tonics.

The bedrooms and bathrooms, all featuring white-washed walls, antique furnishing and the snowiest of white bed linen and towels, were mostly on the first floor, except for the master bedroom: this suite, with its huge, ornately carved mahogany four poster bed, also had a dressing room with ample storage space, and the modernist of bathrooms that boasted a whirlpool bath and double porcelain washbasins that were enhanced, exquisitely, by gold plated taps and fitments. Gold plate had been used for further detailing in the opulent bathroom as well. This suited area of the house, situated on the ground floor, had the use of a large open-air terrace that gave access to the garden and the pool.

The house was very well cared for. And its occupants were treated the same. Antonio and Anna, a husband and wife team, kept everything under their control in their roles as butler/concierge, housekeeper/cook. The couple were not live-in, which was a perfect scenario for their guests who wanted a well catered for holiday with privacy included.

'I would much have preferred to stay in this evening, Don. I wish you'd asked me first, before letting Anna go!' Seated at the three-mirror mahogany dressing table that was part of the fine old furnishings in the master bedroom, Maureen tried to mask her annoyance as she called out to her husband.

'I thought it would be nice to eat out, our first night!' Don called back from the comfort of his reclining chair, which was positioned on the bedroom's terrace so that he could watch the setting sun.

She heard him setting his glass of beer onto the small black wrought iron table, and knew he was probably coming back in to the bedroom. She was right: Don entered through the billowing white voile curtains that gave a moderate amount of privacy to their terracotta tiled floor bedroom. He came to crouch at her side.

'Sorry, hon. But Antonio had already made the reservation for us. He thought we'd enjoy dining out, next to the sea. And he said it was the most perfect restaurant. And the village, Cala…something or other, I forget its name, is *spectacular*. I couldn't say no to him, now could I? *Hmm?'* He spoke to her through the mirror.

Applying a second coat of mascara to her eyes, Maureen, with a careful shake of her head, agreed that he couldn't. Screwing the top back onto the eye make-up wand, she sighed, and then leant sideways to rest her head next to Don's.

Seeming to take this as a sign that he was forgiven for not explaining any of this to her earlier, Don took her hand and asked her to join him on the terrace, saying that they had the time—no one ate early in this part of the world.

Seated next to her husband in an identical reclining easy chair that was patterned with lush flowers against a cream background, Maureen sipped her iced gin and tonic that Don, bar tender for the night, had thoughtfully garnished with a thick slice of lemon.

'Isn't it peaceful?' Maureen laid her head back against the back of her chair, savouring the tranquillity of the evening, watching the huge orange sun as it dipped and dropped behind the mountains that looked, for all the world, like the craggy back of a sleeping dinosaur. The silence was peppered every now and again by the tinkling bell that hung from the neck of a lone goat as it nibbled on the stubbly grass of adjoining farmland.

'How did you *find* this place, Don? It's *so* perfect.'

'Oh, some colleagues recommended it. They've stayed here—and thought it would be ideal for us. And it will be, won't it darling?' Don stretched out his arm to catch hold of his of wife's hand as she smiled and nodded her agreement.

They sat so, watching the wondrous sunset paint the sky with vivid colours. There was still not a cloud in sight, and the night promised to be balmy and star studded.

Antonio's knock at the bedroom door announced the arrival of Miguel and the black Mercedes.

As Don helped her into the silk red jacket that matched her strapless, knee length evening dress, he whispered, with merriment dancing in his eyes…'Your Spanish Knight awaits, dear.'

'Good evening, Senor, tonight, no radio, eh? You sing a for me, si? I not know a who you are before. *Now* I know a, I very happy, *very* happy. Senor, you sing, par favor?'

'No, Miguel, I will not be singing. I need to rest to rest my vocal cords. I'm on vacation…*Sorry.*'

Miguel did not seem too *put out* that his request was no to be granted. The Spanish man, who was probably in his late twenties, but looked older, was not shy of his famous passenger, either. His commentary was as non-stop has it had been earlier.

'We soon in de Cala…Maybe it too dark now to see, but it is very butiful…The playas are good: Very good for de swimming. And the restaurant I take you…A very good food…Very nice a people there…'

Miguel's monologue continued, until they drew up alongside the entrance to the restaurant where a table had been reserved for them to have dinner.

As Maureen stepped from the car, a breeze that carried the sea sir caught her face. She closed her eyes, embracing the familiar fragrance. She loved the sea. Had lived close by it for most of her adult life and tonight welcomed its tantalizing haze: she realised with some surprise that sea-smells were the same the world over.

Don also seemed to be exhilarated. Grabbing her hand, he led her away from the entrance to the restaurant and up a short flight of steps that appeared to give access to the terrace. They did. And they also led to a well-lit swimming pool that was graced with palm-fringed umbrellas.

Skirting past the pool, they came to a stop at the railings that guarded the terrace from the sheer cliff drop below.

Even in the darkness of late evening, the huge waves that came crashing and foaming onto the golden sands of the cove were clearly visible. A salty, wind borne spray whispered the air.

'This place must be magnificent in the daytime. What you say we come back tomorrow, and swim, eh? Is it a date, huh?' Don hugged her close as he suggested the plan.

Saying that would be fine with her, Maureen linked arms with her husband as they made their way back to the restaurant's main entrance. Maureen was now more than eager to sample the culinary delights she hoped the restaurant had to offer.

In the restaurant's sea facing dining room, all heads turned as Maureen and Don were shown to their table. Maureen's glossy black hair, her shimmering red dress, complimented her handsome husband's well-groomed silver hair, and his immaculate black dinner suit. They would have made a striking pair even if Don had not been what he was: a famous celebrity.

Excitement rippled the air as seated diners' nudged each, recognising the singer, who was as equally known for the films in which he'd starred.

However, Maureen's anticipation of an enjoyable evening was dispelled when she noted that their table, set near open French doors, was set for four. She was even more indignant when the headwaiter announced that indeed another couple would be seated with them this evening. Don's casual acceptance of all this made her eyes widen with dismay, her finely arched eyebrows nearly touching her hairline.

'*Don…*' She was mortified that Don was going along with all of this.

The maitre d' fussed around her, guiding her into her seat, opening her napkin and gently laying it across her lap, whilst all the time Maureen was trying to get her husband's attention. And failing.

Don, who seemed oblivious to his wife's discomfiture, looked incredulous when she finally managed to make her feelings known.

'Sorry, hon. I'd have said something if I'd known. But what the heck, I'm sure they'll be nice folk…'

The sommelier had arrived at the table and, much to Maureen chagrin, Don accepted the wine menu, slipped on his reading glasses, and gave the listing a thorough investigation

When the drinks had been ordered—an aperitif of champagne cocktails, and to go with the main course a Crianza Reserve, a local red wine from the nearby town of Binnissalem—they were momentarily left alone. Maureen used the time to whisper her utter annoyance with both the restaurant…and her husband.

'I can't *believe* this. There are other tables we could sit at, surely.' She took a second to look around the room, but in honesty, couldn't see an empty table. 'Lets go, Don. I don't *want* to sit with people I don't know. Not tonight. It's our first night here. *Don*, please do something. This is *so* not like you…'

Don's nonchalance towards the situation was really beginning to bug Maureen. And the stares and smiles from nearby tables were also very intimidating. Her husband's offer of his hand across the table, and a simpering smile did little to make her feel any better. In fact it did the opposite: her cheeks flamed, and she felt quite close to tears.

Maureen withdrew her hand, turning her burning face towards the gentle breeze that floated in through the open doorway. The waiters' returned with the ordered cocktails, and a plate of canapés. Out of the corner of her eye, she could see all this happening; being well mannered, she even murmured her *gracias*, but her stomach was not the slightest bit interested in the food or the drink…or husband of six days.

It was obvious to Maureen that Don couldn't care less whether they dined alone, or with others. And this knowledge hurt. She felt even more pained when Don trilled...

'Oh, *here* they are.'

With Maureen's emotions already straining to stay under control, the sight of the couple being ushered across the room, decidedly being lead towards Don, who was now on his feet and grinning, burst the dam of her tears.

Standing to enthuse her own welcome, Maureen had to make use of the pristine linen napkin from her lap to dab at her eyes. The tears were two-fold: relief and disbelief.

Hugs were exchanged. 'Look at you? Don't you look well...' aplenty. Laughter, though not on the menu, was also plentiful. Great whoops of it were given and received.

Taking their seats, the interloping couple beamed their happiness. The small, slightly plump woman, dressed in floating pale green chiffon, her dark hair immaculately cut and styled, sat down and immediately grabbed hold of Maureen's hand.

The tall, stoutly built grey haired man, dressed in evening clothes that were just as impeccable as Don's, took his seat, bellowing his amusement. Shyness seemed to be a word that neither of the pair knew.

Maureen managed to steal a glance at her husband. It was a look of pure adoration. Don saw it, and accepted it with a wide grin and a slight tilt of his head.

The couple that had joined them noticed this, and they too were visibly pleased. It could have all gone so very wrong: Joining honeymooners was not the usual route for meeting up with old friends.

But this surprise had been so well planned, so much looked forward to, the three people who had known of its existence had also been fairly sure it would execute well.

It did. Maureen was shocked but completely delighted to be in the company of her dearest friends: she would welcome Chuck and Mary Lou at any time, and in any place. That they had chosen to meet up with them on the small Spanish island of Mallorca, well, if it puzzled Maureen, she certainly wasn't showing it.

Now, as the four of them drank and ate in complete enjoyment of each other's company, it was if they had never been apart. As if they holidayed together, always.

'So, Mrs Sommer, what do you think of Cala San Vicente?' Chuck leaned back in his chair as he posed his question.

'Is that what this place is called?' Maureen's eyebrows rose again. Maybe she was being kidded, you never knew with Chuck Vicente.

'Yep. It sure is.'

Being kidded or not Maureen decided to go along with it.

'Well, what little I've seen of it, it seems marvellous. And the people...there're pretty okay, too.' Then she had a thought, 'Hey, are you two staying here?'

Chuck and Mary Lou exchanged a quick, furtive glance.

Mary Lou answered. 'Tonight, we are. We're leaving Mallorca tomorrow. You see, Maureen, we've been on the island for nearly a month.'

The enormity of what she was being told sunk in quickly. Maureen felt herself deflate with disappointment. She voiced it. 'You *have*? You were so near to England, then...all this time? Then why on earth didn't you...'

Mary Lou interrupted, knowing what Maureen was going to say. 'Come to the wedding...?'

'Well, yes.' Maureen looked across to Don for backup. But it was not forthcoming. She went on alone...'Yes, Mary Lou. Of *course* I'm now wondering why you didn't attend. For heaven's sake, you were so close.'

'Yes, we were, and that was the reason we thought it best not to come...' Chuck answered, reaching to catch hold of Maureen's hand, stilling the way she was nervously twisting the stem of her wine glass. 'Maureen, listen, hon, we wanted to be a part of your future, not just the *past*. We thought, heck, Maureen, don't look at me like *that*...'

Maureen was indeed looking incredulous at what she was being told.

'Don't make this an issue, Maureen, please, huh? We just thought it best to meet you here. When you were Mrs. Sommer,' Chuck squeezed her hand...'we want to be special friends...to you, *and to Don*. And we wanted it to start here, and *now*.'

Maureen looked from one to the other of the people sat with her round the table. They were all looking a little sheepish, perhaps even a little afraid. She slowly grinned, shook her head: they were right of course, these special people, these wonderful human beings were, as usual, quite right. She watched as, in turn, they caught each other's eye, nodding that all was well...and then shoulders relaxed and laughter came. As it always did when Chuck and Mary Lou were about.

Don beamed his own approval, his eyes sparkling. Maureen leant close to him, her head touching his as they studied the dessert menu in front of them:

what should they have?

When crème caramel for the women, and almond pudding for the men, had been ordered, the head-waiter popped open a frosted bottle of champagne and, amid much talking and laughter, toasts were made: to friends; to family; to life; to Mallorca.

'Before you leave, I hope you will have time to come and see the house we've rented in, er...Where is it, Don...?'

He told her.

'Yes, Font la Mer. Can you come for breakfast, do you think?'

'I don't see why not. We'll come and see your little hacienda—the Casa Blanca, I'm told.' Chuck's eyes were full of mirth, mischief, really.

Maureen could see that Chuck could hardly contain himself...*What was he up to?*

'Yes...the White House,' Maureen answered slowly, as something began to dawn on her...'Charles Vicente. You've done it, haven't you? You've really gone and done it. What are you like? You've *bought* yourself the White House, haven't you...? *Yes?* The villa belongs to you, doesn't it? Oh...my...goodness...'

It was three-thirty in the morning before Maureen and Don flopped into their bed in the *White House*. Exhausted, but very happy, they were still chatting and tipsily giggling over everything that had happened. The evening had been a splendid occasion, a great success, and Mary Lou and Chuck had promised to breakfast with them in the morning.

'But come back here,' they had said. 'Come back to the Cala, have breakfast with us and we'll show you round the village.'

And now, with the warm morning sun climbing high in the sky, Don was driving the black Mercedes down the narrow winding lane that led to the gates of the property and their exit onto the not much wider roads that would lead them back to Cala San Vicente.

Behind them, standing forlornly outside the front door of the farmhouse, was Miguel: from the look on his face it was obvious he could still not understand why the couple did not require his services as driver for the day.

'Please, Senor, let me be driver, eh? The roads here, a very difficult, the car, she like a her master at the wheel, si?'

But Don had been adamant.

'I'll be careful, Miguel, don't worry. We'll be okay. You take the day off. Go see your new son. Play with him awhile. We'll have the car all day.'

From the rear view mirror, Don watched a sullen Miguel mount Antonio's bike and then pedal up behind the car until it was time for him to wave a sorrowful goodbye and turn into the opposite direction heading for his Pollensa home.

Don had been right in his assumption that Cala San Vicente would be magnificent by day: it was. To reach the golden-beached village, they had to travel through the glorious open countryside lanes of Font la Mer.

Entering the village of Cala San Vicente was breathtaking: they were met by the vivid blueness of the Mediterranean Sea and the cove of Cala Clara. The cove, sheltered by a rugged headland, was fringed with honeycomb coloured sand. A few small fishing boats were moored in an inlet.

As the road they travelled came to a T-junction, Don steered the car left, following the curve of the road as it curled like a hairpin towards the top of the headland. Now, surrounded by the hypnotic turquoise-blue sea, it was hard to see where the calm, sun shimmering waters ended and the sky began. They were spellbound, and Don slowed the car for them to revel in the early morning beauty, before they drove on down towards the Cala's second sandy cove, across the small square and then turning left to drive the few hundred yards up yet another rocky headland.

Here, perched magnificently, architecturally triumphant and facing the sea was the restaurant where, once again, they were meeting with Chuck and Mary Lou.

The four friends, clad in cotton shorts and t-shirts, breakfasted on delicious pastries and strong black coffee before setting out to explore the small resort. As they climbed the paved steps that sided the splendid hotel where Mary Lou and Chuck had stayed overnight and which led to the centre of the village, they huffed and puffed, joking about their health and fitness. In truth, it was Mary Lou who was finding the ascent the hardest; Chuck held out his hand to assist up her the final few steps and, as she panted, wafting a hand in front of her face in an effort to catch more air, she voiced that she was going to get fitter—indeed, that she was going to lose some weight. And then, looking at Chuck she boldly stated that he was going to diet, too.

They found the heart of the village to be quite small and easy to explore.

Mary Lou and Maureen stepped under the shade of the gift shop's awning, keeping out of the sun. The shop was also the newsagent. The newspapers racked inside the shops entrance were a couple of days old. Together, the four

286

of them scanned the various headlines that told of world events. One front page held a grainy photograph of Don and Maureen coming out of their wedding reception, looking elegant and sophisticated, nothing like they were looking at present—sucking on quickly melting iced lollipops, pointing and giggling and being thoroughly loud Americans. As the jubilant foursome tried on umpteen straw sun hats and modelled a large selection of sunglasses for one another's amusement, the shy smiles and felicitations of the friendly shopkeepers enticed them to further frivolity.

By ten-thirty their exploration of the village's shops was complete and, sporting new hats, and Maureen a new pair of sunglasses, they called their 'adios' and made their way back down to a palm roofed beach bar, settling at a small white table that was so close to the sea it felt as if they were almost aboard ship.

Served immediately with ice-cold beer, a popular Spanish brew, they relaxed back in their chairs in companionable silence savouring the refreshing drink and at the same time watching a group of young children splashing and squealing as they ran in and out of the lapping tide.

Don was the first to speak, asking what was on the agenda when Chuck returned to the States.

'I'm still very much involved with the big shopping complex project. Seems there's more plans in the offing for future shops and restaurants. And I'm scheduling the building of a new hotel in Galverston.'

Maureen turned to ask her friend Mary Lou some questions of her own. 'Do you think you'll be able to get over here very often...?'

'Sure will. Lydia is flying over when you leave; and Roy and his girlfriend hope to join her, later. We're coming back in September, if all goes to plan, that is. What about you? Will you live in Palm Beach? Or does Don have other ideas?' Mary Lou was aware that *where to live* was a difficult topic with the newlyweds. It had been a problem even before their wedding day.

Maureen turned her gaze to look out to sea as she quietly answered her friend. 'Don wants us to go live in Montport. He'd like us to try living there, for a while, at least. Although he's not actually lived there himself for years.'

'And you're not too enthusiastic about, yeah?'

As Maureen slowly shook her head, Mary Lou glanced quickly at Don and her husband and, when satisfied that both were deeply involved with their own conversation, she said, 'Surely Don knows how you feel?' Getting no reply, she went on, in an urgent whisper...'You've *got* to tell him, Maureen.'

'No. It wouldn't be fair.' Maureen whispered back. She pulled her chair nearer to that of her friends, her back to the sea. 'Leave it be, Mary Lou. Don't worry, I'll get used to it; I really have no other choice...' Maureen frowned a warning glance at her friend. The last thing she wanted was for Don to overhear any of this conversation.

A disgruntled Mary Lou sipped on her beer.

The beach began to fill. Families rolled out blankets to support all the paraphernalia that went with a full day in the sun. Bare-bottomed toddlers squatted, heads touching, earnest in their digging before wet sand, caked onto their small hands, found its way into cherubic eyes, bringing with it blinking bewilderment and wailing cries.

Older children splashed in the rolling frothy waves, their voices an echoing chorus of squeals and laughter.

Men sat on colourful towels, on guard, on duty, protecting their territory, whilst their womenfolk smothered lotions onto the milky smooth young skins of their infants, before turning their attention onto their own skins. These female bodies, soften and rounded by childbirth were in all probability undernourished now by the desire to shed the unwanted poundage—winter hunger pangs had been fulfilled at a cost. But even so, with a swiftness born of embarrassment, flowery sundresses were shed, lotion applied and covering one-piece swimsuits were wrestled into under the cloak of a large towel, and for a few, the begrudged help of bikini-clad teenage daughters...the 'Oh, Mum, do I have to?' brigade.

Ready at last, these same women then lay prone and stony-faced, their eyes following the antics of the lone, long-legged blonde mother-of-four, who had joined her brood, all aged under seven, in the digging of a hole that would find Australia but whom had, in all innocence, found the eyes of most of the men on the beach.

Yet oblivious to all of this, the four friends sat on. The palm roof of the bar was a perfect shade against the glaring heat of the now almost overhead sun. Don, who seemed to be more observant than the others, remarked that the mountain sheltering the right-hand side of the cove had the appearance of a 'Dinosaur on sentry duty.' Lifting their sunglasses in unison, all three agreed. Their attention was then drawn away from the mountain by the sight and sound of a dinghy trying to moor close to the rocky shoreline. Crowded with maybe six or seven swimsuit clad people who had left their sumptuous yacht further out in the bay, the four friends spent an amusing few minutes watching the passengers alight before Chuck said, with a light chuckle in his voice, 'Time to make our exit, folks: The raiding party is here.'

Chuck's joking announcement had the friends on their feet, glasses drained and bags shouldered. It was time for them to take to the sea themselves: the Port of Pollensa beckoned where Chuck's hired cabin cruiser and a crew of two was waiting to take them round the bay to Formentor, and lunch at the resort's world famous restaurant.

The glorious day passed all too quickly. After a sumptuous lunch, they had boarded again and cruised into the port of Pollensa. Being on the luxurious white boat, named *The Shadow* was a perfect way to while away the hot afternoon.

Maureen and Don said that they would like to visit Formentor again before they left Mallorca, and this seemed to be the perfect time for Chuck to tell the couple that the boat and crew were at their disposal for the rest of their stay. He also suggested, to his thrilled friends, that they all take a walk down the tree lined avenue that nestled next to the sea.

As it was nearing five o'clock, he lead them towards a bar that was positioned at the far end of the paved walkway, and here, on a slate tiled patio that promenaded out to sea, a five piece band played and jugs of red liquid graced every wrought iron table.

'Perfect, isn't it? We found this place the first week we were here. Hey, try this...' Chuck poured from the glazed jug, filling four glasses with Sangria, a cold drink that was a mixture of red wine and lemonade blended with sparkling water and, as Chuck informed them, 'Maybe a mere *hint* of brandy...' The potent local punch, choked with sliced fruits, was both aromatic and irresistible.

One taste, and they all agreed that the Sangria was just delicious. And once again Maureen and Don found themselves seated at a table that had the Mediterranean Sea almost lapping at their toes.

Mary Lou sat sipping her drink listening to up-tempo music and also hearing the pride and pleasure in her husband's voice: he was elated to the fact that it was he who had first *found* Mallorca and that it was he who had suggested it would be an ideal place for Don and Maureen to spend their first few weeks as husband and wife. Silently, she blessed him for all that he was. Though they had had their share of difficulties, in the main their marriage had been a good one. And in the past few weeks their relationship had rekindled onto a more loving partnership. The island of Mallorca was definitely responsible for the romance that once again was part of their life.

And to this effect, Mary Lou was as delighted as her husband that they were able to share some of this romance with the younger woman by her side: over the years, Maureen had become more like a sister than a friend.

Now, with departure imminent, Mary Lou was sad to think that these special few weeks had come to an end. But it made her smile to think how furious she had been when Chuck had first muted his desire to come to the island at all...

'Just because you've found a place with a resemblance to your name—it doesn't mean we have to go there, Chuck! Why on earth do you want to travel thousands of miles to some hole-in-the-corner island...?'

Thankfully, Chuck had been firm. With the knowledge that his ancestry was Spanish, he had traced his great, great grandfather back to the Balearic Islands. With the passing of his father, and his own mammoth workload, Chuck had found himself to be overwrought, overworked, and very much overweight. His doctor had voiced his concern and had suggested that Chuck took time out to unwind both his mind and his body.

With Mary Lou decidedly against the trip, Chuck had been unsparing with the truth, 'Look, honey, I need some time out, and it's got to be away from the States. In fact, far away from *everything*—since Pop's death, it's been one long slog. And answer me this, Mary Lou? When was the last time we spent any time together? Just the two of us, eh? I mean *real* time?'

'But the *baby*, Chuck: I want to spend some time with Lydia and the baby.'

And though Chuck had conceded to her wishes—baby Michael was their first grandson, and he was also thrilled by his birth—to Mallorca they had finally come.

And Mary Lou was glad that they had. It had been wonderful to just laze about. Exciting to find and make the farmhouse in Font la Mer a home they could return to again and again. The weather had been pleasant, not too hot, nor too cold. And the lack of humidity was an extra bonus. Not only Chuck's health had improved, so had her own. The local food she had found to be delicious. The mountain air, the tranquil countryside had been so beneficial. And Chuck had slowly started to lose the extra pounds that had been threatening to damage his health.

Now, a good few pounds lighter than when he had arrived, her husband's weight loss, and his new vigour, had made Mary Lou adamant that she too would take stock of own punishing routine of too much work. The entrepreneurial years had been successful: success at the cost of their marriage...nearly. A truthful statement from an old acquaintance, an ex-school friend of both of them, had finally saved their long union from ruination at the hand of gossip.

'Mary Lou, listen girl, I don't know how to tell you this, but honey, I *have* to. Chuck, well, gee, honey, this is hard...he's having an affair.'

Mary Lou had vehemently denied the allegation. And the woman, a true friend, had back-peddled from passing on any further information regarding Chuck's infidelities, of which, according to hearsay, were many.

However, the gossips were right about one thing: Chuck had spent time with many women who were not his wife. And Mary Lou knew of every one. Chuck Vicente's passion was well known to his wife. Chuck was a collector. Her husband collected people in the same manner he collected properties; if he liked the look of them, and they could be put to use, Chuck had no hesitation in acquiring the property...or the person.

With more than thirty years of marriage behind them, Mary Lou knew every foible of her husband. When he had returned from his war years spent in England, Mary Lou had known, even then, that her fiancée would want to return to the people who had taken his fancy. Later, as his wife, they had indeed returned to England, visiting those people and it had not surprised Mary Lou, in any way, that Chuck had made Stuart his target. Chuck Vicente had many qualities and one of these was his ability to motivate others. Years afterwards, it was Chuck who installed into Maureen the ambition to be her own boss. Fuelling her, finding the right premises in which to set up her business. As he had already done so with his own wife: Chuck had ignited Mary Lou's ambitions to magnificent proportions, for wasn't she now the owner of many fashionable clothing boutiques situated near, and within, most premier hotels on America's eastern coast?

And, of course, these shops were managed by elegant and ambitious young women, all enlisted by Chuck Vicente, who thought nothing of approaching a person, either man or woman, who caught his eye. 'Informal management,' Chuck called it. He always head-hunted and would stay by the side of that person until the next challenge came along.

But with these challenges came the accusations and gossip. All of which was unfounded. Mary Lou could and would swear on the Holy Bible that Chuck Vicente had never been unfaithful to her.

Nevertheless, the gossip had to stop. During their month long stay on the island of Mallorca, Mary Lou had brought the matter to her husband's attention.

'You're a grandfather now, Chuck. I cannot keep defending you, looking over my shoulder, explaining to people. Folk will believe what they want to believe…and it hurts, Chuck, it really does.'

Chuck had been dismayed by what she told him. Could not take on board that one and one had been added…to make three. He was in business, that's all.

For a time, the knowledge of his bruised reputation demolished his usual assurance; he'd been shaken by the revelation of what people were saying. He was hurt, too. He avowed to Mary Lou that he was innocent of any philandering,

'Mary Lou, darling, I've never even *looked* at another woman. Surely you know that…?'

'But you have…*looked!* Don't you see, Chuck? It's because you look…and then do something about it, that *all* of this has come about. And you might as well know, even Lydia has asked me…Don't look like that! You spent a whole week in the company of Jane Gulliver…People talk.' Mary Lou had been determined to make her husband see the error of his ways. Especially where this latest collectable person was concerned: Jane Gulliver was indeed Chuck's latest conquest. Undoubtedly she would manage their newest state-of-the-art boutique in Galveston with the aplomb of Cleopatra, for not only did she look like the legendry queen, Jane had the necessary warrior business finesse. Sadly, though, the time Chuck had spent at her side had caused the ripple of gossip that had been just one accusation too far. Mary Lou had had enough…

Now, as she sat beachside in the Port of Pollensa, slightly tipsy from the heady drink, the warm sun of late afternoon mellowing with a golden light the faces of her husband and companions, Mary Lou felt totally at peace and very satisfied with her life. Though saddened that these were her last few hours on the island she had come to love, another potent passion had crept to the forefront of her mind: baby Michael. Mary Lou was smitten by her first grandchild, and couldn't wait to have him in arms again. She was ready to leave.

Arm in arm, Maureen and Don waved until the black car disappeared from view.

The Mercedes, with a happy Miguel back in the driving seat and Chuck and Mary Lou sat squashed between the umpteen packages and gift-wrapped boxes in the rear, sped off into the night. With its trunk also loaded to capacity, the vehicle was heading for the city of Palma where the Texan couple would board a midnight flight that would take them back to the US via

London.

'Will you miss them?' Don's warm breath brushed the crown of his wife's head as he spoke.

'No...' Maureen turned to look up unto her husband's face that was illuminated by the coach lamps that lit the main gate at the end of the farmhouse's driveway. She put her arms round his neck, pulling his face nearer to hers. On tiptoe she kissed his mouth, tasted the wine they had drunk earlier, traces that were still on his lips. Happiness exploded within her; a giddy burst of delight thrilled her thoughts...*He's mine. Don Sommer is mine. Don Sommer...Don Sommer...*

With their arms entwined behind their backs, the newly weds walked the gravel, lantern lit driveway, the sound of crickets chirping being the only other sound save their footsteps. The early summer night was star-lit, warm and balmy. As they stood for a moment or two outside the front door, savouring the mountain air, an owl hooted, and the bell of a lone goat jingled once, twice: A good night call.

But as they stepped inside the potpourri and wood-polished fragranced hallway, closing the heavy front door behind them, both were oblivious to anything or anybody. The kissing began in earnest, the caresses, as they made their way to the bedroom, urgent. The long night ahead of them would be wanton, seductive, tender, loving...and private.

*

27

They were tanned, fit and relaxed. Indeed, they were the perfect example of the old saying—they looked good enough to eat. And Maureen had jokingly asked her husband of six weeks if that was what he intended doing during the love-making that had taken place yesterday morning...

'Every...last...bit,' Don had huskily replied, in between nuzzling the various naked parts of his wife's body.

At the first light, they had woken and had lain in a subdued silence of it being their last day, before reaching for each other, entwining warm, sleep rested limbs that invited and flamed the passionate intimacy they had come to accept as normal. They had enjoyed an idyllic honeymoon. Forty-nine days of love, sun, sea, good food and wines, laughter and unparalleled joy...

They were now mid-air on the long journey that would take them from the balmy climes of Mallorca, to the steaming heat and crowded streets of New York. To Don's Manhattan two-bedroom apartment that overlooked Central Park. Then from New York, maybe as early as one week later, after Don had put the finishing touches to his latest album in his recording studio, they would take up residence in the mansion in Montport, Rhode Island.

Rockfort House...The very thought of the grand house that was soon to become her home terrified Maureen. A perhaps irrational terror that she had not discussed in any depth with her husband; ignoring Mary Lou's insistence, Maureen had still never broached her fears to Don.

Truth was, she was ashamed. Ashamed of her thoughts regarding the house: Elizabeth's house. For that was how Maureen thought of the Rhode Island mansion: Elizabeth's.

As the plane touched down on the tarmac at Kennedy airport, she brushed her anxiety aside in preparation for the onslaught of photographers that came in the wake of Don's travelling.

Wearing the lemon linen trouser suit she had worn at the onset of her honeymoon, Maureen was aware that she had made another mistake regarding her outfit: her clothes would have course be noted by the eagle-eyed journalists who lined the pavements outside the airport terminal...*I must learn that wearing the same thing twice is not acceptable in Don's business...the journalists will make him out to be a miser...*

Thankfully, Jake, who had taken it upon himself to be at the airport to greet the honeymooner's return, had his silver Mercedes parked ready to whisk them from the melee.

'Thought I'd get you out of there quick; it was like a circus. Phew, fame—who wants it?' Making light of the chanting crowd that had pressed itself close to the couple, Jake grinned into the rear view mirror, to be rewarded by a shy smile from Maureen and a thumps-up sign from Don.

'The fame would be okay, Jake, if the paparazzi would just leave us alone! Are you all right, sweetheart? I know it must be hard for you; all the pushing and shoving.'

Maureen, a little shaken by their rushed exit, nodded that she was fine, squeezing her husband's hand to let him know that she was.

'Don't worry about your luggage, Maureen; Jerry will see to it.' Jake successfully manoeuvred the car through heavy traffic, swapping lanes frequently in doing so, negotiating into the fast lane of the Manhattan bound, vehicle clogged freeway, as he spoke.

The three drove on in silence. Maureen was looking out of the window and thinking about Jerry: Don's butler. Jerry was also her husband's valet, driver, housekeeper, some-time cook...Jerry, well, Jerry just was *the man,* invaluable to Don and the singer's lifestyle.

However, unbeknown to Maureen at this time, or to Don, Jerry was retiring. And though Jake *did* know, he didn't say anything. It wasn't his place to do so. Jerry would let his employer know in his own good time...

As Jerry Fontaine had chauffeured the courting couple through the streets of London in the hired Bentley the previous winter, and then again in the spring, he had known, instinctively, that his days of being Don's major-domo were over. And he had been pleased.

Jerry had been by Don's side for over twenty years, and he was more than ready for the break. Ready for retirement. Ready for his cabin in Vermont. A two-bedroom, but very substantial log cabin, that had been made possible by the large salary paid to him by Don Sommer. As long-timed widowed Jerry neared his sixty-fifth birthday his thoughts often lingered on the cabin and the acre of ground that surrounded it

Now he was retiring. Bowing out. And the timing was perfect.

His reasoning had plenty to do with Maureen. It wasn't that he didn't like the new Mrs Sommer. On the contrary, Jerry was quite taken by the quiet elegance of the petite dark haired woman who had stolen his boss' heart. She knew about loss, being a widow herself, and Jerry was sure she was the perfect partner to make Don Sommer happy.

But Jerry was also very much aware that the life the newly weds would be living had no place in it for himself. He was part of the old life. Not the new.

Now, driving Don's silver grey Mercedes, its trunk weighted by the many suitcases belonging to the couple, Jerry barely noticed the bumper-to-bumper downtown traffic of Manhattan. He was on autopilot, his thoughts on his own flight that would take off at the end of the week: A flight that would herald the end of his service within Don's empire. Jerry had taken it upon himself to secure that his replacement would be on hand with immediacy the moment he handed over the baton—or in his case, the keys.

Maureen had only been in Don's New York apartment once before: that was the night before they had flown over to England for their wedding.

The apartment was splendidly proportioned. On the seventh floor, its elevated windows took in all the views Central Park had to offer. And Maureen loved it. Loved its masculine furnishings: the deep burgundy decoration and walnut panelling, the deep cushioned leather suites, polished floors and oriental rugs. Loved its many airy rooms, rooms that were filled with photographs and trophies of Don's recording successes. She loved the apartment because it was Don's home. Loved it for that very reason. And that in itself answered her question of why she didn't want to live in the house in Montport: Rockfort House was *not* Don's home. It was Elizabeth's, and always would be. No matter what Jake wanted—no matter how great the sacrificing gesture, the mansion house could never be her home, or Don's. It could never be theirs.

Since she had known Don (not even a year yet,) he had made it obvious that the house in Montport held little enchantment for him. However, on the eve of their wedding Jake had requested that they share the mansion with him—for them to become a family. Jake had pointed out that he would be travelling extensively with his own work. That being so they would invariably have the house to themselves. When Don had started to decline the offer, Jake had hushed him, saying that it would greatly please him if they would at least consider the suggestion.

Much to Maureen's dismay, Don had done little considering. His immediate answer to Jake's request was an emphatic, 'Yes.'

Weeks later, in Mallorca, she had voiced her unease at his easy acceptance of his stepson's offer. Especially in light of the fact she had known that his first thoughts was of refusal.

Don had stated clearly his reasons for accepting. Reasons that Maureen found difficult to find fault with. Indeed it would have been unforgivable of her to voice further objections.

She and Don had talked long in to the night, sitting side by side under the star filled Mallorcan sky. In truth, Don had done most of the talking, she the listening. Don told her of Jake's childhood. And though Maureen's own childhood flashed through her mind that night, she had to admit to herself that nothing she suffered was as bad as what Jake had endured...

Jacob's formative years had been hell. After the loss of his father he had been enrolled into a military academy. His mother, Elizabeth, had not been callous in doing this: it was a course often thought best for youngsters of privileged backgrounds.

But far from being good for the boy they were wasted years: he endured cruel, even barbaric years under the unequivocal domain of sadistic men.

That the school had finally been closed, it came too late to help young Jake who had lost his father and was soon to lose his mother.

A mixed-up teenager, abused by those whose care he had been placed in, Jake had taken his revenge by ravaging his own body.

Don had traced the absconding young man to a commune on the outskirts of San Francisco urging the bearded and drug-addicted teenager to seek medical treatment and to take his offer of help...

It was at this point in his recall of that dreadful harrowing time, that Don seemed too choked to go on talking. Maureen, who was moved herself by her husband's obvious distress as he reminisced that dreadful era, chastened him not to upset himself any further.

But Don had wanted to tell Maureen everything: he wanted his wife to have first-hand knowledge of what had gone before...

Jake had finally accepted Don's help. And treatment that was just in the nick of time. Jake was hospitalized for over a year: A year in which he lost his mother to Leukaemia. Although Elizabeth's death was a dreadful blow to the recovering young man, who was now technically an orphan, it appeared to be the catalyst of emotion that brought the two men closer.

Don encouraged his grieving stepson to take up writing. At first it was a good way of putting down pent-up feelings, loss, anger, stress, sadness, the things that were difficult to talk about. Later, when Jake's talent became obvious, Don nurtured the young man further. So much further as to write a melody to fit Jake's lyrics. The song, recorded by Don, was an immediate success both is America and Europe.

Five years on, Jake had his first novel published: *A Stranger Stalks Within Us* stayed on the New York Times bestsellers' list for more than nine months. Jacob Adier's own demons stalked no more. They were laid to rest in the pages of his blockbuster book.

Jake's healing was complete. And the affection for the man who had made the recovery possible was ever-growing: Jake made it quite clear, to everyone, that he would always be indebted to the man who had shown the unconditional love and foresight that had been required to save him.

Rockfort House had been left to Jake in his mother's will, along with a vast fortune. Nevertheless, Jake had needed more than money could provide: he needed a base to call home. And he'd had that, by living in the same Manhattan apartment block as Don. The arrangement had worked well: Jake had his own lifestyle, but on the odd weekend or two, would ask Don to accompany him to Montport where, with other invited friends, of both of them, they slowly learnt to enjoy all what Rockfort House and its extensive grounds had to offer...

As midnight passed on that hot Mallorcan night, Don had continued telling Maureen even more...

Jake had become fond of a young woman called Harriett. It seemed as though the young man had found the girl of his dreams. Harriett was a classic New York socialite: brunette, bossy, independent and quite an amusing young woman. They had met at a nightclub, and became inseparable.

However, Harriett had ended the relationship abruptly. Within weeks she was married to a lawyer from Cincinnati. The only contact with Jake was an annual Christmas card which each year would herald another arrival to a thriving nursery.

So, like his stepfather, Jake had been alone, probably for far too long. That he would form or trust another relationship—Don feared that this would not be happening. And the upshot of it all was that he still felt responsible for his stepson.

And how can I go against all I've been told...? These were Maureen's thoughts that night, or, more rightly, that dawn, when they had finally moved off the terrace to the bliss and the comfort of their farmhouse bed...

Every window in the apartment was open, allowing the entry of a slight breeze that was accompanied by street sounds. Sounds, noise, which could only belong to a busy city: Sounds that could only belong to New York.

'Close the damn windows, Maureen! Let the air-conditioning do its work!' Don called from his study.

He heard Maureen walk out of the kitchen, cross the black and white tiled foyer to his study.

'Sorry. Is it too noisy?' She asked the question from the doorway.

Don, who was seated behind his walnut desk, took off his gold-rimmed glasses and smiled at his wife. 'No...it's not that...But these papers keep blowing all *over* the place,' Don pointed to massive piles of opened letters that practically covered every inch of the large, leather topped desk. 'This room always catches the wind if windows are open round the place...and I don't want to close the door...I *like* to hear you moving round, hon. Sorry if I sounded a bit *grouchy;* but it will look as though we are having a ticker-tape parade if this little lot has its own way. Its been flying off in all directions. *Look...*' Don banged his large hands down on to papers that were indeed trying to fly off the desktop.

Maureen smiled at his performance, but looked bemused.

Don felt guilty then, it wasn't as if a hurricane was blowing. The gist of what really was making his so grumpy was his workload...and anything that was making it worse, was getting the flak.

'Okay, then, Don; let's compromise. You stop working say in, what, half an hour, yes? And I'll close the windows. Don, *I* need some fresh air, *before* it gets dark...' Maureen was now leaning against the door frame, her arms folded across her breast, the stance letting her body language spell volumes: she too was getting a bit fed up of being cooped up.

'You're a bossy *broad.*' Don grinned as he rocked back in his chair, his elbows resting on the padded burgundy leather arms of his swivel chair. A walnut framed chair that matched the desk and the other cabinets and book shelves in the well-furnished room.

'Yep, and this *broad* would like to be romanced. We only have a few days left, and you still haven't taken me for that carriage ride through the park.'

'We'll do it tonight. *Promise.* But for now, me darling, I have to carry on with my work—there's letters to be answered, bills to be paid—let alone a script or two to read. I've been away *too* long...'

Don was plied with scripts. The pity of it was, only the odd one or two were worth reading. But he felt that he had to scan everything that was sent to him to be fair to the sender and to himself—and he was always on the look out for that special manuscript. Over the years, the singer/songwriter had appeared in many movies. Most were memorable, even very memorable, but times had changed: most scripts that came his way these days were third rate and often included too much bad language and violence.

The fact of it was that Don wasn't really too concerned whether he ever made another film again or not. Don was happy just to sing, happy to write. His heart had never really been in the movie business.

However, like most successful people, Don was always looking for new material. Always had his eyes open for genius.

But now, albeit it he was this studious and efficient man, he was keenly aware that he had to save time and space for his wife. Though they had been away on honeymoon for many weeks, Maureen was not going to be ignored. And she didn't deserve to be stuck in the apartment, wiling away endless hours whilst her husband worked. They had both planned to take things easy their first year as a married couple. There was still a lot to learn about each other. Don knew he would have to compromise. And in truth he *was* willing.

'Hey, come here, *you...*' his request, his masterful beckoning brought an indolent smile to Maureen's face. She sashayed across the room and onto his lap.

'M*mm,* you feel good.' Don ran his hands up and down his wife's back—as she was wearing a slip of a summer dress, the top part of her back was bare. He kissed her ears, her throat. 'Close the door...' he murmured into her ear.

Maureen laughed as she slid off his knee.

'No! You finish in here, first; Jerry's in the kitchen making something very special for tonight's dinner. You've not forgotten that it is his last night with us, have you, Don?'

'No, I've haven't forgotten. And we *will* go for that ride...later. For now, you are right. Get gone, and let me *get* on. Remove your sassy presence from my place of work, you delectable creature…'

At the doorway, Maureen turned and blew a kiss and then said, 'Make do with that for now, *fellar.* And be quick, 'else I'll go for that ride on my own or, better still, I'll take Jerry. I'm sure Mr Fontaine knows how to treat a *sassy broad.'*

And before Don could summon up a cheeky retort, the door was closed and his wife was gone.

Jerry had not only cooked the meal he had also enjoyed it. Maureen and Don had insisted that he join them at the table he had previously set for two. From the candlelit table, the threesome had unparalleled views of Central Park as it shadowed in the coming twilight.

The ambience in the low-lit apartment orchestrated well with the fine food Jerry had placed before them. Thick juicy steaks, leafy green salads, sour cream filled baby baked potatoes. The finale had been crepe suzette. Jerry's culinary masterpiece had been ladled with brandy and orange liquor, and had left them replete.

Nevertheless, as Don poured vintage champagne into their glasses, they toasted each other with boisterous enthusiasm.

They toasted to Jerry's retirement. They raised their glasses to married life…the best life anyone could have. They saluted absent family and friends. They toasted each other. And, finally, Jerry stood to say a few words about his boss, Don Sommer: He raised his glass to the finest man anyone could work for. He said that he had been blessed to have spent the past twenty years in the man's company.

Tears glazed all eyes as Jerry sat down. But before the atmosphere could become further maudlin, Don made them laugh again by telling them of a child that had been named after him.

'Straight up, no kidding! The guy's named his daughter after me: *Donna Fitzgerald.* I opened his letter this afternoon. Wait a minute…I'll go and get it.'

Don returned from his study waving a piece of paper. Seating himself back at the table, he held in his hand the blue airmail letter he had first read during the afternoon.

'It's a long letter; hang on, where is it about the child…? Ah, yes, here it is. First he wishes me…*us,'* Don nodded his head towards his grinning wife, 'a happy married life. Then he goes on to tell me he has had his own study fitted out to resemble the one I have here, in this apartment, no less. Apparently my fan club members know what every inch of this place looks like...a bit creepy, I know, but there you go. This is what fame is all about. Anyway, I digress. Yep, here it is, I'll read exactly what's written...*I have been blessed by the birth of a daughter. My very own Cathy gave birth to our nine-pound darling two months ago and Cathy has agreed that no other name would be suitable. We are to call her Donna. Donna Fitzgerald. Perhaps you would be good enough to raise a glass to the daughter of Declan Fitzgerald*...Okay, then. Let's do it! Can we be upstanding, lady and gentleman, *please?*'

Giggling, Maureen stood.

With a wry grin, Jerry did the same.

Raising their near empty glasses, they clinked in unison as Don led them into a toast.

'To Declan Fitzgerald's daughter, may God bless her. May her life be full of love, laughter...and *my* music...'

'Hear...hear!' Jerry tossed back the remainder of his champagne.

Maureen added her own salutations, 'To Donna Fitzgerald. May her devotion to Don Sommer be as strong as that of her fathers.' She too drained her glass.

Don followed suit. He then became more subdued. 'Hey, you know what? All kidding aside, I *do* wish my fans good luck. Heck, where would I be without them, huh? Though in all honesty, one or two of them take their devotion too far. He's one of them: *Fitzgerald*. His has cost him a small fortune. Yeah, sure has. He was the fan who paid to see me back-stage at the Castle Theatre. Do you remember...? He was an intense little man...? No, you *won't* remember him, Maureen, because you'd gone to the hospital with Vi. Yep, he was a strange man. Very humble, said he'd collected *every* recording I've ever made. Said he was my truest fan...he sure was old enough for that to be so...Hey, when I come to think about it, hell, he must be old enough to be celebrating the birth of a granddaughter! Still, he was very generous; I'll give him that. And his money will be put to good use in the Leukaemia Fund...'

Don's words altered the ambience around the table.

Jerry stood, collecting the used glasses and dishes.

Maureen excused herself on the pretence of needing to get ready for the carriage ride, which Don had arranged for ten pm.

Don sat on, staring out of the window, his thoughts tinged with emotion;

the melancholy of losing Elizabeth still with him: the impending farewell of Jerry, his loyal employee, who had also been a consistently good friend was very unsettling: Don disliked goodbyes. And, of course, Don was, once again, battling with the thought that he would never be able to father a child himself. It plagued him. It was an emotion he could never come to terms with. An emptiness that he had tried to put down into words; had tried to write music for...and had failed...as he had failed to give life to his own child.

Thankfully, though, Don was not given to too much brooding and, with minutes, he became his old self again, extolling the virtues of Jerry (Jerry was pleased to accept the praise, if it got Don out of his sombre mood,) and at the same time calling for Maureen to be quick if they were to keep their twilight appointment with the park!

The carriage ride, the clip-clop of the horses' hooves, the mellow glow of the park's many lamps brought the romance Maureen had yearned for during her weeks' stay in Manhattan.

Snuggling closer to her husband, she revelled in her extreme good fortune. Her life. And she decided...*no more sad thoughts...for either of us. I'll manage Montport! I'll make the mansion a proper home: I'll make it our home...*

*

28

'The baby's crying…'

'I'm going. I'm *going*…' Malcolm threw back the bedclothes, swung his bare feet to the floor and sighed as he pulled on his dressing gown. Third time in three hours…*why can't he sleep…?* Malcolm Greenwood was finding being a father for the second time round very trying. And tiring. He could not remember Julie being so much trouble. But then, Malcolm had not been a hands-on father when Julie was a baby.

'Shush, son, *hush*, now.' Malcolm lifted his son out of his blue painted cot, urging the six-week old baby to be quiet. 'Do you want to feed him again, Patsy?'

'No.'

'What should I do, then? He's already been changed *twice*.'

'Nurse him.' Patsy turned over, pulling the bedclothes over her ears.

As Malcolm paced the floor, hushing the wailing eleven-pound infant in his arms, he wished for life to go back to normal: Back to the quiet life. That life, with his pleasant natured daughter, his hard working wife and his well-run garden nursery, seemed to be lost somewhere back in time. Sam had seen to that.

A break in the crying brought father and son into eye contact. In the gloaming darkness of the bedroom they stared at one another. Malcolm felt a rush of love...*my lad*...He kissed his newborn son's brow, and whispered his request, 'Samuel Gerard Greenwood, son and heir, go back to sleep, for pity's sake.'

Patsy woke him, and at the same time their son opened his eyes.

'Good *morning*, my darling, precious boy; did your daddy let you sleep in his arms all of the night...?' Patsy cooed baby talk to her son as she gently took him from the pins and needled arms of his drowsy father.

Rubbing his arms to get some life back into them, Malcolm realised that he was stiff all over. His overweight body had been crushed into the white wicker chair since three in the morning, when the baby had finally fallen into a hiccupping sleep. A fragile slumber that Malcolm had not wanted to disturb, and so he had sat on, the baby cradled in his arms.

'Holy Moses, is that the time?'

It was six am.

'You'll not have time for breakfast.'

'Tell me something I don't know...'

'Mornin' Mam...Dad...I've made you some tea.' Julie entered her parents' bedroom with a steaming mug of tea in each hand.

'Bless you, love...'

'You sound like a priest, Dad.' Julie said as she left the room.

'You wouldn't have thought that last night if you'd have heard him carrying on about our Sam's crying...!' Patsy called after her.

'I wasn't that bad, was I?'

Patsy gave her answer to the baby who was suckling at her breast. 'It's a good job you can't understand your daddy yet, Sam, the air in here was as blue as your cot last night.' And with her statement, Patsy pursed her lips and stared in the direction of her husband.

Ignoring his wife's comments, and the murderous look he felt was being thrown like a dagger, Malcolm turned to the wardrobe, dressing himself hastily in his dark green work overalls.

'See you at dinner-time,' Malcolm bent over his wife, who had taken his place in the chair, kissing the top of his son's head and inadvertently kissing the blue veined mound of Patsy's right breast.

'Yer can cut *that* out...' Patsy's diction was always rougher when her dander was up.

'Sorry, love, me mouth slipped…'

'And my hand will slip round yer ear hole if yer don't watch yourself.'

The husband and wife exchange brought with it a mirth that dispelled any tetchiness. Malcolm kissed his wife's lips and felt an overpowering happiness…*I've got it all.*

'It's the christening next week, Jake.'

'Sam's christening? Can I go with you…?'

'That's what I was going to ask.' Beth pulled herself into a sitting position.

'What do you think your Mom will say?'

'Hey, I'm a big girl now, Jake…'

'I know, I know, but it worries me all the same…'

'What *worries* you is what Don will think, right?'

Jake also sat up. 'I don't want *either* of them to think I've taken advantage of you.'

'Have you?'

'What? Taken advantage of you? Is that what you think?'

'No.'

'Good. Because I haven't.'

'And I haven't. Been a big girl before, is what I mean. You are the first…'

'And the last…?'

'Is that what you want…?'

Jake got out of bed and moved so that he was knelt at Beth's side.

'Beth Greenwood, will you be my wife?'

'Yes.'

'*Yes?*'

'Yes…yes…*yes.*'

Jake jumped onto the bed, to the delight of his wife-to-be. He whooped his joy before diving under the covers and smothering Beth with kisses. Coming up for air, he caught his breath and kissed her lips, tenderly. 'You'll not be sorry,' he said, breaking the embrace, momentarily, 'I'll make you the *happiest* woman in the world.'

Beth returned the kisses before answering, 'I *know* you will.'

'Will *they* be happy for us?'

'I hope so.'

They snuggled together, the bedcovers up to their chins.

'So do I. God, so do I.'

'Jake? Are you scared?'

'Of your Mom, *yes...*'

Beth sat up again, to look at him. 'Why?'

Jake folded his arms behind his head; he wanted to answer truthfully, but he knew he would have to take care. 'Because she doesn't like me...'

'Jake! Don't talk stupid. You are so *wrong.*'

'We'll see.'

Beth pulled her knees up under the covers, hugged them to her chest. She sat thoughtfully. 'I don't want to get married sort of straight away...you know what I mean?'

'Yep, I know. And it's *okay*, Beth. Lets keep it a secret for a while, eh?'

'Let's have a long, romantic courtship.'

Jake stroked her arm, 'As long as you like, sweetheart. You're the boss. And it will give *them* time...'

'Mum and Don?'

'Yes. Let's give them a year.'

'Okay. It's a deal.'

They shook hands. Laughed. Beth flopped back onto her pillow, turned to face Jake. 'Now that's settled, Mr Adier...*Junior*...Oh, my, that's awful. We are not doing that to *our* kids. You are the last of the juniors...Hey, big man...let's make love...'

'Are you awake, love? It were our Beth on the phone.'

'Well, then, is she coming, or what...?'

'Yes she is, Sid, and she's bringing that Jake with her...'

'*Who...?*'

'You remember Jake, Sid. He's Don's stepson...Yes, you'll remember him, love, he was at the wedding.'

'Is he still in England, then, Vi...?'

'Must be, love. I'll just pop down to our Malcolm's, to tell Patsy. Will you be all right for a while?'

''Course I will. I'm not a baby, you know...'

'You could have fooled me...'

'It's not my fault I have to be fed.'

'I know, love, I know that...' Vi knew only too well that it wasn't her husband's fault that he had been rendered so helpless through the strokes. But the saving grace, for Vi at least, was the fact that Sid had not lost all his faculties, nor that much of his speech.

'Vi? Does Maureen know about Don's lad...?'

'That he's coming to the christening? *Probably;* why?'

'I just wondered like…if she knew…knew that he was her fellow.'

'Don's lad, you mean? You think he's Beth's boyfriend, or something? Don't talk *wet*, they are just friends, that's all.'

'Am telling you: He's her *fellow*…'

'He's not.'

'He is.'

'And how the devil would *you* know, hey…?' Vi was beginning to feel uneasy.

'I saw the way they were at the wedding…'

'Well, you saw more than I did…'

'I know, Vi…I always do.'

'Listen to your daddy, Donna.'

The two-month old baby gurgled, reaching out her chubby, dimpled hands, pulling at her father's face closer, tugging at his thin cheeks.

Declan put his nose to hers, and gently rubbed it backwards and forwards, and was rewarding with a smile.

'You're going to be a *princess*. Daddy's going to give you the moon, and the stars, me precious girl. Oh, my Donna, you are *so* beautiful. I'm going to ask him to write how it feels to be a daddy.' With his statement, Declan gently tickled his daughter under her chin, and thought to himself…*I'll pay him to do it…*

This very morning Declan had been made aware that his huge cheques had been noted. It had thrilled him.

The baby gurgled again, and then chuckled. It was her first laugh, and Declan, joyous that he was the first to hear it, was overcome with emotion. He had never felt like this in his whole life. It was ecstasy being a father. A daddy to a wonderful little girl whom he was going to give the world to…

'Are you listening, my Donna, the world and *everyone* in it. And I've already started.' Declan tenderly lay his daughter back in her pink-gingham frilled Moses basket, and reached again for the package that he had opened earlier. A pink and white dress, the cutest thing, with broderie anglaise at it's tiny collar and trimming the puff sleeves, nestled between layers of white tissue paper. The small white card that was placed with the gift stated that it was from a Fifth Avenue store, New York. The personal message read: *For your daughter, with best wishes, from Don and Maureen Sommer.*

*

308

29

The Bentley crawled up the gracefully curved, balustrade driveway before coming to a gentle stop outside the columned façade of Rockfort House. And though Maureen's heart lurched in her chest, she said nothing of how nauseous she was feeling.

At her side her husband of two and a half months sat quietly, too. As the hushed ambience of the luxurious car stole around them, neither made any immediate attempt to either speak or to alight from the limousine. *If* Maureen had known that Don's stomach was churning and that his own heart was beating too rapid for comfort, she would have asked to be driven back to New York: with immediacy. Whatever, at this moment, neither knew the others' thoughts.

It was Andrew, the chauffeur new to them both, who opened the rear doors of the car, enabling first Don and them Maureen to step out onto the gravel path that led to the marble portico and massive front door of the mansion.

Lena and Louis Grant, the couple who had been waiting in the shade of the cool portico, and who had been with the house for more than twenty years, moved forward to greet them.

A tight-lipped Lena was the first to speak.

'Good morning, Mr. Sommer...*Mrs. Sommer*...Oh, Mr Don! Can I just say how good it is to welcome you back to Rockfort House.'

Don let go of his wife's hand to enable him to shake the outstretched ones of his housekeepers; he also pecked a kiss onto Lena's cheek before turning to beckon his wife forward to receive her welcome.

Maureen shook the woman's hand, and felt the hostility. Louis's welcome was only slightly warmer. The insincere reception did not surprise Don's new wife in any way. From what she had been told, what she had gleaned, the Grant's, who had lived in Rockfort House for most of their own married life, treated the sumptuous residence very much as if it was their own. Until recently, these employees had been left entirely to their own devices and, though in reality they were only entitled to three rooms, three exceptionally spacious rooms that faced the sea at the rear of the property, they had more or less had the entire house at their disposal. The occasional weekend visits from Jake—and the less frequent ones from Don—had been pleasant interludes into the Grant's contented way of life. Now, that would all change.

In the past week, Jerry Fontaine had answered many of Maureen's questions regarding the housekeepers: she knew that Lena had adored Elizabeth, that she had nursed the sick woman as if she were her own family. Jerry had also told her that Lena liked to have her own way. That she was an excellent cook, a good homemaker, and ruled her husband with an iron rod.

Maureen was also aware that Lena liked to look good. Jerry had said that the woman had a passion for sunbathing...in the nude if she thought no one was about.

'It's lovely, isn't it?'

'It really is, Don. I hadn't *expected* it to be like this. I thought it would be dark and gloomy, for one thing...which, of course, it's anything but.'

'Yes, the house retains its light even mid-winter, and I've seen some cruel winters here, Maureen, *believe* me.'

They were outside, in the grounds that backed the house. The lawns were pristine, the shrubs thick and healthy. Don had steered Maureen to the swimming pool that was sheltered by thick privet hedges. Maureen immediately thought of England: *Funny*...she thought...*how certain things transported her back to the land that had not been her home for years...*

But as she sniffed the air, she realised it was the smell of the greenery that reminded her of hawthorn and holly trimmed country lanes, and the many well-to-do houses she used to pass on her way to school when she lived in

Warrington Clough, Cheshire: Cheshire was a very verdant county; its patch work land and fields were tended to with pride and farmed well.

With the ache of nostalgia for England and times past very much in her mind, Maureen remained silent as Don continued the tour of the grounds, which finally gave way to a pathway that led to the rocky shoreline.

But Don had plenty to talk about, things to show, plans to make. 'You can change *anything*, Maureen. Jake will not mind. In fact, he'll be pleased to see that you are making the house your home!' he gushed.

'*Our* home, Don; *you* will also have plenty of say...'

What Maureen meant, but didn't but into words, was that Don had always very much seen the house as Elizabeth's property. Then, after her death, the house had become Jake's territory. If they were going to have any life in Montport, Don would have to start thinking of the house as his home, too.

When they were back in the mansion, making their way up the grand staircase, Maureen let her husband know what was in her mind. 'Don, there's something I need to say straight away. I have to say it! We are *not* taking over the master bedroom...I think you and I would do best to make just *one* wing of the house our home. That way, when Jake does comes home, he will have the run of the main part of the house. What do you think?'

Don stopped for a few moments, obviously taking stock of what she had said.

Just a stair ahead of him, Maureen stopped, too. She looked down at her husband and offered, 'Sorry, Don, if I've offended you. Perhaps I'm wrong...' she was beginning to feel nervous again.

But Don grinned, and stepped up to join her on the wide and thickly carpeted stairs. 'There is nothing wrong at all, my darling. Far from it: I think it's a *perfect* idea!'

Before Lena announced that she had a light lunch ready for them, Don and Maureen had selected a suite of rooms with interconnecting doors. It was an *apartment* that would soon become known as the Tower Suite because of its position on the first floor section of the house that took in the huge arched window overlooking the front lawns and the gravelled forecourt. However the rooms themselves, three in all: lounge, bedroom and adjoining bathroom, plus a smaller room they would use for storage, also offered magnificent views of the grounds that sided the house, and the one they had chosen for their bedroom took in a glimpsing view of the sea.

After sitting outside on the patio of the dining room where, seated at a dark green wrought iron table they had quickly demolished a delicious spiced chicken salad, a glass of chilled chardonnay and two cups each of Lena's special coffee, Don was enthusiastic about spending the afternoon with the back-and forth task of establishing their belongings in their newly allotted rooms: Louis was roped in to help with the lifting and shifting.

Maureen, after offering to help Don, and was declined, "Darling, you don't know where things are—where they are kept...*you* just relax this afternoon; have a swim; leave it all to us," was further rebuffed by Lena when she had, in a lets-try-to-be-friends gesture, suggested she assist the woman tidy away the luncheon dishes.

Idly venturing back into the gardens, she seated herself next to the inviting looking pool. It was a very hot day, though much fresher than New York. Maureen would have like nothing better than to strip off her cream coloured slacks and her sleeveless caramel coloured shot-silk blouse, put on a swimsuit, and dive into the pool—as Don had released her from an afternoon of grind to exactly do. Yet she rejected the idea. She had already made the blunder of offering her services to the housekeeper—what would it look like if she was caught splashing about in the pool while her husband was left to do the unpacking?

Some hours later, bored beyond belief, she was gingerly exploring the downstairs rooms in the house, when she found Don in the study. He told her that Jake had been on the telephone insisting that his stepfather make good use of this room, too.

'I'll take you down to the basements. We have a recording studio that Jake uses mostly as his office: that's why the study will be *perfect* for me.'

Don seemed *so* happy now to be back; Maureen found herself hoping that she too would soon begin to feel the same way. But she doubted it. Nothing felt like home. And she had spent the best part of the afternoon trying to keep out of everyone's way: especially Lena's.

Maureen was aware that during the long afternoon the housekeeper had run up and down stairs as agile as a teenager, her arms laden with linens and other sundry items that would be needed in The Tower Suite: *her* services had definitely not been declined. And though Maureen had heard Lena chatting, calling amenably to Don and to Louis, the woman had barely uttered two words to her new mistress in passing. Not that she had been rude; on the contrary: Lena had been all smiles and quite condescending when, re-entering the house from the garden she had inadvertently got in the housekeeper's way. The reason for the woman's smugness was obvious: She had dealt herself a winning hand when earlier, after she had poured them their second after-lunch coffee, which was just seconds after refusing any offers of help from the newcomer, Lena had ventured to say, a cunning smile plastered to her face, that the move to the new suite would be no trouble at all; that it was ideal, really, for now she could return Miss Elizabeth's memorabilia back into the master bedroom...where it belonged.

Maureen had noticed that Don had seemed to wince at these words. However, perhaps because he was embarrassed, he managed to avoid eye contact with her in his swift departure from the table, and so it was now, late afternoon, before she had the chance to talk openly and discreetly to him.

The sound proof recording studio was an excellent place for just that. And some much needed kissing. Though Maureen was petulant when she said, 'I feel as though I'm always being watched! Oh, Don, will I ever get used to it? Having live-in staff?'

'Of course you will, darling! Lena and Louis have been round our feet all day because we have only just arrived. Give it a couple of days and you won't even know they're in the house; they are truly very professional, believe me!'

Maureen wasn't too sure that any of that was right. Lena seemed a bossy woman; and an inquisitive one, too. She was also too fixated on her dead mistress.

'Anyway, I'm glad that we are not going to sleep in the master bedroom, Don. Ghosts of the past and all that...' She'd finally said it out loud; her thoughts and fears of living in the shadow of Elizabeth had been broached.

Don's reply was not what she had been expecting.

'I'm glad, too, honey. This house *can* be ours, you know. And we've started right. Don't think that I wasn't worried about Elizabeth's shadow, because I was. But, Maureen, since I've been back, I have to tell you...she's *gone*.' Don pulled her into a tight embrace. 'Please remember this: Elizabeth was a *good* woman. She was kind, thoughtful, and quite a lot of fun...until she became ill. And one thing I know for certain is that she would have liked *you*. So, my darling, let's think and act positive. Jake wants us here: it's a family home; let's make it that! We can, you know, we can. And I'm sure that Beth will love it, too. And Vi...and Sid...and the rest of them when they pay us a visit.' Don kissed her cheeks, her forehead, her lips. He was so obviously excited, and wanted his new wife to feel the same way.

*And, if that's what he wants, he can have it...we'll MAKE it work living here...*Maureen was determined to make her marriage a happy one: But not at any cost. And she was still unsure about a couple of other things, and if

313

there was a time to air them it was now…

She was straightforward with her request, 'Don, I don't want to sell my Palm Beach apartment.'

Don hugged her, firmly. And agreed. 'Okay, if that's what you want. It will be a good base for visiting with Beth, her place is far too small for the three of us, anyway.'

Now for the next: 'And I don't want *you* to sell the New York apartment, either.' She was worried she'd gone a bit too far.

'You being a bossy *broad* again, by any chance, Mrs. Sommer?'

They both laughed.

'Yep, sure am!'

'Well, okay then, so be it! Your wish is my command, oh mighty one. But you do have to do one thing for me, right…?'

Maureen felt a chill of unease climb up her back, even though Don's warm hands were round her waist. 'What?'

'Sell the salon.'

'Sell *my* salon? Why…?'

'Because you will hardly be there.'

'But Vera can manage it. *Does* manage it…and well!' Maureen pulled away from Don, but he grabbed her hands and kept her close.

'Hey, don't get upset. It's just that Vera would do better *buying* it.'

This time, Maureen managed to get out of her husband's embrace. She took a step backwards, leaning against a filing cabinet, she flared, 'How can you say *that*. You don't *know* that's the case at all…'

'I do, because I've asked her.'

'*When*?'

'Last week; when we were in New York.'

'Why didn't you *tell* me she'd rung?'

'She didn't. I rang her when you were out shopping for that baby stuff…'

'*Don…*'

'I did it for the *best*, Maureen; you wouldn't have broached the subject with her, would you?'

'No. Because I don't *want* to sell! To Vera or *anyone*…' Maureen felt tears prickle behind her eyes. She couldn't believe what Don had done behind her back…'Oh, Don! I spent *years* building that business…the clientele base…'

'And now you can have *years* to do what you like. No more working long hours. You will have enough to do just being my wife…' His statement seemed to echo in the air. He did have the good sense to look contrite. He murmured that he was sorry. That he hadn't meant for it to come out that way. Of *course* she could do what she liked. If the beauty shop meant so much to her, *sure* she should keep it. It was just that being married to a singer, she would spend many months on the road. Travel came with his job. And he had thought Maureen had planned to travel with him…

In all honesty, Maureen had given the latter little thought. What with the excitement of the wedding, the selling of her house, the adjusting to live in her Palm Beach apartment, and then their long honeymoon, Maureen had not stopped still long enough to think what the future—married to an international singing star—would entail.

They both stood in silence. Don, the first to move, began turning off lights, readying for them to leave the recording studio.

Maureen, not wanting this, their first day at Rockfort House to be embedded in their minds as the day of their first real argument, said, without much conviction in her tone, that she would give the matter some thought.

'All I *ask* is that you think on it, Maureen. And it's no hardship to know that you have a ready buyer…now is it?'

As they made their way up the back stairs, Maureen knew what she would do. Hadn't it already been arranged? And, for the first time, she felt well and truly married…*From now on I will always have to think of another person's welfare before that of her own*…Being a widow had been awful. But the truth of it was, she had been in command of her own day-to-day affairs. Now all that had gone. In front of her was a dream lifestyle, the envy of many: and she would have to get used to living it.

The wood tread spiral stairs, leading from the basement recording studio, emerged into what had been a conservatory: When Elizabeth and her first husband had purchased the grand house, the conservatory—the *Glass House*, as it was then called—was often too cold to sit in during the winter months and far too hot for much usage in the summer. Alterations had been made: the room was now banked by large picture windows to the rear and the side glass had been replaced by walls of sand coloured stone. Two stained glass arched windows, which were set into the rustic stone, were responsible for the kaleidoscopic dazzle as the afternoon sun came peeking through. Tall potted palms, cane furniture cushioned with floral fabrics; glass topped tables (now laden magazines and monthly journals,) gave the room a European air, and the cream and terracotta tiled floor, covered by rush-weaved rugs, further enhanced this feeling. .

Today, with the huge wooden fan, which hung high in the cathedral ceiling, doing its job, the *Sunroom*, as Maureen was just being told that this room was now called, was very inviting.

Don, seeming to have gotten over their spat very quickly, appeared to be thoroughly enjoying giving his wife a history lesson on her new home as he opened the French doors and bade her to follow him out onto the terrace.

The terrace, which ran the entire length of the back of the house, was surrounded by a white stone balustrade, which, at three intervals, gave access to the gardens. Maureen was pleased to hear that every ground floor room, except the kitchen, had access to this paved area: a promenade setting for the magnificently shaved lawns.

Maureen liked this aspect of the house. Having lived the best part of her life in the sunshine state of Florida, she enjoyed being in the open air: most days, when she had lived in her Larson house (and at this moment she felt the tug of wanting to be back there,) she had spent time either at breakfast, or later in the day at dinner, making full use of the patio and decking area of her neat back garden.

As it neared five o'clock, the housekeeper appeared at the open doorway of the library announcing that afternoon tea was ready to be served: and would they be taking it inside or out? If out, she would pull down the awning.

Don, making his response without asking Maureen's preference, said inside would be just fine.

Lena seemed pleased: she had already set it out in the library. 'Well, then, I'll leave Mrs. Sommer to pour, shall I? You, *Mr. Don,* have a telephone call to return: Mrs Howarth. She phoned asking if you could arrive earlier than planned. She has people she would like your, er, *wife* to meet; and she says she would like to do it *before* sitting down to dinner...I said you'd ring back; let her know if that is possible.'

Maureen did pour the tea. But she ignored the plate of pastries, as she herself had been ignored (even Don had not excused himself as he left the room with a chattering Lena by his side.) Taking her cup of tea with her, she walked outside feeling utterly miserable, and to be honest, tearful: she was not at all looking forward to the dinner party that had been especially arranged so that Don's new wife could be launched into the Montport social scene.

Their hosts this coming evening, Julia and Ben Howarth, a couple who had always been extremely good to Beth, were their nearest neighbours here on Rhode Island. The busy pair spent most of August and September in their

Montport home. It was something that Maureen had felt thankful for—she liked all three Howarth's very much, and the thought of them living so close, if indeed for only a short period of time, was both comforting and pleasing.

But now, with the late afternoon sun warm on her face, as she stood gazing over the lawns, watching the busy gardeners clip the privet hedge that surrounded the swimming pool, she felt close to despair, and quite out of her depth. She felt outside of herself: lost.

The past months she had spent with Don had been superb: he had been easy, loving, generous and totally loyal to their commitment of one another. He had been a joy. It was only when they had arrived in New York that she had begun to see another side to his character: Don was making very little changes to his lifestyle. It was *she* who was making the changes: and most of them were being foisted upon her: she appeared to have little say in anything that mattered; her whole life was altering, drastically.

And change did not come easy to Maureen. It was, and always had been, something she feared. That the voice at the back of her mind (it was haunting her again) didn't help matters much, either; it was so invasive and tantalising: irritatingly familiar. Almost recognisable, but at the same time as distant as a radio programme tuned with the sound too low...*God, it drives me mad at times!*

It didn't help that she was also missing Beth: This was the longest time they had ever been apart; England had the strongest pull on Beth's career for the moment, which was, of course, a splendid accolade for her daughter's future in the music business. But though she was pining for her only child, Maureen would never let any one know this...*what would it look like? I'd come across as an overbearing and possessive parent*...And she could honestly say to herself...*I have never been that...!*

As she made her way upstairs to get herself ready for the dinner, Maureen thought...*maybe having Jake around will be okay, after all*...But she knew that for now Jake's arrival would not be forthcoming—it seemed that England was indeed the flavour of the day, though Maureen had no idea what Jake's real reason for being Europe-based entailed: the daily telephone conversations had been between stepfather and stepson. Since the wedding, Jake's messages of 'Best regards to Maureen' had been relayed *via* Don.

'How's your beauty *empire* these days, Maureen?' Ben Howarth's eyes twinkled with mirth. Even after just a short time in Maureen's company he knew he could breathe easily around her. Knew she had her feet planted

317

firmly on the ground—and could take a bit of jesting.

Earlier in the evening, Ben had made sure that he was seated next to Don's new wife. Having known Beth for many years, through the special friendship with his own daughter, Sonia, Ben had spoken on the telephone numerous times to her mother but, until tonight, they had never previously met in person.

When Maureen had walked in, on the arm of her husband, Ben realised that he would have known her anywhere: her photographs did not do her justice—she was the image of Beth and, perhaps, even more beautiful.

'Empire indeed! That would be the day…Ben, you *know* I only have small salon; my clientele could easily fit around this *table*.' Maureen, too, was pleased with the seating arrangement: delighted that Ben was her dinner companion. Beth had said that he was a good man, great fun, and now, after being in his company for the past hour or so, Maureen heartily agreed: both her hosts had gone out of their way to make her feel comfortable tonight. The other couples seated round the table, five to be exact, seemed to be enjoying the night just as much: it seemed that Julia and Ben chose their friends with care. The evening so far had been a great success.

'*Any* business, *any* size is an empire these days, Maureen…the lists of what you can and can't do, who you can hire, who you can fire is getting to be like a business itself. We all need to be as clever and as canny as lawyers to survive…'

Maureen, thinking back on her distant troubles with training Vera, and of how she had had to grovel on a few worrying occasions when a dissatisfied client (usually the type who had gone against advice and had made a wrong choice of hair colour, etc.) had made un-just claims that the salon was 'badly run' and 'inefficient,' nodded that Ben was probably right: being in business, you had to think on your feet and have powers of persuasion that was sometimes taken to breaking point; making a wrong decision could be costly. Making a right connection was what business was all about. Maureen had to agree: Ben did have a point—whatever business a person was in, it *was* their empire.

'Whatever, what I am really saying, Maureen, is that *you* are probably very good with your customers: people are your business. Yes?' Ben sipped from his wine glass whilst waiting for Maureen to answer.

'I *listen,* Ben, if that's what you mean. You *have* to in my profession. And I do give advice, if it's asked for. But, hey, it's only concerning their hair colorants and perms.'

'So, then, if they trust you in advising them how they look, they could possibly trust you on other judgements...get my drift?'

'Not necessarily, I think in the main people should be left to make their own judgements, look after the own affairs. I think advice can be taken two ways...like it could be good for the person who proffers it, but quite catastrophic for the person who asked.'

'You seem to have specific thoughts on the matter...'

'I suppose I have. The person who advised me to open my own salon, and I must add that, in reality, it was good advice...well, this person, these *people*, actually, because there was two of them, well they advised what they knew *they* could be good at...I was the guinea pig. Don't get me wrong...I've loved every minute of being in my own business; well, mostly!' Maureen laughed lightly, shaking her head, remembering some of the downsides: especially the tired legs and aching back of standing all day. 'But, Ben, the friends who gave the advice soared at doing *exactly* what they got me to do first: Theirs was done on a grander scale.'

'So...then, what you are saying, Maureen, is, perhaps, that folk *use* each other in the guise of counsel, hmm?'

Thinking on the profoundness of this last question, Maureen sipped on her chilled Chablis before answering. 'I've never thought about it like that before, but *yes*, I suppose I am.' Maureen was so deep in conversation with Ben, she didn't notice Don's frown.

Don, who'd been placed opposite Maureen for the candlelit dinner, had been watching his wife most of the evening. And by the look on his face he had not like what he had seen, or what he had heard.

Ben saw this, and made a quip that was voiced for more than Maureen's ears. 'Maureen. *Forgive* me. I think my recruiting skills have been *snared.*' He patted her hand, consolingly, nodding a truce across to Don.

'Recruit...?' Maureen was puzzled. She too looked to Don.

'He wants you to campaign for Julia.' Don didn't beat around the bush. It wasn't and never had been his style.

'*Me*?' Maureen's question was said loudly. The buzz of conversation that had been babbling on around them ceased.

'Yes, *you*, Maureen! Ben doesn't waste time, not when there is an election on the horizon...'

'Don, really! You make Ben sound so *callous*.' Julia, seated next to the singer, rounded on him.

'He could have waited, that's all. A day, at least!' Don retorted, his eyes steely with annoyance.

'There's no problem here, Don. Ben and I have been discussing my life, not *Julia's*. Julia was never even mentioned…' Maureen spoke across to her husband louder than she intended. She was *so* angry. And because of this, she had inadvertently insulted her hostess. Don had caused a scene for no apparent reason. The conversation with Ben had been very pleasant. She had found his openness refreshing. And as for Julia—Maureen already knew of the woman's campaign to become Governor, and had already pledged her own support through other channels: *Beth.* Tonight or any night, she did not need Don telling her who and who not she could speak with; nor the content of the conversation. She was livid.

'*Whoops*…! Sorry, Don, if you think I've come on a bit *strong*. But I'm sure you can see that Maureen wasn't offended; so lets drop it, hey? Now then, shall we move on outside to the terrace. Brandies, port, anyone…?'

It was a beautiful evening, the sky an ebony black, the air carrying a soft breeze.

Maureen, who had excused herself from the dining table after the diabolical display of bad behaviour from her husband, now made her way out onto the terrace after spending a good few minutes in the ground floor bathroom that had been designated as the ladies powder room for the night.

'Here she is! What would you like to drink…? Brandy, cognac…champagne?'

Ben escorted her to the marble topped table where Don was already seated, and in conversation with a couple who had previously been sat at the opposite end of the dining room table; a couple Maureen had barely spoken more than a few words to other than when they had been first introduced at the commencement of the evening.

Don stood, and with a hand to her elbow guided his wife to the vacant, yellow and cream striped garden chair, positioned next to his own.

'Sorry…' he whispered into her right ear as he helped her to settle, taking her handbag and placing it under the white wicker chair.

Maureen smiled at her table companions, looking about her and liking what she saw: the long terrace, similar to the one at Rockfort House, was lit by torch candles and the effect against the white stone pillars that supported the white wrought iron of the terrace's veranda gave the setting a Roman inspired ambiance.

As she ordered a glass of champagne, Maureen thought how well her dress fit in with the surroundings: a dress she had bought whilst in Madrid. The white crepe de chine halter-neck evening gown was ankle length and very flattering against her deep suntan. Tonight, with her black hair swept back by a gold and white velvet band, the small diamonds at her earlobes her only jewellery, she knew that at least she had made the right impression with her clothes...*but heaven knows what my companions think of my earlier demeanour*...

Don, who held on tightly to her hand, openly, on the tabletop, was dressed in a white dinner jacket over an immaculate pale blue shirt, that was now, because of the warmth of the summer night, open at the neck. Maureen was aware of the fact that Don, as usual, would look perfect in any setting. And his conversation, which he was making every attempt to bring his wife into, was both confident and entertaining.

With her annoyance with him somewhat abating—he made no fuss about telling John and Sadie (Maureen could not remember the couple's surname,) whom they were now seated with, that he would have to watch out for his jealous tendencies in the future. And this very open apology (he had brought her hand, that he was still holding, to his lips and said "sorry," for all to hear...including issuing a nod in the direction of Ben, who had accepted the reparation with an incline of his own head together with an exaggerated salute.) and due to the fact that it had been Julia herself who had also made her excuses to leave the dining table, in hot pursuit of the guest she feared was close to tears, Maureen felt herself begin to unwind...

Maureen had been very close to tears: she had fought back the urge to weep with humiliation. After excusing herself, and hurrying from the dining table, she had become somewhat at a loss in the hallway of the enormous, chandelier lit house. There were so many doors leading off the opulent foyer, that she could not remember which one opened into the ladies' bathroom.

But Julia had been close at hand and, linking her arm through her Maureen's had led the way.

There, whilst Maureen repaired her eye make-up, Julia had asked whether or not Ben *had* offended.

'Certainly *not*.' Maureen had stated, looking back at Julia through a large, crystal framed mirror of the cream marbled bathroom. 'Don's the offender! He made me feel so *stupid*.'

Julia had been very frank in her own condemnation. 'Don't worry, honey. Everyone knows you are not. And if *anyone* is to blame, it's me, I'm afraid...'

Maureen had turned to face Julia and, taking in the woman's own style—

Julia wore a sleek, midnight-blue, ankle length shift dress, that was as conservative as it was elegant, and complimented the dark blonde hues of her hair, and the startling blueness of her kind eyes—had wondered why on earth her hostess would say such a thing.

'It's true, Maureen, it's *my* fault. In defence of Don, he was looking-out for you. Ben can be *so* tactless! And you see, Maureen...I had set Don's guard by something I mentioned to him within *minutes* of you being here tonight. And Ben had heard what I said, too. So, here goes: It was *I* who said you had the right potential...the right attitude for the campaign trail. Sorry, Maureen—it was thoughtless and selfish of me. And Don was quite right; you shouldn't have been being *sized* up! Not that Ben was actually guilty of doing it. Like I said, it was *me*...I'm afraid it got Don's back-up, and poor Ben, and *you*, got the flak...'

They had spent a further ten minutes in chat, Maureen assuring Julia that no offence had been taken; they had then turned the conversation to their daughters both confiding that they hoped and prayed that each girl would find the right man to settle down with. Julia had also been emphatic that Beth was a delightful young woman, a daughter to be proud of. She also said that she wished Maureen and Don "every happiness" in their new life together.

Again linking her arm through Maureen's, Julia had escorted her back from the powder room and into the company of the other guests seated outside in the balmy, hot August night.

Now, with Don's apologies ringing in her ears, champagne on her lips and the grand golden *Roman* ambiance wafting the air, Maureen felt a thrill run down her spin....*Julia thinks I'd be a good asset in helping her achieve high office...wow!*

Music filled the night air. Don beckoned her to her feet. Everyone applauded as they danced. Whistles, stamping of feet, and calls of 'best wishes for a long life' accompanied their steps. Maureen felt radiant, and as if her life was finally taking on another dimension. She was also aware that she had taken back control of her own destiny.

And as she danced into the early hours, fear and loneliness became a thing of the past. Maureen felt alive...Truly, alive. And so much in love...

'So, the christening went well, then? Did Patsy like the outfits I sent over for Sam? Good. I'm glad the weather was fine. Even August can be cold and wet, in England, you know. Pity that the newspapers got wind of it. Were they great pests, the photographers? I know, I know; no matter *how* accommodating you are, they always want that one more...On the whole, I think you treat them well, love...Just remember, you are not completely public property! *What*? Jake was with you? Oh...' Maureen swallowed hard, and gripped the receiver closer to her chin, 'I thought he was in San Francisco...Oh, The Cotswolds...Did you go with friends...? Just Jake...Oh, right...No, love, there's nothing the matter...*I sound funny?* No...' Maureen swallowed again, the palpitations of her heart making her feel faint...'no, I'm not unwell, I'm fine, darling...Just tired, we've travelled so much, recently...By the way, Beth, I'm selling the salon...Yes! It's true: Vera's buying it...Of *course* I'll miss it. But Don seems to think I'll have little time to spend...No. I'm not *too* bothered. Not now. What I'm not *sure* about is living here...yes, *darling*, I *know* you love it...' Maureen laughed at her daughter's exuberance regarding life in Montport, 'guess I'm just a Floridian country bumpkin at heart! So, tell me, is Jake still in England? New York! Yes, oh, all right. That's *great*. When will you be there? Sunday...? Do you want to stay in the apartment? You can get the keys from...*what*? No, Beth, absolutely not! *No way*...Beth, you can't stay with *Jake*...*Why*? Because you can't! People will talk...It's not right, sweetheart...what do you mean, "you're a big girl now"? Please listen to me...thank you...*thank you, darling*...No, it's not because I'm old fashioned...Just being sensible, that's all. No, nothing...Beth, I have *nothing* against Jake. For goodness sake, Beth! Aren't I living in his *house*? Okay, you're right, let's not argue...it's stupid, yes. Wow, a screen test for Disney! Fingers crossed, then. Ok...okay...give my love to Aunt Vi, Uncle Sid...Tell them I'll speak to them at our usual time...Bye, bye, my love...Take care...Yes, Don's just fine...Love you, too...'

Maureen sat staring out of the bedroom window for a long time after replacing the receiver into its cradle. Her heart had finally stopped banging, though it still felt heavy. Loaded with doubt...*Beth, Beth...no, please...no...*

Maureen's thoughts were troubled by the telephone conversation with her daughter. Her anxieties were increased further as she watched Lena Grant practically skip across the lawns that graced the rear of the house. The housekeeper, tall and stately and hardly showing any signs of her fifty-five or so years, appeared more the mistress of Rockfort House than Maureen could ever be. And in her subtle way, Lena had made it quite clear that she was aware of this fact herself.

It was nothing that Maureen could put her finger on, no insubordination, sneer or bad looks of any kind: Lena undertook all her duties with aplomb.

But, nevertheless, the housekeeper made it quite apparent that Maureen did not deserve her respect: that she was not moneyed. And money was what Montport prided itself on: Old money. Class. No flashy clothes, no really flashy cars (Bentley and Rolls were just part of the scene.) Good stock. That was essential. To be well bred and moneyed was what it was all about. The newly rich were merely tolerated. And the servants and staff knew the difference between the old and the new. Lena Grant was going to tolerate the second Mrs. Donald Seymour Sommer. And that was all.

With this knowledge firmly installed into her brain, Maureen moved from the window, picked up a pen and a note pad from her side of the canopied bed, and began furiously writing down a list of changes she wanted to make to the rooms that would be known as their apartment: it would be a home within a home, and Maureen's only chance of surviving being here in Montport at all.

Two hours later, when she joined Don for afternoon tea, a ritual that was always served in the red-flock wallpapered library on the dot of five, Maureen informed her husband that she had made earnest plans to make Rockfort House their home. And, further more, she was also going to assist Julia Howarth in her campaign to reach high office.

This latter news brought a wary smile to Don's face as he sipped his Earl Grey tea.

But, not wanting to jeopardise Maureen's newly found commitment to living on Rhode Island, he said nothing.

Following suit, Lena, who had been in earshot of the two pieces of news, also remained quiet; after all, it wasn't the housekeeper's place to say that no matter what plans the new Mrs. Sommer had, no matter what changes she did to the house, or to Montport itself, if it came to it, she would never belong. As the interloper would find out, soon enough...

*

30

'She quit, Mary Lou…just like *that.*' Seated next to her friend, Maureen clicked her fingers to emphasize her words.

'And now Beth thinks Jake would be a good manager? Is she *sure* that's what she wants?'

The waiter had brought a fresh pot of tea to the table; the conversation between the two women was silenced whilst he poured.

Maureen took a sip of her tea, which Mary Lou noticed she had started to take with lemon. It was obviously too hot, and she winced. Placing her cup back into its saucer, Maureen answered truthfully that she had know real idea what was going on at all, or how her daughter felt about anything.

'Oh, Mary Lou, I just don't know. I don't seem to know anything, anymore. Cynthia has been with Beth for so long, it's hard to come to grips with what she is doing. And I *still* can't believe she can let go…leave it all behind: It was her…*life.*'

Mary Lou had never seen Maureen so agitated. Had never noticed the lines, dark smudges that now ringed her large blue eyes: Maureen had aged, drastically, and in a few months…*If this was being married to a super star…forget it.*

'You can't blame her, not really. I mean Cynthia has always been up front; she never hid the fact that she was on the look out for love. She was man *mad*. We *all* knew that. Now she's got what she wanted…She got her man.'

'But, Mary Lou…Fernando is so…*old.*'

Mary Lou had to laugh. 'And so*oo* rich…'

'No. She says she loves him.'

'Well, Maureen, maybe she does. Maybe she *wants* to live in Argentina. Maybe she is a cow-girl at heart.'

'Bull!'

At that, both women started giggle, reaching for their teas to smother their mirth. After all, they were in the one of New York's most elite hotels: afternoon tea here had to be reserved months in advance. Unless, of course, you name was Don Sommer.

Maureen's humour was short lived.

'What *am* I going to do, Mary Lou? I hate the idea of Jake being her manager.'

'The idea? Or Jake? Which is it, Maureen?'

'What do you mean?' Maureen reached for her teacup again: a crutch, as far as Mary Lou could see…

'You really dislike Jake, don't you?'

'No.'

'Then why does the possibility of him becoming her manager bother you so much? Come on, Maureen…I've *never* seen you like this before…'

Maureen was saved from having to explain her feelings to Mary Lou by the arrival of their husbands: a late arrival and another reason why Maureen was so worked-up this November afternoon.

The two couples had agreed to meet in New York for the earlier part of the week prior to Thanksgiving Day.

Don had been so excited by the prospect: Chuck Vicente had invited him into a business venture: an apartment block facing the beach on the fringes of South Miami. Don was thrilled by the partnership deal—his first venture into the business world. And one that was sure to be a guaranteed triumph: Chuck Vicente's name was synonymous with success.

Whilst the two women had spent the cold wintry morning shopping, the men friends had been ensconced in a warm lawyers' office going over and finalising details on the documentation.

Maureen and Mary Lou had whiled away the best part of an hour waiting for their men folk. That the afternoon date had been Don's idea in the first place, Maureen was festering a grievance: her husband was well aware that she was loathsome to all these afternoon-tea drinking rituals. The fact that he was late, and, from the wide grin on his face, late without a care in the world, infuriated Maureen more than she was already...*Don couldn't care less about anything other than himself...six months married and he thinks nothing of standing me up for hours...*

However, as Mary Lou was giving her eye contact, that spoke volumes, Maureen smiled a welcome, though her thoughts remained anything but agreeable...*what the hell is Cynthia thinking of, leaving us in the lurch like this...! Why would she ever want to marry a sixty-nine year old Argentinean rancher...? And what's Beth playing at? Jake Adier to take Cynthia's place...? Never...*

It was the following day, Thanksgiving Day, that Maureen's anger finally exploded.

Seated at the long, refectory styled dining table in the Manhattan apartment that she loved so much, and in the company of Don, Beth and Don's stepson, Jake, her fury was stoked to full blaze as the last mouthful of turkey was being swallowed.

'What do you mean..."So you can be together more"...?'

'Just what I said, Maureen. Beth and I enjoy each other's company. And I *know* the business, far better than Cynthia did as a matter of fact; do you know that Cynthia had no real contacts in California, for instance?'

'And you have, I suppose?'

'Mum!'

'Yes, actually, Maureen, I have *plenty*. And it's what Beth needs right now...'

'Don't *you* tell me what Beth needs, *young man*. Because I'm telling you that she doesn't need a bunch of half-crazed...*hippies* meddling in her life...'

'Steady on, Maureen...' Don stood, throwing his white linen napkin onto the table and walking round to stand at the back of his wife's chair.

'I don't need your help to move away from the table, Don...But I do need help in keeping...*him*...' Maureen jabbed her right index finger into the air, directly in front of Jake's face, '...away from my daughter!'

Beth began to cry. Lowering her head, her tears fell silently.

'Maureen! Enough! Come into our bedroom...you've gone too far with this...'

From behind her chair, Don grabbed hold of his wife's arm in an effort to persuade her from her seat. She pushed him away. But stood anyway.

'Tell *me*...' she looked across the table to where her daughter sat next to Jake, '...are you...lovers?'

Beth lifted her head, a look of defiance on her face as she said, 'Yes.'

Maureen flopped back on to her seat 'I knew it...I knew it...*Knew it*...'

Don stared at his stepson, at his stepdaughter. 'Is this true?'

Jake answered. 'Yes, Don, it's true. I love Beth...' he reached for Beth's trembling hand, '...and Beth loves me, too. Tell them, sweetheart, tell them.'

But Beth wanted to speak to her mother, only...

'Mum? Why are you being like this? Hey? *Why*, Mum?'

'*Why*...? After all I've done for you! All the *sacrifices:* All the time and money spent on singing lessons...dancing lessons...driving you here, there...working long hours in the salon. Never going out...never having a date: ALL FOR YOU! And now...*now* you tell me you have taken up with this...*degenerate*.' There was spittle on her lips.

'Hang on a minute, Maureen; this has gone far enough...'

'Shut up, Don! It's got nothing to do with you...She is *my* daughter.'

Don walked out of the room.

Beth and Jake stood. Jake put his arms around Beth's shoulders as they moved away from the table, Jake whispering soft, comforting words, ignoring the stony faced Maureen who sat perfectly still.

Then they were gone. And Don slammed the front door hard, as he also left the apartment.

It was three am. Maureen heard Don re-enter the apartment. She lay rigid, fully dressed on top of the bed she had only recently so lovingly shared with her husband. Now, Don failed to even open the door of the room.

Dry-eyed, she lay for hours, seeking solace. Seeking guidance: *Dear God...please help me...Please show me the right way...*

Maureen lay awake all night long. And throughout those long winter hours she knew that she was wrong. Knew that God could not help her. That Don could not help her. And she also knew that she had lost her daughter.

As the dawn crept across the sky outside the tall windows, Maureen finally wept. The tears came from deep within her. And the crying brought with it a longing: an ache that now she fully accepted, the truth she had hidden for far too long, not wanting to hurt her Aunt Vi's feelings: She wanted her Mam. She wanted Ethel. The gentle, pleasant woman who had been the only mother she had ever known. She wanted that unconditional love.

Maureen cried long and hard. She wept for her lost little brothers...*oh, how often I've thought of you both, Timothy and Christopher*...She cried about the bad years under the hateful hand of her stepmother, Iris: never before had she shed tears for that dreadful time. But the scars were etched deep into her heart, and now she was acknowledging that they were still so sore...*why did you hate me so much? I was so willing to be part of that new life...so why did you hurt me? What had I done...?* She sobbed too for Gerard, lost so young. But most of all she cried for the help she would never have again; from the person who would have gladly given it to her...Stuart.

She woke to street sounds. Turning her head, she looked at the bedside clock: twelve forty five: Lunch time.

She lay still. Listening. Trying to hear whether the pleasant Mexican woman who came in to do their cleaning was at her chores. She craned her neck, cupped her ears for any evidence that Don was in the apartment. But the stately roomed apartment was still, silent. Life was going on outside, only.

After her bath, she felt almost human again. Staring at herself in the full-length bathroom mirror, she coloured with embarrassment when she remembered her behaviour of the previous evening: Thanksgiving Day...*and what had I been thankful for? Nothing.*

The need to atone was great. Maureen dressed carefully, then sat in her bedroom to wait: Neither thirst or hunger made her venture into the body of the apartment. Night fell. No Don. She sipped water taken from the bathroom taps, and waited. Later, she lay fully clothed on the bed. Waiting.

Morning came. Maureen was stiff. Cold. Alone. She ventured down the hallway and into the lounge, then the kitchen, the study, the dining room, the guest bedroom: all were empty of human form.

That night she slept in the bed: Earlier in the evening she had made and had eaten a stale tasting sandwich and had drank a glass of cold chocolate milk. Then, wearing one of Don's shirts, she snuggled under the covers and slept well.

The long weekend was almost over. It was obvious that the cleaning lady had been cancelled from doing her chores. The telephone was silent. This puzzled Maureen. *Surely someone would phone...?* But then she remembered: it was Thanksgiving Weekend: a four day holiday. Most people were with their families, their friends; the people they loved most. Giving thanks. Receiving thanks.

Monday came and with it a decision. Maureen took a taxi to the airport and from there, a flight to Miami, heading for Palm Beach. She flew home. To her home: her small apartment facing the Atlantic Ocean. It was a place she had spent so little time in. Now she had all the time in the world.

Putting the key into the lock, emotion welled up inside her: Now she was here, she realised it was not what she wanted. What she wanted was her family. She wanted her heart back. She needed her husband, Don. Her lovely daughter…and yes, even Jake…*he's never done me any harm…quite the opposite. Dear God, what have I done…?*

Maureen turned the key, opened the door, entered the hallway, and then closed the door behind her. The white and cream furnished apartment was still. Silent…*I have come all this way for more silence…*

Her thoughts were interrupted by a noise. Her heart beat faster. She swallowed hard before moving slowly down the hallway that led into the lounge: the wide windowed room that faced the sea. Her sea: The vast Atlantic that for so long had been a part of her life.

Hearing a cough, she froze. Fear almost paralysed her movements. But she opened the door…

'It took you long enough to come home…' Don called from the small balcony terrace that graced the living areas.

'Hi, Mum! You're just in time for my famous Spaghetti Bolognese…' Beth called from the kitchen.

'With *hippie* made garlic bread to accompany it…' shouted Jake, who was also in the small, hardly-ever-used kitchen of Maureen's ocean viewed apartment.

Maureen cried. She sobbed. She laughed. She hugged. She kissed. She said she was sorry. Over and over again she said how sorry she was.

In return, they cried with her, hugged with, kissed with her. But most precious of all, they forgave her. They loved her enough for this to be possible. Maureen was truly home.

*

31

As they crowded into the small, low-beamed bedroom, each had their own thoughts. Each their own memories. And as they looked at the man who lay so still, so shrunken, these thoughts and memories were haloed in a golden light. For that was what this man had been, to all of them. A bright and beaming light, a constant ray of sunshine, be it his dry wit, his open honesty or his sanguine humour.

Most of all, Sid Greenwood had shown them, and in turn had taught them, that an indomitable spirit and unquestioning love could conquer all hardships life could muster.

This being so, not one of them had questioned their motives—their urgent need to be by the man's bedside for his final hours.

This bright spring morning, as they clustered around the bedside of the dying man, each had a need to let him know that they were there.

In the hushed ambiance, they glanced around the bedroom and were pleased to see that nothing had been changed in the years that they had been gone. Years which had changed their own lives, though not their hearts. Their hearts, as always, were full of love for the man who now had so little time left on this earth.

A globe that had been travelled from east and west, as Sid's twin sons and his beloved niece had journeyed back to the little town of Warrington Clough to pay their final dues. Their farewells to a man they had sincerely hoped would always be amongst them, had not visualised a time when he would not: Until recently, Sid had battled valiantly with ill health. He had made massive inroads to an almost full recovery from the strokes he had suffered. And that had not surprised his family in the least. Their memories of this man would always be of him being a robust, hard-working, vibrant family man, who, until the first stroke, had never had a day off work through illness in his life.

Maureen's Atlantic journey from the west had been made in the company of her cousin Barry, one of Sid's twin sons. Barry, a restaurateur and very popular figure in the community where he lived in southern Florida, had not seen his father in quite some time. In truth, Barry had not seen the importance of a passage back to England until now. Before, it had been enough to pick up the phone and chat to his *old man* as if he were in the next state. Even after Sid's second stroke, Barry had never doubted that his father would pull through. And he had been right. Sid had made a remarkable recovery. It took the third, fourth and finally the fifth stroke to render Sid helpless, bringing him to his deathbed.

Bobby Greenwood, Barry's twin, and the most aloof of the Greenwood boys, had travelled from the east to be with his stricken parent. He had journeyed from the town of Bergendorf, which he now called home, situated a few minutes outside the city of Hamburg, Germany.

The quiet and quaint suburb of Hamburg was where he had lived the many years since his marriage to Liselle. Now, the strapping, blond haired man had the appearance of a well-fed German, his stature straight and tall, his girth wider than anyone would have ever thought possible on a man who looked, and was, so fit and strong.

Bobby and Liselle, a childless couple, had recently inherited the bakery that had been in Liselle's family for nearly a century. And because of this, Bobby had travelled to Cheshire alone: Liselle had been left behind in Germany to manage their profitable business.

Malcolm had travelled the least distance to be at his father's bedside: his home was still just down the lane. Of Malcolm it could be said that, even though father and son had rarely seen eye-to-eye, that he was the son most suited to be following in their father's footsteps. And those who had not been home for quite some time, where astonished to see how much the Greenwood's market garden business had flourished under their youngest brother's green thumbed hand.

The thriving business, which had only recently added the *Garden* to its name, had prospered more than any of them could have imagined since Malcolm had been at its helm: Malcolm had purchased extra land and had also bought the cottage that had once belonged to their neighbours, Flo and Percy Fielding.

The derelict cottage had since been demolished and the ground levelled. In its place a modern, light and airy construction had been built to house the many healthy plants and shrubs that Greenwood's had become well known for selling.

Malcolm had also been responsible for fencing his parent's cottage, and giving them the privacy they desired in their retiring years by diverting the Tarmac entrance to the business through the opening that at one time had been their next door neighbour's side garden.

And as the family, grouped together in the sick room, stole glances at the outside world going on below the bedroom window that overlooked the rear of the cottage, they could see a steady stream of vehicles entering and leaving the thriving garden centre, manned this day by the ever-efficient Patsy and a handful of loyal, though deeply saddened part-time employees.

From the kitchen, directly underneath the flimsy floorboards of the sick man's bedroom, they could hear the hum of voices as the doctor and the district nurse arrived for the second time that day and were greeted by Vi; then the clomp of feet as, in single file, the trio mounted the steep wooden stairs.

'I think we had better go down. There's not enough room for any more of us in here.' Malcolm took control as the new party, headed by the solemn looking doctor, entered the room. He herded his brothers and his cousin onto the landing, before they, again in single file, clomped down the familiar stairs.

Sydney Greenwood died on 13th of May 1980. He drew his last breath cradled in the arms of his beloved wife, Vi, and surrounded by his family.

His funeral took place on a glorious blue skied May day, the nursery ablaze with colourful pansies, begonias, wallflowers, indeed all the early summer plants and flowers that Sid had so enjoyed nurturing from seed to bloom.

He was buried in a plot of land that held the remains of his adored sons, Stuart and Gerard, and where two well-tended rose bushes held the promise of summer blooms.

The after-the-funeral meal had been a noisy affair; the church hall had been packed with the many people who had attended the service. Vi had done the rounds of thanking everyone for their kind thoughts, cards and beautiful floral tributes. She had done her duty dry-eyed, saying, in a matter of fact manner, that she had been married for so long, she could hardly remember her life before Sid had come along. She spoke of Sid as if he was just in another room. Her dignity, her ability to put others at ease (and they were not at ease: not when they were in the company of two famous people—Beth Stuart and Don Sommer were, of course, amongst the mourners—though in paying their respects to the deceased, none had approached either entertainer seeking autographs,) impressed the gathered together mourners; all told, Vi was holding up well.

Outwardly, she was. Vi moved amongst them with a composure few thought they would be able to match under the circumstances. Only those closest to her knew just how bereft she really was. And they too watched her; but with anxious eyes, and worried thoughts...*what will she do, now...? Where will she go...? Who will she live with...?*

The family were grouped round the table in the kitchen. Vi was at the sink, washing cups and saucers in readiness for another brew of tea. The wake over, only close family had come back to the cottage.

The conversation going on between them had her blood boiling...

'What do you mean, *live with*...? There's only one person I'll be living with and that's *me!* Sodding *hell, you*'re talking about me as if I'm an imbecile.' Vi blustered, her anger mounting, although her words fell on deaf ears. She banged the filled kettle onto the stove in disgust.

'She can always live with us...' Malcolm spoke across the table to his brothers, ignoring his mother's outburst.

'Aunt Vi? Don and I would *love* you to come over and spend time with us...' Maureen was earnest in her invitation. Don, sat next to her (his eyelids drooping with weariness, he'd taken an overnight flight to England and had little sleep) nodded in agreement with his wife.

'Now *that's* a good idea, Gran! Then you'd be able to stay until the wedding, if you wanted to, of course.' Long before her grandfather's death, Beth had set her wedding date. And it was date that would have to be cancelled if Vi was not to attend: Beth had already made it clear that the wedding would have to be postponed if her grandmother was not present.

Vi had heard enough She moved to stand behind Barry. 'Will you lot give over! This is my *home*,' she banged her hand on Barry's chair to emphasize her words, 'and here is where I will *live*...Got it, have you?'

All faces turned to look at her.

Vi was really storming. It was like the Vi of old...the Vi of their childhoods, at least for most of them.

And as usual with Vi, after the clap of thunder, came the momentary calm. 'Look, my loves, I knows you are only being kind...But...'

Bobby interrupted his mother. 'But you have never been in this predicament before...'

'Predicament? Bloody *predicament!* It's not a PREDICAMENT losing your husband...of a *life time*.' Vi's sobbed statement brought a silence.

Barry stood up and made for his mother to sit in the chair. 'It's all right, Mam, there now, it's all right. Don't cry; come on, sit down. Our Bobby here, he didn't mean any harm.' Ever the peacemaker, Barry tried to soothe his mother, and cover for his brother's blunder.

'Vi will be okay. *We'll* see to it, no fret. And she'll be *here*, in her own home; right, chuck?' Patsy reached across and patted her mother-in-law's hand. 'She'll be all right, then, won't you, Mother?'

They all watched as Vi grabbed hold of her daughter-in-law's hand, and held on to it, firmly.

'Well, then, now *that's* settled, I've got work to do.' Malcolm stood, moving across the kitchen, making for the back door of his mother's house.

At the door, Malcolm turned to look back into the kitchen; there was a note of sarcasm in his voice when he asked whether any one was for joining him at his chores, 'Like, don't knock me over in the rush; but are there any takers, or what...?'

'I'll come, Uncle Mal.' Beth was on her feet.

'Show us the way, little bro...' Barry's choice of words, and his own laughter at them lightened the air.

Bobby also took his cue, moving with more uncertainly towards the back door and the unknown quantity of work awaiting him in the nursery.

Don, with a quick glance in his wife's direction, understood at once the movement of her head, and joined the others who had enlisted.

The women left seated at the table smiled conspiratorially at one another. Maureen was the first to speak...'And then there was three...'

The laughter that exploded with the remark would have seemed remiss to many who had been to the funeral: disrespectful, even. However, those who knew the three women well, would have known different: they would have known the laughter would soon turn to tears: As it did.

What followed the mixed emotions was also what would have been expected: Each had a remembered tale of the man who had been uncle, father-in-law, and husband. Anecdote after anecdote tumbled from their lips, their eyes remaining wet throughout with laughter and with sorrow. There was so much they had to say, so much to tell: a fitting epitaph to the ordinary, unassuming man who had left in body but not in spirit.

'I've said this before, and I'll say it again—Sid didn't mind you having a laugh on his account…aye, he'd chuckle himself, most of the time. When I think of some of the times we've had…*Dear God,* I had a good one…Hey, and I'll tell you something, our Maureen…' Vi dabbed at her eyes with a soggy, crumpled white handkerchief as she spoke, '…you know when you sent us that drawing of what your new house will look like, when it's finished, like…?'

Maureen nodded that she did, and her thoughts fluttered to the Palm Beach house that at this moment in time was at foundation stage: as late as yesterday evening, Don had been overseeing the work at the construction site. The very thought of the house was a joy. But she chastened herself away from her own good fortune and back to putting the needs and care of her Aunt Vi to the foremost of her mind.

'Well, anyway, love, Sid looked at them drawings for ages. Turning them this way and that. I don't think he could understand much, but whatever, he said he could see it was going to be a blooming *palace* of a house. And do you know what else he said, love…?'

Maureen shook her head.

Vi leant forwards, and gestured for Maureen's hand across the table. When she had it, she said, 'He said, "Now my princess will *really* need a tiara"…'

Maureen and Don were indeed having a home built. And as Sid had surmised, it was going to be a palace of a house.

After Maureen's near breakdown (they had come to realise that was what had happened,) Don was so relieved to have her back to normal that he had asked her to talk through her problems. Maureen had been just as relieved to pour out all her pent-up emotions regarding living in Montport.

What transpired after these many hours of talks, under-taken, mostly, in the cool of early morning as Don partnered Maureen on her daily beach walk, was pleasing to both of them: Don was to keep his Manhattan apartment, but Maureen was to put her Palm Beach apartment on the house market. However, they both agreed that Florida was an ideal place to have a home, and that Palm Beach area fit the bill. And a brand new house was what was needed: A dream home, built to their own specifications.

When it came to choosing a builder, Vicente's was given instruction to build a house that would last generations. And Chuck Vicente was only too happy to oblige.

A two-acre, ocean front building plot was purchased. The new house, which now, in mid-May, and while Maureen and Don were staying in a small, discreet bed and breakfast hotel during their sad two (Don was staying just one) week stay in Warrington Clough, was only at the foundation's stage, but was on schedule to be completed by early September: Maureen's birthday had been set as the goal.

And as June moved in to July and July into August, with each brick laid, each wall constructed, the couple were like expectant parents, excitedly awaiting the birth of their new...*home*. A home of splendid proportions: A pink stuccoed, white marbled, many-roomed palatial abode: as the late Sid Greenwood had forecast so astutely.

With its back lawns sweeping down to the sea, Maureen and Don's new residence would be an ideal venue for a wedding.

And a wedding was indeed planned. The date was set for late September. A ceremony had been planned not unlike that of Beth's own parents, which had taken place, uncannily similarly but without elaboration, on the lawns of the Vicente's home so many years before. And, like that wedding day, which had come on the heel of Gerard's death, Beth and Jake's day would have a similar tinge of melancholy for those who had passed away.

*

32

Overhead, a helicopter hovered under the skilful guidance of its pilot, steadying his craft in readiness for the photographer's zoom lens.

On the ground outside the locked and guarded white columned front gates of the ocean front property named Strand House, other cameras were readied and waiting. The competition was fierce regarding who would get the best shots, the closest photographs, that would then be wired, world wide, to appear on front pages of newspapers and magazines.

Beth Stuart was hot: Beth Stuart marrying Jake Adier, stepson of Don Sommer, was even hotter news. Especially since Jake's first, block-busting novel had been scripted for film—a movie that would star his new wife and his famous stepfather. The hoped for photographs of Beth in her wedding dress would be priceless: the singer's second record in succession had recently reached the number one spot both in America and Great Britain. *Shout it Clear* was hailed as perhaps Beth's Stuart's finest recording. Her calendar was filling with tour dates as the record sales kept soaring.

However, today was the date the singer/actress had eagerly awaited more than any other. Today she was be become Mrs Jacob Adier.

The weather was doing its best to make the day special, too. The sky could not have been bluer; there was not even a hint of cloud on the horizon. The newly laid lawns had captured the early morning dew, and looked almost like an emerald green carpet twinkling with diamond sequins.

Borders of colourful flowering tubs added to the Technicolor splendour of the occasion and the many eight-seating round tables, dressed with pristine rose pink linens, sparkling crystal and polished silver, set the ambiance for what was to come.

The rows of cerise velour, gilt framed chairs were quickly being taken as the eighty or so guests began to take their seats in readiness for the ceremony. Chatter buzzed, laughter trilled, and excitement stirred the mid-morning air.

Under the white trellised arbour, which was graced with white lilies and pale pink roses, the Reverend Thomas waited. His presence stilled the congregation. The scene was set for the most perfect of weddings, back-dropped by the vast Atlantic Ocean.

Heads turned, as the groom and his best man were the first to walk down the deep pink coloured carpet. At the arbour, they, in turn, shook hands with the minister.

The groom, Jake, dressed in grey morning suit, looked slightly nervous as he turned to smile his welcome to his invited guests.

The best man, dressed similar, looked anything but nervous: Don Sommer's pride about the forthcoming union was obvious to all in attendance. That Beth was about to become his daughter-in-law (besides being his stepdaughter) he thought to be amazing. He was often quoted as saying that it had "the makings of a great movie."

As the ten-piece orchestra began playing melodies from some of Don's Broadway shows, the bride's mother, Maureen, looked as nervous as the groom. Dressed in a shell pink, pearl buttoned, figure-hugging knee length silk suit, and wearing a pill-box hat of the same silk, she sat in her appointed front row seat with apprehension on her face. Smoothing the skirt of her suit over her knees, it was easy to see that she was hoping that all would go according to plan: Maureen had found that being the mother-of-the-bride was far more difficult and demanding than she would have thought possible: So may arrangements, so many lists.

Vi Greenwood, majestic in flowing pale blue chiffon, her abundant greying hair swept up and held in place by a rhinestone encrusted blue butterfly clip, sat comfortably in her delicate chair, her youngest son,

Malcolm, on her left hand side and Patsy, her devoted daughter-in-law, on her right. Since first arriving in Florida, Vi had thought of her late husband often, as was to be expected, although her long dead son Stuart was in her mind the most. And this morning he filled her thoughts completely...*Oh, son, you'd have been right proud today, lad...I hopes you are looking down, like, and enjoying it...I hopes you are celebrating with your Dad and our Gerard...*

Malcolm's mind was a jumble: Stuart had been flitting in and out of his thoughts during the morning, especially when he'd been dressing. The morning suit and white dress shirt, which had been hired for him, had been a devil to work out how it should be worn, notwithstanding the difficulty he'd had with the many button-studs on his shirt; and his palest-of-pink cravat had been re-knotted many times over to get it right. Whatever, he knew he looked grand, now. He felt proud that he looked the part: part of all this...*What a blooming place...what a setting...what a wedding...*

Malcolm, as usual, was overawed by everything and everyone; from the white jacketed, black tie staff, to the row after row of celebrity. His thoughts were giddy...

I could pinch myself...I can't believe that this is happening...that I am here...and that it's real...

Patsy had never felt so smart in all her life. The day after their arrival, Maureen had taken her shopping on Worth Avenue to buy the lavender coloured crepe de chine suit she now wore so elegantly. Purchasing the outfit, that had cost the best part of a weeks' wage (Patsy had vehemently declined Maureen's generosity in offering to pay,) it had been the first time that she had acknowledged that, in truth, she could afford it: Greenwood's had been making money hand over fist in the past year or so: and all due to the back-breaking long hours and hard work that both she and Malcolm had put into the enterprise.

Leaning forward in her chair, Patsy stole a glance at her husband. He looked very handsome today. Not that she would be telling him that...*No way! He's big headed enough...and I don't want him to start any of his shenanigans again...*Patsy's thoughts were self-centred, and with reason: Malcolm had not always been the best of husbands...

Chiding herself for her thoughts of the past, Patsy sniffed, and settled back into her seat her head held high. She had a lot to be thankful for. Especially to Maureen...and Don.

Patsy felt a thrill run through her. She and Malcolm were going to have a few days in Key West. They'd stay for four nights in an apartment owned by Barry. Maureen and Don had offered to care for Julie and Sam whilst their parents took the trip...*I hope our Julie behaves herself today...keeps her gob shut, and that. She can be quite a madam when she wants to be! But she'll be beautiful bridesmaid, none the less...It's Sam I'm worried about, though...I'll miss my little lad...Still, it'll be nice to have some time on our own...Key West...*

With the orchestra playing the traditional bridal melody, Beth walked towards her groom on the arm of her Uncle Barry. As they strolled, in step with the music down the petal-strewn carpet, every head turned to watch her arrival.

And they were not disappointed by what they saw: Beth's beauty this day was ethereal. Made from white silk organza, her billowing gown seemed to float as she glided towards the arbour. The wedding dress, made more exquisite by the silk spun, crystal-embroidered veil that both covered her face and trailed behind her, seemed to shimmer under the rays of the late morning sun. And, although misted by the sheer veil, her face, her petite features were visible; her porcelain skin glowed with youth and the radiance of love. Her glossy jet black hair, newly cut into a fashionable *pixie* style, was adorned by a band of white freesia, which matched the trailing bouquet of white freesia, lily of the valley, and pink orchids which she carried.

As Beth joined her groom at the arbour, Julie Greenwood, who had been walking behind, holding the gown's long train, moved forward to take the bride's bouquet. Julie's strawberry blonde hair was set in ringlets and was crowned with a band of pink rosebuds. Her bridesmaids' dress of pink silk organza, cut low at the bodice and graced with short puff sleeves, was, except for the colour, a perfect replica of the bride's gown though, of course, it was minus the train. Two more completed the bridal entourage: Sonia Howarth, dressed similar to Julie, was the Matron of Honour. Beth's closest friend looked enchanting in her Victorian styled bridesmaid's dress. Her white blonde hair, which today was swept from her face, and held in a chignon festooned with pink rosebuds, gleamed sleekly in the sunlight. Tall and very elegant, Sonia brought a regal bearing to the occasion.

Michael Landon, Lydia Vicente's infant son, was behaving impeccably as he, dressed as a young courtier in dark blue velvet with white frilled cuffs and collar, proudly carried a blue velvet cushion. The cushion had been intended to be the vehicle to carry the wedding rings to the altar. However, with Michael's young years being taken into consideration, the cushion was now being carried empty (good thinking, really; Michael, as of now, had taken to swinging the cushion up and down in the air, accompanied by his infectious giggles) the rings having been firmly ensconced into the best man's trouser pocket before the ceremony had begun.

Mary Lou and Chuck Vicente had been beaming with pride, before the cushion flinging began.

Now, with young Michael on his knee, Chuck was whispering for him to be quiet, and to stop wriggling, so that he could hear Beth and Jake taking their vows: candy was proving to be an effective bribe for his grandson.

Sonia's parents, Ben and Julia Howarth smiled at each other, and held hands. They too had whispered during the bride's arrival: they had whispered that Beth looked radiant. Joyous. They also whispered their cherished desires for their own daughter: they hoped that when it is her turn, she would choose well.

Roy Vicente, Chuck and Mary Lou's bachelor son, who was seated next to the Howarth's, had never been introduced to Sonia. In fact he hadn't even known she existed. Now, though, he hoped an introduction would be soon forthcoming. Roy, who stood well over six foot and was dark and handsome with it, (swarthy, some said) was smitten, bowled over by the Scandinavian-style good looks of Beth's Matron of Honour. *Wow...* he thought...*got to get some of that...*

Until today, Roy had been every bit of the playboy character: love them and leave them had been his motto. And if Ben Howarth could have read his seating companion's thoughts, he would have thought all his wishing and hoping for his daughter's future was doomed: Roy Vicente was a known womanizer, with a reputation to boot.

Night had fallen. The tables had been cleared and moved so that they now clustered round the open-air dance floor.

Each table held a centrepiece of pink and white roses and was lit by candlelight.

The flower borders of the lush green lawns glowed in shades of deep golden yellow, their colours and shades mellowed from the light of the many stanchion torch flames.

The strains of the song regaling the merits of a early autumn morning, brought Mister and Missus Jake Adier to their feet.

They took to the dance floor, smooching, gliding, shyly smiling their acknowledgments to the various cat-calls and whistles that came from the people seated at the various tables around them. Even the orchestra members, resting in a much needed interval time, smiled and clapped with enthusiasm.

Beth had detached the long train of her wedding dress and now, by the light of a hundred or so candles, the dress had become a stunning, waist hugging ball gown.

Maureen and Don were coaxed to the dance floor, and they too were treated to the whistles and applause. They held each other tightly, swaying to the melody that was written for lovers—lovers of all ages and all creeds, and especially for an occasion such as this, surrounded by a loving family and loyal friends.

And as Maureen and Don danced into the small hours of the velvet-aired night, each had thoughts of their homeland: Maureen glanced at her daughter, when, encircled in the protective arms of Jake, she was swept by, laughter on her lips, love in her eyes...*Look at her...Stuart? Are you watching...? Doesn't our daughter have so much style...? You would be so proud of her...she is so beautiful, in every way...*

Don, who nodded his encouragements as Jake and Beth danced by, held his wife more tenderly, and thought...*Jake and I both have a so much, now: Our very own Brits...*He kissed the crown of Maureen's head as they waltzed, and was rewarded with a radiant smile in return.

Don felt so good, dancing with his lovely wife, his son and daughter-in-law on the very same dance floor. Everything felt just right. Perfect...*America*...he thought...*God bless it; this grand US of A is a place where wishes and dreams have a habit of coming darn true...*

'*America*. Is there anywhere else like it...?'

Patsy and Malcolm were walking down a Key West street, as the latter posed his question.

Patsy shook her head, laughing her reply, momentarily deafened by the loud clash of cymbals and heavy drum beats coming from the bar they were passing. A bar that was one of many that lined the Key West thoroughfare.

The linked-armed couple were walking the late night streets stopping here and there when a bar or a souvenir shop took their fancy. After a while, they

343

found themselves in a quieter, quainter, more historical section of the town.

'Hey, Pats...! Look at this. This *house*,' Malcolm had spotted an information board placed close the tree-lined property's gate.

Patsy turned to see what her husband meant.

'Hey, this was that famous writer's house. It says: open for visitors during daylight hours.'

Malcolm pulled his wife in closer as he continued reading the printed information:

'*For...*'

Patsy interrupted. 'Okay, ok, clever dick! So you can read a notice board...Big deal! Come on, let's be getting back before our bell's rung. And besides, you can't be *that* interested. You've never read a blooming book in your life...'

'Wrong there, love, I have you know, read books. And plenty of them...Aye, I've read the one about the little girl who pals out with bears, and about that little fellow that lives in a kind of dream town...now *that* one was brilliant...'

Patsy laughed with her husband, and cuddled him close. 'It feels as though we are in a *dream town* here, doesn't it, Mal?' She had taken to calling her husband Mal since they had first arrived in America. He had retaliated with *Pats*.

'You're not *kidding*. You know what, Pats? Once the first shock of how different it is wears off...I mean, I know you were as bowled over as I was, when we first arrived over here...but it's funny, like, isn't it? Funny how soon you get used to it.'

'Yep.' Patsy's answer was pure Americano.

Malcolm pulled her closer, and kissed her lips.

She fought him off, '*Malcolm*...Stop it! I'm not *necking* with you here, in the street...'

'Patsy, we're on our second honeymoon. Who cares what we do, it's a free *world*...'

At that moment, two young men, smartly though casually dressed, passed by. And Malcolm's eyes nearly popped out of his head when he saw that the men were holding hands. Wide eyed, he turned to his wife; she, having also noticed the same thing, looked dumbstruck.

Reaching for his wife's hand, Malcolm urged her to a fast walking pace. 'Shit! Did you see that? As the American's would say...let's get our ass out of here...'

Malcolm and Patsy ran, panting, and out of breath with laughing, all the way back to their apartment

'Is he asleep?' Don whispered his question as his wife tiptoed into their bedroom, and was closing the door quietly behind her.

'For the *moment*,' Maureen whispered back as she climbed in to bed, 'poor little mite, he's missing his Mum...'

'And *you* are missing your sleep,' Don interrupted, his voice not so low now that his wife was back beside him.

Maureen snuggled close to him. 'Oh, I don't mind, Don, not really. It's only for a few days. And Vi's so good with him during the day.'

'Which means you volunteered for the night shift...' Don planted a tender kiss on his wife's lips, 'But if that's what you want, it's okay with me...*nanny.*'

Don was asleep again within seconds.

Maureen lay awake longer. Though her eyes were heavy with tiredness, she had no intention of closing them. She lay tense. Listening. Listening for cries. Listening and waiting to be called to duty..."He has you between two slices of bread, our Maureen" Sam's Grandma Vi had said. And it was true: fourteen-month old Samuel Greenwood had his carer alert to his every need. And seemed to be making the most of the attention. "Aye, he's a clever little monkey, our Sam is," Vi had chuckled, "he has all the women in his life at his beck and call. And that's what's surprised me about his mother leaving him in the first place. Patsy must think right highly of you, our Maureen, that she must! Make no mistake, she wouldn't leave her precious little lad with anyone else, I'm sure of that."

And that was it. Maureen *was* aware of this trust and was terrified of making a mistake in the care of the infant. Julie and Vi were on hand during the day, but at night, the sole responsibility of Sam was left to Maureen. And in truth, as she now lay fretting, it was more of a burden than she would admit to anyone...*two more days...then they'll be home...* With these thoughts, her eyes began to close—until a wail from the next room had her bounding from the bed for the fourth time this long September night.

'I thought it was too far to travel, for so short a time; but I'm *sure* glad we did.'

'Mmm...yes, so am I. Is it time to turn over?'

Jake smiled indulgently at his wife's question. It was a question she asked

345

every quarter of an hour: Beth wanted a suntan, but not a burn.

Removing his sunglasses, Jake sat up and placed them on the small wrought iron table at his side. Picking up a bottle of suntan protection cream, he unscrewed the cap and poured white lotion into the palm of his left hand and then leant over towards his bikini-clad wife who lay face down next to him on a similar sun bed.

With mischief in his eyes, Jake let the cold lotion drip onto his wife's bare back.

Beth let out a squeal...but then laughingly shouted her admonishments.

'You swine; you horror! You could have *warned* me you were going to do that! What sort of a person have I married...hey? A *cruel* one it seems.'

'I'm only getting my own back for yesterday...'

The tomfoolery had started the moment they had arrived. And yesterday, Beth had stolen Jake's shorts, and his towel, after a late night swim on the beach.

Now, the young couple threw mock punches at each other, shrieking and yelling as they tussled together on Jake's about-to-collapse sun-lounging chair.

The din had reached Anna's ears as she worked in the kitchen, and the dark haired, slightly built woman had ventured onto the sun-baked terrace, wiping her hands on her white apron, smiling broadly, shaking her head at the young couple's antics, before moving back inside to continue with her preparations for lunch. A lunch that would be served within the hour to the honeymooners who were so very pleased to have taken up the Vicentes' offer of a week long stay in their holiday home on the Spanish island of Mallorca.

Eating their paella at a shaded table on the terrace of Casa Blanca, with the heady scent of bougainvillea all around them and the majestic purple mountains towering behind them, Jake and Beth enthused about the sumptuous food set before them, sipping alternately from glasses of iced water and local wine, revelling in the exquisite romantic setting. The weather so far had been lovely and, though it was as hot as Florida, they were finding the lack of humidity to be splendid.

With just two days left, Jake was as eager as his new wife to spend the time idling under the cloudless blue skies of a Mallorcan afternoon.

Lunch over, the couple had shed their towelling robes and had returned to lie in the sun, Jake just wearing a pair of red shorts and Beth a tiny white bikini. Well oiled and well fed, they looked the epitome of good health and good living.

And as a golden skinned Beth lay on her back reading, her face shaded by both the book and her sunglasses, Jake crossed his hands behind his head and lay with his eyes closed but his mind very alert. He was so excited. Not only was he bowled-over with joy to be on honeymoon with his wife Beth Stuart (Jake still found it hard to believe that she had consented to marrying him…and that the happiness he now experienced, every minute of every day, was here to stay,) he was simmering with an intense excitement that his novel was about to be made into a movie. The shoot was to commence the first week of October, in California: *A Stranger Stalks Within Us* was to be made entirely on location. And the location was the streets of San Francisco. A place Jake knew well. Intimately. It was the city he had set his first novel in and around. It was also a place were he had finally put his demons to rest.

The icing-on-the-cake was that both his wife and his stepfather were starring in the film. Jake had thought himself lucky that he had been chosen to write the script. But the casting pushed the project past joy: He was ecstatic.

However, it had not been all plain sailing. Jake had had to work hard to convince both the financiers and the producers that no other writer could do justice to the script.

True to his word and to his book, Jake had only slightly altered the script from the original manuscript. And he now thought of himself as a lucky man. He was lucky in love, in family, and in his talent. That Don Sommer had been instrumental in him obtaining all of this, Jake would be eternally grateful.

Hearing a light snore, he opened his eyes to see that Beth had let her book slip to her chest, and was snoozing under the glare of the late afternoon sun. Jake sat up and moved from his chair, quietly. Uncapping the sun lotion, he warmed the cold cream in the palms of his hands before tenderly rubbing it onto the satiny skin of his wife's arms.

And as Beth murmured her sleepy 'Thanks,' Jake's eyes misted with his own good fortune: that this beautiful young woman was his wife; that the fine man, Don Sommer, was his father; and that through the generous kindness of friends they had been allowed this week in paradise. After years of a living hell, Jake finally knew who he was…and what he was: Blessed.

Roy Vicente had tried just about everything in his attempt to get Sonia Howarth into his bed. But the lady was not for laying.

Roy stared up at his bedroom ceiling, his thoughts troubled…*She is such a lady...And I think I love her...Crikey, I know I love her...!*

He swung his legs out of bed, reached for the phone and placed a call through to Sonia's hotel.

'Hello? Sonia...?'

A sleepy voice, inarticulate because of being woken in the middle of the night asked who was calling.

'It's *me*, Sonia. Roy.'

'Oh, right...*Roy*. Hey, do you *know* what time it is...?' Sonia, wide-awake now, sounded angry.

'Yes, it's three forty five...'

'In the morning...'

Ignoring the fact that Sonia was disgruntled to have be woken, Roy went on:

'I wanted to tell you something...'

'Listen, Roy...I think I've heard just about enough from *you*...'

'No, Sonia, don't put the phone down, *please*? Just listen to me, hear me out. There is something important I want to tell you,'

The line was silent. Then Sonia said, with a sigh, and weary tone in her voice, 'Go on, then, spit it out. *Then get off the phone...*'

'Okay. Yes, but...well...Oh, *Sonia*. Can we start again? That's what I wanted to say...Can we *please* start again...Look, I know I've been a jerk...'

'You can say that again...'

'Jerk, jerk...*jerk*. There; is that enough...?' Roy could sense that Sonia was smiling. He held the phone closer, closed his eyes; and was rewarded with a 'Maybe,' from Sonia. Then she added a rejoinder, 'But a *dirty* jerk would be a better description...'

'Would it really, Sonia? I had a bath before I got into bed...'

'See? See what I mean? You are always talking about *bed*.'

'Meet me tomorrow, before you leave for your flight home, and I promise, faithfully, that I'll not mention the *B* word...'

There was another silence. Roy feared that Sonia would just hang up. She didn't.

'Well, Roy, your usage of the B word has certainly ruined my vacation, here in Florida. I'd thought it would be so nice to come to the wedding; spend time with my parents. Then take some extra days to chill out, relax...Even play a bit of tennis. Yet all I've had is...*you*. You've tried to get into my bed, or get me into yours for the last five days...'

'Six, actually.'

After his statement, the silence returned.

'Sonia? Are you still there…?'

'Yes.'

'Sonia? Sonia—I think I've fallen in love with you…'

'Oh.'

'Oh…?'

'Yes…*oh.*'

'Do you mean 'oh' like, *oh dear, isn't this just…awful?*' Roy let his voice rise high as he finished the sentence. He sounded like a maiden aunt.

Sonia giggled. The she said, 'I'm going back to bed, now, Roy.'

'That's not fair…'

'What's not fair…?'

'You can mention the B word—but I can't.'

Sonia chuckled. There was warmth in her voice when she said, 'Good night, Roy. See you tomorrow…'

'What? Do you really mean it? *You'll see me…tomorrow?*' Roy's maiden aunt voice was back.

'I must be crazy…Yes, *Roy.* I'll see you in the morning…'

The line clicked. Sonia had replaced her receiver.

Roy Vicente felt like doing somersaults. Instead he roared, 'Yes! *Yes!*' Punching the air as he did so. The echo of his voice floated round the immense bedroom which was just one of four in the beachfront apartment owned by his parents on the shores of the Atlantic Ocean.

Alone in the well-appointed property, Roy had found what he hadn't known he had been seeking. He had found his lady. He had found the same love match his parents had shared for over forty years.

Climbing back into bed, Roy slept at once. His dreams were filled with Sonia: his first lady. And fate would make her his last.

*

33

Declan sat in the waiting room. It seemed as though his entire life had been lived in waiting rooms: Doctors' waiting rooms.

As the tall, sandy haired, white-coated man approached him, Declan stood and reached out his hand in greeting.

'Hello, Christopher; it's been a long time. Could we go back into your office...please?'

'Declan! How are you? I didn't believe that it could actually be you when my receptionist said there was a *Mr Fitzgerald* waiting to see me. Yes, come on in...'

Declan was ushered into a small room. The grey and white painted room was clean and smelled nice. Light poured in from a window that had its light grey Venetian blind rolled to the top. The office was furnished with a paper cluttered teak framed desk; a couple of grey-metal filing cabinets and two black vinyl swivel chairs. Utilitarian. Nothing like the usual consultation suites that Declan had become all too familiar with of late. But the necessity to be here was dire.

Doctor Christopher Grady took his seat behind the desk and watched as

Declan settled himself on to the facing chair. It was obvious that his stepfather was distressed. It was also as clear as day that the man had aged dreadfully since they had last met. But ever the professional, Christopher was warm in his approach.

'Well, then. Yes, sit down. Make yourself comfortable. Would you like some tea?'

Declan waved the request off. 'How's your mother keeping?' he asked.

'You should know, Declan. I send you all the reports, and the clinic bills.' Christopher was taken aback by his stepfather's question: to date, the man had shown little interest in his wife's welfare, though the medical bills had always been paid: prompt.

However, the edge of any mirth on Christopher's part was soon dispelled by Declan's next statement.

'To be sure, I'm not interested in your mother. I was trying to be polite. I've had enough of the woman's ailments to last me a lifetime; her wellbeing is in your hands now, so it is. Muggings here just pays the bills, that's all. I'll get to the point: My baby, my Donna...the little one...she has...*cancer.*'

Christopher was immediately aware that Declan was struggling with his emotions. He had hardly been able to say the word cancer: the cankerous malady, that put the fear of God in most people, had done its best to destroy Declan, that was for sure.

'I'm sorry to hear that, Declan. I know the little girl means so much to you. How old is she now...?'

'Sixteen-month. Aye, and she walked at ten month...and she can hold a conversation now...that she can. She is so clever...so bright...and so...very...*ill*'

Declan began to sob. His thin body was doubled in grief.

Moments passed. Christopher knew it was better not to speak. He'd been in the medical profession long enough to know how to behave in an emotional crisis. He let Declan control his emotions; gave the man time to compose himself.

When he did speak, it was with the up most kindness, and with thoughts of how he could be of help. 'Is there something that I could do, Declan? Surely you have a specialist, though? And you do know, don't you...? That cancer can be cured, especially in the young, *and*, more importantly, if it has been caught soon enough. Has it, Declan?'

Declan blew his nose. Leaning sideways to put his handkerchief back in his trouser pocket, he shook his head. 'It's not curable. And yes, we *have* tried everything and everyone, well, nearly…'

Christopher looked surprised. 'What age was she when she was diagnosed?'

'Six month.'

'And the prognosis…?'

'A few months, a year, if we were lucky…'

'She's done well, then, so far.'

'Yes, and that's why I'm here, Chris. There's no one else to ask…See, there's a new drug…not been tried on humans…but I've read the papers on it…It will work, I know it will! And Donna, she's a fighter.'

'When will it be available? Any idea…?'

'That's it. Two years, perhaps a little longer. The tests have not been finalised. But you've got to help me, Christopher…it *will* work for my Donna.'

'What form of cancer does she have?'

'Hodgkin's disease.'

'Declan. I'm *so* sorry. It's quite rare; especially in a child.'

Christopher was genuinely sorry. Sorry for the little girl. Sorry for Declan; in his time, the man had been a good stepfather. The young doctor had no doubt that Declan was a devoted father to his little girl.

Declan moved forward in his seat. His face was haggard with worry, lined with fatigue. Though when he spoke again there was passion in his voice…

'I'll pay, Chris. *Anything.* You know that, don't you?'

Christopher began to feel very uncomfortable; he pushed himself further back into his chair.

'What do you want me to do…?'

'Get it. Get the drug. No matter what it costs. Get it. Please.'

Christopher felt himself break out in a sweat. He knew his forehead looked damp.

'But Declan, you have said yourself that it is not available…'

'To *me*, it's not. But you are a doctor. Think man; think what I've done for you. You would *never* have been a friggin' doctor without me…and me money.'

'I know all that, Declan. And believe me, I'm grateful. But I can't do what you want; it's impossible.'

Declan was almost out of his chair, his arms, the whole top half of his body was forward on the desk as he implored his stepson for the help he so drastically needed.

'Nothing is impossible, Christopher. Surely I taught you *that*…?' There was an edge of seething anger in Declan's quietly spoken question.

'But what you are asking *is*.' Christopher was now as distressed as his visitor. He was also becoming more fearful by the second. He tried to hide his own emotions by consoling and offering a more rational way to help find a good treatment for the baby girl.

'Look, Declan. I *will* help you. Give me a couple of days. I'll ring around; find another specialist. Have you tried America? I know for *sure* that they have done some excellent work over there…'

'I wouldn't be here if anyone else could help. Believe me. America is *out*. So it's down to you…and remember, Chris, you *owe* me…'

Christopher wiped his brow on the sleeve of his white medical coat.

'Declan, I can imagine how distressed you are, really I can. But I'm afraid I can't help you in the way you want. If the drug is not available, that's it. There is *nothing* that I can do…'

'Coward! You always were a bloody little coward. To think how brave my babe is, and what she's been through. And you, you snotty nosed *nothing*…you won't even pick up the bleedin' phone to see what you could do…'

Christopher stood. He moved round from his desk as he spoke.

'Declan. I know *you* well enough, too. You must have tried every avenue before coming to me! Face the facts: If you can't get access to the drug, I most certainly can't.' He was now standing next to Declan. He stretched out his hand, offering friendship, offering his best service. 'Declan, I'll do all I can for you, and for Donna. But please don't ask the impossible. Let's get the girl's medical records and go forward, together…'

Declan stood, knocking Christopher's hand out of the way as he did so. His fury reddened his neck, seemed to choke his words; he loosened his collar and tie as he almost flung himself to the door.

'Bastard! That's what you are…A *bastard*. No more. No more, *no more*. Your mother can *rot*. Get her out of that fucking expensive clinic! I'll be paying no more bills. There's nothing friggin' wrong with her. She's a drunk, a stinking, lousy, whoring drunk. *You* can pay for her, from now on. You pay to keep her…insane…and may all the evilness in this vile world fall on your shoulders, *Doctor*. Aye, I hope you *rot* with her…'

Declan slammed his way out of the surgery.

Christopher moved back to his seat behind the desk; his thoughts were very troubled…*Declan will ruin me for this*…

Doctor Christopher Grady was well aware of Declan Fitzgerald's powers. And he also knew that only time would tell what the Irishman could do to harm his stepson's career.

As he sat in a numb silence, he rubbed his hands across his face, trying to obliterate the scene that had just taken place; the young doctor knew that the distraught man was capable of just about anything...Except, it seemed, to be able to save the life of his beloved only child.

*

34

This time round, Lena Grant had been happy to welcome the new mistress of Rockfort House. And a mistress she could address as Mrs Adier made her smile even wider.

However, from the spring months through to late summer, Lena had probably had cause to rethink her ideals. Now, as the colder days of autumn approached, the housekeeper was kept busier than she had ever been. Having always been smart in appearance, of late Lena was finding it difficult to fit her own needs into her busy schedule: she had not been to the hairdressers in months, and her nails both on her hands and her feet were badly in need of some attention. The truth was, Lena had been run ragged with the continual round of chores that made up her day since Jake Adier and his new wife had taken residence.

As the stresses and strains of her daily *load* brought a pained expression to Lena's face and slowed her pace, it was not only her husband who had worried for her health—Maureen Sommer had too.

The newly-weds liked to entertain. For the past year, weekend after weekend brought with it an assortment of visitors: musicians, actors, writers, financiers, accounts, friends; it seemed that both Jake and Beth knew everyone there was to know.

'Seems like my daughter likes to party, Lena.' Maureen's statement came one Saturday afternoon in early October when, arriving at Rockfort House, for what Beth had said would be, "a quiet weekend for just the four of us," she had been somewhat taken aback to find that the quiet weekend for four had tripled to twelve.

Maureen had noticed how tightly Lena's thin lips had stayed sealed and had been impressed that the housekeeper had been loyal enough not to nag about the massive workload placed on her thin shoulders by the young couple's impromptu invitations.

Nevertheless, Maureen had been quick on the uptake and voiced her concern to Beth...

'Do you want to lose Lena, darling?'

Beth, dressed for tennis, had been rushing out of the front door in her eagerness to get to the courts, expressed total surprise, her huge blue eyes widening at the question put to her.

'No, Mum! What a strange thing to say. You know that Lena's been with the house for years. *Why* would she want to leave?'

Maureen had placed her arms round her daughter's shoulders and explained the reasons. 'Well, my love, you and Jake are tiring her out. And to be honest, I think she'll *quit* if you burden her much more...Beth, you have too many houseguests. And from what I can gather, you don't even inform Lena has to how many you are expecting. It's practically 'Open House' these days...'

Beth had stared open mouthed at her mother for a second or two, before she shrugged off the accusation. 'Oh, Mum! Don't worry so much; Lena can *more* than cope. And listen...even *I* don't know who'll be here most of the time. I invite people...Jake invites people...and then I sort of *forget*. But it's no big deal—we eat out most Saturday nights. And Lena does have all week to wind down. Honestly, Mum, you do fret about the strangest of things!' Beth had hugged Maureen, as a comfort to the older woman's worries, a *there, there*, nothing's wrong, pat on the back, and then bent to re-tie her white plimsolls.

But Maureen had not let up on the matter...

'But after you come back from dinner, you *party* all night. True?'

Beth had straightened up, tucking her white polo tee shirt into the waistband of her tiny white tennis skirt as she had answered...and there had been a hint of irritation in her voice. 'If Lena *had* any complaints, surely she would have come to me. I can't believe she has been bellyaching to you! I was under the impression that there was no love lost between the two of you...?'

'She *hasn't* complained. Not a word. But believe me, darling, she's close. And don't look like that, Beth: pouting never suited you. Anyway, I'm just airing my observations, and I think the first *you'll* hear is when she hands you her notice and her bags are packed. And of course, if Lena goes, so does Louis...'

Beth had seemed to take this information on board with immediacy, knowing that her husband would hate to lose either: Lena and Louis were almost family to Jake.

'Okay, Mum. Point taken. But I'll have to run, now. Sonia is back this weekend. Roy's with her and we have doubles booked for this afternoon. I'll make it right with Lena. I *promise.*'

With a hasty kiss planted on her mother's cheek, Beth had rushed off to her appointment with her closest friends. Maureen had been left standing in the opulent hallway of the house she herself did not care for, with a bemused look on her face and accommodating thoughts in her mind...*she's only young...young and carefree with the world at her feet...She has time enough to grow old...She'll grow into her responsibilities...That will come for certain with children...*

As Maureen had made her way into the kitchen, she'd felt a thrill run up her spine...soon she would have grandchildren...*Wow.*

That weekend brought a change of heart to Lena Grant: without any fuss, Maureen Sommer had rolled up her sleeves and had worked side by side with the housekeeper. At first Lena had resented the intrusion. But later, after making and serving afternoon tea for fourteen and changing the linens and towels in the doubled-up bedrooms and bathrooms that were to house the unexpected visitors, all done with the constant good natured assistance of Don Sommer's petite wife, Lena had to admit to herself that Beth's mother had more to her than meets the eye.

A mutual respect began to enter into the early stages of friendship. And it could be said that Lena Grant, as the autumn weeks passed into the bitter cold days of winter, would often find herself hoping that Maureen Sommer had been invited to the weekend gatherings organised to herald the forthcoming festive season.

'*Happy New Year,* my love.' Maureen had made sure that she would be the first to wish her husband all the very best for the New Year.

'And a Happy New Year to you, too, my darling: Can you *believe* it is 1982?' Don kissed her long and hard before releasing her to answer his question.

Breathless from the passionate embrace, but glowing with happiness, Maureen shook her head. And before she had the chance to catch her breath to answer properly, she was caught up in the flurry of hugs and kisses bestowed on her from their dinner guests.

The Sommers' had invited a select group of people to their New Year celebrations. The party of twelve had feasted on smoked salmon canapés, lobster bisque, rare fillet steaks, and Maureen's speciality, English trifle. The latter had been laden with sherry, loaded with raspberries and groaning with thick white cream.

Ushered outside to watch a firework display, the camaraderie between the friends, both old and new, was relaxed and informal. Jokes flew, laughter rippled and the New Year started in a joyous atmosphere.

The felicitations and fireworks over, the party settled into the soft padded, rose patterned patio chairs that graced the terrace of Strand House, Maureen and Don's beautiful beach front Floridian home.

Cradling a balloon glass of brandy, Ben Howarth brought up the topic of their forthcoming vacation.

'It's such a *pity* that Beth and Jake aren't coming.' Ben had already let it be known that he was very much looking forward to the ski trip arranged for the following weekend and that as far as he was concerned, the more in the party, the merrier it would be.

'I know. They were so keen to take you up on your offer. But the film still isn't finished. And it's *way* over budget. They have been waiting for bad weather and, as you know, in San Francisco that only comes when you don't want it.' Maureen felt, yet again, the need to apologise and explain the need for her daughter's cancellation. She was also very aware of how fraught her son-in-law was with the non-completion of his first film and how Beth, understandably, wanted to stay by her husband's side.

'The weather will turn; San Fran can have some dreadful weather. Is it the storm scene on the bridge they need to complete...?' Julia Howarth had spent her childhood years in Lafayette, a suburb of San Francisco, and explained that the climate could change in a matter of hours. The fact that for the past few months there had been no rain was very unusual. Julia, who had read Jake's novel when it had first come out, was aware that many of the scenes would need fog and heavy rains. Now, Maureen confirmed that she was right: rain was being prayed for.

'Well, I for one am glad not to be coming with you on the trip...I hate snow!' Chuck Vicente liked his creature comforts. Texan by birth, and a lover of Florida's climate, the big man thought they were all crazy to be flying to the snow of Colorado.

'To be truthful, I'm a bit wary. I've never skied before. I'm not used to snow, so I'm sure I'll make a right fool of myself.' Maureen was worried about the trip: and she too preferred warmer climes and gentler exercise.

Roy seemed to sense this, and thought to comfort his hostess.

'No you won't, Aunt Maureen. You'll do just fine. With your slight figure you'll ski like the wind. And you'll love it! They'll start you off on the beginner's slope. But believe me, it won't take you too long to tackle a steep run.'

The silence that followed Roy's statement said it all: Roy Vicente was an all round athlete. What he thought of as easy would be mind-blowingly difficult for most who'd been listening. Except for his fiancée, Sonia: the Howarth's only daughter was an excellent sportswoman.

As this was now spoken of, Sonia's prowess as a skier and her abilities to be good at most things, it was not for the first time that everyone on the terrace agreed that the forthcoming wedding, calendared for late June, between Roy and Sonia was just about perfect.

The compliments brought a flush to Sonia's cheeks, and glow of pride to her parents.' Roy had to be told to be quiet; indeed Sonia herself clamped a hand over his mouth, to everyone's laughter.

Like her politician mother, Sonia Howarth had a clear idea of what she wanted from life; this last year had been very trying in that respect. Her courtship with the impetuous Roy had been turbulent. That and having to study for her law degree had left her ready for a break from routine. Part of the problem with her union with Roy was that like many in the Vicente clan, Roy liked his own way. And he had wanted her to quit college.

She had not relented to his wishes. When, finally, the engagement was announced, Mary Lou was still in the dark of who really wore the trousers in the relationship...Sonia had overheard her future mother-in-law's whisper to her women friends attending the duo Thanksgiving and engagement celebration...'She should have quit college. She'll *never* practice law. She'll be having baby after baby if Roy has his own way...' But Mary Lou's statement was way off mark: Sonia Howarth had every intention of practicing law and very little intention of starting a family until in her late thirties. Though Roy knew of this plan, he had not mentioned any of it to his mother. But it wasn't rocket science to know that Mary Lou, who so enjoyed her role as grandmother to Lydia's offspring, was more than eager to add her son's to the collection.

As the early hours of the first day of January began, the yawns began too. Couple by couple, the tired but happy New Year revellers made their way to waiting cars that would whisk them through the sleep quiet streets of Palm Beach to their own homes or hotel accommodation.

Don pulled Chuck into a manly embrace, thanking him profusely for his generosity: the Vicente's twelve seating private jet was going to be the mode of travel for the ski trip.

'Hey, you're welcome! I won't be using it—not until the end of January. In some ways, I'm sorry that I'm not coming with you, but, hey all that snow…no way. Craig Gowrie is a good pilot. You'll *love* it, pal!' It was then Chuck's turn to embrace Don. And as Don's eyes rolled into his head after receiving the bear hug, he was left in no doubt that Chuck Vicente was a powerful man, in every way.

It appeared that their world had become full of *ifs*.

If only Maureen had left the clearing of the celebration debris to those who were being paid to do it, she might not have broken her left ankle.

'Mum…' Beth chuckled, 'you're supposed to break a leg on the ski holiday—*not* in your house just days before…'Beth playfully admonished her mother down the telephone line.

Maureen took the joking in good stead: it was a stupid thing to have happened. Polished floors and high-heeled shoes had never been the best of partners. Add the fact that she'd had more than her share of alcohol, plus her willingness to be always helpful, and what do you get: a broken ankle.

Later that day her unselfish approach to life was once again to the fore: Maureen insisted that Don continue with his plans to go skiing, 'Darling, please go, if you want to. I don't mind in the least…really I don't.'

When her husband flatly refused, stating that he wasn't going anywhere without his wife by his side, Maureen had been quietly relieved…*if Don should break a bone, or his back…*these thoughts had been playing on her mind since the trip had first been muted.

If the truth be known, Don was somewhat relieved, too: he'd been thinking on the same lines and had even said to one or two that perhaps he was "Too long in the tooth for any shilly-shallying on ski slopes."

So it was a party of six who, six days later, took off from the West Miami airport. Ben and Julia Howarth, both good skiers where delighted to be once again in the company of their daughter Sonia and her fiancé, Roy Vicente. The others in the party were the two security officers that always travelled with the Howarth's.

If Maureen had not been sat on the sofa in the den, her plastered ankle resting on a padded footstool. If she had not chosen to watch (and cry over) an old black and white movie, she would not have seen that the film was interrupted by a newsflash:

'It has been reported that a light aircraft has crashed near Denver airport. The plane—thought to belong to Charles...Chuck...Vicente, a millionaire property tycoon—disintegrated on landing. Debris was thrown in a two-mile radius. There are thought to be two survivors, although at this moment in time they have not been named...An eye witness report said that the plane seemed to be approaching too fast...'

If Don had not heard the blood curdling screams of his wife, she may have further damaged her foot: the grave news had made her leap from the sofa, without thought of her infirmity. Don had lifted her from the floor, completely bewildered at first by his wife's hysteria.

If Beth and Jake *had* have heard the news flash, they probably would not have boarded their secret flight that would take them to meet their friends at the ski resort: the rains in San Francisco had finally come, the shoot in the can. The couple had thought it a good plan to surprise their friends with their arrival, especially in light of the fact that the ski party was already two-down due to Maureen and Don's absence. The tragic news of the crash was broken to them by the captain of their flight after their aircraft had safely landed.

Ben and Julia Howarth were the two survivors. Ben had broken his neck, Julia, miraculously, had suffered just a broken arm. The others on the flight had all perished: Roy Vicente and his fiancée Sonia Howarth, Craig Gowrie, pilot, and his co-pilot Mark Hampton. Adrian Jackson and William Brown, Vice President Julia Howarth's two security guards, were named as the dead. The death toll numbered six.

The funerals were well attended. Each had a separate day. In total, most of the grieving relatives, colleagues and friends spent over two weeks travelling the country to be present for the burials: Roy Vicente was buried in the family vault in a grassy cemetery in San Antonio, Texas.

Sonia Howarth was buried in Boston. An icy cruel wind blew as she was laid to rest.

Craig Gowrie was buried next to his stillborn son, in a small, winter white graveyard in Maine.

Mark Hampton was buried in a similar graveyard in frosty New Jersey.

Adrian Jackson was given a military funeral in freezing Washington.

William Brown's funeral, the next day, was given the same honour. Snow was thick on the ground as the flag was folded and handed to his wife.

Those who by fate's hand had cancelled their involvement with the ski party, or who had travelled secretly, were inconsolable; and guilty...*Why were we spared...? Thank you, God...But why? What is your purpose for me? What should I do with my life...?*

The answers to many of these questions would never be known. What they did know was that they had to carry on, to live their lives fully and enjoy the precious gift that it was. Those who cared for the ones who had been spared begged them to put aside all thoughts of guilt, and to live with good memories of those who had perished.

Easier said than done.

Chuck Vicente, who was built like a powerful workhorse, suffered a massive heart attack later that spring. An attack he would never fully recover from.

Mary Lou busied herself with constant demands of her invalid husband and the company of her grandson, Michael. To keep herself sane, she let her thoughts think forwards and onwards to the autumn months when Lydia would give birth to her second child. A child they all hoped would be a boy.

And their hopes were fulfilled: Roy Charles Landon was born on the fourth day of October.

Ben Howarth was making a slow recovery. Paralyzed from the neck down, he had been told that he would probably never walk again.

His wife, Julia, who was kept busy with her duties as Vice President (an office that had so thrilled her only months before, was now just a routine job that gave her little time for despair,) took all the support she was given. She took counselling, she took on more staff; and she took more and more pills. Pills that she had first taken to ease the pain of a broken arm, were still being used daily, nightly, to combat the affects of a broken heart.

It was a bright June morning. Julia had been at her Washington desk since first light. Her food intake had been just her usual black coffee and a water biscuit. And the benefits of this inadequate diet were showing well on her gaunt face. The hollows under her eyes could not have been blacker; the pallor of her skin could not have been greyer. In another life, she and Sonia would have been excitedly planning the wedding that had been due to take place on the last Sunday of the month.

It was with these thoughts in mind that she answered her personal phone after she had let it ring far longer than necessary. It was the hospital. Ben had moved his foot. Replacing the phone back into its cradle, Julia let the tears falls. They started as a smarting trickle, and then they gushed and flowed as if they would never stop. Grief that she had tapped for months washed her cheeks, cleansed her mind, and collapsed the dam of emotion she had kept erect and strong since January.

If her staff heard her keening wails, they did nothing about it. They let her be. And rightly so: Julia Howarth had been strong too long. Now it was her turn to wallow in what she had lost, and what she was being given back: Ben would make a complete recovery, of that she was now sure.

And as her tears finally stopped, part of her grief had been washed away. She opened her desk drawer and withdrew the photograph of Sonia that she hidden away. She stared at her daughter, her beautiful, radiant daughter. She brought the glass to her lips and held it there. And then she made her vows. Vows she knew she would keep. She promised her daughter that she would never take another pill; that she would take up an exercise programme again; that she would eat regular, and properly. That she would be the best wife in the world to Ben. And that she would become the first woman president of the United States of America.

Julia Howarth had often spoken of her ambition. And it was an ambition that both her husband and her daughter had readily supported her in. She would not let them down. But first she would have to ensure that Ben, who had been her childhood sweetheart and to whom she had been married to for thirty years, got well. When it was time to take her oath of office (and this morning, right now, the revelation that this would come to pass had made itself known to her) Ben would be standing by her side.

Beth decided it was time to make babies: Lots of babies. And Jake agreed.

By the winter of the year that had started so badly, Beth had suffered two miscarriages. Though deeply traumatised, she had recovered enough to attend a prestigious award ceremony early in the new year of 1983. At the well-attended gathering, Beth was presented with, to rapturous applause, her award for her performance in *A Stranger Stalks Within Us*.

Don Sommer was named as best supporting actor.

Jake Adier best screenplay writer.

However, the very best was yet to come: By spring, Beth was pregnant again. The baby expected late September.

Much was done to ensure that this baby was not miscarried. Beth rested in Montport for most of the summer. And as she bloomed with good health, so her stomach swelled.

Charlotte Elizabeth Adier was born on a beautiful sunny September morning. A week earlier than planned, she arrived, unexpectedly, within an hour of her mother's labour and at home in Rockfort House.

The birth attendants had had no training. But both Jake and Maureen did a splendid job of delivering the child.

And it was grandma Maureen who put the wailing brown haired infant to her mother's breast and encouraged her to suckle. The baby stopped crying instantly, which caused the other three to burst into tears of relief...and joy. As Maureen glanced around the bedroom, that looked as if a massacre had happened, she shook her head in disbelief: she and Don had taken the early morning flight to Montport. As it was now only eleven, it had been quite a morning.

Later, when Don first held his first grandchild, as he nursed her and kissed her, savouring her newborn, downy scent, he whispered to her that her entry into the world had the makings of a grand film. Maybe even a musical...

In England the early part of the eighties decade had been particularly difficult for Declan Fitzgerald. The devoted father had tried everything in his power to find a cure for his sick daughter.

But Declan's heroic efforts had been in vain: Donna Fitzgerald, aged two years and eight months, died in her daddy's arms on a bleak early January morning in 1982.

At the end of the following week, the London newspapers reported the tragedy that had be-fallen the Vice President of America: she had lost her only daughter in an air crash. It made front-page news, with grainy photographs of the wreckage taking precedence. On the second or third pages they printed a story of another death. It was just a small article, a few lines, though for it to be told in most newspapers, the editors must of thought it held merit enough to be newsworthy:

Declan Fitzgerald, wealthy property developer, who made his name and his fortune repairing Blitz damage caused by the Second World War, fell to his death yesterday. It is reported that Fitzgerald plunged sixty feet from the roof of one of his city central properties. His secretary and long time friend, Miss Cathy McDowd, said that Mr Fitzgerald had been inconsolable since the death of his two-year old daughter. Donna Fitzgerald had been suffering from Hodgkin's disease. Her burial took place yesterday morning. Mr Fitzgerald's wife, Iris, was unable to comment on her husband's death as she is suffering from a debilitating illness and is herself hospitalized. Foul play is not suspected.

*

35

Charlotte Adier was not a good baby and this made caring for her needs very trying. Lena Grant secretly thought that perhaps there was something really wrong with the child who never stopped crying, be it day or night.

For six, wearily long months, Charlotte made her presence very much known. Then, like a turn of a tap, the crying stopped. From the moment she could sit, unsupported, the brown haired, brown-eyed infant beamed at everything and everyone. At last she was the child the family, and the household staff, had craved.

By her eighth month she was a bouncy, chuckling, energetic crawler. Her delighted parents joked with family members that their daughter could be an Olympic crawler, if there was such a sport, taking a gold medal for being so clever and nimble at the activity.

What Beth and Jake didn't joke about, as their daughter reached her first birthday, was the fact that she possessed a very strong will, a frenzied temper and an intense dislike of music. Any music.

'Happy birthday, sweetheart! Come to grandma. *Come on;* you can do it. Walk to grandma...' Maureen bent low and held her arms open, beckoning for Charlotte to toddle towards her across a short expanse of lush green lawn. She laughed, though in truth was a little embarrassed, when the child, impervious to her grandmother's wishes, fell to her knees, and moved at the speed of lightening, in the opposite direction.

Straightening to her full height, Maureen watched her granddaughter with ever-anxious eyes: Charlotte could get into mischief as quick as she could do her famous crawl.

Backing into her seat on the floral patterned, swing-action garden sofa, she once again became her Aunt Vi's companion—not that the older woman was such sweet company this gloriously sunny September afternoon. Charlotte's great-grandmother was in a foul mood; the birthday girl herself being responsible for the heavy scowl and muttered grievances.

'She's a little *villain*, that one is. She has you all running rings round her. A good smack bottom would put her right, no mistake.'

Vi had been a guest at Rockfort House for just one week. But it had been long enough for her to do some plain speaking about her great-grandchild: Vi thought the little girl to be a "ruined brat" and now, as she watched Charlotte reek havoc in one the herbaceous borders, she felt justified in speaking her mind.

Maureen, irritated by both her aunt and her granddaughter, jumped to her feet yet again, and raced across the lawn just in time to stop Charlotte from stuffing ripped up roots into her mouth.

'Charlotte, no! *Naughty* girl. Don't do that, you'll make yourself sick.' Bending to her haunches, Maureen scooped the dirty-faced baby into her arms.

Apoplectic to have been thwarted in her plans, the chubby toddler struggled, red-faced with fury, frantically trying to riddle out of her grandmother's arms. Bubbling both spittle and the dirt from her mouth, she shrieked her annoyance, grabbing hold of Maureen's hair in her attempts to free herself.

The fierce strength of the child's grip forced Maureen to topple backwards, tumbling them both onto the grass.

Charlotte's eyes sparkled. She'd found her escape.

But great-grandmother Vi was on hand to capture. Hoisting the writhing child into her arms, she held onto her firmly, though became breathless with the exertion of the screaming toddler's battling arms and flailing legs.

'This...child needs some...*discipline*...' Vi's panted words were rewarded with a smack in the mouth: Charlotte, as young as she was, had a vicious energy when her temper was aroused.

Maureen was quick to whip the child from her aunt's grip.

'Give her to me, Aunt Vi,' Maureen took a blow herself as she rescued the now screeching child. Pained as she was by the shoe-shod kick in the throat she had just received from the hysterical youngster, she still felt the need to be loyal. 'She doesn't *mean* to hurt. She's just having a bit of a paddy, aren't...you...*darling*...?' Charlotte, stiffened with rage, was practically horizontal in Maureen's arms.

Rubbing her top lip, Vi let the lid blow off her own anger...

'Bloody *paddy* my foot! She's spoilt *rotten*. No child should get away with what she does...'

Maureen tried valiantly to hush both her aunt and her granddaughter. 'Oh *do* give over, Aunt Vi! She's just a *baby*. Hey, now, *Charlotte! S*hush, shush, sweetheart, you'll have your mummy thinking you're being...*murdered*...Ouch! No, Charlotte! No! Let *go*...'

It was Maureen who was being tortured: Charlotte's closed fist clutch had the strength of steel: now it was her grandmother's hair that she now trying to rip from its roots.

Beth's face was stern as she stepped out into the garden from the open French doors of the dining room.

'Charlotte! *Charlotte*...Stop *that*. At once!' Beth had to raise her voice to a shout to be heard over the uproar her daughter was making.

Trying to cradle and pacify the writhing child in her arms, Maureen tried also to make allowances at the same time:

'I thinks she's over-excited, Beth. We tried to stop her from getting into mischief; but she'd already spoiled her dress. *Sorry.*' Apologetically, but with a relief that was obvious, Maureen handed the sobbing child over to her daughter.

And as she watched Beth quieten her daughter, and then turn and slowly walk back into the house, hushing the child, talking rhythmically as she calmed and comforted with words of firm admonishment and then instructively as she told of the forthcoming birthday celebrations, which needed her to be a very good girl, Maureen conceded to herself that she was hopeless at handling her own grandchild.

With a heavy sigh, Maureen plonked herself down next to Vi on the soft-upholstered comfort of the wood framed hammock seat. Moving her heels backwards and forwards, she set the swing in motion and was calmed by the rocking movement. And as Vi sat swaying silently, too, she felt grateful for the older woman's refrain from conversation, knowing that once a dialogue did begin, she would have to come up with some answers. Fast.

As it happened, they both began to speak at the same time, which made them laugh, easing the tension.

'Look, Aunt Vi, I *know* what you are going to say. Believe me, I'm worried, too...'

When Vi tried to interrupt, Maureen hushed her to listen more...

'They do *not* spoil her. Honestly, Aunt Vi, they don't. To be honest, well, this might sound strange, but, well, I think they are afraid of her—what I mean is, *for* her. You see, Charlotte is extremely bright, and her intelligence is...'

Vi did interrupt. 'Bloody twaddle, Maureen, and you know it. I'm surprised at you, that I am! Don't *insult* me with all your philosophizing. I've not reached my seventies without recognising when a child is a brat; aye, an a *spoilt* brat at that!'

'Keep your voice down, Aunt Vi, *please*. They'll hear you...' Maureen patted her aunt's knee to emphasize, re-enforce her words. But Vi, in full flow, took little to no notice.

'I don't bloody care if they do! It's about time someone said something, because since I've been here they've crept around her, and her bad behaviour...I'll give it that she's a bonny lass. Her smile, when she wants to, can break your heart. True enough, she's me own flesh and blood and all that, but *someone's* got to say it: she's a little devil. The little demon bit me last night. The first kid *ever*...I bent to give her a kiss, and she bit me *blooming* nose.'

Turning to look at her aunt, Maureen could see the red mark evidence on the tip of her aunt's snub nose. Her nervous giggle at what she saw was out of place: it wasn't really funny. Charlotte had bitten once or twice before. She herself could vouch for that.

Not daring to air her personal knowledge of Charlotte's taste for skin, Maureen hugged her aunt close, begging her, 'Leave it be, Aunt Vi; for or the time being, *please*?' Maureen felt the need to keep the peace: To be the pacifier at every turn. Though she did go on to say that when Don arrived— he was expected within the hour—she would ask him to have a quiet word with Jake. But, seeing as today was Charlotte's first birthday, and numerous guests were about to descend for the celebration, it would be better to let matters lie...

Vi grudgingly agreed to Maureen's request, and the two of them spent the next quarter of hour in a contented hum of conversation regarding other things and other events, whilst around them Lena and the catering crew (brought in just for the day,) laid tables and set places at balloon flying, gaily clothed party tables in readiness for Charlotte's birthday party. A celebration that would commence as the Montport afternoon sun lowered in the sky and shadowed the manicured lawns and sparkling blue swimming pool of the infant's palatial home, Rockfort House

*

36

'Just after she was admitted into the clinic, your mother's malady brought with it a series of delusions. Mrs Fitzgerald insisted she had a daughter. And yes, your stepfather, when I finally telephoned him, was as bemused by it as you are now. However, Mr Fitzgerald put me in the picture: it seems that Iris—we do like to use Christian names as often as we can, your mother knows me as Len—did have a stepdaughter…perhaps you were too young to remember her…?'

Christopher Grady, who'd rubbed his hand across his face in sheer bewilderment of his mother's imagination, was now beginning to see that there was a smidgeon of truth to her ramblings; he nodded that was aware of the girl's existence, saying, 'Though I don't personally remember her, my mother spoke of her often when we were in our teens…'

'Yes, well, that's another bone of contention: "in our teens," you were referring—you mean you and Timothy, right?'

Christopher nodded again.

'Still no trace of him I gather?'

Christopher shook his head this time. With sadness in his voice he said, 'We haven't heard from him in a long time. I'm beginning to think that he might be dead. Tim was heavily into the drug scene. LSD…pot. Heroin…'

'Tragic. I'm sorry to hear that. Anyway, back to the *girl* business. Your mother insists that the, er, *Maureen*,' the doctor looked down at his notes to make sure he had the right name, '…yes, that Maureen was her *own* child. Her natural daughter sired by your stepfather, Declan Fitzgerald.'

Christopher looked down at his hands clasped in his lap, and shook his head again and thought…*my mother would have said anything to keep hold of Declan*…

'However, the late Mr Fitzgerald was completely honest with me, about everything—his involvement with Miss McDowd, and the birth of their daughter. It's been a terrible time all round, for you all, I'm sure. A death is always traumatic, but a *baby's,* dear, dear…and then Mr Fitzgerald himself. How is Miss McDowd coping, by the way…?'

'Managing, I'm told.' Christopher, though he was saddened by the deaths, had not been in touch with Cathy McDowd; he'd left all that business to the lawyers.

The psychiatrist, Doctor Leonard Barnes (Len to his patients) leant forward in his chair, leaning his tweed-jacketed elbows on the neat leather-topped desk that was a barrier between himself and the man sat before him.

'Look, Christopher—you don't mind me calling you that?'

'By all means; whatever you want'

'Well, Chris, I'm not *too* sure you know what you are taking on, your mother is still, how can I put it…confused.'

'Nothing new in that.' Christopher actually grinned; the statement was true.

'Exactly. And it would *confuse* her more, at this stage in her treatments, if you were to take her away from our care.'

'She'll be okay. I'm sure of it. And she wants to come home: And why not? The Hampstead house is hers. Declan never divorced her, you know…Now, with his death, the property and the businesses go to my mother.'

'Well, then. She can certainly *afford* to stay here…'

'I want her home.'

'Mr Fitzgerald signed all the forms: he committed her…'

'And I'm un-committing her. Fitzgerald is dead. And I believe my mother is well enough, now, to leave…' Christopher then added a rejoinder. 'Of course, if you prefer, I could get another opinion on her condition…'

As he had thought, this statement brought a silence to the proceedings.

Doctor Len seemed to be sizing up the situation. He had earned excellent fees for the treatment of Iris Fitzgerald. But in truth, not much could be done with her problem: once a drunk always a drunk seemed to fit the woman's character and medical assessment with aplomb. And he was also probably thinking that, if he were to be honest, which *Doctor Len* rarely was where money was concerned, that over the years of him being her psychiatrist, he'd had a good enough return for the upkeep of the difficult-to-handle woman.

'Will she be cared for? A nurse, perhaps?'

'I'm moving my own practice to the Hampstead Vale house. There will be everything my mother needs; constant, round the clock care.'

'She is quite delicate...' Doctor Len was having one last stab, 'as you know, she has always been that way, both in mind and in body, although, I must say, that since her husband's death, she has seemed more settled. She seems very content, at peace. Somewhat. But it could be that she has found her religion again...you do *know* that, don't you? That she has returned to her faith? Your mother is a devout Catholic.'

When Christopher confirmed that he knew of this, the psychiatrist seemed to resign himself to losing his monetary well-endowed patient...

'Though I will need to see you mother from time to time,'

'That will be done.'

'Right, then, shall we go and see her? Give her the happy news? Hmm, yes, let's see...' he looked down at his heavy gold wristwatch, 'yes, it's twelve fifteen; she will probably be in the dining room. I'll show you the way, Doctor Grady...'

'We're flying back to England with you, Aunt Vi.'

'Are you love? What, the both of you?'

'Yes...we *thought* you'd be pleased.'

Vi Greenwood *was* pleased. Being with Maureen and Don these past months had been a real treat. And now, as she was pampered with the service of breakfast in bed: hot buttered wholemeal toast, a boiled egg, a cup of steaming English tea and a tall chilled glass of Florida's freshest orange juice, Vi had no hesitation in showing her appreciation.

'By, lass, your *too* good to me. I'll miss all this, our Maureen, that I will. It's like being in a long-running film, aye, like the ones I used to take you to when you were a youngster. Who'd have thought it, hey? Who would have *blooming* thought it?'

Vi was still in America. It was the longest time she had ever been away from home. And she had loved nearly every minute. The trip to California with Maureen and Don had been wonderful. They had stayed in a very famous hotel, situated on Sunset Boulevard. Vi had been so excited as they had travelled down the famous *Sunset Strip*, looking out for number seventy-seventy. During its long run on British television, Vi had tried never to miss an episode of the detective series that had been made in Los Angeles and had famed the *Strip*. However, her disappointment at not catching a glimpse of any members of the cast was short lived: Los Angeles' other sights and attractions were a great compensation. She had been truly drop-jawed by the many film stars and celebrities breezing in and out of the world-class hotel.

Christmas had been spent in Palm Beach Florida, at Maureen and Don's beach side home. From there she had travelled with the couple to Las Vegas where Don had been booked to perform for the first seven nights of the new year of 1985.

Now, as she sat in bed, cosseted by the many soft pillows at her back, Vi devoured her breakfast, watching the television at the same time. Outside her bedroom window, the Florida sun was already heating the January day. But Vi was glad to be going home. She was ready. And now that she knew that Maureen and Don were going to be her companions on the long-haul flight, and indeed were going to be in England for the best part of two weeks, she felt more than satisfied. If only the problem of Charlotte, Beth's girl, could be so easily sorted...

Vi had arrived in America at the beginning of the previous September in time for the christening of her great-granddaughter Charlotte, and the infant's first birthday celebrations which was to follow two days later.

Staying as a guest of Beth and Jake in their home in Montport for the week prior to the baptism ceremony, Vi had had the time to get well acquainted with the almost one year-old youngster.

Beth and Jake had wanted the christening to be just family members and close friends, especially in light of the fact that most were still mourning the loss of those who had perished in the plane crash disaster.

When it had come to choosing Godparents for their daughter, Beth and Jake had decided that Barry Greenwood was an excellent choice, and had also thought the same of father of two, Pete Landon, Chuck and Mary Lou's son-in-law. Both men had been delighted to accept the honour, which had then left just the matter of who would make the best godmother. And here both Beth and Jake were immediate with whom they thought would be ideal: Julia Howarth.

Julia had said that she had been overcome with emotion when the invitation was first put to her, for didn't everyone know that if things had been different it would have been Sonia's role? However, the politician was also immediate with her acceptance: Charlotte would be the nearest to ever having a granddaughter of her own, and Julia had told Vi she was delighted to think, and to hope, that in the coming years both she and the youngster would grow to become very close.

The christening had taken place at St Mary's Church, Montport. Harry Sommer, Don's brother, was another family member who had flown in for the occasion; though he had never had children of his own, Don had mentioned to Vi that he felt it was important that his stepson and his wife Beth were well acquainted with his only brother. And that he now hoped for the same for his granddaughter.

Cynthia Martinez (nee Paton) was also on the invitation list. Senora Martinez arrived very much on the arm of her husband, Fernando. The oddly matched, chatty couple were obviously very well suited, and as usual, flame haired Cynthia had no compunction in telling Vi, and everyone else gathered together for the child's baptism that she was gloriously happy in her new life in Argentina. The healthy sheen to her skin suggested that the climate suited her; her well toned arms and legs displayed by the pillar-box red shift dress (Cynthia thought nothing of wearing red, even though most red-heads avoided the clash of colours,) though sleeveless and simple was the epitome of understated elegance and, if her abundance of jewellery was anything to go by, her husband's wealth suited just fine, too.

Vi, never a fan of Beth's one-time agent, found herself seated next to the woman. She also found, within minutes of her company, that Cynthia had the same leanings towards Charlotte as, quite frankly, she herself did:

'Sorry and all that, Vi, I know that you are her great grandmother, but hey, the kid's a child from hell! And she bites like she means it.' Cynthia had the marks on her arm to prove her statement true.

Both women, united with the battle scars of reaching out to the celebrated infant, had been deep in conversation when Maureen had come across the lawn to offer more champagne. And Maureen had become indignant, indeed quite angry when Cynthia had asked, in her loud booming voice,

'What are they *doing* to the child? Aren't they teaching her *any* discipline? She's a wild cat. And Beth was such an angel as a child...'

Maureen had seen the two women sitting together, becoming as thick as thieves, and was infuriated by Vi: hadn't it been she who had instilled in them all to "always stick up for your own." That statement had been Vi's mantra. And now here she was, agreeing with an outsider, *conferring*, no less, that her first great grandchild was, "a bit of a monster."

But Maureen's harsh words were for Senora Martinez,

'Cynthia! Since when have you been an authority on children? If I remember rightly, they were just a *meal-ticket* to you and your agency.'

Smarting under her own words, Maureen tried to mask her burning cheeks behind her champagne glass.

However Cynthia was made of sterner stuff. The rebuke rolled off her, 'Come off it, Maureen! You can't kid *me*. You held Beth in an iron rein. She was a *doll*. Adorable. And she still is, for that matter…'

Maureen's eyes followed Cynthia's. And Cynthia's gaze was on Beth. Attractive as ever, Beth was dressed for the christening in a sleeveless, square-necked, figure hugging dress that was complemented with a colour matching cream chiffon wrap which was draped loosely round her tanned arms and shoulders. Deep in conversation with friends of her husband's who had flown in from New York, she was giving her guests her undivided attention.

But as the sapphires in her earlobes (the first gift from her stepfather, Don) caught and reflected the afternoon sun, those who knew her well noticed that the strain lines that now circled her brilliant blue eyes, were becoming deeper by the day.

Ever the perfect hostess, Beth smiled and chatted, moving across the lawns of her home, exchanging pleasantries, thanking people for their attendance, their gifts, her worries on hold for a short reprieve: shrieking Charlotte had been taken out of ear-shot and was upstairs in her nursery, accompanied by her father, Jake, who without doubt would likely to have been wringing in sweat as he and the latest nanny wrestled with his daughter's stiff legged fury and screaming temper as she was being laid down for her much-needed afternoon nap.

Two days later, once again a screaming and red-faced Charlotte had been carried, stiff-legged, up to her bedroom after the candle blowing of her birthday cake had been ruined by one of her tantrums: In the silent awe of the handful of other children invited to the party, which included the Vicente's two well-behaved grandchildren, Charlotte's wild temper fit had seen her smash her dimpled fists into the un-cut, butter soft celebration cake. Even the attending adults gulped at the child's audacity on such an occasion; the whole downstairs rooms of the house, including the garden, had been gaily decorated with banners and balloons and an air of festivity had prevailed. What should have been such a joyous afternoon in the golden sunshine of a late summer's day, was marred by the birthday girl's lack of normal excitement and curiosity: she had ignored everything—from her gifts to the jubilant squeals of delight that accompanied the other more playful children as they frolicked on the lawns.

It had been the chorused singing of happy birthday wishes that had set off the one-year old's frenzy.

With the echo of Charlotte's screams filling the air, the partying children were bidden farewell; bumper-sized gift bags in hand, the unusually subdued youngsters climbed into the backseats of the various cars that would take them home.

After other guests had also made a quick get-away, Don had beckoned his stepson to one side, motioning that they move on outside again through the open French windows of the dining room. They had to wait a few moments whilst the collapsible party tables were cleared before they could have any privacy. Hurrying the procedure, both men tucked in to help.

When they were finally alone, Don and Jake seated themselves at the patio table and, for a time, sat in silence...

Don had known what he wanted to say, but couldn't quite find the right words. He didn't want to appear to be interfering, though none the less, something had to be done.

Jake, who was dressed quite similar to his stepfather in khaki shorts and white, short sleeved polo shirt, sandal footed for comfort, looked across the lawns and onwards to the brilliant blue sea with a look of dejection on his face.

Turning to take a glance at his stepson, Don was upset to see how distressed Jake actually was. The younger man's hair was flecked with grey at the temples, and his mouth, perhaps one of his best features, as it more often than not graced with a wide smile, paying the best of compliments to his strong white teeth, showed little evidence that that had ever been so. Today, the lines round Jake's full lips had taken a downwards turn; even the skin round his eyes seemed drooped with sadness.

Noticing all of this, Don felt angry and said as much...

'This is *not* normal, Jake. You will have to do something. The child is completely out of hand.'

'I know. *We* know. We've talked about it for weeks; in fact, we talk about nothing else. There is something wrong. Beth wants to take her to New York; have some tests done. She thinks she is probably autistic. Oh, God, Don! Do you think Charlotte's problems have anything to do with the past? My past? You know what I mean, through the *drugs*?'

As Don looked at the anguish on his stepson's face, he was filled with pity...*Guilt, there is always some kind of guilt lurking, and we all suffer for it.*

Sighing deeply, Don stood and moved to stand behind Jake's white wrought iron chair. Placing his hands on Jake's shoulders, he squeezed the man's tense muscles as he spoke, 'Listen, Jake, whatever is causing Charlotte's tantrums will have to be seen to. Personally, I don't believe that it will have anything to do with *you*.' Don gave Jake's shoulders a firm squeeze to emphasize his words.

Jake stood up from his chair; relief swept his face as he turned to speak.

'I hope you are right...it's been worrying me so *much*. They say the past always catches up with you: Sins of the father and all that. But I don't want it to ruin my *baby's* life.' There were tears in his eyes.

Seeing the emotion, Don felt that any further comment would be useless. He placed his arm round Jake's shoulder and both men began to walk the length of the terrace.

The early evening air was fresh and balmy, scented as usual by the sea and the many trees, plants and shrubs that graced the magnificent grounds of Rockfort House.

Breathing deeply, taking in the good air, Don said, 'You know, Jake,' he hoped he sounded quite matter-of-factly, 'it *could* be that she is just hyperactive. I've read quite a bit about this lately.'

Jake's laugh had hollow ring to it.

'What you mean, *Don*, is that you have asked around and that's what people have come up with...'

Both men had stopped walking. Don found that he couldn't look into Jake's face...*Guilt, again...Mine this time...Jake is worried enough without the added burden of gossip...*

'Charlotte *will* be okay. You'll see. Perhaps she just needs a brother, or a sister, other children to play with, constantly. Kids are like young pups...they need to learn discipline from each other. Oh, I don't know, Jake! Kids, babies for sure are a new territory for me.'

The walk continued until Don spied the more comfortable patio chairs and plonked himself down.

Jake did likewise.

'I'll tell you what, Don. I'm *glad* that we only invited the neighbourhood kids and family to her birthday party. The christening was bad enough, though thank God, she didn't bite either Julia or Barry! She did have a go at Pete, but he said that he was used to kid's and handled it well—he nibbled her back. So I suppose you are right: she needs to be *shown* who's the boss.' Jake seemed to have found some of his lost humour.

The humour was short lived: Even on the terrace, Charlotte's piercing screams could still be heard.

'You know we will be travelling back with Vi?'

Don had said all there was to say; his change of subject was obvious...

Jake, recognising Don's mood change, made an heroic effort to push his own troubled thoughts aside. Noticing that Lena was still in the dining room, clearing the final debris of the party, he called out to her asking if it was possible for her to get them a couple of beers.

The two men sat sipping their cold beers. Don talked of his plans to give Vi a whistle-stop tour of California. Then, after his New Year appearances in Vegas, he was booked on chat show in England, so he and Maureen were going to travel back with Vi. But they were keeping that part of the plan a secret from the woman: it was to be her New Year treat: apparently the television chat-show's presenter was well-known for his informal interviewing; apparently he could be uproarious with his guests, and that made for it to be one of the best rated programmes in the UK: Vi loved the show; it was one of her favourites.

Listening to all of this, Jake couldn't help think that people these days, even family, seemed to want to be anywhere rather than Rockfort House. Indeed, they fled at the earliest convenience.

Ten minutes earlier, as he had watched a stony-faced Lena come out onto the terrace carrying a tray with two cold beers and ice frosted glasses he had known, with a certainty when she poured the beers without a word or a smile, that she too was about to flee. And she would not go alone: Louis would leave with her. This imagined scenario was set to come true...

The following day, one hour after the departure of Don, Maureen and Vi, and the Vicente/Landon family, Louis Grant gave notice.

'I'm sorry, Mr Jake, but the work is too much for Lena. I've tried to help her all I can, but, with regret, this is our only choice. We will leave as soon as you have a replacement for us.'

Jake knew that Louis was finding it difficult to cut his ties with the Adier family. However, Lena was a different story. Lena had quite simply...*had enough*. And couldn't wait to flee from her reins.

They had been in the library, all four of them; this time it had been the housekeepers who had done the summoning.

Upstairs in her playroom, in the company of the young woman who was the third in a succession of nannies, Charlotte was quiet, for once.

Jake knew that he had to do something, say something, and quickly.

'Louis, Lena, sit down, *please*. Let's talk about all this,' taking Lena by the arm, Jake guided his housekeeper to a seat on the plush, red velour sofa. Louis, following, took the space next to his wife.

Beth remained standing where she had been when Louis dropped his bombshell; the tall grandeur of the heavily draped French windows in the high ceiling room seemed to emphasize her petite figure. Dressed in soft green lightweight slacks and a matching short sleeved cashmere sweater, Beth anxiously watched the couple take their seats, her hands playing nervously with the gold chain at her throat.

Jake took centre stage, choosing to stand in front of the huge, white marble fireplace. A fireplace that was graced with a slab of oak for its long mantel that—even today—had been polished by Lena to a lustrous shine. Jake put forward his case for why the couple should not give notice to quit.

'Rockfort House is as much your home as ours. So listen, I have a plan: Beth and I will be leaving next week for New York. While we are away, just lock up the house and take a rest. Go away for a few days, if you like. And when you come back, I...*we* would like you, Lena, to engage some help. It's a big house, too much for one person to manage...'

Lena interrupted. 'I'm sorry, Mr Jake, but our minds are made up. We will not be changing them, *or* our plans. We'd like to travel a little, while we are still young enough and fit enough to enjoy it.'

Beth, who had stayed silent, now spoke up.

'It's Charlotte, isn't it, Lena? You are leaving because of our daughter, aren't you?'

Lena, dressed in her usual navy blue, had the good grace not to answer, either way. She sat, looking down, her work roughened hands clasped on her lap.

It was Louis who said, 'You must understand, the child has certainly brought a lot of extra labour, not for me, really, but for Lena...' Louis grabbed hold of his wife's hand, 'Lena has been having trouble sleeping. Her nerves...'

Lena turned on her husband, her grey eyes blazing at him, 'It's not my nerves, and well you know it! It's the noise, the tension. The house *steams* with tension...'

Contrite, Louis agreed with his wife. 'Perhaps it's *my* nerves, too. I've had enough. We both have. And it's our time, now. We are ready. We have savings, good savings. We'd like to take a long vacation. Mrs Greenwood has kindly offered for us to stay in England for a few weeks as her guest. We'd like to do that; and see London, too. And Jerry; we'd like to visit with Jerry in Vermont; he's been practically *begging* us. And of course, Lena, here,' Louis turned and smiled at his wife, as if he was responsible for the sheer indulgence of next treat, 'Lena wants to see Italy: Venice. Like I said, it's *our* time, now, Mr Jake.'

Both Jake and Beth were visibly shaken. The world as they had known it was falling around them, going down like a line of ten pins. It was bad enough that their family and friends had made early exits. Now, to think that their own staff were quitting...they looked at each other but remained speechless.

The awkward silence was shattered by shrieks and cries coming from the room directly above them: the playroom.

Lena and Louis excused themselves from the library, terminating the meeting they themselves had called. Sheepishly avoiding eye contact with the despairing young couple, they closed the door behind them with the softness of a whisper.

The week that followed left all four of them wondering what would happen next: Charlotte, of course, was responsible. The one year old behaved impeccably. She gurgled and giggled, played quietly and contentedly for hours, slept through the night, and also managed to grow her three front top teeth. If that was not enough, the smiling child let it be known that she could quite easily say, 'Mamma and Dada.'

The tension had vanished to be replaced by a soothing even reverent ambiance.

Lena was having some surprising thoughts; she spilled them to her husband as they were readying themselves for bed.

'Perhaps there were always too many people around. She's been fine this past week. I even got a cuddle from her yesterday…and I have *no* bite marks to prove it.'

Lena was herself amazed that she could find some mirth in a situation that had been intolerable just days before.

Louis, in bed already, laid down his newspaper and watched his wife cream her face.

'Having second thoughts, are you?' he took a sip from his mug of cocoa after he spoke.

'No. No, not really. But, well…well *maybe* we should wait until the spring. England's not the place to visit in the winter, is it?' Looking through the dressing table mirror, Lena caught her husband's knowing smile, and returned it, benevolently, with a grin of her own.

In her heart, Lena knew that Louis had never wanted to leave Rockfort House. But being the good spouse that he was, he had supported his over-worked and distressed wife the best he could. And he would have left, of that she had no doubt. But whether he would have enjoyed retirement was another matter altogether.

As she climbed into the huge walnut framed bed that she shared with her very nice husband, Lena wondered just how long their savings would have really lasted.

'It's as if she *knows*,' Beth spoke quietly to her husband. They had been in bed for the best part of two hours and, as yet, neither had found sleep.

'We are still going, Beth. One week doesn't make that much difference.' Jake's whisper was louder than his wife's.

She hushed him…'I know, I know. But it's been a good week, hasn't it?' Jake agreed with the fact.

Beth voiced the question that had been at the back of her mind all week. 'Do you think Grandma Vi actually *did* smack her?'

'No. No, she wouldn't have done that…*Why*? Do you?'

'No, I don't really think so; but she did threaten to a few times.'

'Do you think *we* should…?'

'Smack her…?'

'Yes. Especially if she has another one of her *paddies,*'

'I'm not sure, Jake. I don't think *I* could do it…'

'Me neither, not after *my* schooling: I'm just not into violence…But, I have to admit, it *is* a thought, short term, though, perhaps. Anyway, maybe it's over. Maybe she's passed the *shrieking* stage. We'll ask the doctor tomorrow, because, Beth, like I said before, we are *still* going.'

Jake turned to face his wife. He moved closer.

'Beth?'

'Yes...?'

Jake kissed her.

Beth kissed back.

'Beth...' Jake gave another kiss, 'Don thinks that Charlotte should have a brother or a sister; or even *both*.'

The kissing was in earnest now; lips touched lips, breath mingled with breath. Heat flowed through their entwined limbs. They removed their nightshirts.

Beth kissed the hollow at the base of Jake's throat. 'When should she have them...?' Her voice, famous for its timbre, was sultry. Kissing her husband's throat again, she felt him swallow before he spoke.

'*Now*. Let's make our family tonight. Beth, let's make our son...'

Daniel Seymour Adier was conceived in an act of love, and hope.

*

37

Christopher had made sure his mother was very comfortable. Happy to be back in her own home again, Iris was more than agreeable to her doctor-son's ideas. Especially when one of his plans meant that she could live in her own little flat within the large, many roomed Hampstead Vale house.

Now, as she sat in front of her twenty-six inch colour television, cosseted in a pink fleecy dressing gown, surrounded by the cosy ambiance of her small sitting room, Iris was very much at ease.

Her three-room apartment was situated at the top of the house; the windows of both her sitting room and her bedroom overlooked the long gravelled driveway and then across to the heath beyond. Iris felt that, at last, she was home: In her own home. The first one she could truly call that in all her sixty-one years.

As a child, Iris had lived in the mansion house her stonemason father had built as a showcase for his work. The house, though it looked magnificent, became a cold and heartless home after the death of her mother.

Her teenage years had seen her moving from rented room to rented room; home was something everyone seemed to have, but she.

On her marriage to ailing Bill Grady, she had taken up residence in the back-to-back terraced house in Littleton where the ambiance, the ghost of his first wife, had very much prevailed.

Although her second marriage, to Declan Fitzgerald, had brought her back to the grandeur of her early childhood, this vast house had been, without doubt, more her husband's home than it was hers.

Yet an unparalleled twist of fate was to change all this: Declan's last will and testament should have bequeathed everything to his daughter Donna; then maybe Cathy McDowd, the mother of his child, might have had some claim. However, apparently not having planned to die so soon after his baby daughter's death, his estate, in its entirety, had automatically gone to his estranged wife, Iris. And it was an ownership she was going to use and enjoy to her best advantage.

Having agreed to Christopher's request to move his medical practice to the house, Iris had been adamant that he rented the rest of the vacant rooms to other practitioners: Iris was well aware that medical consultants needed just a couple of spacious rooms in which to see their patients; an exclusive address, of course, being an important criteria.

This had been done, has had the re-naming of the property: *Moira House, Hampstead Vale, London,* was beginning to be noticed on the classified pages of various high quality glossy magazines. Iris had chosen the name with her own long deceased, beloved mother in mind.

One or two of the magazines had found their way to the coffee table in Iris's flat. And now, as she sat waiting for her favourite programme to begin, she flicked through the pages of the one she had taken onto her lap. Her face displayed an ironic smile when she read the advertisement: *Moira House offers the very best in medical care.* Underneath the caption, details of the various treatments and services were listed. Iris herself had worded the article, for she had learnt well in the tranquil comfort of her expensive clinic years: The years of *drying out,* years of sedation, medical tests and electric shock treatments: years and years of therapy. And then, when Declan had refused to pay any further bills, in what was to be his final months of his life, she had been told that her problems were caused by her delicate frame of mind—and her obsession to have a child with her husband. So she had told them, told them straight, but as usual, would anybody believe her...*No, no...no.*

'Bah. Bah...bah...bah! Sheep! They are all bloody sheep, bleating on, thinking they know best. I'll bloody show them. I'll show them all.'

Iris chortled; a chuckle came from deep in her throat as she raised her beer glass to her lips. The froth tickled her nose, delighting her senses. Christopher had agreed to her having two glasses of beer at night. In truth, he had no choice. His mother was now the boss.

Sitting in the comfort of her wing chair, her feet on a small gold fabric pouffe that matched the armchair and the other deeply upholstered soft furnishing in the television lit room, Iris contentedly sipped on her ale watching the programme she had looked forward to seeing for most of the day.

Usually, the chat show gave her a lot of pleasure: she liked the lively, sometimes boisterous banter that went on between the astute broadcaster and his invited guests. But not so tonight; tonight, her eyes were stony as she watched the programme's amenable host shake hands with his guest: Don Sommer, still as handsome and striking as he was years ago, was being loudly and enthusiastically applauded by what appeared to be a fan-based studio audience. Twice the presenter barracked the assemblage to 'Shut up, and let the poor man sit down, for heaven's sake.'

Watching Don as he became animated in conversation, Iris seethed. And she shouted out her thoughts...

'You'll not be getting anymore money from the Fitzgerald's, that you won't!'

As Don and his host chatted and laughed, Iris shouted her abuse...

'Leukaemia Fund my *foot*...I'll bet it all went in your own bleedin' pocket...' Iris continued berating the television screen, shouting and bawling, drowning out Don's voice.

When Christopher let himself into his mother's apartment, he was in time to hear her own rendition of *Blood's No Thicker Than Water*, out of time and way off key, with the voice of Don Sommer as her backing vocal: Iris had turned the volume of the television set to high, and the noise of both his mother and the set was chaotic and deafening.

'Mother...*Mother!* What the hell are you playing at, hey? I could hear you outside when I was parking the car...' Christopher marched to the television set, and adjusted the volume.

'Look. Look at him! You know who that is, don't you?' Iris waved a bony finger at the screen.

'Yes, of course I know who it is; it's Don Sommer,'

'Aye, it's Don-robbing bastard-Sommer...Declan's bloody idol...'

Christopher, who was the living image of the Greenwood twins, and could easily be mistaken for either Barry or Bobby, sat down on the vacant sofa, his eyes focused onto the television screen.

'He's still very good looking. He's getting on a bit, too, isn't he? Is he about the same age as you, Ma?'

'Never mind his age. He's got *my* money...Do you think we could get it back?'

Christopher gave a snort of a laugh, then said,

'You mean the money Declan donated? Not a chance, Mother. Anyway, you don't *need* it. You own this house, and when the businesses are sold, well, you'll be a very wealthy woman...'

'I do need it! I could give it to you, then. I'd rather you had it than his family. *Bloody Fund*...I bet every penny landed in his pocket.'

Christopher grinned, shaking his head in denial of his mother's accusations.

'Maybe Declan would have done that. But I don't think Don Sommer needs to pinch money, Ma. These funds are dead legit. They have to be.'

'Humph.'...Iris took a long drink from her glass.

Son and mother sat on, watching the programme and commenting, even sharing a wry smile every now and then: the show's presenter was very quick with his repartee.

Christopher hoped his mother's edgy mood had been lulled by the laughter. Not so...

'His wife's called Maureen.'

'Is she.' Christopher, who'd been out for an early evening meal in the company of his latest lady friend, loosened his tie and sighed, dreading what was to come next...

'I had a Maureen...' Iris stated it flatly.

'I know, Ma, I know. She was your stepdaughter.'

'She was my *babee*...' Iris began to have a wail in her voice.

'Come on, now, Mother. Don't get upset. No tears, tonight, hey...?' Christopher reached from the sofa to pat his mother's hand that was resting on the arm of her chair.

'I nearly killed her, you know...' Iris's lamenting was picking up speed, '...I locked her in the shed for days...And I pushed her down the cellar steps...and all the time she was my girl. And...*Declan's*.' The sobbing was now in full flow.

With a cheek-filling sigh, Christopher stood up, exhaled, and then walked to the television set, switching it off. Moving back to his seat, he took hold of his mother's hand, again.

'Listen, Ma, listen. I've an idea. Would you like to see babies? See them here? New born babies, in *this* house…would you?'

Iris stared at her son through teary eyes.

'You see, Ma, I was thinking of making this house into a home: A first class nursing home. There's plenty of money in the scheme; better than renting out rooms…what do you think, hey? We have the grounds to extend the house, if we needed to. Come on; tell me what you think? Because, well, the thing is, *you* could be a bit involved in it all, if you wanted to…'

Christopher had been toying with the idea for weeks. His mother's outburst this evening had catapulted his plans, and his thoughts… *The old girl wants to believe that she had a baby with Declan…Well, she'll get to see plenty of babies this way…*

Iris's thoughts were indeed on the baby she had conceived with Declan Fitzgerald…

It's not fair, I've come clean about the girl and no one believes me! They all think I'm making it up to get my own back on Declan…No one ever believes me, they think they can just stick a needle up my bum and I'll stop saying it…But there's no medication that can mend what I have done…none! Even the booze doesn't help…Oh, Maureen…Maureen! Where are you…?

The one person who knew that Iris was telling the truth was Violet Greenwood. And the woman had said, categorically, that she would take the knowledge to her deathbed without breathing a word to anyone.

Iris had indeed done some checking up—and it appeared that Maureen had disappeared off the face of the earth: not even the electoral role of the whole of the Cheshire area offered a clue. And, even if she did find her, she wouldn't stand a chance of being believed: Iris knew that it was on record that she was an alcoholic and a pathological liar. She also knew that this stigma would be with her till the end of her days.

*

38

Beth and Jake's son was stillborn. Daniel Seymour Adier, although perfectly formed, never took one breath on this earth. His parents were distraught. His grandparents were grief stricken. In England, his great-grandmother wept for the boy she would never know.

Only his twenty-one month old sister was dry eyed at his funeral. Sitting between her grandmother and grandfather, Charlotte, well advanced for her age, wanted to know where her baby was.

'He's in that little box...*there* darling, near the altar.' Maureen, aware of her granddaughter's intelligence, told the truth, pointing to the small white coffin that, adorned with a simple bunch of blue forget-me-nots, looked so surreal, so out of place near the steps leading up to the high altar.

'Why doesn't he cry, like Jamie?' Charlotte's voice seemed so loud in the quite reverence of the church, even though the congregation numbered well over a hundred, the youngster's voice rang loud and clear.

'Shush, darling...' Maureen squeezed her granddaughter's hand and looked to her left to see Don's reaction to their granddaughter's questioning.

But Don's face was unreadable. Eyes forward, he seemed to be lost to his own thoughts as they all waited in a difficult silence for the pews to fill and the service to begin.

Seated directly behind them were the Vicente and Landon family. And with the latter family was two-month old Jamie, Lydia and Pete's third child.

Turning to look again at the snuffling, mewling baby in her Uncle Pete's arms, Charlotte tugged on her grandmother's hand and repeated her question,

'Grandma...? Where's *my* baby...? I *want* to see Danal...'

Maureen bent her head low to whisper to the child,

'We told you, sweetheart, that you could only cuddle Daniel just the *once*. He's sleeping now, there, in that pretty box.' Maureen, once again, pointed her finger to the small coffin, hoping that for the moment Charlotte would try to understand and remain quiet.

'Hush, now, darling, we are going to sing him a lullaby, so that Daniel stays fast asleep.' Maureen smiled down at the glossy haired, wide-eyed child she had grown to love so much; her fast growing, ever inquisitive granddaughter, the energetic toddler who had been pronounced as being "both hyperactive and extremely intelligent" by the child physiologist in New York. The eminent specialist had also told her growing-less-anxious-by-the-minute parents that their daughter would eventually grow out of her tantrums. He told them to teach her new things every day, to engage her interest, to take her travelling with them...

'She is a bright and active child, give her lots of different experiences; and have patience with her. You *will* be rewarded...'

And they had been. Beth and Jake, so very relieved that their daughter was normal, had taken all the advice, which included removing wheat and dairy produce from her diet, and had been delighted to report, six month later, that Charlotte, though still a handful, was everything and had done everything that was expected of her: the tantrums had lessened, she'd become more inquisitive and was showing signs that her intelligence was above average. She had walked at thirteen month, was dry at seventeen month, and now, nearing her second birthday, was fluent enough in her speech to hold and conduct a conversation. And Charlotte loved to ask questions. Beth had recently told her mother that she had counted, on one day, that Charlotte had asked one hundred and nine questions.

'Mum, she is so *excited* about the baby. She rubs my tummy, bends her head and whispers to her baby. And when she heard that Jamie Landon was born, she wanted her baby *now*...' Beth had been so happy to report all of this down the phone line from Montport to Palm Beach.

In reality, of course, they had allowed Charlotte to see lifeless Daniel just once, and, because the child had very much wanted to, they had also given permission for her to hold the blanketed still bundle in her small arms for a second or two...

Now, on this summer-bright late afternoon at the end of June, with the sky outside a flawless blue, so inappropriate on so sad a day, the brown haired, brown-eyed child, dressed today in a bodice-smocked, puff sleeved, white cotton dress, her chubby legs tanned and healthy against the frilly white ankles socks and black patent shoes, sat playing with the pretty white butterfly clip that firmly held back her jaw length straight hair, keeping it out of her eyes. Obediently quiet, she swung her legs, focusing her keen attention of the unfolding scenario of the church service. Craning her neck, she looked down the pew past the bowed head of her grandfather, and saw that her parents were holding hands, and that her daddy was crying Her thoughts were puzzled...*where is my baby...? Mummy said I could hold him, lots...Why is Daddy crying...? They don't like me crying...they shout at me...*

Charlotte looked at her mother. But her mother did not look back...*Mummy hasn't kissed me today, but she is kissing daddy...*

The little girl watched as her mother pecked her husband's cheek, before dabbing at her eyes with a white handkerchief. She saw her give the hanky to Jake, and clutch his hand. And then they looked at one another, and smiled. Just a tiny smile, but it was a smile.

Charlotte reached for her grandmother's hand and brought it to her mouth. She kissed the knuckles, hard. And her grandmother smiled down, and then started to cry.

Charlotte was going to do the same with grandpa Don, but he held on too tightly and wouldn't let Charlotte bring his hand to her mouth. Instead, he just squeezed her hand, firmly. Charlotte knew this meant...*be quiet.*

Charlotte wanted to please her grandfather; she wanted him to be happy. Everyone was standing up now; and they were listening to music. As young as she was, the clever little girl knew what she had to say...

'Grandpa? Grandpa, I like *this* music...'

Jake gritted his teeth...*of all the days...'*

Beth cried, even more.

Through tear filled eyes, Maureen looked down at her small granddaughter and was pleased to know that at last there was *some* music that didn't bring on a tantrum.

Don stood, face forward, the set of his mouth grim. Although he knew that the child was watching him, waiting for his approval, he thought it best not to acknowledge her statement, as the organist played on.

The strains of the lullaby brought a brilliant smile to Charlotte's face and a loud hum to her lips.

As the evening sun streamed in through the stained glass windows, the darkly dressed congregation shuffled with embarrassment as Charlotte Adier began to clap her small dimpled hands in time to the melody

*

39

Charlotte was three years old when Nathan was born in the autumn of 1986.

Arriving so close on the heel of her own birthday, Charlotte believed that the baby was her special present.

Nathan Benjamin Adier was born in hospital in Palm Beach County, Florida on the fourth day of October. The perfect, eight-pound baby boy had a pair of lusty lungs, much to the delight of his proud and thankful parents.

Beth had been in Florida since the onset of the summer months, under the watchful and ever-alert eyes of her mother, Maureen.

Beth had enjoyed the latter stages of her confinement. Florida was the place she had always called home, and a feeling of contentment had prevailed: she had slept late into the mornings, strolled on the white sandy beach before the mid-day heat had become too strong, and then had rested, reading under the shade of a palm tree, as the sun had gone down on what had been picture perfect, idyllic days. Worries about the imminent birth were lessened under the care of her mother, who had made sure that Beth took all the necessary vitamins, fresh fish, meat and salads, whilst taking enough gentle exercise to keep strong both in body and mind for the approaching labour and strains of child birth.

Charlotte had enjoyed being in Florida, too. The heat seemed not to affect her; she played on the beach from morning till night and thoroughly enjoyed being in the constant company of her grandparents. Indeed, the three year old had grown very attached to her grandmother. Should Maureen's time need to be spent elsewhere, Charlotte let it be known that she was very upset.

It was then that Don would take control. Ignoring the girl's shrieks and pitiful crying for her grandmother, he would admonish her with stern words whilst at the same time engaging her attention onto other things.

And his perseverance at his task of *taming his granddaughter* had had some success: Although the sun drenched beach was not the place he would have chosen to spend endless hours, the singer/songwriter kept his boredom firmly to himself as he built numerous castles, forts and even a small village out of the sugar white sand, his reward being the endless chatter, and the jubilant squeals of pleasure coming from his running-to-and fro, bucket and spade in hand granddaughter.

Charlotte had no fear of the sea. She loved to splash in the shallow lapping tide, hand in hand with barefooted Don. Taking this enjoyment into consideration, he had been quick to capitalise on her fearlessness in water by teaching her the rudiments of swimming, usually undertaking the lessons after supper, which appeared to be the best time of day.

And now, due to her grandfather's constant vigilance and care, Charlotte was not only the sister to a healthy little boy, she was also an able swimmer, who could master the full length of her grandparent's ocean front swimming pool. The tantrums of the past, though still raising their head from time to time, had somewhat diminished in the time his granddaughter had been in Florida.

Jake, who always fretted for Charlotte's future where her behaviour patterns were concerned, had little choice but to put his worries to the back of his mind. Having used the time his wife and daughter had been absent to stay behind on Rhode Island and to finalise the last draft of his second novel, *Forever To Be Young*, Jake's only contact for the past six weeks or so had been by telephone.

However, he *had* been present in Florida for the birth of his son. Now, ten days later, he was back in Montport, seated in front of his typewriter.

Jake had not been happy to fly back alone. But it had made sense: his wife and young family were better off in Florida: Beth and the new baby were being thoroughly pampered by Maureen; and Charlotte appeared to be thriving and happy in the beachside residence of her grandparents. Even Don had suggested it a good idea that Jake take the time to finish the novel in the peace and quiet of the house on Rhode Island.

So Jake was once again spending many hours in his study, sometimes working long in to the night. Lena Grant was the only person he saw on a regular basis. His agent called once or twice. But apart from that, Jake's only other human contact was with Louis—the jack-of-all-trades man would put his head around the door of the study to ask, 'How's it going?' every now and again—plus the occasional hand—waved acknowledgment from the garden where Eric Morse, their full-time grounds and maintenance man, spend most of his own days.

Well into the second week of his lone vigil, and taking a break from his task at the keyboard, Jake's attention was drawn to the window by the sound of loud shouts and laughter coming from the garden.

Looking out, Jake saw that the rumpus was being made by the gardener and his young grandson; the seven-year old boy, named David, was often seen tagging along with his granddad during the long summer months; even when he was back at school, David often helped his grandfather at his early evening chores.

This unusually hot, late afternoon, the pair were larking around with a hosepipe; or it should be said, that David was the one larking and laughing and Eric was the one shouting, good humouredly to, 'Turn the darn thing off…!' Jake watched the antics of the drenched duo, and he smiled, too. But his thoughts soon fell foul: although he was delighted to be the father of a fine healthy boy, and relieved that the anxiety of the child's birth was well over, his uneasiness with regard to Charlotte was as sharp as ever…

The New York doctors had done their best to re-assure both he and Beth that nothing was seriously wrong with their daughter. The psychologist report was similar. But Jake had not been convinced. He feared that something had been missed. Overlooked. A gnawing anxiety had plagued him constantly. Even though Charlotte was growing well, and learning new skills daily, her overall behaviour had not drastically changed: she was still a difficult youngster; still given to outburst of temper tantrums.

After Daniel's funeral, Charlotte's behaviour had become a bone of contention between the grieving parents. Beth had decided to take temporary retirement from the limelight of show business and had taken the care of her daughter very much under her own wing.

And it had been she, Beth, who had said that it would help matters no end if Jake could immerse himself into a project, too; that the brooding and worrying about everything and everybody had to stop.

Jake had taken the advice and had used it well. But because of this, and the time he had needed to take in the grafting of his second novel, he had not been on hand in Florida to see how much Charlotte had thrived under the loving but firm control of her grandfather.

Now, as he watched Eric ruffle the wet blond hair of his grandson, and accept the waistline hug of the giggling boy in return, he marvelled at the closeness of the pair, despairing at the same time that it was something that perhaps he might never get to have with his own children: Jake could not turn off the feeling foreboding…

'Come and visit *soon*. Promise?' Beth held her mother close, savouring the familiar fragrance of the eau de toilette she always used: lavender.

'Oh we *promise*. You just try keeping us away…' Maureen hugged her pony-tailed daughter, then pulled back to look into her face, knowing what she would see; and she was right: Beth's blue eyes were shining with unshed tears…*she's frightened of being on her own*…Maureen's thoughts were tinged with guilt. But it was time for the new family to go back to their own home, to settle into a new routine: A new life.

Maureen hugged her blue jeans and dark sweatshirt-attired daughter one more time before letting go. She then moved to embrace the similarly clad Jake, who had blanket wrapped Nathan cradled in the crook of his left arm.

'Take great care of them, Jake,' she stood tiptoe to kiss the man's cheek, and then bent to her grandson in his arms, '…and *you*, Master Nathan, be a good little boy for your Mummy and Daddy…' Maureen grazed her lips over the sleeping, dark haired infant's forehead…'see you at Christmas, my precious boy.'

She then squatted to her haunches, pulling Charlotte into a tender embrace.

'Will you promise to look after your Mummy? And Nathan? And will you promise, also, to be a *very* good little girl…?'

Looking very sullen, Charlotte, wearing a beige corduroy pinafore dress over a soft wool, polo-necked red sweater, entwined her arms round her grandmother's neck and buried her face against her shoulders.

Maureen could feel the youngster's tears wetting the fabric of her own pink suede jacket. She stroked her hand up and down the child's back, whispering into her ear, 'Don't cry, darling, Grandma will see you again; *soon*. We'll have a lovely Christmas. And then Charlotte, if you are very, *very* good, Grandpa and I will take you to England...And we will see Sam, and Julie, and Nana.'

Charlotte's head came up immediately. 'Not Nana.'

Flinching at the girl's animosity towards her great-grandmother, Maureen stood again; smoothing the creases from her cream cotton twill slacks, she was at a loss as how to handle the abhorrence that she knew was mutual between the infant and Vi.

As she and Don stood in the driveway of their Florida home, waving and blowing kisses to the departing winter-clothed foursome, Maureen slipped her arm through that of her husband's, overcome with emotion. When the final wave came from Jake, who was in the driving seat of the silver coloured Mercedes estate car, Maureen let her own tears flow...*I'm going to miss them all so much...I do already...*

The melancholy was hard to lift. It wound itself round Maureen like a sea mist. She had busied herself with housework since the departure of her daughter, but now, two days later, there was little left to do. Even the two cleaners, who came in daily, had left for the day after the laundry had been ironed and stacked back onto the linen cupboard shelves. Strand House, which she had always thought to be so perfect, seemed much too large for them now that they were on their own.

Don, on the other hand, was well content to be back to normal. After a late breakfast of unsweetened grapefruit, a half toasted bagel and a cup of English tea, he closeted himself into his small studio: the lyric writing for which he was so famous had been neglected for the past two months. Now, dressed for his day of work in beige shorts and a lemon coloured tee shirt, he was eager to *get back to the grind.*

Maureen walked round the house in a sombre mood. She opened door after door looking into silent, tidy rooms that, so recently, had been filled with the chaotic presence and belongings of her daughter and her young family. Finding no comfort inside the house, she ventured outside.

The month of November, so cold in many states and countries, was a perfect month in Florida. The late morning air was gentle; a pleasant breeze rustled the leaves on the many evergreen trees they had planted in the grounds of their new home. Maureen took a deep breath and made her way to the beach…and the sea.

Looking out across the sun shimmering water of the vast blue ocean that divided her two most favourite countries, Maureen tried to curb the gnawing unease, the foreboding that had settled around her for the past few days.

Thinking that exercise would help, Maureen decided to walk along the shoreline. With her sandals in one hand, she tucked the other hand into the side pocket of her white cotton, mid-calf slacks. Even on the lone beach, and wearing her oldest of clothes (her peach coloured tee-shirt had been bought when she had accompanied a young Beth on her tours,) she looked elegant. Too small to ever be classed as haughty, Maureen's slim frame and quick agility gave her a quality of femininity that was ageless. Her hair, still dark, still cut short and bob style, was lifted away from her small-featured face by the light wind as she paced the tide-frothed water's edge.

She was aching for the company of her daughter. She was missing the easy chat, the spontaneous laughter; the camaraderie that only a mother and daughter knew. A keen, knowing relationship built over the years, through infancy, though childhood, through the difficult and trying years of adolescence. In truth, it started from the womb.

With the sun directly overhead, Maureen turned, and headed back for her home. Her thoughts had moved on. Or, perhaps, back…*where are you, my mother? How could you have given me away…? Have you ever thought of me? Do you know of Beth's fame…? Do you know that you have great-grandchildren…? Will I ever know anything about you? Ever hear from you…? Are you still alive, even…? And will I ever stop wondering if you'll show up on my doorstep…or do something for me, one day…?*

Maureen whipped her sunglasses from her pocket, and quickly slipped them on, hiding her tears behind the darkened lens. She had nearly reached her own home. And she felt guilty. She had so much in her life—and yet here she was, crying and being thoroughly miserable…*forgive me, Lord. Forgive me for being so ungrateful. Teach me; please teach me to stop yearning for what I've never known…and what I'll never have…*

As she opened the heavy wooden gate onto the crazy paved pathway that led to the lush green, flower bordered gardens of Strand House, she felt more troubled than ever. The voice was back. And this time, there was no mistaking the echoing words: 'Maureen…Maureen…*Maureen.*'

*

40

The air in Montport seemed more chill than usual after the heat of Florida and Beth fretted for her son's health.

'Penny wants to take over the night feeds, Jake, but I'm a bit worried that Nathan's room is too cold.'

Sat in bed, Beth continued bottle-feeding her son while waiting for her husband's response.

Jake called his answer from the bathroom. 'You're both right, hon... Why have a nurse for the baby if you won't let her do her job? And yes. Nat *is* too young to be on his own in his big cold nursery. So, compromise...'

Looking down had her milk-guzzling son Beth wanted to know how that could be done. 'How can we...*compromise*?'

Jake entered the bedroom, naked, except for a fluffy white towel wrapped round his waist. Flopping on to the bed beside his wife and son, he grinned as he answered.

'By letting him sleep with his first woman! Let Penny take him into her room.'

They both laughed as they gazed at their still feeding two-month old son.

Jake played with the baby's tiny fingers as they curled and uncurled around his own index finger.

Beth voiced her reservations. 'Oh, I don't know, Jake, it doesn't feel right, just handing him over. But then *you* are right; what *is* the point in having help if we don't take advantage of it. I suppose we could give it a try. He could still sleep in his crib. To be honest, Jake, it's the large cot I'm fearful of; when I tried him in it, he looked so lost, poor darling.'

Beth put her sleepy son on her shoulder to burp him. She kissed the side of his dark head, inhaling his special smell, his wonderful newness.

Still mulling over the problem of where the best place was for Nathan to sleep, she lay the slumbering infant into the blue-ribbon basket crib that was positioned at the foot of their king-size bed. After making sure he was on his side and well tucked in, Beth returned to her own nesting place and into the waiting arms of her naked husband.

The answer to the Nathan's sleeping quarters problem came the very next day.

'Let him sleep in the playroom. It's a warm and cosy room. My room leads off it…and you are just across the hallway.' Penny Adams, twenty-nine years old and unmarried, was gem. She had been with the Adier family since the week prior to Charlotte's first birthday. The third in a succession of nannies, she had been the one who had stood her ground with Charlotte, eventually gaining the youngster's affection and some-time respect.

A local young woman, Penny lived *in* during the weekdays, moving back to her parents' home at the weekends. As a fully trained nurse, and a lover of children, Beth had snatched at the chance of employing the *golden girl*. For that was how they all thought of Penny, with her vivid ginger hair, her freckled glowing face and her abounding energy. With a character bereft of malice or jealousy, Penny Adams brought friendship and a keen understanding of human nature to her position as nanny to the Adier children. And both Beth and Jake trusted this caring woman implicitly with the care of their infants.

'Can I sleep in the playroom, too, Mommy?'

It had just been explained to Charlotte that, for the time being, Nathan was going to be sleeping in the room for the remainder of the winter months.

'No, sweetheart, but you *can* help us move Nathan's things in there. Penny and I are going to do it in a minute or two. Anyway, why would you want to sleep in the playroom? When you have your own lovely warm bedroom, eh?'

Charlotte continued eating her breakfast, taking a bite of toast before she answered her mother: This time taking habit was known to all who had dealings with the three-year old: Charlotte never answered quickly, always formulating her replies with care.

Beth was amused by her daughter's earnestness. Masking her smile, she continued eating her own breakfast of a softly boiled egg and a slice of wholemeal toast. But her thoughts mirrored the grin she was hiding...*Look at her. I can almost see her brain working. Those eyes. I'm sure they are going even browner...*

Charlotte's eyes were a deep chocolate brown. Today, in the bright winter sunlight that shafted in through the morning room's window, they looked almost black. Fringed by a double row of lashes, they were the child's greatest asset—until she smiled: Charlotte was blessed with the most radiant of smiles. They were a joy to behold.

Unfortunately, these smiles only rarely graced the little girl's even featured face. Charlotte was a sombre child. And Beth hoped that her daughter would never need to wear spectacles: without the beauty of her huge brown eyes, Charlotte would seem quite unattractive. No amount of shampooing, cutting or styling could stop the child's hair from hanging limp. Pretty dresses vexed the little imp, who much preferred the freedom of trousers and sweaters, or tee shirts and shorts.

Now, as she formulated the answer to her mother's question, Charlotte sat comfortably at the red gingham clothed breakfast table dressed in denim coveralls over a bright blue turtleneck sweater.

'Mommy, I would *like* to sleep in the playroom so that I can give Nathan his toys when he throws them out of bed.'

'Nathan is too *young* to play with toys, Charlotte. And he certainly doesn't sleep with any, darling...'

Charlotte was quick with this reply, 'I could teach him to play...'

'Thank you, sweetie, that would be nice,' Beth patted her daughter's hand, 'and you will be able to do just that, when he can sit up and watch *you* play.'

Charlotte chewed her last bite of toast.

Beth drank her coffee.

'Okay, Mommy, but can I hold him while you bring his things into the play...his bedroom?'

'You sure can, for a little time, anyway. Now come on, lets finish here and go and say good morning to Daddy. He's been writing since very early this morning; and then we will go and see what our other boy's doing with Penny.'

'Daddy's not a boy. Daddy is a man, Mommy.' Charlotte was stern in her reproach. Where other children of her age would possibly have giggled to hear their father being called a *boy*, Beth's daughter could see no humour in her mother's choice of words. As she would have seen no reason why she would have to leave her nursery bedroom. Notwithstanding that Charlotte's bedroom would have been the ideal place for Nathan to have as his own sleeping quarters, the idea of moving their daughter from the nursery had never been muted.

However, the large bedroom that had been kitted out for Nathan as his nursery was, in reality, too big, too draughty and too far away from either his parents or his nanny's rooms. Hence the dilemma of where he actually would sleep at night.

Penny's idea to use the playroom worked well. Most nights of the week it was Penny who did the early hours of the morning feed. And maybe because he was sleeping in a room of his own, the infant soon made this his only waking call for food. By the end of the second week, Nathan took his two a.m. feed and then slept through until as late as nine a.m. some mornings.

'I'm glad it's all working well, Beth. I must say, I'm enjoying staying in my bed until ten...' The arrangement was working like a dream: Penny bathed both children in the early evening and then left them to the care of their parents. She was delighted to be able to have most evenings to herself and watched television in her room, chatted on the phone to her friends, before getting a few hours sleep until her call to duty for the middle of the night feed. After that was done, she usually slept until late morning.

Because Beth's sleep was not disturbed, nor that of her husband's, both parents were more than happy to rise early and see to the needs of their young family. Penny usually took over the reins at eleven, which left Beth free to go about her daily business and for Jake to hole himself up in his study for a long day of writing.

Beth had been out of the house since the morning. With Christmas on the horizon, there was a lot of shopping and gift buying to be done.

Penny, with Nathan in her arms, the baby looking very much like a young Father Christmas in his red romper suit, was the one who met her as she came in through the front door, snow on her coated shoulders and bags and packages weighing her down.

Handing the contented baby over to Lena, who'd come into the lamp-lit hallway to see what was going on, Penny went outside to help Beth bring in the rest of her marathon Christmas shop.

'Brrr...it's freezing out here...Let's be quick! I think I'll leave the car where it is; I'll get Louis to drive it into the garage later. I need a hot drink.' Beth couldn't wait to get inside out of the cold afternoon. Christmas shopping was an exhausting task; especially in the inclement weather of a Rhode Island winter.

The two women emptied Beth's dark blue Mercedes. Penny, dressed in a black polo neck sweater and dark jeans, her ginger coloured hair pulled from her face and tied back in a high pony tail, was shivering as she hurried into he warmth of the lamp glowing house with the last of the packages.

Beth rushed upstairs to change from her heavy outside clothes. When she came back down, comfortable in a forest green velour jump suit, her feet encased in thick warm matching coloured socks, she was pleased to see that Lena had moved the Christmas booty out of the hallway, and that it was now tucked out of sight in the store room that led off from the kitchen. Beth was also pleased to hear her car start up, and be driven round the side of the house to the garage...*what would we have done if Lena and Louis had have left...?* She shuddered at the very thought.

It was Friday, and late afternoon. The snow that had started around lunchtime was now beginning to fall heavier and faster.

'Would you like me to sleep in this weekend, Beth? I thought that with Mr and Mrs Sommer arriving, you might like extra help...?'

'No, Penny, it's okay. But thanks for the thought. You get yourself off home...Fancy a hot chocolate before you do...?'

More like good friends than employer and employee, the two women walked into the bay windowed, rather old fashioned kitchen. Though Beth wanted to re-model the dark wood cabinets into something more light and streamlined, Lena seemed to be very much against the idea. And now, with the winter white landscape outside the window, and the soft glow of the room's three tiffany lamps illuminating the scene, Beth could see some merit in Lena's request that the kitchen be left alone: it was a comfortable domain, and Lena's empire.

Charlotte seemed quite content, too. Sitting at the scrubbed white oak table, she was head down, intent on crayoning in her colouring book. Her brown hair was parted in the middle, and had been divided into two side ponytails; and it suited the child very much. Dressed in a tartan skirt, white

403

tights and a white turtleneck sweater, the girl hardly lifted her head when her mother came into the room.

Taking Nathan from Lena's arms, Beth motioned for Penny to take a seat at the table with her, and then asked Lena to make hot-chocolates all round.

Her task done, white-apron clad Lena had even run up the stairs with a cup for Jake, who was working in his study, before returning to the kitchen where she sat down at the table, too.

The three women chatted of this and that; they took it in turns to hold Nathan, and did the same with encouraging and praising words to Charlotte. Their conversation turned to decorating the house for Christmas.

'We'll start on Monday. Mum will enjoy helping, too. No you get off, Penny. And enjoy your weekend...'

Penny interrupted saying again that she didn't mind staying on, that she had nothing planned.

'No! Now no arguments, get *going,* before I do change my mind...'

On cue, Nathan started to cry. And Charlotte began to whinge that her crayons were 'Wearing out...'

Bundled up in his outside clothes, a thick padded navy blue anorak that was hooded for total protection against the cold, Louis made his lumbering, fresh air fragranced entrance into the kitchen at the same time as Penny was leaving. He said that he thought that there was a problem with the electrics in Beth's car, and offered to drive Penny home in the vehicle whilst he was taking it for a test run.

And, seeing that Penny's mode of transport was her bicycle, she jumped at the chance to travel in warmth, and style.

Charlotte disliked the dark. She had never mentioned this fear to her mother or father, although there was one person who knew. And that *person* was her teddy bear; and that was what he was called: Teddy

The three-year old really believed that Teddy was a person. Sometimes he whispered to her: Like now. He whispered that Mommy was with Nathan. He whispered that Nathan was a naughty boy to wake Mommy and want a drink. He whispered that Nathan must be a really bad boy to wee-wee his pants. And Teddy also whispered that perhaps Nathan should sleep in the box that was next to her bed.

Charlotte thought that was a good idea. All her toys slept in the big box at the end of her bed. And then she remembered Daniel. Daniel slept in a box and he never cried and woke Mommy.

Charlotte tried hard to stay awake.

Teddy whispered to her when Mommy went back to her own bedroom. Charlotte waited. Waited for Nathan to cry again. He didn't.

Teddy whispered again and Charlotte got out of her bed. She was frightened, but Teddy said he would go with her.

Charlotte's bedroom door was always left open. Mommy said that was okay because then the light from the landing could shine in.

The light was off, now, but Teddy said not to be scared. She crossed the landing and went into the playroom.

The baby was awake. Teddy said to pick him up, but Charlotte was worried she might drop him.

Charlotte did try to lift Nathan, but it was difficult with her teddy bear in her arms already.

Teddy whispered that he would sleep in the crib, just for tonight.

Charlotte laid the teddy bear down next to the baby.

Nathan cried a little and pushed Teddy in the face.

Charlotte tried very hard to carry Nathan just like Mommy did. She put him up to her shoulder and patted his back. On the way back to her bedroom, Nathan began to whimper. She whispered to him not to be scared; she also explained her plans.

'Mommy will be able to sleep, now, Nathan. You can stay with my toys tonight. It's all right. Teddy said it would be all right. He's going to sleep in your bed. Mommy doesn't like you having toys in your bed, but you are not there, now, are you?'

Charlotte found it hard to open the padded ottoman with Nathan in her arms; very carefully she laid him down on the floor.

The baby opened his eyes and looked at her, jerking his blue sleep-suited arms and legs excitedly.

Charlotte beamed her brilliant smile. 'You will be very happy in the box, Nathan. And in the morning, we can tell Mommy that you like playing with toys, now…and we can tell Grandma and Grandpa, too; they are coming tomorrow.' Charlotte was enjoying whispering to her little brother. And he *did* seem very happy. She could tell by the way his arms and legs were jumping about. And his gurgle; Mommy said that was his way of laughing.

Charlotte laid the baby down deep between her softest toys.

'Night, night, Nathan, you can play with Mr Seal if you like; he's my second best friend after Teddy.'

Charlotte picked up the fluffy grey seal toy and put it on Nathan's chest.

She blew the baby a kiss and then closed the ottoman lid. She then went to her bathroom, had a wee-wee, washed her hands, and then jumped back into her own bed and fell asleep immediately.

Beth woke early. Without disturbing her sleeping husband, she slipped out of bed and quickly dressed in her fleecy white dressing gown and put her feet into her white bedroom slippers.

Making her way down the sweeping stairs, she shuddered; the house felt very cold. Even though the heating was left on low during the night, the air was chill.

Hugging her robe closer to her body, she walked into the kitchen and towards the bay window where she then lifted the blinds. The snow lay thick on the ground in the silent outside world. It was a beautiful sight, and Beth stood for a moment or two mesmerised by the wonder of nature. Dawn had just lit the sky, and there was a slight hint of pink beginning to come through the heavy low clouds.

Beth made busy. She filled the percolator with water, added a good few heaped spoons of ground coffee and was just about to go into the fridge for milk, when Lena made her entrance. It was six forty five and time for the housekeeper to begin her day.

'Well, good morning! You're up bright and early this morning, Miss Beth.'

Lena was always formal in her address to her employers: Jake was always, Mr Jake.

Beth, eager for her first cup of the aromatic coffee, poured herself one.

'Oh hi…Good morning, Lena. I woke early, and then couldn't get back to sleep…Mmm…that *hurt*…' Beth had scalded her lips with the steaming beverage. After running her tongue over her smarting lips, she confided in her housekeeper. 'Guess I'm excited about Mum and Don's arrival. I'll take my coffee upstairs, now; leave you to get on…See you later.'

As Beth left the kitchen, Lena went over to the heating thermostat and turned it to high. It was very cold and she was glad that Beth had talked her into wearing trousers first thing in the morning. Being a skirt sort of person, Lena had thought that wearing trousers would be very uncomfortable. Now she knew the opposite. And this early morning she was more than glad to be wearing a warm pair of navy blue coloured slacks and a beige cable-knit sweater—both of them a gift brought back after her young employers had spent time in England—and the thoughtful present had been, and was to this day, very much appreciated, too. With her feet cosy in a pair of fleeced lined ankle boots, that she had bought locally, Lena was ready for what was going to be an interesting day: she too was pleased that the Don and Maureen were on their way.

In the morning room, she set the table for the family's breakfast and found herself humming: she admitted to herself that she was excited. Lena had a soft spot for Don Sommer... *Well...* she thought... *and why not! Oh, I'm so glad we decided to stay; things have turned out all right, after all...*

Upstairs on the landing, all was quiet. Beth took a peek in to her daughter's bedroom. Her little girl lay still beneath the warmth of her bright yellow quilt.

She crossed to the playroom. All was still in there, too.

Returning to her own bedroom, she stopped suddenly with her hand on the door's brass handle. Her thoughts were troubled... *what's Charlotte's teddy bear doing in Nathan's crib...?*

Turning, Beth sped back to the playroom, gasping as she approached the crib. With terror mounting, she flew across the landing and flung open the door into Penny's room. The room was empty, the bed made and no sign that it had been used.

Strange noises came from her mouth as she rushed into her own bedroom, her catapulting entrance shocking Jake awake.

'Beth... Beth! What is it...? What's the matter...?'

Beth blurted, 'I can't find Nathan! I can't find him, Jake... He's not in his crib.'

Jake leapt out of bed, covering his nakedness as fast as he could. Struggling into his navy blue towelling dressing gown, he followed Beth out of the room.

Lena was on the stairs.

'Mr Jake... What's the trouble...? Miss....'

Beth ran at the bewildered housekeeper. 'Lena! Do you have Nathan with you in the kitchen...'

Lena's shake of her head was what the wild-eyed Beth had expected to see.

'For God's sake, he can't have just *disappeared...*' Jake sounded angry.

The three made their way down the thickly carpeted stairs.

'I'm going to get Louis... Mr Jake, I think *you* should call the police.'

He's been kidnapped... With this thought, Beth felt her hand go to her throat.

Seeming to have come to the same conclusion, Jake ran into the kitchen and to the wall mounted telephone. With Beth by his side and Lena standing next to oak table, he was in the process of dialling for police assistance when Charlotte appeared in the doorway.

'Why is everyone shouting...?'

As Beth looked at her daughter she thought...*Teddy? Charlotte never goes anywhere without Teddy...*Her voice was steady when she asked, 'Charlotte, why was your teddy bear in Nathan's crib?' Ice ran though her veins as she waited for Charlotte to reply.

Jake's shaking fingers stopped dialling.

Lena actually said, out loud, 'Oh dear God, *no...*'

'They swapped places, Mommy. Teddy said that Nathan would like it in...'

Beth flew at Charlotte, knocking the child to the ground as she ran past her heading for the stairs. She was screaming to know where Nathan was...

'Where...have...you...put...him...? Damn you to death...*Answer me...*you *bastard...*'

Charlotte whimpered.

'*Charlotte.* Where's the baby? Where *is* Nathan?' Jake's voice was full of dread.

'He's in my room, Daddy. He's asleep; he's not being a naughty boy...'

Lena started to cry.

Jake ran up the stairs two at a time. He too was hollering to Charlotte, 'Where, Charlotte? *Where* in your room...?' he rushed past his wife.

In his daughter's bedroom now, Jake took in everything, but could not see any sign of his baby son.

Jake tore the yellow bedclothes from the bed. He looked under the bed, behind the heavy, lemon coloured velvet curtains, in the white wood wardrobes.

Beth just stood in the open doorway. She stood stock still as she watched her husband tear the sunshine yellow bedroom apart. She watched as Jake opened the hinged lid of the gold velvet padded ottoman that housed Charlotte's cuddly toys. She stood and watched as Jake crumpled to his knees. She fell to her own knees when her husband lifted the lifeless body of their son out of the box.

And from somewhere, somewhere that seemed to be in the distance, Beth could hear harrowing screams. With her mouth open as wide as it would go, she noticed that the sounds were not coming from Charlotte: her daughter was kneeling on the floor, at her side. Silent.

Beth knew also that the sounds were not coming from Lena either, because the housekeeper had a trembling hand clamped to her mouth as she stood leaning against the door-jam of the bedroom.

The screams Beth could hear were her own. And they chorused with the similar ones coming from her husband's mouth.

*

41

Vi shuffled across the blue tiled floor of her kitchen. Her new kitchen, gleaming white and electric blue, was very nice, if you liked that sort of thing; the trouble was, Vi didn't.

Her brilliant white, brand new cooker was electric; the white and chrome kettle was electric. The fluorescent blue-white brightness that flooded the kitchen was electric. Anything in the kitchen that was another colour was blue: Electric Blue: Patsy's favourite colour, which was most definitely not pleasing on the eye to Vi.

Still in her Greenwood's Garden Centre uniform, a light green sweatshirt with the business motive embroidered at the top left hand side, heavy-duty dark green corduroy trousers, and a pair of stout, well polished black boots, Patsy was sat at the white breakfast counter that had been installed in place of the old table in Vi's modernised kitchen.

Perched on a high-backed chrome stool, the seat under her bottom padded in blue vinyl, Patsy watched her mother-in-law move at a snail's pace as she opened and closed cupboards in an attempt to make a pot of tea...*when did she start walking with a shuffle...? I've not noticed that before...* Shaking her head at her thoughts, Patsy tried to placate.

'I know you are not best pleased with the kitchen, Mother. But you will get used to it, given time. It'll make your life much easier, once you get the hang of things. The sugar is in the white canister marked SUGAR.'

Patsy, who now wore her dyed red hair very short, almost manly, was determined to stay put on her stool, and to make her mother-in-law find her way around the newly installed units.

Patsy sighed, none to pleased with the state of affairs. She had put a lot of time and effort into making Vi's kitchen more up-to-date: More in line with the new decade...*after all, it's nineteen ninety-one, not blooming nineteen fifty-one*...

Patsy's temper was steadily rising. It was nearly four o'clock and she still had a lot to do this November afternoon. And yet here she was, twiddling her thumbs and waiting for Vi to stop being awkward and make a simple pot of tea.

When a cup of watery tea was finally placed in front of her, Patsy had begun to concede to herself that the stools were very uncomfortable, and unpractical for the old lady's use...*they'll have to be blooming well replaced...But by what...?* Patsy was vexed by her costly mistake...*ordinary kitchen chairs won't be much use at the high counter; so that will have to be removed, too*...

Vi's voice pulled her from her reverie.

'I'm taking my tea through,' Vi headed for the comfort of her front parlour, the lounge as Patsy kept telling her to call it.

Following her mother-in-law, Patsy would have had to have been blind not to notice the scowl on Vi's face as she settled herself into her favourite armchair that faced the television set.

'I'll be going now, Mother.' Knowing that her presence was none too welcome this early evening, Patsy was ready to oblige.

'I just wanted to make sure you could find your way round the kitchen. Anyways, I'm off, now...we're taking Sam to the bonfire at six. Can I get yer anything before I go?'

Vi shook her head. And she actually smiled, 'Well, tat tar, then love. Don't let me keep you. And thanks again for all you do for me. You've done me proud here these last few weeks. I suppose the old kitchen needed a bit of a seeing to. And I like the new staircase, that I do. But, hey, love, I'm getting too old for the new fancy gadgets you're a wanting me to have. I'll make good use of that there micro-whatsit...thingy-me-bob. I'll warm that there lasagne up for me tea tonight…Thanks for showing me what I have to do. And Patsy, I *do* appreciates you cooking for me, like you do.'

As Patsy went out into the dark wet night, rushing back to her own house, she was thankful that Vi appreciated something…

Pleased to be left to her own devices, Vi dozed in her chair. The heat from the coal effect electric fire always made her drowsy. Loud music blared from the television set. But it didn't interrupt its owner's sleep.

Outside the parlour window, evidence that it was Guy Fawke's Night could be heard and seen. Multi coloured fireworks illuminated the black, rain heavy sky. Excited teenagers chased one another with hand-held fireworks, and some that weren't. The noise, the loud cracks and bangs, mixing with the cacophony of shrieks and screams, laughter and yelps of fear, filled the night air, the acrid smell of gunpowder and burning wood polluted it further. Younger children—thrilled to be out in the dark, no matter the weather—squealed and shouted their pleasure as they made their way (their warmly clad parents in tow,) to the recreation ground and the massive, organised and ticket-only bonfire.

November the fifth, Bonfire Night, was now very different from the ones Vi's own children had celebrated in their childhood years. Then, the unguarded and often huge fires were fed by a copious supply of wooden crates, old doors, fencing, tree trunks and branches, anything that could have collected and carried by children as young as four years old.

It was a different era altogether, when children were not as cosseted as they were today. Back then, in the Greenwood boys' formative years, danger meant the bogey man (ghouls and ghostly apparitions) and getting hit in the eye by a catapult or an out of control football; there had been order in the way children looked after children, an unwritten law that came naturally to brothers and sisters: they looked out for one another; took responsibility. Perhaps it had not always worked but, in the main, it had. Muggers, rapists and child molesters were unknown then to the outdoor playing youngsters. It was a time when old women could sleep peacefully in their beds without fear of a being robbed, beaten or raped: A time when children were content to be children. And when those children knew the difference between right and wrong.

Vi woke to a loud bang. She muttered to herself as she made her creaking-gate way into the hallway of her small cottage. Something lay on the coconut-mat behind the front door. Vi bent to see what it was…

'A bloody banger; they could have set my bloody house on fire, the silly little beggars!'

The firework was still smouldering. Vi rushed into her kitchen for water—and couldn't find the jug she wanted. She opened and closed cupboard after cupboard, panicked to be at such a loss. Finally, in desperation, she ran water from the tap straight into a glass.

By the time she was back in the hallway, the firework had burnt out leaving the charred evidence on the brand new doormat.

Clearing up the mess, Vi felt very close to tears...*what's happening to the world...? Kids these days, they're murdering villains. The parents are scared stiff of them all...aye, they'd no more give them a good hiding than...*

Vi was thinking that today's parents would fly to the moon rather than smack their offspring; teaching them right from wrong with the old fashioned sharp-shock treatment of a clip round the ear hole was now frowned upon; illegal, even, she had been told

Turning off all the downstairs lights, Vi moved slowly upstairs to her bed. She felt very old and thoroughly depressed...and she also felt like weeping.

Vi never mentioned Charlotte. The others, Malcolm, Patsy, Julie and even little Sam would go over the tragic events of Nathan's death; but never in Vi's presence.

When the verdict of accidental death was recorded, Vi had stated that she never wanted to hear Charlotte's name mentioned again. Not ever. And she said the same to the grieving grandparents, Maureen and Don, and to the devastated parents, Beth and Jake.

Don had argued Charlotte's case.

'Vi...she's a child! An infant. She thought she was doing right...Thought she was helping her Mom. And it was because of Daniel...Daniel's coffin...Vi, the truth is that no one explained that baby Daniel was *dead*...Charlotte thought Daniel was asleep. When she'd asked about him, Beth, and Maureen had *both* told her that Daniel was sleeping...And when Charlotte had asked where, they told her, over and over again...they'd said, "He's asleep in his box in the church..." No one, not even *me*, ever used the word *dead.*'

Daniel and Nathan's great grandmother would have none of it. Down the telephone lines, Vi had repeated, often, what she thought:

'No explanation can excuse evil. The child's a devil, so she is! And I *knew* it. I knew it the first time I clapped eyes on her. Aye, a baby not yet christened, and I said then...*she's a little monster.*'

What Vi couldn't say, what she *had* to keep to herself, was the root of her unforgiving: Iris, the girl's natural grandmother. Vi's thoughts on the woman had never changed...*Aye, that Charlotte is as evil as her grandmother...She looks and thinks like Iris...The devil's handmaidens...*

Strangely, Vi never associated Maureen with Iris. It never crossed her mind to do this. Maureen was Maureen. Iris was Iris. Even knowing all the facts, Vi steadfastly believed that Maureen had not been tainted by the woman's devilish ways—nor had Beth, for that matter. But then, it was true that neither of the women favoured Iris in looks. Not the way Charlotte did.

Tonight, though, as she undressed for bed, laying her pleated tweed skirt and brown jersey wool jumper and matching cardigan on the back of a chair in readiness for the morning, sniffing, automatically, the under arms of the jumper for traces of sweat before doing so, the thought of Maureen's ancestry did cross her mind...*Nay, our Maureen probably takes after her father and, if it was that Fitzgerald bloke, he didn't seem such a bad sort from all accounts. But why he got caught up with the likes of Iris is beyond me...! And our Bill...in God's name, what did he see in the wicked woman...?*

She lay staring at the ceiling. Fireworks were still cracking, whooshing and banging into the night sky outside her closed curtains bedroom window. She wiped the cold tears from her cheeks. She missed Sid so much; so very much...*listen, my love, I'll be coming soon. Look after the lads for me until than...and take care of our Beth's boys, too...*

Vi's sleep was fitful and full of dreams. This was often the case when she went to bed on an empty stomach. The once vibrant and bonny, hungry for life woman was fast becoming a tiny framed, bony old woman.

Across the Atlantic, in America, Guy Fawke's Night did not exist; the fifth day of November was just an ordinary day in November.

It was a humid afternoon in Florida. The sun shone fiercely through the window of the doctor's office. Don asked for the blind to be lowered. When it had been done, he said, 'Will it kill me...?'

The doctor, seating himself back at his desk, blew out a long breath before answering. 'I'll not beat around the bush, Don...Yes, eventually. Motor Neuron Disease doesn't usually take survivors on board for long.'

'*How* long...?'

'You will certainly have another four, five years; maybe as many as ten.'

'Treatment. Is there any? Will I be able to sing?'

'There isn't any treatment, as such. The weakness will become progressive. What you are experiencing now, in your hand and legs, will continue. Eventually it will affect other muscles. Yes, I'm afraid your voice will be damaged, you will lose it, in time.'

'Will it destroy my brain...Will I become a damn cabbage, Bern?'

'No. Not all, far from it, in fact. Your intellect will be intact...'

'Holy Mother of God! I'll have a fucking brain, but won't be able to move or...*speak?*'

The doctor remained silent for a frisson of time. The air between him and the famous man seated in front of him was electric. Shocking.

'Look, Don. You have *years* ahead of you. You asked me to be honest, and I have been. The prognosis I have given you today could change with the new developments in science that, truly Don, are happening practically overnight. Each passing day, more answers are being found...Look at the treatments for cancer, now.'

Don stood, and made his way to the door. His face ashen, his hand trembled as he tried to grip and turn the doorknob. Turning, the sweat glistening on his brow, he faced his doctor, a long-time acquaintance from the golf club.

'Thanks, Bern...I need to get out of here...some air...Guess I've got a lot of thinking to do...I'll be in touch...'

Bernard Bowstein stared at the closed door long after Don had gone...*I hate this...I absolutely despise this new fashion of telling the patient everything. Sometimes I wish...*

But Bernard, Bern to most people, didn't know what he wished. This was when his profession as a medic made him wish he was anything but a family practitioner. It felt so wrong to tell people they were going to die. To read out diagnostic reports that predicted death. Horrible deaths. Especially when he had to also explain that death would come after years of a wasting muscle disease that, for some unfathomable reason, did not affect the brain tissue...*Don will be trapped in a useless body, and know all about it.*

'Will Grandpa be back, soon? Like he promised.' Charlotte was impatient to speak with Don. Eager to remind him of what he had promised.

'Drink your milk, Charlotte, and stop dilly-dallying. And Grandpa did *not* promise, you remember very well what he did say—he said he *might* take you shopping.'

With her back to her granddaughter, Maureen was wiping the crumbs from the kitchen counter. Although silently amused by the eight-year old's ingenuity at seeking her own way, she too was also a little concerned by her husband's lateness. The one promise Don had made for certain was that he would be home in time to take Charlotte for her after-school singing lessons.

Maureen glanced at the clock on the wall: Four fifteen.

'It looks like *I* will have to tackle the traffic. Come on, Charlotte, drink up your milk and finish your sandwich. Denise is expecting you at five.'

Charlotte groaned about the milk, though she did obey her grandmother and drained the glass. Popping the last of her chicken sandwich into her mouth, she jumped down from her pine stool, pushing it back into line with the three others that nestled under the long breakfast bar. Wiping her mouth on her napkin, she admonished her absent grandfather.

'Grandma; he did so promise. I *do* remember. He said he'd take me to Denise this afternoon, and then, after, we'd go to the mall to look at the baby grand pianos...'

Listening to her granddaughter's chatter, Maureen placed her arm round the youngster's shoulders and walked with her from the kitchen towards the wide stairway that rounded its way to the first floor of Strand House.

And as they stepped their way upstairs, Maureen was filled with a feeling of completeness. She loved her home. The sun filled house, a pretty pink and white on the outside, was mellow and golden within. When first choosing the carpets and furnishings, Maureen had kept the glorious sunny days of Florida in mind, making sure that the house was decorated to reflect its position on the shores of the Atlantic coastline.

All the floors in the house were laid with polished pine. Pink and cream rugs, patterned with deeper pink cabbage roses, complimented the golden wood they lay upon.

The ground floor rooms were furnished in soft pastel tones. Huge sofas and squashy armchairs, upholstered in lightweight fabrics of cream, gold and blues, exuberated a light heartedness. And that ambiance of wellbeing continued through to the dining room. Here, varying shades of green and cream stripes brought a European elegance to the golden teak, twelve seating dinner table that took centre stage.

Next door to this room was the den: here, a huge television set, a state-of-the-art hi-fi system plus a well stocked bar offered the best in entertainment. It was often to be found in a state of disarray. As the family room, it was a place to come to relax, and maybe even read one of the many books lining its trophy laden shelves, or the newspapers or magazines stacked on the massive coffee table that was placed in front of the deep buttoned, caramel coloured leather sofa and wing, deep backed armchairs. Very much Don's domain, his sandalwood fragranced aftershave often lingered the air.

The large kitchen had floor to ceiling pine units and cupboards, white and chrome utilities and black and white marble worktops. This room, overlooking the back of the house, and onwards to the sea, was enhanced by a huge picture window. The pine breakfast bar was placed so that its seated occupants could gaze through the glass pane and watch the ever-changing glory of the sugar-white beach and the mesmerizing activities of the sea.

Like most American homes, the basement of the house was also much used. Here Don had his soundproof studio. There was also a games room, fitted out with a full-sized pool table, another suite of two guests room and bathrooms, and the laundry and storerooms that in turn gave entrance to the three-car garage.

The hallway of the house was magnificent to walk into to: a spectacular crystal chandelier, imported from Venice, Italy, hung pride of place from the vaulted ceiling. The floor, tiled in creamy marble, was cool under foot and perfect for the climate conditions of east coast Florida. Maureen's affection for the scent of lavender was very much in evidence in the twin basined cloakroom, where cream hand towels as thick as blankets hung from gold plated heated rails. The opulence was completed by a magnificent wide-step stairway that wound its cream carpeted way up to the first floor.

This top floor of the house was where most of the bedrooms were located. In each room, huge windows were graced with drapes made of magnolia coloured heavy cotton and floating white voile. The décor, though individual from room to room, followed a similar design: white walls were enhanced by pictures of seascapes, or family portraits, and the beds, some four poster, some canopied and curtained, were adorned with floral patterned bedspreads or exquisitely fashioned story-telling handcrafted quilts; furnishings were simple and chosen for comfort: Every bedroom was serviced by its own bathroom, and most had a balcony overlooking the lush greenery of the palm fringed front driveway or the vast blueness of the Atlantic Ocean. Those rooms that faced the sea, also looked down onto the kidney shaped swimming pool and the terrace and lawns that backed the fabulously positioned house.

Now, reaching Charlotte's bedroom, Maureen urged her granddaughter to quickly go in and change out of her navy box pleat skirt/ primrose yellow blouse school uniform, in readiness for their dash to the studio of her voice coach, Denise Powell.

'I don't know what's keeping your Grandpa...But hurry, sweetheart, we don't want to be late...'

Charlotte played for time, standing half in half out of her room.

'Grandma? Do I really have to go?' There was a whine in Charlotte's voice.

Maureen sighed. 'Darling, you know it's what your Mommy wants; and your Grandpa, too. Go on in; get yourself ready...*Shoo*...' She gently pushed her granddaughter further into the turquoise and white room, closing the door firmly behind the sulky young girl.

However, through the closed door she knocked and called...'Hey, Charlotte...? Last one down *stinks*.'

Smiling to herself when Charlotte called back, 'Pong! I can smell you already, Gran...' Maureen rushed to her own bedroom, the master bedroom suite she shared with Don.

Entering the sumptuous lilac and white room, Maureen's thoughts turned to her husband...*Where is he? He did say he'd take Charlotte this afternoon. And she is right, I remember that he did promise to show her the baby grand piano he was thinking of buying; his bribe to keep her interest in music...*

Changing out of her pink short-sleeved tee-shirt and white shorts, Maureen chose to wear a pair of light-blue slacks, teaming them with a blue denim, long sleeve shirt.

Before she had even stepped into one leg of the trousers, Charlotte was knocking on the door calling that she was ready.

'Put extra perfume on, Grandma...You *really* smell...'

And into this frivolity strode Don: Neither Charlotte or Maureen had heard him come home.

'Were you going to go without me...?'

'Grandpa!' Charlotte rushed at her grandfather, causing him to wobble, unsteadily on his feet.

'Whoa there, young lady! You're not only getting taller each day, you're getting stronger, too. You nearly bowled me over...'

Charlotte giggled, delighted with her grandfather's presence.

'Will *you* take me, Grandpa, *will* you...?'

At that moment, Maureen came out of her bedroom onto the wide landing.

'Where *have* you been, Don? I was getting worried...'

'Oh, you know, I got talking...I called into the club. No bother, hey? I'm here now, aren't I? Are you ready, then, my lady?' Don posed his question to his granddaughter, although it was his wife who answered.

'Thanks to you, we are *both* ready. So you might as well have two ladies with you. Any objections?'

Don glanced at his wife and said, 'None at all.'

Maureen indicated for the three of them to make their way down the stairs.

'Come on, then. Lets hit the road, shall we? And I think afterwards, we'll go for pizza...' she caught her granddaughter's eye, and winked, adding, 'that is, of course, after you have shown us this *bambino* of a piano. Okay with you, Charlotte?'

The music studio was within walking distance of Vera Malone's hair and beauty salon: Vera's newly opened shop, the third in what the woman hoped would be a chain.

After installing Charlotte with her singing coach, Don and Maureen walked the few yards that brought them within inches of the salon's front door.

'I'd rather not go in, Don.'

'Why not? Vera loves to see you, you know that...' Don was surprised by Maureen's reticence, especially since she had been so delighted by the prospect of her one-time employee becoming her own hairdresser again.

'She'll not be in; she does have *other* shops, after all, Don. Let's just go and sit in the car. I think we need to talk...'

Thankfully, the silver grey Mercedes was parked in the shade of the numerous trees that lined the elegant avenue. Don eased himself into the driver's seat, troubled by what it could be that Maureen wanted to talk about.

Maureen came straight to the point. 'What's wrong, Don?'

Don stared at his wife...*did she know? How could she know? Had Bern called to tell her...? No. Doctors' swore an oath of privacy, didn't they...?*

Maureen was saying, 'Don, I know that you have not been feeling too well, recently. Were you at the doctors today? Is *that* where you've been...?'

Don could not quite believe his wife's insight. He truly had never mentioned a word of how he'd been feeling; her woman's intuition no doubt had been beavering away...

Don glanced into his rear view mirror, edging for time...*should I tell her...?*

'Well, Don—I'm obviously right. What *is* it, darling? Please tell me? I'm your wife, and I *need* to know what's been worrying you for the past few weeks...'

Don remained silent, stalling for more time. He had intended to tell her his

419

grave news later: how much later, he had not decided on—until now. Now, Maureen was forcing him to tell all. And he wasn't too sure he was ready. The news had hardly had time to sink into his own senses without inflicting it on his beloved wife.

Maureen's thoughts were filled with searing panic...*how old he looks...I thought it was because he had grown the moustache that he looked older, thinner. But it isn't. Dear God, let everything be all right. Please! Don't let me lose him now, don't take him away from me. Please let us have more time—time for Beth to come completely to terms with having Charlotte back...Oh God, are You listening...?*

Maureen was terrified of any further developments coming into their already deeply scarred life. After Nathan's death, Beth had not been able to have Charlotte anywhere near her. Jake had taken the same attitude. No amount of persuasion had altered their feeling towards their young daughter...

It had been Don's idea to take Charlotte back to Florida with them. That had been five years ago. Five years, which Beth had used to forge ahead with the career she had put on hold to make a family: Her infrequent visits to Florida left them all fraught. Though Jake would take time to talk and play with his growing daughter, Beth made far fewer attempts to get to know her child.

When Charlotte had reached school age, it was agreed that it was the most logical step for her to be educated in Palm Beach. The child was enrolled into a private day school and the years had swiftly passed. Now, at eight, Charlotte saw her parents in the school holidays. Left to Beth, even this would not have happened. However, Jake had taken the matter firmly in hand.

Notwithstanding this, their daughter had visited them in Montport just once since that dreadful December morning. And that one visit had not been a success. Beth and Jake's solution for Charlotte's school vacation time was to either travel round Europe together, the three of them, or to stay in the Manhattan apartment, where with New York's many places of interests, the time slipped by more quickly.

Beth's demeanour had changed drastically. Her once sweet nature was now prone to a quick temper. Her manner in dealing with her daughter was brittle, to say the least...

Now, as she waited for her husband to compose himself enough to reply to her fearful question, Maureen became instinctively aware that her life was about to change, yet again.

And if anyone had taken much notice of the dark haired, middle-aged woman and the rather older, silver haired man, who sat in the comfort of the classy car, they'd have thought that an illicit meeting was taking place.

In the little privacy available to them in the roadside parked car, Maureen cradled Don's head to her breast, burying her tear stained face into his distinguished and famous silver hair.

And when Don finally lifted his head, they had tenderly traced fingertips over each others faces, removing the tears with a whisper's touch, encouraging each other to take strength; to take what was left of their lives together, and to use it wisely.

When Charlotte came bounding out of the studio, rushing to the car, eager to get off to the shopping mall and see the piano her grandfather had promised, Maureen and Don took their first steps into the rest of their lives.

Surprisingly, the evening was a great success. Don bought the french polished baby grand piano, although it was sent to the Father Christmas room for delivery by a reindeer; hopefully it would be Rudolph pulling Santa's sleigh on Christmas Eve.

With Charlotte skipping hand in hand between them, they had gone into the pizza restaurant where they devoured loaded pizzas, garlic breads, green salads and coca-colas. Charlotte even had room for a slice of chocolate fudge cake.

Later that evening, when the happy little girl was tucked up in her bed, Maureen and Don sat down in the air-conditioned living room of their home and talked (and cried) into the small hours.

Both decided it was time for Beth and Jake to take their daughter home. For now it was their time. Time for Maureen and Don to spend what was left of the best years of their lives in their own company; to do as little as they wanted, or a lot of what they wanted, at their own pace and in their our space. They had done more than had been expected of them. Now it was their children's turn to stop the grieving and to get on with making a go of their family. No more time to be wasted, maudlin for what had passed. Life had to be grabbed with two hands.

'And for now,' Don smiled, has he pulled his teary eyed wife into a fierce embrace, 'let's enjoy ourselves, whilst I am still capable of doing just that.'

*

42

'**I**, Julia Howarth, do solemnly swear…' Suited for the ceremony in figure hugging black, a Jacquard and cashmere knee length skirt, the jacket trimmed with ivory silk at the cuffs and on the lapels, tailored especially for the day by one of America's top designers, and also wearing her deceased daughter's eighteenth birthday gift—a present that she herself had given Sonia: a choker necklace and matching earrings of diamonds and pearls—and with her long shapely legs encased in fine mesh black silk and her feet warm as toast in Italian leather black court shoes, Julia could not truly believe that it was happening; that at this very moment, on this cold January day, she was swearing her allegiance to the highest office attainable.

And Julia could also not credit that, even to her own ears, her voice sounded so loud, clear, precise and strong when her insides were quaking and her heart was thumping fast enough to break through her chest…

'…That I will faithfully execute the office of the President of the United States…'

Sonia…? Oh, my darling girl, are you listening? Are you watching? I've done it! Like I promised! Are you watching your Mom being sworn in as the fist woman president of the United States…?

Julia's thoughts continued as she took the oath. With her hand on the Holy Bible, she vowed openly and silently; and she also prayed.

As the applause began to rise to a thundering, roaring climax, and the twenty-one-gun barrage fired its salute to the new Commander-in-Chief, she opened her eyes and turned to face her husband, Ben, standing by her side.

The eye contact and the wide smiles on both their faces said it all...we did it.

And it was true: both of them had triumphed. Each had won: Julia Howarth had attained her long awaited and well earned place as leader of one of the greatest countries on earth. Her husband, Ben had, against all odds, learnt to walk again.

It was her husband who took her icy cold hand and brought it to his lips.

'I love you, Madam President.' His voice was barely audible as he kissed his wife. Dressed in a heavy navy blue coat, a thick wool red scarf round his neck to combat against the time spent in the wintry weather, Ben was overcome with the emotion of the occasion and his thoughts (blatantly obvious to those who knew him,) were probably of the very special person who was sadly missing from the ceremony.

Today, their beautiful daughter Sonia would have been so very proud: Of both of her parents.

After President Howarth's Inaugural speech, which lasted for a snow falling twenty minutes, the Sommer/Adier party moved inside, out of the frostbitten day. The next part of the proceedings, the Inaugural Lunch, was set to be a much warmer affair.

Charlotte Adier noticed that she was the only child in attendance. But at five foot six inches tall, the fourteen year-old, wearing an ankle length, double-breasted military styled dark red coat over a long straight skirt of a similar material and colour, which she had teamed with a white cashmere polo sweater and knee length, black fashion boots, realised, with a haughty acceptance of the fact, that she could quite easily be taken for a young adult.

Sipping a glass of chilled cola, the keen eyed teenager also noticed the attention her mother and father was receiving. Her grandfather, too, was being greeted with the same enthusiasm: The crowd gathering round Don Sommer were loud in their praises and compliments regarding how well the singer looked and in their pleasure that he was amongst them. The scenario had the effect of making Charlotte feel invisible...*why did they insist that I come here...? Or my Gran, for that matter! Nobody's the least bit interested in either of us…*

Later, when her mother and grandfather sang their duet salute to the new President, notwithstanding that Beth, dressed in a stunning sapphire blue silk suit, was a good eight inches shorter, and many pounds lighter than her illness-stricken singing partner, Charlotte (and most of the people present,) could see that the diminutive songstress was allowing the dark-suited Don to lean his weight against her as they stood together in front of the well-placed microphone.

The touching and well-sung tribute was rapturously received. Everyone took to their feet to applaud: All except Charlotte. Though she did rise to her feet, Beth Stuart's daughter excused herself to her grandmother, Maureen, and started to make her way to the ladies' powder room, her thoughts peevish and flaming with anger…*She thinks she's the most important person here! The pygmy…Singing dwarf…*

As she was about to exit the clamorous stateroom, Charlotte glanced back to her grandmother, whom she thought looked very glamorous for her age, dressed as she was today in a skirt and jacket of soft jersey wool in a shade of beige that, because of the golden thread woven into the delicate material, now, under the soft light of the chandeliered dining room, looked a glowing pink, and was rewarded with a wide smile from the hand-clapping woman. Warmed somewhat by this show of affection, Charlotte returned her own flick of a smile, one that was gone as quickly as it had come.

Unaware of Charlotte's moodiness and anger, Maureen herself was giddy with happiness; her thoughts reflected her gaiety and her thankfulness…*I'm so very lucky…What a family I have…! And what good friends we have, too…*

Maureen fingered the gold necklace with the teardrop pearl and diamond pendant that she was wearing with so much pride. It was a thoughtful memento, a gift from the Lady President, delivered in time to be worn this very day.

She had not been alone in receiving a gift: Charlotte was wearing a gold wristwatch, its numerals highlighted with tiny diamonds. Julia had had the back of the bracelet watch inscribed, making it worth a small fortune in the future.

Beth had been sent a pearl choker, similar to Julia's own, except for the fact that sapphires had been used in place of the diamonds.

Maureen's thoughts were joyous; they were also invoking…*Just look at my Beth. Isn't she gorgeous! I'm sure she grows more beautiful with every passing day. And Don—he looks so well, today. I hope Charlotte is enjoying herself. She is so lucky to have been invited to such an historic occasion. And to think, the first woman president is my granddaughter's godmother! I feel like pinching myself...it's all so unreal...! Oh, that was a nice smile. I've always said Charlotte should smile more; she becomes quite lovely when she does. Oh, God, please give me more time with Don, just a little more. And help Beth and Charlotte to become closer. They are getting there, but it's going to take time...Let us have the time, Lord, please...*

*

43

Charlotte was in love. His name was David. David Morse was the nineteen-year old grandson of Rockfort House's head gardener.

Now a boarder at her school in Florida, Charlotte was at home in Montport for the holidays. And she had spent most of her vacation time in hot pursuit of the handsome college boy.

David, blond haired, tall and athletic in build, supplemented his meagre college allowance by working alongside his grandfather in the massive grounds and formal gardens of the Rhode Island mansion house whenever he could. And during the long summer break, he spent most days toiling at the more mundane chores required in the upkeep of pristine garden maintenance.

Sweating under the hot summer sun, David had tackled his chores knowing that his every move was being watched and followed. And now, with the stalking well into its second month, David was truly annoyed by its intrusion: the puppy-like devotion of Charlotte Adier was becoming intolerable.

It was mid-September, one week prior to Charlotte's departure back to school. Clad in a lime green, miniscule bikini, the girl lay by the side of the pool, soaking up the last rays of the afternoon sun. She had also been trying, unsuccessfully, to catch David's attention by practising her stretching abilities and doing acrobatic manoeuvres with her long legs.

'You'll have to watch yourself with that one...' Eric Morse, quite aware of Charlotte's infatuation, quietly joked with his grandson.

'Come off it, Gramps...she's just a kid...'

David, stripped to the waist, his bare upper body deeply tanned by his own many weeks of working in the outdoors, coloured even more when he realised that his grandfather had noticed Charlotte's very obvious and provocative behaviour.

As the teenage girl sprawled on a yellow and white striped padded sun bed, her skin glistening by her over use of oily sun-protector cream, blue jean clad David continued with his hedge clipping, a smirk on his face as he listened to his grandfather's chirpy whistling rendition of a song that was about only have eyes for that special someone...

From his study window Jake had been watching his daughter, worry creasing his brow...*I hope she isn't into boys*...With what he had just been witnessing, coupled with his thoughts, Jake was not a happy man.

Beth was well aware that her daughter was besotted. And it was she who walked onto the pool terrace, beckoning her daughter in-doors...

'Come and get changed, Charlotte. I want you to drive into town with me and help choose a gift for Lena. It's her birthday next week, and you should get her something, too. Be quick, now...and put your robe on. Don't just saunter back to the house like *that*...for heaven's sake, girl, cover yourself up!'

And as Charlotte sullenly obeyed, half-heartedly wearing her lemon towelling beach-robe, letting it slide down off her shoulders as she slouched towards the house, Beth gave inwards thanks for her own ability to think fast. The trouble was, she was running out of ideas to get Charlotte away from the house...*Thank God it's for just one more week*...

Beth smiled at the gardeners as she tidied up after her daughter, collecting the wet towels and the numerous glossy teen magazines that were always in evidence when Charlotte was around. The one she had been reading last was left open on the oil-stained sun-bed.

As she made her laden way back indoors, Beth's attention was drawn to this particular magazine. Walking slowly away from the pool, skim reading the article on the page, she felt her cheeks redden: it was an advice column on how best to perform some sex acts: Charlotte had pen marked the advice on oral sex…

'What's wrong with having a wheelchair? An electric whiz one at that.' Maureen tried to keep her voice light. In truth, she was as distressed as Don. She tried again, 'Come on, darling, at least *try* it.'

Don's full-time nurse, Australian born Pete Gregson, guided and assisted his charge into the brand new, chrome wheeled chair.

'It's motorised, Don. Probably faster than your Mercedes.' The well-built, very blond and healthily tanned male nurse had an amusing quip for even the most awkward of moments.

'Ha…bloody…ha…' Don panted his words, the exertion of moving just a few steps taking his breath away.

'There, Don. It suits you, darling; it's a lovely machine.'

'You have it then, Maureen, if it pleases you…so…much.'

'She prefers her bike, I think, Don.' Pete winked conspiratorially at his seated patient, who gave a feeble smile in return.

Maureen cottoned-on to Pete's cajolery, and was thankful for the young man's quick thinking.

'You can both make fun of me all you like—it keeps me *fit;* and it's better than going from the house to the car—the car to the shops. I *enjoy* my rides…and I meet interesting people…' Maureen stated all of this with mock indignation.

'I keep telling you…that…we should…entertain more…'

'Why do we need to entertain, Don, when we have Pete's company to keep us laughing…?' Maureen realised that she had inadvertently opened a topic that was close to Don's heart: her husband was very aware that Maureen's life was a little lonely. He'd said, and said often before today, "you are still so *young,* Maureen. Get out and about more. You don't want to be stuck at home with an old man—an ailing old man at that…Bring people in for dinner. Entertain; like we used to."

But Maureen had been firm. She told Don, and told him daily, that if they went out, they went together. And as for having people over for dinner, well, it was not all it was cracked up to be. Maureen told Don that she liked it as it was: the two of them. And Pete just down the corridor in his own apartment suited their requirements fine.

As a live-in carer, the nurse had been given the en-suite bedroom next door to the master bedroom. Another bedroom had been converted to be his living room. Pete ate with the couple, aiding Don, and, because Maureen insisted that he have the run of the house, he had full use of the kitchen, den and pool areas when he was not on duty.

Today, Maureen had not been entirely truthful in the reason for her taking up bicycle riding. True, it was a good way to exercise. And true too, she did meet some very interesting people when she was cycling out and about. However, the bike riding had another side to its usage.

Doctor Bernard Bowstein, visiting Don on a weekly basis, had also been concerned by Maureen's blood pressure. Maureen's very high blood pressure...

'The tablets I'm going to prescribe will help. But get some exercise. Walk, swim...cycle...Get it *down*, Maureen, we don't want you suffering a stroke.'

Maureen had taken her physician's advice. In return, she had asked the doctor to keep her hypertension problem away from Don's ears.

Bern had conceded to this, knowing that Don had enough to contend with; the Motor Neurone Disease was relentless in its progress.

'What *is* your exciting news, Gran?'

'Grandpa has his wheelchair; so you'll have company travelling back to Montport—we'll be with you. It's going to be a fun Christmas! I do hope it snows.'

Charlotte agreed about the snow bit. As to it being exciting that her grandfather was now in a wheelchair, well, Charlotte thought it all a bit sick. Grandpa Don was getting worse by the day; and Charlotte could find nothing exciting about any of it.

That aside, she was enjoying her weekly telephone chat with her grandmother. With only two weeks before term ended for the Christmas break, the school-boarding teenager was keen to get back home. If she had travelling companions, so be it.

The school Charlotte attended ruled that each boarder could make three telephone calls per week on a set day and at a set time. This term, Charlotte's slot was allocated to Friday and between the hours of six and eight in the evening. It was normal that her grandmother received the first of the telephone calls, and some weeks, that was the only call the teenager made: Charlotte found that, although she had lots to tell her grandparents, there was very little she had to say to her parents.

This Friday night, after saying goodbye to her grandmother, and sending her best love to her all ready in bed grandfather, Charlotte made one other phone call. It turned out to be a wasted call: David Morse's roommate said that his college friend was not available. That he had gone into Boston with his date.

David, who was not in Boston, his pal had been coaxed to tell a down-right lie, groaned, his thoughts in overdrive...*Where in hell did she get my phone number from? I'll have to go round and see her when I get home...put a stop to all this nonsense*...Charlotte Adier had called him three times already. He had spoken to her just the once, and that was three weeks ago.

'Okay dark horse. Seeing that *that's* the second time I've fabricated the truth for you...who is she?' David's roommate was intrigued.

David, who was lay flat on his back on his paper strewn single bed, sighed. 'Some little rich kid...My Gramps works for her parents.' He sat up as he continued, a nonchalant smile on his face; he knew he was about to name-drop.

'Actually, she's Beth Stuart's daughter.'

'Wow.'

David really smiled as he thought to himself...*I suppose it really is a bit of a wow...I guess I'm just used to being around celebrities*...

'Yep, she's Beth's kid. And guess who her Pop is...'

'Who...?'

'None other than Jake Adier.'

'You mean *the* Jake Adier? As like *A Stranger Stalks Within Us,* and *Forever To Be Young*...fame?'

'The one.'

'And you said to say that you weren't in—that you were out on a *hot date*...?'

David didn't answer his friend; he let out a long sigh and flopped backwards again before saying, 'She's a kid, Jon...Just a kid...'

'Kids grow up, fast.'

David lay silent, thinking. His roommate went into the bathroom to get himself ready for bed. When the dark haired young man returned, just in his white boxer shorts, David turned to watch him as he climbed into his own bed.

'Want to know who her granddaddy is, Jono?'

Jonathan stalled at switching off his bedside lamp.

'Don't tell me, let me guess...heir to the throne?'

'Almost. Her grandfather is the one and only Don Sommer.'

'No shit! My Mom's been crazy over the guy for years...and her Mom, too.'

'He's old, now; and ill.'

'But, Davey, man, his little girl isn't, is she? Think on it...'

David grinned into the darkened room. It was true; Charlotte Adier wasn't such a little girl any more.

As light snores came his way from across the room, David's mind went back to the summer—and Charlotte's blatant attempt at looking sexy.

With his hands linked under his head, his feet crossed at the ankles, David felt a fluttering of desire at the base of his stomach. The feeling began to grow the more he thought...*Okay, Jono, I'm thinking...*

*

44

David could not believe how easy it had been. Next to him Charlotte lay asleep, curled into a ball, her knees drawn up to her small naked breast, obviously unaware of the penetrating cold.

Having nothing to use except a thin piece of floral patterned material that had been a picnic tablecloth at some time in the past, David covered the girl's slim hips and began to feel very guilty.

It was freezing cold in the old, now used for storage *Summer House*. It was two days after Christmas and two in the morning.

As he quickly dressed himself, David began to shiver. His breath fogged in front of him when he said, with some urgency, 'Wake up, Charlotte; get dressed. We'll freeze out here, otherwise!'

David became quite fearful of being found. Fastening his shirt, he squatted down, nudging Charlotte to wake up and move herself.

'No...I want to *stay*. To stay with you...' Charlotte reached for David, putting her cold hands inside the warmth of his shirt near his belly. With a quick movement, her face replaced her hands and she nipped his warm flesh.

'Give *over*...' David pushed her away; then, more gently, more quietly he said, 'get some clothes on, Charlotte, before you freeze. Shit, man, it's *cold.*'

Charlotte made no attempt to move, though she did sit up.

'Why, David? Why do you want me to get dressed? Come and lie down again, *I'll* keep you warm…'

David felt a surge of exasperation…*She's acting like a kid. My God, she is a kid…*

'Charlotte, we have got to move. Enough is enough. What are you crying for…?'

'Because you are shouting; you don't want to be with me anymore…David? I thought you *loved* me…'

Panicking, David knelt at Charlotte's side on the dusty cold wooden floor. Around them, floor to ceiling, there was neatly stacked tables and chairs, deckchairs, folded sun-chairs and all the other Rockfort House paraphernalia that needed to be stored during the long months of winter.

David held the sobbing girl in his arms. He soothed her, urging her to dress, kissed her hair, her temples, finally her mouth. And he felt the desire mount. Charlotte was quite the temptress. There earlier lovemaking had been frantic, erotic and…

Now David realised that he wanted more.

The kissing lead to caressing; touch became taste, as tongues licked and nipped and the cold was forgotten. The heat of their bodies fused together as they made love again.

Their intimacy had left its scent on both of them. More gently than the first time, David had urged his young lover to dress herself, kissing her, hugging her, promising that they would meet again the following night.

And as he made his way home, in the white pick-up truck belonging to his grandfather, David couldn't help but grin. Warmed by the car's heater, David found that the guilt and panic had vanished. He'd had a fantastic night. Fantastic sex. When Jono heard about it all, his eyes would pop out of his head. Charlotte had not been afraid of doing anything. Nothing had been taboo. And she had done most of the instigating.

Nearing his home, David's face grew hot with the memory of the erotic lovemaking. It was a great feeling to know that there was more on offer. It had been his first time, too…*What a stroke of luck to have Charlotte as my teacher. The girl is insatiable…*

As he quietly parked the truck on the driveway of his wood-built home that he shared with his divorced mother and her widowed father, David had the urge to roll around in the deep snow. He felt on top of the world. Giddy. This Christmas vacation was going to be one to remember.

*

45

Christopher Grady's Christmas had been stage-managed from start to finish. Whom he ate with, whom he drank with, whom he celebrated with had been totally organised by his wife of four years: Carol. It could be said that the doctor was not too keen on married life.

However, his avaricious wife, who at one time had been his receptionist, had revelled in the company of the people they had spent the festive season with. But then Carol was like that. Christopher Grady's wife thoroughly enjoyed her married life, and the social status that came from her union with the mild natured doctor.

Carol had not been idle, either. The four years had been used to upturn the fortunes of Moira House, which no longer advertised itself as a nursing home.

Now, the well proportioned and much extended Hampstead Vale property had become a private clinic. It's sought after services were expensive and exclusive. It specialised in discreet sterilisation, vasectomy, and abortion.

Carol Grady was a woman of her time. Tall and elegant, she kept her nails well manicure and polished deep red; her blonde hair, short, highlighted, and shampooed daily. The suits she wore were sleek, tailor-made and business like. She walked briskly, spoke quickly and effused efficiency: an efficiency that had been responsible for bowling Christopher over in the first place. As his receptionist, the grey-eyed woman had made it impossible for him to function without her.

And as much as Christopher thought that he could not live without Carol as his wife, he was finding it equally as difficult to live with her.

Carol never rested, unless asleep in her bed at night. She never took a day off. She never stopped working, planning, scheming. Their appointment book was full, but not overflowing; their bank account nicely in the black and their reputation steadily climbing in the right direction.

Iris, Carol's seventy six year old mother-in-law, worshipped the ground her son's wife walked on. She idolised Carol's no-nonsense manner, her brittle-bright conversations and her caustic humour. Iris had found her match. Had recognised it as soon as Carol had come into their lives.

In exchange, Carol was as swift with her summing up of Christopher's mother. And the power the woman had wielded over her son. Within days of becoming the nursing home's receptionist, Carol had the measure of Iris Grady.

Quite simply, Carol had then taken over the reins, but not the power. To date, she had never crossed the old lady and had no intention of ever doing so. They were allies, and very useful to each other.

In her late teens, Carol had been a gentle and quite unassuming young woman. But all that had been ripped from her, along with her illegitimate unborn child, by the services of a back-street abortionist who had charged exorbitant fees to mutilate her womb, rendering her to be childless for the rest of her life.

Now, fourteen years after the national health emergency hysterectomy, that had saved her from the tunnel light of approaching death, Carol had finally come to terms with the fact that she would never become a mother.

And, two years into her marriage, when she had come clean with Christopher, she strived to make him see some sense in the fact that they would never have children to hinder them...'And besides, Chris,' she had said, '...what good can *you* remember of your childhood, hey? Come on, be honest, there's nothing, is there? Absolutely *nothing*. Kids always feel that they are in the way. Ours will never feel like that, because they will never exist.'

Carol had a way of winning an argument; even one that made no sense. Over the years, Carol had found that it was always the best policy to insist that she was in the right, and everyone else in the wrong.

Settled into her favourite armchair, crystal goblet of ruby red claret in her right hand, Iris glowed with contentment. By her side, on a small, highly polished table, the white china plate holding the remains of her fillet steak dinner sat next to the half-full bottle of wine.

Never a big eater, Iris had thoroughly enjoyed the tender beef, but had not been over enthused with the potatoes gratin, nor the el dente broccoli. She would much have preferred chips, but Carol had said that French fries were too full of fat to be included in anybody's diet.

Not that Iris was on a diet: Far from it. Always having been thin, Iris was now not much more than skin and bone. However, this was of no concern to her. Nothing really bothered Iris anymore. Though Carol made sure that her mother-in-law's grey hair was shampooed and blow-dried every week, by the hairdresser who came to the house to style her own sleek blonde locks, Iris wouldn't have minded if her hair was left unwashed for a month.

Notwithstanding that she wasn't grateful for her daughter-in-law's care, Iris proudly patted her just cut, well-kept, jaw length hair, eagerly looking forward to the nights' television, which was set to be very special seeing that it was New Year's Eve.

And she was not disappointed by what was being screened on her huge television screen: *Ghosting* was her favourite of all times film; the re-running of this movie was a perfect start to her evening.

Sipping her third glass of wine, Iris used the remote control to turn up the sound, blotting out the hub of conversation which was floating up from the room directly below: the dining room was in use for a New Year's dinner party. The guest list included all four of Carol's most influential friends.

The Grady's guests enjoyed a memorable meal: the before-dinner canapés, mostly fish in a light filo-pastry, were delicious; the perfect textured duck pate and wafer thin toast fingers, delectable. A main course of apricot and prune stuffed pork loin, served with baby roast potatoes, butternut squash, and mange tout was said by all to be divine. The dessert was a masterpiece of culinary skills: coconut ice cream had been blended with kirsch and served on an icing-sugar dusted chilled glass plate in the shape of a snowman. A half glace cherry was in place as the nose, a thin strip of liquorice had produced a smiling mouth and a thicker blob of black liquorice, shaped to be a trilby, had been placed on top of the snowman's head. There were gasps of admiration from the diners, which soon turn to murmurs of "wonderful" when the creation had been tasted.

When twelve o'clock struck, everyone was on their feet, kissing, laughing and toasting the New Year of nineteen ninety-nine.

Three hours later, when Carol had finally climbed into their king size bed, after clearing away the debris (most of the food had come in containers from one of London's most famous stores, save for the dessert which Carol had truly concocted herself,) and making the dining room appear to have never been used, she still had the energy to proposition her slightly drunken, slumbering husband.

'Chris...I need to talk to you. Wake up! Come on, this is important.' She shook her husband's shoulder, vigorously.

Christopher did as he was told. Opening his eyes, he sighed, wearily.

Carol creamed her face as she spoke, 'Gloria was very upset tonight. Oh I know she wasn't showing it, but *believe* me, she was close to tears a lot of the time.' She leant out of the bed to throw her used tissues into the wastebasket.

'Seems they've been turned down, *again*. The adoption people have said a definite no. She's asked us to help.' She poked Chris in the shoulder to make sure he was listening.

Christopher, struggling to keep his eyes for closing—the prodding had helped momentarily, wanted to know why they were being asked for assistance...

'How on earth can we help? They don't need funds, they're loaded; at least Alec is.'

Alec Braithwaite was the Grady's solicitor, and, as Carol often put it, a very useful person to have as a friend. And Christopher's wife now wanted to make sure the friendship lasted.

In actuality, Carol liked twice-married flame haired Gloria. She was glamorous, fun and well connected and, being long-time bachelor Alec's trophy wife, had the man's utter devotion and listening ear. It was because of the two women's friendship that *Moira House* had so many prosperous clients. Offering a discreet service, Doctor Christopher's name was passed round with the greatest of confidence: Gloria, and Alec, had many acquaintances willing to pay for some very intimate treatments.

But what Gloria had no control over was her own desire to have a family. At nearly fifty, Alec was desperate to father a child. At forty-eight, Gloria knew that was impossible: At least with her. And she was terrified of losing her second husband

Gloria had married for the first time in her early twenties. Both she and her city bigwig husband shuddered at the thought of having children. Gloria had found the best solution: she was sterilised. By the time she was thirty six, her husband had left her, fathered two children, married the mother, and was living a happy family life in the garden of England: Kent.

With Gloria's tale of woe firmly planted in the fore of her mind, Carol was ruthless in her eagerness to help the couple attain their greatest wish.

Turning out the light, Carol, her skin slippery with moisturizer, and clad in a coffee and cream shoelace-strapped silk nightdress—which immediately began to dig into her shoulder, and was, unceremoniously, whipped off over her head—snuggled down, naked, next to her pyjama wearing husband. But she wasn't silent; even though it was close on four in the morning, she continued talking...

'They want a baby so much, Chris. They could foster a child, but that is not ideal, is it?'

Though Christopher didn't answer, she carried on, 'Yes, it's a baby or nothing. And Gloria can't face *nothing*...Alec wants her to try the reversal operation again, but I don't think so, do you?'

Christopher's eyes flew open again. Gloria Braithwaite had undergone two operations already in her quest to have the sterilization reversed. He knew all about them, having been the person who had arranged for them to take place.

Having made sure her husband was now thoroughly awake, Carol thought it time to spit out what her plan of action was. It took her thirty minutes to enlighten Christopher as to what they were...

As his wife slept, Christopher Grady was wide-awake and wondering what on earth he was going to do. Though he had adamantly refused to have anything to do with his wife's middle-of-the-night outlandish idea, he knew, by the tingle at the back of his neck, that ultimately, finally, he would agree.

Vi wished they'd just leave her alone, New Year's Eve or not.

'Come with us, Mam, *please*?' Malcolm was having one last try.

'No, lad! Go on. Be off with you. You don't want an old woman at your *do*...' Hoping that this would be the end of her son's badgering, Vi moved from her chair with great difficulty, summoning up the energy to wave her walking stick in the direction of her front door, indicating for her son to get going.

439

Back at his own house, Malcolm relayed the conversation to his wife, who was sitting before the mirror at her dressing table, readying herself for the evening ahead.

Applying mascara she said, 'Well, Mal, you tried. But I told you it would be no use...your mother's too old to go *gallivanting*, as she puts it.'

'But it's *our* party...'

Patsy turned to face her husband, taking in his belated handsomeness...*I'm glad he got his womanizing over when he was younger...Look at him now...so bloody handsome. I see the way some of the girls give him the eye...but, thank God, he'll have none of it...*With these thoughts, Patsy continued her make-up artistry, urging Malcolm to, 'Get a move on,' waving him off into the bathroom to get showered and ready.

Satisfied that her face looked the part, Patsy rose from her seat at the dressing table and went to the wardrobe where she withdrew a polythene-covered, moss green velvet evening gown...*I hope Mal likes my frock. Our Julie says it takes years off me, especially with my blonde highlights...*

Malcolm did indeed like his wife's dress. He thought she looked stunning, and had no hesitation in saying so.

'Come here, Mrs Greenwood...' he pulled his wife into his arms. Avoiding her newly applied lipstick, he kissed her fragrant forehead. He gazed into his wife's eyes and said, 'Do you know what...'

'What?'

'I'm the *luckiest* man in the world. Straight up, Pats, I am...I really am.' He kissed her again, this time pecking at her glossed lips, too. Hugging her as close as he dared, without getting into trouble for creasing her finery, he felt overcome with emotion regarding his life.

'We've had a good life together, haven't we, love? Blessed, really, when you think on it...'

Leaning back, adjusting his black bowtie, Patsy agreed with him that things had worked out well...eventually.

And later, as they danced cheek to cheek, their staff applauding them, Malcolm once again was thankful. As the singer with the ten-piece band crooned, Malcolm hummed along, acknowledging the encouraging smiles and hand clapping good wishes of the many staff members and their choice of guests who had come to celebrate the New Year in one of the function rooms of the golf club: an all-inclusive dinner dance, paid for by the directors' of Greenwood's Garden Centre.

Now, as he whisked his wife across the dance floor, Malcolm was pleased that she had seen the sense to make the evening happen...

Yes, once again, Patsy has led the way...*what would I do without her? To think, I nearly buggered it all up...*

Malcolm felt the tears brim behind his eyes...*I'm so lucky. I have good health and strength...a blooming marvellous wife. Two strong, clever kids...*

Malcolm and Patsy had achieved many things in their long marriage. Not only was the business a success, so were their two children.

Julie Mason, as their strawberry blonde married daughter was now known, was nearing her thirtieth birthday. And she and her television producer husband were expecting their first child in the early spring. Motherhood was set to be combined with her return to television news reporting, for Julie's face was well known in the North West region of England. After returning from maternity leave, Julie was also going to be presenting a ten-minute crime-watch programme, which at the moment was very hush-hush.

Of rugby player build, and still having the reddest of hair, Samuel Greenwood, just out of his teens, was in his final year at Leeds University. Studying for a law degree (though Patsy often said it was a drinking diploma her son was after, with all the boozing that went on,) he had not ventured home this Christmas; with his regular job as a part-time bar man as the excuse, he had decided to stay in Yorkshire in the company of and, as often as possible, the bed of his first serious girlfriend, a young woman who also had high hopes of one day practicing law.

At midnight, as the champagne flowed, Malcolm's thoughts moved on to his mother...*Happy New Year, Mam...Keep well...Stay with us a little longer, I couldn't imagine life without you...*

In her bed in the cottage that had been her home for over sixty years, Vi lay wide-awake.

The bed was the same she had shared with her husband, Sid. Though the mattress was different, the bed frame was the old one, and nothing and nobody could get her to part with it. The cottage had undergone many changes over the years, new kitchen, new staircase, new furnishings and decorations, but Vi had been adamant that the bedstead stay put.

At the stroke of midnight the church bells pealed, the fireworks soared and a new year dawned.

As Vi lay still, it was her thoughts that were roaming. She thought of

Malcolm and Patsy and hoped that their party had been a great success. This year was the second time the event had taken place, and she knew that it was an event eagerly looked forward to by the nursery employees: all twenty eight of them. The garden centre was proving to be a thriving business, not for the first time she wondered why, with all the money they had in the bank, Malcolm had not moved into a grander house than the cottage they'd lived in since they were first wed. Though Malcolm had said that he didn't really know why they hadn't moved, Patsy had been more forthright saying, simply, 'Because I don't want to, Mother.'

With that statement Vi had realised that she herself was a fortunate woman, and a very lucky one to have the likes of Patsy in her life. Malcolm's wife had staying-power; there was no doubt about that. She'd put up with Malcolm's shilly-shallying; she'd been, and still was, the mainstay of the business; she was a wonderful mother and would no doubt be an excellent grandparent. Patsy was a daughter-in-law who showed love without pampering words, laughter without malice and care without payment.

And with these thoughts it came to her... Vi realised that she loved Patsy. She was now as sure of that as she was that she had lost Maureen. Lost her to the great-granddaughter that she loathed. Although Maureen still telephoned weekly, there was a void in their communication: Charlotte.

As Vi finally drifted in and out of sleep her thoughts were tinged with other sad issues: Barry. The son who was now laid to rest with his father and two brothers: Barry had died of Aids in the summer of nineteen ninety-seven.

Bobby had been present for his twin brother's funeral, but had not been in touch since save for the card he sent at Christmas time.

The boys that had swelled her stomach waiting to be born and then had filled her arms, her days and her life, now all so distant or gone. Except for Malcolm... *who would have thought it...?*

And, as always, when she dwelled on those who had gone, her thoughts moved on to the infant sons of Beth and Jake: Daniel, the stillborn baby whom she never saw. Of Nathan, who perished under the hand and actions of his sister: a picture of his tiny face, framed in silver, gracing the mantel of her electric fire, being the only reminder of the other boy she had never had the chance to know.

In the silence of the small hours of the night, Vi thought of Don Sommer... *Poor Don... So helpless, and just waiting... just waiting, like me, to... die.*

Vi could not form a mental picture of Don in a wheelchair. Try as she might, the image would not materialise. Instead she could see Stuart. Stuart in his wheelchair...

Oh, Maureen, love, another husband in a wheelchair...how can you stand it...? With her thoughts bringing tears, Vi knew that the rest of the night would be long.

Maureen knew. Knew what was going on with Charlotte; that the girl was head-over-heels in love with twenty-year old David Morse.

Thankfully, though, what she didn't know was that a relationship had actually started; or of how sexual and wanton it had become. Earlier today, she had taken her granddaughter to one side, and had explained to the fifteen-year old teenager that everyone got crushes. That it was a normal part of growing up.

Maureen had been pleased by the way Charlotte had accepted the pep talk believing that the nods and relieved smile was because the girl was comforted to know that her feelings and longings were just a usual episode in the day-to-day life of an attractive girl in her teens.

Now, as her mother and father, her grandmother and grandfather, raised their glasses to toast the New Year, Charlotte hid her smirk behind a glass of lemonade.

Seeing the over-bright smile on her grandmother's face, as she bent to kiss her wheelchair-bound husband, Charlotte felt a frisson of guilt: she did so love her grandmother.

But the guilt lasted a mere second or two. Knowing that any minute her mother would chime up with, 'Okay, Charlotte, now it's bedtime for you...' Charlotte got in first with her 'Goodnights.' After all it was *bed*time...

Later, in the strong arms of her lover, on the warm plaid blanket they'd laid over the dusty floor of the *Summer House,* Charlotte brought him to an ecstatic climax. His second of the night: the first time was for the old year, this time, for the new.

David said, when he'd caught his breath, that Charlotte sure knew how to celebrate.

Charlotte, smiling seductively in reply, thought that teenager or not, she could teach the oldies, tucked up now in their narrow-minded beds, a thing or two about real loving.

*

46

Maureen's Aunt Nellie died on the eighteenth of September, not making it to the new millennium had she had hoped. The old lady was in her ninety fifth year.

Donald Seymour Sommer died one week later, exactly a month before he would have celebrated his seventy fifth birthday.

Maureen, his widow, was inconsolable. Jake, his stepson, was more grief stricken than he would ever have though possible.

So it was Beth who had the dreadful task of telling relatives and friends, the press and the television networks. The latter sent camera crews to the Rhode Island house as soon as the grave news was received.

News reporters camped outside the mansion, hoping to capture the many arriving celebrities and dignitaries coming to pay their respects to the bereaved family.

Charlotte was deeply distressed, more so than was expected of her. But then, of course, her grieving family didn't know everything about the girl.

Summoned to the *Summer House* for an early evening rendezvous, David now sat with his head in his hands as he listened to what Charlotte had to say, and the despair and tears in her voice.

In England, Patsy wept. Nellie's death the previous week had made her remember her own mother's demise with a deep sadness. Now, with the dreadful telephoned news of Don's passing, Patsy was crying as though her heart was breaking.

Don Sommer had been such a kind and thoughtful man. A gentleman: a true star in every sense of the word. He would be so very much missed, and by so many people. His music had brought joy, hope and love. Over the years, he had been told often, and by many couples, that their children had been conceived with his songs playing in the background. Patsy had been so very proud to think that this special man had been a part of her family.

And she knew, in her saddened heart, that he was the reason her own children had so much confidence out there in the big wide world.

Finally drying her tears, Patsy snuggled closer to her husband. They lay in the dark of their bedroom, holding hands, keeping close; knowing that time was precious. Knowing it was their duty to make the most of their own good health and relatively trouble free lives.

What was a problem was how they would break the news to Vi. Fearing that it would not be good for her to hear the news at bedtime, they had made sure that the old lady was tucked up in bed away from radio and television in the hope that after a good night's sleep, the grave news would not be too much of a shock coming as it were, in the light of day.

Although Don's death had been expected, the end, when it had come, had been sudden. Her husband's death was mourned worldwide. Maureen was touched by the massive show of affection that came by mail, by telephone and by personal contact.

It appeared that no one had forgotten the singer-songwriter who had brought so much to their lives with his lyrics, his melodies and his powerful singer/acting voice. Maureen was humbled and very proud and, without knowing it, seriously ill.

Lena and Louis Grant came out of retirement to help with the funeral arrangements. A memorial service was arranged, and an interment date calendared in at the Boston Cemetery. Lena knew that it was Charlotte's birthday. But she decided to say nothing.

Rockfort House was full. Filled with people, filled with hushed conversations, filled with grief. Palatable grief. Maureen, looking much older than her sixty years, seemed smaller and slighter than ever. A diminutive figure, she now constantly brought a hand to her forehead as her brow creased as if under the strain of a nagging headache.

Charlotte, observing all of this, waited her time. She had thought to confront her grandmother with her problem on the morning of her own sixteenth birthday.

But when the day came, and no one congratulated her, no one noted or even mentioned that it was her birthday, Charlotte became too sullen, too broody and too sick to care.

Vi Greenwood, now well into her eighties, took the news of Don's death badly.

Comforting her mother-in-law, Patsy urged her to think back on the good times. To bring to mind the memories of the love and laughter, the music and good fun Don had bestowed on them all.

Vi would have none of it. She wept most of the day; quiet tears, dignified weeping and when she had tired herself out, she slept.

Crying and then sleeping was the pattern Vi's life took for the two days after Don's death. It appeared as though the man's passing was the final straw in Vi's ability to go on living.

Even the sight of six-month old, Max, Julie's sandy-haired baby son (Patsy and Malcolm's grandson—their pride and joy,) gurgling and guzzling in his breast-feeding mother's arms did not have the power to lift Vi out of her depression.

It took a phone call from Maureen for the elderly woman to find a grain of hope for what was left of her future. When Maureen said that after the funeral she was coming over to England, and was planning to stay for an indefinite time, Vi's veil of despair lifted enough for her to tickle the toes of her newest great-grandson.

*

47

The day she'd married Don she had wondered whose name would be on her lips this day. Soon she would know.

Loosening the top button of her grey silk blouse, she lay back against the soft linen pillows, hoping for ease from the pain.

That was not to be. It worsened. The excruciating pain was iron strong, leaden; it began to sink deep, impervious to any human frailty in its destructive downward journey. It wetted her mouth in its wake; banged against her palpitating heart as it sunk and then sought to anchor.

Closing her eyes, she lifted a trembling hand to her damp forehead. Her icy fingertips traced the throbbing, clammy skin across to her left temple, whilst the bile, gathering at the back of her throat, rose, gagging the panicked scream that instinctively gurgled from her.

Choking on the vomit that was flooding her mouth, she jerked upwards, her eyes screwed tight against the tidal force of pain. Her body began to spasm, her arms flailed, as she made a frantic attempt to leave the bed.

Her efforts were in vain. The weighted onslaught, plunging through her veins, abruptly stopped.

Maureen fell back against her pillows, and was still

The elegant mellow bedroom, the bedroom she had chosen to be their own, so many years before, settled into the stillness. No ghosts pervaded its gloaming, melancholic ambiance, for the long windowed south facing room had always enchanted her, and had pleased Don

This bedroom and its adjoining sitting room had been their domain. Their love had blossomed under the curtained canopy of the huge, oak-posted bed. The soft cushioned sofas had been the perfect setting for a cosy night for two in front of the television set, housed in an aged-oak cabinet in keeping with the rest of the room's furnishings.

The lilac and white linens, curtains and upholstery, the crystal chandeliers (that they had excitedly found in Italy in the early years of their marriage,) and the massive oak mantled fireplace, where in the depths of a Rhode Island winter, when they were in residency for perhaps a week or two, a roaring fire had been lit from morning until night, had all gone into making the small apartment an oasis of peace: it had been a place of privacy where, even in the midst of their extended family, their own companionship had not been disturbed.

The love experienced between Maureen and Don had been so envied by many. It had been battered in the gusting winds of jealousy and resentment, yet had flowered, majestically and unblemished, to be so cruelly cut down as it entered full bloom. Their Indian summer of marriage overpowered by a cyclone of death.

The motorcade crawled up the gracefully curved, balustrade driveway like a giant black insect, lethargic in the heat of late afternoon; the sombre faces hidden behind the glinting, darkened windows, its mournful, captured prey.

The leading limousine glided sleekly to a halt outside the columned façade of Rockfort House; a nineteenth century mansion, designed and built by a wealthy businessman who had been inspired by the grandeur of the White House in Washington DC.

From her vantage point, the huge and arched staircase window that overlooked the lush front lawns and gravelled forecourt, Charlotte watched, unseen. Watched as the soberly attired mourners stepped from the various cars, the murmuring of their voices growing louder as they assembled, demurely, their usual prominent personae subdued for this lugubrious gathering.

On cue, the couple that had been waiting in the dappled shade of the cool marble portico moved forward and out into the brilliant sunshine to greet them.

He, tall, athletic, his brown hair lifted slightly in the soft wind that was blowing in from the southern end of the island's rocky shoreline. As he shook hands with first one and then another, his well-tailored stance was dignified: some he kissed, exchanging the usual pleasantries, speaking low and confidentially, smiling with sincerity as he accepted their condolences with an incline of his head, before they moved on to shake the outstretched hand of the woman.

She, as small as he was tall, her petite dark suited figured haloed by a glossy crown of jet black hair, seemed more fragile than usual and, though she was gracious in her greetings, her grief was obvious.

Charlotte sneered as the woman came into full view. Mounting anger, intense and suffocating, glazed the girl's dark brown eyes, and her thoughts leapt into action...*Ah, shit! No...! What the...? Huh, yeah, look at her...preening prima donna...And he's no better. Sick. The pair of them...performing puppets...*

The loathing for her parents intensified as she watched the unfolding scenario taking place below the window: the massing of family and friends for the memorial service of her late grandfather. A ceremony that the sixteen year-old had thought would be taking place at St. Mary's Church later this evening. As usual, no one had told her that the gathering would begin at the house.

But the truth of it was, as she was now faced with the consequences, her behaviour these past few days had been so diabolical that few had wanted to be in her company. Even if they had informed her about the timetable of events, which in all probability they had, she had been too steeped in her own worries and miseries to be receptive,

And today, none of this had changed. Confused and shaken, Charlotte turned from the magnificent window, her limbs stiffening with frustrated rage, her mind racing...*Oh God, no! No, no, no! What am I going to do? It's too late to speak to grandma now...* Her agitated thoughts ignited her tongue, 'Bastard!' She was referring to her mother. 'Well, she can go to hell! They all can! They'll have to wait. I need Gran, *first*.' She hissed the latter word, her teeth grinding in her tightened jaw as she hurried up the remaining sumptuously thick, beige carpeted stairs, taking the steps two at a time, heading in the direction of her grandparent's suite of rooms on the first floor.

Those who knew the girl well would have raised their eyebrows, recognising the tell tale signs: the fury, the blanched face that was mottling red; the vile profanities uttered not quite under her breath; the rigid way she held herself as she tore down the wide, oak panelled hallway that led to her grandmother's apartment. She was having one of her infamous tantrums: a Charlotte paddy.

What those who knew the girl did not *know* was how much she suffered, too. They did not know that she was tormented and terrified to exhaustion by the roaring venomous fray. Combustible emotions that seemed to have a life of their own, her slender body the vehicle for their survival. When a rage erupted it was volcanic, the lava, hot and thick, destructive, possessive; she was deafened by its roar. The heat seeped into her scalp, her skin, even her eyes. And when the surge slowed and steamed, a fleeting glance of another time, another place, flitting images, tantalised her mind, taunted her thoughts; an echoed voice willed her to be wild, directed here to hurt the ones who loved her most. Only in the presence of her maternal grandmother could these turbulent tirades be soothed and stilled.

And, even then, in the aftermath, they lurked, waiting to be provoked; a low rumbling, a simmering stock of molten grievances brimming close to the edge, always ready, a boiling force of lethal words and actions that threatened to destroy all that was good; to punish.

Why...? In the midst of these red-hot frenzies, even she wondered... *Who is it...? Whose voice rules my mind? I know it's a woman...But who is she...?*

Hurrying along the hallway, Charlotte's thoughts were running wild. But as she neared her grandmother's room, her step began to falter. She stood still for a moment, uncertain. From downstairs she could hear the sounds of people gathering, clustering together in groups, the hub of conversation rising louder by the second.

All of a sudden she felt quite faint. Eying the gold brocade chaise lounge placed outside her grandparent's room, she decided to sit and regain a little of her equilibrium.

Breathing deeply, using the technique that had been drilled into her by her singing coach, Denise Powell, Charlotte tried to focus on what she had to do, and the manner in which she needed to do it. She knew that directly below her, in the cream and white Siena marble hallway, people were genuinely mourning the loss of her grandfather. She also knew that her grandmother was far from well due to her bereavement.

But Charlotte also knew that, though she was at this very moment resting in her room, readying herself for the emotional trials of the memorial service and committal of her beloved husband, Grandma Maureen would be pleased to see her granddaughter, and that, no matter what, she would take the time to soothe and guide her through her problems. Her grandmother was like that. It was no wonder that Don Sommer had made her his wife.

Charlotte was very aware that Don and Maureen had experienced a great love match. Not like her own parent's marriage: Charlotte was under the strong belief that Beth and Jake, though compatible, were just a poor copy of her grandparents.

Calmer now, and more able to put her wandering thoughts onto the here and now, and her present dilemma, Charlotte stood, and walked across the hallway to where a full length crystal framed mirror had been hung for those who wanted to make a last quick check that they looked well groomed, immaculate, before heading downstairs to whatever the business of the day or night happened to be: an essential accessory in a household where show business people resided: looking good was paramount.

Taking in her reflection was not the best thing to have done. Charlotte thought she looked awful… *Well, wasn't that what I intended…?* Not known for her complete honesty, the pale skinned teenager was at least truthful with herself.

Now, of course, seeing that the Gothic styled dress, fingerless gloves and clumpy lace-up boots, all black, looked gross, she chided herself for being so stupid. It was one thing to annoy her mother, as she had intended to in rebellion of, "Oh, Charlotte, you will wear something suitable tomorrow, won't you darling…?" But stirring up her grandmother's animosity on such a day was unforgivable.

Running her fingers through her lank, unwashed hair, Charlotte became furious again…*it's all her fault. Perfect Beth. Miss never-do-anything-wrong.*

Charlotte had little time for Beth Stuart. Over the years, she had become adept at hiding the hostility she felt towards her mother. Especially when she went for her monthly sessions with her psychiatrist.

As a condition of the *accidental death* decision recorded at Nathan's inquest, his three-year old sister was made a ward of the court. It was made known to Charlotte that her actions had caused the suffocation of her baby brother. It was also made public knowledge that there was no medical or psychiatric evidence that the youngster had used malice or aforethought in what she had done; the child had truly believed that a baby could sleep in a box.

Her grandmother and grandfather had always talked to her about what had happened. But her own parent's steadfastly refused to ever mention a word about the incident or the baby who had died.

It hadn't taken Charlotte too long to understand that her mother felt little to no love for her surviving daughter. Her father tried. She was aware of that. But after living with her grandparents for more than five years after the tragedy, with little contact with her mother, being suddenly taken back under the still-grieving woman's care had been traumatic.

Being a boarder at school had helped. But the unspoken antagonism between mother and daughter had fuelled to almost hatred where Charlotte's feelings lay. Her mother's off-hand and indifferent approach had made her feel isolated and lonely. And the loathing had grown to mammoth proportions of late.

Taking a black hairgrip from the hip pocket of her monstrosity of a dress, Charlotte prised it open with her small, neat and very white front teeth, deftly twisting her hair up into a knot at the back of her head, securing it into place with the one clip. A smile made a fleeting appearance across her face as a thought struck her…*At least I have one of her abilities…I can do my own hair…*

With her own mother being a hairdresser, Beth had indeed picked up some of Maureen's skills: it now seemed that Charlotte had, too.

Charlotte posed in front of the mirror, her mood somewhat lighter. Smoothing loose strands of hair behind her ears, she backed away from the mirror, and with a positive step, strode back towards her grandmother's room.

'Charlotte…? *Darling*…?'

Charlotte turned round, startled to hear her mother's tinkling voice behind her.

'I've been *looking* for you…*Oh*, are you going to get your grandmother? I was just coming to bring her down, and I'd wondered where *you'd* got to…' Moving closer to the sixteen-year old, Beth's tone of voice soon changed…

'For heaven's sake, Charlotte! What *is* it that you are wearing…? Didn't I *ask* you last night to make sure you looked nice today, hey?' Obviously crestfallen by her daughter's appearance, a look of despondency swept across her face. Her shoulders sagged. Her forehead creased.

Seeing all this, Charlotte felt pleased. But she stood defiantly silent—and sullen.

However Beth was not rising to the bait.

'Please get changed, sweetheart. If not for me…then do it for your Gran. Black is so not necessary, these days…' Beth's words tailed off.

Charlotte realised that her mother was frightened to say too much in case it caused a scene…*One up to me…She'll have to tread warily, now…*Her eyes were bright at the thought.

For a second or two there was a standoff.

Charlotte used the time to blatantly stare at her mother, weighing her up and down. As usual, Beth looked lovely. Her black hair, that was cut short and neat, was going platinum at the temples. It suited her. Underneath her dark Armani suit, she was wearing a deep turquoise silk blouse. Her eyes took on the shade and, because she was distressed, they shimmered a little making them seem soft and yielding. In her ears, as often was the case, were the sapphire earrings that she treasured.

Petulant at her mother's attractiveness, uneasy in her own choice of clothes, Charlotte went on the attack, 'Sorry, Mother, dear, but we can't *all* be perfect. We leave that to the superstars…' Knowing that her words were like bullets, she continued firing, '…besides, I *like* this outfit. And so will Gran: She likes me to be individual…Just because you'd look like a Black Widow Spider if you tried to wear black…don't get at *me*…'

Beth felt herself reeling under the verbal attack. She wanted to turn and flee, to get as far away from her daughter as possible…*A black widow…God forbid that I should become a widow. I'd go crazy without Jake…She is a monster. My own flesh and blood, and she's rotten…Nothing gets through to her…Oh, God, what have we done? What have I done to have a daughter like this…? Will we ever get on? Will we ever be a proper mother and daughter…?* Aware that Charlotte would take little notice of any request to dress more conservatively, Beth's thoughts were wearied. She let out a long sigh, gazing at the girl. She was rewarded with a sneer.

Charlotte was the taller by a good few inches. Beth moved nearer, until she was stood at her daughter's side. She reached out, and placed her arm round the girl's slim waist, gently tugging her close. It was an offering of truce: An olive branch.

'Well, darling, it's not me that is the widow. It's Gran…And Mum needs us *both* today, Charlotte. You know that. Look, forget the dress. It doesn't matter. Daddy and I are proud of you, no matter what you wear…'

Beth could feel that her daughter was leaning away from her. But she hadn't objected to the arm around her waist…*a start.*

453

'Always remember that, darling. Remember that we *love* you. We'll get through these bad days...we have before, haven't *we*...?' Beth felt herself suck in her breath. She had never mentioned that terrible time to Charlotte...She'd never been able to find the words.

Now, as her daughter shot her a look, Beth soldiered on.

'You know something, Charlotte? I believe that you are going to be the *only* person who can really help Gran, now,' she gently tugged her daughter closer, tried for eye contact, but didn't get it. Dropping her arm, she stepped back slightly before saying,

'You go and fetch her, Charlotte. *You* bring Mum down. Tell her that everyone is here, and that we'll be ready to leave in about a quarter of an hour. Look, darling, I'll have to go back to our guests, but I hope we can have a talk, soon. I think we both *need* too, don't you?'

Getting little response, Beth still tried, valiantly...

'If you won't give *me* a smile, have one ready for Gran. Yes? She'll need it, darling. Tell her that I hope her headache has cleared. And that I'll send Lena up with a tray: aspirin and tea—that should do the trick, don't you think? Do you want a drink sending up, too?'

When Charlotte nodded that she would, Beth smiled with relief, feeling that she had gained a small victory: there had been no tantrum.

Charlotte had no intention of returning her mother's smile...*Let her think she's won me over...She'll soon learn different*...

Watching Beth as she walked back towards to the stairs, Charlotte grinned, slyly. Her mother paused for a moment to straighten her jacket, touch he hair, lift her shoulders, circling them to relieve the tension before heading down to the massing of sympathetic friends and court followers. Even from the back, Charlotte could see her mother's distress; her loss of poise, of confidence was clearly visible. Observing all of this, Charlotte had the urge to shout after her...'Not so cock-sure about anything today, are you...? *Bitch!*'

But letting the aggression pass, unspoken, Charlotte mulled over something that her mother had said. And she decided that perhaps the pathetic woman was right about one thing; and that was her thoughts on Grandma Maureen and who indeed was best placed to offer help and assistance to her in her hour of need.

Charlotte knew that the memorial service, followed by the Boston interment tomorrow morning, was going to be a traumatic time for her grandmother. They had been warned that the television networks would have camera crews at the scene of both services, and that the pictures would be screened world-wide via Satellite and cable: Don Sommer's music was known as far a field as China. If fact, his following in the Orient and Asia was massive.

With all of this in mind, Charlotte stood outside her grandmother's suite confident that she was the one person who could aid the grieving woman. She was also supremely assured that because of this her own need of help would be confidentially and loyally granted.

No answer to her first knock, Charlotte had tried three times. Now, with only a slight hesitation, she turned the round brass handle and entered the darkened sitting room.

'Gran? Gran, it's *me*...May I come in?' Pushing the door further open, Charlotte realised that she was calling in a whispering voice. If she was to wake her grandmother, she would have to be a little louder, 'Gran. *Grandma*, it's me: Charlotte!'

With the lilac coloured velvet drapes drawn closed against the afternoon sun, Charlotte found it difficult to focus in the half-light. But the scent of the room was as familiar as ever: lavender; Maureen's favourite fragrance was used in the potpourri-filled Wedgwood bowls gracing the bureaus, the scented candles on the mantel, and the lotions, cream and soaps that adorned the dressing tables and adjoining bathroom.

Tiptoeing across the soft beige carpet, the hushed and tranquil ambiance quietened Charlotte's agitation. She felt safe, secure, as she always did in her grandmother's presence. This apartment, made up of two, high ceiling, tastefully furnished rooms, and an opulent, gold-fixture bathroom, had always been a haven to Charlotte in much the same way it had for her grandparent's.

Innumerable times she had asked, begged, for her grandmother to move back permanently, to stay and life year-round in Montport. But Maureen had always drawn her into an embrace, hugging her close whilst declining, explaining that as much as she loved to visit, she needed to live in her own home. She had always joked that perhaps Charlotte would not have the same feelings if they were to make Rockfort House their home, repeating a wise mantra, "Guests are like fresh fish: after three days of being out of home waters, the rot begins to set in..."

However, Charlotte had eventually got her wish. Her grandparents had spent the last five months in Montport. The Rhode Island air had been better for Grandpa Don, and then, of course, it had become all too late for them to undertake the journey back because of his fast and severely declining health.

And now Charlotte was more determined than ever that her grandmother would stay in residency, one way or another, for what was there to go back to Florida for, now?

Armed with this determination, the teenager felt confident in her approach. Hadn't her grandmother always said, "No matter what, Charlotte, you can always come to me…you can tell me *anything*, darling, I'll always be here for you."

Charlotte had often wondered why her own mother was not like this. She had also always wondered how someone with her grandmother's qualities could have ever given birth to the likes of Beth.

For as long as she could remember, Charlotte had loathed being in the company of her mother. And that loathing had bred the purest of hate; a jealousy-fuelled hatred that had reached saturation point on a cold January day; the day her mother and Don had performed at Julia Howarth's Inauguration Lunch.

Though she had been proud of her grandfather, as he had valiantly rallied against the disease that was smothering his voice, paralysing his body, her mother's performance, and the way she had allowed Don the prop against her whilst they had sung their salute, gaining wide respect and praiseworthy accolades for both of her generous deeds, had made Charlotte become envious and also vividly aware of the power her family had attained. Their talent, solely and jointly, had reaped friendships from the highest ranks.

And, although she herself had benefited from all of these privileges, the new President was, after all, her own godmother, Charlotte knew that she had little to offer in way of return. The diva style beauty of her mother, the fine temperament of her grandmother, had not been passed down maternally. Nor had the ear for music, or the penmanship of Jake, paternally. Even Don's tutoring, the hours and money her grandfather had spent teaching her to sing, had been fruitless. And with Beth recently having written her autobiography, after being acknowledged as one of America's finest performers, seeming now to possess *all* of these qualities, Charlotte felt cheated and, worse than that, dispensable to the dynasty.

Now, as she took in all the cards and messages of condolence neatly arranged on the mantle of the oak fireplace and on the highly polished occasional tables in the apartment, Charlotte, once again, began to doubt her own significance within the family that was so well-known, well respected,

456

and so very famous.

Charlotte knew that her parent's marriage had been threatened by the loss of their infant sons. Nathan's in particular. She also knew that there was no doubt that she was to blame for his tragic death.

When, at the age of eight, she had returned to live with Beth and Jake, here in Montport, Lena and Louis Grant had retired from their positions as housekeeper and butler, making it very clear whose presence was responsible for their hasty exit. And, before she had left her duties, Charlotte had heard the woman say, on numerous occasions—and to anyone who would listen, "That child has problems: She's either schizophrenic, or has this new, fanciful, multi-personality disorder. Or it's like I think is true: she is just plain *evil*."

Charlotte had asked her mother what schizophrenic was, and did she have it?

And Beth had answered, "No! No you are not, Charlotte. The doctors are certain you don't suffer from *that*."

The youngster had often wondered what indeed she did suffer from, then, as it was apparent that she was unlike most girls of her own age. Friendships had never come easily to Charlotte. And the children she did play with often left her to her own devices, moving off to romp and jump around with others in the company.

Charlotte had one or two school chums. But, when term finished, none were invited to Rockfort House, and she was not asked to visit with them in their homes, either.

Living with her grandparents in Florida had been so different; there had always been children to play with on the white beach that backed their home. And Don and Maureen, famed also for their hospitality, had many acquaintances; when they came visiting they often had their offspring or grandchildren in tow. Life in Florida had been full of gaiety, full of fun, yet her grandmother had always stated that it was family that mattered the most…"Remember this, Charlotte, always: family comes first! Having good friends is important; but it's family that you need in times of difficulty. And we must always look out for one another."

Grandma Maureen had told Charlotte about her own beginnings, of how she had been adopted by a very kind lady. And of how she had never known who her real mother was…"Your great-grandmother, my Aunt Vi, is the only *mother* I have known since I was a little girl, about the same age as you are now…*You* are a lucky girl, darling, you have your very own mummy and daddy."

Knowing this to be true, Charlotte had been left wondering why she lived with her grandparents. She had also felt very sorry for her grandmother: bad enough that she had no parents of her own—but to have that very old and very smelly woman, Vi, as her surrogate mother…

Thinking back on all of this, Charlotte felt aggrieved again. Having no parents had not hindered her grandmother too much. Maureen's life had been pretty wonderful when you came to think about it: she'd travelled; she'd made a home in a foreign land. She'd found love—twice.

Charlotte thought that it was all a little unfair. In fact nothing was fair…*why can't anything go right for me…?*

With a sob catching in her throat, Charlotte left the sitting room and gingerly entered her grandmother's bedroom. The door had been left slightly open, so she didn't feel the need to knock. In truth, she never gave a thought to good manners: Charlotte's own need was greater than showing respect for any privacy.

Blinking back her tears, she was surprised to see that her grandmother was still sleeping. Charlotte could also see that Maureen had not completely undressed; she had slipped her jacket onto the back of a chair, her black court shoes were on the floor next to the seat. Without a covering blanket, her grandmother lay in stocking-feet-comfort in just her dark suit skirt and her dove-grey, long sleeved silk blouse, resting on top of the lilac and white quilted bedspread.

Biting her lip, somewhat concerned for what she was about to do, Charlotte couldn't help but notice that her grandmother seemed so small and vulnerable. Her tears brimmed over…*Will Gran be able to help me? Or will she be very annoyed with me for crying about it all, on today of all days…?*

But Charlotte knew that this was her chance. It was imperative to catch her grandmother in a receptive mood: In *any* mood. She needed the woman's protection, her sole and discreet assistance. In the grief of losing her husband, Charlotte was hoping that her grandmother would be more understanding of her granddaughter's dilemma. And it came to her, also, that it would seem so much better if she *was* crying: Grandma Maureen would think that the tears were for Don.

Not for one moment did Charlotte blanche at the idea of disturbing her bereaved grandmother with more distressing news.

Allowing her hot tears to flow, Charlotte sobbed openly, and loudly. It was a relief to let out all her pent up frustrations and to know that her worries would soon be shared and dealt with. Reaching the canopied bed, Charlotte threw herself to her knees, her head coming into contact with the lavender scented bedclothes, and was jolted a little by another smell that wafted towards her. Whatever, she lifted her tear stained face, extended her black-gloved right hand and, none to gently, shook the slim, delicately boned shoulder of her sleeping grandmother, wailing, 'Gran, Grandma! Wake up! Oh, Gran, they're all *here;* and I wanted to tell you something. *Please* can we talk? *Gran…Grandma…? Grand…ma!*

When seconds later Charlotte screamed, and then screamed again, her cries went unheard for what seemed the longest time.

*

48

Patsy Greenwood saw to everything. Every detail, every cancellation, every new arrangement; night and day she manned the telephones, welcomed visitors and ran the house: Rockfort House.

Beth and Jake were inconsolable. The grief had paralysed their ability to function normally. They had been desperate for help. And Patsy and Malcolm, shell-shocked themselves, had not hesitated in offering their services.

Already in Boston in readiness to pay their respects at Don Sommer's interment, they had been whisked by limousine to Montport the minute the tragic, staggeringly unbelievable news had been received.

Maureen Sommer had suffered a massive stroke on the afternoon of her husband's planned Memorial Service and had died, in hospital, in the early hours of the morning on the day she would have buried him.

The funeral of her husband had been postponed. As had his memorial ceremony that should have taken place the night before.

Now, a double interment had been arranged: Don and Maureen Sommer would be laid to rest together. They would spend eternity side by side, very much in the manner they had been in life.

Those who had been left to carry on their own lives without them were distraught beyond words. The shock had been colossal. Maureen's death had come so sudden. Few knew of the woman's hypertension problem. And fewer still had any idea that she was gravely ill.

For Maureen herself, the end had not been so quick. The headache had been with her since the day of Don's death. A relentless pain that had slowed her step and crippled her thoughts. She had mentioned it to Don's nurse, Pete, and he had suggested that he give her a head and neck massage and that she should perhaps get in touch with her doctor.

Maureen had accepted the massage, and had enjoyed the half-an-hour interlude with the man who had been by Don's side, constantly, for the past few months: Pete Gregson had proved to be a dedicated carer for her husband's many needs.

During the massage, the two had taken time to share a few minutes of quiet contemplation of the deceased man's life whilst at the same time the male nurse had un-knotted some of Maureen's paining and tense bound muscles.

An hour later she had eaten a light lunch, and then had dressed for her husband's memorial service.

After receiving one or two of the early-arriving mourners she had excused herself, withdrawing to seek sanctuary in the comfort of her bedroom.

Lying on the bed had done nothing to ease the pain. In fact, it had worsened it. When the stroke had taken grip, its hold was unshakable. The pain then had been excruciating.

Behind her closed and trembling eyelids she had known that she was dying, and had felt the irony of it; for to die on the day of her husband's burial was what most widows would fervently wish for.

Maureen had first hand knowledge that with time, grief lessens. Hadn't she finally come to terms with Stuart's death? Now, in her own last hours of life, Maureen wondered whether she would have ever have come to terms with losing Don.

Don Sommer had not only been her beloved husband, he had been her soul mate, her closest friend.

So when Maureen became aware of the bright light, felt its pull, its warmth, she had moved towards it with a surge of excitement that pushed away the raging, plunging pain. She could clearly see the outline of the person waiting for her within the brilliance. The blurred image grew stronger, more definite, and more familiar. When Maureen realised who it was, she was filled with great joy. She felt herself soaring; her body seemed to explode, splintering the air, as she floated into the arms of the figure waiting with outstretched arms; waiting to comfort, to cuddle and to love.

And on Maureen's lips was just one word. 'Mam.'

Ethel had been the one waiting.

Malcolm Greenwood was deeply distressed by the death of his cousin. He was also extremely proud of his wife. Patsy had been remarkable in the way she had taken over every thing. She was a rock: strong, solid and always there when needed.

As he watched her attending to mundane things like making sure there was food in the refrigerators, or overseeing the cleaning ladies, he became aware that she was just as capable at arranging the funerals that would ensure that his lovely, already so very much missed cousin Maureen was buried next to her famous husband, Don Sommer.

Last night he'd heard Patsy talking on the phone for the best part of an hour to Julia Howarth, the President of the United States of America.

His ingenious wife had shown compassion, whilst being authoritative. She had used dignity when faced with bureaucracy. Indeed it had been Patsy who had taken the helm of all things that mattered, handling it all with a firm hand when around her the grip of reality was lost in others.

Charlotte was one of the lost souls. Being the first person to see that Maureen was gravely ill, she had run into Lena as the elderly woman had been entering the apartment, her arms laden with a tea tray.

That was when the screaming and ranting had started. And it seemed (to most who had taken residency in the house,) that during the two weeks it took to get the results of the post mortem, and Coroner's Report, that the teenager was either raging round the house or silently wandering it like a caged animal. Charlotte was, once again, unbridled. And her grief brought with it a torrent of abusive and foul language, and screeching and shrieking fits of anger.

Throughout the harrowing two weeks, Malcolm knew that both Beth and Jake had become fearful for their daughter's sanity.

Finally, in desperation, Jake had taken the decision to bring a doctor in to sedate the girl.

The medication had seemed to work. Charlotte attended the funeral of her grandparents without speaking a word to anyone. The fact that she was silent and aloof was passed over by most in the congregation. Her parents and their extended family were indebted to their thoughtfulness at not mentioning the girl's odd behaviour.

During the agonizing two-week wait before the funerals, Malcolm had been Charlotte's only ally. The man had done his best to befriend the often violently tempered girl. And, in some ways, he had won her over: at the church service a sullen Charlotte had seated herself next to him, and at the graveside, she had leaned against him as if for physical support as well as moral.

But now, with the funerals over, it was time for him and his wife to return to their own home, and their own country.

Malcolm was worried for the welfare of his mother. Too frail to undertake the journey across the Atlantic, they had left the grief-shattered woman in the care of their daughter, Julie.

As he stepped aboard the flight that would take them home, Malcolm wondered just how much time Vi had left on this earth.

They had only been back in their Cheshire home for an hour or so when they were told, by telephone, that Charlotte had disappeared.

But minutes later, upon entering Vi's cottage and seeing the deterioration of the elderly woman, the problem of the sixteen-year old's vanishing trick was put on a back burner. After all, Charlotte Adier was young, healthy, and extremely wealthy. And though she acted liked a wilful spoilt child, she was, without doubt, a very intelligent young woman who probably knew exactly what she was doing.

Whispering together, as they got Vi ready for bed and a visit from the doctor, Malcolm and Patsy both agreed that Charlotte would be found, but only when she wanted to be found.

A week had passed. In England it had been a week where Malcolm and Patsy battled to save Vi's life, urging her, tempting her, imploring her out of the shadow of death.

In America, Jake and Beth had notified every police station in the country. Charlotte's photograph was shown on the pages of most newspapers for a couple of days or so, with the hope that it would trigger some information regarding her whereabouts. By the end of the week, it had become a smaller picture in the middle pages before it too, vanished: old news seemed to be no news where the newspaper editorial lay.

Even the police were giving up the search. Charlotte was fast becoming a statistic along with countless other runaways and missing persons.

There had been one glimmer of hope. On the tenth day they found out that Charlotte had flown from Boston to Ireland, landing in Dublin. She had then travelled up to Belfast. There the trail ended. If Charlotte was in hiding in Northern Ireland, she had made a good job of keeping her identity secret.

Jake had come clean, telling the police that his daughter had taken a large sum of money with her. Along with her passport, his daughter had stolen thousands of dollars from her father's personal safe. Wounded that she was a thief, Jake was, however, thankful to know that at least his daughter had enough cash not to have to resort to living on the streets of wherever she had absconded to.

Beth felt herself to be a total failure. None of her children had survived as far as she was concerned. For in truth, the day Nathan had died was the day her love for her daughter died too.

Over the years she had tolerated Charlotte. From time to time she had found herself growing fond of the girl; but that feeling was usually soon shattered by her daughter's wicked temper, and bouts of peevish behaviour. Charlotte was a difficult child to be close to.

However, Beth had always been pleased to see the good relationship that existed between her own mother and the girl. Now that Maureen's loving care was no longer available, it was no wonder the teenager had fled.

Beth's days began to be filled with remorse. Maureen had always been super-human at being a parent. Even after the death of her first husband, Stuart, she had been steadfast in her care and dedication to her daughter. Beth knew that she herself lacked the necessary qualifications to be an all-consuming parent. In fact, she had been a lousy mother to Charlotte, blaming the girl for being alive in place of her brother.

There was no doubt that Charlotte had been responsible for Nathan's death. But it had been a tragic accident. Beth could very well remember telling her young daughter, and telling her often, that baby Daniel was asleep in his box in the church.

And as for Charlotte's babyhood abhorrence of music, it had taken Don and Maureen only a matter of weeks of having the little girl in their care to find that she had hearing problems. And painful ones, too: a small operation, to insert Grommet tubes, had made a remarkable difference to Charlotte's behaviour and dislike of loud music.

All of this had been told to Beth over the phone. And she had not been the slightest bit interested. Out of sight, out of mind, was the way she had treated Charlotte from being aged three until she was eight.

Beth was aware that, over the years, she had shown her child very little love. And this fact, coupled with the tragic death of her mother, following so quickly on the heel of Don's demise, left her feeling both bereaved and despairing.

Beth now truly believed that Charlotte had had no choice other than to leave home. For without the love of her grandparents, the girl's life was bereft of affection.

David Morse kept silent. He had been questioned by Charlotte's parents, and then by the police. He told them all that he had not seen Charlotte for quite some time. He was honest when they asked whether he was aware that Charlotte had a teenage crush on him, answering that yes, he had been aware of the fact, but that he'd not been interested himself because she was only a bit of a kid.

He had seen the look in his grandfather's eyes, and wondered whether his Gramps knew the extent of his involvement with the missing girl. If he did, the old man was keeping the faith and saying nothing to contradict his grandson.

Now, as David was wending his way as far away from Montport as possible, to Chicago and his placement in a downtown lawyer's office, he was glad to be leaving the anguished environment of the Adiers' behind him. And more than pleased that Charlotte was at last out of his life. She had become a liability. And a dishonest one at that, too

When their relationship had first started, before it had become sexual, he had asked her what precautions she wanted to use regarding contraceptives. Charlotte had told him that she was already taking the pill and that it had been prescribed to her to help with her painful periods. Arriving at their rendezvous of the *Summer House* with the proof in her hand—a strip of birth control pills, showing that the day's tablet had already been taken—David had felt secure enough to take what was on offer: Charlotte.

Little did he know that months down the line she would come to him begging for help, and screaming that the pills had not been hers. That she had stolen the strip from her mother's purse. And that during their elicit love-making sessions—and there had been many—no contraception had ever been used.

David had not believed a word she'd said. He knew that she was not stupid enough for that to be true. By then, the summer break from boarding school, which also marked the end of his college life, he had begun to realise that Charlotte was a dangerous, cunning, devious, cheating, liar. And that her problem was not that she was pregnant it was the very fact that *he* was leaving Montport to start a new life in Chicago. Charlotte had been hysterical when he had told her his news.

As he pulled on to the freeway in the ten-year old red Ford Escort he'd bought yesterday from a car lot, David felt relief sweep through him as his old life was left behind. That he would miss his mother, his grandfather, was nothing to the fact that he was delighted to be as far away from the menacing Charlotte Adier as possible.

But as he put his foot down on the accelerator, gathering speed to switch lanes, it came to him that Charlotte could have disappeared deliberately...*No! Please don't let her be waiting for me in Chicago...Shit...!*

Julia Howarth was distressed to learn of the run-away. But it didn't come as a surprise. Though she had discreetly put her own *feelers* out to trace the girl, she felt declined to get too involved.

Julia had not had much pleasure from being Charlotte Adier's godmother. She saw the girl perhaps a couple of times a year. As Charlotte had turned down the offer of spending a few days of her school-break with her at the White House, which was a staggering snub, she'd continued to just send birthday and Christmas presents, and to speak occasionally by telephone to the teenager; but that had been all.

President Howarth had been in attendance at the funerals' of Charlotte's grandparents, who had always been such dear friends. But with the pressure of her High Office duties, and the overseeing of the day-to-day care of her own ailing husband's health (Ben was into his second round of chemotherapy for the bone cancer that was breaking his body along with his wife's heart,) Julia had little time for worrying about her gone-walk-about godchild. She was also convinced that Charlotte was safe and well and just on a thoughtless adventure. Jake had assured her that Charlotte was not without funds.

As Julia waved to the gathered press before climbing into the helicopter that would fly her to an early morning United Nations meeting in New York, she only hoped that the wayward teenager would not get involved in anything that would bring repercussions not only to her still grieving family, but to the reputation of her position as a world leader.

When the helicopter moved off the pad, Julia found tears gathering behind her eyes: her life was very hard, very lonely. Not for the first time she thought how gladly she would swap all of this just to have Sonia back.

Back in Texas, the Vicentes' had spent their time since the funerals of their dearest friends recuperating from the journey. Mary Lou and Chuck very rarely left the Yellow Rose State these days. Jaunts across the Atlantic and onwards to the Spanish island of Mallorca, set in the Mediterranean Sea, had been suspended indefinitely, though their daughter, Lydia, and her husband, Peter, flew there often with their own three children.

The Landon couple had once taken Charlotte with them for a six-week holiday. But since that time, Charlotte's godfather and his wife had given up trying to get close to the girl: the vacation on the paradise island had been a disaster from start to finish—Charlotte, then aged eleven, had developed an ear infection on the long haul flight, which was worsened by her dissipation to show her prowess in the villa's swimming pool to the three on-looking Landon children. Told time and time again that the pool was out of bounds whilst she was in recovery, Charlotte had thrown tantrum after tantrum begging to be taken home.

Though there had been initially a lot of sympathy shown towards Charlotte and her ear problem, by the end of the second week, Peter and taken steps to fly Charlotte to Manchester, England, where she was met at the airport by her Uncle Malcolm. It had been a grey and miserable day in the middle of July, and Peter had been eager for his return flight away from the inclement weather and relieved to be going back to his own well-behaved youngsters. Charlotte had flown back to the USA the following day, chaperoned by her cousin, Julie Greenwood.

Mary Lou (who still battled with weight gain, but looked very good for her age since being aided and abetted by two face lifts,) thought that there was little chance that Charlotte would turn up in Texas.

Chuck, wheelchair bound most of the time, due to him having suffered three major heart attacks, didn't think anything: he wasn't that interested.

Peter and Lydia said they hoped that Charlotte would not show up. Lydia was pregnant with their fourth child, and, well, try-as-they-might they could never forget what happened with Nathan. Even on that infamous vacation, they had made sure that their own children slept close by them at all times, and, after Charlotte's tortuous two week stay had ended, Lydia told her parents, by Trans-Atlantic telephone, that she was mightily relieved, saying that, "One way or another, I've not had a wink of sleep for the past fourteen nights or so…she had me on tenterhooks…"

Beth and Jake tried to get their life back on some sort of normal footing. But it was difficult with so many of their family either dead or missing. Charlotte's disappearance took the edge of their double grief. The couple's thoughts and words were constantly centred on their daughter.

Though they both felt instinctively that she was alive. But whether they would ever see her again was very debateable.

Jake said he thought she'd arrive home when her money ran out.

Beth hoped she would. She *prayed* she would. She also knew that if her daughter wanted to be found, she would be. And if she didn't…

Vi said, 'Good riddance!' A spark of Vi Greenwood of old, glinting in her eyes.

Patsy was going to tell her mother-in-law that she was being unkind; all said and done Charlotte *was* her very own great-granddaughter. But she held her tongue. Patsy also held her breath: she most certainly didn't want the girl showing up in Warrington Clough, thank you very much.

Malcolm did not have the time to think. The business was thriving and now they were opening seven days a week, and twice a week for twelve hours a day, there was little time for further problems. The weeks he'd taken off to be in America had put him very much behind with the ordering and whatever.

Still, he wouldn't have done anything different. Not where Maureen was concerned. He was going to miss their Maureen. She'd been like a sister. A sister to all the brothers…and now there were only two left. Malcolm knew it wouldn't do for him to look as if he was going to burst into tears at any minute. Not in the shop, it wouldn't. And, truth was, he wasn't one for maudlin…*Too much has happened…Perhaps I've grown hard in my old age. Aye, and if that bloody Charlotte turns up, by, I'll give her what for, no mistake…Little madam! Buggering off with her dad's money. My Mam's right, she's a brat…! And maybe she's dead right about her coming from bad stock…Our Maureen never did know who her mother was…*

*

Epilogue

[London, England]

Charlotte found it strange that she had never liked the taste of milk, especially as it was now her favourite drink.

Draining the glass, she placed it back on the tray before picking up a small triangle of lightly buttered wholemeal toast and taking a good bite.

As she contentedly munched, she gazed out of the window and remembered an old saying her grandmother had taught her about the cruel winds and snow of the month of March and how the bird population found it difficult to find food. She could remember sitting in the sun-filled kitchen of her grandparent's Floridian home and feeling sorry for the poor birds that lived in cold climates. Especially the red breasted robins.

And now, as she slunk back down into her nest of pillows, the wholesome breakfast settling nicely in her stomach, she thought...*that's a good name...Robin...*Charlotte rolled the name off her tongue.

'Robin.' Spoken out loud, it was even better.

Of late, names had become important to Charlotte. It had been imperative to choose one that she liked. And the reason she had settled on Zoë for herself was because it was short. Easy to remember: Zoë Morse? And excellent choice; it was snappy. It also, to her own ears, sounded Canadian.

Zoë Morse had arrived in England by ferry: The hourly boat service that sailed from Belfast to Liverpool. Then, after being directed to Lime Street station, she had taken the train to London. Once there, she had booked into a small, quiet hotel in Bayswater. Situated close to a small park, the hotel had been recommended to her by one of her travelling companions on her Atlantic flight.

The elderly woman, Noreen, had also said that she was pleased to have such a nice girl for a seating companion. Though Noreen had talked non-stop, Charlotte had been more than happy to let her rattle on. And in the long run, it had paid off.

Noreen was making her annual pilgrimage to Ireland to visit the graves of her parents. During her seven-hour monologue she had told Charlotte that long ago, before migrating to firstly Canada and then America, she had been fortunate in life: Her shop-keeper parents had seen to it that she had been well educated, and that she had eventually taken a university degree in Dublin. And asking if her travelling companion was at university, Charlotte had been quick to answer that she was on her way to take a years' placement at the very same one.... Wasn't *she* lucky, too?

Talkative Noreen was a generous old soul. Charlotte had gleamed much from her airline companion; the woman had been a font of useful knowledge and her reading materials had been inspirational, though Charlotte had had to wait close on six hours for the woman to tire herself out and fall into a light doze before she could quietly glance, skim-read through the glossy magazines and journals.

The name *Zoë* came from one of Noreen's loaned magazines. It was in an article about a brave young woman called Zoë Bannister. The heroine had beaten all odds at surviving. Buried alive after an explosion, Zoë had spent five days without food or water, and in terrible pain. The rescuers had been about to give up their efforts when they heard a tapping. Zoë was finally brought from the rubble and, although she had to have her left leg amputated, she was full of good cheer and hope. She said that during her ordeal she had remembered that her name, Zoë, meant *life*.

Reading the true story had helped Charlotte come to terms with her own problems and what she had to face. Flicking through the rest of the magazine, another article—an advertisement in reality, caught her attention.

By the time the flight touched down on the tarmac of Dublin airport, Charlotte knew what she was going to do.

And it had all been so easy. Civilised. It wasn't until she came out of the anaesthetic that she was thrown off balance, again.

'What do you mean, "it's too late"…?'.

'You were too far advanced in your pregnancy. It's not ethical. Sorry, but you must have told me the wrong dates.' The doctor had been quietly spoken, but firm in his decision.

'Well, what will I do, *now*?' Lying flat on her back, Zoë had felt the tears trickle from the corner of her eyes, run down the side of her cheeks and into her ears.

'Eh, there, come one now, don't cry. Is there someone you could talk to: A family member you can trust?'

'No. I told you. There's *no one*…'

The doctor was silent. He moved away from her and had stood looking out of the window.

Zoë knew that the view would be over the extensive lawns of the clinic's grounds. Gardens still colourful with late flowering red roses, even though it was early November.

The man had turned, smiling kindly at Zoë.

'No frost, yet…but it won't be long. Now, then, you will have to give some thought to your problem, Zoë. It won't just go away, you know…'

'I wish it *would*. You said it would be okay. Two days here and then I'd be able to leave. No hassle. No worries…' Zoë had been surprised that she had felt quite calm. She noticed that she was speaking softly, no rage in her voice, even though the news she'd been given was bad.

The doctor had sighed. Walking toward the door he'd said,

'Sleep a little, for now. I'll be back to see you in an hour or so. And don't *worry*. We'll sort it out, somehow…Okay, Zoë?'

She must have slept for quite some time. When she had woken the curtains had been drawn, the room lit by two large, silk shaded table lamps. A pale pink glow mellowed the oyster coloured walls of the single-bedded room and the lull of muted music filtered the air. The music seemed to be was coming from the room above.

Zoë had sat up, taking in her surroundings. It was pleasant on the eye: white wood furniture, brass fitments. Framed landscapes in pastel shades graced two walls. The third wall, where Zoë knew the window to be, was masked by heavy, rose pink damask curtains; looking very much like a stage setting, Zoë felt that at any minute they'd be whisked open and the show would start. That thought had made her smile.

And she had been smiling when the door had opened and a woman she had never seen before entered the room. Smart suited, sleek blonde hair, she introduced herself as the doctor's wife.

'Well, Zoë, how are you feeling, now? Had a good sleep? Are you hungry?'

So many questions fired at her, but Zoë had had the feeling that answers were not important.

She had been right. The doctor's wife had seated herself on the bedside chair and had answered all the questions herself: And efficiently, too. Then Zoë had been led to the bathroom, helped to bathe, had been pampered with thick, sweet smelling towels and a fleecy white bathrobe and then afterwards, back in her room, had enjoyed a light supper of poached salmon in dill sauce, a crisp green salad, raspberries and vanilla ice cream, and a tall glass of chilled fresh milk.

Later, when she was warm and comfortable in bed, after having been wished a very good night's sleep, it seemed to Zoë, as she drifted into a pleasant slumber, that it was as if she was meant to be ensconced in the pink glowing room, as if it had been planned, previously. Which of course, it had been anything but. Now, as sleep lulled her body, she felt calm and serene; trouble free. Behind the closed eyelids it was light and airy; it was a new sensation for her. And one she was finding to be pleasant. Her mind and thoughts were unburdened...She had enjoyed being spoken to—ever so softly—by the elegant and very likeable doctor's wife, who said Zoë must call her Carol.

Everything Carol had said had made sense. Everything Carol had suggested seemed plausible. Made to order. The answer.

After the whirlpool bath, when Carol had left her to go and see to the supper, she had snuggled into the fleecy robe and had felt something she had not felt for a long time. She'd felt safe. Wanted. Needed. And most importantly, at home...

It was February, and the last day of the cold month. And the only thing Zoë had to think about today was names: Boy names, girl names, Gloria Braithwaite had insisted that Zoë did the choosing.

'Please, dear; we want the baby to have its name chosen by *you*.'

That had been said on Christmas Day, when Zoë had been invited upstairs to share lunch with Doctor Chris and his family, and two of their closet friends. The doctor's mother had suggested a name, as she had been warned that she would...

'If it's a girl, you should call her Maureen!' The old lady seemed to be as eager as anyone for the baby to be born.

Zoë had tactfully declined the name, though her heart had thumped hard in her chest at the mention of it. Though she had felt sure that no one knew her real name or true nationality, she had been made uneasy by the coincidentally use of the name of her late grandmother.

Everyone sharing the delicious roast turkey lunch had been told that Zoë was Canadian. They also knew that she had spent some time in Ireland. However, because of the situation they were all in, very little else had been asked about her background.

When they had sat to watch and listen to the Queen's speech, Zoë had thought that perhaps Canada was not such a bad move: Vancouver, probably, especially as Queen Elizabeth seemed to be singing its praises.

But as a plateful of tempting mince pies, dredged in white icing sugar, was placed on the coffee table in front of her, Zoë had put all thoughts of the future out of her mind. It was pleasant being part of a family: And wonderful to be the centre of everyone's attention. The Hampstead Vale clinic had been tastefully decorated for the festive season with swags of holly, berries and tiny white fairy lights. Upstairs in the Grady family's private rooms, very much of the same had been in evidence. Zoë had felt loved and wanted—and happy...

Zoë had been dozing when the old lady came in.

'Carol said that I wasn't to disturb you...'

'Oh, it's all right. Please, come on in, it's *nice* to have company...' Zoë knew all about the grey haired old woman's problems: She was an alcoholic. But as far as Zoë could tell, she was a harmless one.

The two spent a pleasant morning watching television and talking. Chatting mostly about babies and different names—the name Robin was discarded—whilst outside the first floor window, snow began to fall from a leaden sky.

The labour pains began in the early evening of that day. By midnight the contractions were severe.

Carol stroked Zoë's hand and Gloria and Alec took it in turns to massage her back.

By four the next morning, they were all exhausted. The old lady came into the room, and was shooed away by everyone. She tottered out, clutching her fleecy pink dressing gown tightly to her chest.

By daylight, all except Zoë could see that Doctor Chris was becoming worried. But he put them at ease, whispering there was nothing much he could do. That first delivery's could take hours.

Gloria mentioned that it was now the first day of March.

'It's St. David's Day!' she exclaimed brightly.

In the throes of pain, Zoë heard the statement. It coincided with the timing of the final, gruelling push. And as the baby travelled down the birth canal, heading for its first breath of life, she knew, without doubt, that the child was a boy. And she knew that she would name him David.

David was born on the dot of eleven and in the middle of the heaviest snowstorm that London had witnessed for many years. By the afternoon it would have stopped all traffic.

The baby boy, weighing in at a hefty ten pounds two ounces, was perfect. An astonishingly beautiful newborn, being neither red or wrinkled, he had a mop of black hair, and eyes that were almost violet in colour.

Gloria and Ben were ecstatic. Even Carol shed a tear. Doctor Chris seemed grateful it was all over, but looked on with pride as the baby was cradled in his mother's arms.

The old lady had re-appeared in the room, and she stood quietly watching the scene.

It was Gloria's idea that David be breast-fed:

'Always the best for baby; keeps them free from infection.'

Nevertheless, so that she could bond with the infant, it was Gloria who undertook the night feeds after Zoë had painfully expressed as much breast milk as possible.

And through all of this, Zoë still felt safe. Still felt wanted. She also felt very proud when she looked at her son and the happiness she had achieved for the Braithwaite couple. The only person who made her feel uneasy was Doctor Chris' mother.

Well into the second week after her son's birth, Zoë had been taking an afternoon nap when she woke to find the old woman by her side.

'Are you sure...?' That's all she said.

Without a moment's thought, Zoë knew what the woman meant. And her safe world fell apart.

'No.' She whispered back.

The old woman straightened, smiled shyly at Zoë and said, 'Good.' She then shuffled out of the room.

Later, when Zoë was giving David his early evening feed, Carol came into the room announcing that she and Chris were going out to dinner. The Braithwaite's had invited them to their home for a celebratory meal—and to see the new nursery.

'We'll not be back late...It's Sarah on duty tonight. And we can trust Sarah...she knows. Ring her if you need anything. Oh, and Zoë, we'll get your flight tickets organised tomorrow. You can fly back to Canada on Saturday, if you like.'

As Carol left the room, Zoë was seized with fear. It felt icy. And it ran through her veins at a hurtful speed.

She went to look out of the window. It was still snowing. She would have to get used to snow. There was a lot of it in Canada.

At about seven thirty, she heard the doctor's car's wheels crunching down the driveway on the hard packed snow and ice. They were on their way to meet with David's new mother and father. Zoë, who'd peeked through the curtains to watch the car drive away, shivered as she moved from the window and went over to the white crib where her innocent, contented son lay sleeping.

A feeling of great dread began to fill Zoë. Her thoughts wandered. Her grandmother, her grandfather came to mind: Even her parents. She thought of the warmth of Florida: The hot sunny days of her childhood. She thought of the love and care she had received throughout her life, no matter what. And was humbled...*what have I done...?*

The door opened and the old lady entered wearing a long and heavy fur coat, a garment that was much too big for her slight frame.

'Be quick...'

That was all she said. But Zoë knew what to do.

The taxi took a long time to get to Heathrow. The old lady cradled the baby all the way, crooning to him, peppering him with kisses.

Zoë's ticket was waiting for her at the Service Desk. She panicked. The baby was not on her passport.

The old woman didn't look worried. 'No problem,' she said, 'you are only flying to Ireland tonight. Sort it out tomorrow. Phone your family, they'll help. It's...different...these days...' she broke down crying as she spoke. And she cried even more when she handed the sleeping infant to his mother.

As Zoë walked to the departure gate, the old lady trotted behind at a distance. And she shouted something. Whatever she was shouting was unintelligible against the background noise of the airport.

But Zoë stopped rushing for a moment. Turning to look back, she froze...*That was the voice...it sounded like the shrill voice that had plagued her for most of her life...*

The old lady called out something, again; Zoë couldn't quite hear what it was. Then she called out again—loud enough for anyone one to hear...

'Zoë...Zoë, or whatever your name is. Love that baby! Now that you have him, *never* let him go...

It was Beth that answered the phone,

'Hello...?'

'Mom...*Mom*...It's me, Charlotte.'

'Charlotte...? Charlotte...! *Is* it you?'

'Mom, oh, *Mom*, can I come home...*please?*'

'Charlotte. Where *are* you...? Where have you been...?'

'To...*Mom*...Oh, Mom...*Mommy*...I'm so *sorry*...'

Listening, with her heart banging in her chest, thumping in her ears, Beth steadied her own emotions as she tried to speak calmly, clearly.

'Charlotte...come home...Please, *yes,* come home...' all her efforts of keeping calm were in tatters. Tears began to pour down her face. She heard Charlotte sobbing too. And she thought her daughter said, 'Mom, I need your...*help*...'

The line went dead.

Beth waited. She felt as though she had stopped breathing. Jake came into the kitchen and stood by her side.

'Was it *her*...? Was it Charlotte...?'

Beth nodded. Jake pulled her close. They stood in silence waiting for the phone to ring again. The seconds passed. Minutes, too.

'She said she wanted to come home...that she wanted help...Oh, Jake, suppose she doesn't ring again! Suppose she thinks...'

The phone shrilled. Beth grabbed it.

'Charlotte? Oh, thank God...Listen, Charlotte. What can we do? What do you need...? I'll come anywhere...*we'll* come anywhere! Daddy's here, by my side...'

Beth held onto her husband's hand as she gripped the telephone receiver with the other, 'where are you, darling...?'

'I'm in Ireland...Mom? Will you *really* come...?'

'Yes, of course I'll come. We'll both come...now...*today*...this minute!'

Beth heard her daughter laugh. It was a splendid sound. The best music ever heard.

'Mom, the thing is, I'm not on my own...Mom, oh, *Mom*...I've had a baby. I have a son...'

Never in her life had Beth had to think so quickly...

'Charlotte. I don't care if you have a *moon*. Dad and I will be on the first available flight. We are coming to get you. Darling, are you well...? Where are you now...? Let me get pen and paper...' Beth motioned for Jake to hurry with the writing materials. Writing down the address of the hotel, which Charlotte was saying was the same hotel she had stayed in when she had first arrived in Dublin, she also answered some of Charlotte's anxious questions...

'No, Charlotte, I am *not* angry with you. There is no *point* in any of that anymore...*Pardon*? What will your dad say...?' Mischief danced in Beth's eyes as she looked into the puzzled ones of her husband. Never taking her eyes off Jake's face, Beth answered her daughter, truthfully, 'Charlotte, your dad will say that he is so glad to have his daughter back. *Really* back, this...time...' a sob caught in Beth's voice, but she held it back to continue talking with her daughter.

'Mom, I have to go now. The baby is crying. Mom, are you *really* going to come? You are not sending someone to get me...you're coming *yourself*...?'

'Nothing will stop me.'

'And the baby? You don't mind about my baby? I called him David...*Mom*...'

Charlotte was crying. The baby was crying...

Beth had never heard a more beautiful, natural, sound. Then the line went dead, cutting them off.

Beth collapsed into her husband's arms. Jake had gathered most of what had been said. In between sobs, Beth confirmed it.

'Jake, she's had a baby. On her own, she's had a baby: a little boy. Oh,

Jake…she *wants* us…'

'And we want her, too. We always have. But had to lose her to get her back. I've been a *dreadful* father, Beth.'

Beth agreed that she too had not been a good parent. They cried together, long and hard. Cried for all they had lost. Finally, the tears came from relief. Their daughter was coming home.

And as they rushed around, flinging items of clothing into an overnight bag, reality struck home. Jake called to his wife who was in the bathroom gathering toiletries together.

'Beth?'

'*Yeah*…'

'You're a grandma…'

'And you're a *grandpa*…' she called, loudly.

Beth walked back into the bedroom, dressed in a heavy knit, pale blue turtleneck sweater and blue jeans.

Jake's eyes were fixed on hers.

'I love you, Beth.'

Beth's eyes filled again as she replied, 'And I love you too, Jake.'

Jake shut the lid on the suitcase. He went to the wardrobe and took out a tan coloured leather jacket. Shrugging into it over his own warm blue check shirt and blue jeans, he said, 'We'll be a family…'

'We have always been a family, Jake. And thankfully, Charlotte has remembered that. And what Mum always said, she must have thought of that, too. My Mum always said that family came first. Families turned to each other in a crisis. Mum was so good with Charlotte. And she was *always* there for her. Now it's our turn…'

Beth hurried her husband from the bedroom and rushed him down the wide sweeping stairs that would lead them into the future.

*

The end…or is it another beginning?